PAPA'S WIFE

PAPA'S DAUGHTER

MAMA'S WAY

A Trilogy by Thyra Ferré Bjorn

NEW YORK   Rinehart & Company, Inc.   TORONTO

To Dr. Nels S. F. Ferré, a
great theologian, but to me a wonderful
and beloved brother, this trilogy is
fondly dedicated.

A NOTE TO THE READER

It was many years ago, when I was a young housewife and a mother. Life was rich and exciting and every day was filled to overflowing with those little tasks that belong to a happy family life. As I think back to this special day I remember that it was springtime and I had company—a house guest who was more than a guest. She was the wife of one of my beloved brothers. Because this day was so enchanting, we decided not to spend it indoors but to take a trip to the lovely Forest Park, in Springfield, Massachusetts, where I was living at that time. We must have walked for miles, enjoying the first spring flowers that peeked up from the black dirt, the freshness of the air and the mystery of new life being born all about us. After a while it was good to sit down on a bench by the waterfall, facing a smooth green lawn, and hear the birds sing and see young lovers strolling up the lanes.

Presently a lady came walking along and after a moment's hesitation she sat down on the bench beside us. We all smiled a friendly smile of new acquaintance and soon the three of us were engrossed in watching a little blonde girl playing on the lawn with her doll. She was a busy little thing, completely lost in her own world as she danced and skipped, stopping once in a while to turn her big blue eyes our way and give us a great big smile.

The world about us was beautiful, but more than the loveliness of nature, the beauty of the little girl captivated us. Suddenly I could not contain myself any longer; to the amazement of my sister-in-law, I turned to the stranger beside me and words burst from my lips: "Have you ever seen a lovelier sight than that little girl? Isn't she adorable?"

The strange lady smiled. "I was just thinking the same thing," she said. "I was wondering to whom she belongs?"

Without one moment's hesitation I said, "Why, she is mine!"

I do not know if my sister-in-law thought it was cute to speak that way or if, in her heart, she felt I was bold and ill-mannered. I did not dare to ask her, but I shall always remember the strange look on her face as she exclaimed, "I never before heard a mother speak like that to a stranger about the beauty of her own child!"

Her words left me wondering: Is it not proper for a mother to voice delight in something so precious as this gift of gifts from the Creator—a beautiful child?

And I wonder now, as I introduce to the world this new creation of my three books as a "TRILOGY," if I am forgiven because the words "It is beautiful!" again spring from my heart. These three books are also my children, born from my heart and from my brain. Once, long ago, they were thoughts living deep within me, beautiful dreams longing to be fulfilled. My first-born, PAPA'S WIFE, was to me truly a miracle . . . that words of romance and humor and happy family life could appear on paper through me. Surely the words were not mine. They were God's words coming through my brain. Like sunlight dancing on water the pages looked to me as I delighted in the wonder of feeling a book being born. "Read it!" I told my public. "You will love it . . . it is beautiful!"

A few years later my second brain child, PAPA'S DAUGHTER, came to take its place beside its sister, and I knew that much of the very best of me had gone into it. As I wrote it, I lived my own life over again. There were sun and shadow, joy and sorrow, all mixed together; and as it stepped out into the world, I felt I had grown a little in wisdom because I had given of myself to share with others, and I hoped the world would find in receiving the same joy as I found in giving.

The third book, MAMA'S WAY, is my baby! It is the youngest and the smallest and my heart dearly loves it. The first two were a gift from God to me. MAMA'S WAY is a gift from me to God.

It is my big "THANK YOU, GOD" for talent and dreams. I want the world to know my God as I know HIM. I want them to love HIM because HE is so wonderfully good to HIS earth-children. And I hope someone will know God a little better because MAMA's WAY was written.

Indeed, a great honor has been given me—my three books being made into one. It makes me feel very humble as I think this must be God's plan and somehow it seems that my heart has known it for quite a while. A few months ago a letter came to me from my brother, Dr. Nels Ferré. He had written:

Dear Sister,
Last night I had a dream and I want to share it with you. I dreamt I came into a bookstore and there it was . . . a great big book . . . your three books made into one volume, and I, your brother, just glowed in the glory of it.

Yes, in God's eternity it was already accomplished. May He richly bless those who read this book and share it with others. It is hard for me to express in words the feeling of joy this creation gives me. All I can say is that I am blessed and happy.

To the fine staff of The Christian Herald Family Bookshelf who conceived the idea of this threefold volume and to my own wonderful publisher, Rinehart & Company, Inc., I want to express my deep gratitude. My cup is so full it runneth over.

My warmest greetings to all!

Thyra Ferré Bjorn

Longmeadow, Massachusetts
February 14, 1960

Papa's Wife

THYRA FERRÉ BJORN

CHAPTER I

How Mama Got Papa

Papa was an old-fashioned preacher. He preached the word of God straight from the Bible, without regard for personalities or consequences. Perhaps his method was a bit severe, but when his congregation heard his sermons of hell and its forever burning fires, they shivered in their boots. If they needed to repent, it was done right there and then, after the service. The Church, to Papa, was the House of God. He expected reverence from the oldest to the youngest.

If Mrs. Nelson whispered to Mrs. Backlund about the price of her new hat, Papa would stop in dead silence. "When you ladies are through talking," he would announce in an even voice, clipping short each word, "I will continue."

You may be sure there was no more whispering that Sunday morning. But Mama was furious. "Do you have to say a thing like that right in the middle of Job's patience? If only you had a bit of it yourself, then you might be able to teach others!"

Papa insisted that what was right was right. He certainly would not tolerate a couple of gossipers in the house of the Lord who had placed him there to preach.

He brought up his children the same way, a stick in one hand and the Bible in the other. Still the eight of them sinned in any way they could, just to get even with him. Although Mama wanted her children to behave properly and walk in the ways of the Lord, she often helped them in harmless schemes, which was probably her way of revenge on Papa for making her wait so long to become Mrs. Pontus Franzon.

Mama and Papa both came from the old country. It was Mama's greatest triumph that, in spite of arguments and tears, Papa had finally consented to resign his pastorate in Lapland, a far northern province of Sweden, and cross the Atlantic Ocean to take on the ministry of a small church in New England where the Swedish language was spoken.

When the church secretary sent his letter to the Conference in Sweden, requesting Reverend Franzon to come to Berkley Hills, he did not know there were eight children in the family, most of them of school age. He had learned, through correspondence, only that Papa was a gentleman of fifty-nine years, and hadn't even thought to ask about his family. How could he have known that Papa was forty-three when he married Mama, who was only twenty-one, and that thereafter, about every year and a half, there arrived either a bouncing baby boy or a squealing little girl?

When Papa had his blue days, he could not quite forgive Mama for coming into his peaceful life and making him ten instead of one. But Mama was the one to get Papa to America and, until the day he left this earth, she tried to replant him in American soil. She never quite succeeded.

Papa had been a bachelor, not by choice, but because of a hopeless love for a lady who would not marry a minister, when Mama, at the age of sixteen, had come to work for him as a maid. To mend his broken heart, Papa had accepted, a few years earlier, the "call" to a small village in Lapland where the sun shone day and night during the short summer. Here Papa had found a new challenge in life.

For a man of his standing, Papa had one fault which, strangely, often ruled his better self. He dreamed of possessing a large bank account. This could be achieved only by hoarding even the smallest coin and adhering to the most rigid frugality.

So, despite Mama's exceptional qualities as a maid, Papa made it very clear that the prestige of working in a parsonage would have to make up for the very small salary which she would receive.

But Papa compensated for his "sin" by being a very handsome man, with a tongue from which eloquence flowed as rushing waters. Many a maiden's heart caught fire during his preaching. Mama's burned from the start. She felt a definite calling to become a minister's wife. How, she did not know, but her mind was made up. And when Mama made up her mind, neither heaven nor earth could stop her.

Papa did not know her determination, so he hired her, gave her a small sum of money to do the buying for the household, and at once laid down the rules. He warned her to be careful with the draft in the wood stove. He allowed absolutely no waste in any form. Mama must also keep her place. If she didn't mind, Papa suggested, she was to walk on the sidewalk across the street from him. It just did not look right for a man in his position to walk on the same sidewalk as the maid.

Mama obeyed all his rules and suggestions, but she did not forget her determination. She kept Pastor Franzon's house as well and as proudly as though it were, indeed, already her own. It was a fine house, five spacious rooms, all expensively furnished in spite of Papa's interest in a large bank account. Perhaps Papa reasoned then, as he did throughout his life, that the best was the cheapest in the long run.

Salen, which was only for company, Sundays and Christmas Eve, was a magnificent room. Here were the handsome organ which Papa loved to play after a day of work in the Lord's vineyard, and the huge upholstered gray-and-rose divan with its heavy silken tassels on each arm. In the center of the room stood a large round dining table above which hung the great crystal chandelier. On the serving table against the wall, the silver coffee service and two large candlesticks, polished to mirror brightness, stood in perfect order on a large silver tray; above it hung

the gold-framed picture of the King and Queen. On the opposite wall, over the organ, hung a magnificent painting of Jesus
before Pontius Pilate, a sober reminder of the sins of man.

Mama ventured into the study only in the interest of
cleanliness. This was Papa's private domain. Here he would sit
for hours in the high-backed upholstered chair behind the huge
carved mahogany desk, pondering his sermons. Mama's task was
to keep the desk shining and to see that the white-tiled fireplace was clean and its brass doors polished. A rich red hand-
woven carpet covered the floor. Altogether there was an air of
dignity and restful quiet in the room.

Although Papa was single when he furnished his house, he
had given particular attention to his bedroom. It was an enormous room. It had to be to accommodate the massive furniture.
There was a double bed with elaborately carved mahogany head-
and footboards. The night table, also mahogany, held an ornate
kerosene lamp, candle and matches. The washstand was very special, with a marble top on which stood the porcelain basin and
pitcher, both decorated with large red roses. Underneath were
two doors, one for the porcelain pail and the other for Papa's
porcelain chamber.

Across the room were two massive dressers, heavily carved
in the same design as the headboard. Above the dressers were
two ornate mirrors reflecting the paintings on the opposite wall
—*Jesus Blessing the Children* and *Jacob's Dream*. Near the window, overlooking the hills, was an overstuffed chair which in an
emergency could be made into an extra bed.

But the kitchen was Mama's special pride and joy. It was a
pleasant room with a wide window overlooking the valley. Geraniums bloomed on the window sill the year round. Papa had seen
to it that his house, unlike most homes in Lapland, had running
water, although this luxury extended only to the kitchen. The
rest of the plumbing was outside. All kitchens in Sweden at that
time had a large wooden sofa, and here, for the two years she
acted as maid, Mama slept. It was not an ordinary sofa. The top

part was loose and could be lifted off at night and the sofa made
into a double bed. During the day the bedclothes were stored in
the sofa-bottom. In front of the sofa were a table and two
chairs. A maid did not eat with her master any more than she
walked on the same side of the street with him.

Saturday was Mama's busy day, for no work was permitted
in the parsonage on Sunday. When the baking was finished, Mama
scoured and polished and cleaned. And there was plenty to polish.
The reservoir attached to the huge wood stove was of copper,
and this had to be shined to gleaming gold every Saturday.
Above the stove was the *kåpa* which held the copper pans and
covers. The big copper coffeepot always stood on the back of the
stove, ready for chance or expected guests. Even the woodbox
had a copper cover. Mama had little time on Saturdays to think
about her ambitions.

By the end of the second year, Mama had done such a good
job of keeping Papa's house that she graduated to the position
of housekeeper. Now she did not sleep in the kitchen in the big
sofa, but in the *vardags*-room, a kind of den furnished with all
the odds and ends of furniture. And now, too, she was allowed the
great honor of walking on the same sidewalk as her master.

"I am making headway," Mama assured herself. "But this is
only the beginning. Someday I shall wear *two* rings on my finger and sleep in the same bed as the Reverend Pontus Franzon."

But two more years passed and Mama was still housekeeper.

Then one summerlike spring day, Mama was sure the
moment had arrived. She was called into Papa's study for a special talk.

"Maria," he said, "you are the best housekeeper the Lord
has ever made. I am humbly thankful that He gave you to me.
The years we have lived under the same roof have been good
years. I have come to a very important decision."

He stopped for a moment. Mama's heart was beating like a
bell clapper.

"Maria," Papa said with deep emotion in his voice, "I have

decided that I shall never marry and you can stay on as my house-keeper for the rest of my life."

"Thank you, Pastor Franzon," Mama finally managed, tears choking her, "thank you very much, I shall think it over." She left the study so fast that her shoes hardly touched the floor.

In her own room, between sobs, Mama faced facts. The first half of the game was played and she had not made a gain. Would Papa always remain a bachelor? Well, she had no intention of being a housekeeper the rest of her life. More than anything Mama wanted children, a whole houseful of them. In fact, she had already named most of them. All their names were picked to go with Franzon. Papa just couldn't do this to her. Mama dried her tears and started dreaming again.

She imagined herself Mrs. Maria Franzon, opening the door to the parsonage, letting people in. The caller would not turn up her nose and say, "Please tell the Reverend I am here. My appointment was for two o'clock."

No indeed! Instead, the visitor would curtsy and say, "My dear Mrs. Franzon, I am so glad to see you." Mama would call out, "Pontus dear. Mrs. So-and-So is here to see you." She might even cook coffee and serve them company cookies.

Oh, no, Mama was not licked—yet.

A plan started to take shape in Mama's mind, a web, but she must weave it very, very carefully. Men were dumb when it came to their *own* hearts. Papa might love her and never even know it himself. Somehow she must kindle the flame to life, if it existed, and she was now sure it did.

How Mama would have played her cards if she had not met Mrs. Johansson, no one knows. But she did meet her—at a church auction—and they became friends. Mrs. Johansson had a terrific problem to solve. She was planning to leave for the United States, late in the summer, to join her husband, who had gone before and secured a job as a plumber in Joliet, Illinois. Mrs. Johansson was looking for a young lady, preferably one with

America fever, to assist her and her five children across the ocean. This was the opportunity Mama had been waiting for. A weapon with which to shock Papa.

Mrs. Johansson left the church with Mama's promise that she was the young lady she was looking for. But in her heart, Mama expected the very next day to tell her she had changed her mind. She planned to spring the news on Papa at the breakfast the following morning. The scene was set in her imagination, and she was sure her news would hit like a snowslide. Papa would gather her up in his strong arms and beg her to stay, as his wife, forever.

So Mama laid her plans very carefully. If the way to a man's heart is through his stomach, she would prepare the most elegant breakfast. Yes, it must be Papa's favorite—fried herring and potatoes in their jackets. And the coffee—why she would even use the high-priced company coffee and put a few extra beans in the grinder. She was singing as she set the table with special care, using gleaming white linen and a bouquet of wild flowers which she had picked in the woods behind the parsonage earlier that morning.

When Papa entered the dining room, the air was filled with cheerfulness, Mama smiled demurely. Papa returned the smile. It was a happy morning, and the breakfast progressed pleasantly without comment as Mama waited for the right moment. She chose the time when Papa was buttering his third slice of *limpa* and had just swallowed the tail end of a crisp, brown herring.

"Pastor Franzon," said Mama softly, "I have important news for you this morning."

"It must be glad news, you look so happy."

"It is. I had the most amazing offer to go to America." And Mama painted Mrs. Johansson's offer in vivid colors, expecting the big moment to arrive.

But Papa was very calm about it. America was a wonderful

country, he agreed. Mama was young and had her life ahead of her. If this was what she wanted, he could only wish her God-speed—and look for another housekeeper.

Six weeks later Mama was on the Atlantic Ocean. She had almost given up the idea of becoming a minister's wife. The anticipation of the golden land in the West was gradually replacing her intense desire for Papa. Mama entered the United States of America as an immigrant.

In spite of the thrill of standing on American soil, Mama was lonely. She had never before seen people bustle about so. She felt very small and insignificant as she stood by a large trunk surrounded by the five children, while Mrs. Johansson went through customs. A rather overstuffed lady, gaily dressed, spoke to Mama in a strange tongue, pointing to the children. Mama smiled helplessly and the lady went on without receiving an answer. The tears were on the verge of breaking through, but Mama held them back. So this was New York with its skyscrapers and swift traffic. And here she was because of Papa. Her heart ached as she pictured in her mind the peaceful parsonage in faraway Sweden. She wondered if Papa was missing her—or at least her cooking. What a fool he had been to let her go! Even thinking about it made her furious. By the time Mrs. Johansson returned, Mama had banished even the thought of tears. Mrs. Johansson thanked her profusely.

"Here is where we part, my dear. You certainly have been an angel to me on that boat. My husband ought to be here any moment now and after that we will get along fine."

She explained to Mama about the Swedish-American Employment Agency and there was where she left her. Mama found herself with a dozen other "greenhorns," waiting for a fairy godmother to touch them with her magic wand and make them millionaires overnight.

Mama could speak only nine words of English; however, by mixing, pouring and stirring certain ingredients, she could create the most tempting dishes. Soon her aching heart found solace among pots, pans, and mixing bowls in an enormous kitchen on Fifth Avenue. She was now second cook for an old American family related to the Vanderbilts.

But the biggest part of her heart was still across the Atlantic in a red-and-white parsonage, and she was forever wondering about Reverend Franzon's new housekeeper. Would she try to become Mrs. Franzon, too?

After a week, Mama sat down and wrote a very formal letter to Papa, informing him that she had landed safely at her destination. She marked her address very plainly. Then she waited.

Months passed and at last there came a letter from Papa. Mama put it unopened in her apron pocket, impatiently waiting for the afternoon, when she could sit down in the wicker chair in the servants' dining room, to read it.

My dear Maria,

The fall here in Sweden has been very rainy, in fact there have been only two days of sunshine this month.

The fruit soup you cooked before you left was very good. I ate it every day for two weeks.

My health is not too good due to the fact that my housekeeper keeps the house too warm, with the result I catch cold when I go out in the cool air. It also makes a very visible hole in the woodpile.

Her cooking is not satisfactory and she is very careless with the dishes. The blue coffee cups are either without ears or nicked.

The church is progressing. Last Sunday I took in three new members, including Olga Ström, my new housekeeper.

If you would consider coming back to work for me, my offer of long ago is still good.

May God bless you!
Pontus Franzon

"I hope she breaks all his dishes!" stormed Mama through her tears. "I hope she finishes his woodpile in a month. I hope she burns all of his food and cooks it so badly he gets indigestion. His offer is still good! Well not that offer. . . . *Never*."

But Mama answered his letter promptly.

Dear Pastor Franzon,

I am sorry it is raining in Sweden all the time. Here in America the sun is shining every day. It is a wonderful country and I plan to stay here.

If I should ever decide to come back to work for you, it will never be as your housekeeper. If you have a better offer to give me, let me know.

I am feeling fine.

God bless you, too!
Maria

There now! She had told him. He could think whatever he wanted. With over three thousand miles between them, she just didn't care.

Mama did not receive any more letters from Papa. She mended her broken heart, learned some English, bought many new clothes, and almost gave up marrying Papa. A year passed.

Then one beautiful summer day in June, on her afternoon off, the second cook, Maria, took a stroll in Central Park. The sun was shining brightly on her new parasol. She felt quite like a lady, with money in her pocketbook, wearing a new white eyelet dress that reached to her ankles, but did not hide the new white leather shoes.

She tripped along gaily, aware of admiring glances. Then suddenly she stopped. There on the park bench, in a gray linen suit, sat a man so like the Reverend Franzon that Mama's heart jumped into her throat, and she stared. Then the man arose from the bench and came toward her.

"Maria!" cried Papa, extending both hands. Mama took one outstretched hand and shook it hard. Finally she found her voice.

"Pastor Franzon," she stammered. "Whatever are you doing in New York?"

"I have my vacation month," said Papa. "Crossing the ocean and seeing New York is not a bad way of spending it. I had planned to look you up tonight, but this saves me the trouble."

Fortunately Mama had the evening off. They went to a little restaurant, called "Just Like Home," for a supper of Swedish meat balls and a talk. Mama expected any moment to hear what she had been waiting five years to hear, and Papa was very talkative, but not in the way Mama hoped for.

"The ocean trip was most invigorating, Maria," he said looking past her. "The salt air certainly is a tonic for your lungs."

Well, Mama was just not too interested in Papa's lungs at that moment.

"How is everything at home in Lapland?" Mama looked dreamily out the window.

"Everything was fine." Papa stopped eating and stroked his forehead. "You know," he said, "just being in America makes you appreciate Sweden. Everything is so peaceful over there and people don't run around like mad. I am not at all in sympathy with all this rushing to and fro. What in the world is their hurry?"

Oh, heavens! He is almost in a preaching mood now, thought Mama, but out loud she said, "It's in their blood, I guess. After a while you start running yourself and it is sort of fun after you get used to it."

"I am sure that I would not enjoy it," snapped Papa.

Mama was sure that he wouldn't either.

Papa talked about Lapland, the church, the people and finally ended up with the parsonage. He will tell me any time now, thought Mama. To her disappointment, Papa only reminded her of his offer made that spring day long ago.

"You shall always have a home with me. Maria, please come

back," he pleaded. "My stomach is all upset from bad cooking, my furniture is scratched. I gave my housekeeper a permanent vacation. Things have not been right since you left."

Mama's heart sang. If that was not love, what was? She became bold.

"Pastor Franzon," she said, without pretending, "the only way I will go back with you to the old country, is as your Mrs."

Papa gasped. "But I don't want to marry you or anyone else. I need to be free! Furthermore, you are young, there might be children. They would disturb me when I prepared my sermons."

"Poppycock," answered Mama more boldly. "Don't you think I could keep half a dozen children quiet while you are studying?"

"Half a dozen?" Papa was astonished. "Would there be that many?"

"Who knows?" Mama looked mysterious. "I will give you until tomorrow to think it over."

She really had not meant to propose, but everything is fair in love and war. Besides, the poor man did not know what was best for him.

In spite of her triumph so far, Mama was worried. She knew that Papa was a man of principles and that when his mind was made up it did not change very quickly.

But the next morning Papa said "yes" to Mama and arranged for the ceremony to be held the following Thursday.

Mama was dancing on clouds. Now she could put her hand on his arm and call him Pontus! He had not kissed her yet, but she was on her way to becoming a minister's wife.

But on Thursday Papa was ill. The strain had been too much for him. Poor Mama had to wait another day. Even then Papa looked pale and dejected when he appeared before the preacher with Mama beside him.

"Pontus August Franzon, do you take this woman to be your lawful, wedded wife?"

Beads of perspiration formed on Papa's forehead.

"No," he said, "I had better not, I am not sure, I only wanted her as my housekeeper."

Mama's brave heart trembled.

"Pontus," she whispered without looking at Papa, "I am warning you. I at least expected you to be a man of your word!"

The preacher refused to marry them.

"Marriage is a holy and solemn sacrament. It should never be entered into lightly." With a side glance at Papa, he said, "A minister ought to know that. I feel obliged to ask you to wait until you are both sure."

Once outside the preacher's house, Mama looked at Papa for a long while, and then, instead of crying as she wanted to do, she spoke her contempt with dignity.

"I thought of you as a new, beautiful top hat. But you are not. All you are is an old worn-down slipper! I think it is better for both of us if you don't ever see me again."

Mama turned quickly on her heel and walked down the street as proudly as any minister's wife could have done.

Papa stared after her. This was a Maria he had never seen. Her eyes had been like two glowing coals plucked from the fire. She had been furious and still had spoken with dignity. Never had she been more beautiful and desirable. His feet did not move, but his cold, hardened bachelor's heart broke its shell and tumbled down the street after Mama.

"Strange," he spoke out loud, "I love Maria, and I think she is a most wonderful woman. Now I must not let her slip through my fingers."

The next morning Papa telephoned Mama.

"Maria," he said in the same voice in which he would deliver a sermon, "I discovered something yesterday afternoon."

"You did?" said Mama, in no mood for guessing games. "Well wasn't that clever of you! I told you, Pastor Franzon, not to bother me any more."

But Papa continued as though he had not heard a word Mama said.

"You have the bluest eyes I have ever seen, Maria, and I'm in love with you."

Mama could only gasp. Pastor Franzon was not given to flowery compliments.

Papa's voice became weak and humble. "Maria," he said tenderly, "will you kindly inform me if you are in love with me too?"

This was too much for Mama. What could she do but give Papa an honest answer?

"You are the strangest and most conceited man I have ever known, and for the life of me I can't figure it out. But I do love you, Pontus Franzon, although I'm not sure if I want to marry you after yesterday."

"Now," said Papa, "don't let us waste time. We must be married as soon as it can be arranged."

That afternoon at two o'clock, Mama became Mrs. Pontus Franzon.

Her heart was filled to the brim with happiness. The only drawback was that she must leave her new-found country with all its glorious opportunities for a cook like Maria.

We will be back, she promised herself, Pontus, myself and all the little Franzons-to-be.

It took sixteen years for Mama to make up Papa's mind for him. In that space of time, eight of her dreams had come true.

CHAPTER 2

~Papa Makes a Resolution

If Mama had grieved over the lost opportunities for a good cook in America, she soon had other things to fill her mind. Being a pastor's wife presented very different duties from those of a maid of all work. She still kept the parsonage (her own home now as she had dreamed it would be) in perfect order and was just as vigilant about waste or unnecessary expense. But she slept in the big double bed upstairs, occasionally accompanied her husband on sick calls, and on Sundays walked arm in arm with him to church. On Thursdays she received any of the ladies of the church who wished to call, serving coffee and fresh-baked pastries in *salen*. This was always an especially happy time for Mama, for she loved company.

But by the end of the first year as Mrs. Pontus Franzon, Mama knew one thing had not changed: a pastor's duty to his church always came first. She discovered this, with disturbing emphasis, one spring morning when Papa announced that he would attend the Church Conference in Stockholm. This in itself was not surprising. It was an annual event. What disturbed her was that she was expecting the first of her "dreams" almost any day, and Pontus didn't seem to regard that as of first importance.

A tear rolled down Mama's cheek as she closed Papa's suitcase. She had hoped against hope that even in this last minute he would change his mind.

"Pontus," she said once more, "please don't go to Stock-

holm to the conference. I know how important it seems to you
for the good of the church. But this is our *very first* baby. What
if it should come in the middle of the night? Who would get
the midwife for me?"

Papa seemed so distressed Mama took a bit of hope. He
placed his hand under her chin, lifting it up, and looked into her
pleading blue eyes.

"Maria," he said tenderly, "do you suppose a soldier in war
can go home because his wife is having a baby?"

Mama shook her head, her throat too full of tears to speak.

"God's work is even more important," Papa continued now
in his ministerial voice. "You knew before our marriage that I
could never let home life interfere with my duty as a pastor. Believe me, Maria, I wish with all my heart this conference were
not at this time and so far away. But I hope you will go your full
time, then I'll be sure to be back. Now let's consider the matter
closed and let me go in peace."

Mama choked back her tears as she opened the suitcase again
and packed four more handkerchiefs. It would do no harm to put
them in. Sometimes things *did* happen at childbirth. It might
serve Papa right if—if—no, it was a wicked thought. Nothing
must happen to the baby or to her. They'd just have to get
along without Papa.

"All right, Pontus," Mama agreed, tossing her head in-
dependently, "go along! If our baby should arrive before you
come back, I'll just have to sort of excuse your absence. 'Don't
worry, little one,' I'll say, 'you *have* a father and when he is
through with his *duty* he'll gladly be back to look at you.'"

Papa smiled bleakly. "Don't be ridiculous, Maria. I shall ask
Tant Renberg to stay with you while I am gone."

Mama's head went up again. "No, thank you, Pontus *lilla*.
I just can't stand the way her false teeth rattle when she talks.
And besides, her hands are rough. What would our baby think
having Tant Renberg's rough hands touch its soft skin?"

"Maria!" Papa was losing patience. "Babies don't think or

form opinions. Really, sometimes I wonder if I married a *child*."

Mama laughed, but the next minute she was crying again. "Don't mind me, Pontus. Women are queer at a time like this. After all, I still have two more weeks to go, and you'll be back before that."

But when Papa kissed her good-bye at the door, she clung to him, trying hard to keep from crying. He released himself tenderly. "I'll be back as soon as I can, Maria."

Mama watched him until he disappeared around the bend of the road, then she let her tears flow freely. But even as she wept, she knew Pontus was right. She was being ridiculous about the whole thing. Women all over the world had babies. Some of them had no assistance whatsoever. She must stop acting like a child.

She dried her tears, suddenly aware of the heavy silence. How empty the parsonage seemed without Papa. This was the first time he had left her in the ten whole months of their married life. It scarcely seemed possible ten months had passed since that morning in late July when they had boarded the Swedish-American liner in New York to return to Sweden and Papa's pastorate in Lapland. What a wonderful honeymoon it had been even if they had had to occupy quarters at opposite ends of the boat. For by the time Papa had made up his mind to marry her, there simply was no space left on the boat except an upper berth in a cabin occupied by a schoolmistress returning to Stockholm. It hadn't been easy to say goodnight at the door of her cabin to a brand-new husband, and, though he tried not to show it, Mama knew it wasn't easy for Pontus either. So they would meet for breakfast in almost the same manner they had in Lapland when she had been only his housekeeper. And sometimes Mama wasn't sure that Papa remembered she was now his wife. But she was so gloriously happy she didn't mind his absentmindedness.

I'll make him the best wife in the whole world, she promised herself. Pontus will never, never regret that he married me.

Only one thing had disturbed her. Papa disliked emotion.

Even his good-night kisses were reserved, and Mama was sure if she hadn't put her arms around his neck and kissed him, he would have just tipped his hat to her and gone to his own cabin.

Never mind, she had consoled herself, watching him disappear into the shadows at the other end of the passageway, Pontus will get used to love.

And when, the next day, her arm linked in his, they walked miles around the deck, the salty spray and the wind in their faces, Mama was convinced his education had already begun and that he was as happy as she herself.

"Isn't this wonderful, Pontus?" she had cried, shouting to make herself heard above the wind.

Papa had holloed back, clasping her arm a little tighter. "It's like climbing Gellivara mountain in the wintertime."

Later, when they sat in their deck chairs, away from the wind, Papa had spoken of their homecoming. "It is going to be a shock to all the church people, Maria," he said, looking wistfully out over the white-capped waves, glistening in the sunlight. "No one had an inkling that I crossed the ocean to get married. In fact, Maria, I have to admit it is still a surprise to me."

Mama laughed gaily. But Papa continued soberly, "It will be awkward for me to tell them. They might even belittle you, Maria. You know marriage between a pastor and his housekeeper does not often take place in proud Sweden."

For a moment Mama's spirit sank. What Papa said was true, of course. A man of Papa's standing in the community did not marry a mere maid. And that is what she had been, even though he was kind enough to call her a housekeeper. But she also knew that she loved him more than anything else in the whole world, and was going to be the very best wife any man ever had. She would *make* the church people like her. She had to! But would that be enough? Her great love for Pontus must never bring him sorrow or humiliation.

A young couple swung by, laughing happily. Mama looked

after them until they were out of sight. Then, "Pontus," she said softly, "how do *you* feel about it?"

He had taken both her hands in his with more emotion than he had ever shown before. "I love you, Maria," he said gently.

"Then we will tackle them together, Pontus. And if they don't like it, we'll just go back to America!"

Papa had not seemed as sure they were equal to the battle alone. "We'll leave it in God's hands, Maria," he said.

But Mama had known he was more worried than he admitted; and, in a strange way which was difficult for her to understand, he was a little ashamed. A man of forty-three, and a pastor, just didn't run off and marry his former maid who was only twenty-one. Mama was quite aware that wasn't an easy situation to face, but, as for herself, she could face anyone with Pontus beside her.

They had arrived in Lapland on a Saturday night about eleven o'clock. In the saffron twilight of the never-setting sun, a gentle peacefulness lingered over the western mountains and the low houses with their well-kept gardens. Mama was thankful that the road which lead to the parsonage was deserted. It would be better for Pontus to feel the good earth of his own garden beneath his feet before he had to face the townspeople.

At the door of the parsonage, Papa stopped. "Oh, it is good to be home, Maria," he exclaimed fervently. "Is there a place in the world as beautiful as Lapland?"

"I think America is very beautiful, too," Mama said simply.

"But it is dark there in the summer," argued Papa. "Imagine, lamplight in the summertime. Why here in Sweden we can pack our lamps away until fall."

"You are forgetting the awful long winters, Pontus, with only a few hours of daylight. In America it is more evenly divided."

Papa had looked at her for a long time. "You do love America, don't you, Maria?" he said, a note of disappointment in his voice. Then as if to impress upon her that this was *really* her home, he had taken her hand in his. "Come, let us kneel in prayer right here on our doorstep before we enter our home."

Mama had knelt with him in silent prayer. She would never know what Papa had prayed for that day, but it must have been, like her own prayer, for their happiness together. For when they rose from their knees and hand in hand stepped over the high threshold, the sun broke from behind a cloud, bathing the parsonage in a stream of rosy light like a heavenly benediction.

When Mama opened her eyes early the next morning, bright sunshine flooded the bedroom. It took her a moment to remember she was back in Sweden, in the parsonage. She rubbed her eyes and looked over at Pontus sleeping heavily beside her. The quilt, rising and falling gently with his breathing, covered half his face. Mama peeked at the clock. There was still half an hour before she had to get up and start the coffee. She settled back for a few more winks. Suddenly she remembered. Why, this was *Sunday* morning and she was a married woman now! Mama almost chuckled aloud. Would Pontus remember, too, that a husband was supposed to bring his *wife* coffee on Sunday morning? For years as a housekeeper she had brought Pontus coffee *every* morning. On weekdays she had used the brightly painted wooden tray; but on Sundays she had carried the silver tray with a very special coffeepot and Papa's favorite *vienerbröd*. She would knock softly at his door, then wait for his sleepy voice to answer before she entered.

Now she glanced over at him again, sleeping so soundly. What if he didn't wake up in time to bring *her* coffee? Well—she better make sure that he did. Cautiously she touched his leg with her toe. Papa slept on. She "touched" a little harder. This time he stirred and threw back the quilt from his face.

"Pontus," she whispered softly. "It's morning—our *first* morning in the parsonage."

"So it is—so it is." Pontus stretched luxuriously. "And our first *coffee*, too. It will taste good, Maria."

Mama's heart sank. He *had* forgotten. But there was still time if only she could think what to say.

"It's Sunday, Pontus," she ventured.

"Well?"

Mama settled back against her pillow and closed her eyes pretending to be sleepy. "Don't you remember what husbands do on Sunday, Pontus *lilla?*"

Papa sat up suddenly and stared at her without speaking.

"This is *my* day, Pontus," Mama murmured sleepily. "You are to bring *me* coffee this morning."

Papa pushed back the quilt reluctantly and threw his legs over the side of the bed. "Of course, Maria, I never thought of it," he said, and started for the kitchen.

Mama smiled as she watched him. He looked so funny in that nightshirt, with his carpet slippers flapping. But she loved him so much. She was glad she had made everything ready in the kitchen the night before. The *tyre-wood* lay beside the stove, along with the exact amount of regular wood needed to make the coffee boil. (Pontus had always been very particular about how much wood she used; and only enough *tyre-wood* to make sure the regular wood caught fire quickly.) She had filled the coffeepot last night, too, and measured out the right amount of coffee. Even the tray had been prepared—the big silver one, for she had completely forgotten that *she* was the one who would be honored.

Mama snuggled into her pillow and waited. Presently Papa pushed open the bedroom door. The coffee smelled so good. Maria sat up brushing back her hair from her face. "You are a real husband, now, Pontus," she cried.

Silently Papa placed the tray on her lap and sat down beside her. Maria poured out two steaming cups.

"Maria," Papa said after several moments, "I've been thinking it would be best for us to go to church separately this morning."

Mama almost dropped the cup and saucer.

"I don't want them to think I have come to church with a strange woman," Papa hastened to add with a smile. "No one would know you in those stylish clothes!"

Mama smiled back, but some of the Sunday morning joy went out of her. Hadn't she dreamed for a long time of walking to church arm in arm with Papa? But when she saw how concerned he was over the situation, she tried to hide her own disappointment.

"You just come early, Maria," Papa directed, "and sit down as a stranger. I will break the news in my sermon."

The little church was filled to the doors to welcome back Pastor Franzon from his vacation. Maria had arrived early, as Papa had requested, and sat quietly as the church people filed into the pews. When Papa rose to preach, she prayed that he would be given the right words.

"My text this morning," began Papa solemnly, "is from the thirteenth chapter of First Corinthians and from the fifth verse: *Love seeketh not her own.*"

Mama's heart almost stopped. Was this Papa's way of telling her before his congregation that she shouldn't have proposed to him and that he was sorry he married her? She did not hear much of the sermon. Her heart was too full of sorrow for herself—and Papa's eloquence. Finally when the sermon was finished, Papa had not said the usual "Amen." He had paused significantly, looking out over the congregation, and smiled.

"Today I have a confession to make," he said slowly, and Maria held her breath. "I have preached a sermon against love seeking its own, yet I myself am guilty of that sin."

A rustle of surprise passed through the congregation. Questioning glances were exchanged.

"In our midst here today sits a beautiful young lady," Papa continued, a little twinkle in his eyes. "I guess you have thought her a tourist from America. Well, her lovely clothes are American, but her *heart* is Lapland. She is an old friend to all of you. Let me present the woman I love and had to go three thousand miles to tell her so—Mrs. Maria Franzon."

Mama's heart had almost burst with pride and happiness. The church people were all looking at her and smiling. Mama stood up and smiled back with her warmest, sunniest smile—and all the congregation stood up too. They couldn't cheer or applaud in God's house, but Maria knew this meant the same welcome. Deacon Lund had spoken then for all of them.

"Our warmest congratulations and God's blessing over our pastor and his bride."

Mama had taken her place beside Papa after the service and received the handshakes and curtseys as the church people filed out. At last her dream had come true. She was Mrs. Franzon for all the town to see. God had been very good to her.

As they walked back to the parsonage, arm in arm, Papa had said, "They all love you, Maria. We must be grateful for the spirit in which they received you." But there was a note of relief in his voice.

Mama had smiled up at him. "That's because God made us for each other," she said softly.

Life in the parsonage as Mrs. Franzon was even more wonderful than Mama had dreamed. Oh, there were times—when Papa had things on his mind perhaps—that he forgot she was no longer the housekeeper and started ordering her around. Then Mama had only to look at him and smile, and he melted like butter in the sunshine.

It was the week before *Lucia Day* that Mama was finally ready to tell Papa about the baby. She had wanted to tell him immediately she knew about it herself, but a miracle as wonderful as this had to be told in a special way. And what day could be more appropriate to break the news than the day all Sweden honored—"*Santa Lucia*," the Queen of Light? She had always thought it the loveliest celebration of all, and this year the parsonage could have its own *Lucia* in the old tradition.

Mama was up before daybreak on December thirteenth. By the time Papa should be awakened, she had everything ready. She chose the prettiest cloth for the coffee tray, and on a special plate arranged the fat *Lucia cats* which she had baked secretly the day before. The crusts were nicely browned in butter, cinnamon and sugar, and the raisin eyes looked almost alive. "They are so real I could just hug them," Mama laughed to herself.

On the table beside the tray was the crown bearing its thirteen tall burning candles. Just as the first light of dawn broke over the horizon, Mama fastened the crown over her golden hair and marched ceremoniously to Papa's bedroom. Gently she pushed open the door and started to sing the funny little song which she had made up for the occasion:

> "Awake, awake my sleepyhead
> So I might know you are not dead
> I'll bring some coffee to your bed
> My darling, lazy sleepyhead!
>
> As a beautiful Lucia I come to you
> To whisper a secret so very new
> A sweet little angel with eyes so blue
> Shall soon come to live with me and you!"

Papa stirred in his sleep and turned over. Mama put the tray on the little table and knelt beside the bed, singing the song again, close to Papa's ear. He sat up then rubbing his sleepy eyes.

"Pontus *lilla*," laughed Mama, her eyes shining as brightly as the candles in her hair, "*it is Lucia*. Have you forgotten?"

Papa was wide awake now and saw the burning candles. "Maria," he cried, "how dare you put all those burning things in your hair? Remove them at once, *please!*"

Mama only laughed at his scolding. "Not until you have

heard my secret," she whispered. "I have told you already in my song and you never heard a word of it."

"Told me *what?*" asked Papa.

"Pontus, the most wonderful thing in the world has happened. *You* are going to be a *papa.*"

For a long breathless moment, Mama did not know whether Papa was pleased or not. Then silently he removed the burning candle-crown, and her head was against his shoulder and he was smoothing her golden hair.

With her own secret happiness, Maria fairly danced through the Christmas baking and preparations. She even refused to be disturbed that Papa seemed embarrassed about the baby and blushed each time she called him Papa. Well, she would just talk so much about the baby that Papa would *get over* his shyness before it arrived.

One evening a few weeks later, Mama decided it was time she talked to Papa about a name for the baby.

"I am sure it is going to be a boy, Pontus," Mama said, "so we got to think of a real special name for him."

Papa had looked up from the sermon he was preparing.

"I have been thinking, Maria, that Engelbrekt would be a grand name."

"Engelbrekt!" Mama gasped, then quickly controlled her disappointment. "Isn't it a rather long name for such a little fellow? What would he ever do with it?"

"He would try to live up to it," Papa answered proudly. "Engelbrekt was one of Sweden's greatest men. If it weren't for him, we might still be subjects under Denmark. Have you forgotten your history, Maria?"

Mama had not forgotten. "But that was way back in fourteen hundred and thirty-five." She smiled, hoping she could make him think of something else. "Pontus, I bet you never thought I would remember!"

Papa did not answer her directly, but she knew from the

softness of his voice that he was pleased she was so smart. "We can give him more than one name, Maria, can't we? You find one for him."

"I think he should have one name from the Bible. How about David? And then Pontus after you. One name for the Bible, one for Sweden and one for his father!"

"Engelbrekt David Pontus Franzon," Papa repeated slowly. "I think that will be very fine, Maria."

The winter had seemed longer than ever to Mama that year. On mild days she took brisk walks up the mountainside, breaking little narrow paths in the thick fleecy white carpet that seemed to cover the whole world. Spring was not far away she knew, for underneath the snow she could hear the low-voiced song of the mountain streams. And her heart would beat a little faster, for her baby would arrive in the springtime. Often she would talk aloud to her baby as though he were already born. "Little one," she would say, "your father is a very strange man. Sometimes it is very hard to understand him. But he loves us and we just have to love him a lot."

Maria wouldn't have admitted it to anyone, but deep in her heart there was a yearning. A wish that Pontus would be more romantic. Sometimes she felt she would just burst with this love she had to keep bottled up inside her. Love for Pontus, the baby that was soon to be theirs, and for the whole world. As spring drew nearer, a strange kind of restlessness possessed her. Soon young lovers would stroll the crooked little mountain paths. The budding new world would be filled with gay songs and happy glances, and love words whispered cheek to cheek. Sometimes Maria dreamed that Pontus was a young and ardent lover. "My dearest darling," he would say, "in all the world there is no one so beautiful. My love for you is like the skylark rising high above the earth in the cloudless sky." And then Pontus would take her in his arms and their lips would meet and he would hold her close, whispering sweet love words. Oh, it was wonderful! Then almost at once Maria would chide herself for this yearning. Wasn't Pontus the husband she wanted most in all the world? He was just timid about love. Hadn't she promised herself that day on the boat that she would love him so much he would get used to love? Anyway, how could Pontus know that at a time like this a woman needed more affection? She would have to go on making believe, and when the baby came Papa would love them both so much his heart would just run over with it. . . .

Suddenly the grandfather's clock in the hall chimed the hour. Maria came out of her dreaming with a start. My goodness! Here she sat like a *herskaps-fru* although there was work to be done. She hurried into the kitchen. Tant Renberg would be coming to look after Pontus when the baby was born, and Mama wanted to make sure there were plenty of rusks even if Tant Renberg didn't lift a finger. By midafternoon the baking board was piled high with cinnamon rusks. "I've enough to feed a whole army." Mama laughed as she packed them away in tins. "Pontus won't starve while I am in bed, that's sure."

From the ceiling, in a corner of the kitchen, hung the thin-bread on a wooden pole covered with a clean white baking sheet. Why, thought Maria, there would be almost enough to last all winter! And there was a whole crockful of fruit soup. Mama smiled as she pictured Pontus relishing his favorite food. "This is a meal for a king," he would say as he broke a whole round cake of thin-bread into his plate.

When the kitchen was cleared up and the stove polished and shining, Mama went into the bedroom, where the many tiny new clothes were stacked on the bed. Tenderly she caressed the soft woolly sweaters, holding them against her cheek. The baby stirred within her. Suddenly she was uneasy. "What if God sends the baby before Pontus returns?" For a fleeting moment she was afraid; then almost at once her heart was so full of gratitude for this baby that God was giving to Pontus and her that she just couldn't worry about anything. By the time she blew out

the lamp that night, she felt safe and happy with all fears
banished.

In the darkness, Maria sat up with a start. How long had she
slept? Her forehead was wet with perspiration, though the room
was cold. Suddenly she grasped the sides of the bed with both
hands. She hadn't imagined pain could be so sharp—a strange kind
of pain that tore at her like frantic fingers. Dear God! It had
come—her time—her hour and she was all alone!

"Oh, Pontus," she cried into the darkness, "how could you
do this to me?"

And Mama buried her face in her pillow and sobbed with
pain and fear.

All afternoon on the train Papa had been restless. Too many
thoughts, crowding like swarming bees through his brain. Over
and over he tried to discipline himself. He was supposed to be
thinking of the speech for the conference, but he could not get
Maria out of his mind. Unseeingly he stared out the window,
oblivious to the majestic beauty of the rugged mountainside.
He could see only the pleading in Maria's eyes as she begged him
not to leave her and clung to him like a frightened child. She
had been heavy in his arms. And Papa smiled, thinking how each
day Mama looked more like a big round rubber ball! And how
dear she was. It was not the way she looked now that bothered
him; it was her melancholy mood. One moment she would be looking at him with those big eyes and they would be full of laughter;
then suddenly her arms would be around his neck and she would
be in tears. "Oh, Pontus," she would say, "Oh, Pontus." Just
that, over and over. No matter how hard he tried, he couldn't
understand her. A woman's ways seemed a bigger mystery every
day.

Papa stirred uneasily in his seat as the train rumbled through
the early night. He was sorry he had to leave Maria when her
time was so close. But this conference was very important. He

couldn't seem to make her understand that. Ministers of small churches could not run the risk of letting larger ones swallow them up. He had seen this happen too often. No, a pastor's duty was to look out for his parish; to be at each conference and see and hear what was going on. A small church's vote was as important as a large one's. Why couldn't Maria see that?

But even as he argued with himself, Papa could not get the picture of her off his mind. How warm and alive she was, and what a gift from God to have her sunny disposition in the parsonage. He recalled the morning she had told him of the baby. She had almost scared him to death with all those burning candles in her beautiful hair. Why, there should be a law banning such foolishness. Quickly he had taken the crown from her head, realizing how very precious she was to him. And then she was in his arms, her arms about his neck, and her golden head on his shoulder. "Darling," she had whispered, "I'm so happy I think I am going to die. And I *will* if you don't just about eat me up this minute."

Papa squirmed uncomfortably. He loved Mama with all his heart, but he just couldn't get used to the way she acted and talked sometimes. He had tried to express his feelings to her, but the words just wouldn't come out of his mouth. Years ago he had given up emotional things for the sake of his high calling. And now, when he wanted to tell her how much he loved her, he couldn't. But when she was in his arms, her lips soft and sweet upon his, Papa found that he was a fool and a weakling like other men.

That *Lucia-Day* had been one to remember. It had snowed all night, and the village looked like a toy town made of cotton. That afternoon he and Maria had taken a long walk and stopped to visit a Lapp family where a baby had recently arrived. Mama had taken the tiny bundle in her lap and cuddled and cooed with it until Papa was red-faced with embarrassment. Especially when she had asked him to hold it. When they reached home again that evening, they had celebrated with an extra special Lapland treat—a supper of *soursmelts* and *tatemilk* with thin-bread.

"What a crazy meal this is," Papa had joked, feeling care-free and lighthearted. "The fish tastes as good as it smells *bad*—the bread is thinner than the butter—and the milk is so elastic that when you try to eat it, it snaps right back into your plate!"

Mama had bubbled over with laughter. "Maybe we could roll it into a ball like yarn, Pontus. How could it ever get this long?"

"All I care about is how good it tastes," Papa had replied, his mouth full of fish. . . .

Presently Papa was aware that the train had stopped and new passengers were boarding. Filing into the seat opposite him was a family—a rather young man with five small children and a baby in his arms. The children were clean and well behaved as they shyly cuddled close to their father.

"Nice children," Papa remarked to start the conversation. "How old is the baby?"

"She'll be three weeks old tomorrow," the man said as he pulled the pink blanket around the small head.

Papa smiled friendlily. "Quite a job handling all those little ones alone, isn't it? Where is the mother?"

The young man swallowed hard a couple of times, before he tried to speak. Too late Papa realized how he had blundered.

"I'm so very sorry," he said kindly. "I should not have asked. Forgive me, please."

The young man lifted sorrow-filled eyes. "How could *you* know? She just isn't with us any more. Somehow we shall have to get along without her. We did all we could, the midwife and I, but something went wrong, and there was no doctor within miles."

Papa could feel the tears of sympathy moistening his eyes. "And now what will you do? You can't care for this little one alone."

"I am taking them to my wife's mother for a while. After

that I don't know." He sighed deeply as the baby stirred fretfully in his arms.

"May the good Lord send you strength," was all Papa could say. His heart was suddenly heavy with anxiety.

As the train clicked over the noisy rails, now it seemed to be whispering over and over, "Maria—Maria—Maria." And then he would hear her voice, "Pontus—Pontus—Pontus."

Suddenly he could stand it no longer. What a fool he had been to leave her. He would get off at the next station and go back as quickly as he could. Even then it would be hours before he could get home. He prayed to God it wouldn't be too late. Meantime he would send a telegram to Tant Renberg to go to Maria at once.

"How long will it take?" Mama asked, her voice weak from pain.

Tant Renberg's rough hand wiped the perspiration from her forehead, and Mama followed her glance over to the midwife, sitting in the big easy chair having a good nap. How *could* she sleep? Didn't she realize, thought Mama anxiously, that her baby was about to arrive?

"I had twelve," Tant Renberg was saying. "It was different with each one. But the first is the hardest. It might take hours."

Mama gave a long deep sigh. Hours of this pain—and no one seemed to care. Then instantly she regretted her thought. She was so grateful that Tant Renberg had come when she did. And so very, very happy Pontus had worried about her enough to send the telegram. If only he himself would come. But of course he couldn't. The conference was so important. She was acting like a coward, expecting him to turn back from his first duty. Then as the pain began again, Maria wondered which *was* his first duty—the Church or their first child? She glanced at the tiny clock by the bed, seeing it dimly through the pain that gripped her. Almost nine. The past hours had seemed like a million years. And Tant Renberg said it would be hours more.

Suddenly a sound reached her ears. No, it couldn't be! But it sounded so like Pontus's footsteps. He had a way of scraping his feet just before his hand touched the doorknob. Was she imagining things because of her pain? And then before she could even think the answer, Pontus was in the room tossing his coat on a chair. In another instant he was on his knees beside her bed and would have taken her hands in his had not Tant Renberg cried out a sharp command. "Keep your cold hands off her, Pastor Franzon! She has pain enough."

Never had Mama wanted so much to feel the coolness of his hand on her forehead and to throw her arms about his neck and tell him how happy she was that he had come back in time. What had happened to her voice? It seemed lost somewhere in the forest of her pain, and she was aware of the tears on her cheek.

Gently Pontus brushed them away. "Oh, Maria," he cried, "I never knew it would be like this. Never, never will I permit you to go through this again."

In spite of the pain, Maria smiled at his dear foolishness. How could she tell him that a baby—their own little baby—was worth all the pain she might have to suffer? Weakly she lifted her hand and placed it in his.

Then the midwife was bending over them. "Please," she ordered curtly, "you must go, Pastor Franzon. A man is just a nuisance at a time like this. What a woman has to suffer she will suffer. A husband can't help." Then as he rose from the bedside she added wryly, "But I am sure if he had to have just *one*, the population wouldn't multiply so fast."

Mama watched Papa moving slowly away from her, his head bowed in anxious prayer. "Don't mind her, *lilla* Pontus," she wanted to call after him. "All midwives are just old crosspatches!" But no sound came from her lips.

As the night deepened, the pain increased. Maria bit her lips to keep from crying out. For endless hours it seemed to her,

Pontus's footsteps had been going back and forth, back and forth, outside her door. She wanted to tell him to go to sleep—not to worry. God wouldn't let anything happen to her or their wonderful baby. Soon, soon they would have a son.

Now it was morning and Tant Renberg stood at one side of the bed with a little woolly bundle in her arms, Pontus at the other. When she opened her eyes, it was like seeing the sunlight pass across his face. Mama laughed in spite of her weakness. He had looked so forlorn and worried.

"Come to your Mama, precious," she murmured. "Welcome to the Franzons'! My goodness, I never dreamed you would be such a funny-looking little fellow. But I do believe you look just a *little* bit like your handsome father."

Papa leaned down and kissed Mama tenderly. Almost fearfully he touched the baby's tiny hand. "Thank you, Maria," he said softly, "thank you for giving me a son."

All the pain of yesterday was forgotten. Such happiness as she had never known welled up in her heart. "Oh, Pontus, isn't he wonderful! Just look at him. And to think he is *all* ours." Mama pulled back the blanket from his tiny head so that his father might have a better look at him.

"Maria," Papa exploded. "He has *red* hair!"

Mama laughed gaily. "So he has, Pontus."

"But—but," Papa stammered, "I—I don't like red hair."

Even Tant Renberg laughed this time. Mama snuggled her baby closer. "I'm afraid we shall have to take little Engelbrekt the way he is," Mama said. "And Pontus, I don't think it says in the history books, but it *could be* that the great Engelbrekt had red hair. Did you ever think of that?"

It was Papa's turn to laugh aloud. "You always have an answer, don't you, Maria? I guess you are right. We'll just take little Engelbrekt as he is. And very wonderful he is, too."

Mama caressed the soft head, smoothing down the few golden hairs. "I hope we haven't hurt your feelings, little one," she whispered, "but I better tell you this right from the beginning: Your *father* is *definitely* the head of this household."

Papa smiled proudly. Outside the window the bright May sun was shining. Spring had come to Lapland, the most beautiful, glorious spring that Lapland had ever seen.

CHAPTER 3

∾Papa Sees Red

For a week or two Papa was so busy receiving congratulations on his first-born that he forgot about his son's red hair. Gradually the baby became an accepted member of the family. But as the excitement subsided, Papa began to worry.

At first he endeavored, sternly, to push his worries aside. A minister who truly believed in God and His teachings, knew very well that superstitions were the work of the devil. He reasoned, however, that *customs* and *superstitions* were two entirely different matters. Of course he didn't believe that seeing the new moon for the first time through the trees was bad luck for the entire month; or that singing before breakfast was a sure sign of tragedy before the day was over. Such things were rank superstition and the work of the devil. But a son with red hair. . . !

Papa walked up and down the length of the study, his hands clasped behind him, his chin on his chest. He could always think better while walking, especially when he had a problem to solve. And this one was knotty indeed. There was some *reason* why his first-born son had red hair and he just had to find it. But the miles he had walked in the past hour or so had brought him no nearer the solution.

The furrow between Papa's brows deepened and he pulled thoughtfully at his mustache, trying once more to reason it all out. So far as he was concerned, no true-blooded Swede begat red-haired children. Why, as far back as he could trace the

Franzon line, there had never been *one* with red hair. His own
rolled back from his forehead like sun-ripened wheat rippling
in the wind, and Maria's hair was bright as a summer morning.
Yet here they were with a redheaded son. It was unthinkable.
Perhaps, he decided sorrowfully, this was God's way of punishing him for yielding to the desires of the flesh after so many years
of single devotion to his calling.

Presently Papa stopped as though a brake had been applied.
It was just possible! Why hadn't he thought of that before? But
how did it happen? Quickly he climbed the stairs to ask Maria
about it, and, as he climbed, some of the anxiety left him. Marriage, he reflected, had its problems, but Maria certainly made
up for most of them. And Engelbrekt *was* a wonderful son. If
only he didn't have red hair.

Sunshine lay in a golden mantle over the bedroom. Maria
sat in a high-backed rocking chair near the window, nursing little
Nim (as she had already nicknamed him), and singing as she
rocked. Papa paused in the doorway, caught by the picture they
made. Maria looked more like a child than ever with her hair
falling loosely over her shoulders, held back from her face by a
blue ribbon that seemed reflected in her shining eyes.

She stopped singing as Papa came into the room, and
smiled, holding little Nim closer to her breast. "Isn't he adorable,
Pontus?"

Papa gazed tenderly down at them. "He is growing fast,
Maria. Tomorrow he will be three weeks old and already he is a
little man."

"No wonder he grows so fast," Maria laughed. "He's always
hungry as a little bear. Why this morning I was sure he would
gobble me up."

When Papa said nothing, Mama glanced up. The deep frown
was still between his eyes. "Pontus, darling. Whatever is the
matter?" she cried.

Papa crossed to the opposite window and stood looking out
for a long moment before he spoke. Then, "Maria," he said

irrelevantly, "can you see Larson's old barn from this window? *I* can of course, but I'm taller than you."

Mama was puzzled. "Why, Pontus, I never even thought of Larson's old barn. It certainly is nothing to look at."

Papa began pacing the bedroom floor. "I just thought it could have been that," he finally said in a disappointed voice.

"Pontus," Maria said sharply, "will you please stop walking up and down and explain yourself? What has Larson's old barn to do with me, I'd like to know?"

Papa stopped abruptly and stared down at the baby. "Because, Maria, it is *red*, that's why—like our baby's hair!"

Mama laughed. "Oh, *lilla* Pontus, I thought you were serious."

"How can you laugh, Maria?" he asked tensely. "And how can I ever explain having a son with red hair?"

All the love of her heart was in Mama's voice as she said softly, "Darling, *please* don't fret so. You don't have to explain anything. Engelbrekt is a beautiful boy even if he does have red hair. And I just guess he is going to follow right in his father's footsteps and be a wonderful man."

Papa was a little ashamed, but not yet pacified. "But it is so ridiculous, Maria—so utterly ridiculous. How can we be sure all our children—*if* we have any more—won't have red hair too?"

"Of course we will have more children. And if they have red hair we'll love them just as much." Mama looked down at Nim sleeping quietly in her arms. "He is so wonderful I wouldn't care if he was twins. Pontus," Mama suddenly cried, **her blue** eyes wide, "*I bet I know.*"

"What, Maria? What?"

But Mama took her time. Gently she wrapped the **blanket** about the sleeping baby and placed him in the cradle, pulled the window shade and motioned Papa to follow her down the stairs. Only when they were seated on the parlor sofa would she speak.

"You know, Pontus," she began excitedly, "our church janitor has two boys with *flaming red hair*. But that is not all. You know that every Sunday morning those little boys sit on the front bench."

"Well?" asked Papa eagerly.

"Don't you see what I mean Pontus? Every Sunday while I was that way, I sat and *stared at those red heads* while you preached for a whole hour. No wonder our little Engelbrekt has red hair."

Papa gave a deep sigh of relief. "Maria," he said proudly, "you have found the answer." Then as a new thought struck him he cried, "But, Maria. What has happened to *you* can also happen to others. Why, in a very few years our church will just be filled with redheaded children."

"You are right, Pontus," Maria agreed in an awed whisper. "What can we do?"

Papa took a turn around the room, his head lowered thoughtfully. "I shall have a *talk* with that janitor, Maria, this very day."

It was midafternoon when Papa knocked at Lars Erickson's door. Lars himself answered the knock, delighted to see Papa.

"Welcome to our humble home, Pastor Franzon. Come in and be seated in the best room."

He ushered Papa in, talking briskly in his quaint manner. "Emma is out doing *Patron* Karlberg's washing today, so Pastorn have to kindly excuse the house. But I assure him coffee I am expert in cooking. I shall get the *coffee-petter* on right away."

Papa sat on the edge of the wooden sofa and stared for a moment at the two large pictures of King Oscar and Queen Sofia in imitation gold frames. In the center of the room stood a large table, covered with the lace cloth Maria had made them for Christmas. The small table near the window held the many flowering plants and the family Bible. It was a comfortable room and Papa relaxed a little. He could hear Lars poking about the stove, preparing the coffee.

Presently two small faces, topped by flaming red hair, peered around the doorframe. Timidly they came inside. For a moment the boys stared at Papa, then as if on signal marched to the sofa, shook hands and bowed almost to the floor.

"Good day, *Farbror Pastorn*," they said as one voice. And, as suddenly as they had come, disappeared toward the kitchen.

Papa smiled and shook his head in dismay. They certainly have red hair. No wonder it had been catching and poor Maria had been the innocent victim.

Lars came in with the *coffee-petter* and a plate of *pepparkakor*. They talked pleasantly of the repairs the church needed, until coffee had been drunk. Then Papa cleared his throat. "Erickson," he began tactfully, "I have come here today because I need your help."

Lars beamed. "This has not happened before, Pastorn—that you come to me for help. I am happy you ask."

Papa crossed the room and took up the family Bible, opening it expertly to the passage he had been thinking of this morning, then handed the open book to the janitor.

"Please read the thirtieth chapter of Genesis, starting with the thirtieth verse, to the end," he said kindly.

Lars Erickson read. When he had finished Papa asked, "What do you make of it, Erickson?"

The janitor scratched his head. "Good," he said. "Very good indeed, you have to give him credit. That Jacob was a smart one."

Papa took the Bible and settled himself on the sofa again. "You miss the point, Lars." And in his best Sunday-morning voice he read:

32. I will pass through all thy flock to day, removing from thence all the speckled and spotted cattle, and all the brown cattle among the goats: and of such shall be my hire.

37. And Jacob took him rods of green poplar, and of the hazel and chestnut tree; and pilled white strakes in them, and made the white appear which was in the rods.

38. And he set the rods which he had pilled before the
flocks in the gutters in the watering troughs when the flocks
came to drink, that they should conceive when they came to
drink.

39. And the flocks conceived before the rods, and brought
forth cattle ringstraked, speckled, and spotted.

Papa closed the Bible quietly and placed it back on the
table. "That all happened thousands of years ago, Lars. But it
could just as well be today. Basic principles never change."

Lars stared at him as though he wondered if the Pastor suddenly had lost his wits. Papa plunged on. "This morning, for
instance. Mrs. Franzon and I had a little talk about our baby
having red hair. We came to the conclusion, my good man, that
you are to blame."

Erickson almost leapt from his chair. "I beg your pardon,
Pastor Franzon. I am but a poor janitor, but I am a man with
honor and respect for God and man."

Papa blushed in embarrassment. "Indirectly, I mean, Lars.
Please don't misunderstand me. That is why I wanted you to
read that chapter. You see it even makes a difference what a
woman *looks* at at such a time as Mrs. Franzon has just been
through. And that is why I need your help."

"I don't understand, Pastorn."

"Well, you see, your two little redheaded boys sit in the
front pew every Sunday. And Mrs. Franzon, who attended
church even though she was in that condition, had to sit and
look at them. Result—our baby has red hair. Now do you think
you could kindly move them to the back seat for the benefit of
others who might not want their children to have red hair?"

The janitor looked up helplessly. "I'll be glad to do anything
you suggest, Pastor. But what puzzles me is how *my* boys got
red hair. Emma had no redheads to look at."

Papa had no answer for that, but he could never let Erickson
know he had stumped him. "I guess women have strange ways,
my good man. Just now suppose you try to help *me*. Will you

do what I asked? Or, if you prefer, you might have their hair dyed."

Erickson laughed relieved. "I'll put them in the back seat, Pastorn. You see I don't care what color their hair is if they are good kids. I guess you just don't like red."

Papa rose and warmly shook Erickson's hand. "Thank you, Lars," he said. "You are a fine man—the salt of the earth. May God bless you."

But as Papa walked home, glad that the mission was over, he pondered certain church reforms. Matters like this should be handled by the conference. It would save a lot of embarrassment. He would propose that a church law be made, forbidding people with red hair to sit in the front pews. Yes, that would take care of the situation splendidly. It would, he suddenly realized, *if* he was not minus an excellent janitor.

"Don't go so fast, Pontus," Mama called as she reached the top of the hill, puffing for breath.

But already Papa had topped the hill and was on his way down. "I can beat you to the clearing, Maria," he shouted back. "You never could ski very fast."

Mama watched him skimming gracefully and effortlessly down the hill and around the curves, gliding in and out among the trees as easily as if they had not been there. Papa was certainly an expert skier, she thought. No wonder she had a hard time keeping up.

"Wait for me at the clearing, Pontus," she shouted after him, her voice echoing across the snowy hillsides.

Papa had the thermos bottle of coffee in his knapsack. It would taste good right now, but he had said, "Let's wait for the clearing, Maria," and she hadn't wanted to tell him how tired she was or the reason for it.

Now she took her time. From this high point she could see endless miles across the glistening hills. It was so beautiful she just wanted to hug the whole world. It wasn't only the view that

made her happy. Mama knew both her happiness and her tiredness were for another reason. And she wasn't sure Papa was
going to like it at all. Nim was only nine months old. All summer
she had been confined to the parsonage a good deal. Pontus had
looked glum when she couldn't go berrypicking with him, but
finally would set off by himself. On Midsummer's Day, Tant
Renberg, who vowed she was too old for hill climbing, had
looked after Nim. And once Papa had insisted that Nim was old
enough to go picnicking, and Mama had laughed and packed
him in a big basket like a lunch. Papa had carried Nim in the
basket, and Mama had looked out for the lunch.

Today Tant Renberg was nursing a touch of rheumatism and
was glad enough to stay by the fire and watch over the baby. He
was such a good boy. Maria smiled, remembering how Papa
would beam when little Nim held out his chubby arms to be
taken up, squealing with joy at the sight of him. But no matter
how much Papa seemed to love his son, he would still tease
about his hair.

"Engelbrekt," he would say, loud enough for Mama to hear
in the kitchen, "you are a fine big boy. Smart and good-looking,
too. If only you didn't have that red hair!"

Mama knew he was just joking, but she couldn't help being
hurt. Somehow she felt she had bungled the job with Nim; that
she should have made sure God sent a golden-haired baby—not
one with red hair.

Mama sighed happily and examined her skiis. Well, she
wouldn't have to worry about that with the new baby, now that
the janitor's boys had been moved to the back of the church. The
next little Franzon would be blond, and Papa would be so happy
he wouldn't even mind how fast it had happened.

Papa was waiting in the clearing in the woods. He had
already removed his skiis and taken the thermos from the knapsack.

"Let me help you with your skis, Maria," he said. "This
coffee is going to taste good with some of your fine *bullar*."

It was wonderful to get the skis off and stretch out a bit. They hadn't seemed heavy when she started out earlier this afternoon. Mama sat on the tree stump and sipped the coffee slowly, nibbling on a *bulle*. The coffee warmed her and chased away some of her tiredness. She looked up as she felt Pontus's eyes on her.

"You look tired, my dear," he said gently. "Are you not feeling well?"

"I *am* tired Pontus," she answered hesitantly, deciding this was as good a time as any to break the news. "I guess I have to expect to tire quickly these days."

For a long moment Papa just stared at her, and when finally he spoke it was with sharpness in his voice. "I hope, Maria, you are not telling me you are 'that way' again so soon."

Mama's eyes filled with anxious tears. How could Pontus talk so about their new little one? He should be happy as she was. Somehow she must make him—but *how* she did not know.

Papa finished his coffee in silence. He packed the cups in the knapsack and strapped it on his back; then he tied the two pairs of skiis together and hung them over his shoulder.

"Come," he said kindly taking her hand in his. "We'll have to walk all the way home. You should know better than to go skiing in your condition."

Mama's anxiety vanished. Pontus wasn't angry. This was just his way of showing her how much he loved her. As she crunched over the snowy trails, her hand in his, Mama had never felt so safe and cherished. Occasionally Papa would press her hand tightly and look down at her with a smile full of love.

It was not until supper was over and little Nim had been tucked in the cradle that Papa mentioned the new baby. They were sitting before the open fire, silently watching the sputtering flames that made an endless bright chain up the chimney.

"I am afraid it is going to be hard on you, Maria, with Nim still a little baby," he said softly.

Mama knew he was remembering the long hours of anxious

waiting and the agony of her pain. She too had thought of that. But the joy of having another baby pushed the memory of pain out of her mind. Suddenly she wanted more than anything else in the world to assure Pontus—dear frightened Pontus—that everything was going to be all right.

"Oh, Pontus," she cried, "it is just going to be wonderful having a new little baby. It won't be hard at all. You know Nim is good as gold. He just coos and laughs and sleeps. I won't mind to manage two of them, not a bit."

"We'll have to make the best of it, Maria," Papa said, caressing her hair. "I guess I never expected them to come so fast."

Poor Papa looked so perplexed that Mama's heart went out to him. After all it had not been easy to adjust himself to one baby in the house—and now it would be two. Her arms went about his neck. "Pontus *lilla*," she whispered in his ear, "do you think it could be because we love each other so?"

But as her time drew near, Mama was frightened. Hard as she tried not to remember, the memory of those long painful hours before Nim's birth swept through her like a nightmare. She must not let Pontus know, she told herself, and when he looked at her anxiously, she would push away her own fears and smile. "It is nothing. Don't you worry even a little bit. It is only the first baby that makes trouble. Why having the next one will be just like a song."

And it *was* almost that easy. Tant Renberg had just stepped inside the door and the midwife hadn't even had time to take off her coat. Little Charlotta Maria arrived with a lusty cry.

Mama was all smiles when Papa came in. "Didn't I tell you it would be easy, darling? You see! It was nothing to worry about. And look, Pontus," she cried excitedly, "what we got. A beautiful little girl with *blonde* hair."

Papa kissed her tenderly, and Mama folded the covers back from the baby's tiny face. The happiness that shone in Papa's eyes more than made up for any doubts she might have had.

"Maria," he whispered with awe, "she *is* beautiful."

And because Papa's joy was overflowing and he wanted to
say something very special to his little golden-haired daughter,
he covered up his embarrassment by speaking in English. "You
sweet little thing," he said, "that nose of yours looks just like a
tiny pink button."

Mama's laughter was triumphant. "Oh, Pontus, that is ex
actly what we shall nickname little Charlotta. Button. Won't that
be the cutest name in Swedish?"

"Nim and Button," he repeated slowly. "Maria, I think that
will sound very special."

She had been right after all, Mama rejoiced silently. Papa
had forgotten all about his redheaded worries.

But their joy was short lived.

Before little Button was a week old, even Papa admitted
there were worse things than red hair. Button had a pair of
lungs that would have made a mountain yodeler proud. And
what was more, she used them day *and* night. The peacefulness
of the parsonage, in one short week, had become only a memory.
The lamp burned in the bedroom throughout the night while
Papa and Mama took turns walking the floor with Button, so
little Nim could sleep.

"Is this going to keep up, Maria?" Papa asked wearily after
the third week of nightly floor walking.

"It looks like it, Pontus," yawned Mama.

"How shall I ever prepare my sermons? All night I walk the
floor and all day I'm so sleepy I cannot keep my eyes open."
Papa stopped walking and Button began to cry.

Mama was so tired she could not help speaking crossly.
"You didn't think redheaded babies were good enough, Pontus,
so the Lord sent you a beautiful blonde one that *cries* all the
time."

Papa wasn't going to blame the Lord for this. "Don't let us
be too hard on her, Maria," he said sleepily. "It might be she has

pain and can't tell us. We will just have to give her time to adjust
to this big world."

Mama waited.

Every day Button seemed to grow more beautiful—and more
troublesome. She screamed during the day if you picked her up,
and she screamed at night if you didn't. She would sleep all day
like a little angel, and cry all night like an imp from the other
world. As if that were not enough, she began cutting teeth at an
early age. Mama was almost afraid to nurse her.

"You see, Maria," Papa said when the first tooth manifested
itself, "she did have a pain she couldn't tell us about. Soon she
will be all right."

Mama just looked at him for a long time. She put Button
into the cradle and gave her a *socka* to chew on. Cutting teeth
took a long time, and it would be months and months before
Button would be all right. How could babies be so different? Nim
had been no trouble at all after his first tooth. He would sit all
day and chew on a *socka*, and if he had pains he kept them to
himself like a little man.

For a few minutes now there was quiet. But only for a few
minutes. Presently the sharp cries filled the room again. Mama
took the baby from the cradle and walked up and down, patting
her gently. Button would not be pacified.

"Believe me, Pontus," Mama exclaimed in desperation, "the
next one is going to be a good baby—*red hair* or not."

It was a full minute before Papa could make himself heard
above the din. "Maria!" he almost shouted, "how can you even
think of a next one?"

Mama did not answer. Little Button had finally fallen
asleep.

Winter gave way to spring. Icicles dripped and fell from the
eaves of the parsonage, and the coverlets of snow vanished from
the hillsides. The twilight grew longer and longer, each passing
day. Silvery buds fattened on the fruit trees and shrubbery. Nim

toddled happily about the house, and Button, on all fours, seemed to be everywhere at once. Usually she slept the night through now, except when a new tooth was starting. But she found other ways to disturb the peace of the parsonage. If she couldn't crawl forward, Button crawled *backward*, wriggling outside any protective barrier Maria set up. She was into everything within reach. Mama couldn't leave her alone a moment.

"Why can't you be good like your brother?" she scolded as she put Button back on the floor blanket for the tenth time that morning. Button gazed up at her with wide blue eyes, her golden curls like a halo, and Mama melted. She sat down on the blanket and cuddled the child to her. The baking and cleaning would have to take second place this morning. Papa was working on his sermon, and she wanted to keep the children quiet. Nim would amuse himself for hours with never a sound. But not Button.

"I think you will grow up to be an explorer, Button," Mama said. "You never want to stay in one place a minute."

At least she wasn't crying, Mama thought as she went back to her baking. On the window sill above the baking board, the rows of geraniums flaunted their bright red blossoms. Beyond, the greening countryside stretched invitingly. Soon, Maria thought, it will be warm enough for picnics. This year they would take both the children. What fun it would be!

Suddenly an earsplitting crash behind her brought her out of her dreams. Button, screaming loudly, sat in a pool of milk, surrounded by broken dishes and baking tins. She had caught the end of the tablecloth which hung too near the floor and had literally brought it down about her head. Papa came rushing in from the study just as Mama picked Button out of the clutter, examining her for injuries.

"What in the world!" Papa cried. There was more fright than anger in his voice.

"I just turned my back for a moment. Thank Heaven, she isn't hurt." Mama handed the baby to Papa while she mopped up the milk and gathered up the pieces and pans. "Whatever are we going to do with her, Pontus?" she asked when she had finished.

Button was quiet again. Papa was bouncing her on his knee and she loved it. "I've been thinking about that too, Maria," Papa said. "I guess you are right. Perhaps God is punishing me for asking Lars to put his fine little boys in the back seat just because they have red hair. I think I better have another talk with Lars Erickson."

When Mama arrived at church the following morning, Lars and Emma Erickson and their two little boys were sitting in the front pew. Mama couldn't help feeling proud of Pontus. It took character and courage for Papa to admit, especially to his janitor, that he had offended God. But still Mama worried. More than anything else in the world, she wanted to please Papa. And though he had said now that he didn't care if all his children had red hair, Mama knew that deep inside he did care. It was up to her to give him the kind of children he wanted. But how could she be sure with the janitor's redheaded boys in the front pew?

All the following week Mama wrestled with the problem.

It wasn't until Saturday night, when she was putting Button to bed after a particularly trying day, that the answer came to her. Nim had been asleep in his crib for an hour, but Mama had to sit beside the cradle and rock Button, until her arm was numb. Now the baby had finally closed her eyes and Mama rose from the chair. She moved about noiselessly, not to waken her. It was hard to believe that this baby, who looked like a little sleeping angel, could be so different when she was awake.

And suddenly Mama knew what she had to do.

She wanted to rush right down to tell Pontus. But he might not approve. She had better wait. All day Sunday Mama went about with that twinkle in her eyes that should have told Papa she was guarding a secret. She was sure he was thinking she was that way again, but she just let him think. He would find out soon enough.

It took Mama almost another week to find what she wanted. Then one evening when Papa came in from making a call on old

Mrs. Nelson who was down with rheumatism, Mama was ready with her surprise.

"Come with me, Pontus," she said taking his hand and pulling him up the stairs after her.

On the bedroom wall, beside the two large mirrors, hung a large picture of a beautiful angel.

Mama stopped in front of it still holding onto Papa's hand. "See," she cried like a child before a lighted Christmas tree.

"It *is* beautiful, Maria. But don't you think we had enough pictures in this room?"

Mama laughed. "I guess I just got too excited to explain, Pontus *lilla*. But you see, it worked with Nim when I looked at the janitor's boys. And it worked with Button too, for I never thought of anything except she must *not* have red hair. Now I shall look at this beautiful angel with the next one, and think of goodness, and she will be just perfect."

It was Papa's turn to laugh. "Maria, always you are a surprise. Is there no end to your fanciful ideas?" He put his arm around her and hugged her to him.

Mama's excitement was almost more than she could bear. "Oh, Pontus, I'm so happy you like it. With both of us looking at it, we'll just have the most wonderful children in the whole world."

CHAPTER 4

～Mama's Model

What Papa really thought of Mama's model he never revealed, but her own faith in it, he was fully aware, was steadfast.

The long Swedish winter gave way to the brief twilight which heralded the coming of spring. Gradually the twilight hours lengthened to the full brightness of day, the days themselves became increasingly longer, until by the middle of June, the sun did not set at all.

Twice, since the advent of the model, this cycle of seasons had completed itself. Summer lay on the Swedish hills like a gentle hand. Inside the parsonage on this bright morning all was peace. Nim played contentedly with the cat. Papa went about with a happy smile. Even Button was behaving these days as a good child should. It had been this way, Mama reflected, ever since she had hung the picture of the angel in the bedroom as a model of perfection for the next child. So far, the model had proven a good influence in every way—except one. The one for which it had been bought. Almost two years had passed now and still there was no sign of another child.

A little frown grew between Mama's brows. Maybe God had decided not to let her have any more children. Maybe it was punishment for not being pleased with the babies He had already sent her. It was an awful thing to think about—never to have more than two children. Silently Mama prayed for forgiveness. She hadn't really meant to be displeased with her children; she just wanted them to be good. Surely God would understand that. Surely it was not sinful for a wife to want to please her husband who was one of God's chosen.

But more weeks drifted by. Soon Button would be three years old.

It was on a midsummer day, when they climbed Gellivara mountain, that Mama knew her prayers had been answered at last. She had been almost too tired to reach the top of the mountain. But, as always, she kept her secret until she was really sure. This time even Papa seemed pleased. Maybe, thought Mama, he was getting used to love—and children. She was happier than she had ever been in her life. Eagerly she waited the day, for by now it held no terrors for her.

When the day finally arrived, everything went on schedule. The midwife was snippy as usual and sent Papa for a long walk. Since no one ever crossed midwife Eklund, Papa went. Mama watched him reluctantly put on his hat and coat and, with a backward glance at her, walk slowly out of the room. She wanted to tell him to stay, but suddenly her throat was too full of love for words.

An hour later he returned. By that time it was all over. Tant Renberg met him at the door.

"Go right in to Maria, Pastor Franzon, and take a look at your little angel."

Mama's eyes were sparkling as Papa came into the bedroom. "Oh, Pontus," she cried, "it worked. Our new little baby is the *picture* of that angel."

Papa kissed Mama and then gently pulled the quilt back from the baby's face. "I'm so happy, Maria. You really got your little angel this time. Now I just hope she will be as good and sweet as she is beautiful."

"Oh, Pontus, there is only one thing. It isn't a *she*," said Mama softly.

Papa's eyes almost popped out. "Don't tell me, Maria," he demanded needlessly, "that this angelic-looking child is a *boy?*"

"I do tell you just that, Pontus." Mama twinkled.

"Don't you see what you've done? Just tell me how will a boy with a face like an angel get along in this world? What can he *do?* If only you could be like other women, Maria. But always you have to do something no one else ever heard of. We'll get rid of that picture at once."

Mama only laughed. Nothing could dampen her spirits today. "Don't be so silly, Pontus. It won't hurt him to be beautiful, and I assure you he will grow up to be a real he-man. And why not with a handsome Papa for *his* model."

As always Mama had had the last word. But when it came to naming the baby, it was Papa who had the final say.

"Peter Gabriel Franzon," he announced the next morning, when they discussed the baby's Bible name.

"Why *Gabriel*, Pontus?" Mama had asked. "There are so many fine names in the Bible."

"That's for the angel part of him, Maria," Papa answered firmly, with a little twinkle in his eyes. "You made him *look* like an angel, didn't you?"

Mama said no more. From the first the baby was nicknamed Pelle.

The picture of the angel remained on the bedroom wall. If God had sought to punish either Mama or Papa, He must have relented, for thereafter about every year and a half the parsonage was filled with the excitement, cries and laughter caused by a new baby. And each one of them in one way or another, Mama assured Papa, resembled the angel.

Now there were seven. If Papa tired of the happy confusion, Mama would send him off to meditate in the church.

"They got to make noise and be happy, Pontus. Someday they will all grow up, and then you and I will just sit here and remember their shouting happy voices."

But Mama knew there were days when Papa wished they were grown up already. On such days it was hard to convince

him that she still wanted one more. Uneven numbers were un-
lucky! One more and she would be satisfied.

"Well I certainly *hope* so, Maria. But it seems to me you
have more than plenty of work with the seven we already have,"
Papa commented dryly.

"Why, Pontus. It doesn't seem like work at all to me. It is
such fun to watch the children growing up like little plants need-
ing love and sunshine."

And they were growing up. The days and weeks and years
seemed to float by, so filled with love and happiness that Mama
couldn't believe there was another woman in the world as happy.
Of course there were times of anxiety and strain when illness
struck; when the rest of them spent long hours in prayer and
waiting and tender service. But always when these dark days had
passed, there was even greater happiness and a deeper love.
Then Mama would sing more softly as she went about her work,
as if this were another way of saying, "Thank you, God!"

The house seemed to expand with the years without the ad-
dition of rooms. Sometimes after supper Papa would play the organ and everyone would sing. Even the littlest one would join in.
And then everyone would laugh at the cracking notes in Nim's
changing voice. These were gay and happy days, indeed.

But for Mama, Saturday nights were the best of all. This
was the time she felt nearest to her children; when she could
plan and think about their futures.

This was the night she shined the shoes.

It was the last task of the busiest day in the week. For Saturday was a day of preparation in the parsonage. By nightfall every room in the house was in order. The hand-woven rugs were
bright splashes of color against the newly scrubbed white floors.
The copper pots and pans and all the silver had been polished.
White-tile fireplaces gleamed. The pantry gave off tempting
odors of pre-cooked meat for Sunday dinner. Prepared vegetables
stood in bowls of water. On the baking board, covered with a
clean towel, were Mama's pride—coffee bread and a special

dessert. No cooking ever was permitted on the Lord's Day. Even the table was set on Saturday night. It was Nim's job, just before he went to bed, to place a chair at each place.

Truly for Mama it was the end of a perfect day. From the back hall came the spicy fragrance of fresh spruce-mats. on which nine pairs of shoes were carefully wiped before daring to step on Mama's scrubbed floors.

Finally, when the children were in bed, and Papa was busy in the study, Mama would sit on a low footstool in the kitchen and shine seven pairs of shoes.

"Why don't you let Nim and Button tend to that?" Papa had asked. "Surely you have enough to do on Saturday."

But Mama only smiled dreamily. "I shall always do this, Pontus. As long as the children live at home. When they grow up and move away, one by one, most of all I think I shall miss this beautiful hour on Saturday night, shining their shoes."

Papa did not quite understand it, but he had to admit that for some mystic reason shining the children's shoes made Mama happy.

Mama always shined the shoes according to age. How like Nim was the first pair. Strong and sturdy. And a little bit slow, for Nim was never in a hurry about anything. Except his scissors! By the time he was five he managed to find the scissors wherever Mama hid them, and had tried his skill on everything from Papa's best white church shirt to a perfect barber job on the tail of Kurre, the cat. Sometimes, even when she was most exasperated, Mama couldn't help wondering tenderly what great talent was hidden for him in a pair of scissors.

But it was Papa who worried most.

"Maria," he said sternly, when Nim had chopped off half of Button's beautiful golden braids, "he will never amount to anything. The best I can figure for him is the life of a barber!"

"And what's so tragic about that? Barbers do an important job in the world."

"How can you joke about it, Maria. You know I have dedicated my first-born to be a great missionary. Why, imagine a man with a noble name like Engelbrekt being just a barber."

Mama's eyes began to twinkle. "Maybe he could be both."

"Don't be ridiculous, Maria."

"But it isn't, Pontus. With a razor in one hand ready to shave a man, he would only have to say '*My good man, are you ready to die?*' and he would have a convert for sure."

Papa had to laugh. He should have known better than to criticize one of the children to Maria. "Well, perhaps he will outgrow it," he said consolingly.

But Nim didn't. Now he was twelve years old and still cutting up everything in sight and reach. Something had to be done, but what? Mama made suggestions, but Papa was convinced that the best system was the application of his right hand to a certain bottom.

It wasn't long before Papa had a chance to test his theory.

It had happened on a Saturday when Mama had been especially busy. Not only were there the regular duties of cleaning, polishing, cooking and baking, but there was to be a special guest at Sunday dinner. Pastor Mickelson from Haparanda was passing through on his way to Stockholm and would attend Sunday morning service, saying a few words after Papa's sermon. Then he would have dinner at the parsonage.

As soon as Papa had received the news, he had set about preparing a special sermon for the occasion. His pastorate might be smaller than Pastor Mickelson's, but Papa would not be found wanting when it came to preaching the Word of God. For three days now he had been shut up in his study, scarcely coming out for meals. Maria had been asked to keep the children quiet, and she was especially careful to make as little noise as possible herself.

It was almost noon when Maria heard the study door open. Papa had just finished copying, in his clear and precise handwriting, the most powerful sermon he had ever prepared. At least so he assured Mama as he came into the kitchen where she was putting a pan of coffee bread into the oven. Nim and Button were playing quietly at the big table as Mama had commanded them to do.

"I tell you, Maria," Papa said reverently, "sometimes I think that, of all the disciples, John was the greatest. His words are as appropriate to our times as if they had been written to-day."

Before Mama could tell him that she thought St. John would have been pleased with the way Papa delivered his word of redemption, there was a knock at the kitchen door. Papa put his sermon on the table and went to answer it. It was Lars Erickson about the arrangements for tomorrow. Mama went on with her baking. Both had forgotten Nim and Button. When Papa came back after several minutes with Lars, Nim was proudly showing Button his handiwork.

"See, it's a deer head!" he cried excitedly.

Button had taken the cutout from his hand. "Let me see what's written under it," she said, and then read aloud, "'*We shall all come short of Glory!*' What a silly thing to write under a deer head."

Papa was across the room in a stride. His powerful sermon was now a pile of scrap paper.

"Come with me, young man," he said firmly, "and we shall see who will come short of glory!"

Mama tried to be a peacemaker. "Oh, Pontus, he didn't *know* it was your sermon. Please don't be too hard on him."

But Papa had already departed, with a protesting Nim, in the direction of the woodshed.

By virtue of considerable midnight oil and his remarkable memory, Papa's sermon was rewritten in time. The church was filled for Sunday-morning service, and Papa had never been more eloquent. Afterwards, Pastor Mickelson spoke for ten minutes. Nim thoroughly chastened, sat next to Mama, as unhappy and quiet as a wounded deer. Mama's heart ached for him, remembering the severity of Papa's "laying on of hands." Perhaps

a child did need a spanking once in a while, but she was sure
Nim was cured of his cutting habit. Just the same she resolved to
ask Pontus to deal gently with him if ever there was a next time.

It was November before Mama was confronted with a reso·
lution of her own.

On a particularly cold day, Mrs. Lund, who daily exercised
her little French Poodle, Sippan, regardless of the weather, had
stopped in for a visit at the parsonage. Mama loved company.
Quickly she made a fire in the open stove in *salen* and served
coffee and company cookies. The time passed so pleasantly that
it was late when Mrs. Lund shook hands, thanking Mama for a
lovely afternoon. At the door she called, "Come, Sippan! We
must be going."

Sippan came bouncing into the room—and Mrs. Lund let
out a scream.

"Sippan! What has happened to you? You are naked in the
middle of the winter," she cried, wringing her hands and throwing her scarf over the denuded little dog.

But Mama knew too well what had happened. When she had
pacified Mrs. Lund with profuse apologies and sent her on her
way home with promises that she would knit Sippan a coat, she
went in search of Nim. She found him behind the sofa in the
kitchen, scissors still in hand. Her resolution completely forgotten, she did not wait for Papa. Firmly she took Nim's scissors
and, with tears running down her own cheeks, sheared off every
red hair on his head.

"Now, young man," she said sternly, "perhaps you will understand how Sippan is going to suffer without a coat in the middle of winter."

But that night Mama was a little longer over her prayers
for Nim.

Gently Mama put Nim's shoes on the floor and picked up
the small narrow boots belonging to Button. It was easy to see
that they belonged to restless feet. Button was eleven years old

now and, while she had outgrown her baby temperament, she
had developed new tendencies that kept Mama on the jump
most of the time. In Papa's eyes she could do no wrong. But hard
as Mama tried, there were a good many quirks she just couldn't
understand. One was the child's interest in "magic."

"When I grow up," Button would announce, "I'm going to
join the circus."

Mama would look at Papa and say nothing until Button
had performed one of her disappearing acts, which she did whenever something happened Button didn't like. Then Mama would
ask, "How in the world, Pontus, could she ever get such an idea?
Why, she has never even *seen* a circus."

"It's beyond me," laughed Papa. "No circus would ever lose
itself in this part of the world."

Mama could only pray a little harder that the child would
forget about this silly dream, for, as the apple of Papa's eye, Button *had* to turn out right or it would break his heart. But Button
went right on practicing magic and disappearing, especially
when there were dishes to wash, or it was time for prayer meeting.

How long this might have continued Mama would never
know, if Button had not begun disappearing from the supper
table during grace. At such times, Papa's eyes were closed, and,
if dinner consisted of something Button did not like, she would
slide slowly from the chair under the table and quietly disappear
on hands and knees into the *vardags*-room. When Papa opened
his eyes, her chair would be empty. After several such occasions,
Papa resolved to say grace with his eyes open.

One night when there was *rot-mos*, turnips and potatoes
mashed together, which Button particularly disliked, she waited
her chance. Papa bowed his head, but Button failed to note that
his eyes were not closed. Slowly she began to slide under the table. Papa's prayer, to the amazement of the rest of the family,
had a very strange ending:

"Crawl back, my sweet. It won't work. The devil may tempt,

but just now I have caught him by the tail. . . . May this food be blessed and our hearts made grateful. Amen."

Mama smiled now as she put Button's shoes, brightly polished, into the line and picked up Pelle's. How completely he lived up to his real name, Gabriel. Five of her children had had the angel as a model and all of them were wonderful children. But Pelle was goodness itself. As a baby, he had given her no trouble at any time. Later, when the other children quarreled over who would be served first, or would get the biggest piece of *appel-kaka* Pelle would stand aside, with wide clear blue eyes looking up at her. "I'll wait, Mama." It was, Maria, reflected, this big heart that had got him into the only situations he had ever created in the family.

From the time Pelle was old enough to read, he had been fascinated by the Bible. At first Papa had read the stories to all the children, and Pelle would sit in the little circle which they had formed at Papa's feet, his eyes wide and his mouth a small "O." But when the others had tired, or gone off to bed, it was Pelle who asked for more. Then Papa would take him on his lap and Pelle would trace the lines with his tiny finger as Papa read. As soon as he could read them himself, he did more than read; he began to live what he read. This, Mama and Papa agreed, was wonderful, until a certain winter day when Pelle had come home blue with cold. He had given his warm coat to a little Lapp child who had been scantily dressed. Later, when spring had loosened the ice on the streams, Nim had rescued Pelle from the swift-flowing waters and tried to explain that not everyone could walk on the water like Jesus.

It was not until Pelle had suggested, as a remedy for Nim's cutting and Button's acting, that "the Bible says to cut off the hand and foot that leads into mischief," that Papa knew something had to be done. He forbade Pelle to read the Bible alone. But Pelle only listened more intently to Papa's sermons.

Then had come a special night. Mama chuckled now remembering it, but at the time it hadn't seemed funny at all.

She had been fixing *råraker* for supper. The whole family loved these raw potato pancakes, and she had just finished grating a large bowlful. Pelle came rushing in from outside, happy and excited.

"I better grate a whole lot more potatoes for you, Mama," he panted, taking off his cap. "We will have lots of company for supper. I did just what Papa preached last Sunday."

Mama's heart sank right into her shoes. Frantically she tried to remember what Papa had preached, but she couldn't.

"Pelle," she finally asked slowly, "what *did* Papa preach last Sunday?"

He was surprised. "You don't remember, Mama? He asked if any one of us, when we gave a dinner, ever invited the poor and the lame and the blind. And if we did, God's blessing would smile down on us."

Mama trembled as she realized what he was saying.

"Oh, Pelle," she whispered while her heart stopped, "you didn't!"

Pelle had just looked at Mama with eyes as clear and deep as a mountain lake. "Yes, Mama, I did. Only five, though. One lame, two poor and one crippled. And do you think one with a glass eye is just as good as a really blind man, Mama?"

In her heart Mama cried, Oh, Pelle, Pelle, what shall we do with you? But aloud she only said, "Well, you better start grating lots and lots of potatoes."

When the "party" was over that night, and the last of Pelle's guests had gone, Papa had considerable explaining to do to his second son. Something to the effect that even *his* preaching shouldn't always be carried out *too* literally.

Vickey's shoes were long and narrow. Aristocratic, thought Mama, like the child herself. She was only six, but already quite tall and, according to Papa, the perfect result of the angel model. Indeed, Mama had to admit that, much as she loved all her children, Vickey was certainly the most beautiful. She had been named for two queens, Victoria Sofia, and, as though she had understood the significance, the child had seemed to live up to her queenly namesakes almost from the day she opened her deep blue eyes upon the world. Now, young as she was, her lashes were long dark fringes accenting the depth of her eyes and the petal-like skin of her slender oval face. She walked like a little princess and never showed confusion or excitement. Sometimes Mama thought Vickey was almost too kind, too quiet, too restrained. It wasn't always good for a child to suffer so intensely in silence.

Mama's heart still ached when she thought of what had happened at the Christmas "robbing" party last year.

Christmas in Lapland, as in homes over most of the world, was the most festive season of the year. From December twenty-fourth to January thirteenth there were parties and celebrations. Every home, however modest, had its Christmas tree party. While everyone took part in the games, only the children were allowed to "rob" the tree. Then there would be coffee and many kinds of cookies for the grownups, and finally, to the gay accompaniment of folk tunes and laughter, the Christmas tree was "danced" out. This was the gayest ceremony of all. Papa would take the top of the tree, Mama the trunk. Everyone else at the party would hang onto the branches, scrambling happily for the best position, and "dance" the tree into the back yard.

It had been an especially happy Christmas last year. Mama as always had spent weeks getting ready. In the center of the floor in *salen* stood the tree, loaded with good things to eat. There were candies wrapped in all colors of fancy paper, and unwrapped candies shaped like Santas, bells, hearts, angels, and stars. And most important of all—*julbocker* and gingerbread men, that belonged only to Christmas. Under every candle hung a red shiny apple. On the big table, which had been pushed aside to make room for the tree, was a pile of white paper bags.

When the time for the robbing ceremony arrived, everyone formed a circle and danced around and around the tree. Even

Papa completely forgot his dignity and joined in the games, dancing and laughing with the children. Then suddenly the grownups dropped out and the children pounced upon the tree, robbing it of its goodies and piling them in a great heap on the table. When the tree had been picked clean, Mama gave each child one of the paper bags, counting the number of children aloud as they circled the table. There were sixteen, so the big heap of candies and cakes were quickly divided into sixteen little heaps, and on top of each was placed a red apple.

When Mama gave the signal, each child began filling his or her paper bag with one little heap of goodies. Suddenly Mama noticed that Anna-Lisa Lund, who was next to Vickey and a year older, was taking Vickey's goodies as well as her own, popping them all into her paper bag. But Vickey was making no protest at all. Instead she was quietly putting into her own bag the few candies and cookies that remained, and the red apple. Then she slipped away into the *vardags*-room.

Mama started to follow her, but the line around the refreshment table was forming. Mama poured the coffee and Button handed each guest a plate for the many kinds of cookies Mama had made. Gay voices and laughter filled the room.

"No one makes *spritz* like Maria," Mrs. Lund exclaimed.

"Or *mandelformar*," cried Mrs. Nelson.

"One day I shall start a bakery," laughed Mama, "then we will *see* how good I bake." But Mama's mind was not on the gaiety.

When the plates were filled and the coffee poured, she went in search of Vickey. She found her curled up in a corner of the sofa in the *vardags*-room, crying bitterly. Mama picked her up and held her close.

"Darling," she comforted, "you mustn't cry so. I saw Anna-Lisa take your goodies. Why didn't you ask her for them? She would have given them back."

"She—she—wouldn't, Mama," Vickey sobbed, "she doesn't like me."

"Of course she likes you, darling. You're a fine little girl."

Slowly Vickey dried her tears. "Papa says we must love our enemies, Mama. I couldn't tell on Anna-Lisa. She would get a spanking and then all our fun would be spoiled."

For a moment Mama's throat was full of tears. Vickey adored Papa, and to her whatever he said was next to the voice of God. She had preferred to suffer in silence rather than bring punishment even to one who was guilty.

"Papa is right, darling," Mama agreed. "God does want us to love our enemies and forgive them."

Vickey threw her arms around Mama's neck. "I feel better now since the tears came out. I have forgiven Anna-Lisa, and God will give me a new bag of goodies when I get to Heaven."

Yes, thought Mama now as she put the shoes aside, that was little Vickey, too kind for her own good, but willing to wait a whole lifetime for Christmas goodies, rather than to hurt others. And all because Papa said it was right!

Greta's shoes were short and stubby. Greta was the nickname for Margareta Kristina—names which Mama had picked from the royal family in Stockholm. But there was certainly nothing regal about Greta. She was small and round, with twinkling eyes and quick easy movements. She was always happy about something—and hungry.

"Can I lick the cake pan, Mama? Please, Mama, make me a special little cake." This was Greta's song every Saturday when the baking started.

When Mama passed over the cake pans from which most of the batter had been scraped, Greta would get three or four spoons and head for the back porch steps. In a moment, as if by signal, she would be surrounded by her playmates, all dipping in for a "taste."

Mama, watching through the open door. would smile with special fondness.

"Greta is always the little mother," Mama remarked proudly to Papa one morning.

As usual Papa laughed with his eyes before he spoke. "Just you wait, Maria. Greta will grow up and get married and have as many children as her Mama."

"Won't that be wonderful, Pontus? What could be nicer than just loads and loads of grandchildren?"

Papa didn't seem to agree. "Maria," he chuckled, "Greta is only four and already you are counting *her* children."

But Mama had wondered if Papa might not be right, the day she had left Greta to "help" Tant Renberg look after her two baby brothers, while Mama took Vickey to buy new shoes. She had thought this would teach Greta a sense of responsibility, to "help" Tant Renberg. But as it turned out, Greta had had her own ideas about the meaning of the word. When Mama and Vickey returned, the parsonage was in a turmoil.

In the forbidden *salen*, four-year-old Greta presided over a very fancy tea table. Mama's best silver and her finest lace cloth had been spread, and Greta was serving lump sugar and cream and company cookies to four wide-eyed little girls. Tant Renberg was not in sight, but she most certainly could be heard. From the direction of the bedroom came loud cries and pounding.

At the sight of Mama and Vickey, four frightened little girls scurried out, leaving Greta to face the music alone.

But Mama released Tant Renberg first and learned what had happened. Greta had brought in four of her little playmates and asked her "to make a party" for them. Tant had told her she was too busy and left the kitchen to look after the two babies. Greta had followed and turned the key in the door, and all Tant's pounding and screaming had done no good.

"How could you do such a thing to Tant Renberg," scolded Mama. Greta hung her little golden head, but kept silent. "You know sugar costs very much money and you have used the cream for Papa's board meeting tonight. What do you think Papa is going to do about that?"

Still no answer. Mama brought the switch from the kitchen *kåpa*, but she used it as sparingly as she dared and still hope to teach the child a lesson. Only when the spanking was over and her tears had been dried would Greta talk.

"It was the black angel, Mama. It whispered it would be fun to lock Tant Renberg in." And then to Mama's amazement Greta began to laugh. "And it was fun. Tant Renberg screamed, 'Open the door or the black angel will take you.' And all the time it was the black angel doing it."

In the front hall the big clock struck nine resounding chimes. Only two more pairs of shoes—busy little baby shoes—and this most loved of all Mama's tasks would be finished for another week. Calle was a year old and Torkel two. Almost twins, Mama thought as she watched them trotting unsteadily about the house, following Greta wherever she went. And Greta never seemed to tire of mothering them.

Tenderly Mama placed the four little shoes in her lap, caressing each one before she started polishing it. Soon there would be no baby shoes in the row on Saturday night. Soon—much too soon—the children's shoes would be carrying them into the world, leaving the parsonage hushed and empty. Mama sighed deeply. Suddenly she couldn't bear to think of the house without a dimpling little baby to care for. And she knew Pontus loved them as much as she did. He just didn't say it so often. Mama's heart swelled with happiness and love, thinking of what a wonderful Papa Pontus was.

Now seven pairs of shiny shoes stood in a row on the kitchen floor. Mama knelt reverently, folded her hands and bowed her head. Aloud she prayed a little prayer that she had made up once while shining the shoes—a special prayer for a special night.

> "God bless the step each foot will take
> Of each dear child a staunch soul make
> Help them to grow to do thy will

And with Thy love my children fill.
Amen."

Mama arose, tiptoed to the study door and knocked softly.
"May I see you just for a moment, Pontus?" she asked.

When Papa opened the door she whispered, "Come, darling, I want you to see how many children we have."

Papa looked annoyed. "I think, Maria," he said sternly, "I
have reason to know how many children we have."

Mama only laughed and led him into the kitchen. "If we
count all their feet, it makes fourteen."

"And if we count all their hands too it will make twenty-
eight. And how about their fingers and toes?"

Even Papa was laughing now with Mama. "Oh, Pontus," she
cried, "I think we are just the luckiest Papa and Mama on the
whole of God's earth!"

CHAPTER 5

~ Mama Stands in Papa's Shoes

Papa had very strict ideas about most things. He was particularly definite about the place God had allotted in this life to men and women. He permitted Mama to run the parsonage as she thought best and proper, so long as she gave due consideration to his bank account. But when it came to matters of the Church, they were entirely within his domain.

At least so Papa thought until he awoke one spring morning with a headache and a fever.

Papa let his head fall back onto the pillow and pulled the quilt up over his shoulders. It was no use. He was really sick. And what was worse—it was Sunday.

Outside the brightness of the day mocked him. The past three Sundays it had rained. Now when the late spring sun was high and warm in a cloudless sky and he had prepared a fine sermon, he had to be flat on his back with a fever.

"Please, Pontus," Maria pleaded, "stay in bed and be sick in peace. And don't fret, dear. I have a thing or two to tell that congregation and I might as well do it this Sunday morning."

Papa sat up again horrified. "Maria! You can't do that!" he shouted hoarsely.

Mama only pushed him gently back onto the pillow and tucked him in. Papa submitted weakly; he was too sick to argue.

Anyway, he might just as well try to stop the midnight sun as to argue with Mama. She always managed to get her own way. As a preacher he could soften the most rebellious hearts, make men confess their hidden sins and women weep over erring lives. But when it came to handling Mama, Papa knew he was lost. If he blocked her in one place, she would loophole through another. If he thought he had her cornered, she would miraculously squeeze by his all-seeing eye.

Now he stared gloomily out the window, only too well aware that if Mama had made up her mind to preach, she would preach, one way or another. Desperately he wracked his brain. If only he could get in touch with Deacon Lund. But Mama had refused to call him—just kept repeating that ridiculous command, "Stay in bed and be sick in peace." Surely there was some way to make her listen to reason. But even as he hoped, Papa knew he was helpless. Maria had a way of twisting him to her wishes no matter what he said or did. Oh, why had the Lord ever created Eve in the first place? She was a thorn in Adam's flesh, a chain around his neck—a weight on his foot.

For the hundredth time since his marriage Papa asked himself why he had been such a fool as to get married. He might now be serving one of the large churches if it were not for a wife and seven children. It was a bit odd—and Papa admitted that he himself did not understand it—that the larger churches objected to calling as their pastor a man who had obeyed the Lord's command to propagate the earth. So he had to be content with a small church and the small salary that went with it.

Suddenly he was ashamed of himself. Maria had never complained. She *was* hard to handle, but that was only part of Mama. Most of her, he thought warmly, was bighearted, loving and beautiful—and she was only half his age. Without wanting to, he remembered that morning on the boat so many years ago, when he had spoken of his fears that the congregation would not welcome her easily. "We'll just tackle them together, Pontus," she had said, her eyes shining like a child's.

Papa sighed. Of course he loved his children and he loved Mama with all his heart. But if Mama insisted upon preaching this morning, he would lose even this small church and its small income. His heart pounded with fear; his head and body ached. If only he *could* be "sick in peace." But there was about as much chance of that as jumping over Gellivara mountain.

Mama came in with a glass of water and a small white powder-envelope. "You'd better take this before I leave, Pontus. It will take away your headache."

Papa sat up obediently and took the medicine. "Maria," he barked, "don't you know that to be able to preach you have to have a text?"

Mama smiled and showed her dimples. "Don't get so excited, darling," she soothed. "I have had a text for years. It is about those fishermen that fished all night and caught nothing. Of course I might change it just a *little bit* and make it "His Twelve Lean Years.""

Papa gasped and sank back on the pillow. "You can't do that, Maria," he wailed. "You'll preach me right out of a church."

"Pontus," Mama said firmly, "our bank account is leaner than a rabbit's front tooth, and I intend to do something about it. Just you wait and see."

Mama set about dressing with special care in her finest black dress with white trimmings. Her blonde hair was piled high on her head and held in perfect order with two simple combs.

"How do I look, Pontus *lilla?*" she asked when she was ready.

Papa did not answer. He turned his face to the wall and closed his eyes, but it had no effect on Mama.

"Now I'll put Torkel and baby Calle to bed for their morning nap. The other children can go to church with me. You see, Pontus, there isn't a thing to worry about."

Nothing except ruin, thought Papa, as he heard the front door close.

Beads of perspiration formed on Papa's forehead. It was lucky for him that his occupation was not an engineer on a fast passenger train. Mama, being Mama, would have taken over that job just as confidently.

After a while Papa turned over again. Through the window, he could see the white church down the street. It was a homey church, friendly and inviting. The doors were wide open. Up in front was the pulpit he had occupied all these years. Today Mama would be standing there, slim and blonde—*and preach him right out of a job.*

Papa watched the family procession until it reached the church. Mama and Greta were in front, then Vickey and Pelle, and finally Nim and Button. All in their Sunday best. Any other time Papa would have been proud, but he was not in a mood this morning. Now Mama was smiling a greeting to everyone as she guided the children ahead of her into church.

Papa sighed and closed his eyes. What a stubborn woman! She would never know how to handle that congregation. They were a touchy bunch of people, especially about money. Hadn't he hinted for a raise for the past three years? And hadn't they completely ignored the hint? Such a thing as a raise for their underpaid shepherd had never even been taken up at a board meeting. Now what would happen when Mama suddenly appeared in *his* pulpit and preached about "His Twelve Lean Years?" Gooseflesh covered him at the very thought.

Papa tried to pray. He tried to sleep. He succeeded only in counting the minutes until Mama would return to the parsonage. Never had an hour seemed so long. His body felt old and his soul discouraged.

At last he heard Mama's laughter in the kitchen, and the eager chatter of the children. Mama was telling them stories as she prepared their dinner. Why didn't she come into the bedroom. Didn't she know he wanted to know what had happened? Even if the roof of the church had fallen in, Maria would only smile and find some good reason for the catastrophe. Today Papa was just tired of being Mama's husband. She was too young for him anyway, and too full of tricks—and stubborn.

By the time Mama opened the bedroom door, carrying the bowl of hot broth, Papa had worked himself into such a rage that his temperature was soaring.

"If I were a well man, Maria, I would turn you over my knee," he said grimly. "You know you have completely gone against my wishes."

"Drink this broth while it is hot," Mama commanded, ignoring his remark. "As for preaching—Pontus, I wouldn't undo that for a barrel of gold."

This was too much. "Preaching," he almost shouted. "What do you know about preaching?"

"I know this," said Mama sweetly. "*I simply love it.* And if it weren't for the children I think I would go into the business."

Papa was completely paralyzed with anger. He tried to speak, but only managed to sputter inarticulately. Mama patted him on the cheek, utterly oblivious to the destructive effect of her words. "You should be very proud of me, Pontus." There was a twinkle in her eyes that could only mean more mischief. What more had she done to destroy his career? She is keeping something from me, thought Papa. She always looks like that when she has a secret. Well, he decided as he finished gulping down the broth, she could keep her secret. He'd never give her the satisfaction of asking her about it.

And for the rest of the day Papa lay with his face to the wall, sulking. Several times he heard the door open softly and knew that Mama was peeking in to see how he was getting along, but he pretended to be sleeping.

It was late afternoon when Papa heard the doorbell. After a few moments his door opened.

"You have a visitor, Pontus," Mama whispered as she touched his shoulder gently.

Papa turned over to find Deacon Lund standing beside the bed. When Mama had gone out and quietly closed the door, Lund said sympathetically, "You don't look so well, Pastor Franzon." And he eyed Papa critically.

"This is the first time I have missed a Sunday in *twelve* years," Papa almost snapped, "except of course for my vacation Sundays."

"Sorry. I didn't mean to offend."

The deacon sat down on the chair next to the bed, tapping his foot up and down on the floor. Papa's nerves were jumping and his head ached, but he forced himself to speak more kindly.

"I'm sorry I was unable to preach this morning," he said, watching the effect upon Lund.

"Of course," the deacon hastened to say, "I understand."

Papa was getting nervous. Obviously this wasn't just a social call. Deacon Lund had something on his mind. Something he was finding very difficult to say. Inwardly Papa groaned. It would be hard to leave the church and Lapland; they had made up the happiest years of his life.

"When a man is sick, Deacon Lund," Papa ventured after several minutes of unbearable silence, "sometimes things happen over which he has no control."

To Papa's utter suprise the deacon smiled sympathetically. "Indeed they do, Pastor Franzon. I know I speak for the entire congregation when I say we are very sorry you are ill. But we made out just fine this morning. Mrs. Franzon did a splendid job." He chuckled to himself. "She has a most engaging way of putting things over, you know. In fact she made us remember certain responsibilities which I'm afraid we have overlooked."

Papa couldn't believe his ears. Was it possible that Deacon Lund was *praising* Maria's outrageous behavior? Or was he merely trying to ease Papa's embarrassment? If that were the case, thought Papa, he had better let him know where he stood on the matter.

"A woman's place is in the home. I assure you, Deacon Lund, it was not by my choice that Mrs. Franzon preached this morning."

"Well, that is beside the point. Mrs. Franzon is a very gifted lady—very gifted indeed. We feel you are a lucky man, Pastor. And the church is mighty lucky too to have two preachers."

Papa stuttered, "T-*two* preachers!"

The deacon cleared his throat before he continued. "I am here to bring you good news, Pastor. We were so impressed by Mrs. Franzon's sermon this morning that we called a meeting of the board right after the services. The vote was unanimous to raise your salary twenty *kronor* a month."

Long after Deacon Lund had departed, Papa lay very still and stared at the ceiling. Somehow he could not rejoice over that longed-for and much-needed raise. Mama had done it again as she had said she would. He would never hear the last of it. He could just see her strutting about the parsonage like a crowing rooster. No, if he was to have any peace in his own house, he must never let Mama know how that raise came to be. Why, she might even think it her duty to do half the preaching. And, being Mama, she would gradually take over the ministry. Papa could almost picture himself in a pink gingham apron cleaning house, tending the babies, and washing diapers, while Mama sat in his study and wrote sermons.

The horror of such a thing caused Papa to exclaim aloud, "That must never happen—never."

Too late he realized how loudly he had spoken. Mama rushed into the room. "Did you call me, Pontus?" she asked anxiously.

"No," snapped Papa, angry with himself, "I did *not* call you."

"That is strange. I was sure I heard you calling." Mama sat down on the side of the bed. "Are you sure you are all right, Pontus?"

"Of course I'm not all right, Maria. I am a sick man."

"Did Deacon Lund upset you, darling? You look so flushed."

Mama's eyes were big and very blue. Papa wished she would stop looking at him that way—like a child who had been scolded. As always, he melted as though he were on a hot stove.

"The Deacon was very kind, Maria," he said gently. "He just paid me a friendly visit, that's all. Nothing about that to upset me, is there?"

Mama moved a bit closer. "Pontus," she said leaning over him, "could you stand to hear some news? I mean if you are well enough and won't get too excited."

There was that secretive twinkle in her eyes again. Could she have already heard about the raise?

"Well or not," he said warily, "if you have news I better hear it."

Mama tilted her head a little to one side and smiled her sunniest smile. "Pontus, darling," she whispered, "we are going to have an increase."

Papa was speechless. She did know. Somehow she always outwitted him.

"I saw midwife Eklund yesterday and had a little talk with her," Mama continued, "I didn't want to tell you until I was sure, Pontus *lilla*."

It was several seconds before the full truth of what she had said hit him. Then Papa almost exploded. As if seven children were not enough for a poor preacher to bring up. How much good would the raise do him now?

He stared at Mama knowing he had to say something. Suddenly a thought struck him. A broad smile quickly erased the gloom of a moment ago. What better luck could have happened? For now, with another baby on the way, Mama would not be able to preach. She would have to step right out of *his* shoes and back into her own—and just be a wife.

All his ill temper vanished, and miraculously he felt almost well again. "Maria," he said softly taking her hand in his, "I think that is fine news—very fine indeed. Now I shall immediately *demand* a raise from that Church Board."

With Maria's arms about his neck, Papa felt a bit guilty because of the fib. But a husband *must* prove himself important before his wife. Even the Lord, he was sure, would understand that there were certain things a Papa could not tell a Mama.

CHAPTER 6

✦Mama Makes Up Papa's Mind

They were a happy family. If Papa was too strict at times, Mama softened his severity with gentle humor and warm understanding. The boys, especially Nim and Pelle, planned what they would be when they grew up, changing their ambitions with the whim of children, which they still were. But none of them worried much about education. Especially the girls. In Sweden, at that time, it was not considered important to educate girls. They were supposed to marry, bear children and make fine homes for their husbands and families. What need had they for higher education?

But just as Mama had dreamed, while a preacher's maid, of the time when she would marry the handsome minister and have a large family, so now she moved on to her next dream. Education. She had not forgotten her promise, sixteen years before, to return to America, although she had been too busy during the years to talk about it or give it much special planning. With eight children and the parsonage to care for, and her many church duties, Papa believed Mama was as happy and contented as he was.

Then one winter morning, when his oldest son was about fifteen, Papa learned just how long a woman's memory can be —especially Mama's.

Papa leaned back comfortably against the pillowed head-board, munching a piece of *bulle* and sipping his morning coffee. Between bites and sips, he watched Maria vigorously brushing her hair. It fell like a golden veil below her waist, shimmering in the lamplight with a million refracted rays. And for the millionth time, Papa silently thanked God for the wonder of her.

"Just think, Pontus," she said peeking bright-eyed through the veil, "the Lord in all His goodness has given us *eight* beautiful children. Healthy—and *smart,* too. It is up to us to see they get a chance at education. And where can they get a chance, but in America?"

Papa did not answer. Irritation swept all the loving thoughts of a moment ago from his mind. Mama had talked of nothing else but America for months. How could a man hold his tongue against this ceaseless pounding of words? Wasn't it a father's right to think about the welfare of his family and do what he thought best for them, with the help of God?

"Nim will be fifteen years old in May," Mama went on, not even noticing that he hadn't answered her first question. "He is almost too old now to go back to the first grade in America to learn English. Education just can't wait forever, Pontus."

Papa set the tray on the side table, threw back the quilt and stepped out of his warm bed. Still he did not speak, but walked past her to the washstand and poured cold water into the basin. Suddenly he felt embarrassed standing there in his short nightshirt. He waited for Maria's usual giggle and her remark about how "unpreacherlike" he looked, but it did not come. She is so full of America, Papa fumed inwardly, that she can't even see how funny I look in my nightshirt! Well, he'd have to settle this America talk one way or the other soon, but he did wish Maria would let him handle it his way for once.

Cautiously he glanced over his shoulder at Mama. She had stopped brushing and now twirled the golden veil into a mass on top of her head, securing it with large yellow pins. Papa dressed hurriedly, picked up the coffee tray and started toward the stairs.

"I shall go for a walk before breakfast, Maria," he announced before she could continue her speech. "I am getting nowhere with that sermon about Daniel for Sunday morning, and I can always think better on an empty stomach."

Mama's laughter stopped him. "Empty," she cried. "Oh, Pontus! What happened to the three *bullar* you ate with your coffee?"

Papa continued in silence down the stairs. He put the tray on the kitchen table, then slipped into his heavy fur coat and pulled the fur laps on his cap down over his ears. "Good-bye, Maria," he called from the front door.

The morning was clear and very cold. It was past nine, and the first rays of the sun were lifting rosy fingers into the bright sky. Snow-covered bushes bordering the garden gleamed like jewel-coated guards. Under Papa's overshoes the frozen path sang a morning song. After a while all irritation left him. The crisp high air gave his steps wings.

Desperately Papa tried to meditate on the Prophet Daniel. But all he could think of was America and Mama's urgent pleadings. A hundred times during the past few months he had been tempted to tell her about his letter to the Conference, but always caution stopped him. It would be too great a disappointment to her if the American pastorate, which he had requested, was not given to him. Lately he had become more than little concerned. It was now almost three months since he had written and no reply. What could he tell Mama? Suppose there was no pastorate available, or that an American-born pastor was preferred? Would she give up her pleadings to go to America and be content in Lapland? There were many days when Papa sincerely hoped so. The thought of leaving the land he loved, and the little white church that had been like a gift from God when his very soul seemed lost, was almost more than he could accept.

Papa paused and looked back over the path he had come. His throat filled with emotion. The tiny steeple of the church seemed very tall this morning and the parsonage across the way especially dear. For there he had first met Maria, and there she had given him eight wonderful children. At the thought of her, his heart pounded like a young man in love for the first time. Yet she had not been his first love. Was it possible that there had been a girl named Alvida who had broken his young heart and caused him to vow that he was forever through with love and women? How had life *been* before Maria?

Truly, thought Papa, God moves in mysterious ways.

It had been Papa's first year at the University in Upsala. He was young and very much in love. For who could help being in love with the beautiful Alvida? Tall and stately as a queen, she walked with regal grace. Her hands were lily-white and her voice like the mellow tones of the organ she played so perfectly. Her father was very rich and much pleased with the engagement of his daughter to a "rising young lawyer," though that young lawyer-to-be had very little money.

"Don't ever worry about money, dear," Alvida had whispered one evening shortly after they had become engaged. "Father will lend you as much as you need to finish at the University."

"I do not like borrowing money, Alvida," he had told her, more worried about finances than he dared let her know.

"But my dear, you can repay him when you are prospering as a practicing attorney-at-law." She did not speak banteringly, but rather with a fleeting note of annoyance that he would allow anything to disturb her smooth and perfect way of living.

Papa had not known how to answer her, but even now he recalled the strange tumult within him. He needed the loan very much, but somehow he could not let himself accept it. Perhaps later, if there were no other way, he would have to consider the loan, but first he had to try to earn it himself. They had come close to quarreling over the matter.

Nevertheless, when the term ended, he had taken a job as a farmhand on a friend's farm near Gnesta in the beautiful Södermanland. He had missed Alvida terribly. But gradually, as his health improved and he gained physical strength from the hard farm labor and long sweating hours under the summer sun, he found himself thinking less and less frequently of her. Often when the day's work was done, he would walk slowly back across the fields, golden with God-given harvest, and a peacefulness would pervade his heart such as he could find no words to express. And suddenly he had felt himself a part of earth and sky—and God. And it was good.

And so the summer had passed and he had come finally to the last night on the farm. He would not have believed leaving could be so difficult. It was almost as though he were leaving a big part of himself here, so that never again could he be a complete and a whole man. Slowly he had packed his few belongings while conflict swirled within him. Then to still the turmoil, he had set out along the narrow path beside the small lake, walking briskly. It was a night white with moonlight, and an almost unearthly stillness surrounded him. After a while he had paused, gazing out across the silvery expanse of water and the silent fields beyond; then upward into the misty blue-white of the heavens. And suddenly it was as though he were alone in the universe. For a seemingly endless time he stood motionless, knowing not fear, but a sense of utter quiet. Then a voice that was not a voice, but rather the gentle stirring of the night wind seemed to speak to him, and in that moment he knew what God wanted him to do. He had dropped to his knees, his face lifted to the heavens, and signed his contract with God.

Papa had returned to the city, eager to tell Alvida of the wonderful call he had received. But she had not thought it wonderful at all. She had stared at him with contempt in her beautiful eyes.

"Pontus," she had said in that perfectly controlled voice which betrayed no emotion, "are you telling me you are not going to be a lawyer? That you intend to become a *preacher?*"

Desperately he had tried to explain what a great honor it was to be called to the Lord's work; that her position as a minister's wife would be even more important. Alvida had listened quietly, and for a moment he felt he had won her understanding. Then she had *laughed*. And the next moment stripped his ring from her finger and handed it to him. Automatically Papa had taken off the ring she had given him and held it out to her. The fingers that touched his were cold. Then she had walked away from him, tall and straight, and unbelievably graceful, without a backward glance. For weeks he had been numb with pain, for she had been the other half of his life. But it had never occurred to him to change his mind. If it was God's will, she would come back to him; if not, he would devote his life to a higher calling—service to his God.

By the time he had completed his work at the theological seminary in Stockholm and received his first pastorate, he expected Alvida would be married. But she wasn't. With hope still in his heart, he furnished the parsonage with the finest of everything, though it took most of his savings. But when three more years had passed and still there was no word from her, he knew that his long and cherished hope was dead.

Now a bitter restlessness possessed him, one which his most fervent prayers failed to dispel. Surely God was testing him. Somehow he must meet the test. As the months passed into years and his wisdom increased, he began to feel that at last he had won the battle with himself and that God was pleased. Then had come the "call" to a small village in Lapland, in the ore-mining country of the rugged northern part of Sweden. Once more he would be close to the earth where he might draw strength from the everlasting hills. A tremendous sense of thanksgiving filled him.

It had been an arduous undertaking, moving his fine furniture so great a distance. But once there, the neighbors had helped and soon he was comfortably settled in the parsonage.

Slowly, with God's help, he had found peace and contentment. . . .

Papa had been so absorbed in remembrance he hadn't realized how far he had walked until suddenly he found himself
on the mountainside. It had been a long and bitterly cold winter.
Hunger had driven the wolves close to the village—closer this
winter than he ever remembered their venturing. Only a few
nights ago he had been awakened by their howling. For a long
time he had listened to their eerie wail, hoping Maria would not
be awakened by it. But she had awakened.

"Pontus, the wolves," she had whispered as though they
might hear her. "It must be a whole pack from the noise—and
they are so near."

"Yes, Maria, it sounds like a pack, but they won't come any
nearer. They must be very hungry to come this close."

Mama had clung to him. "Oh, Pontus," she cried, "let us
move away from here. Let us go to America. There at least all
the wolves are in the zoo."

It was difficult not to tell her then about the letter to the
Conference. But he had resisted the temptation and, pulling the
quilt up around her ears to shut out the howls, had told her
to try to go back to sleep and not worry.

"Promise you won't go on the mountain road, Pontus, until
spring. Promise me, please." And he had promised.

Quickly now he turned back along the path he had come,
glancing up from time to time cautiously. Even now in the
morning sunlight, these mountain roads were dangerous. After a
few minutes he was back in the village and beginning to be
hungry from his long walk. He hadn't meant to walk so far.
Mama would be worried about him.

How good God had been to send Maria to him. Again he
wondered how he had lived without her. From the moment he
had looked up from the sermon he was preparing, that long ago
summer morning, and saw her coming up the road to the par-

sonage, his life had taken on a brighter glow—a richness he had never dreamed possible.

It had been one of the first really warm days of that summer. Maria was wearing a blue dress, which later he noticed matched her eyes perfectly. At the little bend in the road she had stopped and surveyed the parsonage and its garden and the little white church as proudly as a traveler returning home. Then she had smiled, and it was as if suddenly she stood in reflected light. Presently she took from her pocket a white handkerchief and wiped the dust from her high-button shoes, then squared her shoulders and marched straight to his front door. In a moment the knocker sounded three sharp raps.

"I am Maria Skogberg," she announced as he opened the door and stood facing her. The smile was still in her eyes, but there was a firm almost determined set to her mouth, which in an older person would have been offensive, but which, in one so young as she apparently was, was rather amusing. "I have heard through *Patron* Karlberg that you are looking for a maid."

"So I am," Papa had answered with proper dignity. "Step right in and be seated while I interview you."

Strangely enough it had not occurred to him at all to show her into the kitchen where a maid properly should be interviewed. Instead he had led the way to *salen*. Timidly she had seated herself on the rose-colored divan and twirled the large silk tassel on the arm until he feared it would fall off in her hand. But he had said nothing, sensing her embarrassment; only sat opposite her on the organ chair and questioned her as directly as he could. Even then, there was something about her that disturbed him and caused him to feel more like the one being interviewed.

"Have you ever worked in a household before?" he began. "You seem rather young."

"I was sixteen last March, Pastor Franzon. My mother, God bless her soul, died when I was seven. Since then I have taken care of my father's household. Until last spring." She stopped and her lips quivered. "You see, Father was killed by a train last spring."

"I am truly sorry, Maria," he said gently.

"Thank you, Pastorn. You are very kind." She brushed away the tears that were about to overflow. "Mrs. Karlberg has permitted me to help with her children for my keep, until I could find a place."

Papa was aware that he was becoming too concerned about the girl's welfare. This would not do if she were to work as a maid and keep her place in his household as befitted a minister's servant. So he had cleared his throat and made sure that his next words carried dignity.

"Well, you seem like a capable girl and I might consider you for the position. But first I want you to know that the salary is very small, and working in a parsonage will mean that you must be especially careful to live a godly life, avoiding frivolities."

"Oh, yes, *Pastorn*. I do understand how important that is. I will try my very best."

For a moment Papa was apprehensive. Being godly should not be an effort for a girl so young. But when he had looked into Maria's honest blue eyes, it was as though he were looking into her heart, and he knew that this girl could never be anything else but kind and godly.

To change the subject he cleared his throat again. "My household, you understand, must be run with great economy. I permit absolutely no waste. You must watch the draft in the wood stove. It must be kept at a minimum and still maintain enough fire to throw plenty of heat. Can you light a fire in the morning noiselessly, using only three sticks of *tyre-wood?*"

Maria had moved to the edge of the divan and now stared at him as though he had accused her of a serious crime. But there was no fear in her voice when she spoke.

"Pastor Franzon," she said firmly, "my father was not a skinny man and we lived on only seven *kronor* a month, foɪ that is all he earned at the railroad. He was a strong man and his job was to shovel coal all day long. He did not believe that heat should go up the chimney either, but he liked his house to be always warm and cozy. We never had *tyre-wood*. I lit the fire with bark."

It was Papa's turn to stare. Why the girl was a little wonder! He had almost stammered his next question. "Did you dry the bark in the oven first?" He realized too late that he had released a torrent.

"Only if it was sour. And, Pastor Franzon, I know how to split a match in two. I can make soup from an almost meatless bone. If you like *råraker* I can make them light as a feather, without egg, and crispy brown with almost no butter." She paused and tilted her head knowingly, "You see it is the egg that makes *råraker* heavy. I save the egg for mashed potato cakes; it makes *them* light."

Already she had him dreaming of delicious food that he had never had a chance to taste in his household. Tant Renberg had her own large family to take care of. He could only expect the simplest food or cleaning service from her. He pulled himself back to the interview and carefully explained to Maria that it was most important for a bachelor pastor to avoid all suggestion of gossip. Therefore she must walk on the opposite side of the street from him in public and conduct herself with utmost dignity at all times.

She had laughed then, and there was a touch of sarcasm in her voice when she spoke, unbecoming to one of her age.

"I understand, *Pastorn*. It is right to *live* in the same house with a bachelor pastor, for goodness knows a man needs a woman to look after him. But it is wrong to walk on the same sidewalk in public."

Color flooded his cheeks. "Well," he had stammered, "not wrong really. Just looks wrong to some people." Then almost before he realized what he was saying he had blurted out, "I think you may consider yourself hired, Maria. Can you start tomorrow morning? I shall ask Tant Renberg to show you your duties."

She had beamed with happiness, and then come up with another surprise. "It is going to be wonderful working for a minister."

"And why is that more wonderful than working for Mrs. Karlberg?"

She had raised shining eyes to his, with an expression akin to awe. "Because that is almost like working for the Lord God," she said sweetly.

And the wonderful thing about it, thought Papa now as he turned into that same road leading to the parsonage, she had meant it. All through their years together, even when there were arguments and she had had the last word, there was still that little note of respect and sometimes awe which she had expressed that first day.

Well, now he must try to be patient and understanding with her. It was not much wonder that Mama pestered him about America after the winter she had had. First baby Kerstin had the whooping cough; then Nim had come down with the mumps and of course Greta and Torkel had caught them. And before they were out of bed, Vickey and Button caught the chicken pox. And all through it, not a word of complaint from Mama—just tenderness and hours of prayer with never a doubt but that God was looking out for all of them and would not fail her trust. Just watching her had made Papa a little ashamed of himself for much as he tried, he had never quite achieved that perfect faith which, with Maria, truly moved mountains.

Now as he reached the front step, the delightful aroma of fried herring reached out to draw him into the warmth of the kitchen. Breakfast would taste good after his long walk—particularly the way Mama fried herring to a crunchy brown.

But before he could open the door, Calle and Torkel came racing around the house. Seeing him, both stopped abruptly and bowed a polite good morning.

"What are you playing so early in the morning?" he asked.

"It is a new game Mama taught us," Torkel replied courteously. "It is called 'Going to America.'"

"It is fun, Papa," explained Calle. "You just run around the house seven times without stopping and the one that does it fastest gets a cooky from the Statue of Liberty."

Papa glanced around him. "But I don't see the Statue of Liberty."

The boys laughed. "Oh, she is in the kitchen," declared Calle.

"She is just Mama," confided Torkel.

Papa went into the kitchen, his appetite of a moment ago somehow not so hearty. What would Maria think of next?

Papa was to learn the answer later that evening.

All day he found it difficult to concentrate on the preparation of his sermon. He kept wondering if there might be a letter at the post office now, deciding his—and his family's—future. He consoled himself with the promise that after supper he would walk down to the post office. Postmaster Olauson lived in the back rooms and would be glad to get the letter for him if it had arrived. But when he had gone into the *vardags*-room to tell Mama that he was going out for a while, he had found all of them sitting on the warm brown carpet in front of the cozy fire, playing with matches! At first he couldn't believe he was seeing properly. Then Mama had looked up.

"Oh, Pontus. Come play the game with us. It is so much fun."

He started to excuse himself, but the pleading look in Mama's blue eyes melted him as always. Presently he was sitting with them on the floor before the fire, feeling most undignified.

"Where did you learn this game, Mama?" Nim asked as he dumped a box of matches onto the carpet.

"In America, of course, darling. Now listen carefully while I explain how the game is played. First I will divide the box of matches equally. Then each of us must build a house of matches. When all are finished, each of us blows softly on the house. The secret is to see whose house will stand the longest. The one whose house stands the longest gets a wish, which is sure to come true."

"Really come true, Mama?" asked Calle.

Mama winked at Papa. "Well, I remember playing this game one night in New York City with a little Swedish maid. *I* won and *my* wish came true."

"What did you wish, Mama?" asked Vickey.

Mama's eyes filled with dancing lights. "I wished that a tall handsome blond man would come from across the ocean and take me back to Sweden, and he did!"

Greta jumped up and down with glee. "I know who the pretty man was. It was Papa!"

"I shan't give away any secrets," laughed Mama. "Come on, let's start the game."

Papa wouldn't have believed the game could prove so exciting. In a moment he had forgotten about the post office and the hoped for letter from the conference. With much laughter and squeals of delight, one by one the match houses were finished, and a sudden quiet settled over the room. Only the whispering sounds of soft blowing pervaded the room.

Papa had tried to blow softly, but his house was the first to fall; then Nim's and Vickey's. Next Mama's. By this time everyone was laughing so hard it was impossible for anyone to blow softly. The rest of the houses fell in rapid succession. Finally only Kerstin's house stood.

"Kerstin wins!" Papa thought the shout would lift the roof.

Button protested, "Baby shouldn't count. She hasn't any wind to blow with anyway."

"Be fair, Button," Papa said firmly. "Kerstin's house stands and that was the point of the game. Now let us hear her wish."

"Yes, little one, tell us your wish," urged Mama.

Kerstin pulled at her hair in excitement, then looked at

Mama with her big blue angel-eyes. "Oh," she said, as if repeating a lesson, "I wanna go 'Merica on big boat."

Papa pulled Kerstin up on his knees. "And who told you to say that?" he whispered.

Kerstin pointed her chubby finger at Mama. "You did, didn't you, Mama?"

Early the next afternoon Papa set out to make his weekly calls on the sick. But first he would inquire about the letter. It had been too late last night when the games were finished to call on Postmaster Olauson. Papa had intended to go early this morning, but there was his sermon. It wasn't going well and already it was Thursday. Sternly he told himself that if a man could not discipline himself, what right had he to feel he could guide others—or, indeed, serve the Lord at all?

Now as he hurried along the snowy path toward the post office, he gave full rein to his eagerness. And as if to reward him for self-discipline, the letter was there. For a moment he held it unopened, keenly aware that its contents, whatever they were, would greatly affect the rest of his life. It was, he thought fleetingly, like opening a strange door not knowing whether light or darkness waited on the other side. Finally with clumsy fingers, he tore open the envelope:

Dear Brother Franzon:

We are happy to inform you that word has reached us from the Swedish-American Conference in Saint Paul, Minnesota, that a small church in New England is seeking a pastor from their native land. As the immigration is at a high point, there would be great opportunity there for a man of your qualifications.

Berkley Hills is an ideal location for a man with a family. It has an excellent high school and a small college.

The church is without a pastor at present. Therefore, we earnestly request that you advise us immediately of your decision. If you accept, we trust you would be able to begin service in Berkley Hills by the first Sunday in May.

We shall, of course, regret losing so excellent and zealous a preacher as yourself from the Lord's work here in Sweden but the education of your children, the reason for your request, is of great importance and, I am sure, a worthy one in the sight of God.

Yours in the Master's service,

Harald A. Backlund
CONFERENCE SECRETARY

After a long moment in which he seemed unable to think or feel, Papa slowly folded the letter and put it into his pocket. And then suddenly excitement possessed him. He wanted to rush back to Maria with the glad news. He wanted to see her eyes open wide with surprise and then melt into a thousand dancing lights when she finally realized her dream had come true. But again the stern hand of discipline held him. His duty must come first. He remembered that Mrs. Nelson was very ill with lumbago; that Farmer Larson, a godly man, had a broken leg, and dear Miss Asp, the schoolteacher, was suffering from an infected ear. Why, he wondered, did so many saintly people have so much sickness and the sinners stay so well? Truly, "Whom the Lord loveth He chastiseth"! He must remember to preach a sermon on this very soon.

Papa's calls took longer than usual. Mrs. Nelson had asked him to read two chapters from the book of Job, and Mrs. Larson insisted he must have a cup of hot coffee and some of her newly baked coffee bread before going out into the cold again.

It was after six and many hours past darkness when Papa arrived back at the parsonage. Reflections from the open fire in *salen* threw purple shadows on the snow beneath the window. Papa stopped, surprised. Why should there be a fire in the best room in the house on an ordinary week night? Important unexpected company must have arrived. His wonderful news forgotten for the moment, Papa hurried through the door. Inside all was strangely silent. By the door, motionless as a statue, stood Button in her best dress. Wordlessly she took his coat, hung it on the coatrack, then with sweeping dignity, ushered him into *salen*.

Papa gasped. The whole family dressed in their best was seated about the big table which glowed with "company" silver and linens. But there was no company.

"Sit down, Pontus *lilla*," said Mama, her eyes laughing at his surprise, "this is a very special night."

Papa sat down.

"The children and I have planned this night to tell you why we want to move to America," continued Mama. "We call it America Night. See, Pontus, even our food is American hamburgers, scalloped potatoes and Harvard beets. *And* the biggest surprise of all—American apple pie. I made it from dry apples and it smells just like America! After dinner we shall have a program."

Papa was too overwhelmed for speech. Now the silence which had greeted him was transformed. The familiar family noises restored a little of his usual poise. He realized that he was very hungry. Even an American dinner would taste good.

When the last crumb of the apple pie had been devoured, Mama signaled for quiet. "Now we are ready for the program, Pontus," she said, settling back comfortably in her chair. "Each of us will tell you why we want to go to America."

Papa started to speak—to tell them there was no need for this. They were *going* to America. It was all arranged. Then, as he looked about him seeing as if for the first time tonight the shining, eager faces of his children and the proud affection with which Maria met his gaze, he was silent.

"Come, Nim. You are the eldest. You may speak first," said
Mama.

Nim arose. Awkwardly he smoothed his unruly red hair.
He was tall for his fourteen years and, as Papa watched him
wavering, as it were, on the threshold of manhood, he could not
help seeing a mischievous little boy cutting up everything in
sight with his wicked scissors.

"I have a special wish to go to America," Nim began, looking straight at Papa. "You see, last summer I suddenly knew
what I want to be when I grow up. I had been down by the
brook and found a dead frog and I cut it up with my scissors.
Not in pieces—just one big cut. Then I knew I wanted to be a
doctor—a surgeon who would help people by cutting out the
sickness." Nim blushed in embarrassment and sat down quickly.

Of course, thought Papa meeting Mama's eyes for a moment, that was it. A doctor was what he was meant to be. Papa
almost laughed aloud, remembering that he had thought him
destined only to be a barber.

Now Button was on her feet, her eyes sparkling with mischief. "With your permission, Papa, I shall read you a poem I
have written telling you why I want to go to America." She
cleared her throat and read:

> "America is a country where we will go some day
> That is—I am sure we will—if Mama has her way
> They have no King or Queen or such
> You just get rich by a magic touch
> They have more fruit than you ever know
> You eat yourself sick if you don't go slow
> You are free and happy and gay of heart
> And I am asking Papa—when do we start?"

Everyone was laughing now. Button sat down triumphantly.

"Oh, Button," cried Mama, "that was perfectly wonderful!
Just think, Pontus, so far we have a doctor and a poet in the
family."

Now it was Pelle's turn. He stood up, his angel-face beaming with excitement. "I want to go to America because I can go to school and read a lot of books, but if Papa doesn't think we should go I know that is best and I shall just stay in Lapland and read only a few books."

"Thank you, Pelle," whispered Papa. The lump in his throat too big to permit him to say more.

There was no embarrassment in Vickey's manner. She stood as poised and regal as a little princess beside her chair and spoke in a low, vibrant voice. "The streets in America are very wide and there are many store windows filled with pretty clothes. I want to grow up and be very beautiful and marry the President."

The burst of laughter that followed did not disturb her at all. Even Papa tried to suppress a chuckle and think of the proper thing to say. This was not the time for reprimand. "You don't want very much, do you, little Vickey? But to me you are beautiful now, and I guess I wouldn't mind having a daughter in the White House."

Greta was giggling so hard by this time she could scarcely make her speech. "In America I can have all the cream puffs and ice cream I want and when I grow up I shall marry a baker so I can lick all the bowls in the bakery."

The merriment was in full swing now and, as always Greta was a good target. "You'll get so fat," teased Button, "that nobody will want to marry you. Certainly not the baker. You'd eat up all his cakes."

"And how can you wear pretty clothes if you are fat?" chimed in Vickey.

"Too many cakes are bad for your health," put in Nim, the doctor-to-be.

"Come, come, children," laughed Mama. "It is time for Torkel's speech."

Torkel seemed to have forgotten whatever speech he had prepared. He stood for a moment twisting the corner of his coat into a roll and finally the room was quiet as a church.

"I think," he finally said in a high, singsong voice, "that in America there are lots and lots of trains. Some of them run under the ground and some in the air. Most of all, I want Papa to take Calle and me on the train under the ground." He wriggled back onto his chair and sat looking down at his plate as though expecting jeering laughter.

"I'd like that, too!" cried Calle who always followed in Torkel's footsteps.

The smile that suddenly flooded Torkel's small face, thought Papa, was like a light turned on inside.

At last it was little Kerstin's turn. She stood up in her chair and curtsied daintily to Papa. "Go—go! 'Merica on big boat," she said. At the laughter which followed, Kerstin jumped up and down, clapping her tiny hands.

Then as if by unspoken command, sudden silence settled over the festive room. Mama stood up and for a moment her eyes rested lovingly on each of her children and finally on Papa. "Pontus *lilla*," she said softly, "now you know how much we all want to go to America. We hope we have convinced you America is the right place for us. But if you still think we should stay in Lapland, we shall stay and be very happy, for we all love you very much."

Mama paused. Her eyes held the brightness of tears. "And now," she continued, "a speech from the most prominent speaker in all Lapland, Papa Franzon!"

The family applauded as Papa got to his feet. For a quick moment he remembered his excitement this afternoon when he had wanted to rush home with the letter to break the news to Maria and the children. How grateful he was now that he had not done so. Why, at that very moment the children probably were busy with their speeches and Maria joyously planning this special evening. He wanted very much to tell them he hadn't been blind to their wishes, that their happiness would always be first in his heart; that he had wanted only to be sure of his surprise for them. But to tell them this now would destroy the triumph which shone with radiant eagerness from the dear faces around the table. He would just let them think *they* had convinced *him*. What did it matter whose idea it was, so long as they were always as happy as now?

"Dear family," he began, including them all in his smile, "let me thank you for a most enjoyable evening and for all your very fine speeches. I think you will all grow up to be orators, for you have *completely* convinced me that we should go to America. I shall write a letter to the Conference this very night. Now I would like to ask Mama a question. How soon can you get ready?"

For a moment there was utter silence. Mama's blue eyes were big as cookies, staring unbelievingly at Papa. Then everyone started talking at once. Papa sat down, amply rewarded for the sacrifice of his own simple triumph.

Suddenly Maria's arms were around his neck. "Oh, Pontus, thank you, thank you."

Jubilantly the children formed a circle and began marching around the table singing "America" in high-pitched voices. So, thought Papa, Mama had been very sure of herself, using that song as a climax to this special evening.

Later, when the children were in bed and Maria was busy with her mending, Papa went to the study to write his letter of acceptance to the Conference. Finally he sealed the envelope and stamped it ready for mailing at the railroad station in the morning. Then he leaned back in his big chair and closed his eyes, giving himself over completely for the first time today to the turbulent emotions within him. Soon spring would touch with flowering hand the Swedish hillsides. The silvery birches beside the little white church would sway gently in the soft wind. A new pastor would be standing in his pulpit. In the garden across the way, the cherry and plum trees would be lavish with bright blossoms. Other hands would smooth the paths of his sand-yard and tend his cherished strawberry plants.

Other childish voices would echo in the red-and-white parsonage and other happy feet would climb Gellivara mountain on Midsummer Day. Their eyes would mirror the excitement of roaring waterfalls, salmon jumping, the wonder of huge logs floating downstream and finally the miracle of a flame-tinted June sky in which the sun did not set at all.

For a moment Papa felt it was more than he could relinquish. His roots were deep in Swedish soil. How could he tear them up and hope to replant them in a strange new country? Suddenly another picture imposed itself—the circle of happy faces around the table tonight when he had told them they would all go to America. There was no longer room in his heart for selfish desire.

He got up and crossed the study to the wide window which overlooked the hills, now snow-garmented and sparkling like silver in the starlit night. And suddenly it was as though God's hand, reassuringly, was on his shoulder.

The clock in the front hall sounded ten long strokes. As Papa came back into the *vardags*-room Mama put aside her mending. "Oh, Pontus darling," she cried, her arms around him, "I'm just one big heap of happiness."

And two large tears rolled down her cheeks to prove it.

CHAPTER 7

❧ Lost—One Preacher

The next few months were busy ones for the whole family. They lived in a state of breathless excitement. For each of the children the big journey to America carried an individual significance. Parting with small but to them very important possessions was a major problem. Leaving forever their friends and the places which were especially dear to them—a woodland path, the ski run on the snowy hillside, the river where in summer they boated or picnicked on the grassy banks—all required the courage of sacrifice. How many times they sorted their toys and books, selecting an increasing number which they simply *must* take. And just as often Mama reasoned gently with them, until at last they were happy to leave most of them behind, as presents to their best friends.

As the months sped by, Mama was quite sure that the children had begun to regret the decision. Education just wasn't that important. They were happy and doing very well, they thought, without it. Button had always had a gift for light verse and rhymes, and a few of them actually had been published in a small church magazine. She doubted that America—or education—could offer greater happiness. So it was Button who sowed tiny seeds of rebellion, which Mama carefully dug up before they had a chance to take root.

Early in April the new pastor arrived and Papa arranged to sell him all the furniture. Departure now became an inescapable

reality. Up to this time Mama had kept her own emotions carefully veiled behind a cheerful smile for the benefit of the family.
Of course she loved Sweden; but education was *important*, and
important things required sacrifice. But parting with her home
was not easy. Her eyes lingered lovingly on each separate piece
of furniture as she followed Papa and the new pastor from room
to room. When she came to the picture of the angel which had
served as a model for the virtues she hoped her children would
acquire, she touched it gently and for a moment her eyes filled
with tears.

But when the day of departure finally arrived, Mama was
determined that no note of sadness should creep into their final
farewells, whatever emotions tugged at their hearts. All must
eagerly look toward the future—and education.

Even Mama might have lost some of her eagerness for education had she known then the severity of their first "lesson" in the
new world.

The whole Franzon family waited on deck of the big
Swedish-American liner, peering through hand-shaded eager eyes
toward the famous skyline. It was early morning. Mist, like a
rose-gray veil dropped from Heaven, hung over the choppy waters, and, far beyond, the first faint flame-tints of sunrise touched
the horizon. Soon they would land in a magic new world.

"And those mountains way in the distance," Mama whispered excitedly, "are not mountains at all. They are just tall
buildings in New York City."

There had been little sleep last night. Everyone had eaten
too much at the sumptuous "Captain's Dinner," and the dancing
and games had continued until long after midnight. Not even
Kerstin had been put to bed early. Now, wide-eyed at Mamma's
remark, the children stood in a quiet little group apart from the
other sleepy passengers on deck, awaiting with awe and suppressed excitement the first glimpse of this unbelievable land.

"Are they really as big as mountains, Papa?" asked Torkel.

"Well, not exactly," answered Papa winking at Mama. "They just seem that big when Mama talks about them."

Mama laughed softly. She was so happy she wanted to tell all the people on deck how her wonderful dream had come true. Tense with inner excitement, she kept her arm about Vickey and held on to Kerstin's warm little hand. Nim and Button were leaning on the rail now, quiet but so eager she had to watch that they didn't lose their balance and fall overboard.

"I bet it would take a lot of faith to move them, wouldn't it?" asked Pelle solemnly.

"Move what, dear?" asked Mama who had been busy with her own thoughts.

"Why, the houses big as mountains," Pelle replied.

Everyone laughed, as much at his earnest big eyes as at the question.

But Papa put his hand on Pelle's shoulder and swallowed hard before he could speak. "It would indeed, Pelle," he said softly. "But just remember, nothing is *too* big for faith to move."

The mist began to lift now. Slowly, thought Maria, as though the hand of God was raising the curtain of night to reveal, especially for them, this wonderful new world. In the distance the famous skyline gradually emerged, at first like a faded etching, then clearer and clearer until at last the tall towers stood sharply engraved against the bright spring-morning sky.

Mama was awed to silence at the wonder of it. Then she placed her hand gently on Papa's arm. "Oh, Pontus," she whispered, "isn't it beautiful? I think we should all say a little prayer of thanks for our safe journey."

"Of course, Maria," agreed Papa, his voice husky with emotion. "Come children, let us form our family circle and all say 'Thank you, God, for a safe journey.'"

For a moment all eyes were closed and heads bowed. Then Mama linked her arm in Papa's. "Thank you too, Papa *lilla*," she said quietly. "Now we are ready to enter our Promised Land."

Papa smiled down at her and she saw the brightness of tears in his eyes. For a second she wondered if it was because he was happy too, or was he already homesick for the little white church and the red-and-white parsonage in Lapland? It was not going to be easy for him, she knew. But she loved him even more for sacrificing his own desires, so that she might have her dream and the children a chance at education.

Landing was even more thrilling than the first time, decided Mama, as she watched the eager excited faces of the children and listened to the gay laughter of the other passengers now crowding the deck.

Papa lined up the children in pairs. "Now hold on to each other's hands," he directed when the big gangplank was down and everyone began trying to reach it at once. "And stay close to the pair ahead of you so we won't get separated. I shall walk ahead of the line and Mama will follow with Kerstin so the other passengers will not crowd between us. Nim will end the procession. It would not be good to get lost in the crowd."

Finally they were safely on the pier, waiting in line again for customs inspection. Mama could not help remembering that first time she had stood here with Mrs. Johansson's five children. How long ago it seemed! Now there were eight children around her and—even more wonderful—they belonged to Pontus and her. God had heard her prayers and indeed had showered her with His blessings. And now they were all in *America*. Mama's eyes were dripping tears, but her heart pounded with happiness.

At last the inspector reached their pile of trunks and suitcases. He frowned heavily at the huge stack. If only she could assure him, thought Mama, that there was nothing in all those trunks and bags but a few household items and their clothing, most of which she had made herself. But it was his job to look, so she better not interfere. Then, as though he had heard her wish, he looked her way. Mama smiled. She couldn't bear for anyone to be unhappy this day, especially because of them. Maybe,

thought Mama, he had come from another country, too, and
now was remembering how he had felt when he arrived.

An hour later they were in taxicabs on the way to Grand
Central Station where they would get the train for their new
home. One cab was not enough so Papa and Nim rode in one
with the luggage, and Mama and the other children followed
in a second cab.

"Wait for us in front of the station, Pontus," called Mama
as the first cab pulled away. "We just might get separated."

All the way uptown the children chattered and gasped at the
incredible sights and sounds. "How will we ever find Papa in all
these crowds, Mama?" worried Calle.

Kerstin took up the cry. "Papa's lost! Papa's lost!"

"Papa and Nim are right there ahead of us. See," assured
Mama. But they weren't listening.

"Oh, Mama, look. The man is all *black*," cried Calle.

"Yes, darling," whispered Mama, realizing that the children
had never seen a Negro or even a dark-skinned person before.
"There are lots of people in America with dark skin. Some
brown and some black skins as well as white. And they are all
God's children."

"If I touched him would it come off, Mama?" asked Torkel.

"Of course not, silly!" said Vickey disgustedly.

Mama smiled, trying to remember *her* impression the first
time she had seen a dark-skinned person.

There was so much to see, no one thing held their interest
very long. From the taxi they could not see the tops of many of
the buildings.

"Are all the houses in America that tall, Mama?" asked Calle.

"Will our house be that high?" wondered Torkel.

"No, yes, no." Mama couldn't answer the questions fast
enough. Only Pelle was awed to silence and little Kerstin snuggled close in Mama's arms, frightened by the ceaseless noise and
confusion.

But it was *good* to be here in America.

At the station Papa learned that it would be several hours before the next train to Berkley Hills. "I better send a telegram to Mr. Olson to let him know we have arrived safely." Mr. Olson was head deacon of his new church.

When Papa came back from the telegraph office, although it was not yet eleven o'clock, he took all of them into the big station restaurant.

"What funny long names they have for food, Mama," laughed Button as Papa gave the order in English to the waiter.

"But it will taste just like our ham and eggs in Lapland," smiled Mama.

After lunch Mama found a long, unoccupied bench in the station and settled the girls about her to wait until train time. Papa had taken the boys to the washroom. Kerstin slept in Mama's arms. Greta leaned against her on one side and Vickey on the other. Beside her Button sat erect and wide-eyed, not missing a thing.

"Mama," said Vickey suddenly for no apparent reason, "is the Statue of Liberty alive?"

Mama laughed so gaily that people in the waiting room turned to look at her. "Whatever made you ask that, Vickey?" she asked.

"Well I heard you *talking* to her when we passed her this morning."

Mama hesitated a while before answering. "The Statue of Liberty, darling, is not alive, but it is very real. So real it is easy to *think* of it as alive. I call her Lady Liberty, and we have been friends for years."

"Aw, how could you, Mama, if she isn't alive?" scoffed Greta.

"You see, darlings," Mama said softly, "a long time ago I asked God please to send Papa and me a lot of wonderful children. I knew He would, for God always answers our prayers if we *really* want what we ask. So when Papa and I left America, I told Lady Liberty some day I would come back and show her all my "dreams." That is what I called all of you in my heart. And today I kept my promise to her."

Greta still was not satisfied. "Papa says the Statue of Liberty is just a hunk of steel—and things."

Mama slipped her arm about Greta and hugged her closer before answering. "Little one, that is true if you look at the outside. But inside that steel lady I think there is a very big heart —big enough to love all the thousands and thousands of children that come from all over the world to this beautiful country."

"Nim says he wants to shake hands with Lady Success," said Button.

"And I'll bet he will, too," said Mama. Then she added softly, "But if you want to meet Lady Success, you must first place your hand in God's. And that is just what we all did this morning when we thanked Him for a safe journey."

Papa and the boys had returned now, so Lady Liberty was momentarily forgotten.

"Maria," asked Papa, "what would you think about my taking the boys for that subway ride they wanted? It is still almost three hours before our train leaves, so there is plenty of time."

"Oh, Pontus, I think that would be fine."

"I'd better stay here and take care of Mama," said Nim importantly.

"I want to stay too," cried Pelle. "I don't want to go under the earth. Nim says the trains go right under the buildings and everything."

"They do, indeed." Papa smiled. "All right, son, you and Nim stay here and help Mama. Come, Torkel and Calle! We better get started."

Mama watched them cross the high-ceilinged station. How American the boys looked in their short blue pants and sweaters, thought Mama proudly. At the subway entrance they turned and waved before disappearing into the dark cavern.

After a while the younger children began to get sleepy and

curled up on the seat for a nap. Mama let her own head rest against the back of the seat and closed her eyes. She wasn't sleepy; she was far too happy for that. But she still found it hard to believe they were in America at last. Maybe for the rest of their lives.

At that thought Mama sat up quickly. Somehow it hadn't occurred to her before that they might never see Lapland again.

I guess I didn't have time to think about that, she thought, seeing dear old Tant Renberg's wrinkled face again as she handed her her most precious possession—a small alabaster statue of the three graces. Tant had wept unashamed. It had been hard for Mama not to cry, for she knew how much Tant Renberg loved that statue. She had given it into Pelle's care for the journey, promising the old woman it would have a cherished spot in their home. How could she ever have managed all the years without Tant? Her hands were rough and her voice often sharp, but her heart was always big and full of love for everyone.

It had seemed the whole town had come to the station to say good-bye. Even Kurre the cat, who now belonged to the Ericksons, and Sippan, Mrs. Lund's poodle. Mama smiled, remembering how Kurre, at the sight of Sippan, had tried to make himself as big as a lion and as ferocious. But Pelle, who had been saying good-bye to the cat for the hundredth time, stroking its sleek sides, had quickly scooped him up in his arms and held him. Sippan, a haughty, well-bred little dog, had marched stiffly past them as if to say, "Don't you know better than to start a *fight* at a farewell party?"

Everyone had brought some kind of special food for the long train ride. Three dozen hard-boiled eggs, new-baked coffee bread and thermos cans of hot coffee. There were big bags of cookies for the children and dozens of cheese and ham sandwiches.

But the flowers were the most wonderful surprise of all. Mama had not expected anyone to observe the Swedish custom of giving flower wreaths to America-goers. It was too early for garden flowers and the greenhouse flowers were much too costly. But that hadn't made any difference. It seemed they had emptied all the greenhouses in Lapland!

Mrs. Lund placed a lovely wreath about Mama's neck; then a more dignified one around Papa's. Deacon Lund called for quiet.

"Anna-Lisa wants to say a few words to the children," he explained.

Anna-Lisa Lund, as spokesman for the young people, came forward carrying a pretty braided basket filled with small flower-wreaths. Solemnly she placed one about the neck of each of the children, even little Kerstin. Then she curtseyed and spoke her piece.

"We shall miss you all very much. God's blessing on you in your new home across the ocean."

"Thank you, thank you," chorused the children. The boys bowed properly and the girls curtsied as Mama had taught them to do.

It seemed no time at all after that until they were on board and the train was pulling away from the station. Mama's last sight of all their friends and neighbors was a sea of white hand-kerchiefs waving good-bye, the beautiful melody of their song, "God Be With You 'Til We Meet Again," slowly fading in the distance.

"Oh, Pontus," sobbed Mama, "if only we could take them all with us."

"Heaven forbid, Maria," Papa had said soberly. "I am glad they will all stay in Lapland where they belong."

There was so much sadness in his voice that Mama knew his heart must be very heavy. She had begun talking rapidly to the children about the two days they were to spend in Stockholm, seeing all the wonder of Skansen Park with its fine zoo, and the old, old houses with grass growing on their rooftops. And the fun of watching the folk dancing on the green lawn with every prov-ince represented in its own costume. Soon Papa was smiling again and joining in the fun and anticipation, and she knew, at least for the present, he had put aside his heartache. . . .

Button's hand on Mama's knee awakened her from her daydreaming. "Nim and I would like to go and look around in the station. Is it all right, Mama?"

"Of course, dear. I'll be right here keeping an eye on you. Don't go out of sight."

Vickey and Pelle were getting restless too. "May we get a drink of water from the fountain, please, Mama?" Mama nodded, and they pattered off across the stone floor, holding on to each other's hand. As proudly as if they were going out to conquer the world, thought Mama. Well now that they were in America they would soon be doing just that.

When they returned Mama glanced at the clock. Almost two o'clock. Papa and the boys should be back soon. Then they would be on their way to their new home. What would it be like? Mama wondered. She hoped the church would be white, with a steeple, and there would be a big garden where Papa could grow strawberries and lots of flowers; maybe then he wouldn't be too homesick for Sweden. After a while, she was sure he would be so happy in America, he would be glad she and the children had made up his mind to come to this wonderful country.

Papa was trying very hard to get into the spirit of adventure as he crossed the huge vaulted station. The two boys held onto him excitedly as they descended the subway stairs. Perhaps, he thought, if he could just regard this arrival in America as a vacation like the other time, it wouldn't seem so *final*. Then he might be able to swallow the lump in his throat, which had been there ever since the train had left the small village in Lapland, and really enjoy the subway ride with the boys. So far he hadn't been able to pretend very well, but the boys hadn't noticed; they were too busy trying to see everything at once and asking a million questions.

Suddenly Torkel grabbed his arm and pulled him to one side. "Papa," he almost shouted to make himself heard above the roar of the trains, "are those people kidnapers?"

"Why of course not, Torkel. Whatever made you think such a thing?"

"Well, Nim told us in America every hundredth person you met would be a crook. We must have passed a hundred people by now, and a kidnaper is the meanest crook of all, so I just thought . . ."

Papa wanted to laugh. Instead he said sternly, "Nim should not have said such a thing, in the first place. There are bad people in America as there are in every country. But why would any bad man want to harm you or me. Now let's get that subway ride before it is too late."

"Nobody can kidnap us while Papa is around," boasted Calle.

Both boys clung to a hand and said nothing more until they were down another flight of stairs. Then: "Papa, if a kidnaper tried to take all your money, would you let him have it?" asked Torkel.

This time Papa did laugh. "Are you still worried about kidnapers?"

"Well, if he took all your money, how could you buy furniture for the new parsonage?" put in Calle.

Papa stopped again. "We better settle this right now. First of all, a kidnaper steals the *person* and then tries to get money for returning him. I don't look like a rich man, do I? So how could they get a lot of money for returning me? Now do you see how foolish this kidnaping idea is?"

"I'd pay a—a *hundred* dollars to get you back, Papa. Honest I would," promised Torkel who could just count to a hundred.

"Me too, Papa, honest," echoed Calle as usual.

Papa didn't think it wise to ask where they would get the

hundred dollars, so he changed the subject. "Come now, boys. One more flight of stairs down under the buildings and we'll find the subway train."

Papa had forgotten how crowded a subway platform could be at midday. He cautioned the boys to stay close to him as they edged their way through the packed masses. The deafening roar of incoming trains made conversation difficult. It was impossible after a while even to walk side by side, so Papa pushed the two boys ahead of him as they neared the yawning mouth of the train. Like a hungry giant, it gobbled up the crowd in one big bite.

Torkel and Calle were part of the bite, but not Papa.

Just as the door was about to close, a huge workman had forced himself in between Papa and the two boys. By the time Papa realized he couldn't act like a gentleman in the subways of New York, the train was halfway down the platform on its way to Brooklyn.

Papa had always considered himself a brave man. But now he was scared. Scared and helpless. He tried to think as the hurrying crowds pushed him about like a piece of paper in the wind. Faces, faces, faces. Everywhere strange faces. People too busy with their own affairs to tell him what to do or even to listen to his questions. Anxiously he looked about for a policeman, but there was none.

"Dear God, help me," he whispered, almost too frightened to pray.

Panic left him. Of course. The boys would get off the train at the next stop when they missed him. If he hadn't been so filled with fear he would have thought of that sooner. Now he hoped it wasn't too late. Poor little chaps! They must be frightened half to death alone on a subway and—the thought almost paralyzed him—unable to speak a word of English. Papa didn't stop to be courteous this time. He pushed his way into the first train that came along.

But the platform at the next stop was just as crowded. Anxiously, hopefully, Papa worked his way from one end of the platform to the other. No Torkel or Calle. He tried the next station and the next, with the same result. For hours he rode the subway and prayed. At each station he got off and searched the crowd, then on to the next station. But it seemed now even God had deserted him.

By five o'clock Papa had reached the end of the line in Brooklyn. Still there was no clue to finding his lost boys. Several times he had considered returning to Grand Central Station. Mama always had good suggestions. She would know what to do. But how could he go back and tell her that he, a grown man who had been in America before, couldn't even take two small boys for a subway ride without losing them? No, he *had* to find them himself! So he had continued the search. Now his stubborn pride wilted. Pride! That was why God hadn't answered his many prayers this afternoon. Didn't the Bible teach that "Pride goeth before a fall"?

Papa staggered a little with relief at the thought. Humility, deeply sincere, swept through him. "Forgive me, Lord," he whispered half aloud over the lump in his throat. Just let him find his children unharmed and he wouldn't care if Mama reminded him of his carelessness the rest of his life.

He started across the platform to get the first train back to Grand Central station. Suddenly a headline, in bold black type, stared up at him from the newstand. MINISTER FEARED KIDNAPED.

For one awful moment Papa just stared at the newspaper, then he snatched it up and started toward the subway.

"You savin' yer money, Bub?" shouted a heavy voice.

Papa stopped, realizing what he had done. "I'm sorry, sir. I wasn't thinking. How much is it?"

He put down the pennies requested, stuffed the paper into his pocket and pushed into the train just as the door was closing. Jammed in with the evening rush crowd, it was impossible to get at the paper in his pocket. But the headline had told him two things: *He* was supposed to be kidnaped; but his boys were safe; where else but from Torkel and Calle could the paper get such a ridiculous story?

Papa squirmed in the unyielding crowd. Why Mama must be frantic with worry! He only hoped she hadn't seen the paper.

Then suddenly the gravity of his own situation struck him full force. He could never go to Berkley Hills now. He would be the laughing stock of the whole town. Deacon Olson must have been worried when they were not on the train they were supposed to be on, and by this time, with news traveling so fast in America, no doubt he had read the story. He'd better send him another telegram as soon as he could get out of this sardine can. Why hadn't they all remained in Sweden where they belonged, where people were content to travel slowly, not on underground lightning, with crowds acting like madmen?

For two endless hours Mama had watched the enormous clock in the center of the station ticking off the minutes. And with each vanishing minute her anxiety grew.

"What has happened to Papa and the boys, Mama?" questioned Nim, and Mama knew he was worried too.

"It takes longer to get places in New York," she said consolingly. "They will be along any minute now."

"But, Mama," put in Greta, "Papa said the subway goes like lightning."

"It does, dear, once you get on it. It is getting *to* it that takes so much time. See how big the crowd is in the station now? Well, that is the way it is almost everywhere in New York City." Mama smiled reassuringly though she did not feel like it.

Three o'clock came. Still no sign of Papa and the boys. Now they had missed the train to Berkley Hills. With one corner of her mind Mama remembered that Deacon Olson was to meet that train, but she was too troubled by this time to give much thought to the Deacon or the good church people of Berkley Hills.

What if something had happened to Papa and the boys? No, she must not think that. God wouldn't *let* anything happen to them. They were good and God was good. But she couldn't help wondering just a little what she would do with six children and not a penny for food and shelter. In New York you had to pay for such things. There were no kindly neighbors to help you when in trouble. Mama prayed silently.

The hands of the big clock moved like the arms of an evil giant waiting to destroy them. Half-past three. The children were restless and hungry. Nim and Button's faces were white with anxiety. Mama could stand it no longer.

"Here, Button," she said quietly, "you hold Kerstin for a while."

Button took the sleeping child without question. Mama hoped she would think she was just going to the rest room, as they were called here in America, so she wouldn't have to explain. But she prayed there would be a telephone somewhere beyond that protecting wall. Inside the big anteroom a woman in white uniform sat at a small table. Mama approached her and in her best English explained the situation. The woman picked up the telephone. "Please give me the Police Department," she said importantly.

Mama was speechless. Was it a crime to let one's children and husband get lost in New York? She had been away from America a long time. Maybe things had changed since she had lived here.

"Please, Miss . . ." she began. But someone on the other end of the line was answering the woman in white.

"Give me the Missing Persons Bureau," commanded the woman. "Sergeant Malm."

Relief swept through Mama, but her knees felt weak. She had forgotten about special places like that in New York. Why in a way, New York *did* have good neighbors to help you. But there must be so many people to be helped, they had to do it like a business.

The woman was speaking to her. "What's the name, Madam?" Mama spelled it out for her. "Sergeant Malm? Mary Mullen at Grand Central. A little Swedish woman with eight children seems to have lost her husband and two of the children. Name's Franzon. Reverend Pontus Franzon. Kids' names, Torkel and Calle. Got anything on it?"

She waited. So did Mama, breathlessly.

A little frown appeared between Miss Mullen's eyes. "Well, be on the lookout, won't you. What's that, Sergeant? Okay?"

She hung up. "Sergeant Malm—he's Swedish too, you know —says to send you and the children down to the Bureau."

"Do they—have they—found them?" gulped Mama.

"Not yet, but they will. Now don't you worry. Meantime, you'll be better off there than sitting in the station all night."

"All night!" exclaimed Mama, terrified at the thought. "Oh, I'm sorry. I didn't mean to be discourteous. You are so kind. But suppose my husband and the boys come back to the station and we aren't here? Then he will have to look for *us*."

"Well, that could happen. But the sergeant said to send you down there, and I guess I better obey him."

Mama did not want to break any laws, but she just couldn't take a chance that Papa and the boys would return and find them gone and not know where they were. Anxiety gave her courage. "Would it be all right to leave the children in the station with Nim and Button, and I will go talk to the police officer myself? They are big children and very reliable. They will take good care of their sisters and brothers."

Miss Mullen hesitated. "I guess that would be okay. I'll keep an eye on them for you too. Now where are they?" She followed Mama back to the bench where the six children waited.

As they walked the short distance, Mama tried to think what she would tell them. If she expected Nim and Button to be big enough to look after the younger children, they were big enough to know the truth, she decided.

"This is Miss Mullen, children," she said in Swedish. "She

will stay with you until I come back. I have to take care of something." Then she took Nim and Button aside and explained, assuring them she wouldn't be gone very long. Miss Mullen would know how to get her if Papa and the boys came back before she returned.

Mama got out of the taxicab before an imposing-looking building and paid the driver with the money Miss Mullen had given her. Inside the lights were very bright, and many men in blue uniforms stood about, talking and laughing together. One young officer separated himself from the others and came toward her. "And what might I be doing for you, young lady?" he asked cheerfully.

Mama smiled in spite of her worries. He was so friendly, and he had called her "young lady." What would he say when she told him she had eight children and a lost husband?

"I'm Mrs. Franzon—Maria Franzon. Sergeant Malm is going to help me find my husband and missing children."

"Glory be to God, now," exclaimed the young officer. "Imagine a husband running away from a pretty little thing the likes of you. And kidnaping the kids, too."

Mama did not know whether he was taking God's name in vain or not. Some Americans, she thought, had a funny way of talking. But she certainly didn't like him accusing Papa of running away from her and stealing his own children.

She started to tell him so, but stopped in time. It would only make matters worse. Maybe he just meant to be kind, anyway. In New York some husbands *did* run away from their wives and children. How could the officer know how much she and Pontus loved each other and their children?

"Please take me to Sergeant Malm, officer," she said with dignity; then smiled again.

He jumped to attention. "Right this way, young lady." Mama was sure he winked as he smiled back at her, then led the way down a brightly lighted hall.

He knocked on the door. When the voice inside said, "Come

in," he swung the door open and stepped back for Mama to enter. "Sergeant Malm," Mama began, but got no further. Two flying arrows came at her faster than she could think.

"Mama, Mama, Mama," cried Torkel and Calle throwing themselves into her arms. "Oh, Mama, we thought we would never see you again."

When Mama could get her breath she looked around for Papa. He was not there. "Where is Papa?"

At that the boys began sobbing so hard they could not speak. Mama's heart almost stopped. "Torkel, Calle," she commanded in Swedish, "where is Papa?" She hated being severe with them, but it was the only way to stop their tears.

Sergeant Malm, who had had no chance to speak before, came forward. He spoke to Mama in Swedish. "The children were found by Officer Murphy on the subway in Brooklyn an hour or so ago," he explained. "He could not speak Swedish and they could not speak English. He *could* understand they were lost. So he brought them here. Luckily Miss Mullen had just telephoned me a few minutes before. I hoped they would be your children. They insist their father has been kidnaped by a big hoodlum. That is all I have been able to get out of them."

Mama sat down on the straight-backed chair and pulled the boys to her, an arm about each of them. "Please, boys. You must stop crying and tell Mama everything that happened. Don't you know God wouldn't let anything happen to Papa? He just got misplaced, that's all. Now tell me right from the beginning."

Torkel got control of his tears first. "The big train came roaring in, Mama, and millions of people got on and the door shut fast. When I looked around for Papa he wasn't there. Then I knew that big man kidnaped him! He *did*, Mama. I just know he did!"

"What big man, Torkel?"

"The one that we saw on the way to the subway. I saw him first, and I tried to warn Papa, but Papa said nobody would want to kidnap him. He said kidnapers only wanted money to bring you back."

Mama held onto her patience. So far none of it made any sense. Poor little chaps. They were so upset their imagination was playing tricks. Gradually, with much patient questioning while Sergeant Malm listened, Mama got the story.

When the boys had realized that Papa was not with them they were very frightened. Calle had tried to ask a man standing next to him if he had seen Papa, but the man only shrugged and looked at him and said something in a strange language. Suddenly they realized that no one could understand them either.

By this time the train was traveling through the underground tunnel with the speed of an angry dragon.

"Do you think we might ride on and on for years, Torkel?" Calle had asked.

"Of course not," Torkel had answered, trying to be brave enough for both of them. "It has to stop sometime."

"Maybe we'll be in—China—or—or India by then," speculated Calle.

"Of course not, repeated Torkel. "Trains can't run under the ocean."

Frightened and trainsick, the boys had huddled together for comfort and stayed on the train. After what seemed like a long time to them the train stopped and a lot of passengers got off and more got on. Eagerly they had looked for Papa. One passenger had a round collar and looked very kind. He had smiled at them and Calle had wanted to ask him if he had seen Papa, but he remembered in time that he could not speak English.

Again the train rushed on, jolting and rocking in its speed. More stops and more people. None even looked like Papa. Finally almost all the people left the train.

"Do you think we should get off too?" asked Calle.

"No, we better stay on," Torkel said hesitatingly. "I've been thinking, Calle. Papa says the world is round so maybe in a year

or two we'll come right back to New York station and find
Mama and Papa."

Calle settled back in his seat. "Won't we be awfully hungry?"

Torkel had not thought of that.

The train rumbled on, stopping and starting at intervals.
Hundreds of people coming and going, but none of them Papa.
Again the train was almost empty.

"Torkel," whispered Calle, "my stomach feels awful funny."

Torkel looked at his brother. He was white as milk. "Calle,
please! You can't be sick here."

Calle only rolled his eyes back and forth.

"And the next moment, Mama," Torkel related, "Calle's
sickness was running down the aisle."

Two men at the other end of the waiting train, attracted by
Calle's groans and what had happened, tried to help them.

"But we couldn't understand them, Mama, and they
couldn't understand us."

The train had started again.

At the next stop one of the men took them off the train. "I
thought we were being kidnaped like Papa," explained Torkel,
"but I hoped the kidnaper would take us where they kept Papa
and then we could fight the kidnaper and get away and come
back to you."

But presently the man had stopped beside a policeman and
after a lot of words which they did not understand, the policeman had taken both of them by the hand and led them away.

"He's taking us to jail," Calle had sobbed. "We'll never see
Mama again."

Torkel had not been sure he wasn't right, but he had to be
brave and look after his younger brother.

After a while they emerged from the cavern of the subway
and presently found themselves in a brightly lighted room with
many policemen. Several of them tried to talk to the boys without success.

"Finally one policeman led us to a bench and then went away. When he came back Mr. Malm was with him and he could talk to us," finished Torkel.

"That was about half an hour ago, Mrs. Franzon," explained Sergeant Malm. "They were too frightened, I guess, to tell me very much except that their father was kidnaped. I was sure then they were the children Miss Mullen had telephoned about."

"But where is my husband?" asked Mama in English, fears crowding in despite her prayers. "Could the boys be right? Do things like that happen in New York City now in broad daylight, Sergeant Malm?"

"Lots of unfortunate things happen in New York City, even in broad daylight, I am sorry to say, Mrs. Franzon," said Sergeant Malm.

Mama's eyes filled with tears, but she managed a faint smile. "I must go back to my other children now. How grateful I am that you found my boys. I am sure my husband will come back, soon, too. It might be he is at the station now."

But Papa was not at the station.

The children sat close together on the waiting room bench, trying not to cry. They were hungry and too concerned about Papa to talk about the subway adventure. Sergeant Malm had instructed Miss Mullen to telephone him if Reverend Franzon had not shown up.

Mama watched the big clock, praying silently as the minutes ticked off an hour—then two. She knew Sergeant Malm was trying to find Papa. She must not worry.

"Mama, I hope Papa will give the kidnaper the money so he can come back soon," Pelle said and Mama's heart wept because of the ache in his voice.

"Darling, please don't worry so. God will take care of Papa and bring him back safely to us."

"We never should have let go of Papa's hand," Torkel regretted with half-stifled sobs.

Mama put her arm around him and pulled him close to her.

Torkel's anxiety was reflected in the faces of all the others. "Everything is going to be all right, children. Remember, trouble is just *luck* turned inside out. It will turn back again very soon now. Just you wait and see."

Mama tried to feel as cheerful as her words. She would just wait and pray and have faith so the children would not be so frightened and worried. How patient they were. Not a word of complaint, though she knew they were hungry. Now Pelle was praying a little too loudly and people were looking his way.

"Tell him not to pray so loud, Mama, please," Nim protested. "After all, God is not deaf."

Mama smiled. "Indeed He isn't, Nim." And immediately she felt better. *Out of the mouths of children*, thought Mama. She *had* been acting as though she believed God were deaf—not hearing her prayers. She had wanted to have faith, but deep down she had been doubting. Now Nim's innocent words of criticism of his brother had made her realize the truth. Mama closed her eyes. "Lord, forgive me my unbelief," she whispered fervently under her breath.

It was as though God had been waiting for her humility.

"It's Papa! It's Papa!" shouted Calle.

Mama opened her eyes quickly and there was Papa almost running across the station waiting room. Mama didn't care if it *was* Grand Central Station. In a moment her arms were around Papa's neck and, for the second time that day, tears of happiness were on her cheeks.

"Oh, darling, darling," she cried, "I don't care if they stole all your money. You're safe—you're safe!"

Papa squirmed uncomfortably. "Maria, people are staring at us." He loosened her arms from about his neck and wiped the tears from her face with his best pocket handkerchief. "Of course I'm all right, Maria. I'm so glad the boys are safe." Mama noticed there were tears in his eyes too.

The children were all trying to talk at once and hang on to Papa. All but Torkel and Calle, who stood back a little and seemed to be waiting for Papa to scold them for letting him get lost.

Papa pulled them both to him. Instantly their arms were around his neck like little ropes. "Oh, Papa, Papa! We didn't mean to let you get kidnaped," they cried.

For the first time in hours Papa laughed. "How would you boys like to go for a subway ride?" he asked, winking at Mama.

"No, no. Let's go home," both agreed at once.

"We're hungry," said Greta. "Did the kidnapers leave you any money?"

Papa assured them again that he had not been kidnaped, and that his money was safe. With full stomachs, life seemed right once more. The children were eagerly listening to Torkel and Calle's adventure. At last Papa could talk to Mama without being overheard.

"I'll never live this down, Maria," he sighed. "It is bad enough having my name smeared all over the front page like a common thief——"

"Pontus," exclaimed Mama, "what are you saying?"

Only then Papa remembered the paper still crammed in his coat pocket. He hadn't intended to mention it if Mama hadn't seen it. Now he took out the paper and unfolded it, displaying the headline.

"Story on page 6," directed the small print under the black headline.

Papa turned the pages reluctantly.

"Here it is," said Mama. Then she started to laugh.

"I don't think it is amusing, Maria," snapped Papa.

"Oh, Pontus. It's not *you* at all: it's a minister in someplace called Kokomo."

Papa seized the paper and read. By the time he had finished, his face was almost as red as Vickey's hair ribbon. He had *assumed* the headline referred to him, apparently because of Calle's ridiculous remarks earlier, and he had been too upset by it to take time to read the facts. He had had only one thought—

to get back to Grand Central—and of course there had been no chance to read on the subway. Mama certainly would never let him forget *this*.

Quickly he changed the subject. "That still doesn't excuse us for not notifying Deacon Olson in time about our delay. He's probably waiting for us right now at the Berkley Hills station." And suddenly Papa realized he had forgotten to send the second telegram.

"Pontus," Mama began thoughtfully, "maybe Deacon Olson wasn't expecting us."

Papa stared at her. "Why of course he was. I sent him a telegram as soon as we arrived. Don't you remember?"

"I mean maybe he won't be expecting so *many* of us."

Papa opened his mouth to ask "why," then stopped. Good Heavens! Mama was right. He had neglected to mention that there were eight little and not-so-little Franzons. Now he realized that the matter of the children had never been mentioned by the Church secretary either. Apparently they *assumed*, knowing his age, there would be just himself and wife.

"I'm afraid you are right, Maria," Papa admitted finally. "Well, probably we will soon be on our way back to Sweden— where we should have stayed in the first place," he finished sharply.

Mama patted his hand. Poor Pontus. He had had a very tiresome day, and she couldn't blame him for being cross and depressed.

"You'll feel better after a good night's sleep," she said gently.

"You mean what's left of the night by the time we get there," answered Papa, glancing at the big clock. "And we had better not miss *this* train."

While Mama assembled the children and the baggage, Papa hurried across the station to the telegraph office. He hoped Deacon Olson was a God-fearing man and wouldn't mind meeting a train in the middle of the night to welcome a lost preacher and his family.

CHAPTER 8

❧ Button Goes Wild

The adjustments to be made in a new country were excitement enough for all the Franzon family during the next few years. How they struggled with the language and the seemingly unreasonable and strange customs! Even Mama, who had lived in America before and now spoke the language quite well, had to learn many American ways all over again.

She was thinking of this as she surveyed the dozen white sheets on the long line in the parsonage garden, blowing softly in the May morning breeze. How easy washday was in America. Here, every Monday was washday. *Every* week, instead of twice a year as it was in Lapland. Of course, in Lapland she had not done all the work herself on those twice-a-year washings which consumed an entire week. Tant Renberg and Emma Erickson had helped. All the white clothes were boiled in *lut* and pounded vigorously with a *klappträ* on a board in the brook, until they were white as the mountain snow. Twelve dozen sheets and several times as many towels and pillowcases. Now she had only two dozen of each.

Mama laughed softly thinking how shocked dear Tant Renberg would be to know that. Why, in Sweden, no girl would have thought of getting married until she had twelve dozen sheets, pillowcases and towels, all marked in lovely embroidery with her own first initial and the second initial of her husband-to-be. But even more important were the bride-sheets. The bride-to-be worked almost a year on them. Every stitch by hand and delicately embroidered. With these she herself prepared the bridal bed.

American girls missed a lot of fun, thought Mama. Then suddenly she realized that she had too. *She* had had no bride-sheets. She had slept alone on ordinary sheets, in a bed made by a stranger on a ship. And even when they reached Lapland, there had been only sheets made by Tant Renberg, who had no idea that a bride was to sleep in the big hand-carved parsonage bed.

Mama grunted apologetically. What was a girl to do when the man she wanted to marry could not make up his mind until two days before the wedding.

Mama gathered up the clothesbasket and bag of clothespins and went inside. Never again would they have a home as lovely as the parsonage in Lapland, even if she had not had bride-sheets. She loved being in America, but sometimes she had to admit that she missed the parsonage almost as much as Papa did.

"Maria," he had said one evening, walking up and down the living room, "it was indeed kind of the church members to furnish the parsonage before we arrived, but sometimes my heart aches for our beautiful home in Lapland—our own furniture instead of this weird mixture of everybody's leftovers."

Mama had forced herself to answer cheerfully. "Don't worry, Pontus. Some of the furniture is too old to last very long. And maybe the owners will want it back when we have worn out our newness. Besides, we must never forget how thankful we were that first night, when we arrived at two o'clock in the morning. to come to a home instead of an empty house. Why, Pontus, this furniture is really 'love' furniture, and anyway in a few years it will be just memories like Button's curtains."

Button had looked up from the English paper she was work-ing on, and laughed. "Curtains!" she said disparagingly. "Why they were straight from Mrs. Lindström's ragbag. Every time the wind blew on them they developed a new hole until they looked like a spider web."

"But now you have beautiful ruffled curtains, dear," Mama reminded her. "And some day we'll have those fluffy-ruffle curtains at every window. You'll see!"

Button had gone back to her English paper, but Mama stood looking out the window, a dreamy smile curving her lips. "Just like a bride . . ." she murmured to herself.

Papa had quickly changed the subject. "Anyway Button is a lucky girl to have a new maple bedroom set in her room."

Button giggled. "You mean lucky for me that the Widow Beck fell in love at the age of sixty-five and was the first to ask for her furniture back!"

"That was Papa's first marriage ceremony," exclaimed Mama, for in Sweden only the State-Pastors could perform wedding ceremonies.

Papa chuckled softly. "If I only had a chance to perform one for Miss Lilja so she would ask for her desk back. Can you imagine how difficult it is, Maria, to write *sermons* on an old-maid schoolteacher's desk?"

Mama put the clothesbasket away, smiling over her happy memories. What a funny and dear parsonage this was. Even if the house was a bit on the tumble-down side, it was big and the rooms were large and spacious. To be sure, the furniture was odd, a conglomeration of strange pieces, most of which had seen far better days. But it had been source of much merriment in the new parsonage.

"Please don't lean too hard on the Anderson table, boys. The leg might fall off again," Papa would warn.

Or it was the Almgren chair, or the Hanson rug, or the Frilen stove.

All these had been given under a keep-it-as-long-as-you-need-it policy, and Mama would remind them, before the merriment reached a point of ridicule, that these things had been given in a kindly generosity and they must never forget it. But even as she spoke, she could not help remembering longingly all the lovely things she had left in Lapland.

But if the furnishing of the parsonage left much to be desired, the garden made up for it. Loving hands had designed the garden and planted the flowers which bloomed lavishly every year for each pastor and his family that lived in this old house.

Mama tidied the kitchen, now, removing all traces of washday. When lunch was over and the children had gone back to school and Papa set out for his afternoon calls, she went into the sunny garden with her sewing and mending. The red and yellow tulips, bright against the picket fence, were dropping their lovely petals, making a gay patchwork quilt of the dark soil beneath. Soon lily of the valley and bright purple iris would take their place. Near the house, the lilac bushes were in full glorious bloom, shedding their nostalgic fragrance over the whole garden.

Mama buried her face in the lavender blossoms. "Oh, you sweet beautiful things," she whispered to them. "You're almost as beautiful as our white lilacs in Lapland."

Indeed, she thought, as she sat down on the rustic garden bench beneath the big elm tree at the far end of the garden, life had been more than wonderful this first year in Berkley Hills, in spite of the longing they all felt for the good life in Lapland. Even Papa, who, Mama was sure, had not really wanted to come to America, now seemed reconciled and happy. But this had not happened easily. At first he had seemed to live entirely in the past, and it had taken a good deal of planning to keep him too busy to think about it more than was good for him. All those first months Mama had gone with him on his sick calls, so he wouldn't have too much time alone to think about the past.

Until last October, when her strategy had almost brought about a tragedy.

Miss Temple, the schoolteacher, had given Torkel and Calle each a small jack-o'-lantern for their first Hallowe'en in America.

"You must wait until dark, and then light the little candles in the lanterns and place them in the windows," she had directed.

The boys had run all the way home, too excited to talk coherently. Mama had not had time to listen, for she and Papa were ready to leave on a sick call. Vickey, Greta and Kerstin had gone to a party, and Nim, Button and Pelle had little after-school jobs. Torkel and Calle would have to stay home alone.

"Now be good little boys," Mama admonished as she kissed them good-bye, "and look after the house like little men. Papa and I will be back soon."

Torkel and Calle, as Mama learned later, had sat down dutifully at first, waiting impatiently for darkness. In each small lap rested a bright orange jack-o'-lantern with its single candle waiting to be lighted.

"I wish the dark would hurry," said Calle, when half an hour had passed.

Torkel glanced at the window. Outside the soft rosy light of Indian summer lingered. "It will be a long time, I'm afraid," he sighed.

"If only we could *make* it dark," said Calle hopefully. "Do you think if we pulled the shades it would be like night?"

"Let's try." They had pulled all the shades, but it still was not dark enough to please them.

"Perhaps we can find a dark corner," suggested Torkel. "It won't be as good as night, but when night really comes we can put our lanterns in the window too."

It was Calle who finally cried, "I've found one! Under the Ekdahl sofa." The boys got down on their knees and peered speculatively underneath.

"It sure is dark under there," agreed Torkel.

They had scrambled up and run to the kitchen for matches. Soon two small candles glowed from the lanterns. Trembling with excitement, they pushed the lanterns under the sofa, then sat back admiring the flickering light from the funny faces of the jack-o'-lanterns.

"Look, Torkel," shouted Calle after a moment, "my lantern shines a lot brighter than yours."

Torkel looked. "Calle!" he exclaimed, "I think your whole lantern is burning."

Calle's eyes filled with tears. "Save it, Torkel! Save it!"

"I can't." Torkel's face was ghostly white. "The Ekdahl sofa is smoking, too. I am afraid it is getting burnt."

Calle got to his feet. "I'll get some water."

"No, Calle. Go for the fire engine. I'll get the water," said Torkel taking command.

Calle had been only too eager to agree. "I might get a ride on the fire engine," he yelled, starting for the door.

"Wait, Calle, I'll go with you," decided Torkel. "I want to ride on the engine too."

And the next moment they were racing down the street, leaving the Ekdahl sofa to its fate.

Mama and Papa had arrived home a split second ahead of the fire engine.

When the fire was out and the fire engine had gone, Papa had taken the boys into his study, and a few minutes later two very unhappy little boys, lanternless and with very sore seats, had gone to bed without their supper. Mama had examined the furniture for damages. The Ekdahl sofa was badly burned, and there was a great brown hole in the Hanson rug. But she was thankful that was all that had burned, and she was sure the boys had learned a valuable lesson in patience. . . .

Mama dismissed the memory and picked up a pair of Nim's socks that needed mending. Not just Nim's socks, but a whole basketful of socks and stockings. Well, it took a lot of mending to keep up with a large family. Mama chuckled softly. No wonder the welcoming committee that had met them at the station, in spite of the late hour, the night they had arrived in Berkley Hills, had been openmouthed in surprise!

Deacon Olson had found his voice first. Red-faced he had stammered, "Are—all—these—children yours, Pastor Franzon?"

Papa had stared bleakly at him for a moment, then answered, a note of irritation in his voice. "I should hope I would not bring eight children that did not belong to me, all the way from Sweden!"

"I'm—I'm sorry, Pastor Franzon," stuttered the Deacon, "you see we were under the impression you were an older couple past the age to have so many children." Then apparently realizing he was only making matters worse, he lapsed into flustered silence.

Mama had extended her hand to him, feeling sorry that the poor man was so embarrassed. "It was thoughtless of us, Deacon Olson, not to write you about our children. But it won't be long before you know us all. We're really a very nice family."

"Of course. Of course." The Deacon beamed. "We are happy to welcome you to Berkley Hills, Pastor Franzon—and family!"

"We are happy to be here," said Papa, a little more gently. "And it was most kind of you to meet us at this unearthly hour. Now would you please show us where we are to live. The children have had a very tiring day, I'm afraid."

The next morning, Pontus had been able to laugh with her over the shocked faces of the committee.

"And Deacon Olson will never forgive us for making him forget his speech," laughed Papa. "Well, tomorrow the whole church will have a chance to look us over, Maria."

"They will like us, Pontus. You'll see!"

Mama went back to her mending. Six pair of socks for Nim and three for Pelle. It was the same almost every week. Such busy feet, thought Mama, but her heart was full of pride for the way those boys worked. Nim had a paper route, and Pelle searched for odd jobs which they both worked at when the papers had been delivered. Now they had regular window-washing and floor-scrubbing jobs on Wednesdays after school, and on Saturdays. And the money they both earned went into the big tin box on Nim's bureau. Mama knew that Nim was saving up to become a doctor, but that didn't explain Pelle's contributions.

"Don't you want to save for something special, too, darling?" she had asked Pelle one evening when he had emptied his pockets of his day's earnings, into Nim's tin box.

"I'll wait, Mama. It's awful important for Nim to hurry up to be a doctor, don't you think?"

Unselfish as always, thought Mama, hugging him. "It is, indeed, Pelle. Papa and I are very proud of you both."

"Just think, Mama," he boasted. "Sometimes we earn as much as *four dollars* a week. It won't be long now 'til Nim can start."

But even a fortune like four dollars a week hadn't been fast enough for Pelle and Nim. A few days later, when she was finishing the supper preparations, Pelle had come bursting in, too excited to remember his manners and almost too excited to talk.

"I got it, Mama! I got it! We'll earn *three dollars* just there. We'll be rich pretty quick now."

"Well, that's fine, Pelle. But suppose you catch your breath and tell me what is going to bring about this miracle of riches."

"It's Doctor Davis, Mama. I got a job for Nim to wash windows in his office and scrub the waiting room two nights every week."

"Why, Pelle, that's just wonderful."

"But that's not all, Mama. I told Doctor Davis all about Nim and I spoke very good English. I know he understood every word I said. I told him how Nim is going to be a great doctor, too, some day, and he promised to let Nim help on Saturdays when he has lots of sick people."

Mama smiled and patted his eager little face, her own heart ready to burst with pride. "Does Nim know about this?"

"Oh, yes, Mama. I ran all the way to Mr. Ekdahl's where he was washing windows, to tell him. He says maybe Doctor Davis will let him peek into his black bag to see how much tools he will need to save up for."

"That's just fine, dear. Now get washed up for supper. Papa will be coming in soon and you can tell him all about it."

It had been Papa's idea to let the children work at odd jobs. Mama had thought it might not be looked upon as proper for a minister's children, but Papa had insisted. "Best way for them to learn English, mingling with people who speak nothing else." And Mama knew he was right.

Nim and Pelle loved it, and Mama had to admit they were learning the language very rapidly. But with Button it was a different story.

Sometimes Mama was sure that Button just naturally rebelled—against *what* made little difference so long as she stirred things up. Even as a baby, Papa often reminded her, she had rebelled against order, keeping him up half the night walking the floor to quiet her yells.

Papa had arranged for her to help the Rogers family, who lived a few blocks down the street, an hour or two each evening after school. There were only Mr. and Mrs. Rogers, so the work wasn't heavy, and it gave Button an excellent opportunity to learn English and American housekeeping methods. Button hated it. And after several months, Mama realized Button wasn't learning English. Several times she determined to speak sharply to Button, but one look at her confused face, when she came home from her afterschool work, melted Mama's heart, and, instead of scolding, she would try to make the child smile again.

Papa conducted classes for the younger children three evenings each week, and they were making remarkable progress. After a while Button was so far behind the others, she refused to speak English at all unless forced to do so. Mama was worried. This might prove harmful to Button in more ways than one. Button had always been high-spirited, gay and happy. But lately she seldom smiled and no longer made up the little songs which she used to sing at the top of her voice.

"We must do something, Pontus. I just know inside her

heart is heavy. She is so ashamed she can't speak English as well as the others, she just refuses to talk at all—even in Swedish."

Papa hadn't said very much at the time, but a few days later, when the family was gathered for breakfast, he had made an announcement.

"Starting tomorrow morning, all of us will speak English during mealtime. Anyone speaking Swedish during meals will not be recognized," he said solemnly, including all of them with a sweeping glance. "And by tomorrow morning I trust you will make sure you are prepared."

It had proved a wonderful plan for all the children—except Button. Mama was deeply concerned now and again mentioned her concern to Papa. But this time he only frowned. "I'm afraid, Maria, she will just have to adjust herself to America, like the rest of the children," he said calmly and went back to his reading.

How, thought Mama, could she make Pontus understand that some people just couldn't learn *some* things as fast as others? Why Button was a perfect housekeeper and a wonderful cook. It was just English that was hard for her.

The mending was done and Mama walked slowly across the soft green grass, her thoughts still on Button. Must there always be an ache in my heart for that child, she was thinking, and is America the wrong place for her? She would have to pray a little harder that Button would be happy like the rest of them.

One evening, a week or so later, when Mama had just finished the supper dishes, Button came into the kitchen, her eyes bright with tears.

"Button *lilla*," exclaimed Mama, "whatever is wrong?"

Button ran into her arms sobbing. "Oh, please, Mama, help me to make Papa see how wrong it is to make me work for the Rogers. They laugh at me, Mama. It's awful. I wish—I wish **we** were back in Lapland."

Mama held her close to her heart. "Please, Button, don't cry. Just tell me all about it if you want to."

"It's awful, Mama. I won't go back."

"Now, now, dear. Dry your tears and come upstairs with me and tell me what happened."

Mama closed the door softly to Button's room. Button sat down on the bed and for several minutes just stared at the floor, fighting her tears.

"Well," she finally began between sobs, "this afternoon Mrs. Rogers was showing me how to iron a shirt."

"Why, Button, you know how to iron a shirt."

"Oh, no I don't, Mama. Not according to Mrs. Rogers. She doesn't want anything done the Swedish way."

Mama smiled. She was beginning to think Button's problem wasn't serious after all.

"We were in the laundry in the basement. Suddenly I looked up and right in front of me, on the wall, was a spider web with a little spider in the center."

"Button! Don't tell me you were afraid of the spider."

"Of course not, Mama. But Mrs. Rogers pointed to it and said, 'That is a *spider*, Button.' I guess she wanted to help me with my English. So I said it over and over, ten times, so I would be sure to remember the word."

"I think that was kind of Mrs. Rogers, darling."

"I know. But that is not all. Later when I was getting supper, she called to me from the dining room, 'Please put the spider on the stove. I'll be in in a minute.' I didn't know why she wanted to cook the poor spider, Mama, but they do funny things in America. So I went down in the basement hoping the little spider would still be there and it was. I caught it in a towel and put it in a pan of water on the stove."

Mama wanted to laugh, but this was serious to Button, so she kept silent.

"Oh, Mama," Button sobbed, "when Mrs. Rogers came into

the kitchen she looked in the pan and asked me what that was. I was so proud I had remembered, and I told her. Then she laughed so hard she cried. And she called Mr. Rogers and they laughed some more. Then she picked up the frying pan and tried to tell me *that* was a spider. Oh, Mama, I'll never go back. Tell me I don't have to!"

Mama put her arms around Button. She didn't blame Mrs. Rogers for laughing, and someday she knew Button would laugh about it too. But right now she was heartbroken. She had to do something to make her see the whole incident in a different light. Suddenly she remembered some of her own experiences when she had come to America the first time. In a few moments they were both laughing together over the stories.

"See, dear," explained Mama, "it is funny when it happens to someone else. That is the way you must feel when people laugh at your mistakes. They don't mean to be unkind. And anyway, don't you think it is wonderful to make people laugh, even if it is because of your funny English?"

"Well, I didn't think about it that way before," said Button. "I guess I am just hurt because I am so stupid, Mama."

"Of course you're not stupid, Button. Why, look at all the things you do very well—better than most people. English is not easy to learn."

For the next week, Button was more like herself, even humming her little songs as she helped with the late evening chores at home. Truly, thought Mama, God moved in mysterious ways.

But just how mysteriously, Mama did not understand until later.

Button came bursting into the house, one evening ready to explode with excitement. "The circus is in town. And look! Mrs. Rogers gave me two tickets. Oh, Mama, isn't it just wonderful? At last I'm going to see a real live circus!"

Long before Mama had begun to insist upon education and had transplanted her family to American soil, Button had had a burning desire to join the circus. What put the idea into her head in the first place was a mystery. She had never even seen a circus. At the time, Mama dismissed it as merely the normal desire of any child for color, gay music and excitement, which the circus stood for, or perhaps a natural rebellion against the restrictions which surrounded girls in Sweden, especially if they happened to be part of a minister's family.

Now, as she regarded Button's joyous excitement, she wanted to agree that seeing the circus would be wonderful, but she wasn't at all sure Papa would permit her to use the tickets. But she didn't voice her doubts, and Button was too jubilant to notice her silence.

"There's a beautiful dancer, too, Mama. Princess Mitzi in her fire dance. I saw a big picture of her on the signboard. Oh, she is so beautiful, Mama."

For the rest of the evening Button floated about on dreamy clouds. Fortunately Papa was attending a church meeting and did not return until after Button had gone to bed. He went directly to his study to work on his sermon.

Mama waited an hour, then knocked on the study door.

Inside, Mama hesitated. Now that she was here she wasn't sure how to begin. She waited a moment for inspiration.

"Don't you think it is wonderful how American the children are, Pontus?" she began. "Even Button is working very hard on her English."

"Maria, did you interrupt my sermon just to tell me how remarkable our children are?"

"I've been thinking, darling, it would be nice to give the children a little reward for working so hard to be good Americans. Maybe do something specially American—like the hamburger supper we had the night the children convinced you to come to America."

Papa cleared his throat, a puzzled frown between his brows. "Maria, you have never consulted me before about the kind of meals to serve. I'm sure if you think a hamburger supper would please them, I shall enjoy American food."

"Oh, I don't mean food this time, Pontus. I was thinking of something even more American—like—like the circus, maybe."

Papa jumped up from his desk and stared at her.

"Maria! I can't believe my ears. Surely you're not suggesting we take *our* children to a *circus*."

"I don't know why not, Pontus *lilla*. It's just *animals*. It would be educational for the children and do us all good. We could make it a family party."

Papa was walking rapidly up and down the study. His frown had grown into a very big scowl. "I am surprised at you, Maria. In Lapland we had no such temptations. America is full of cheap entertainment. I trust you have not suggested this to the children. Besides costing a great deal of money which we cannot afford, what do you think the church board would say about their pastor and his family attending a *circus?*"

Mama laughed. "Oh, Pontus! I bet Deacon Olson—and well, just everybody will go. Besides, it won't cost much. Mrs. Rogers gave Button *two* tickets."

Papa strode across the room and back, then stopped in front of Mama. "We shall not attend the circus, Maria," he said quietly as if he were announcing his Sunday morning sermon. And Mama knew the subject was closed.

"Very well, Pontus," she said softly and went out, closing the door behind her.

If Mama expected Button to receive the verdict with tears of defeat, she learned how wrong she was the next morning. There were tears—but they were tears of rebellion, not sorrow. Button stamped her feet and stormed.

"I don't care what anyone says or does. *I* am going to that circus."

Mama said nothing.

"Papa is just an old-fashioned preacher! Everything that's fun is wrong," she raged. " 'Don't, don't, don't'—that's all he ever says. 'Don't talk so loud—don't wear make-up—don't go to the movies. Remember, you must be an example for others.'

Well I don't want to be an example. I want to live like other girls."

"Of course you do, dear," Mama said softly.

Button stopped pacing the floor and stared. "Aren't you going to scold me for acting like a heathen?"

"No, darling. This is no time to scold you when your heart is breaking with disappointment."

Button threw herself into Mama's arms and wept stormily. Mama let her cry until the tears diminished to controlled sobs. "Now dry your eyes, little one. I shall talk to Papa again. Perhaps he will go *with you* to the circus."

"Oh, Mama, please try! I'll be the happiest girl in the world, and I won't ever complain again about working for Mrs. Rogers."

"Now run along, dear. You'll be late for school."

But when she was gone, Mama wasn't at all sure that the miracle of getting Papa to change his mind could be accomplished. Perhaps she was wrong, as Pontus had suggested, in encouraging the child to want to go. Well, she would ask God's guidance, and everything would turn out right.

It was Friday, the day before the circus, that she got the inspiration.

Mama waited until the children had left for school. Papa was getting ready to go to town. "I've been promising Nils I'd come in and inspect the seats for the Sunday School room the first chance I had," he remarked, as he took his hat from the rack in the front hall.

"I'd like to talk with you a minute before you go," Mama said.

Papa came back into the living room and sat down, his hat in his lap. Mama sat down on the sofa beside him.

"Isn't it wonderful, Pontus, how God sets an example for us in just everything?"

Papa stared questioningly at her, then spoke sternly, "I think we are all aware of the goodness of God. But I fail to see why it is so important to remind me of it at this particular moment."

"I've been thinking, Papa *lilla*. Do you realize it was God Himself who started the first circus?"

"What a ridiculous thing to say, Maria."

"It's true, Pontus. God commanded Noah to bring all kinds of animals into the ark. Not just one, but two of every kind."

Papa got up and started toward the door. Then he turned, and Mama could see a tiny smile nibbling at the corners of his mouth. "You do think of the queerest things, Maria. Long ago I should have learned that when you make up your mind, an earthquake couldn't shake it."

"Oh, Pontus, it isn't *bad*. I know it isn't. And the children will have so much fun. Seeing all kinds of strange animals—and the clowns—and horses. . . ."

"And the naked dancing girls like the advertising?"

"Of course not, darling. Besides, that's just advertising. If there are dancers, they will wear beautiful costumes."

However difficult it had been to change Papa's mind, it was worth it, Mama decided that evening when she broke the news to Button. The child was simply transformed.

Saturday afternoon was declared a holiday for the whole family. Nim and Pelle hurried through their window-washing jobs, and Doctor Davis assured Nim nobody could be very sick with the circus in town, so he wouldn't need him that afternoon. Mrs. Rogers gave Button the afternoon off. When finally they were on their way to the big circus grounds, Papa seemed almost as excited as the children. Mama and Button used the two tickets from Mrs. Rogers, and Papa took his place in the long line to buy tickets for the rest of them. Then they all entered the big tent together.

It was cool and shadowy inside, and the blare of bands made it almost impossible to talk. But the children were too excited to talk anyway. The dancing clowns, the elephants, the prancing horses, and the colored streamers and balloons everywhere kept their eyes so busy Papa had difficulty getting them into their seats. When they were lined up at last on the long benches, Mama glanced at Button, next to her, to see how she was taking all this. She was sitting like a stone image, on the edge of her seat; only her eyes moved, trying to see everything at once.

Suddenly there was a blare of trumpets. The circus began.

First the parade of animals, followed by the clowns, playing pranks and turning somersaults every few minutes. Papa was laughing with the rest of them as each act appeared. He had just opened a big bag of popcorn and was passing it among the children, when the trumpets let out a mighty blast, the drums rolled, and the spotlight flashed in the center of the circus ring onto a color-draped elevated stage.

Button clutched Mama's arm. A chariot entered, drawn by prancing white horses, bearing, according to the announcer: "That greatest of all dancers—the most daring—the most beautiful—the magnificent *Princess Mitzi!*"

Button sat transfixed. As Princess Mitzi swept into the opening measures of her dance, Button exclaimed, "Oh, Papa, isn't she just divine?"

"You mean that girl jumping about like a wild woman? Button, don't let me ever hear you call a human being divine. Only God is divine."

But Button wasn't listening, for now the sensational part of the dance had begun. Suddenly a circle of leaping flames appeared in the center of the stage. The music rose to a throbbing, intoxicating rhythm. Twice Princess Mitzi whirled on her toes around the outer circle of flames. Then with a wild cry, she leapt into the fire. Through the encircling wall of flames, the audience could see the frenzied dance of death, until, apparently overcome by the fire, the dancer sank like a dying bird into a motionless heap.

The lights went out, leaving the little stage in semidarkness, and the big spotlight swung to the trapeze act which was just beginning.

It was during the intermission that Mama leaned across Button to whisper to Papa, "Look, Pontus. There's Deacon Olson, just two rows ahead of us. You see. Everyone is on a spree today."

"And *Mrs.* Olson," said Papa. "She was too sick to attend prayer meeting this week. But she seems to have recovered remarkably. We must go down and shake hands with them."

"Oh, Pontus. She could have been really sick on Wednesday and still be well enough to be here today. Now don't spoil her good time by mentioning her health." She turned to Nim. "Please look after the children, darling, while Papa and I speak to the Olsons."

When they returned to their seats, Button was not there.

"Nim, where is Button?"

"Oh, she just went for a drink of water, I think."

The lights went down and the second part of the show began. But Button had not returned.

"I'm worried, Pontus. Maybe she is having trouble finding her way back. I think you better look for her."

Several minutes later, Papa returned, looking worried "There is no trace of her, Maria."

"Oh, Pontus. What shall I do? Something awful could have happened to her in all this crowd." And Mama began to pray.

"We had better send the other children home, and you and I will start looking for her," Papa decided.

"Nim will take care of the others, Pontus. No use to alarm them. I'm sure we'll find Button without trouble." But she did not feel as confident as she hoped she sounded.

Papa went back and spoke to Deacon Olson, making an excuse that would not excite him, and the Deacon agreed to see that the children got home safely when the circus was over. Then Mama left the tent with him. Outside, Papa asked, "How do we know where to start looking? Perhaps she got sick from the excitement and is in the rest room. You look there and I'll go back to the fountain. If she isn't either place, we'll meet at the door and decide what to do."

Button was not in either place. Mama found a worried Papa when they met again at the door. Then suddenly she remembered Button's enthusiasm for the dancer.

"I bet I know, Pontus. That dancer! What's her name? Princess something. Let's go find her tent."

"But surely, Maria, Button would have more sense than to go there."

"It isn't a matter of sense, dear. Button is young and young people sometimes get strange ideas. I think we better hurry."

It took Mama some time to locate the dressing-room tent of the star performer. Papa was about to pull back the tent flap, when Mama stopped him. Loud angry voices came from inside. "You dirty devil," screamed a woman's voice, "I told you not to come back here. Get out and leave me alone."

Mama's heart almost stopped. Did the woman mean Button?

Papa tore aside the curtain. On the dirty tent floor lay Button. And across the room a frowsy woman and a drunken man faced each other in anger.

Quickly Papa gathered Button into his arms. "What have you done to her?" he demanded.

"So she's your kid, eh?" growled the man. "Well, get her out of here. We didn't ask her to come. And we didn't do nothing to her. She fainted."

Neither Papa nor Mama waited to learn more. With Button in his arms, Papa hurried through the crowd to their car.

Hours later, with Button in her own bed, conscious, though still shaken by the experience, Mama sat beside her, changing the cold wet towels on her head. Papa was downstairs with the other children.

"Oh, Mama," sobbed Button. "I didn't mean to spoil everything. Honest I didn't. I just wanted to see Princess Mitzi and ask her to let me join the circus with her."

"Everything is all right now, darling," comforted Mama. "Try not to think about it."

"It can't ever be right again, Mama. Poor Princess Mitzi! She was so afraid of her husband and I know he will kill her. Can't we do something to save her?"

Mama had not realized until now that a good deal must have gone on in that tent before Button fainted. She had to erase it from the child's mind, but she could only do that if she knew all that had happened.

"Button, darling. Would you feel like telling me everything from the beginning? Sometimes it helps to talk about it."

Button just looked at her with vacant eyes for a long time. Then she shut them tightly and a big tear rolled down each cheek. "All right, Mama."

It had been during the fire dance that she had made up her mind to see Princess Mitzi in person. But the problem was getting away without Papa seeing her. When he and Mama had decided to greet Deacon and Mrs. Olson, she knew her chance had come. She waited until Nim was busy watching the clowns, then she had slid out of her seat and stolen from the tent. There were so many little tents she hadn't known which direction to go, so she just wandered around looking at everything. It was almost as much fun outside as inside the tent. So many exciting things happening. Finally she had met a boy with two pails of water.

"I'm Princess Mitzi's cousin," she had said politely in her best English. "Would you kindly direct me to her tent?"

The boy stared at her for a minute then pointed to a large ornate tent. Above the entrance hung a huge silver star. "Right over there. But you better be careful. She's pretty nasty after a performance."

Button had tossed her head and laughed confidently. "Oh,

she won't be nasty with me!" She set off in the direction of the tent.

She knew it was wrong to lie and run away from Mama and Papa, but they would forgive her when she was famous. She would beg Mitzi to let her work with her, take care of her; and maybe Mitzi would teach her the fire dance, so she could do it when Mitzi was tired or wanted a holiday.

Outside the tent she stopped. It did not look so beautiful close up. But she stepped inside, trembling with excitement.

Mitzi's back was toward her. She was taking off her beautiful costume, and her golden hair fell over her bare shoulders almost to her waist, like the pictures of the fairy queen Button had seen in books. Mitzi had not noticed her yet. She had flung her costume onto the cot and sat down at a small table, littered with dishes, glasses and bottles. To Button's horror, she saw her idol pour half a glass of what looked like whiskey and drink it at one gulp.

Button took a step toward her. Mitzi turned quickly at the sound.

"Hey, kid," she snapped in a scratchy voice, "what the hell you doing in my tent? How'd you get here?"

She was staring with cold, hard eyes at Button. Button's knees began to tremble. She tried to speak, but no sound came. Mitzi was getting up now and moving toward her. Suddenly Button saw the long hair fall to the tent floor, revealing straggly strands of gray. Mitzi's face, which had seemed so divinely beautiful as she danced, Button now saw was deeply lined and scowling. She wanted to turn and run, but she couldn't. Mitzi was standing before her now. Button had to find her voice.

"I—I—only wanted to tell you how beautiful you are."

Mitzi glared at her for a second, then let out a loud harsh laugh.

But having found her voice, and for the first time forgetting her difficulty with English, a torrent of words burst from Button's mouth. "I want to work for you. I'll do anything you tell me. I'll take care of you, wait on you. Oh, please let me stay! I want to learn to dance like you."

Mitzi sobered. "Well, I must say that's a new line." Then her face twisted into a rage. "What did you steal? Tell me before I call a cop!"

Button was stunned. "I—I didn't steal anything, honest!" And suddenly she was afraid. She began to cry. "How could you think I came here to steal? I just wanted to see you."

But her tears and compliments had no softening effect upon Mitzi. "Don't you move an inch," she snarled, "until I've checked my money and trinkets."

Button obeyed, wondering how she could ever have thought Mitzi was divine. Mitzi went to the battered trunk standing next to the entrance and clawed through her belongings. Then she came back and faced Button.

"I guess you are right, kid," she said more kindly. "You didn't steal anything. So you want to work for me, eh?"

Button wasn't so sure now. She didn't know what to say. She just wanted to get out of there and die.

Mitzi dropped down on the cot. "It's no good, kid. You better run home to your folks if you have any. This racket ain't for a sweet kid like you. I *was* beautiful once, and I was a great dancer. But not any more. You better go."

Suddenly Button was sorry for Mitzi. She wanted to tell her she was sorry, but her throat was like cotton. Then she saw the man crawling under the side of the tent. Mitzi must have heard him, for she jumped to her feet and yelled, "Get out of here! Get out before I call a cop."

The dark evil-looking man stood up and looked at her and laughed. "Not even the law will stop a man from seeing his dear wife."

"Wife," sneered Mitzi. "That ain't what you came for. You know I got paid yesterday. Well, you're not getting a dollar, do you hear!"

"Don't be so sure about that," he said and started toward her.

Button had been standing in the shadows near the entrance. The man apparently had not seen her until now. He stopped. "Who is she?" he snapped suspiciously.

Mitzi smiled calmly. "An admirer. Believe it or not, I still have them."

"Get her out of here."

"The kid stays, Max." Even though Mitzi's voice was calm, Button knew she was afraid. She wanted to do something, but her legs were like jelly, and she couldn't make a sound. Her head began to swim.

Then she saw the man coming toward her, his eyes bloodshot and angry. She tried to run, but her knees crumpled under her. She could hear Mitzi yelling, "You dirty devil! I . . ." Then nothing.

Mama did not speak for several minutes. She was thinking, and praying. Praying for the right words to help mend her confused little girl's heart and make her glad again.

Presently she realized Button was crying bitterly, "Oh, Mama, I wish I could die. Everything I thought was so beautiful is just ugly and awful."

"No, darling. Life hasn't changed. Everything is still beautiful. Sometimes God has to let us get hurt because we refuse to listen to Him. You are very young, and I am sure God has wonderful and beautiful work for you to do. Something much nicer than being a dancer. Trust Him, darling, and He will show you the way."

Button stopped crying. Mama kissed her tenderly and turned off the light.

"Now go to sleep, darling. Tomorrow is a new day; a brand-new day God has given us to be glad in."

CHAPTER 9

❧ Any Woman's Privilege

Whatever else could be said for youth, thought Papa, one of its virtues was flexibility. For his children, America, after three years, was still a place of adventure, though even they admitted at times that many of the customs were strange indeed. To Mama, however, it always had been the land of opportunity, and she seemed daily more determined that the children realize that.

But Papa was not finding transplanting so easy. Although he spoke the language with very little trace of accent and was proud of the progress his children were making in education, there were some things he simply couldn't understand.

In Sweden, every man was master of his own home. If he was a minister, he was also the leader of his "flock." Children were polite to their elders, and a wife respected her husband's wishes. But in America, Papa stormed inwardly, it was difficult to tell where a man's authority and responsibility began or ended. America, it appeared, belonged to women. There had been a time when *his* wishes were a law to his family. But no longer—not in America! Here even his *opinions* counted for little.

"Someday I am going to change the marriage vow. I swear I will."

Papa talked aloud to himself in the study. "Do you, So and So, solemnly promise that as a married man you relinquish your own opinion and do and think only as your wife desires?"

He straightened his black bow tie, gave his tailcoat a couple

146

of jerks, then placed the notes for his Sunday sermon on the large family Bible and noiselessly opened the study door. Through the long narrow hall he could see Mama at the table by the window of the sunny kitchen, preparing coffee bread for baking. The sunbeams played in her blonde hair, but there was a deep frown on her forehead.

Papa walked with slow, even steps to the kitchen. She is still boiling mad, he thought. She hasn't even cooled down since our last discussion. But he could try anyway. Even if she was this earth's most determined woman, she looked like an angel and the coffee bread she made was out of this world.

Mama's blue eyes had a glint of steel in them as she went about her work. Papa walked the length of the kitchen floor twice before he stopped and spoke.

"Maria," he said putting some ministerial authority into his voice, "when you are through baking, we shall take the children for a ride. I want you all to have a look at that farm."

Papa waited in vain for an answer. Mama was chopping nuts and raisins. She did not even stop that, forcing Papa to raise his voice on his next words.

"Didn't you hear what I said?"

"I heard," answered Mama softly.

"Well doesn't a question call for an answer?" thundered Papa.

Still Mama did not raise her voice. "That was not a question. It was a demand."

The fragrance of cardamon and cinnamon found its way to Papa's nose. It softened his heart a bit. He changed his tone almost to pleading.

"My nerves need a rest, Maria. I am preached out. A few years on a farm would make a new and better minister of me. If you could only grasp how good this farm idea is for all of us."

Mama placed her hands on her hips and faced Papa.

"Pontus. *I* know what's happened to you. You have developed an evil eye. The Good Book teaches us to pluck it out before it is too late. Just think of it. You want to give up your noble calling as a pastor to become a *farmer*."

Papa's head ached from too much thinking. He knew Mama was an exceptional woman. Few wives could cook, bake, keep a parsonage immaculate, besides tending eight children and accompanying her husband on pastoral calls. Papa was convinced there was not another woman in the world that could be compared with Mama. But as efficiently as she ran her home and children, she tried to run him and that had to be stopped.

"Evil eye," he mumbled. "As if giving up preaching for a time could connect me with evil."

Mama brushed her hair from her forehead, leaving a streak of flour across her eyebrows.

"I married a minister not a farmer, Pontus. And I don't want to become a farmer's wife. Not even a gentleman farmer's wife, or whatever you name it."

Papa was desperate. If only there were some way to talk reason into Maria. She was braiding the coffee rings now, her body moving gracefully back and forth. Carefully she dipped the pastry brush in the beaten egg yolk and penciled the top of the rings. Papa wondered as he watched her if she were through bearing children? Nim was eighteen and Kerstin five. Having babies had seemed such a pleasant, natural process to Mama as though she enjoyed going on increasing the earth. It seemed to Papa that Mama would fit perfectly in the large, spacious farm kitchen with more than ample room for the children to run around. He looked dreamily into space, thinking aloud.

"There is a lake below the farm where I could do a lot of fishing."

But Mama found the words to pull him back on the straight and narrow road.

"Pontus! I think the kind of fishing the Lord wants you to do is not done with hooks and sinkers."

Papa tried once more to convince her.

"Look how much fun the children could have on a place like that, Maria," he said eagerly. "How healthy it would be for them away from city life, with plenty of fresh air and sunshine."

"Yes," said Mama sarcastically, "and look how much fun *I* would have. I can just picture myself as a farmer's wife with a milk pail hanging on my arm. A pair of old shoes with worn-down heels that would smell far from perfume. Oh, yes, I can feel the flies buzzing around my face as I am milking. And I suppose the cow will give me a slap across the mouth with her smelly sharp tail every so often. For of course *I* will have to do the milking. I can't visualize you on a three-legged stool under a cow."

Mama went to the sink and washed her hands energetically under the faucet. Papa heaved a deep sigh. There was not a thing he could say or do to convince Maria. He put on his hat and went for a walk.

Mama stood by the kitchen window and her eyes followed Papa as slowly, with heavy steps, he walked down the street. His head was bent a little forward and his hands were locked behind his back, as always when in deep thought. Mama wanted to be fair, and just now her heart ached for him. She knew how deeply hurt and disappointed he was. She wanted to follow her impulse and rush after him, calling, "Papa *lilla*, come back. I didn't mean a word I said."

If she only could have told him that she had been thinking a lot about the farm idea herself. It must be a beautiful place and it could be such fun. She understood too well how tired he must be of a demanding congregation. She, too, was tired of all the little pinpricks she had to endure as a minister's wife. She would have loved to agree with Papa, but all she could do was to stand there and watch him wander off lonely and dejected.

Poor Pontus, she thought as a flood of love welled up in her heart. But after tomorrow he would know her reason and that had to be her consolation. He would understand then why she could not be a farmer's wife—why she could not leave the city. Mama was running for President of the Woman's Club.

In Papa's estimation a woman's duty was at home with her children. Mama loved her home, her children, her husband but she also loved to "climb the social ladder." To be President of the Woman's Club had been Mama's dream for years. It would give her influence. She would "sit in the council with the wise." She would be respected and honored and invited to every function of importance. Tomorrow the newspaper would carry the story. It might even make the headlines. Mama could already see them in her mind: MRS. PONTUS FRANZON ELECTED PRESIDENT OF THE WOMAN'S CLUB. And then what could Papa do but be proud that he had married a woman who was capable of such honor. He would drop the thought of the farm at least until Mama had served her two years.

Only it was important how Papa received the news. It must come as a pleasant surprise and not as a shock. Mama would arise early the following morning. She must be the first one to put her hand on that paper so she could bring it to Papa when she served him his before-breakfast coffee. Mama still served Papa coffee in bed. It was one habit from Sweden that he had refused to give up.

It was with purpose Mama had baked Papa's favorite coffee bread this morning. (It was not often that she made coffee bread in the middle of the week.) But tomorrow morning it must be extra special with lots of butter and sugar and cardamon. She would also wear her blue dotted Swiss dress which was his favorite, and she would smile very sweetly as she came with the tray. When Papa was on his third *Kringla*-bread and had asked her to pour his second cup of coffee, she would slip him the paper. And there from the front page her picture would smile at him. The rest she would have to leave in God's hand.

When the coffee bread was in the oven, Mama went into the study to be near the telephone. The nominating committee meeting would be over any time now. She sat down in Papa's favorite chair to wait for Miss Thompson to call and to dream about the future. At first she had refused to run for such a high position because of her Swedish accent. But Miss Thompson, the chairman of the nominating committee, had assured Mama that her accent only added to her charm.

"In our democratic country," Miss Thompson had explained, "we disregard such things. If a woman is willing and capable of leadership, we clubwomen are proud to have her serve regardless of foreign birth. And you, Mrs. Franzon, are a born leader!"

Mama had felt better about it after Miss Thompson's remark and had decided to run. If she only could have told Papa and he could have shared her happiness. Still she would handle him when it was all over. First she would point out that the church membership would be sure to increase through her election. It might even double in two years. What an honor for Papa to take a leave of absence and go farming at the height of his career.

The clang of the telephone broke in on her dreams.

"The election is over," Miss Thompson said in a toneless voice.

"Oh," answered Mama with a pounding heart, "how sweet of you to call."

"My dear Mrs. Franzon," Miss Thompson continued, "I am brokenhearted to bring you such bad news. It is my duty to inform you that you lost to Mrs. Rodney. I am terribly, terribly sorry."

Something broke inside Mama. Her whole beautiful world tumbled down. For a moment she was speechless. If she could only think of something to say to Miss Thompson—something to save her face. She must pass it off lightly, no one must ever say she was licked. But what? Then the idea clicked.

"Miss Thompson," she heard herself saying easily, "don't feel badly, please. I am really relieved. You see, Miss Thomp-

son, Mr. Franzon is leaving the pulpit for a rest, and we are
buying a beautiful old estate in the country. If I had won, I
would have had to resign at our first meeting. But thank you so
much for calling, and good luck to Mrs. Rodney from me."

Mama hung up and sadly stared at the telephone, her "wonderful friends" were just a bunch of cats.

Papa had walked past the city limits out toward the open
country. It was springtime and a bright sun shone from a clear
blue sky. Somehow, at this season of the year, Papa was always
especially homesick for Sweden. Today even his soul seemed sick
with longing for the small white church which he had left back
there in dear, beautiful Lapland. In spring the little mountain
streams, chained by icy fetters during the long Swedish winter
months, regained their freedom. Then they would rush from
the mountainsides down the deep ravines and race with lightning speed toward the river. Along the riverbanks the tiny dwarf
birches would be thrusting forth their furry buds and tender
green leaves. Papa longed to fill his lungs with clear, cool mountain air, and once again to feel the "peace that abideth" among
the snow-covered hills of Sweden.

Why had he listened to Mama and left his native land? He
had known he could never be replanted in happy-go-lucky America, with all its noise and bustle. Even here on the highway far
from the city, the noise of traffic never ceased. How could Mama
be so perfectly contented in this screaming world? If only he
could make her understand that it was peace he needed and that
the farm by the lake far from the highway could give it to him.
How well it could have worked out. That farm was one in a
thousand!

Papa sighed and walked on. After a while he left the highway and followed a narrow path through the woodland. At least
this would take him away from the stench of gasoline-smelling
cars that seemed to enjoy making his life more miserable by
blowing their trumpetlike horns as they passed him.

The path led to a little brook gurgling happily through the forest. Papa seated himself on a large rock and gazed down at the water. A fish caught his eye. It must be a brook trout! If only he had his fish line along. Then sadly he remembered Mama's words of the morning, reminding him that his work was to be "a fisher of men." He was supposed to look neither to the right nor to the left; only straight ahead at the road he had chosen. Papa sighed again. Life was hard. Perhaps getting married had been a mistake. A married man could not call his soul his own. He might as well admit that he was licked. Not just licked about the farm, but about everything else in life. Since he had become the father of eight children and had brought them across the ocean, his once quite sizable bank account had become very slim and undernourished. It was all Mama's fault. *She* had made him leave Sweden. For sixteen years she had kept at him and, like the slow dripping of water on a hard stone, gradually had worn him down. He remembered that summer morning, now so long ago, when Mama had *won* her first point. They were having coffee under the white lilacs.

Suddenly Mama had asked, "How do you ever plan to educate our eight children here in Sweden? In America, high school is free. They don't even have to pay for the books. And over there they could all work themselves through college."

Papa knew Mama was right. For education, America *was* the promised land. But Papa loved Sweden; and besides he could not let Mama win *every* time.

"I never wanted eight children in the first place, Maria," he protested. "Three would have been ideal. And I think I could have managed to educate three, *even here* in Sweden."

Mama had been horrified. "Why, Pontus. You ought to bow your head in the dust. You just take a good look at the five you never wanted and tell me if you would really have the heart to deny them their rightful place here on earth. It is wrong, Pontus—very, very wrong. You are playing at high stakes with the devil."

Papa had felt guilty and very ashamed of his hasty words, and he had told Mama so. "Of course I love all the children, Maria. But it isn't good to spread love so *thin*. Don't you agree that eight children are enough, Maria?"

Mama had just looked at him for a long time and, under her steady gaze, Papa had felt very evil. So, to change the subject, he had promised to give America some thought.

But summer in Sweden was especially wonderful that year and Papa hadn't had much time to think of America. It seemed to him that the red-and-white parsonage outshone all the other homes in the village. This, Papa was sure, was because of the garden—his own creation. With God's help of course. He kept the sand-yard neatly raked and the paths where the children were allowed to walk were as smooth and straight as a godly life. Grass bordered the sand-yard like a thick green carpet, and on the outer rim the currant and gooseberry bushes grew in lush profusion. At one end of the garden, three cherry trees and two plum trees blossomed in all their pink-velvet glory.

"They are like a bright fringe on a green shawl, Pontus," Maria had said one morning in early summer. Later, when the bushes were heavily laden with black, red and yellow berries, Maria had called them "old women kneeling in prayers of gratitude for a rich harvest." Papa had agreed, squirming uncomfortably as he always did when Mama got poetic or emotional.

But the strawberries were Papa's pride. Every day during the dry season he had faithfully carried five dippers of water from the nearby well, to each thirsty plant. Even Mama agreed that the fruit was the largest and the reddest and the sweetest in all Sweden.

By the middle of the summer, when it was daylight the clock around, tourists poured into the village from all over the world to see the wonders of the Midnight Sun, and they often stopped at Papa's little white church to pray. He was sure that life had never been so full, so rich in God's bounty and blessings.

Maria, he decided, must think so too, for she hadn't mentioned America again.

On Midsummer Day (the twenty-fourth of June), all Sweden celebrated. That afternoon, late, Maria and he had left the children with Tant Renberg and begun their long journey up Gellivara mountain. At midnight they had stood on its highest peak, breathlessly watching the sun descend to the horizon, linger a moment, then swiftly turn and rise again in majestic glory into a cloudless blue sky. They had knelt in a silent prayer before this vision of everlasting peace that, one day in God's good time, would spread throughout the whole world.

Short as summer was, that last one in Sweden had been especially filled with happy times. Picnics under the tall straight pines beside mountain lakes; long peaceful hours of fishing while Mama and the children scrambled into the little rowboat and went adventuring downstream. America was just a name on a map to all of them, if, indeed, Maria ever thought of that faraway country.

By early September the strong winds had begun to blow their chilly breath over Lapland. The birches put on gay autumn colors, for a time flaunting their brilliance before the spruce trees in somber green. Then the rains, day after day, poured down the mountainsides. Inside the parsonage there were warmth and happy voices and a thousand spicy odors. Gallons of lingonberries simmered in huge pots on the back of the stove. Papa had picked most of them himself, relishing the rich red sauce, which Mama served over mashed potatoes as a substitute for expensive meat.

Presently the cellar was filled with wonderful things to eat. Great barrels of potatoes; and boxes of apples, round and red, to be hung under each candle on the Christmas tree; eggs in water glass, and tubs of brine in which lay hams, sausages and pigs' feet. From the rafter hung great quantities of dry fish, which later would be soaked in strong *lut*-brine for the tradicional Christmas *lutfisk*. Papa could almost taste it now, white and fluffy on the Christmas Eve supper table. Why, it wouldn't have been Christmas in Sweden without it!

So summer and autumn had passed all too quickly, and before Papa realized it winter had wrapped a heavy white coat about the world. Still Mama had said nothing more about America, and Papa was sure even she had now completely forgotten that foolishness. He could settle down and live out his life peacefully in dear Lapland.

Then one winter morning, when the snow almost reached the window sills, and Mama had been busily baking *julbockar*, their favorite Christmas cookies, Papa had glanced up from the sermon he was preparing, to find Mama standing in his study door. Her shining childlike eyes looked past him over the endless white snowland.

"Pontus," she said excitedly, "I was just thinking about all the fruit in America."

Papa's heart skipped a beat. So! She hadn't forgotten America. She had only waited until she thought *he* had. Papa was annoyed. "And what has that to do with us?"

Mama had gone right on talking as though she hadn't heard him. "How *cheap* it is, Pontus. Why it costs hardly anything. I could even buy a whole big bag of bananas and give the children two each. And a big orange for each of them, too. And for you, dear, a heaping plate of grapes."

Papa knew he had to say something, but what? While he was trying to decide, Mama turned, and as abruptly as she had arrived, went back to her work, humming a little English folk song. Papa had been so upset, he hadn't been able to finish his sermon. All the rest of the day he was dreaming of fruit in the middle of winter. Mama was certainly clever. She knew his weakness for fruit and that there wouldn't be any in Lapland until summer; even then it would be very hard on his pocketbook. . . .

A branch from a nearby tree fell into the little mountain stream, reminding Papa that this was America not Sweden, and that his dream of a farm was farther away than ever. Mama always found a way to make him give in to her. If one method didn't succeed, she had another. Both were very familiar to Papa. One, Mama would go around the house with tears dripping down her cheeks, her eyes filled with reproach. That always made him feel so mean that he would do and say almost anything just to see her smile again.

But even worse than that was the other method. Mama would go about with lips tightly pressed together, never saying a word. The house became a tomb. Meals were eaten in silence. If the children spoke, they were hushed up quickly. Any attempt at conversation ended with "yes" or "no." Papa was certain Mama was going into this stage now.

"Well," Papa said aloud, as he arose from the rock, "this time I will surprise her. I will *give up* the farm all by myself. Then life can go on as peaceful as before."

Yes, he would preach until his time was up, then go to receive his reward—*if* Mama did not snatch *that* from him too. Papa was not at all sure how a Higher Power would handle Mama, but then the responsibility would be out of his hands. A preacher's life was not as glorious as some people, especially a preacher's wife, seemed to think.

Reluctantly Papa followed the woodland path back to the main highway. At the intersection, he turned for a last look at the peaceful scene. Early afternoon shadows lay now across the path, and the birds' chorus had become a symphony. Busily they twittered from twig to twig, building their nests, accepting God's promise of a new earth and all things added thereto, with a kind of faith that suddenly made Papa more than a little ashamed of his own doubts. Here he was complaining about Maria and their wonderful children, when he should have been grateful to God for entrusting so many precious lives to his care. Papa was so contrite that he felt like kneeling right there in the dusty high-way and asking forgiveness. But he couldn't do that. The cars were thick on the road now, and he would have to keep to the path along the highway to avoid being hit.

Well, one thing he *could* do. He'd hurry back to the par-sonage and tell Mama that he was sorry, just as he had done that long-ago day in Sweden, and that he loved all of them, even if they did complicate his life, especially his bank balance. He'd give up the farm so cheerfully she would know that he wasn't just giving in to her. He'd be a "fisher of men" if that was what God—and Mama—wanted him to be.

It was long past lunchtime when Papa reached the parson-age. Before opening the door, he stood for a moment outside, listening to the noise of the children, Mama's laughter and Greta's giggle. This morning they would have annoyed him. Now he could feel only humble gratitude. Gently he opened the door. The homey fragrance of newly baked bread greeted him. On the baking-board, the coffee rings were lined up on a clean towel. Mama's cheeks were bright roses, and she wore his favorite dotted Swiss dress.

She looked up from tying Kerstin's hat ribbons and greeted Papa with a big smile. "We are all ready now, Pontus."

Papa couldn't believe his eyes and ears. He just stared. "Ready for what?" he finally managed in a weak voice.

"Why, to go for a ride to look at the farm, of course," said Mama sweetly.

Papa gasped, "But I thought you——"

"Never mind what you thought. We have to hurry if you want to see it in daylight."

Papa sat down for a minute and took a long breath. *One* thing he had completely overlooked in his planning—a woman's privilege of changing her mind.

CHAPTER 10

❧ The Sunny Years

Mama exercised her prerogative to change her mind on more things than buying the farm. By the end of March, when they were ready to move to the country, she was, if anything, even more enthusiastic about the farm than Papa was.

To the children, the farm meant only escape from the rigidly proper behavior which was expected of them as "the preacher's children" and the stern scrutiny of everything they said or did. They had been "the preacher's children" all their lives. To suddenly become "Farmer Franzon's children" was like acquiring a new personality, and for a whole month they planned accordingly. "When we get to the farm . . ." became a common expression among them, a to-be-desired state of existence which compensated for any self-discipline they still had to endure.

Life on the farm wasn't, of course, the perfect state they had envisioned. Few things ever do measure up exactly to dream specifications. Still seeing how much they could "get away with" was a challenge to all of them (with the possible exception of Pelle, who came as close to being a saint as a human being could), and they made the most of every opportunity. Fortunately there was work to be done, which kept them out of too much mischief, and Papa saw to it that personal discipline was quite as exacting for a farmer's children as for those of a minister. Nevertheless, the farm was a new kind of freedom for all of them. Good behavior somehow seemed easier. The chores were fun, and they loved the animals and all growing things.

Even Mama, who had wanted so desperately to be President of the Woman's Club, now seemed just as happy being a farmer's wife, actually enjoying the very chores she had earlier ridiculed.

Mama walked jauntily down the path toward the big red barn, a milk pail swinging on each arm. The sun, a big coal of fire, peered cautiously over the horizon, promising a hot day. But at this early hour the green and golden fields of grain beyond the barn rippled, fresh and cool, in the morning breeze. Birds twittered and sang, flitting happily from tree to tree. Busy with their morning chores, too, thought Mama. What a wonderful new day!

Suddenly Mama found herself listening for the low mellow voice of the cuckoo. Then she laughed softly. At least in this part of America there were no cuckoo birds to foretell the future. In Sweden everyone waited eagerly for the return of the cuckoo in the spring, for you could tell what the future had in store by the direction from which the call first came. Like that spring morning in Lapland so long ago, when she had walked up the road to the parsonage to apply for a job as Papa's maid. She had heard the cuckoo then for the first time that year, and her heart had stood still at the sound. She had stopped and listened, scarcely breathing until she realized that the call came from the west. Then she had known she would have the best year of her life.

With the cuckoo on my side, she had thought joyously, I can't fail.

And as she neared the parsonage, she realized how lucky she had been that the sound had not come from another direction. For had it come from the east, it would have meant she would need to be comforted before the year was up; or from the north, a heartbreaking disappointment. And the south meant death!

Well, it was a good thing there were no cuckoo birds around the farm. In spite of its wooing call, it was ugly and a heartless false charmer, a disgrace to the bird family. The mother cuckoo was so busy all day just cooing "cuckoo" that she had no time to raise her family. And besides, she was a robber and a murderer. First she would steal into another bird's nest, destroy its eggs, then lay her own eggs and fly away, leaving her helpless babies for some other mama bird to take care of.

Just thinking about it made Mama angry, and she walked faster.

It was over a year now since they had bought the farm. And Mama was sure it had been the happiest time for all of them. It was good to be free. Especially good for Pontus. She wondered if church people realized how demanding they were of their pastor and his family. How wearing it was never to have a moment that really belonged to you. Why Papa was like a new man since they came to the farm. Just watching him as he went about the heavy work, laughing even when he was tired, made her wonder if maybe this was not Papa's real calling after all. Perhaps she had been wrong to insist that he remain a preacher as long as he had.

"A man needs to be close to the soil, Maria," he had said one spring night as they had walked together across the freshly plowed fields. "It makes him feel very close to God. Sometimes I wonder if it is not even a closer walk than preaching. Seeing the miracle of creation in nature makes a man stand in awe before the power of the Creator."

A little thread of fear ran through her. "You mean, Pontus," she had asked, "that you might not go back to preaching?"

"No, Maria. I only said I was wondering, that's all."

They had walked for a while in silence, and Mama was sure Papa was remembering, as she was, the offer the church people had made at the farewell banquet the week before they had left for the farm.

"Pastor Franzon," the moderater had said that night, "as a church we have voted not to give you up completely. We realize that working in the Lord's vineyard for so many years and the adjustment to your new country have been very tiring. We know you need a rest. But we want you to come back to us. The minister we have selected to preach during your absence was about to retire, but he has agreed to postpone his retirement for two years. We hope that will be long enough for you to think the matter over carefully, and we hope you will decide to return to us. The pulpit in Berkley Hills will be waiting for you, Pastor Franzon."

Papa, deeply moved by their affection, had promised to think it over and let them know his decision before the two years had passed.

And for more than a year now, Papa had relaxed on the farm, happy and carefree. The farm had prospered remarkably. Already they had been able to pay off the loan from the bank, and now the profits went regularly to nourish Papa's bank account. . . .

Suddenly Mama stopped and almost dropped the milk pails.

The stillness of the morning was broken by the sound of Papa's rich, strong voice coming from inside the barn. It was not the voice of farmer Franzon, but that of *Reverend* Franzon, in his best ministerial tones.

"And I say to you, that to hear with your ears and see with your eyes is not enough in the sight of the Lord. The fires of hell may still await you at the end of your days . . ."

Mama could not believe her ears. Something had happened to Papa's mind. No sane man would preach a sermon on hell at six in the morning to five uninterested cows.

Frantically she pushed open the barn door. "Pontus! What in the world are you doing?"

Papa's voice stopped abruptly. His face was red with embarrassment, and he stared at Mama as though she were a creature from the lower world. Finally he walked slowly toward her.

"No, Maria," he said calmly, "I am not crazy as you perhaps think. I was just practicing. I can't afford to lose the quality of my voice."

Mama drew a sigh of relief. If she had been wondering what decision Papa would make next spring, she no longer needed to wonder. The knowledge brought both happiness and regret. Much as she loved the farm and knew Papa loved it, she had not been able to convince herself that this was his rightful place, that his call to God's work had not been for all his life.

But seeing Papa's embarrassment over having been discovered at his strange preaching, Mama laughed outright.

"Oh, Pontus *lilla*," she said, "for a moment I thought you really expected the cows to repent. But let me ask you: do you always preach to them about hell? Of course I can see the connection. They have the horns and tails and you the pitchfork."

This was too much for Papa. "I don't think it is funny, Maria," he grunted gloomily. He dropped the pitchfork, seized the big broom standing by the door and began sweeping the barn floor vigorously.

Mama was still giggling as she sat down on the three-legged stool beside big, good-natured Albertina and started to milk. Albertina was a very special cow. In fact, all the Franzon cows were special, Mama thought, listening to the soft music the little streams of milk made against the tin pail. And they were lucky too. Papa insisted that Sweden was way ahead of America when it came to farming. He thought it was disgraceful the way American farmers allowed their cows to run about, using up the energy that should have gone into making them good milkers. The Franzon cows were not permitted to remain outside the barns at night, even in summertime. Days, they were allowed to roam the grassy pastures, but at night they were brought back to the barn.

"Cows are not unlike people, Maria," he had said that first day at the farm as the whole family eagerly surveyed their new possessions. "They like attention and they appreciate it."

"Of course, Papa," exclaimed Button, "and instead of saying 'thank you, sir,' they give a couple of extra quarts of milk."

Everyone laughed. Laughter was so easy when there was so much happiness in your heart.

Both Button and Papa had been right. In a few days the children had named the cows, Swedish names which carried special affection, and the cows responded with brimming pails of milk. . . .

The pail was almost full now. Albertina turned her head and looked at Mama gratefully. Just as if she wanted to say "thank you," thought Mama. She patted the cow gently. "Thank you, too, Albertina, for the good fresh milk," she whispered, and picking up the pail and the stool, moved past the next stall—Rosa's stall.

Rosa would bear her first calf in a few months and now was having special care. Mama turned back for a moment and patted her proudly, feeling the satiny sleekness of her bulging sides, and receiving a patient "moo-oo" in response. Rosa was always patient, and Mama thought how right the children had been to name her Rosa, a name which seemed to mean gentleness and goodness. Beside Albertina and Rosa, there were Stjärna, Hjärtros and Lilja.

"Just like their dispositions," Calle had explained to Papa.

And it was true, thought Mama. Albertina was fat and easy-going, and Rosa was patient and gentle. Hjärtros was a snippy little animal. Once she had kicked Mama right off the stool and made her spill a whole pailful of milk. But that was before Mama had learned how to handle her. Now she always patted Hjärtros first and talked to her before she started milking. Stjärna was the hardest. She had a habit of switching her tail which, if Mama did not duck in time, would leave a red mark on her cheek for days. Lilja was the gentlest of all. She would stand as still as a candle while Mama milked her, chewing her cud contentedly. Perhaps it was because Mama always sang

as she milked Lilja. Or did she sing because Lilja was so good?
Mama wondered.

She put the full pail on the low shelf by the door and
took down the second pail. Lilja stood motionless as Mama
placed the stool in the right position. Then to the music of the
milk in the pail, Mama sang:

> "Morgon mellan fjällen
> Klara bäck ock flood
> Sorlande på hällen
> Sjungen Gud är god
> Gud är god."

By the time she had finished the milking, Papa had apparently given up trying to convert the cows to God-fearing
creatures and had gone to the fields with Pelle. Last summer
Nim and Papa had worked side by side, planting and tending
the crops, so that by fall the harvest had been very good. But
this summer Nim was helping Mr. Jones, a neighboring farmer,
with the morning chores, and adding his earnings to the pile of
coins in the tin box for his medical education. So it was Pelle
who now went proudly every morning to the fields with Papa.

With brimming milk pails, Mama started back to the house.
Farm life was indeed a good life. It was good not to have to
worry about what other people thought or said. Especially
where the children were concerned. Here there was no Mrs.
Olson to complain that Button was too young to wear face
powder and to insist that she should be called Charlotta instead
of a crazy name like Button. Or a Mrs. Svenson to contend
that here in America a girl as old as Button *should* wear a little
make-up. And Mr. Skoglund thought it was downright selfish of
Papa to allow Nim, a growing boy, to work so hard; while Mr.
Benson complained that all the children old enough to work
should contribute to the family budget. Even Papa had come in
for criticism. One member thought he did too much house-call-

ing; another thought he should call on every member at least once every month. A minister was supposed to please everyone but himself!

Well, thought Mama, here on the farm the children could work as they wanted to, Button could wear make-up or not as she chose, and, when she and Papa went calling or received callers, it was because they enjoyed them.

Mama chuckled out loud, remembering the first time farmer Jones had called, and the way Kerstin had embarrassed Papa. They had been sitting on the front porch, drinking coffee and enjoying some of Mama's freshly baked *bullar*, when Kerstin had rushed up the steps exclaiming, "Oh, Papa, Papa! Come quick! Rosa is walking in the flower garden."

Papa and Mr. Jones got up and followed her.

"I was under the impression, Franzon, that you had only eight children. I thought I had met them all, but I don't remember meeting Rosa. How old is she?"

Kerstin did not wait for Papa to reply. "Oh," she said quickly, "there are four more."

"Well well, thirteen children. That's a mighty big family these days."

"I'm afraid, Jones," said Papa somewhat sharply, "you are mixing up our children with our cows. We happen to have *five cows* and one of them is trampling down Maria's flowers. We had better hurry."

Later that evening, Papa had laid down a firm rule about the cows. If the children insisted upon calling them by human names, at least they should be sure to make clear that they *were* cows. Thirteen children, indeed! And with a final grunt, Papa had decided to go for a walk.

Mama had to admit that this habit of naming the animals could be confusing. If you added the names of all the animals on the farm to those of the family, Papa would really have some explaining to do. Two horses, two dozen or more chickens, and two pigs. The horses were named Bläsan and Brunte; the pigs Napoleon and Josefina. So far the children hadn't been able to think up enough names for the chickens.

Mama sang as she went about her work in the sunny kitchen. She strained the milk into three huge stone jars. Later she would skim the cream from one jar and put it into small containers for delivery to her customers. Another jar would be divided into quart pails for the same purpose, and the third jar was kept for family use. Two large baskets of eggs, which Vickey and Greta had brought in last night, waited for sorting into dozens—some for market and some for home use. This task held special interest for Mama, for the egg money belonged to her. How surprised and delighted she had been that morning when Papa had announced this decision. She had thanked him properly, but she had not told him the idea that began to take shape at once in her mind. But the chickens received extra special care from that moment, and they rewarded her kindness. The amount in her bank account was evidence of that. And every market day added to it.

The only trouble, Mama thought now, as she counted the eggs into the containers, was that Papa took the milk, cream and eggs to market because she could not drive. How could she keep the surprise she was planning for Papa a secret when he knew exactly how much money she had in the bank?

She had just finished sorting the eggs when the bold idea hit her. She would learn to drive the car herself. She knew this remarkable feat would have to be accomplished in secret—perhaps while Pontus was working at the far end of the fields. It wasn't that she wanted to do anything dishonest. It was just that she knew already Pontus's attitude on the subject. He had made that very clear the first day on the farm. Mama had innocently suggested that he teach her to drive so she could take over the marketing.

"God made woman to cook and have children and care for

a home and love her husband, Maria. He did not intend her to risk her life and every other life on the highway by driving a car."

"Oh, Pontus! I bet I'd be the best driver on the road. Do you think I'd risk breaking the eggs and spilling the milk and cream?"

But for once Papa could not be cajoled into agreeing. "Absolutely no, Maria. The subject is closed." And Mama knew it was. For the time being.

But, she thought now, if she could *prove* to him how wrong he was—well, then he couldn't forbid her to drive. She just had to prove it.

For several days Mama's conscience bothered her. Maybe it was wrong to go against Pontus's decision. But, she reasoned, didn't the end justify the means in this case? She only wanted to make a big happy surprise for Pontus, and somehow Mama felt God would approve of that. A week later, she was sure God had sent her a sign.

They had just finished the morning chores and Papa was about to set off for the south field, when a car drove up. It was Deacon Olson.

"I was hoping I'd get here before you got into your day's work, Pastor Franzon," he said, when he had greeted them warmly. "Old Mr. Stenström passed away yesterday, and it was his last wish that you conduct the funeral service. Mrs. Stenström would like to see you to talk about the arrangements."

Papa did not hesitate. He was especially fond of the old gentleman, and he was pleased by this final expression of regard. He changed into suitable dark clothes, and in a few moments Mama watched the Olson car disappear down the road. Papa's car, for want of a garage on the farm, was parked near the lake under a large oak tree whose foliage was almost like a roof. Mama's eyes fell upon it as she started back into the house to continue her work. Surely this was a sign from God! *This was her day.*

She hurried with her housework, and by noontine the house was spotless. The boys went to the fields, and Button and the younger children set off for Ellen Jones's birthday party. Mama had the farm to herself.

She climbed into the car and settled herself importantly behind the steering wheel. She had sat often enough beside Pontus, watching what he did to start the car, how he shifted the gears three times until finally the car was humming contentedly along the highway. It was very simple. Papa was foolish to think a woman could not handle a car as well as a man.

First, she must turn this little switch, then step gently on the big button on the floor. The car leaped into action. Mama was so surprised that for the life of her she couldn't remember what to do next. Then as she looked up, she realized with horror, that she was headed straight for the lake. Frantically she tried to think what Papa did to *stop* the car. Too late, she realized *that* was one thing she had forgotten to notice. By the time the car stood in two feet of water, reason had returned. She flicked off the switch she had turned to start the car, and grabbed the brake. The car stopped as abruptly as it had started.

Mama sat there shaking with fright. The sign she had thought came from God surely had come from the devil. She had almost drowned the family car, and Papa's wife, too. And instead of proving *her* point, she had only proved how right Papa was. Now he would never let her learn to drive.

At a time like this, Mama would ordinarily have prayed. But she was so ashamed of letting the devil fool her into thinking he was God, she just couldn't pray. There were real tears of contrition in her eyes as she removed her shoes and stockings, climbed out of the car and waded to shore.

How could she ever explain to Pontus what she had done? She had to think of something so he would not be so angry. Maybe God would forgive her if she told him how truly sorry she was for listening to the devil.

By the time she had reached the house, she had an idea.

When Papa and Deacon Olson drove up half an hour later, Mama, barefooted, and with her dress pinned up to her knees, was scrubbing away on the family car as though it was one of the children in the bathtub.

Papa was out of the Olson car in one jump. "Maria," he called angrily, "what in the world are you doing with my car in the lake?"

Mama, all smiles, called back, "Isn't this a wonderful way to wash the car, Pontus? It seemed silly to carry all that water when it was so much easier to drive the car into the lake."

Papa stared, horrified. But Mr. Olson roared with laughter. "Leave it to a woman, Pastor Franzon. They will always find a short cut."

But Papa did not think it was funny. Something else was bothering him. "Maria," he said sharply, "did you say *you drove* the car into the lake?"

"Of course, Pontus. It was easy," Mama announced proudly.

Papa, too surprised to speak, pulled thoughtfully at his mustache, then scratched his head. Finally he glanced at Deacon Olson who was still chuckling over the incident. Mama could not believe her ears when Papa spoke.

"You did very well for a beginner, Maria," he said with dignity, "but I have come to the conclusion that the highway is a much better place to drive. Tomorrow I shall see how well you can drive on the road."

Mama waded back to the shore as fast as she could, and, ignoring Deacon Olson, threw her arms around Papa's neck. "Oh, Pontus! I think that's just wonderful."

Papa cleared his throat in embarrassment. "Very well, Maria. But just promise me one thing. That in the future you will allow *me* to wash the car the old-fashioned way."

By midsummer, even Papa admitted Mama could drive the car as well as anyone. and Mama was quite sure he was glad she *had* learned, for he was too busy in the fields to make the trips to market. And Mama loved it. It was such fun spinning along the highway in the early morning before the sun got too hot, thinking about how much she would add to her bank account that day. Wouldn't Pontus be surprised when she told him she had saved enough money to let him go back to Sweden for a visit? But still, it was going to be a long time before she had saved enough and could tell him. Meantime she had to think of some way to thank him for teaching her to drive and for not getting angry when she almost drowned the car.

Then one morning, as June turned into July, and Mama tore a leaf off the big picture-calender in the kitchen, she knew what to do.

Pontus had a birthday on the twelfth. Birthdays in the Franzon household were always special occasions, for that was the one day of the year that was completely "your day." And this year Pontus's birthday was going to be extra special.

For the next week there was much whispering and planning with the children, everyone making sure Papa was not around to overhear the plans. The presents had to be selected very carefully, and of course there must be a present from everyone. By the end of the week everyone had decided except Pelle.

"I haven't thought of anything good enough yet, Mama," he would say each time Mama asked him about it.

"Well, you better decide, darling, or you won't have time to get it."

But it was not until two days before the big celebration that his decision was made. Actually it was made for him. And Pelle was sure God had a hand in it.

Mama had asked him to bring in the milk pails from the back porch. When he returned, instead of the milk pails, he was carrying a large black cat.

"Pelle," exclaimed Mama. "Where did that come from?"

"From God, Mama. God sent him for Papa's birthday."

Mama wasn't so sure about God's part in the gift, for she knew too well how Papa felt about cats. But she hadn't the heart to dampen Pelle's excitement.

"It is not going to be easy to hide this present, son."

"But I will. I'll keep him in the cellar, Mama, and take good care of him."

Button helped him prepare the big wooden box, which would be the cat's home for the next two days. Then they set about making a cardboard box for the presentation. It was covered with blue-and-white wallpaper and was to be tied gaily with red ribbon. Two round air holes were cut in one side.

"Oh, I hope Papa will like my present, Mama," said Pelle as he started for the cellar. Mama said nothing, secretly worried about the situation.

"I know how we can make him like it," chimed Button.

Pelle stopped. "How?"

"Oh, just call him Lapland. That will do it."

"Why, Button, that's a wonderful idea," cried Mama, relieved. Papa just couldn't help liking anything which reminded him of his beloved Sweden.

Papa's birthday celebration started at five o'clock in the morning, with coffee in bed. The coffee was carefully boiled to just the right golden brown, and the big silver tray—one of Mama's treasures from Sweden—was laden with special cakes and coffee bread. Most important was the *tårta*. It was filled with applesauce and on top, in large pastry letters, Mama had written "sixty-three," surrounded by a huge circle of whipped cream.

When the tray was ready, Mama lighted the two tall candles on the tray. Then the procession started. Mama carried the tray and the children carried the presents. Only Pelle was empty-handed. His present now stood on the kitchen table.

"You better wait, darling," said Mama, "until Papa has had his coffee and opened the other presents. Your present will be the biggest surprise of all, so I think it should come last, don't you?"

Pelle reluctantly agreed, casting anxious glances back at the box as he followed at the end of the procession.

Outside Papa's bedroom door, Mama waited a moment, then signaled for the singing to begin as she opened the door. It was a special song she had made up for this special occasion:

> "Happy birthday, Papa dear,
> So sweet and happy and free from fear
> We love you more than the birds in the tree
> Or the stars in the sky—or the bumblebee
> For Papa—our Papa—so fine and tall
> Is the very best Papa of them all!"

Papa sat up and rubbed the sleep from his eyes. Then he stared for a moment at all the smiling faces and the festive tray.

"Well, well! The whole family up so early, and look at all the good things to eat! My birthday. Sixty-three years old! Do you have to remind me of that, Maria?" But he was smiling and Mama knew he was very proud.

One by one the children placed their gaily wrapped gifts on the foot of the bed. Mama poured the coffee and Papa cut the *tårta*. When the tray was empty, Papa started opening the gifts. Socks, overalls, handkerchief, shirts, books—Papa exclaimed happily over each present. As he started opening the last package, Pelle slipped away and a moment later returned with a big box. His eyes were shining as he placed it in Papa's lap.

"What in the world is this, Pelle?"

"M-e-o-w!" said the box.

"Hush, Lapland," warned Pelle. "Are you going to stop being a surprise?"

Papa opened the lid and was almost knocked out of bed by the big black cat. He glared at the family.

"Is this a joke you are all playing on my birthday? I am sure you know my feelings about cats."

Mama's heart sank. But before she could say anything, Pelle spoke excitedly, "Oh, no, Papa. This is a very special cat God sent for your birthday. His name is Lapland. See how dignified he looks. I am sure he knows he has been sent to serve a minister."

"But . . . but . . ." stammered Papa, "we have two cats already."

"Maja and Kurre are just *barn* cats," put in Vickey. "And barn cats live in the barn and catch rats. Lapland is a *herskaps*-cat. He will be your very special escort."

But it was Lapland himself who saved the day. He jumped up on the bed and curled up on Papa's lap, purring like a motorboat. Papa stroked his glossy black fur, which only made Lapland purr the louder. "So you are Lapland," he said slowly. "I wonder how you happen to have a name like that?" And he winked at Mama.

Within a week, it was plain to see that Papa was as attached to Lapland as the big black cat was to him. The cat followed him everywhere during the day and at night slept in the big cushioned chair by Papa's bed.

One afternoon, about two weeks after Lapland had joined the family, Papa set out for the Jones farm, to help with the repair of a piece of machinery which Nim reported had broken down the day before. Nim and Mr. Jones had tried to fix it but, as Mr. Jones admitted, he never had been much of a hand with machinery. As Papa started down the front steps, Lapland appeared from nowhere and trailed after him. Papa did not discover this until he reached the Jones farm, and then only when he became aware of something white streaking across the Joneses' lawn, followed by a black streak. The white streak was Bunny-Betty, Ellen Jones's pet white rabbit, and the black streak was Lapland, in hot pursuit. Papa stood paralyzed, then caught a thankful breath as Bunny-Betty disappeared through a crack in the barn, too small for Lapland's big body.

In a moment Lapland was back, rubbing himself against Papa's leg, Papa picked him up and carried him to the machine shed where Nim and Mr. Jones were already working on the tractor. He found a wooden box in a corner of the shed and, to Lapland's surprise, put him on the floor and turned the box over him. And here Lapland had to remain until Papa and Nim were ready to go home. That night, at supper, Papa told the story and issued an order that Lapland was never to be allowed on the Joneses' farm. As Lapland was usually with Papa, this order did not seem a difficult one to carry out.

Life went on placidly about the farm for several weeks. Then one Saturday afternoon, while Mama was busy with the week-end baking, the telephone rang. It was Mrs. Jones, inviting the Franzons to Sunday dinner. Mama accepted graciously. As she hung up, she wondered why Mrs. Jones had not extended the invitation earlier in the week. It was all very well for the Joneses who did not have a big family to plan for, but she had already done most of the cooking in preparation for Sunday. Well, thanks to the big icebox, her own food would keep for another day.

When they arrived at the Jones farmhouse on Sunday after church, they found a big picnic table, loaded with food, under a large elm tree on the back lawn.

"A picnic," cried Greta, always interested in food. "Look, Papa, at all the good things!"

Mama began to understand why Mrs. Jones could entertain on such short notice. There was indeed an array of good things. A heaping platter of fried chicken, big bowls of potato salad, coleslaw and pickled beets. Fresh bread and butter and two large apple pies for dessert.

"And ice cream, too, Mama! Ellen said so," boasted Greta.

"Have you forgotten your manners, Greta?" said Papa sharply.

But nothing could dampen their festive spirits today. It was cool here on the big lawn under the elm tree, and the food was delicious. Everyone passed his plate for second helpings. Only Ellen seemed unusually quiet and ate very little. Well, thought Mama, excitement did that to some children. But it certainly hadn't affected her children's appetites.

Mama and Button helped Mrs. Jones and Ellen clear the

table after dinner. The other children were too full of apple pie
and ice cream to do more than stretch out on the grass in the
shade. Papa and Mr. Jones sat by, talking of crops and farm
problems.

Mama was stacking empty plates for Button to carry
into the house when Papa said, "You must let me in on your
secret, Jones."

Mr. Jones looked quickly at Papa. "What secret?"

Papa chuckled. "How to raise chickens. I've never seen such
large meaty chicken legs as your wife served today."

Mama had been wondering about that too, so she stopped to
listen.

Farmer Jones dropped his eyes, then swallowed a couple of
times before answering. "Oh, that," he finally said, "that wasn't
chicken you ate today." Then he sat up straight and faced Papa.
"Yesterday afternoon a murder was committed on our farm. Your
Lapland made an end to our Bunny-Betty. We decided it was
proper to invite you folks to the *funeral*."

Papa was horrified. "You don't mean that—that—chicken
was—Bunny-Betty?"

"That's just what I mean!" snapped farmer Jones.

Even the boys were sitting up now, and staring at Mr.
Jones.

Pelle's eyes got bigger and bigger. Torkel turned white as the
tablecloth. And Nim was not smiling. The good food suddenly
wasn't happy in Mama's stomach.

Papa's face was a thundercloud as he gathered his family together and stalked silently down the dusty road toward home.
Mama almost had to run to keep up with him.

"I must say," said Mama when they were once more in their
own kitchen, "that was an awful way to punish us for Lapland's
sin."

"We could invite them back next Sunday and roast Lapland." Button suggested sarcastically. "Anyway, how do we know
Lapland ki—did it?"

"That's right," said Nim. "Lapland was with Papa all the time."

All eyes went to Papa, slumped morosely on a kitchen chair.

"Wasn't he, Papa?" pleaded Pelle.

Papa did not answer at once. Heavy silence hung over the sunny kitchen.

Finally, "I'm afraid Lapland does not have an alibi," he said sadly. "He hasn't been with me in the field for several days. I just thought it was too hot for him. Thought he was sleeping in some cool spot."

"Maybe he was, Papa," said Pelle. "Just because Bunny-Betty got dead doesn't prove Lapland did it."

Papa put his arm around Pelle and hugged him. "That's right, son, but I'm afraid the circumstantial evidence is pretty strong. Farmer Jones would not tell a lie about a thing like that. But we must not blame Lapland too much. He cannot help it that he was born with cat instincts. We shall just have to forgive Lapland—and Mr. Jones."

Mama almost dropped the pitcher of lemonade she had prepared, she was so surprised that Papa wasn't angry at Lapland or the Joneses. That meant that Papa really loved Lapland, just as Pelle had hoped he would.

That evening, after the children were in bed, Mama sat with Papa on the big front porch, listening to the peaceful sounds of the night—the chirping of the crickets, the low-voiced song of the frogs, and the gentle whisper of the wind in the leaves. God found so many ways to show His love for His children, thought Mama, her heart too full of happiness and thankfulness for words. Out of what might have been the evil of neighbor set against neighbor had come love and forgiveness and better understanding.

"I think I'll take Mrs. Jones one of those extra-special coffee rings, tomorrow, darling. Don't you think she would like that?"

"I'm sure she would, Maria," answered Papa, and there was a softness in his voice that told Mama more than his words.

But if Mama and Papa had expected the Joneses to accept forgiveness for the "fried chicken" dinner and forgive the death of their pet, they found out soon enough that it takes two to make forgiveness.

Early the next morning the telephone rang. Nim answered. It was Mr. Jones, brusquely informing Nim that he would not need his help on the farm. Mama wanted to cry when she saw the hurt in Nim's eyes as he hung up the receiver and told them what had happened. And her heart was still heavy as she watched them leave for the fields. She just had to do something. She would bake that special coffee ring and go and have a good talk with Mr. Jones.

After lunch Mama wrapped the still-warm coffee ring in waxed paper and set out for the Jones farm. It was cooler today, and the light breeze ruffled the ripened wheat in the fields beyond. Mama's spirit rose as she walked. Mrs. Jones was a fine, sensible woman. Together they would be able to bring harmony once more between the two families. Nim would be back to work on the Joneses' farm tomorrow, the hurt look gone from his eyes. The girls and Ellen would be friends again.

Mama climbed the four wide steps of the front porch and knocked. The front door was closed, which was strange on a summer day. She waited, then knocked sharply again. Still no answer. She was about to decide they were all in the fields, or had gone to town, when she saw the lace curtains at the front window cautiously pulled aside for a second, then dropped. The window was closed, so the movement couldn't have been the wind. Mama's heart pounded anxiously. She just couldn't believe Mrs. Jones would refuse to see her. But when she had knocked again and again, and still no answer, she had to accept the unhappy truth.

It was Pelle who took the matter the hardest. After all, he told Mama, he had found Lapland and Lapland's sins were his fault too. Mama tried to reason with him, but nothing she could say brought that happy light back into his eyes. Mama worried, and took her worries to God in prayer. But for once God did not seem ready to answer her prayers. The Joneses ceased to be good neighbors.

With the approaching harvest, everyone was too busy on the farm to give much thought to the problem. Maja became the proud mother of five black-and-white kittens. And a week later Rosa had her first calf.

Papa had kept Rosa tied up in the barn for several days, watching her closely. One night, just before bedtime, he and Nim had gone back to the barn to size up the situation. They were gone so long, Mama decided something was wrong and went to the barn to investigate. Papa and Nim were with Rosa, and beside her was the most perfect little baby calf. The proud mama stretched out her long tongue to lick her baby.

"Oh, Rosa," cried Mama, "what a nice little baby you have. I'm so proud of you!"

But at that moment Papa and Nim took the calf away from Rosa and locked it in a stall at the other end of the barn. Rosa bawled in protest.

"Pontus! What are you doing? Why do you take the baby away from her mother? Can't you hear poor Rosa crying. Bring it back, please."

Papa stormed. "Maria! Nim and I are bosses here, and we know what we are doing. I don't have time now to explain farm laws to you. Please go back to the house and leave this to us."

Mama went, but all the way back to the house she could hear Rosa's sorrowful cries. Maybe Papa did know best about farm laws, but he wasn't a mama and he couldn't know how terrible it was to lose your baby.

Mama went to bed, and when Papa came in an hour later she pretended to be asleep, for she had a plan. She waited until Papa was snoring soundly, then crept out of bed and tiptoed to Button's room.

"Wake up, darling," she whispered. "Rosa has had her calf."

Button sat up, wide awake instantly. "Oh, Mama . . ."

Mama put her finger to her mouth. "Hush, dear. Don't wake the others. Get dressed quickly and come with me. I need your help."

On the way to the barn, Mama told Button the story.

"Papa just doesn't understand, darling. You and I must undo the wrong he and Nim have done."

But it did not prove easy to get the wobbly calf back to its mother. Its long shaky legs kept crumpling under the weight of its body, so that Mama and Button were forced almost to carry it the length of the barn. But it was worth it, thought Mama, to see that little baby calf snuggle up to its mother and enjoy its first good meal.

Papa, however, had other ideas the next morning. He stormed and threatened. Mama would leave the farm decisions to him or he'd just sell the farm right now and take them all back to Lapland, where they should have stayed in the first place. Mama had never known him to be so angry.

"Oh, Pontus, you wouldn't be so angry if you had seen how happy that mama-cow was to have her baby. And besides, just once couldn't hurt. I think Rosa will understand now if you take her baby away."

Papa said no more. A few minutes later he stalked silently back to the barn.

Mama was preparing supper one evening about a week later, when the doorbell rang. She dried her hands and took off her apron, and hurried to the door.

Mrs. Jones stood there, all smiles.

"Good afternoon, Mrs. Franzon. May I come in?"

"Why of course," said Mama, recovering sufficiently from her surprise to unfasten the screen door.

Mrs. Jones sat down in Papa's big rocking chair, and for a few moments there was a strained silence.

"I'm afraid we owe you an apology, Mrs. Franzon," Mrs. Jones began.

"Oh?" said Mama, still more or less speechless over the turn of events.

"Yes. You see Ellen was pretty broken up over losing Bunny-Betty, and I guess my husband and I acted kinda mean about it. Not Christian-like at all. But I guess Ellen is even fonder of Luke now than she was of Bunny-Betty."

"Luke?" echoed Mama.

"The kitten. The one Pelle brought us. Oh, I know I should have thanked you long before this. It was so kind of him to want to make up for your cat's crime. I declare, I never saw a boy so concerned. Why, I think his heart would just have broken if Ellen hadn't liked Luke."

So that was it! Pelle had returned good for evil.

"That's all right, Mrs. Jones. You don't need to apologize. But how did Ellen happen to name the cat Luke?"

"She didn't. Pelle named him." And Mrs. Jones chuckled. "It was the oddest thing for a boy his age. He said we should call the kitten Luke after one of the Gospels because he was sure a cat with a name like that would never even think of killing a rabbit."

Mama and Mrs. Jones laughed together over the story.

"And do you know, Mrs. Franzon, not a single one of my cabbages has been nibbled since we lost Bunny-Betty. I just wonder if she was as good as we thought she was."

"Well," said Mama, laughing, "maybe Bunny-Betty just had rabbit instincts like Lapland had cat instincts."

And when Papa and the boys came in from the fields, Mama and Mrs. Jones were chatting happily over coffee and some of Mama's new-baked coffee bread.

With harmony restored, Nim went back to helping Mr. Jones with the morning and evening chores, and Ellen came to the Franzon farm almost every afternoon to go swimming with the girls. The families visited each other on Sundays and holidays, but no one mentioned picnics. Summer sped. Happy days filled with toil and play. Another leaf was torn from the big calendar in the kitchen. July had passed into history, and soon August was racing to catch up.

And then it was harvest time.

It was wonderful, thought Mama, how the farmers helped each other. One day at one farm and the next at another. And presently the crops were all in, and they were better neighbors for having shared their labors.

Almost before they could realize it, there was a tang of autumn in the air. Papa came in one evening in an unusually happy mood. After supper, Mama learned why.

"Jones is going to help me with the butchering next week," Papa announced. "He thinks Joe Ryan may be able to help too. We'd like to make a day of it. It will mean extra cooking, Maria, and hot coffee all day long."

"Why of course, Pontus," Mama agreed.

"That way, we can get it all done in one day. Nim and I could probably do most of it ourselves, but I'm not sure we could handle Napoleon alone. He's a mighty big hog."

Mama gasped. "Pontus! You don't mean to tell me you are going to make meat out of Napoleon?"

"That's just what I mean. Why do you think we raise pigs?"

A sickness raced through her, and a bitter taste filled her mouth.

"I—I—just thought . . . Well, I just thought it went with farming!"

"And so it does, Maria. Steers and pigs and chickens and turkeys, to have good meat summer and winter."

A new and more horrible realization struck Mama. Did Papa mean that not only was Napoleon and maybe Josefina to be turned into meat, but Hero, Rosa's boy-calf, too? Oh, that was too much! Button and Pelle would be as heartbroken as she was. Somehow she had never thought about where meat came from before. She wished Papa would sell the farm right now and—yes—go back to Sweden where he didn't have to kill help-

less animals, especially animals you had taught to trust you.
Maybe it wasn't right for a preacher to be a farmer too.

Mama sat very still for several minutes, trying to think.
Papa was reading the *Church Quarterly*. Surely, thought Mama,
if he thought it was right to raise animals for food, no matter
how fond you became of them, then it must be right in the sight
of the Lord.

But on butchering day Mama stayed close to the house, and
Button and Pelle received a sudden invitation to visit Mrs.
Jones.

The first snow fell early that year. The evergreens bordering the farm were stately in their white coats, and the lake was
an endless sheet of white paper. The snowy hills beyond might
have been the Swedish hills that rose in cold grandeur outside
the parsonage windows. Even Mama felt a pang of homesickness
for Lapland. But presently she was too busy with Christmas
preparations to think of anything else.

An atmosphere of "work well done" pervaded the farmhouse. The harvest was in. The potatoes had been dug and stored
in great bags in the hayloft where they were safe from freezing,
along with bushels of turnips, cabbage and onions. In the cellar
stood the barrels of pigs' feet, sausages and dill pickles, and from
the rafters hung Napoleon's hams, smoked and wrapped in bur-
lap, ready to be made into Christmas delicacies. Papa had been
able to buy *lutfisk* from the Swedish store in town, and herrings
for pickling, and real Swedish *Bond-ost*. The apple trees on the
farm had yielded several barrels of apples—more than enough,
thought Mama gratefully, for the traditional Christmas apples.
She herself had made *sylta* and *korv*, forgetting entirely that
these were part of her dear Napoleon.

By the week before Christmas, the farmhouse gleamed and
exciting odors of cakes and cookies and spicy delicacies filled
the air. Papa and Nim came in from the hills one evening, carrying a big Christmas tree which they had cut from the forest be-

yond the lake. After supper the tree was set up in the center of
the big living room and the fun of decorating began. Even
Kerstin was allowed to stay up late that night to help deck the
tree. Mama had promised there would be a Christmas tree robbing, just like in Sweden, and some of their friends had been
invited to share in the festivities.

And finally it was Christmas Eve.

The children had taken care of Christmas for all the animals.
The cows and chickens had had special feed. The horses had
been given an extra measure of oats and some sugar lumps.
Lapland had a bowl of cream. And two sheaves of wheat had
been placed outside the kitchen door for the birds. Soon the
guests would begin to arrive.

Mama stirred the rice, which had cooked all day, and
poured in a little more milk to make the *jul-gröt* especially good.
Greta sat on the high kitchen chair watching.

"Will there be enough rice for *Tomte-Nisse*, Mama?" she
asked, her anxious eyes following Mama's stirring.

Mama put down her spoon and gathered the child into her
arms. All the children but Greta had accepted Santa Claus as
the American symbol of Christmas. In Sweden it had been Greta
who always remembered to set out the bowl of rice on Christmas
Eve, so that *Tomte-Nisse* would not be hungry as he went about
the world, distributing Christmas joy.

"Here in America, darling," Mama explained, "there is no
Tomte-Nisse. He belongs to Sweden. Here there is Santa Claus,
who comes in a big beautiful sleigh drawn by eight prancing
reindeer. Don't you remember? Why, just last night Button
taught you the names of the reindeer—Donner and Prancer and
Blitzen——"

"I remember, Mama," Greta broke in, her eyes shining.
"And the sleigh is just filled with toys and everything, and we
hang up our stockings and on Christmas morning every stocking
is filled with just what we wanted."

"That's right, darling. Now isn't that just as nice as *Tomte-Nisse?*"

Greta didn't answer. She squirmed uncomfortably in Mama's arms and stared at the floor.

"It will be a wonderful Christmas, honey. Just you wait and see!"

Greta twisted around and looked up at Mama, her eyes wide with doubt and a little hint of fear. "But just suppose, Mama, *Tomte-Nisse* didn't know we came to America and got lost looking for us. Wouldn't he get awful hungry? Maybe I could set out just a *little* bowl of rice—in case."

Mama laughed, but her heart was warmed by Greta's deep concern.

"Why, Greta, I never thought of that," she exclaimed. "I think we better put out a *big* bowl of rice. It's a long way from Sweden to America."

Greta threw her arms around Mama's waist and hugged her tight. "Oh, Mama! Thank you. Thank you." Then she ran to the cupboard and came back with a large bright-red porcelain pan. "Is this big enough, do you think?"

"I'm sure it is, darling," chuckled Mama. "Even if *Tomte-Nisse* brings a lot of little helpers with him." And she poured the pan half-full of rice.

Later, when the family were all gathered at the table, and Papa opened the big Swedish Bible to read the Christmas Story as he always did, Mama could not help being glad that here on their wonderful American farm, *Tomte-Nisse*, the Swedish Spirit of Christmas, had not been forgotten.

CHAPTER 11

✧ Papa Learns a Lesson

Being one chosen by God to preach His gospel was, to Papa, a heavy responsibility, and he accepted it with great seriousness. He had an unswerving devotion to Biblical truth, believing that the laws of God were unchanging dictates which, if ignored, brought pain and suffering, but which, if obeyed, could result only in peace and happiness.

Outwardly he was more severe than Mama in handling his children, for he was convinced that discipline was quite as important as education, and he desired above all that his children walk in the ways of the Lord always. He endeavored to set a good example, though there were times when he admittedly found life confusing and decisions difficult. On such occasions, he would sternly search his own soul, confess his faults and shortcomings to God, and, with His help, rise above them.

One of these occasions—which was to have a profound effect upon his entire life—he faced on a spring morning toward the end of the second year on the farm.

Papa cut across the freshly plowed garden patch just beyond the house and took the narrow path toward the woods. Over one shoulder dangled a fishing rod, and in the other hand he carried a packet of sandwiches and hard-boiled eggs. It was Saturday and a glorious spring day. Almost too warm for March, he thought. In the far field Nim and Pelle were plowing. He felt a pang of guilt taking a holiday, going fishing when there was work to do. But Maria and the boys had insisted.

Presently the path plunged into the woods, and Papa for-

got his guilt in thinking of the fine perch he would bring home
for supper. Farmer Jones had told him about the little pool in
the woods, and, when he described the size of the fish he caught
there, Papa was skeptical, but anxious to find out for himself.

Well, it couldn't be very far, he thought, filling his lungs
with the tangy spring-scented air. It was good to be alive on such
a day. The trees were faintly green against the silver-blue sky,
and along the path wood violets lifted their delicate heads. Birds
twittered a hymn of joy that winter had passed. Everywhere there
was a clean sparkling freshness, as though the world had been
washed and spread out in the spring sunshine to dry—and grow
to new life.

He came upon it abruptly—a small, quiet pool so clear that
he could see the rocky bottom, mossy-green and red-gold. Beyond
the tracery of soft shadows near the shore, the sunlight made a
diadem of the gently rippling water. Papa dropped his fishing
rod onto the grassy bank, tucked the packet of lunch into his
pocket and sat down on the rock which jutted out over the water.
This was, indeed, a perfect spot for fishing. Now if the fish were
biting well as Jones said, he'd soon have that mess of perch he'd
promised Maria for supper. He was especially fond of perch with
parsley sauce, the way Mama had made it in Sweden.

"Do you still remember how to make that parsley sauce you
made for perch in Sweden?" he had asked this morning as she
fixed the lunch for him.

"Of course I remember, Pontus," she laughed. "You just
bring home the perch and I'll fix it fit for a king."

Mischief had danced in her eyes as she waved him good-bye.
"And don't strain yourself carrying them home."

Papa stared down through the clear water at the big fish
darting merrily among the rocks. Well, Maria was going to be
surprised at the catch he brought home tonight! He slid off the
jutting rock, onto the grassy bank and stretched out, watching
the float bobbing up and down. Any minute now it would disappear and he'd have his first perch. But when half an hour had

passed and still no bite, Papa began to be disturbed. The fish, he saw, were still there, playing tag with his bait, but not biting. If this kept up, Mama would have the laugh on him for sure. He just had to get at least one big fish. Otherwise there would be *plättar* for supper. It wasn't that he didn't like *plättar*. They were all very fond of the little Swedish pancakes. It was just that Maria always substituted them for uncaught fish, and the whole family knew he had been fishing and caught nothing.

Papa lay back on the grass. He couldn't *make* the fish bite. He'd simply have to be patient. Even if he caught nothing, just being here was a tonic to his soul. It was good to lie close to God's earth, to feel the warmth of the sun and listen to the rustle of swaying branches above him in the spring wind. The pungent fragrance of pine made him drowsy. He was glad he had decided to remain a farmer. Tomorrow he would notify the Church Board of his decision.

But even as the thought went through his mind, he was vaguely disturbed. He couldn't explain the disturbance. What was wrong about a man his age stepping out of the ministry when hundreds of young men were waiting for an opportunity to begin their life's service in God's work? Surely he had a right to be a farmer if he felt that was best for his family and himself.

They were all so happy on the farm. Hard as the work was at times, no one complained. It was always a happy tiredness, the kind that comes from the satisfaction of work well done. A wholesome atmosphere in which the children could grow up, close to nature and God's abundant creation. In the fall, Nim would be starting to college. The fund in the tin box had increased steadily, and Papa would add to it if needed; Nim was pretty independent about that. He was proud of his achievement, and Maria beamed every time the subject of college was mentioned.

She wasn't so happy about Button. For Button had firmly refused even to consider college. She would finish high school in the spring and she had made her own plans.

"I am through with lessons and teachers," Button had announced one evening during Christmas vacation. "When I graduate from high school in the spring, I'm going to *live*."

Maria had looked up from her mending in shocked surprise. "But, Button, college education *is* living, darling."

Button just shook her head and smiled. "Not for me, Mama."

But Maria did not give up easily. "Oh, Button, you will love it when you get started. There will be so much fun besides the lessons. And if you don't take the opportunity when it comes, you might be very sorry later on."

"I have my own plans about my life, Mama," Button insisted.

And that was that. Papa had no doubt about Button's meaning it. But he was not worried. Button was growing into a beautiful woman, and a woman's first duty was to get married and make a real home for her husband and give him fine children. Maria would just have to learn that not even in her wonderful America could she sell education to *all* the children.

Papa sat up and examined the line. Still no fish. He stretched out again and let his thoughts return to the good life on the farm. Presently he chuckled, remembering what Jones had said when he told him that the abundant yield of his land had been due to his prayers.

"Well, for goodness' sake, Franzon! Don't hoard all the blessings for yourself. Come over and pray for *my* potatoes."

One of the best parts of farm life, thought Papa, was the security it offered. He would not have to accept charity from the ministers' fund when he grew too old to preach. The farm would take care of Maria and himself even when the children were grown and married and living lives of their own. And they would bring their children on holidays and summer vacations. It gave him a strange happy feeling just to think of himself as a grandfather.

Suddenly Papa jumped and sat up. His line had tightened

and the float had completely disappeared. Here was that fish for supper at last! He got ready for the quick pull at the right moment. But he didn't have a chance.

A sharp voice spoke directly behind him. "Don't move, Mister. Unless you want to land on those rocks at the bottom of the lake. Do exactly as I tell you."

Papa remained motionless. Vaguely he realized that the fishing line had slackened and the float was again bobbing on the surface of the water. The big fish had got away. The voice behind him was speaking again, "Don't turn around. Just take that watch out of your pocket and drop it gently on the ground behind you."

Papa couldn't believe this was actually happening to him. Not here in the peaceful forest. Then he almost laughed out loud. It was Mr. Jones playing a joke on him. Of course! Only Jones and the family knew he had come here to fish. Well, he'd play out the game with him, then they'd have a good laugh over it. Slowly he started removing the watch, pretending fear. Then a terrible thought struck him. Suppose that wasn't Jones behind him? Suppose this wasn't a joke, but the real thing—a holdup? It didn't sound like Jones's voice, but then that could be disguised. His watch was a gift which the good people of Lapland had given him as a farewell expression of their regard. He couldn't bear to think of it in the hands of a hoodlum, ending up in a pawnshop for a few dollars.

"Hurry it up, Mister," commanded the voice, "and don't try any tricks."

Papa's fingers were shaking as he unfastened the thick gold chain, then placed the watch gently on the ground behind him. He knew now this was not a joke; that the man behind him was not Jones. He'd read about crimes like this, and he knew that often they killed the victim after robbing him. The thought so shocked him that before he realized the danger, he had whirled around and grabbed the man as he stooped to pick up the watch.

Taken by surprise, the man tried to recover his advantage.

but Papa was stronger, and after a moment's struggle had him on his back, his hands pinned under him. Only then did he see his face. He was young, not over twenty-five, he guessed, but his face was so dirty and sullen it was hard to tell. He stared up at Papa, anger and defeat in his eyes.

"Now, young man," said Papa, a little winded by the struggle, "what is the meaning of this?"

He didn't answer, but his gaze shifted, and the anger went out of his face. Only a sullen, defeated look remained. Papa wasn't quite sure what to do next. Then he remembered such characters carried a gun. He went through his pockets with one hand, the other on the boy's chest to make sure his hands couldn't get free. But there was no gun.

"What did you do with your gun?" Papa barked.

He reacted to that. But not in the way Papa expected. He laughed. A contemptuous laugh.

"I haven't got a gun. That's what makes it so funny. I got your watch without a gun."

Papa was relieved. But the young man's speech had told him something else. He was educated, obviously not a professional crook. Papa stood up.

"Very well, in that case, you may get off the ground."

The boy jumped quickly to his feet, spitting dirt and leaves. But he made no further move to violence.

"I suppose you know what happens to people who go around stealing other people's possessions and threatening them?" Papa asked.

"What is this? A Sunday School class?"

Papa laughed in spite of the grave situation. "It could be at that. I happen to be a minister."

The hatred returned to the boy's eyes. "That won't stop you from turning me in," he snapped sarcastically.

"What do *you* think I should do with you?" asked Papa.

Obviously this was not what the boy expected. He stared at Papa in disbelief. Papa ignored him and began calmly to retrieve his rod and line, which had barely escaped a watery grave in the excitement. "I guess this is the end of the fishing for today," he finally remarked casually.

Still silence from his "prisoner."

It was when he started to put the tackle into his pocket that Papa discovered the package of lunch. He drew it out and sat down on the big rock and opened it.

"Now, young man, why don't you sit down and share my lunch with me, while we talk this thing over," Papa suggested calmly. "Then you're coming back to the farm with me and we'll decide what to do next."

"I thought you were a minister?"

"A minister *and* farmer," Papa corrected. "Not a bad combination."

A couple of minutes of silence. Papa unwrapped the lunch and spread the paper wrapping on the rock beside him, careful that the eggs didn't roll off into the water. His "prisoner" moved slowly toward him. But this time Papa was sure it was because of hunger, not from the desire to harm him. He handed Papa the watch, then squatted on the grass. He took the sandwich which Papa offered, then picked up an egg and started peeling off the shell.

They ate in silence. Occasionally Papa stole a glance at him. Why, he was no more than a boy, a hungry, confused boy at that, and quite handsome in spite of the dirt. He wondered what he could say to get him to unburden his soul. If he could just make the boy understand that he wanted to help, not hurt him.

"What's your name, son?" Papa asked after a while. "Mine's Franzon."

The boy hesitated a moment then in a low voice, said, "Steve."

"All right, Steve. Now do you want to tell me what this is all about? You don't look like a thief. You didn't even have a gun."

"If I tell you, you'll still turn me over to the police."

"That depends. I want to help you, but if you don't tell me

what made you do this—this holdup, I won't have any choice."

Steve stared at the ground. He picked up a small stick, snapping it in two with suppressed anger. "You don't know what it's like to need money desperately," he exploded.

"Not so desperately I'd commit a crime for it, no. Crime doesn't solve anything."

"It was the only way, I tell you. I didn't want to hurt *you*. I was—well, I was practicing," he blurted.

"Practicing? For what?"

His eyes were still on the ground. "So I could join up with a gang in New York."

Papa was a little shocked. But he still hadn't got to the bottom of this thing. "Why don't you start at the beginning? Why did you want to join a gang?"

"To get money for Terry and the baby," he said defiantly.

So that was it! The boy had a family. This was more serious then he had thought. But he was more convinced than ever that the man was not a criminal. Nevertheless, he *had* tried to hold him up, and that was a crime. If the boy wouldn't talk, he'd have no choice but to turn him over to the police.

"That still doesn't tell me why you decided to resort to crime, Steve," Papa said kindly.

A deep sigh escaped the boy. A sigh of resignation. "All right. I'll tell you everything. Then you can take me to the police. It doesn't matter any more. I'm a failure at crime like everything else."

It was not a pleasant story, nor a new one. Papa's heart ached for the boy as he told it, speaking in a low voice—a story of heartbreak, defeat and desperation.

Steve had been employed on a farm near Lakewood. He had studied agriculture in college and he liked farming. Then he had met Terry Sanders, the owner's daughter and they had fallen in love. But Mr. Sanders didn't think he was good enough for his daughter. He and Terry had eloped and kept their marriage a secret. Steve continued to work on the farm, living with the help as before, and seeing Terry only when they could meet secretly. But when they knew a baby was on the way, they could keep the secret no longer. Terry's parents were furious, threatened to have the marriage annulled. But Terry was of age and they could not do that without her consent. And Terry wouldn't give her consent. After that, Terry was not allowed to see him at all. When the baby came they refused to let him see the child—a boy. He tried to get work on other farms, but Mr. Sanders stopped that. Everywhere he received the same answer: "Don't need any help now."

Steve was frantic. To have a wife he was not permitted to see, and a son he had never seen, was too much. It was then he had decided on desperate measures. There was only one way he knew to get money fast. He'd find a gang in New York that would let him work for them. He could drive a car. That would keep him from actually committing the crimes himself. As soon as he had enough money, he'd clear out and come back for Terry and the baby. He'd slept in the woods last night and was headed for the main road to town when he saw a man fishing, the gold watch chain flashing in the sunlight.

"I know it all sounds crazy now, Reverend Franzon. But . . . I failed even in that. Terry's parents were right; I'm not good enough for her. Terry and the boy will be better off without me. I don't want them to suffer for what I've done."

For a full minute Papa's throat was too tight for words. He wondered what he would have done under the same circumstance. It wasn't an easy question to answer, for as a young man in Sweden he had had no such temptations. It was different in America. The papers were full of crimes, robberies, swindles—all seeming to offer an easy way to get rich in a hurry. Not even the threat of prison or the danger of death prevented young men, every day, from trying to outwit the police. Doing right had to come from a desire for good in a man's heart. Then, with God's help, he would not be tempted beyond his strength to easy riches.

"I don't suppose you ever asked God to help you, Steve," Papa said quietly.

Apathy vanished from Steve's face. He jumped to his feet. Anger glittered darkly in his eyes. "*God*," he shouted. "If there was a God, would he let a man's wife and baby be taken from him by a selfish father? Don't give me that Sunday School stuff! Take me to jail if you want to, but don't start preaching."

Papa said nothing. He got up, picked up his fishing rod and began unreeling the line.

"What are you going to do?" Steve asked, a hint of alarm in his tone.

"Steve, my boy," said Papa briskly, "you've just taught me a lesson about failure. I promised my wife I'd bring home a mess of perch for dinner and I'm going to do it. I was about to give up when you came along."

Papa cast. Out of the corner of his eye he watched Steve. He was just sitting there staring, as though he thought this phony minister had lost his mind.

Presently Steve sat down again on the grassy bank. Only the lapping of the water against the rocks broke the stillness. But Papa was praying. Silently. He needed those perch now for more reason than food. He had to show Steve there was a God—a God who cared what happened to His children. But this was not a time to do it by preaching. The boy was deeply hurt, too bitter against circumstances and his fellow man.

Suddenly the line tightened. Papa waited half a second, then jerked. A big perch lay squirming at his feet.

Steve was so surprised he forgot his anger. "Say, that's a big one," he exclaimed. Then added wryly, "I don't know how good a preacher you are, Mister, but you sure know how to fish."

Papa looked proudly at his catch. God had answered his prayer but he couldn't tell Steve that—yet. "I don't know about that, son. Guess it was just a matter of waiting for the fish to get hungry," he said lightly.

For the first time that afternoon Steve laughed pleasantly.

"The next one is yours," said Papa, handing him the rod. "Look at that big one down there."

Steve hesitated. "With my luck, he'll grab the bait and be gone before I can move." But he took the rod, and Papa noticed how deftly he cast.

And again Papa prayed, "Dear God, Thou knowest how important this catch is."

A few minutes later Papa was realizing once again how much better God looks out for His children than even their fondest desires. A perch, larger than his own catch, flapped on the grass beside Steve.

They took turns after that, and the fish were indeed hungry. It seemed to Papa that the bait scarcely had time to reach the water before the float disappeared, the line tightened, and presently another big fish lay at their feet on the grass. An hour passed. Papa and Steve proudly surveyed the day's catch.

"'. . . full measure, pressed down and running over,'" quoted Papa half aloud.

"What did you say, sir?"

"It's from the Bible, son. I was just thinking how abundantly God answers prayer. Do you remember the story of Simon, the fisherman? Simon had been fishing all night and caught nothing. He was about to give up, but as he turned his boat toward the shore, he saw a Man standing there. And the Man called to him, telling him to cast his nets on the other side of the boat. And Simon did as he was told, and behold the nets were filled with fishes, so many that he could scarcely lift the catch into his boat."

"Sure, I remember the story. But what's that got to do with us?"

"A great deal, Steve. Would you believe me if I told you God sent you here today?"

"Are you trying to tell me *God wanted* me to steal your watch? Not even a preacher could make me believe that."

"I didn't say that, Steve. I said God *sent* you here. He sent you to help me."

"To *help* you?" Steve echoed. "Look, Reverend Franzon, all I did was try to steal your watch, and I failed. God certainly didn't have a hand in that."

"He moves in mysterious ways, Steve. A preacher has his problems too. Yes, I'm sure God sent you to me this afternoon." Papa was speaking more to himself now than to Steve. For he was remembering a decision he had made earlier—to give up the ministry. He had told himself he had a right to be a farmer if he wanted to. Now he wasn't so sure he did have that right. Conflicting emotions surged through him. He got up slowly and collected the fish.

Steve still sat on the fishing rock, saying nothing.

"Well, I guess we'd better get started home," said Papa. "We've certainly got enough fish for supper. No one cooks fish like Maria—my wife." Then he laughed. "She's going to be mighty surprised. You see she's not used to my catching anything when I go fishing."

Steve chuckled. "I see what you mean. The laugh will be on her today."

"But it wouldn't have been without your help, Steve," said Papa.

"I still don't see . . ."

"Never mind that now. Let's go. I'm getting hungry."

The sun was low over the distant hills as they left the woodland pool and took the path toward home, single file with Steve in front. Papa noticed some of the droop had gone from his shoulders. There was new hope in his step. But when they reached the end of the path and started across the plowed field to the house, Steve stopped.

"What will your wife say to your bringing a thief home to supper?"

"What thief? I'm sure my wife will be pleased to have a fellow fisherman as our guest. And besides, don't forget that if

it hadn't been for you there wouldn't be any fish. We'd have
plättar."

"What's that?"

"Oh, it's very good. But it is what my wife always makes for
supper when I come home with no fish."

Steve laughed, but he still hesitated.

"That other incident," said Papa casually, "shall we just
keep it between us for the present? And by the way, you'd better
tell me the rest of your name."

"Hill. Steve Hill. You're very kind, Reverend Franzon," he
said softly. But Papa noticed his eyes were suddenly bright.

Maria opened the kitchen door as they approached. "Oh,
Pontus! You did get them. What wonderful fish."

"No *plättar* for supper tonight, Maria. Thanks to my young
friend here. Maria, this is Steve Hill. Steve, my wife."

"Come in, Steve. You certainly are a good fisherman."

"I'm afraid your husband gives more credit than I deserve,
Mrs. Franzon. He's a mighty good fisherman himself."

"Well, it doesn't matter who caught them. Now you sit down
here and have some coffee. You must both be tired."

The kitchen was fragrant with Saturday baking. Mama
poured two cups of coffee and set a big plate of *bullar* on the
table.

"Well, I have some chores to do, Steve," said Papa, finishing
off his third *bulle* and second cup of coffee. "Would you like to
come along?" He wasn't ready to leave Steve to Maria's questioning.

"I sure would, Reverend Franzon. That is if I can *move*
after eating so many of those delicious rolls. They were wonderful, Mrs. Franzon, and the coffee the best I ever tasted."

"Would you like another cup?" offered Mama.

Steve laughed. "I'm afraid not. Any more and I wouldn't
have room for that perch. Your husband told me what a good
cook you are. Already I agree with him."

Papa was pleased that Steve was talkative. It meant the tension—and the fear—had left him. Later he would tell Maria the whole story and they would decide what to do about this young man.

Button and Greta came in from feeding the chickens. Papa introduced Steve, then he took the milk pails and they left for the barn. He realized at once that Steve was very much at home around a farm. They milked the cows, and Papa told him how the children had given each cow a name according to its disposition. Steve laughed heartily over the idea.

"I never realized that cows had dispositions, but I guess they do at that."

The pigs grunted hungrily as they neared the pen. Napoleon, who was now hams and sausage in the cellar, had been replaced by Oscar. Soon there would be a new litter of squealing little pigs. Steve helped Papa mix the feed and pour it into the long troughs.

When the chores were finished, they walked slowly back to the house, each with a brimming milk pail. Dusk was falling. A short distance away, Nim and Pelle were returning from the field. The younger children played under the big elm tree by the lake, their laughter echoing against the purple hills. In the gathering shadows the farm suddenly seemed to Papa like a giant bud, ready to burst into life, then to full-flowering as the spring winds gentled and gave way to summer. Now there were fields to plow, seeds to be planted, fences and barns to be mended and painted.

Outside the kitchen door Papa paused and placed a hand on Steve's shoulder. "I've been thinking, Steve. There's a lot of work on a farm in the spring. We could use another hand. The job's yours if you want it."

Steve didn't answer at once. Finally, "You mean you'd let me work for you after—after what I did?"

Papa sat the pail of milk on the step. "I told you before, Steve, God sent you to me today. Sent you to *help* me. I mean it."

"I'd be so grateful, Reverend Franzon. I'd be proud to work for you." Steve's voice choked with emotion.

"That's fine. I'll speak to my wife about it first. I'm sure she can arrange a room for you. *Now* I think we can do justice to that fine supper of perch and mashed potatoes, which she has waiting for us."

Supper (not at the big kitchen table as usual on Saturday nights, but in the dining room) was a gay occasion. Having a young and handsome guest added a note of festivity. Papa noticed Vickey was wearing her new dress—a birthday present. Kerstin, who usually had to be reminded to brush her hair, had every curl in place, with a pink bow on top. Even Maria was wearing her best blue home dress.

Papa was very proud of his family.

Everyone praised Papa and Steve for being such good fishermen, and they all passed their plates for second helpings. Papa assured Mama that never had she prepared such delicious parsley sauce.

After supper, while Button and Vickey helped Mama clear the table, the rest of the family gathered in the big living room. Nim and Steve and Papa discussed spring planting, the values of crop rotation and Swedish farming compared with American ways. Pelle and Torkel listened attentively. Presently Kerstin, who had been very quiet until now, interrupted.

"Mr. Steve, would you like to see my baby chickens?"

"I certainly would, young lady. My, that's a pretty hair ribbon. Did you tie the bow yourself?"

Kerstin tossed her curls proudly. "My Mama did. But I bet I could if I tried."

"I don't doubt it a bit," chuckled Steve and obligingly followed her to the back porch where the box of chicks had been placed for the night.

Papa went to the kitchen and was pleased to find Mama alone.

"When you have finished, Maria, I'd like to have a word with you in private."

Mama turned from the cupboard, alarm in her eyes. "What is it, Pontus? What's wrong?"

"Nothing at all, Maria. I want to talk with you about Steve."

Mama finished putting the dishes away, then followed him upstairs to their bedroom and closed the door. Papa told her all that had happened that afternoon.

"I think Steve needs a friend more than he needs punishment, Maria," he concluded. "I can use him on the farm if it is all right with you."

"Oh, Pontus! Of course it is all right. The poor boy! Just to think of having a baby he's never seen. And being separated from his wife, I just don't see how anyone can be that cruel."

"We'll try to do something about that soon. Right now he needs work and understanding."

"Of course. I'll fix up that big room I've been using for storage. It will be quite comfortable. Oh, Pontus, there's plenty of room. Couldn't we let him bring his wife and baby too?"

Papa hesitated. He hadn't counted on adopting a whole family just to get a farm hand. But he should have known Maria would realize it took more than work and money to make a family man content. Steve would do a better job having his family with him.

"I hadn't thought of that, Maria. But I see no reason why not."

"Oh, darling, just think. Won't it be wonderful having a little baby in the house?"

"Well, I'm not sure how wonderful it will be. I just hope he's a good baby. Steve won't be much use on the farm if he has to walk the floor all night with a fretful child."

Mama laughed. "You still haven't forgotten those nights with Button, have you?"

Papa started to open the door. "By the way, Maria, I think Steve's past should be between us and him, don't you?"

"I certainly do, Pontus. We'll be just one big family."

Papa agreed it might very well be that, when he reached the living room and found the children gathered around Steve, all trying to claim his attention. It was strange, he thought. This morning a would-be gangster; tonight, a friend. Surely that was the way God intended it to be.

When finally the children had been sent to bed, and Mama had prepared the guest room for Steve, Papa came into the kitchen where Mama was fixing the coffee tray for morning.

"I think I'll go for a short walk, Maria. Don't wait up for me. You must be tired."

Mama put her arms around him and kissed him. "Whatever you decide, Pontus *lilla*, will be all right with me."

Papa wondered, as he went out into the crisp spring night, if Maria was referring to Steve, or did she sense, as she seemed always to do, that something else was troubling him.

He stood for a moment looking up into the limitless heavens, where stars twinkled faintly, so far away they were like tiny fireflies in the night. Then unbidden, he took the path to the big lake, now a great shadowy mirror, reflecting only the deeper shadows of the leafless trees along the banks.

His doubts had begun even before Steve came. Vague, disquieting thoughts about his decision to give up the ministry and remain a farmer. He had told Steve God had sent him. At the time it had been a half-formed conviction, but now he knew with certainty that it was true. It was God's way of showing him his work as a minister was not finished. But even as he acknowledged this truth, the conflict within him began anew.

He tried to reconcile his convictions with his desires. Was he not serving the Lord as a farmer, tilling the soil, tending the crops, bringing forth the good harvest from the land? Was not the farm also the Lord's vineyard? But as he questioned, Steve's face came into his thoughts—defiant, angry, crying out against a domineering God who made his way difficult. How many such young men were there in the world, tempted to evil, seeking an answer to the mysterious, confusing thing called life? Seeking and, without guidance, never finding. Taking the easy solution which led only to more confusion and deeper sin.

As he looked out across the dark lake, faintly restless under the gentle night winds, he found himself thinking, "And the Spirit of God moved upon the face of the waters. And God said let there be light; and there was light."

Light! God called his ministers to carry that light to all the world. To the seeking, troubled souls who walked in darkness. He, Pontus Franzon, had been one of those ministers.

He remembered another night, long ago, beside another lake. He had signed a contract with God that night, not for a few years, but for *always*.

Papa covered his face with his hands. "Not my will, oh. Lord, but thine," he sobbed, and knew an inner peace which he had not known for a long time.

And suddenly it was as though the floodgates of wisdom were opened to him. The questions which had gone up from his soul earlier were now answered. He knew that his desire to remain a farmer had come not alone from love of the fruitful earth, but from the sense of security which it offered. It was selling the farm that he had resisted. He had not had sufficient faith in God to trust Him to provide so long as he did the work God had called him to do.

Shamed and contrite, he now understood why God had sent Steve to him. Not only to show him the work he must do, but because *he* needed Steve. Steve was part of God's plan for him. An intricate, mysterious, wondrous plan! It was as clear now as though a book had been opened before him.

God did not mean him to sell the farm.

In sending Steve to him, he had provided the way for keeping the farm and reuniting Steve and Terry and their child. In the fall, when the crops were in. he could go back to his pulpit

in Berkley Hills, and be a better minister because of the two
years close to the soil. The boys could help Steve on Saturdays
during the winter, and summers the whole family would return
to the farm, and he would spend his vacation there.

Papa felt like a new man. A young man with a purpose.

Tomorrow he would tell the Board of his decision to return
in the fall. By that time Steve would be able to run the farm
very well alone. And tomorrow, too, he was going to make his
very first call as a minister under his renewed contract with God.
He would have a talk with Mr. Sanders who needed a few things
set straight for his own sake.

The house was dark when Papa returned, except for a light
in the front bedroom. Maria must be waiting for him after all.
He was very glad. He took the stairs two at a time.

Maria was sitting up in bed, her bright hair loose over her
shoulders. The soft glow of the night lamp shed a radiance about
her, which to Papa now seemed celestial.

"Maria," he said softly, on his knees beside her bed, "I'm
going back. I'm going back to my calling."

Mama's hands were gentle on his bowed shoulders. She drew
him into her arms, and kissed him tenderly as she would a child.
"I thought you would, Papa *lilla*. And oh, Pontus, I'm glad—so
very glad."

CHAPTER 12

Man Does Not Live By Bread Alone

Papa was sure he loved his wife and children as devotedly as any husband and father, but there had been times since that day twenty-two years ago when he had married Mama that he had questioned the wisdom of his action.

And never had he questioned it so seriously as on a particular May morning the following year, when he reluctantly faced a shocking revelation: *He was no longer wanted in his own home.*

Papa had scarcely finished breakfast when Mama, smiling, and a little too eager, presented him with a list of sick calls which she insisted must be made that day.

"It certainly is a long list, Maria. Sometimes I think the church people lean too heavily upon a pastor and his wife for prayers. But I suppose when the body is ill, one's faith needs replenishing." Papa sighed, wondering what they thought the minister did when *his* faith weakened or his body was too tired to want to be leaned upon.

He drank the last of his third cup of coffee and pushed back his chair. "I guess we'd better get an early start, Maria. I'll be ready when you are."

Mama's eyes widened. "But, Pontus, I can't go with you to

make the calls. I have *so* much to do today. I'm sorry, dear. Some other time."

It was Papa's turn to look surprised. "I don't understand, Maria. I just don't understand why you are suddenly so busy. Besides, Mrs. Anderson's name is on this list, and you know it's *your* prayers and smiles she wants, not mine."

Mama chuckled. "You know, Pontus, I think Mrs. Anderson just gets sick so her handsome pastor will call on her and hold her hand. Now run along and make her happy."

Ridiculous as Maria's remark was, Papa knew there was no use trying to outtalk her, so meekly he took his hat from the hall rack and left the house.

If it had been the first time Mama had refused to accompany him lately, he wouldn't have been so surprised. But this had been going on for weeks. At first he had accepted her excuse of having too much to do, but now he knew for certain there was another reason. Strange and mysterious things had been happening of late. There was an air of secrecy in the parsonage. Quickly exchanged glances between Mama and Button or Greta or Vickey when they thought he wasn't looking. Whispered conferences he wasn't supposed to hear. And now, suddenly, the number of house calls had increased alarmingly. It all added up to one thing: *His own family wanted to get rid of him.*

Somehow he got through the list of calls and hoped he had said the right comforting word, although he wasn't sure God approved of his half-interested prayers. It wasn't that they weren't sincere; he just couldn't keep his mind on them. It kept returning to the strange behavior in the parsonage.

It was almost one thirty when Papa climbed the steps to the parsonage again. He was tired and hungry, and the delicious cooking odors which greeted him only whetted his appetite. But when he reached the kitchen, he found only a cold luncheon set out for him, and a note propped against the sugar bowl.

"Pontus *lilla*," the note read, "Sorry I couldn't wait and eat lunch with you. Had some errands to do. There is a new list of house calls on your study desk. Some of them seemed urgent, so I assured them you would call *this afternoon*."

Papa's hunger vanished in annoyance. Mama was too busy to accompany *him*, but not too busy to run errands. What errands? What in the world was going on in his own house right under his very nose?

He stalked into the study and almost snatched up the list. Why it would take all afternoon to see all these people, even if he did little more than say "hello" and "good-bye." As he glanced up from the list, he caught a reflection of his scowling face in the mirror on the opposite wall. He was really shocked—and ashamed. He certainly wasn't acting like one of God's chosen. Contrite, he sank into a chair and covered his face with his hands. Silently he prayed for wisdom and strength and understanding; and as he prayed, the tension and anger went out of him. He got up slowly and returned to the kitchen. Half an hour later he set out once more on house calls.

As he closed the door on the last name on the list, he knew God had indeed guided him; for some of the cases had been urgent, and for several hours he had forgotten his own problems in prayers for the really ill and troubled members of his congregation.

It was getting dark when he reached the parsonage. Just as he started up the walk, a car pulled to the curb and stopped.

"Pardon me, Sir," a woman's voice called, "can you tell me if this is the Swedish Home Bakery?"

Papa stopped. "It isn't," he said politely. "This is the Swedish parsonage."

"Are you sure?" the woman persisted. "I am certain this is where Mrs. Appleton bought those *delicious* cookies."

"I'm quite sure, madam," Papa snapped, his patience wearing thin. "And I ought to know. I happen to be the minister who lives here."

The woman left in a burst of speed which plainly said she thought he was lying. Papa stood there a moment in the shadows, trying to get control of his temper. But before he could sort out his thoughts, Greta came hurrying down the front walk, her arms full of boxes and packages, and bumped right into him.

"For goodness' sake, Papa," she gasped. "I didn't see you. I hope I didn't break any!"

"Break any what, Greta? Bones?" Papa laughed.

"No. The orders, of course."

"Orders? What orders?"

To his astonishment, Greta began to cry. "Oh, Papa," she sobbed, "you made me tell!"

Papa put his arm around her shoulders. "Made you tell what, Greta? Are you sure you are all right?"

But Greta only pulled away from him and ran down the street as fast as she could with her arms full of packages. Papa watched her, puzzled. And suddenly he knew! The woman who had just driven away was right after all. Mama *was* baking cookies and selling them behind his back. She had turned the parsonage into a *bakery*.

The very idea made Papa sick. His head whirled, and his stomach felt queasy. He had an impulse to rush into the house and demand that this ridiculous business be stopped at once. But his knees were suddenly weak—so weak he couldn't have run had the house burst into flames. He sank down on the grass in the shadows, momentarily overcome with chagrin and self-pity. Why was Maria doing this terrible thing? Wasn't he a good husband and father? And didn't he try to be a minister of God, worthy in His sight? How could his own Maria—his *wife*—do this to him?

As he questioned, his questions took on the quality of prayer, and he realized he had been jumping to conclusions. Who better than he knew the bigness of Maria's heart? Of course she was baking cookies. But only for charity—not just to make money. Maria would never do that. Suddenly he was very much ashamed of himself for thinking such a thing. He decided to let her have her little secret; she probably thought he would object to her spending the money. In a few days she would tell him why she had given away so many cookies.

Comforted, Papa got up quickly and hurried up the steps. When he reached the kitchen, he saw no cookies—only something bubbling appetizingly on the stove. Maria was all smiles, her eyes as innocent of guile as a child, when he kissed her.

"Supper will be ready in a moment, Pontus. You must be tired and hungry after all those house calls."

"I am, Maria. But I'm glad I went, especially to old Mrs. Aronson. She is a dear old soul, and I'm afraid she isn't going to be with us long. She was so disappointed you were not with me."

"Oh, Pontus! Is she really that sick? I'm sorry I couldn't go."

"Were your errands more important than sick calls, Maria?" Papa asked gently, chuckling inwardly at the way her cheeks were suddenly flushed.

"They were *very* important, darling. But I'll go see Mrs. Aronson tomorrow without fail," she promised. Then added, "Even if my work has to wait."

Papa started upstairs to freshen up before supper. Mama called after him. "Pontus, I forgot! Deacon Olson wants you to call him right away."

As Papa finished talking with Olson, he wondered if there was any way in the world Mama could have had a hand in *this*. For the matter which had suddenly become urgent was not urgent at all. Mr. Stenström who had passed away the previous spring had made provisions in his will for new aisle carpets for the church. The Church Board had decided to wait until the many conferences of the winter and spring were over, then one of the board members would go to Boston to select the carpeting. Now, suddenly, with a great deal of illness among the church people, and a number of important decisions regarding the coming year to be made, the Board had decided it was only proper that Pastor Franzon himself should have the privilege of selecting the carpeting and that it should be done immediately.

Well, no doubt it was merely coincidence, but coming at this time it certainly looked suspicious. And later, when Papa broke the news to the family over supper, he was sure he detected a note of relief in their exclamations, which had nothing to do with the refurbishing of the church.

The selection of the carpeting was accomplished more quickly than Papa had anticipated. He had thought it would be necessary to spend several days visiting various wholesale carpet companies and comparing prices, but on the second morning he found exactly what he wanted in both quality and price and was able to catch an afternoon train back to Berkley Hills. He arrived at the parsonage just before suppertime and hurried into the kitchen, eager to tell Maria about the beautiful green carpets he had ordered. But the sight that greeted him froze his words in his throat.

Mama was sitting at the kitchen table, and before her lay a pile of money—nickels, dimes, quarters, and a large stack of bills.

"Maria," he exclaimed, incredulous, "Where in the world did you get all that money?"

Mama started. Then with mischief dancing in her eyes, she quickly scooped the money into her apron. "Just pennies from Heaven, darling." She laughed and brushed past him on her way upstairs.

Papa was too overwhelmed to protest or insist upon an explanation. He went into his study and closed the door. He had been wrong about Maria. She *was* turning the parsonage into a bakery, and for money. It was hard to believe, but in the face of what he had just seen, he could no longer deny it. He paced up and down the study, trying to make sense out of the whole business. He realized now with a heavy heart that he had *assumed* the baking was for charity.

It seemed a reasonable assumption, for this was the time of

the year when all the church groups were doubling their efforts to complete their pledges before the summer vacations began. But if that were true, why did Maria have the money? And even if she were merely keeping it for the church, why was she being so mysterious about it?

Well, whatever the reason, he had to put a stop to using the parsonage in such a manner. Why it was sacrilege. Almost as bad as the money-changers Christ had found in the Temple. Christ had driven them from the Temple, and he, as a minister of God, must now act with firmness.

He squared his shoulders and went back to the kitchen. Maria was there, preparing supper as if nothing unusual had or was happening.

"Maria," Papa began sternly, "I think it is about time you told me what is going on in this house."

"Going on, Pontus?" asked Mama innocently.

"And don't try to look innocent. I happen to know that you are making cookies for *money*. And from the amount of money I just saw, they seem to be paying you very well."

"Oh, they do, Pontus. I get forty cents a dozen for them."

"Maria. Do my ears deceive me?" Papa almost shouted. "You boldly admit you are turning the parsonage into a *bakery?*"

"Oh Pontus, it isn't that bad."

"Bad! It is sacrilege. Maria, don't you realize this parsonage is as much a part of God's house as the church? I am paid a salary for my services, to support my family. And you, my wife, are neglecting your church duties to earn *money* for yourself. What do you think Deacon Olson would say if he heard of this?"

"Mr. Olson doesn't object, darling," said Mama eagerly. "I asked him."

Papa sputtered. "You—you asked Deacon Olson if you could sell cookies? Maria, what in the world has happened to you?"

Mama came over to him and put her hands on his shoulders. "Don't be so upset, Papa *lilla*. It's just for fun."

"Fun? I don't see anything funny about a minister's wife falling in love with money. And besides, since when does Deacon Olson decide what's right or wrong in my house?"

"Now, now, Pontus. You just got through saying it is God's house. And you won't be able to preach on Sunday if you break a blood vessel. Now calm yourself while I finish supper."

But Papa would not be pacified. He bounced out of his chair.

"This baking has got to stop, Maria. This very minute. I am still head of my own family—even in America."

Mama didn't answer. Calmly she returned to the stove and went on preparing supper. This was the last straw. If he didn't get some air he *would* burst a blood vessel.

"Never mind about supper," he snapped from the doorway. "I'll eat at a restaurant."

Papa sat dejectedly at an oilclothed table in a downtown lunchroom and tried to swallow the beef stew. The meat was tough and the vegetables were soaked with grease. He began to regret his hasty action. Then he started feeling sorry for himself. Maria had done this to him. Why? For money! Money, the root of all evil—a tool of the devil. Something had to be done.

By the time he had paid for the uneaten meal and left the place, he had made up his mind what that something was. He would go right now and have a talk with Deacon Olson. Mama would listen to *him* even if she wouldn't listen to her husband.

Mr. Olson greeted Papa warmly and invited him into the living room. "I'm so glad you stopped by, Pastor Franzon. Did you get the new carpeting for the church?"

But Papa was in no mood for conversation about carpets. He came right to the point. "Deacon Olson, I want you to tell me all you know about my wife's bakery. I understand you gave your *approval* to this sacrilegious action. I am very much surprised and shocked."

Deacon Olson laughed. "Don't take it that way, Pastor Franzon. I think your wife is a mighty plucky little woman. I see nothing wrong with her earning a few extra dollars if she wants to."

"Well, I do," snapped Papa. "It's the work of the devil, and I want it stopped. The very idea of turning a parsonage into a bakery! It's . . . it's . . ." Papa was too upset to go on.

Deacon Olson took time to adjust his necktie. "I am sorry, Pastor Franzon," he said with kindly dignity, "but I am afraid it is too late for me to be of any help to you. I've already given my consent, and so have the other deacons. We agreed that so long as Mrs. Franzon didn't hang out a sign on the parsonage, or do anything that would reflect upon the church, we could see no reason why she shouldn't bake cookies and sell them."

"And you think *that* doesn't reflect on the church?"

"I don't see that it does."

Papa started to speak, then changed his mind. It was no use. Mama had them all on her side as usual. All she had to do was smile, and they forgot the difference between right and wrong. Well, *he* knew the difference. And he intended to see that right was done.

He got up, mumbled a curt "good night" and left.

Outside the cool night wind cleared his brain. He walked slowly, aimlessly, trying to think. Was it possible that he was wrong in his attitude? Why had all the deacons of his church given their approval to Maria's ungodly actions? He had as much respect as anyone for money, rightly earned and rightly spent. But surely it was not right to turn a parsonage into a cookie store. And besides, it was humiliating—made it appear he didn't provide for his family.

"God in Heaven," he prayed unconsciously, "what shall I do?"

He walked on, his shoulders slumped. Suddenly he stopped. Suppose Mama was just playing a joke on him? She hadn't taken him seriously when he threatened to eat in a restaurant. If she had, she would have stopped him. Now she was undoubtedly frantic with worry. Crying. Women always cried when they were worried. The moment he stepped inside the door, she would throw her arms around him and beg his forgiveness. Then she would explain the money, and she would promise to stop using the parsonage as a bakery. Peace would be restored to his home.

Papa hurried. He hadn't realized he had walked so far. But he was happy once more. He felt fine. Maria was a fine wife. His children were fine. Life was fine.

It was ten o'clock when Papa opened the parsonage door. The house was dark except for a light in the kitchen. Maria *was* waiting for his return, worried, just as he had thought.

"Maria," he called softly, "I'm home."

But there was no answer, only the ticking of the kitchen clock. He stood at the kitchen door and stared at the empty room. On the table was a note.

> Pontus, dear—I got tired waiting up for you. I hope you had a good dinner. But if you are still hungry there are meat balls in the oven.
>
> Good night, darling.

Papa's happiness oozed out of him like air from a toy balloon. Mama hadn't worried about him one bit. Meat balls, indeed! Did she think he could *eat* when his home was tumbling down about his head? Savagely he switched off the kitchen light and climbed the stairs to his room. In the soft light from the hall, he could see Mama sleeping as innocently as a baby. He turned off the upstairs light, undressed in the dark, and crept into bed.

Mama awakened on the stroke of five the following morning. Pontus still slept heavily and there was a troubled frown between his brows. Poor dear! It was too bad he had to find out

about the baking business before she was ready. She hated to
have him worry, and think all the wrong things she knew he was
thinking. But soon she would tell him all about it. Until then he
would just have to suffer.

The fragrance of fresh coffee greeted her when she entered
the kitchen. Button was there ahead of her and had a batch of
cookies ready for rolling and cutting.

"Ummmm, that coffee smells good." Mama sniffed. "Thank
you, Button." She poured a cup and sat down at the kitchen table. "You're a wonderful helper, dear. I'd never be able to keep
up with all this work if you children weren't so willing to help."

"We're just as anxious as you, Mama, to get this finished.
Then we can start living again. I don't like the way Papa looks—
as if no one in the whole world loves him."

"I know what you mean, Button. Let's just pray he can hold
out until we get the five hundred."

Button poured herself a cup of coffee and sat down. "How
much more, Mama?"

Mama sighed. "That's the trouble. I don't know. Yesterday
when I was counting Papa came in and caught me."

"Oh, Mama, how terrible! What did he say?"

"I'm afraid he is more upset than is good for him. But I can't
tell him yet, Button. It would spoil the surprise. He's just got to
wait and suffer, I guess."

"Poor Papa. He must be very worried. We will have to hurry,
now, before he has a stroke. But he will forgive us when
he knows. Haven't you any idea how much you have, Mama?"

"Well, let's see. There's a little over two hundred from the
egg money last summer, twenty dollars I have saved from my
housekeeping money, and we've made about a hundred and sixty
dollars from the cookie sale. How much is that?"

Button added silently. "About three hundred and eighty dollars. A hundred and twenty to go. How long do you think it will
take?"

"Well, maybe two weeks, the way the orders are coming in. If we can just keep Papa out of the house that long."

"And if *we last* that long," sighed Button. "I'm so tired by night I'm not even interested in a date."

"I know, dear. But John will understand. He'll wait for you."

Button laughed. "Why John especially? What about Eric and Norman?"

"You know John is my favorite. He's a fine boy, Button."

"They are all wonderful kids, Mama. But I don't like one any better than the other. I can't very well marry all three of them."

"I should say not," chuckled Mama. "One husband is enough to handle—especially if you start a bakery!"

Mama got up and put the coffee cups in the sink.

Button rolled and cut the cookies while Mama mixed new batches. As they worked side by side, Mama was thinking what a good wife Button would make John. John Lambert was a student pastor in one of the local churches, and she hoped very much that soon Button would become serious about him and marry him. She had been so disappointed when Button refused to go to college, but being a pastor's wife would make up for that. There just wasn't anything in the world quite as wonderful as being the wife of a minister. Button was twenty now, and soon she would get tired of working as a nursemaid to other people's children and want a family of her own. Mama felt a warm glow just from thinking about having a minister for a son-in-law. But that started her thinking of Pontus again and how unhappy he looked even in his sleep. She glanced at the clock. Soon it would be time to take Papa's before-breakfast coffee to him.

"Hi, you early birds!" called Vickey, coming into the kitchen. Greta trailed after her, rubbing her sleepy eyes. "We planned on a whole hour before we have to leave for school. Where shall we start, Mama?"

"With some coffee as an eye opener. Then one of you can watch the oven and the other can take cookies off the baking sheets."

"Just like a real bakery," laughed Greta. "But I don't think Papa is happy about the mystery."

"It's no longer a mystery," explained Button. "At least Papa knows something is up. He caught Mama counting the money yesterday."

"Did you tell him, Mama?" asked Vickey.

"Not yet, darling. Papa will just have to wait—maybe two more weeks."

Mama watched Greta as she loosened each cookie from the baking sheet and placed it carefully in the basket. The bakery really had been Greta's idea. Mama had discussed her plans with the children one evening when Papa was at a board meeting, realizing that the egg money she had saved from the farm was not nearly enough for a trip to Sweden. She had tried saving something from her housekeeping money, but that was too slow. Then Greta had suggested baking cookies, and Mama knew that was the solution. Pelle agreed to take orders, the girls would help with the baking, and Calle and Torkel would deliver the orders. Lately there had been so many orders, Greta had had to help with deliveries after school.

At first it had been easy to keep their secret. Papa was very busy with meetings and other church duties which kept him out of the house most of the day. It was when Mama had to refuse to accompany him on sick calls that he had begun to get suspicious. Then he had found her counting money and she had had to tell him about the bakery. But she still hoped she wouldn't be forced to tell him why until she was ready.

When the kitchen clock struck seven, Mama took the tray of coffee and *bullar* upstairs. Papa sat up and accepted the coffee with a gruff "Good morning" and "Thank you." Beyond that he did not seem to want to talk, for which Mama was grateful. She hurried back to her baking.

An hour later, when he came into the kitchen, he still said nothing about the baking, although the aroma filled the room, and big baskets of cookies stood on the baking board. He ate

little, and in silence, then went to his study. The children left
for school and Button for her nursemaid job. Toward midmorning Papa stopped at the kitchen door.

"I think I'll go out to the farm for a few days," he announced
grimly.

Mama knew Papa was hoping she would protest; that she
would explain her strange behavior or suggest going with him.
But she couldn't. This was the reprieve she needed.

"I think that will be good for you, Pontus. You do look a little
tired. Greet Steve and Terry and the baby for me. They have
certainly done well with the farm."

Later, as she watched him walk slowly toward the garage,
Mama was tempted to call him back and tell him everything. He
looked so terribly downhearted. He will get over it as soon as he
knows, she decided and let him go.

Papa sat on a big stone by the lake and tossed pebbles idly
into the water, watching the rings widen on the sunlit surface.
He felt very old and lonely. For two days he had thought
of nothing but Maria and her bakery. He couldn't even concentrate on his Sunday sermon. Still he hadn't been able to figure out
what had happened to his happy home and especially to his wife.
Reluctantly he now concluded that he had lost her to the devil
—and money. How had it started? Bleakly he remembered the
day he had told her the egg money was her own, to do with as
she pleased. That had been the mistake. A woman should never
be allowed to have much money; it went to her head. God intended a woman to be dependent upon her husband.

A crow cawed raucously from the tree overhead. Papa stood
up and threw a stone at it, then watched it fly off to the other
side of the lake, its black wings glistening in the sunlight. The
incident depressed him further. Like an evil omen. To clear his
mind, he forced himself to think of his sermon. Already it was
Wednesday and he had thought of nothing to preach about—except cookies, all shapes and sizes.

And why not? he suddenly thought. "Man does not live by bread alone," he quoted, and the words carried a new meaning for him. His spirit lifted. He'd preach a sermon like no sermon he had ever preached. Maria would hear and cease her sacrilegious behavior; and his deacons who had approved her selling cookies would know their pastor had been right. Maria would ask his forgiveness and he would be gentle with her and understanding. She would never again wander from the right path. Peace would be restored.

Perhaps God had had a hand in this after all, thought Papa. Sometimes He permitted His children to err, so that they were more conscious of the devil's evil ways and of God's mercy and forgiveness.

Papa returned to the farmhouse with lighter step.

For the next two days he worked diligently on his sermon. He was pleased with the way the words seemed to flow from his pen. Surely God was guiding his hand and thoughts. Now that he was sure his sermon would right the wrongs that had beset his household and the church, he was in no hurry to return to the parsonage. He could work better here, and besides it would do no harm for Maria to have time to realize she had driven him from his own home and family.

He enjoyed the evenings with Steve and Terry and the baby. Steve was doing very well on the farm. He was not only making expenses, but was beginning to bank a little each week from the butter and eggs; and in the fall when the crops were harvested, there might be a small profit to divide. Just thinking of the possibility gave Papa a warm, comfortable feeling. It would be only right and proper, he decided, to sell Steve the farm someday, when his own children were grown and married and in homes of their own. He certainly wouldn't want anyone else to have the farm after he was gone from this earth.

Driving back to Berkley Hills on Saturday afternoon, Papa practiced his sermon aloud. The relaxation on the farm had been good for him, and his voice had never been more vibrant and forceful. Truly God was with him.

The spicy aroma of cookies reached out to him as he climbed the steps to the parsonage. Momentarily resentment gripped him. Then he smiled. After tomorrow there would be no more cookies. Not even for home use. He would never be able to eat another cookie as long as he lived.

He expected the house to be in a fury of activity. But only Mama and Greta were in the kitchen. Mama looked up as he reached the door.

"Oh, Pontus, you're home!" She put aside a box of cookies and came over and kissed him. "Did you have a good rest on the farm? You look wonderful."

"I feel fine. Steve and Terry send their love," said Papa, taking in at a glance the many boxes of cookies on the table. The bakery business seemed to have flourished during his absence, he reflected morosely.

"Well, looks like you're pretty busy," he said, suddenly embarrassed.

"Oh, I am, Pontus. Everyone in Berkley Hills seems to want my cookies." She was back at the table, counting cookies into boxes. "But I'll start supper right away."

Papa withdrew to the study and consoled himself thinking of his sermon and the surprise *he* would have for all of them tomorrow morning.

Sunday was everything a spring day should be. Papa hummed contentedly as he dressed for church. On a day like this he could be sure of full attendance. Which was fine. It wasn't every Sunday he had such a powerful sermon. And after today, he'd have a normal home too.

As he had hoped, the church was filled. And when Papa rose to begin the sermon, his eyes were fixed on Maria and the children. This sermon was especially for them. But after the first few words he forgot that his sermon had an ulterior purpose. He felt as though God stood beside him, spoke through his voice, lending it His power and eloquence. It was only when he had finished that he remembered to look at Maria. Her eyes, gazing up at him, were bright with tears.

"Thank you, God," he whispered under his breath. For now he was sure God had heard his prayer and despite his unworthiness, had shown him His mercy.

He stood in the church vestibule and received, humbly, the warmhearted praise of his congregation as he took their hands.

"One of your finest sermons, Pastor Franzon," Deacon Olson commented heartily. Papa was especially pleased.

Sunday was a day to remember—peaceful and *normal*. But Papa awakened on Monday morning to the unmistakable odor of cookies baking. The exhilaration he had enjoyed for a few days drained from him. His wonderful sermon had failed. But no, it couldn't have failed. Perhaps Maria was baking coffee bread. She didn't usually bake on Monday morning, but she might be fixing a surprise for him—a penitent gesture. Papa sat up in pleasant anticipation. Presently Maria pushed open the bedroom door, carrying a well-filled tray. There was no new-baked coffee bread, and her words told him there might not be for a long time.

"Darling, I hope you don't mind, but I've brought you your complete breakfast this morning. The kitchen is too full of cookies and the children want to help as much as they can before school."

"Maria. Do you mean to tell me you are going to continue this crazy bakery business? Even after my sermon yesterday?"

"Of course, Pontus. Why not? Your text was about *bread*, not cookies." Mama's eyes were twinkling.

For a moment Papa was too angry to speak. Then anger slowly melted into black and hopeless disappointment. "Very well, Maria."

Long after the door had closed behind her, Papa lay there staring blankly at the wall. But the wall, to him, wasn't blank. Instead of the usual flower-strewn wallpaper, he saw only a huge red-and-white sign: MRS. FRANZON'S HOME BAKERY. Judging by the boxes of cookies he had seen on Saturday, it wouldn't be long until Maria's baking business outgrew the parsonage kitchen. And once a woman began to put money-making ahead of her home and family, there was no stopping her. And Maria, as he well knew, was the world's most stubborn woman.

Papa had never felt so alone in his life. Even the children were on Mama's side—including Button. He thought at least *she* would remain loyal to him. But the devil had wily ways, and it was obvious that his entire family was under an evil influence.

It was late morning before Papa dared to go downstairs. Even then he avoided the kitchen, going directly to his study. And toward noon he took his hat and left the house without explanations. For the rest of the day he kept busy with various church duties, but the activity did not alleviate his depression. Even God seemed to have deserted him.

The saffron haze of the warm spring twilight cast smoky shadows across the church lawn as Papa started home for supper. He stood a moment gazing up at the slender steeple, now an awe-inspiring finger against a darkening sky. The finger of God. Suddenly Papa was overcome with remorse for his lack of faith. He had prayed, yes, but his prayers had been selfish petitions to the throne of God.

Slowly he turned and re-entered the church and knelt at the altar in complete humility. It was an hour of spiritual communion such as he had known few times in his life. As he left the church, he knew God had heard his prayer. For over and over, like a chorus of responses, his mind kept repeating: "*Resist not evil, but overcome evil with good.*"

He *had* been trying to fight the devil with force. He had tried to force Maria to give up the bakery. Now he would reason with her—show her the evil in what she was doing. Maria would listen to reason. He must act now as her pastor as well as her husband. Give her another chance.

Full darkness had fallen when he reached the parsonage.

After supper, Papa lingered in the living room, scanning the paper and waiting for Mama to finish the last of her baking for the day. He had noticed at supper how tired she looked, and it occurred to him perhaps she would be glad to give up the bakery for her health's sake. As the evening latened, one by one the children came to say good night. And finally Maria, smiling a tired smile.

"Good night, Pontus *lilla*," she said wearily. "If you want to read a while, don't mind me. I'm dead tired."

Papa put the paper aside. "I'd like to talk with you a moment, Maria," he said calmly.

Mama's smile vanished. "Oh, Pontus, please, not again. I don't want you to tell me for the hundredth time to stop my business. I just can't stop now."

Papa got up and stood facing her. "Maria, if you won't sit down, I'll *stand* and talk to you. But I must talk to you now."

"Very well, Pontus." Mama sank onto the davenport. "But please talk fast. I'm really too tired to listen."

Papa talked. He reasoned with her. He pleaded. But Mama sat silent. Papa began to get angry.

"Have you nothing to say, Maria?"

"No, Pontus. I told you I just can't stop my business now. But please don't worry." Mama pulled herself up from the davenport. "I must go to bed. There is so much to do tomorrow."

Papa sat motionless, watching her climb the stairs. He had failed. It was absolutely no use. He felt numb with despair.

The house was eerily quiet. Only the sharp ticking of the kitchen clock, like inexorable doom, broke the stillness. He would have given almost anything in the world to be able to turn back that clock—erase the past few weeks from his life. He thought of all the years Maria had been as close to him as his own heart. Together they had given the Word of God to the people; they had stood beside sickbeds; they had comforted the bereaved. Now all that was over. He had lost his wife to the devil —and money. And what was life without Maria?

Presently, as he sank deeper into the blackness of his

despair, a plan began to shape in his mind. A drastic, irrevocable plan. If Maria wanted a bakery more than she wanted to be a minister's wife, then he'd just resign his pastorate in Berkley Hills and go back to Sweden. Maria and the children could remain in America and run a bakery. Perhaps he could get back his old church in Lapland and find peace in his work until God called him.

Unbearably saddened, he went to bed.

The next morning, immediately after breakfast in a cookie-filled kitchen, Papa left for the farm. Before he had slept last night, he had finally decided to really stop resisting evil, and the only good he could think of to do where Maria was concerned was to leave her alone with her bakery. In the peacefulness of the farmhouse, he'd prepare his Sunday sermon and return in time to make his house calls on Saturday. Perhaps by then Maria would have given serious consideration to his wishes. Perhaps he wouldn't be required to carry out his drastic plan.

But nothing had changed when he reached the parsonage Friday afternoon. Boxes, dozens of them, stood on the kitchen table. Mama was giving instructions about deliveries to Torkel and Calle, while Vickey and Greta packed more boxes from the heaping trays of *spritz*, *peppar-kakor* and *finska-bröd*. They looked so good Papa almost forgot his resentment against cookies. Then the full significance of the scene hit him. *Maria had no intention of giving up the bakery*. His last hope was swept away. When he returned from his house calls on Monday afternoon, he'd tell her of his final and drastic decision.

It was late afternoon by the time the house calls were finished. Papa hadn't felt at all like cheering the sick and comforting the troubled. He needed some comforting himself. It really didn't matter what time he reached home. He thought longingly of other days when he could look forward to a fine supper, the companionship of his family, and Maria's cheerful smile. But those joys had not been part of his life for several weeks, and

now they would never be again. It wasn't going to be easy to tell
Maria that he was leaving her and the children. And that, too,
would be forever.

He climbed the parsonage step slowly, the weight of the future heavy upon him. Even Lapland, without Maria and the children, would be a lonely place.

Inside the parsonage he stopped. Surely his mind was failing
him. All lights were on. The house was quiet. There was no odor
of cookies—only the delicious fragrance of roast beef and onions.
The table in the dining room was set with Maria's best dishes,
gleaming in the soft candlelight.

"Is that you, Pontus?" called Mama from the kitchen.

"Yes, Maria." Even his voice sounded strange to him. Like a
sleepwalker he neared the kitchen door. Slowly his eyes swept
the room. Not a cookie in sight—only two flaky apple pies on the
stove, and Maria taking the golden-brown roast beef from the
oven.

And suddenly the house came alive with the chatter of
happy voices.

"Come, Papa *lilla*," said Mama. "We are eating in the dining room tonight, and the children are waiting for you."

Still dazed, Papa followed her into the dining room and sat
down at the head of the table. Reverently he bowed his head for
the blessing. Often, automatically, he had spoken these words of
gratitude for the food they were about to receive, but tonight
they came from his very soul.

Papa lifted his eyes to the happy faces around the table. Then he started to carve the roast.

"Just a minute, Pontus," said Mama. "This special dinner tonight is in your honor."

"In my honor, Maria?" echoed Papa. "I don't understand."

"You will in a minute. First let me tell you that today I went
out of the baking business."

It was a full second before Papa grasped what she had said.

He just looked at her, then around the table. Was this a game they were playing with him? Finally, "Do you mean that, Maria?"

"I do, Pontus. Six years ago you did a wonderful thing for all of us when you gave up your beloved church in Lapland and brought us to America. We have never forgotten your sacrifice and now we want to show you how thankful we are."

Mama placed a large white envelope on Papa's plate. "Open it, darling."

Inside were five one-hundred-dollar bills.

"But, Maria—what is this?" stammered Papa.

They were all laughing now. "Money, Pontus! Five hundred dollars," said Mama. "It all started when you gave me the egg money on the farm. I began then to save every penny to give you that visit to Lapland. But when you decided to return to the ministry, I hadn't been able to save enough. So the children and I started selling cookies to get the rest of the money."

Papa's throat was too full for speech.

"Now you understand why I couldn't stop the bakery when you begged me to. We are all sorry we had to make you unhappy for a while."

There were tears in Papa's eyes now, and he wasn't ashamed of them. How could he have misjudged Maria and the children, when all the time they were working so hard, not just for money, but for *him*. Working to give him his dearest wish. He was unworthy of such love. He was unworthy to be a minister of God. He preached to others about faith, but failed to practice what he preached. How could God or his family ever forgive him?

Slowly he got to his feet.

"Maria—children—what can I say?" The words caught in his throat. "Forgive me for misjudging all of you. And may God forgive me too. I know now how a condemned man feels when he is granted a pardon. And for the rest of my life I shall try to be worthy of God's grace and such a family. From the bottom of my heart I thank God that you *are* my family."

He paused, momentarily overcome with emotion, and glanced around the table at the joyous faces.

"But grateful as I am for your wonderful gift—and I am deeply, humbly grateful—I can't go to Lapland."

"You can't *go!*" All voices were raised as one. "Why, why, Papa?"

For the first time in days, Papa smiled. "Why? Do you think I could enjoy Lapland without Mama?"

The sudden stillness of the room was electric.

Finally Torkel spoke. "Papa, do you want us to start another bakery for Mama's trip?"

"Heaven forbid," exclaimed Papa above the general laughter. "When Mama is ready to go with me, I will get the money for her fare."

"Oh, Pontus, it will be years before I could leave the children. You *must* go without me."

"Then we will just wait years. Meantime these nice crisp bills will be waiting too in a special 'Home-to-Lapland' bank account. And by that time, who knows, they might have grown as much as the Franzon family."

Papa sat down and picked up the carving set. "And now I think we can all do justice to this fine roast beef!"

But he couldn't help noticing his hand was not quite steady and his carving wasn't as expert as usual.

CHAPTER 13

❧ Miss Franzon
Stands Bride

Mama settled herself in the big chair by the window, her mending basket in her lap. It had been a warm day for late spring, and the cool night breeze billowing the curtains felt good. It was Tuesday, and Papa had gone to a deacons' meeting. The children, except Button, were in bed.

"I'll wait up for Papa, Button, if you're sleepy," Mama said, fitting one of Pelle's socks over the darning ball.

Button, curled up in a corner of the divan with a book, looked up. "I'm in no hurry. This is a very interesting book." Then she laughed. "And I'll probably have time to finish it before Papa gets home if old man Stadling is at the meeting. That man sure likes to talk."

Mama chuckled. "I know what you mean, Button. Poor Papa. He's such a man of peace, but Mr. Stadling can always find some way to start an argument."

"I'll bet Papa will get even with him in the end," prophesied Button. "He'll have him close with prayer."

"I know," laughed Mama. "That is Papa's pet weapon. I guess every minister has to have one."

Button sighed. "Well I certainly wouldn't want to marry a minister," she said emphatically.

Mama put down her mending and stared at her oldest

daughter in startled surprise. "Why, Button! How can you say a thing like that? Being a minister's wife is just the most wonderful life in the world."

"Maybe—for some people. But *I* wouldn't be interested. Being a minister's daughter is confining enough. But a wife! No, thank you, Mama. I'm tired of being a target for everyone's criticism."

"It's different, Button, when you love him."

"Well, I'd have to love him an awful lot to put up with that kind of life."

Mama's heart dropped right down to her shoes. Where in the world would Button find another young man as fine as John Lambert? Not only was he handsome, but smart—really brilliant. Now he was being graduated from Theological School this spring, and already he had been assigned his first church. A minister needed a wife and, now that John could support one properly, Mama was sure he would soon propose to Button. But Button was making clear that when he did, her answer would be no. Children could be so difficult at times. Especially Button. Mama just couldn't understand her. No matter how well intentioned her plans were for her daughter, Button would make up her own mind, that you could depend upon.

A wave of tenderness flooded Mama's heart as she gazed at her lovely daughter. Why, sitting there curled up in the corner of the divan, the blonde soft hair curling around her temples, she looked like an angel. How could she look like that and still turn Mama's world upside down with her stubbornness.

"I'm disappointed, Button," Mama finally said. "I thought you liked John very much."

"I do. He's a grand fellow—smart, and lots of fun to go out with. But there's Eric Björk and Norman Falk. I like them too. Men don't *have* to be ministers, Mama, to be nice."

Long after she had gone to bed, Mama lay awake listening to Pontus's heavy breathing beside her and thinking of Button's emphatic remarks. It was hard to believe that her own daughter didn't even *want* to be a minister's wife. Why, there was no occupation on earth quite as important as being a minister of God. Button certainly wasn't in love with either Eric or Norman. Marriage was a woman's best career. Why, at Button's age, Mama recalled proudly, *she* was a minister's wife and the happiest woman in the world.

Mama forced herself to relax. She certainly couldn't *make* Button marry John. She would just leave it to God. If it was right that Button marry him, God would see that it happened.

She was just falling asleep when *the plan* popped into her mind.

If she made Button's wedding dress now, it would be so beautiful Button would just have to say "yes" to John. Wide awake again, Mama could *see* the dress. It would be of the finest white satin, yards and yards of it, with a train. And of course it would be princess style with a bodice of cut floral lace and a deep scalloped hem to match the long lace sleeves. And a mandarin collar, edged with seed pearls. It would take a long time to make it, especially with the seed pearls, and she would have to make it in secret, working on it only when Button was out of the house or asleep.

Mama became so excited about the plan that it wasn't until the next morning she realized she hadn't enough money to buy the satin and pearls. All the money she had saved from the bakery had gone into the "Home-to-Lapland" fund, and she wasn't at all sure Papa would think her plan a good one—good enough, that was, to give her the money she needed. But there had to be a way. A man, Mama reasoned, would do almost anything for a woman if she handled him just right. And where Papa was concerned, that meant appealing to his gentle side. She would start by making him a special breakfast—*plättar* and lingonberries.

She waited until the children had left for school or their jobs, and Pontus was finishing the last of the little golden-brown pancakes heaped high with lingonberries, before she ventured to speak.

"Pontus *lilla*," she said casually, "have you ever thought how much money it will cost to marry off four daughters?"

"Who's marrying off four daughters, Maria?" Papa asked, not really concerned.

"We are, Pontus."

"Maria," said Papa sternly, now greatly concerned, "please don't start planning the girls' wedding before they have even found their mates. I'm aware one of these days we'll have to arrange a fine church wedding for each of them. And when that time comes, we shall be able to take care of it. I don't see why you worry about it now."

Mama hesitated a moment before she dared try again. Then she looked at Papa pleadingly, and plunged. "Darling, Button is twenty-two years old and I need the money for her wedding dress."

Papa stared. "Maria, have you lost your mind? You know better than to start making a wedding dress before John has even proposed."

"Oh, Pontus, you said yourself John is going to get the church in Littlemont, and he will certainly want a wife, and Button——"

"Never mind. Time enough to make the dress when John has asked her."

"That's because you never made a dress, Pontus. Especially one with seed pearls."

Papa got up and started for the hall. "I'll be a little late for lunch, Maria. I have five sick calls to make this morning."

So—that meant Papa was through talking about the dress. Well, *he* might be, thought Mama, but *she* wasn't.

"Pontus!" she called after him. Then put her head in her hands and began to cry. She hadn't meant to cry, but she had remembered something which in her present state of mind made her feel very sorry for herself.

"Maria! What in the world are you crying about?" Papa came back and put his hand on her shoulders.

"It's just . . . just . . ." she sobbed, lifting her tear-

drenched face to his, "that I never *had* a wedding dress, Pontus.
I even had to sleep in an upper bunk on a steamship on my wedding night, with my husband many staterooms away. All because
he couldn't make up his mind soon enough to get a stateroom together. Oh, Pontus, I didn't even know . . ."

"Maria, don't cry," he said gently. "I can't undo what I did
so many years ago. What is it you don't know?"

Mama spoke through her tears. "I—I didn't even—know if
you loved me—or just married me to get a housekeeper!"

"Oh, Maria. Of course I loved you very much. I was just shy
and you were . . . well, you were so demonstrative. I was afraid
of you I guess. But haven't I proven to you all these years how
much I love you?"

Mama threw her arms about his neck, her cheeks still wet
with tears. "Of course you have, darling. I'm sorry! It's just that I
want the girls to have all those little things in their weddings that
I missed. They mean so much to a woman. And you know how
Button is. One minute she is dead set *against* something, and the
next minute she's all for it. Suppose she decides to get married
quick, and I don't have time to make her dress myself? Oh, I just
couldn't let that happen, Pontus!"

"Will twenty dollars be enough, Maria?"

"You mean——?"

"Yes, Maria. I can't very well marry you all over again to
make up for my shortcomings twenty-four years ago. But I can
see that my daughter has a wedding dress made by her mother."

"Oh, Pontus! You're wonderful—the most wonderful Papa in
the whole world."

For several minutes after the front door had closed behind
Pontus, Mama sat at the kitchen table, feeling ashamed of her
dramatics. She had never in her life resorted to tears to handle
Papa, and actually she hadn't intended to this time. She had just
got carried away by her own emotions. And Button's wedding dress was *so* important. Well, it was done now. She'd hurry
through her work this morning and buy the satin before Pontus

had time to think about her plan and perhaps change his mind.

Saturday was Button's day off from her nursemaid position. She and Vickey were helping Mama with the housework and the baking, when the telephone rang. No one ever answered the telephone on Saturdays but Button; all the calls seemed to be for her. She was so popular. But today Mama didn't mind, for that would be John. Button had told her yesterday she had promised to go with John to look at the parsonage at Littlemont, and Mama's hopes had soared, even though Button had said she wasn't interested in marrying a minister.

But when she heard Button saying, "Oh, I'd love to, Eric," Mama's heart sank. "I'll be ready in thirty minutes," Button finished and hung up the receiver. "I've really done all the dusting, Mama. You don't mind, do you?"

Mama hesitated only a moment. She did mind, but it would do no good to tell Button that. Then she realized Button must have forgotten about her appointment with John.

"But, Button, you promised John today. Remember?"

"I know. But that can wait. He will understand. When he calls, please tell him I'll go with him next Saturday."

"Oh, Button. That isn't right and you know it. You *promised* John."

But Button was already on her way upstairs. In a few minutes she was back, looking as pretty as a picture in her light blue suit.

"I won't be home for supper, Mama. We're driving up to Mountain Lake with Sonja and Paul. We'll eat there." And she was gone.

Mama sighed and went into the kitchen where Vickey was cutting cinnamon rusks for drying. "Don't you ever do a thing like that, Vickey," Mama admonished, not referring to the rusks, but to Button's unseemly behavior.

Vickey smiled wistfully. "Don't worry, Mama. I'll never be as popular as my vivacious sister."

"And don't *you* worry, darling," said Mama. "Your time will come. And I am very thankful you *are* just as you are. Button is so thoughtless of others."

It wasn't until Mama went upstairs again that she remembered the wedding dress—the lovely white satin in her bureau drawer. She had intended to wait until Monday when the children would be out of the house to cut the dress. Now she wouldn't have to wait. She could cut out the dress today, and Monday start sewing on it.

Quickly she made the beds and tidied the upstairs. Then she took the satin from the drawer and spread it lovingly on the cutting table. It was almost too beautiful to cut, she thought, pinning the pattern in place. For one brief moment she was frightened. Suppose she made a mistake and ruined it? She closed her mind at once against the thought, knowing God would not *let* that happen.

Long before Papa returned for lunch, the dress was ready for sewing. She put the satin pieces away again and went downstairs. She had just reached the bottom step when the doorbell rang.

"Why, John," she said, opening the door. Then remembered the unhappy message she had for him. Reluctantly she told him.

"But, Mrs. Franzon, we had a date with my trustees. Button just can't do this to me."

"I'm afraid, John, Button does as she pleases—too much as she pleases sometimes. I'm very sorry. And she won't be back until late."

"Fine," John said heavily. "Very fine for me. Those trustees won't understand. They want the woman who is to live in the house to approve the repairs and select the wallpaper. And they'll never approve of me as the new minister unless I'm to be married. I thought Button understood that."

John sat down, disconsolately, on the sofa. Vickey came in from the kitchen. "My goodness, John, you don't look much like a minister with that long face," she teased.

"Oh, hello, Vickey. That flighty sister of yours is the cause of it. A minister is supposed to have a wife—at least a wife-to-be. How can I select wallpaper without a wife?"

"Is *that* all?" cried Vickey. "Cheer up, John. I'll help you select the wallpaper. Just a stand-in for my sister, you understand."

John looked at her and suddenly a wide grin spread over his face. "Say! That's a very good idea. Would you really do it, Vickey? That old broken-down parsonage has six big rooms, you know."

"I'd love to, really. And we'll take Mama along. At least you'll have a real mother-in-law to show those trustees. That should set their minds at ease. Especially such a lovely mother-in-law."

Mama chuckled. She had never seen Vickey so gay. And her eyes were like a couple of bright stars. Suddenly an appalling thought struck her. Could it be that Vickey was in love with John—had been in love with him all along, eating her little heart out over a man who had eyes only for her sister? Oh, dear! That *would* be a complication.

She had been looking forward eagerly to working on Button's wedding dress this afternoon. But now she decided it was best to go along with John and Vickey, just to make sure things didn't get out of hand.

When Vickey came downstairs ready for the meeting with John's trustees, Mama was surprised at how grown-up she looked. Her hair was swept up in a cluster of curls on top of her head, and she was wearing one of Button's black dresses. She linked her arm in John's playfully. "How does the happily-never-to-be-married couple look, Mama?"

They laughed together. "You certainly look older, Vickey."

"As old as John?"

Mama tilted her head, appraisingly. "M-m-m-m—older, I think."

"Good," cried Vickey. "That ought to please your old trustees, John."

The parsonage in Littlemont was a rambling old structure

which for some reason had not been kept in repair. Possibly, Mama thought, because they hadn't had their own minister for some time. The church until recently had not been prosperous enough to support one without help from the Conference who had let them share an older minister with a church fifteen miles away. But now as the financial problem seemed to be solved, it would be a wonderful place for a new minister, just trying his wings in the service of God. Yes, and a wonderful place to raise a family, Mama decided, when she saw the rustic garden with rope-swings under the old oak trees, and a big fenced-in sandbox. Now of course, there was much work to be done, but what fun a happy young couple could have planting a new garden, and watching the old house take on new life under their hands. Button would love this place, and now Mama was sure everything would turn out all right. With such a home to come to, after her beautiful wedding, Button would settle down and be a good wife to John, just as Mama had hoped and planned.

Mama had been so busy with her own thoughts she hadn't noticed John and Vickey until now. Vickey was just staring at the big old house and the garden, her eyes wide, and bright with tears. "Oh, John, it is simply lovely."

"Lovely," he exclaimed. "A lovely *mess*, if you ask me."

"I mean, it *can* be," Vickey added. "Just *look* at that apple tree at the end of the garden."

That was so like Vickey, thought Mama. Always seeing the beautiful side. For even she had not noticed the apple tree before —a mountain of soft pink blossoms.

"I see," said John pensively. "It is beautiful. But we had better take a look inside."

A car drove up then, and the two trustees got out, carrying a large carton.

"Good afternoon, Mr. Dexter," greeted John. "May I present Mrs. Franzon, my mother-in-law—to be, that is. And——"

"And the happy bride-to-be," exclaimed Mr. Dexter heartily,

extending his hand to Vickey. "I'm delighted to meet you. And this is Mr. Ellison, our other trustee. . . ."

Mr. Ellison shook hands all around. "Now don't you worry about this old house, Miss Franzon. We aim to make it the prettiest place in Littlemont before you move in. It'll be ready by June." And he beamed knowingly at Vickey.

Mama started to correct the error, but when she saw the mischief dancing in Vickey's eyes and the sudden relief in John's manner, she kept silent. It would do no harm to let Mr. Dexter and Mr. Ellison think Vickey was the bride-to-be—just for today. After all, she *was* the bride-to-be's sister.

"Come along inside," suggested Mr. Dexter. "I've a lot of wallpaper samples in this box. It's the wife that should decide on the wallpaper, I always say."

Vickey linked her arm in John's, plainly enjoying this masquerade. And from the twinkle in John's eyes, he wasn't objecting to it either.

For an hour the two young people "ohed" and "ahed" impressively over the samples which the excited Mr. Dexter spread before them. They had made a tour of the house before assembling in the big, dusty living room to select the paper for each room. Mama had been even more delighted with the inside of the house, and its possibilities, than with the garden. She could just see this place, all furnished with soft colors and comfortable furniture, and crisp organdy curtains at the windows. A dream house, indeed! And so big. It didn't take much imagination to hear the happy voices of children ringing through these spacious rooms.

Mama was smiling happily over these thoughts, while Vickey and John selected the wallpaper. Suddenly she was brought out of her dreaming by Vickey's raised voice.

"I should say not, John," she was saying emphatically. "I certainly don't intend to have my little *girls* growing up with boys' wallpaper!"

"And what about the boys?" argued John. "Do you think I want *them* growing up with wallpaper covered with dolls?"

"I didn't select paper with dolls in it," announced Vickey. "*This* is what I selected." And she unrolled a scroll depicting baby angels flying in a blue sky, dropping appleblossoms down on the world.

"But, Vickey! The boys will grow up to be sissies, looking at *that* all their young lives."

"And the girls will be little roughnecks, looking at *trucks and trains and boats*."

Mr. Dexter coughed and looked helplessly at Mama. Mr. Ellison had tactfully withdrawn to the window. Obviously they wanted no part in the argument between their new minister and his wife-to-be. And if Mama hadn't seen how close to laughter both John and Vickey were, she too would have believed the sharp tone in their voices was real.

Suddenly both John and Vickey could restrain their laughter no longer. Mr. Dexter and Mr. Ellison looked enormously relieved.

"We'll let Mama be the arbitrator," said John. "Okay, Vickey?"

"Okay," agreed Vickey, trying to subdue her laughter.

Mama finally selected a paper dotted with ducks, chickens and cows, and little woolly lambs. "This ought to satisfy *both* boys and girls," she laughed, beginning to enjoy this game as much as she knew they were.

"We'll take it," exclaimed John.

"I agree," said Vickey.

And they were still laughing about the masquerade when they reached the Berkley Hills parsonage.

"Won't you come in for coffee, John?" invited Mama.

John looked at his watch. "I'm sorry. I won't have time, I'm afraid. I promised to meet my mother at five thirty, and it is after five now. Thanks just the same. And thanks *so* much for coming along today—Mama!" Then he turned to Vickey. "I don't know how I can *ever* thank *you*, Vickey. You were wonderful. To tell the truth, I almost forgot you weren't my wife."

"It was fun, wasn't it?" said Vickey, but her tone was not as gay as the words implied. "I just love that house and garden, and"—mischief twinkled in her eyes again—"I *still* prefer the paper with the angels."

The following Monday, when the housework was finished, Mama started sewing on the dress, watching the clock against the time the children would be home from school and their jobs. If all went well, the dress would be ready for the seed pearls by the end of the week. And until then she would try to keep it a secret between Papa and herself.

Neither Vickey nor Mama had said anything to Button about the play acting on Saturday, although they had intended to. But when Button returned, she was so full of the good time she had had with Eric, Sonja and Paul, they hadn't been able to get a word in edgewise. And Sunday, after church, they had all driven out to the farm to see Terry and Steve's new baby.

So it was late Tuesday afternoon before Button saw John again. She was in the living room with Mama and Vickey, waiting for John to call for her. Mama decided it was time to speak.

"Button," she began cautiously, "is John driving you over to see the parsonage at Littlemont?"

"Oh, it's so lovely, Button," exclaimed Vickey impulsively.

Button looked at her in surprise. "And how would you know?"

Too late Vickey realized what she had said. The whole story came out then.

"It wouldn't have happened, Button, if you had not broken your promise to John," said Mama.

Button didn't reply for a moment. "Well, if I'm the one who has to live in it," she finally said, "I guess I'd better see it."

Then she *did* intend to marry John, exulted Mama secretly. But when Button returned later that evening, she was anything but impressed. "I think it's a horrid old place," she exclaimed the moment John had left. "Why I'd be scared to death to stay there even *one* night alone. And it will be *years* before the church can afford to do all the repairs the place needs."

Mama's hopes flew right out the window. But now it was for John, more than Button, that her heart ached. He loved Button, and he needed her both because of that love and the glorious life he hoped to share with her as a minister of God's word. How could Button be so unconcerned? Why didn't she see that John was a very fine man, a desirable husband, could have any one of a dozen girls for his wife? And why, oh, why, did poor John have to fall in love with Button when apparently she didn't return his love?

But, Mama decided, hopefully, there was still the lovely wedding dress. And every day it became more beautiful as the satin and soft lace took shape. Just looking at it made Mama wish she were a girl again, planning her own wedding to Papa. Well, June was still a month away. If God meant Button to be John's wife, He would perform whatever miracle was needed. She would just wait and pray.

And so she did—for a full week. And between prayers and tending to the needs of her family, she sewed on the wedding dress. She was grateful that Pontus was unusually busy with church affairs and meetings, and this was the season when the young people's groups were particularly active with parties and socials.

Mama was waiting up for them as usual a few nights later. Button was first to come in, and already it was ten o'clock.

"Any mail, Mama?" was her first question, as it had been for several days now. Mama began to wonder about it.

"Mail? Oh, yes, darling. I put it on your bureau."

"Thanks," she called, already half up the stairs.

A moment later Mama heard a frightened cry. "Oh, Mama! Come quick!"

Mama made the stairs so fast that her heart was not pounding from fear alone, and when she reached Button's room she could hardly speak. "Button . . . whatever . . ." and stopped. For Button was leaning against the wall, her hand clasped to her breast, with the most *rapturous* expression on her face.

Mama was angry. "Button. How could you fool me like that? I thought you were *dying*, the way you screamed."

"Oh, I think I am, Mama." She continued to stare into space with a strange, faraway expression, and Mama wondered if the girl had suddenly lost her mind.

She went to her and took her by both shoulders, shaking her gently. "Button! What is it? What is the matter with you?"

Whereupon Button threw her arms around Mama's neck and hugged her so tightly she almost choked. "It doesn't matter, Mama. Nothing else in the world matters," cried Button. And the tears streamed down her cheeks.

Mama was really alarmed now. Gently she led her daughter to the bed and made her sit down. "Now, Button darling. Try to tell me all about it."

Button dried her tears and turned a beaming face to Mama. "Forgive me, Mama. I'm just crying from happiness. It's my very first story . . . and I sold it!"

Mama sat down heavily as if her legs had been pulled from under her. Button bubbled on, now that she had found her voice. "To a Swedish magazine, Mama! *Kvinnan Och Hemmet*. Isn't it wonderful? And look! A check for *five dollars*. Oh, I'm so happy I could burst. Just think of it, Mama. Your daughter, a *writer!*"

Mama was still trying to adjust to the sudden turn of events, when Papa came home. Button ran down stairs to share her good news with him, leaving Mama with the unhappy realization that now she would never have John Lambert for a son-in-law. Well, God never made a mistake. And surely this was God's will. Slowly she got to her feet and went downstairs.

One by one the children came home and went to bed. All except Vickey. It was unusual for her to stay out so late, but

Mama wasn't worried. The parties at the church often lasted until after eleven. And it was just about that time when Vickey
came in.

"Hello, darling. Did you have a good time at the social?"
Mama stifled a yawn. The excitement with Button had left her
more tired than she had realized until now.

Instead of the answer Mama expected, Vickey ran to
her and threw herself into her arms. "Oh, Mama! I just have to
tell you!"

Now what? thought Mama. What in the world was happening to her children? Must they all reach some kind of crisis on
the same day? Vickey was sobbing against Mama's shoulder and
saying something which surely Mama had not heard right, for it
sounded like, "I'm going to get married, Mama."

She lifted Vickey's head and looked at her tear-stained face.
"What did you say, dear?"

"I'm going to get married. In June. I'm going to marry John."

"But, Vickey. . . !" began Mama, sure now that something
was wrong with her hearing—or her daughter's mind.

"Oh, Mama. Don't take it like that." And her eyes were suddenly like sunlight after a rainy day. "We *love* each other. We
thought you'd be happy for us."

"But, Vickey," Mama finished, "John is supposed to marry
Button. And besides you're just a little girl, barely seventeen."

Vickey sat back on the sofa looking at Mama solemnly. "I'm
not a little girl, Mama. Not any longer. *And besides*," she empha-
sized mischievously, "you told me yourself you were only sixteen
when you fell in love with Papa; and you'd have married him
then if he had asked you."

"But that was different, darling . . ." began Mama again.

"Oh, Mama! All mothers say that. It isn't different. Or maybe
it *is* . . . especially when you love someone as much as I love
John. I do love him, Mama, and he loves me—not Button. We
love the same things . . . his being a minister, that lovely ram-
shackle old parsonage and its run-down gardens, and that lit-

tle nursery with the wallpaper we almost quarreled over, and . . ."

Mama gathered the excited girl into her arms. "My sweet. My precious little Vickey. How could I say anything but 'blessings on you both'? But we still have to ask Papa."

Vickey's eyes popped. "You don't think he'll—object?"

"Only Papa can answer that question, darling. And he's sound asleep now. And so should we be. We'll ask him in the morning."

But when Mama and Vickey confronted Papa in the study the next morning after breakfast, it wasn't as easy as Mama had hoped. He was shocked. "Have you forgotten," he said slowly, "that in any respectable Swedish family it is the *oldest* daughter who marries first?"

For one whole minute neither Mama nor Vickey spoke. They *had* forgotten that old, old Swedish tradition.

"But this is America, Papa," Vickey argued, when finally she had conquered the tears which were about to spill from her brimming eyes.

"Nevertheless," he continued emphatically, "Button must be consulted."

Papa had spoken.

The hours dragged, waiting for Button to come home that evening. And when finally she had heard the whole surprising story, she met it with an announcement equally surprising. "But I'm never going to marry *anyone*, Papa. I'm going to be a writer."

Papa insisted he couldn't see what *that* had to do with getting married. And Button contended she wasn't interested in getting married—especially to a minister—and then added belatedly, "Not *all* ministers are like you, Papa." Button knew how to get around Papa.

Mama knew there would be no more argument. And since Vickey was next to the oldest, Papa gave his consent.

"I'll be happy to see you and John in my study this afternoon," he told Vickey gently, "and give you my blessing. I know you will make him a good wife, and Mama and I will be proud to have John as a son-in-law."

Button placed her arms around Vickey. "I'm *glad* John fell in love with you, Vickey," she said slowly. "You'll make him a much better wife than I would have made him. And he *is* wonderful."

Mama had never seen a girl as happy as Vickey. She floated out of the room on a rose-tinted cloud. And only then Mama remembered the wedding dress, which had been made for *Button.*

"But the wedding dress . . ." she began, forgetting that Button knew nothing about it.

"Oh, I'll help you make it, Mama," said Button confidently. "We'll have it ready in plenty of time."

Mama told her then—of the dress that had been made for her and which now Vickey would wear. For just a moment Button looked sad. Then she brightened with an idea.

"Vickey's *almost* my size, Mama. Why, the dress will only need taking in a little here and there. You'll see! It will fit her as if it had been made for her."

And so it did.

What a lovely bride she will be, thought Mama when, the alterations completed, Vickey tried on the dress for the last time before the wedding. But as she watched the happy child, looking like a little girl playing at being a bride, a sharp pang of anxiety went through her. How young she was for the responsibilities which soon would be hers. In the three weeks that remained before the wedding, she would try to prepare Vickey, with what wisdom she possessed, to assume those responsibilities.

"It's the little things, darling," Mama counseled a few days later while Vickey was helping her with the supper dishes, "that you must learn to cope with as a minister's wife. Big problems have a way of solving themselves, but it's the little foxes, remember, that spoil the vineyard."

"What little foxes, Mama?" laughed Vickey.

"Little foxes of gossip among the church people, for one thing. You must learn to distinguish between gossip and real problems. For you will be required to listen to all kinds of problems, and in most cases from people much older than yourself. Women especially. Sometimes it is easier for a woman to open her heart to a minister's wife than to the minister himself."

"It frightens me a little sometimes," Vickey admitted. "But I do so want to help John in every way, Mama."

"You will learn quickly, darling, for you have the will to learn. That's half the battle. And part of the other half is observing little things when you visit the homes in John's parish, so you will understand the people who live there better. If women only realized how they *reveal* themselves in those little things. Like the woman who doesn't keep her kitchen stove clean . . . *she* is very apt to be careless in what she says about others."

"Mama! You're joking now. Those are just Swedish superstitions."

"Not at all, Vickey. You'll see! And there is the woman who never looks you in the eye when she is talking to you—just don't examine the corners of her house too closely."

"How about the woman who tells little white lies?" chuckled Vickey.

"She is the one who never takes time to fix a strap or sew on a button. More likely *she* is put together with safety pins."

Vickey laughed heartily. "I'll never, never be as wise as you are, Mama. I hope John doesn't expect me to be."

"The way you manage your own home is important, too. Very important. Little things again—like having the table set when John comes home. And making the meal the most important thing in your life at that moment. Nothing lifts a man's spirit like the odor of fresh coffee and meat and muffins baking in the oven. And when you whisper 'Darling, I cooked this especially for you!' Well—that's a big deposit in your happiness-for-life bank account."

Mama opened her eyes to bright June sunlight flooding the bedroom. This was Vickey's wedding day. And what a lovely gift from the Heavenly Father it was.

She lay there a while, torn between happiness and sadness. Happiness for Vickey, and sadness at the thought of parting with the first of her "dreams." *This* part of the wedding had not occurred to her when she started making the wedding dress. She wondered if she would have been so eager, had she known Vickey would be the one to wear it. But she must not think such thoughts. She must be happy so that Vickey and John would be happy, and every moment of this day must be so wonderful they would all cherish its memory the rest of their lives.

For days the preparations had outranked everything else. Papa of course would perform the ceremony, and so it would be Nim, who had now been home a week from school, who would give the bride away. There had been dresses to be made for Greta and Kerstin, and a different one for Button as maid-of-honor, this time soft golden satin. Then invitations, and all the arrangements for the reception. And finally yesterday the decorating of the church with banks of mountain laurel and roses, so breathtakingly lovely that it brought a sob to Mama's throat. It was all so different from what it would have been in Lapland. For Vickey would not have wanted the wedding in the big State Church, where Papa could not perform the service, and where she would have worn the little gold crown to hold her long, sweeping veil. No, Vickey would have wanted the wedding in the parsonage, with only a myrtle crown from Tant Renberg's own myrtle plant. Instead of mountain laurel and roses, the parsonage would have been decorated with newly cut branches. And both Mama and Tant Renberg would have baked and cooked and cleaned for weeks before the wedding, for the celebrations would have lasted three full days. . . .

Mama shook herself out of these homesick thoughts. There was much to do before four o'clock. She dressed quickly and went to Vickey's room to awaken her. But Vickey was already awake, sitting up in bed.

"Oh, Mama," she cried. "It's here at last—my wedding day! Just think, in a few hours I'll be *Mrs. John Lambert.*"

It was impossible not to share Vickey's happiness. After all, thought Mama, she wasn't *really* losing her. And John would be a wonderful son-in-law—just what she had prayed for. God had answered her prayers as He always did—in the right way.

This feeling of deep gratitude to God was still with her as, on Torkel's arm, Mama walked slowly down the aisle, to organ music that was like a chorus of angel voices, and was seated in the front pew. She glanced about her. At John, with Pelle his best man, eagerly awaiting his bride at the altar. And Papa handsome and dignified, in his best black robe with the velvet trimming. Mama wondered if he was nervous. It was hard enough for her to watch without crying. How much more difficult it must be for Pontus! Would he break down in the middle of the ceremony?

Mama closed her eyes for a moment and silently uttered a fervent prayer for Papa.

Suddenly the majestic strains of the wedding march filled the church. Kerstin floated up the aisle in a cloud of pink tulle and lace, then Greta in soft shimmering blue, smiling as if it were *her* wedding. Mama blinked back the tears. This was no time for weeping. Now Button, tall and beautiful, looking almost like a bride herself in the soft golden satin. And finally Vickey, a million stars in her eyes, on Nim's arm—in the beautiful gown that had been made for Button. How precious they all were!

Now they were at the altar. And Papa, his voice husky but so very gentle, spoke the solemn words which, in the sight of God and man, gave Vickey and John to each other "for so long as you both shall live."

"Thank You, God," Mama breathed softly. "Thank You for John, my new son and Your servant."

And because she was truly thankful, she couldn't quite understand, as she stood in the receiving line, shaking hands, hearing the chatter of happy voices about her, and seeing all the happiness in the world reflected in the faces of the newlyweds, why she kept thinking of an old trunk in the parsonage attic which contained snapshots of Vickey from babyhood in Lapland to last summer as a grown-up young lady of sixteen. And those funny little drawings Vickey had brought home from kindergarten her first day in school.

Mother love, thought Mama, was a strange contradiction. But she was sure God understood what was in her heart.

CHAPTER 14

ᕉ Pelle Makes a Decision

Faith, to Mama, was as simple as the word itself. It was never a matter that had to be weighed, nor did it require spiritual ceremonies to achieve it. She merely believed, and it came to pass. If the day seemed dark and beset by problems, her faith in the goodness of God brightened dull skies and lightened the problems. Many times she had beheld, with wonder, the mysterious ways of the Lord, and so never questioned His wisdom. A miracle in the making, she had come to realize, at the time often appeared to be an insurmountable tragedy.

So it was on a particular Tuesday in February.

Outside, dull gray skies threatened snow, and there was a frosty nip in the wind, but inside the parsonage all was sunshine, warmth and cheer. Tempting smells of baking and of roasting meat pervaded the kitchen. Although it still lacked several minutes of nine o'clock, beds were made, furniture dusted and polished, and all the disorder of yesterday's living restored to neatness. Papa had retired to his study immediately after breakfast.

Mama sang softly to herself as she laid the dining room table with her best linen and silver. Today was a special occasion —a luncheon in honor of Pelle's bride-to-be. It was such a pleasure to do things for Pelle. He was always so unselfish, doing for others and rarely asking anything for himself. Not even Mama had known how serious he was about Felicia Bronson until last Sunday night. She had known, of course, that Pelle seemed to prefer Felicia's company to all the other girls he knew in college. Her parents had moved to Berkley Hills two years ago and her father was one of the best doctors in town.

Sunday evening, Mama and Papa had been alone in the living room after supper, when Pelle came in quietly. It wasn't until he cleared his throat that they were aware of his presence.

"Excuse me, please," he began. "I'd like to talk with both of you if you have a minute."

Papa put down his *Church Quarterly* and looked up. "Why, of course, son."

"Is anything wrong, Pelle?" asked Mama, momentarily apprehensive because Pelle so seldom sought counsel.

His laughter quickly reassured her. "On the contrary, Mama," he answered. "Felicia and I are planning to be married right after our graduation in June."

"Married!" Papa sat up and stared at him. "But, Pelle, we haven't *met* this girl. Oh, I've no doubt she is a fine girl, but it is not like you to set the date for your wedding before presenting the girl to us."

"That's what I want to talk about. Could I bring her for luncheon on Tuesday, Mama? That is the day we finish our mid-year exams."

"Why, certainly, Pelle. Papa and I will be very happy to meet her."

Pelle had then explained why they had set the date for the wedding before she had met his parents, or he hers. Felicia's grandmother had died in January, leaving her little home, in the suburbs of Boston, to Felicia. Since Pelle intended continuing his studies at Harvard, they could be together. Later, when he had finished college, he intended to take up teaching as a life work. Until then, he would work during the summers and part-time during the fall and winter as a tutor.

"It is just perfect. Don't you agree?" cried Pelle, and Mama thought that to Pelle the whole world was always wonderful.

She laughed softly. "We do, indeed, son."

"Well," said Papa, "I just hope Felicia is as fine as you think she is, and it isn't the house and the furniture that makes her seem so perfect."

"You may depend upon that, Papa," laughed Pelle, "and after Tuesday you'll love her too."

And so Monday's regular duties had been put aside, while the house was made ready for the special occasion, and odors of cooking instead of washday filled the kitchen.

Mama glanced now at the little gold clock on the sideboard.

Only three hours before their guest would arrive, and there was still so much to do. The table looked lovely, but it needed a festive touch. If she hurried, she would have time to run over to Burke's greenhouse for a centerpiece.

When she returned, she carried a small blue bowl of pink hyacinths. It was just right on the table, and its spicy fragrance seemed to bring springtime into the whole house.

Mama had just finished placing it on the table when a strange sound reached her from the direction of the study. She listened. There it was again—a moan as from someone in pain. Quickly she ran to the study door and, without waiting to knock as usual, flung it open. There sat Papa, his head buried in his hands, moaning and groaning as if he were not long for this world.

"Pontus! What is it?"

"All hell is loose in my mouth, that's what is wrong," cried Papa.

Mama was so shocked at his use of that ugly word that she forgot about his pain. "Pontus Franzon! What an awful way to talk."

"You don't seem to understand, Maria, that I am not responsible for what I say. I'm going crazy. Completely out of my mind. My teeth——"

"Oh, Pontus! Why didn't you tell me before? I'll get an oatmeal pack for you right away. It will ease the pain until you can see the dentist."

"I've *seen* the dentist. I saw Doctor Falk yesterday. He says all my teeth have to come out."

"Never mind that now," called Mama, already on her way for the hot oatmeal pack and a large turkish towel.

When she finished binding the pack to Papa's jaw with the towel, tying it securely in a huge knot on top of his head, she couldn't help laughing.

"All right, Maria, poke fun at me. Laugh at my suffering."

"Oh, Papa *lilla*. You know I wouldn't laugh at your pain," she soothed, "but if you could see how funny you look you'd laugh too, even if you do have a toothache."

"Well, I don't think it is funny. And I'm sure Pelle and Felicia will not laugh."

Mama caught her breath. For a moment she had completely forgotten the luncheon. "Pontus! What are we going to do? You can't meet Felicia looking like that."

"And do you think I could meet her with devils jumping in my mouth?"

Poor Pontus! He must be in terrible pain to keep talking like that. Of course he was right. It was more important that the pain be relieved than that he make an impression on Felicia. But Pelle would be so disappointed, though, being Pelle, he would probably be as concerned about Papa's suffering as Papa was himself. Of all the days in the world for Pontus to get a toothache! Papa simply couldn't appear at the table with a towel around his head. Felicia would decide she was marrying into a circus family.

"Come, dear," she said gently. "Lie down for a while and let the oatmeal pack do its work. Just before Felicia and Pelle arrive, we'll take it off and I'll give you some aspirin. You'll see. Everything is going to be fine."

From the look Papa gave her she knew he never again expected to be fine, but he followed her upstairs and lay down. Mama covered him with a blanket, pulling it up snugly over his jaw, then went back to her luncheon preparations.

If Pontus would just try to make the best of things until after lunch, Doctor Falk could remove the teeth and Papa's suffering would be over. She hated to think of him losing all his nice white teeth, but if that was the only way Pontus could be himself again, it would just have to be done.

As Mama worked, she prayed. If faith could remove mountains, it could certainly remove Pontus's toothache. She just wasn't going to worry about it. God wouldn't let anything spoil this special day for Pelle.

There would be only the four of them for luncheon. The other children took their lunch to school during the week of examinations. But they would be bubbling over with questions when they came home. "Is she pretty, Mama?" That would be Greta. "What kind of dress did she wear?" That from Kerstin whose first thoughts right now centered around clothes. And Torkel and Calle would tease Pelle when he came home about being "an old married man."

A little before twelve, Mama gave the table a last critical glance, then went upstairs to change into company dress. She was pleased to find Pontus sleeping and didn't awaken him until she had finished dressing. The pain, he admitted, was greatly eased, and when Mama removed the pack, she was delighted to find that the swelling too was almost completely gone.

"You look fine, Pontus. But you better take these aspirin anyway, so you can enjoy your lunch. And as soon as Pelle and Felicia leave, I think you should see Doctor Falk."

"Maria! Don't you realize that Doctor Falk wants to *remove all* my teeth?"

"I know, dear. And I'm sorry it is necessary. But we haven't time to talk about it now. The children will be here any moment. Just get dressed and put on your best smile."

Mama's faith, and the good work of the oatmeal pack and aspirin, truly performed miracles. Papa came downstairs smiling, and a few minutes later Pelle opened the front door. The pride in his eyes as he introduced Felicia was all that Mama needed.

But added to that, she saw at once that Papa, true to Pelle's prediction, was very much taken with Felicia. Which wasn't surprising. For Felicia might well have posed for the picture of the angel which had been Mama's model for her children. Her golden curls encircled her composed and perfect little face like a halo, and, when she smiled, it seemed to light the whole room. But the twinkle in her eyes was not quite so angelic. She will be good for Pelle, Mama thought. She is full of fun and Pelle is sometimes too serious. And it was plain to see she adored him.

"Thank you, God, for giving Pelle so much happiness," Mama whispered under her breath. Then aloud she said, "Luncheon is ready, children. I know you have to hurry back to your examinations."

"Only one more exam, Mama. Felicia and I both finish up this afternoon. Then we have ten whole days to ourselves."

The luncheon was a great success. Papa was like his old self, and Mama couldn't remember when he had been so witty. The parsonage sang with their laughter. Afterwards, she served coffee in the living room, while Felicia and Pelle entertained them with stories of college life.

When the door closed behind them, Papa was first to speak, "A fine girl, Maria. She will be a good wife for Pelle."

"I'm so happy for them, Pontus. Pelle deserves the very best."

But already Papa had other things on his mind. "I've been thinking about my teeth, Maria. I just can't let Doctor Falk take them all out. How could I ever face people? How could I *preach* without teeth?"

Mama laughed, despite the stricken look in his face. "Oh, Pontus! You wouldn't be without teeth. You'd have false ones. But of course Doctor Falk is only *one* dentist. He could be wrong. Maybe you should go to another one just to be sure."

Papa's face lit up. "You're right, Maria. Just because Doctor Falk happens to be a member of my church doesn't mean he couldn't make a mistake. I'll talk to Doctor Ruggles, that new painless dentist around the corner."

He set out immediately, and Mama started clearing away the lunch dishes.

Papa had scarcely left the house when the telephone rang. Why is it, thought Mama, a minister could be in all morning and the telephone wouldn't ring, and the moment he left the house everyone seemed to need him at the same time.

"Hello!" answered Mama. "Oh, yes, Mrs. Rydberg. . . . No, I'm sorry he isn't here. . . . No, I'm afraid he won't be back for several hours. Can I help? Well, call me if I can. I'll tell Mr. Franzon you called as soon as he returns."

She hung up and went back to the kitchen. Ten minutes later the telephone rang again. This time it was Mrs. Johnson, and she was in a state.

"Please calm yourself, Mrs. Johnson. Mr. Franzon is not at home this afternoon. . . . Well, that's no reason to be so upset. Girls of fourteen will get into mischief sometimes. No, whipping her wouldn't solve anything. . . . Well, if I can help of course I'll come over."

Of all the days for Papa to be at the dentist's office!

Mama left the dishes in the sink and departed for Mrs. Johnson's. She found the mother pacing the floor and young Sally in tears. The air was electric with the conflict between them. Mama did not know how Papa would handle a situation like this, but she talked quietly with both of them, then they all knelt in prayer, asking God's help and guidance. When an hour later Mama departed, peace had been restored to the Johnson household.

How very little people knew, thought Mama, about a minister's day. Everyone's troubles were his, and it seemed never to occur to them that he might have serious problems of his own. Like today. She wondered what Doctor Ruggles had had to say about Papa's teeth? She did hope he wouldn't have to have them all pulled. Papa was so proud of his even white teeth, and he hated falseness of any kind, even in teeth. It would be hard for him to accept them. She hoped with all her heart that Doctor Ruggles would find some other way to remedy the matter.

There was much to do when she got home. Soon the children would be home from school, and there was still all those dishes to wash. But Mama was so happy, nothing could disturb her for very long. She hummed under her breath as she worked, thinking how beautiful Felicia was, and what a wonderful couple she and Pelle would make. Both of them were natural students. Pelle just couldn't get enough knowledge, it seemed; he drank it like fresh milk and looked for more. And from her talk with Felicia today, she felt the same way about education.

Mama's humming stopped and a shadow crossed her face. Soon—too soon—the children would all be grown and she and Pontus would be left alone in the parsonage. It just didn't seem possible that Kerstin, the baby, was now thirteen. Torkel would probably be the next to go. He had been spending a lot of time the past year at the Joneses' farm, for Ellen had changed from a giggly, almost skinny child, to a slender beauty. Greta had all her dates with Gunnar Olson, and Mama was afraid there would be no college for her either. Only Calle seemed to prefer sports to girls. Nim, of course, was far too interested in medicine to let anything interfere, least of all girls.

With the dishes done and the kitchen tidied, Mama went into the living room to relax a while before she started supper. She had scarcely sat down before Pontus burst into the house as if pursued.

"Pontus! What in the world?"

But Papa could not speak. He could only point to his jaw.

"What did Doctor Ruggles say, Pontus?"

For answer, Papa took the handkerchief from his jaw and opened his mouth. All his teeth were gone.

"Oh, Pontus *lilla!*" She was more shocked than she dared let him know. He looked terrible—not like Papa at all, but an old man.

Papa had found his voice, though it didn't sound much like his. It was thick and indistinct. "That horrible man! Before I knew what he was doing, he gave me gas, and when I came to, he had *pulled all* of them."

Mama was the speechless one now. But as she became aware of the full irony of the situation, she wanted to laugh outright. Papa, hoping to save some of his teeth, had lost all of them. And in spite of the pain she knew he must be suffering, he looked so funny. A sudden thought sobered her. How could Papa preach with no teeth? Already it was Tuesday. The dentist couldn't get new teeth made and fitted by Sunday, and even if he could, Papa would have to get used to them before he dared face a congregation. Mama began to wish she hadn't mentioned Doctor Ruggles; that they had listened to Doctor Falk who would not have removed all the teeth at once. Her regrets were swept away by another disturbing thought.

"Pontus! What will Doctor Falk say?"

Neither of them had thought of that. Falk was one of the largest contributors to the church, and Pontus had sought his advice, then deliberately gone to another dentist, a newcomer and not even a member of the church. At least that is the way it would look to Doctor Falk.

Papa forgot his pain for a moment. "But I didn't ask Doctor Ruggles to remove my teeth, Maria. I just wanted to be *sure* before I let Doctor Falk do it."

"I know that, Pontus. And I think Doctor Falk will understand if you just tell him the truth. And besides, *he* will have to make the false teeth for you."

"False teeth! Oh, Maria, I forgot about them. How can I preach with store teeth?"

"You just have to get used to them, Pontus *lilla*. And the sooner you see Doctor Falk, the more time he will have to make them before Sunday. Do you feel like going now? If he can't have the permanent teeth ready by Sunday, I'm sure he can fix up something temporary."

Papa set out at once. Mama hadn't mentioned the telephone calls to him. Surely this was one time a minister had the right to think of himself first. And when Papa returned an hour later, he was quite cheerful. Doctor Falk had not been hurt, he had just laughed at the forceful methods of the new Doctor Ruggles, and suggested it might be well if he acquired some of them himself. He had given Papa a sedative to ease the pain when it got severe and had promised to fit him with temporary teeth in time for Sunday's sermon. The permanent teeth would take longer to make, but he assured Papa no one would be able to tell them from his own and, when he got used to them, even Papa wouldn't know the difference.

"That's wonderful, Pontus. And no more aching teeth ever again."

Saturday morning Papa went to Doctor Falk for the temporary teeth. When he returned, Mama was surprised at how natural they looked, and Papa was so pleased he could even joke about the ordeal.

"You know, Maria, I believe Doctor Falk collects teeth as a hobby. He told me Scandinavians' teeth have the longest roots of all. I told him that was because we eat so much cinnamon rusk and——"

"And what?" asked Mama.

But Papa did not answer. He couldn't. His jaws were locked as if a clamp had been placed on them.

There was nothing to do but wait for Nim, who was arriving that afternoon from Boston. Papa was in the study when Nim arrived. Quickly Mama told him what had happened, then followed Nim into the study. To her surprise, Nim walked over to Papa and struck him under the chin. What a terrible thing for Nim to do. But she felt differently about it a moment later when Papa could talk.

"You better take it easy, Papa," cautioned Nim. "With false teeth you have to use your mouth the right way. And above all, don't get excited or tense, or it will happen again."

For the rest of the day, Papa could be heard practicing his sermon, carefully speaking each word. Each time he paused, Mama held her breath for fear his jaws were locked again; then breathed easily once more as his voice rose in measured tones.

On Sunday morning, under the circumstances, Mama did not expect Papa to serve her the customary coffee-in-bed. She was up early and prepared a special breakfast for Papa, and carried it upstairs. But Papa was full of gloom. The new teeth, despite the sedative Doctor Falk had given him, were hurting. And when he tried to tell her about it, his jaws stuck again. The blow he struck himself this time seemed to Mama a little more forceful than necessary. But his jaws unlocked. Nevertheless, he refused to eat for fear it would happen again, and only drank his coffee. He dressed, went down to the study, and presently Mama could hear him practicing his sermon. Poor Papa! He was so worried. And Mama was worried too, for as Nim had said, tension was the worst thing for Papa now.

Papa left early for the church. He needed time, Mama concluded, to compose himself. Nevertheless she was uneasy. She would be glad when this morning was over, and for the first time in her life she prayed that the attendance would be small. Which seemed likely, for the skies were heavily overcast, threatening rain or snow any moment.

As she set out for the church, Mama forgot her fears momentarily, in her happiness at having both Nim and Pelle at home. The Franzon pew would be filled this morning, even if many of the other church members decided to remain at home.

Her hope for a small attendance was soon dashed. The church was quite filled when she and the children arrived, and people continued to come in even after the singing had started. By the time Papa rose to deliver his sermon, there wasn't an empty pew in the church.

How handsome Papa looked! So tall and stately and especially dignified now that his hair was completely white. As his eyes met hers she smiled back, encouraging him not to be afraid;

that all would be well. Slowly Papa opened the big Bible and began to read from the seventy-eighth psalm, in a clear, steady voice:

> "Give ears, O my people, to my law: Incline your
> ears to the words of my mouth. I will open my
> mouth in a parable: . . ."

But Papa could no longer open his mouth.

Mama looked helplessly at Nim. Could he go up and strike Papa under the chin before his whole congregation? And what would people think if Papa suddenly struck himself? There was a stir of surprise throughout the church. Then she realized Pelle was on his feet and hurrying down the aisle to the pulpit. Was he going to strike Papa?

Instead, he smilingly motioned to Papa to sit down and without further hesitation, opened the Bible to the third chapter of Ecclesiastes, and read:

> "To every thing there is a season, and a time
> to every purpose under the heaven: A time to
> be born, and a time to die; a time to plant,
> and a time to pluck up that which is planted. . . .
> A time to weep, and a time to laugh; a time to
> mourn and a time to dance. . . .
> A time to get, and a time to lose; a time to
> keep, a time to cast away. . . .
> A time to rend, and a time to sew; a time to
> keep silence, and a time to speak. . . ."

As he closed the Bible, his voice rose clearly. "Today is my father's time to keep silence. But in his zeal to do his duty, his courage has exceeded his strength. With your permission, I shall attempt, in my small way, to take my father's place in his pulpit this morning. I freely confess this is my first sermon. I have no notes, nor have I prepared a sermon. But I have asked God to fill my mouth with His words."

Mama sat spellbound. And so did the congregation. For

Pelle was preaching with the same easy flow of words, the same "silver tongue" which Papa possessed. And Papa sat in silence, his head tilted a little to the back rest of the high-backed straight chair, but there was a faint smile about his lips, and Mama thought she had never seen such a glow in his eyes. It was not difficult to follow his thoughts. His son was preaching from *his* pulpit! At last one of his children had received the call. No longer need he worry about laying down his mantle when the time came, for Pelle would take up his work—be his voice—his mind; or, God willing, be given a greater gift than he himself had possessed.

Presently Mama realized Pelle had stopped speaking. For a moment a stillness lay over the congregation, almost a holy hush. Then the rustling of hymnbooks as they began the closing hymn.

"And now," said Pelle, when the hymn was finished, "Pastor Franzon will speak the benediction."

Mama was stunned. Had Pelle forgotten that Papa could not speak? She held her breath as Papa rose and stood once more before his congregation. He raised his hand, and the congregation stood and bowed their heads. Papa's voice, as he spoke the familiar words, seemed to have a new strength with a deeper significance.

Later, Pelle stood beside Papa at the door to greet the members. Mama's heart was ready to burst with pride, listening to the warm praises heaped upon Pelle. And the way Papa was beaming at each member told her he was so proud of Pelle he had forgotten all about his false teeth.

The parsonage was a busy place during the next week. Nim had been able to stay the entire week end and, because he so rarely could be at home for more than a few hours at a time, the interest centered about him. Pelle and Felicia, their examinations finished, were making the most of their vacation, and plans for the "big day" in June. It was a very happy time for Mama even if there was more work than usual. It was such a joy to prepare special food for the children, things they could not get away from home, so the house was constantly filled with delicious and tempting cooking odors.

Strangely enough, after the events on Sunday morning, the temporary teeth had never locked again. It seemed to Mama that somewhere in all this the hand of the Lord was evident. Just where she didn't quite know.

Then, on Saturday evening, she had the answer.

Pelle was taking Felicia to a concert. He came downstairs after supper dressed in his best blue suit, and there was a glow about him which, at first, Mama attributed to the prospects of another evening with Felicia.

"Is Papa in the study, Mama?" he asked, and she knew there was something special on his mind.

"Yes, dear. He's working on his sermon. Why?"

"Do you think he would mind if I interrupted him? There is something I want to tell you both."

"If it's that important, I'm sure he won't mind."

Mama knocked on the study door, and in a moment Papa opened it.

"Pelle has something to tell us, Pontus," Mama explained when they were seated.

Papa looked at him apprehensively. "You and Felicia haven't changed your minds about getting married, have you?"

"Not exactly, Papa."

"That's a strange answer, Pelle," exclaimed Mama.

"Well, I guess what I have to say is so important I just don't know how to say it. And a minister shouldn't be at loss for words."

"A minister?" questioned Mama and Papa at once.

"Yes. You see ever since last Sunday, when Papa lost his voice and something inside me seemed to tell me to go and preach for him, everything has been different. I had thought my calling was teaching. I guess it is, in a sense. For now I know that the voice I heard last Sunday was not my imagination, but the voice of God, calling me to His work."

The stillness in the room, when he paused for a moment, was

again that holy hush, such as had filled the church last Sunday morning.

Then Mama was out of her chair and had her arms around Pelle. "Oh, Pelle, I'm so glad—so happy!"

Papa got up and put both hands on Pelle's shoulders. "I'm proud of you, son. There is no higher calling than to the Lord's work," he said, his voice husky with emotion. "I *hoped* you would realize you had received that call. Now I am happy, indeed."

"Have you told Felicia?" asked Mama.

"Oh, of course. She thinks it is wonderful, too. It doesn't change our plans for marriage. Instead of continuing my studies at Harvard, I'll enter the Theological Seminary."

Pelle, thought Mama, had always been a joy to her, but never a more blessed joy than at this moment. Now that joy would be given to the world, through Pelle's sermons. Only once before had she been so happy, and that was the long ago morning in Lapland when Tant Renberg had placed her first-born son in her arms. And somehow she knew there was a connection between those two high moments—one that blended into almost unbearable happiness. For today a son had been born into the Kingdom of God.

Hours later, when even the house seemed to be sleeping, Mama lay awake, thinking of all that had happened to her family in a few days. Beyond the open window, the snowflakes drifted slowly to earth, spreading a fleecy blanket over the housetops and casting a white soft glow upon the world. How wondrous, she thought, were the ways of the Lord! For what had seemed a tragedy, only a few days ago, had indeed prepared the way for a miracle.

Suddenly the night seemed filled with a thousand singing angel voices.

Glory to God in the Highest, and on earth, peace and good will.

CHAPTER 15

❧ Nim Finds His Scissors

Late June sunshine flooded the parsonage kitchen. Much as she liked working in a sunny kitchen, it was a little too much for Mama this morning. It wasn't yet ten o'clock, and already it was as hot as a midsummer day. She pulled the shade halfway down and set the big mixing bowl on the table beside the flour and spices, thinking it might be better to put off the baking until Saturday after all. This hot spell couldn't last. It was too early for so much heat. But Nim just might be home this week end, and she wanted to have his favorite coffee bread and cookies ready. Sometimes she wished he would let her know when he was coming home, but Nim was like that—just walking in without warning. And Mama had to admit she liked being surprised. Besides, she guessed he was so busy finishing up the school term, he didn't have time to write, even if it occurred to him.

The quick sharp sound of the postman's whistle shrilled through the house. Mama dusted the flour from her hands and hurried to the door. The mailbox bulged, and when she pulled the mail from the box, Nim's letter fell to the porch. She tossed the rest of the mail on the hall table and sat down, opening the letter eagerly. She did hope he wasn't going to stay on for special work or something. It was so unusual to hear from him when he was expected home.

Before she had finished the first sentence Mama's heart was pounding with excitement. Nim was arriving Friday afternoon —and he was bringing a girl!

264

Nim's homecoming each summer was always enough to set the parsonage buzzing, but this news made it a doubly special event. She remembered that Nim had mentioned the girl, Karin Peterson, a few times, but she hadn't paid much attention then for she knew how little time he had for romance. Now she began to piece together the bits of information she had heard, and they really added up to very little. Karin was a teacher in one of the Berkley Hills grade schools, and her family lived in Blue Falls, a small town in the foothills of the White Mountains, where the girl spent her summer vacations. She recalled that Nim had driven up to the mountains last summer, but she had thought he was visiting the Davises. Now she wondered.

Well, she finally decided, she just wasn't going to worry about it. She had enough to do before they arrived and only two days in which to do it.

She returned to the kitchen and set about her baking in spite of the heat. She was taking a pan of *kringlor* out of the oven when Torkel came in. She hadn't realized it was so late. Papa would be back soon too, and she hadn't given one thought to fixing lunch. As she spread the kitchen table, she told Torkel the news.

Torkel took a big bite of a *kringla* before he spoke. "She must be *very* special," he remarked eagerly. "It just isn't like Nim to be interested in *girls*."

"Any girl a boy's in love with is special, Torkel," laughed Mama. "You'll find that out some day."

Torkel grunted. "Not me, Mama."

"And where have I heard that remark before, I wonder?" chuckled Mama. "Seems to me Button said that too—and what happened?"

"Girls never know what they want," deprecated Torkel.

Mama didn't reply, but she was remembering how adamant Button had been two years ago about a career, until a certain spring night when she had come in from a date with Eric, the same kind of stars in her eyes Mama had seen in Vickey's the year before. And at once Mama had started work on another wedding dress which this time Button *would* wear. After that there had been no more talk of a career. Only of Eric and the wedding and the "simply adorable little cottage" Eric had built for her on a tree-shaded street a few blocks from the parsonage. Yes, love certainly changed things.

But when Papa heard the news about Nim, he was even more disturbed than Torkel.

"Marriage seems to be catching in this family," he remarked gloomily.

"Now, Pontus *lilla*," Mama laughed, "don't you go jumping at conclusions. Just because Nim is bringing a girl home with him for the week end doesn't *have* to mean he is planning to marry her."

"Anyone but Nim, no. But if Nim is interested enough in a girl to introduce her to the family, he is serious about her. How can he support a wife, Maria, and keep up his studies?"

He dropped into a chair beside the kitchen table and mopped the perspiration from his brow. The breeze billowing the kitchen curtains was hot, but it was a breeze. Mama brought a glass of iced tea and a plate of freshly baked *klenetter* before she answered.

"No sense in borrowing trouble, Pontus. We don't *know* that Nim intends to try to support a wife and continue his studies. Lots of young people have long engagements."

Papa sipped his tea in silence. Mama knew he was still disturbed. It wasn't just that so many weddings were making a big hole in his bank account; but he had wanted his first-born to be a minister and it had taken him a long time to become reconciled to Nim's being a doctor. Now the very thought of his taking on responsibility which might prevent his finishing *that* career filled Papa with alarm. Mama had to admit she was a little concerned herself. She certainly wanted Nim to finish his education and be a fine doctor, but she also wanted him to be happy. It was right for a young man to fall in love, and of course she wanted Nim to marry someday and have children. She just hoped if Nim were in love with Karin Peterson, she was the right girl; and if she was, Mama would simply have to convince Papa.

Karin Peterson was a strikingly beautiful girl, with dark curls and mischievous eyes and a manner and smile so warm and vivacious that she walked right into your heart.

"Now do you see why I am concerned, Maria?" asked Papa as soon as Karin had been shown upstairs to her room. "She is far too beautiful to be sensible. Nim is just swept off his feet by her looks."

"Oh, Pontus! The child can't help it if she is beautiful. How do you know she isn't sensible?"

But Papa insisted "lightning didn't strike twice in the same place"; and the fact that Mama had been a beautiful girl and was still beautiful as well as practical didn't mean you could expect that to happen twice in the same family. He was completely convinced that now he not only would have to dig deeper into his bank account to help Nim with his education, but to support a beautiful and frivolous wife as well.

For a few days it looked as though Papa might have a point. Mama liked Karin immediately, but the girl did seem to be almost too gay, too carefree. And whether she wore sports clothes, a housedress or her Sunday best, there was no denying it, she was a picture. It was true, Mama reflected, the devil sometimes worked best through a beautiful face and figure. She certainly didn't want Nim caught in any trap.

Despite the trepidation of the whole family, the week end passed smoothly and happily. Already, thought Mama, as she prepared breakfast Sunday morning, Karin seemed like one of the family. That afternoon Mama packed a huge picnic basket and they all set out for the farm. Even Papa and Torkel now seemed reconciled to Karin, and Mama had never seen Nim so happy and relaxed. Every time he so much as glanced at Karin his heart was in his eyes. Mama wanted to be happy with him, but she couldn't help wondering how being in love was going to affect his studies. It would break Papa's heart if Nim decided to get married now. Then she reminded herself that he had said nothing about marriage, and she felt a little guilty. Here she was jumping at conclusions just as she had criticized Papa and Torkel for doing. There was nothing wrong with a young man's liking the company of a pretty girl. She was not being fair to Karin, or Nim. If he *was* serious about Karin, he couldn't have picked a finer girl.

When they returned to the parsonage late Sunday evening, Papa's fears about Karin seemed completely forgotten. And Karin further confirmed his new attitude about her, when Nim asked Papa for the car to drive her to Blue Falls.

"But, Nim," she protested, "you'll have the long drive back alone. That doesn't make sense. Of course I'd love being with you, but driving back at night alone wouldn't be much fun for you."

"Don't you think it would be worth it to have a few more hours with you?"

Karin wrinkled her nose at him, but remained unconvinced. "Just the same, Nim, it isn't sensible. I'll take the train—but I *will* permit you to drive me to the station."

Nim had to agree. Karin said her farewells, hugged Mama affectionately and followed Nim to the car. As they drove away Mama thought for the second time in two days that love certainly changed things.

With Karin's departure, life at the parsonage settled into its summer routine. That is, it seemed to. Pelle and Felicia drove home for a week end. Both of them were holding two jobs this summer, and for the first time Pelle had to think of his own "tin box" and years of study ahead at the seminary. Mama's heart ached a little. Pelle had always been so kind and now he was working too hard, but he was beaming with happiness. If there ever was a couple made for each other, it was Pelle and Felicia. Greta and Kerstin practically lived at the farm, and as soon as the church summer vacation began Mama and Papa drove up for week ends. Nim worked each summer as a camp councilor, but as his job wouldn't start until the second week in July, he had a little time for himself.

Mama assumed he would spend those few days catching up on his sleep and taking life easy. But she hadn't reckoned with Nim's energy. He was out of the house early every morning and didn't return until suppertime. And a few days later he announced that he wasn't taking the councilor job this summer. Doctor Davis had offered him a position as "helper."

"It will be almost like continuing my studies, Mama," Nim said enthusiastically. "Of course I can't actually tend patients until I have my degree, but I can observe and help Doctor Davis in so many ways. You know he isn't as young as he once was. I can take a big load off his shoulders."

Mama laughed. "You don't have to sell me on the idea, Nim. I think it is wonderful of Doctor Davis to hire you, and I'm sure Papa will feel the same way."

"Sure you don't mind having me under foot all summer?" teased Nim.

Mama thought how good it was to see him in such a light mood. He was always so serious. "I'll try to put up with you, young man."

It wasn't long before Mama began to see through Nim's strategy. Almost every week end he took the train or hitched a ride to Blue Falls. Or drove, if he could prevail upon Papa to lend him the car. He couldn't have been a camp councilor and still spent the week ends at Karin's home. This knowledge worried Mama a little. Already Nim's decisions were being governed by his desire to be with Karin. He had two more years of medical school, then one year of interning, and four more after that to be on the Board of Surgeons. And only then could he set up his own practice. Would Karin—or any other girl for that matter—wait that long? *She* had waited to marry Pontus, but American girls were brought up differently. Marriage wasn't their only career. Karin had her position, and she must meet many young men who

fell in love with her, beautiful and charming as she was. It all
seemed to add up to possible heartbreak for Nim, and that Mama
just couldn't let happen. But there was really nothing she could
do, at least not until Nim confided in her. And again she chided
herself for worrying. Wasn't God looking out for Nim and
Karin?

Nim's smiling face every evening when he came home from
his work with Doctor Davis reassured Mama. Nim's happy mood,
she decided, was not entirely due to Karin; his job had a lot to do
with it. And this conclusion seemed confirmed by Doctor Davis
a week or so later when Mama ran into him on the street. She
was especially surprised to see him, for it was midafternoon, a
time most doctors were the busiest.

"It is good to see you, Doctor," Mama greeted him. "But I
must say I'm surprised to see you on the street this time of day—
and without your little black bag!"

"That, my dear Mrs. Franzon, is because I have the best
helper a man could have." He laughed. "Most of my patients go
away for the summer, but that doesn't mean a doctor can close
his office. He has to be on hand, just in case."

"You mean you leave Nim in charge?"

"Not exactly. But I can get out and stretch my legs and get
a breath of air. Nim takes care of things until I get back. Not
that he couldn't take care of the patients themselves if he were
permitted to. I'll tell you, Mrs. Franzon, that boy is a better doctor right now than I was when I hung out my first shingle."

Mama beamed proudly, but Doctor Davis went on talking.

"You and the pastor are mighty lucky people. What Mrs.
Davis and I wouldn't give for just *one* child, and you have eight
remarkable children. I don't mind telling you I've wished a hundred times that Nim were *our* son. Oh, I know it sounds selfish,
and I don't mean I envy you two. I just don't understand why *we*
couldn't have had a son like Nim to take over for me when I'm
no longer able to practice."

"God's ways are often mysterious, Doctor Davis. Pontus and

I are grateful for the blessings He has bestowed upon us in our children. But sometimes I do feel selfish, being so blessed, when others equally or more worthy are denied even one child." A note of sadness had come into Mama's voice, which Doctor Davis seemed to catch.

"Forgive me, Mrs. Franzon," he said. "I'm not complaining. God has been mighty good to us. I'm grateful to have Nim with me even for the summer. Now I'd better be getting along back to the office. Greet Pontus for me, and tell him those fish are still biting in the mountain lake!"

"I'll do that," laughed Mama.

What a fine man he is, she thought, as she watched him striding down the street, belying his sixty-five years. And how fortunate Nim was to have a chance to work with him.

A few nights later, Nim came home considerably later than usual. Mama was still up, with a basket of mending in her lap, and Papa was busy in his study. Mama looked up as the screen door closed and Nim came into the living room. One glance at him told her something had happened. He was so excited he looked as if he had swallowed a fuse.

"Nim! What is it?" she cried.

"The most wonderful thing, Mama! Is Papa still up? I want you both to hear about it."

"Well, he's working, but if it is that important, I guess we can interrupt him."

She knocked softly on the study door, then opened it. "Nim has something to tell us, Pontus. May we come in?"

"Of course. Of course." Then when both were seated, "Now what has happened, Nim? You look ready to burst."

"I better begin at the beginning," said Nim. "I guess you both know I'm very much in love with Karin and we want to be married as soon as possible. Until this afternoon I thought we'd have to wait years. Now we can be married at once."

"But what happened, Nim? You're not being very coherent," admonished Papa.

"Well, this afternoon after all the patients had left, Doctor Davis said he wanted to have a talk with me, and he offered me a *place with him* just as soon as I finish medical school and my year of interning."

"But I don't understand . . ." Mama began.

"Don't you see? It means Karin and I can get married right away. We don't have to wait even for me to finish school. Karin can continue teaching here in Berkley Hills and live with us in the parsonage until I finish school; then I will be interning at the hospital and we can be together, and as soon as I have finished that we can get a home of our own." He broke off, out of breath.

A heavy silence followed. Mama was as shocked and surprised by his suggestion as she knew Papa was. Young people, once married, should have a home of their own. It just never worked out right, living with the parents of either one. But, if Papa agreed she would not oppose him, and if Karin wanted to live at the parsonage she was certainly welcome.

Papa broke the silence. "I was under the impression, Nim, that you were studying to become a *surgeon*," he remarked solemnly. "You have five more years after you finish medical school. Do you expect Karin to live at the parsonage all those years?"

Nim's eyes dropped to his hands for a moment before he answered. "Well, no. You see I'm not going to be a surgeon."

When neither Mama nor Papa said anything, Nim rushed on:

"I figure good doctors are just as important as surgeons, and working with Doctor Davis I have a chance to become a really good doctor. If I do want to become a surgeon later on, I can do that after I've earned enough as a doctor to take care of Karin." He glanced anxiously from Mama to Papa as he talked.

"But Nim," interposed Mama, "you've wanted to be a surgeon since you were a little boy, cutting up everything in sight. You *can't* give it up now when you are so close to your goal."

"Close," exclaimed Nim, and Mama had never heard so much impatience in his voice. "Do you think seven years is close? It's *forever* when you've found the girl you want to marry. It just isn't fair to Karin to ask her to wait so long."

"Does Karin agree to your plans?" asked Papa quietly.

"She doesn't know them yet. How could she? Doctor Davis just told me this afternoon. But she will. I *know* she will. She is as anxious as I am to be married as soon as possible."

"Then I think you should consult Karin before reaching any decision," advised Papa. And Mama certainly agreed.

Nim lost no time in following Papa's suggestion. Karin was coming down for the week end. Mama refused to worry, although her heart was heavy over Nim's decision. She prayed and left the matter to the wisdom of God in His own time. She hadn't the slightest idea how Karin would react to Nim's proposal, but whatever developed she knew would be right.

When Nim came in Friday evening with Karin, Mama saw at once that Nim had told her about his plan, for both were quite solemn. But nothing was said until after supper when the four of them were together in the privacy of Papa's study.

"How do you feel about this, Karin?" Papa asked as soon as he knew Nim had fully discussed the proposal with her.

"Of course I love him very much, Pastor Franzon," Karin began. "But I think it is unfair to him to give up the career he cherishes or have the responsibility of a wife when he is so near his goal. It isn't that I'm afraid of making sacrifices; marriage demands many sacrifices. But I want our marriage to be a real marriage—one we can build *together*. Somehow getting married and not being together just doesn't seem like marriage."

She was sitting beside Nim as she talked, but her eyes were on Papa. Now she slipped her arm around Nim's shoulders and looked into his troubled face.

"Please understand, darling! I do want to marry you—so very much. I'll wait forever if necessary. But I want our marriage to be right all the way."

Nim said nothing for several seconds, then a reluctant smile spread over his tense features. "All right, Karin. But you won't have to wait forever—just two years."

"Darling, listen to me. I know how much you want to be a surgeon. Why, you've talked about it ever since I met you. You don't have to give it up for me. Don't you know I'd wait ten years—or twenty—to make you happy. It's *you* I want to marry, and only you."

"And marrying you right now would *make* me happy. But if you won't do that, I certainly am not going to wait seven years to call you my wife."

Karin looked at Mama and Papa, her eyes beginning to twinkle. "You've a very stubborn man for a son," she said, sighing deeply, "but I guess I love him anyway. All right Nim, you win half the argument. I'll marry you when you have finished medical school if that is what you want. And, darling, I'll be *so* happy to be your wife."

What more was there to say? thought Mama as she dipped coffee into the percolator a few minutes later. After what they had all been through emotionally the past hour, they needed strong coffee and something to eat. But she couldn't help wondering what Papa felt about Karin now. That child certainly had both feet on the ground. She would make Nim a wonderful wife, and if Nim were going to give up being a surgeon for any reason, Karin was the best reason she could think of.

July melted into what promised to be a hotter August. Nim had been working late almost every night in spite of the heat, and had been spending his week ends in the mountains with Karin's family. He seemed completely happy about the grave decision he had reached, and Doctor Davis was equally pleased with the prospect of having him full time in a couple of years. Already he was saying, "When I retire and Nim takes over. . . ."

But as the humid days of August crept by, Mama noticed that Nim was looking a bit worn. At first she charged it to the heat, but gradually was forced to realize something was bothering him. He was unusually preoccupied, often not even hearing her when she spoke to him. But when she questioned him he insisted everything was fine; he loved his work and was happy. Mama tried to believe that, but her intuition told her differently. Watching him at times when he was unaware of her scrutiny, he seemed a man wrestling with inner torment. Had he begun to regret his decision? Had he quarreled with Karin? Whatever mental emotional battle was going on within him was beginning to show in his face. His cheeks were drawn and at times his eyes looked haunted. Mama's heart broke for him, but she could do nothing. She was sure now that all this stemmed from the conflict between his love for Karin and his desire to become a surgeon which had been part of him for so many years before he met her. She knew, too, that his sense of fairness and right would be sufficient to set up a battle with his conscience that would have destroyed the resolutions of a less determined man.

For two weeks Mama watched him in forced silence—and prayed. This was something in which not even a mother could help. Nim had to work it out for himself, with God's help. And God would help him. She had no doubt about that.

Papa always took the month of August for his vacation. He planned this year, as always, to spend it on the farm with the family; but Mama felt she had to stay in the city and keep an eye on Nim. She did not like the way he looked; if left to himself he might not eat regular meals, and that to Mama was a serious crime. Papa did spend the first week of August on the farm alone, but the second week he was back in the parsonage again.

"If you won't go with me, Maria, I'll stay here, too," he informed Mama reluctantly. "If you insist on being nursemaid to Nim, we'll just spend our vacation in the parsonage garden."

Mama smiled, pleased that Papa did not like taking second place with her, even for his oldest son. But toward the middle of the month Doctor Davis telephoned Papa with an invitation.

"Why don't you and Maria drive up with me to the lake Friday night and plan to stay a couple of weeks. Best fishing in the world, Pontus! And after the hot spell we've been having, the cool mountain air will do you both good."

Mama was reluctant to leave Nim to a bachelor life for two whole weeks, but she knew Pontus wouldn't go without her. She also knew that the prospect of mountains *and* fishing would be more than Papa could resist. The oppressive heat had been like a heavy woollen blanket for days. It *would* be good to breathe cool mountain air once more.

Nim really settled the matter. He announced that evening that he had promised Steve to help with the crops the last two weeks in August when Doctor Davis's office was closed.

"So you have no excuse now, Mama. And anyway I'll be spending the week ends at Karin's place. There will be no one for you to be home for."

"I suppose you are right, Nim, but——"

"No *buts* now. Tell you what, Mama. You go with Papa, and Karin and I will come up for the last week end and drive back with you."

Mama had to give in. "All right. Papa and I will drive up with Doctor Davis and you can bring the car to drive us back."

The Davises' summer home was a rustic lodge, high in the White Mountains. Mrs. Davis opened the place each year the first week in July and remained until the middle of September, and Doctor Davis drove up for week ends and his vacation the latter part of August.

Seeing it for the first time from the foot of the hillside, Mama thought it was like a brown rock which might break loose any moment and tumble down into the valley. But as the car moved slowly up the hill, she saw that it was a rambling structure of cedar logs, sheltered by great pines and elms which cast cooling shadows over the long front porch. Beyond the lodge, wide green lawns sloped down to a natural swimming pool fed by little mountain streams and warmed by the summer sun. And a mile or so away, the mountain itself, towering against the sky like a brooding giant, was reflected in the quiet silvery waters of the lake which lay at its feet. Here, according to Doctor Davis, "ran the best trout in the whole wide world."

Inside, she was amazed at the spaciousness. A huge fireplace stretched across one end of the big two-storeyed living room. At the other end a wide stairway led to a balcony, off which were several bedrooms.

"It's a wonderful place, Agnes," Mama exclaimed. "I can see why Doc enjoys the week ends so much."

"I don't know what we would do without this place in the summer. We both feel the city heat terribly. This lodge has been our sanctuary."

It had been years since Mama had had a real vacation or had been away from the children so long a time at once. But after the first few days she began to relax and enjoy "being company." It was especially good to see Pontus so contented and happy. With the hills and his beloved fishing, it was the next best thing to being back in Lapland.

Nim and Karin arrived midafternoon the second Friday, as planned—an event for which Mama and Mrs. Davis had been busily preparing for days.

"Smells just like the parsonage on baking day," said Nim, sniffing hungrily as he came into the big kitchen with Karin. "Ummmm, hot coffee bread."

"And coffee to go with it," laughed Mrs. Davis, setting the cups and saucers on the table. "You children go on upstairs and freshen up. Take the two rooms at the east of the balcony. We'll have coffee on the front porch when you are ready."

She was pouring the coffee a few minutes later when Papa and Doctor Davis appeared around the corner of the lodge each with a string of perch.

"No *plättar* for supper tonight," whooped Nim. "That's some catch!"

"What do you mean, no *plättar*, Nim?" asked Karin.

And with much laughter, Nim told the family joke about Papa and his no-catch fishing.

After supper that evening—a delicious supper of perch with Mama's special Swedish sauce, and vegetables from Mrs. Davis's garden patch—plans were discussed for the week end's activities.

"The rest of you can make your own plans," Doctor Davis interjected. "As for me, I'm going to show Preacher Franzon I'm a better fisherman than he is."

"Don't forget," warned Nim, "Papa's prayers are pretty powerful. Remember Farmer Jones's potatoes, Papa?"

Mama told *that* story, to Papa's embarrassment. When the general laughter had died down so she could make herself heard, Mrs. Davis said, "Then I suppose you two are not interested in our picnic of fried chicken, homemade ice cream and apple pie? Just fishing!"

"Well . . ." demurred Doctor Davis. "When are you planning to *have* this picnic?"

"Saturday afternoon. But never mind. Maria, Karin, Nim and I will enjoy it. I wouldn't *think* of asking you to delay your fishing trip."

"Oh, that won't be necessary. We'll join you at the picnic and *then* go fishing. All right with you, Pontus?"

"With homemade ice cream and apple pie on the menu? I should say so."

Everyone was up early the next morning. By eleven o'clock the chicken was fried and the pies baked. Nim and Karin had been given the job of turning the old-fashioned ice-cream freezer. No ice cream could compare with what came out of an old-fashioned freezer, Mrs. Davis contended. Mama's homemade rolls, big bowls of potato salad, coleslaw and pickles completed the lunch.

The spot they had selected for the picnic was near the lake, where later Papa and Doctor Davis would fish. Nim and Karin took their bathing suits to have a dip in the lake before lunch.

When the last piece of chicken had been eaten and everyone swore he never wanted to see food again, Papa and Doctor Davis set off along the lake front for their favorite fishing spot—"away from the women."

"How about a little mountain climbing, Karin?" asked Nim, "to work off that full feeling?"

"Just what the doctor ordered. Want to come along, you two?"

"Not me," said Mrs. Davis hurriedly. "I couldn't take a step, let alone climb a mountain. I'm going to stretch out here on this robe and take a nap."

"How about you, Mama?" asked Nim.

"Please come, Mama Franzon," pleaded Karin. "I want to show you *our* mountains."

Mama hesitated, but Karin looked so crestfallen, she finally agreed to go along. The three of them started out along the mountain path which, at first glance, seemed to go straight up, but strangely leveled off as they walked.

"Isn't it the strangest thing?" laughed Karin. "It *looks* too steep for anyone to climb, but somehow you never get to the steep part."

Karin linked her arm in Mama's and, with Nim on the other side, they pressed upward along the narrow trail.

"The view I want you to see is just around the next bend, Mama Franzon. Think you can make it?"

"Karin thinks there are no mountains in the world like the White Mountains," laughed Nim, breathing heavily himself despite his ruggedness.

Mama wanted to boast about the mountains around Lapland, but she was too short of breath to talk. And she was glad she hadn't talked when they reached the turn in the path and the view Karin had been so enthusiastic about burst full upon them. Mama caught her breath sharply. For a moment a sudden wave of homesickness swept through her. She took a deep breath of the cool mountain air.

"Oh, Karin, it *is* just as beautiful as you said it was."

"As beautiful as Lapland?" teased Karin.

"Well . . . I guess to us Franzons no place is quite as beautiful as Lapland. But I got to admit, Karin, it almost takes your breath away. I do love your mountains."

"You see! You see! Your mother admits our mountains are as beautiful as Lapland."

Nim caught her hands and pulled her to him. "All right, young lady. Just for that I'm going to take you to Lapland one of these days and make you eat your words. And when you see the miracle of the midnight sun from the top of Gellivara mountains, you will know what I mean."

Karin pretended to make a face at him, then drew herself up in mock dignity. "Well, of course I can't show you the midnight sun from the top of *our* mountains," she said, her eyes beginning to dance with mischief, "but how do you know what *other* miracles might happen? Especially to us?"

"Only one way to find out," challenged Nim. "We'll climb to the top."

Mama's eyes followed theirs along the narrow mountain trail which seemed endless. But if Nim thought to dampen Karin's enthusiasm, he had been mistaken. "I'm ready, Doctor Franzon," she said firmly, but the mischief was still in her eyes.

"I'll wait here," Mama hurried to say. "It's so beautiful and peaceful, I'd just like to sit on this mossy rock in the shade and enjoy the view."

Karin came over to her. "You sure you don't mind waiting here alone? It *is* a pretty steep climb, I'm afraid."

Mama smiled inwardly, understanding how much Karin wanted to be alone with Nim. "Of course not, Karin. You two just go along and don't worry about me. I'm going to sit here and dream about Lapland."

Mama watched them go, arm in arm, Karin measuring her steps to Nim's. Her own heartbeat quickened just seeing their happiness. How lucky Nim was to have fallen in love with Karin!

She was sweet and gentle and fine—and so very beautiful. She would make Nim a wonderful wife. If only he didn't have to give up being a surgeon to marry her. She knew how difficult it was for a girl to wait years for the one man she loved, and she couldn't blame Nim for feeling it wasn't fair to Karin to ask her to wait that long. But the more she saw of Karin and came to know her, the surer Mama was that she was made of stern fiber and equal to any demands that might be made upon her—even sacrifices.

She tried to put herself in Nim's place and see his side of things, fairly and honestly. When he was with Karin, the restlessness, which seemed to possess him at other times, vanished, and he was like a different man. The hollows were still in his cheeks, and he looked tired, but there was laughter in his eyes and his whole manner was relaxed. If being separated from Karin affected him as it seemed to, perhaps it was God's will that Nim make the decision he had made. She had so wanted him to be a surgeon and she knew how deeply Pontus also wanted that now. But if God wanted Nim to be just a fine doctor, it certainly wasn't right to question His ways.

Mama dismissed her serious thoughts, chiding herself for being so gloomy on such a beautiful day, and especially when before her lay God's beautiful mountains and valleys. She should be "lifting up her eyes" to those hills instead of worrying about Nim and Karin. Life too had its hills, but somehow those hills also leveled off when you reached them, just as the road had done today as they climbed. She let her gaze reach out to the distant hills, now mantled with a silver-blue haze, and realized suddenly that the afternoon was waning. She glanced at her wrist watch and was surprised to find she had been sitting here dreaming for more than an hour. Karin and Nim should have been back by this time. But she must not be annoyed or worried. It was a beautiful day and they were so much in love. Time meant nothing to them. But Mrs. Davis was alone, unless Papa and Doctor Davis had returned from fishing, and it wasn't very considerate leaving her this long. Besides, they should be starting back to the lodge soon.

She looked upward along the trail, and suddenly Karin, alone, rounded the bend and ran toward her, weeping.

Something had happened to Nim! "Dear God, no," prayed Mama.

Karin stumbled toward her, blinded by her tears. "Come quickly, Mama Franzon. Something terrible has happened."

"What is it, Karin? Is Nim hurt?"

"Not Nim. But a man is badly hurt. His foot is caught between two boulders. He's still conscious, but he is in terrible pain. He's been there since yesterday praying help would come, he says. Nim was able to move the rocks and get his leg free, but it is awfully crushed. Nim says he must be gotten to the hospital at once."

Mama was on her feet, her arm around Karin. "Don't cry, child. We'll do the best we can. But how can we get him down the mountain by ourselves? Hadn't I better bring Papa and Doc?"

"I don't know, Mama Franzon. Nim says there is no time to lose if the man's life is to be saved. He's making a stretcher of branches and thinks the three of us can carry him."

"All right, Karin." Mama had thought the climb was too steep for her earlier, but now, with the renewed strength of emergency, she kept up with Karin. When they reached the spot where Nim waited with the half-conscious man and Mama saw the seriousness of the accident, it was difficult to keep from fainting. Nim had fashioned a stretcher of crossed branches and had lifted the suffering man onto it. Slowly and prayerfully they made their way down the mountain to the lake.

"If only Doctor Davis and Papa are there," panted Nim.

And fortunately they were. Their jokes about the day's fishing broke off abruptly as the grim procession reached the camp. Doctor Davis agreed with Nim that there was no time to lose getting the man to a hospital. There was little he could do, for it was pretty obvious amputation was the only way to save the man's life, *if* it could still be saved.

At the lodge, Doctor Davis stopped the car only long enough to let the women out, then started for the nearest hospital some fifteen miles away.

On the porch of the lodge there was silence. Karin stood looking out across the hills. Occasionally a dry sob broke from her, but she did not cry. Poor child! She was having her first taste of what it meant to be a doctor's wife. The anxious hours of waiting when a life depended upon the skill of the doctor; and the agony of spirit that doctor, her husband, must endure when the patient did not live. A wife could be aware of this agony, but powerless to ease it.

"Why don't you lie down for a while, Karin," Mama suggested. "All this has been a terrible shock for you. But there is nothing we can do now except wait until they return. It may be hours."

"That's right, Karin," said Mrs. Davis. "You lie down and I'll fix some hot coffee."

"I'll be all right. I'm sorry to act this way. But if you could have seen the suffering in that poor man's face when we found him. Oh, I'll never forget it."

Mama took her arm gently and led her to a chair. "Try to, dear. It does no good to remember things like that. You'll feel better after a cup of coffee."

It was almost midnight when the men finally returned. The injured man would live, but amputation had been necessary. They had stayed at the hospital long enough to know he was out of danger.

"You did all you could do, dear," Mrs. Davis consoled her husband.

"That's just it, Agnes. *All* I could do was too little—so inadequate."

"Now don't blame yourself. Just be thankful Karin and Nim found the man when they did. Come! Drink this hot coffee and try to eat something. You all look exhausted."

Whatever plans had been made for Sunday seemed to hold

no interest the next morning. Mama knew that Nim was trying
to rise above the experience as a soon-to-be practicing doctor should; to accept it as part of a doctor's life. But it was obvious
he had been deeply affected by the tragedy. He would smile
when Mama attempted a light remark to pull him out of his morbid thoughts, but the haunted look was back in his eyes almost
before the smile had left his lips. Her heart ached for him, but
there was nothing she could say or do.

As soon as seemed feasible after breakfast, Doctor Davis
telephoned the hospital. The man was doing fine; he would probably have a good deal of pain when the anesthetic wore off, but
that was to be expected. He was out of danger and was able to
talk.

"How did it happen?" asked Doctor Davis. "Did you find
out who he is?"

The hospital doctor explained that the man was a summer
resident from Boston. He had started to climb to the top of the
mountain, but had noticed a small cave off the main trail and
decided to explore it. A rock near the entrance had slipped, starting a minor cave-in, in which he had been caught. He had
called for help until he became unconscious. He had just
revived when Nim and Karin passed on the trail, and his cries
had attracted their attention.

"He would like to see the young man who found him," concluded the hospital doctor. "Do you think he would mind coming in?"

Doctor Davis assured him Nim would be very glad to drive
over during the day. And immediately after lunch, Karin and
Nim left for the hospital.

"Don't stay too long, Nim," advised Mama. "Papa wants to
get an early start back this afternoon to avoid the heavy traffic."

But it was long past dark when they returned, and Papa had
been reconciled to going home in the morning. Mama noticed at
once that both Karin and Nim were more relaxed than when they

left. What had the man wanted with them? To reward them? Nim would never accept a reward for saving a man's life. But her intuition told her something had happened. Something more than just relief that the man would live. However, she said nothing. Nim would tell her when he was ready, whatever it was.

So it was a quite normal group who sat down to Mrs. Davis's fine supper. Nim was in better spirits, as though a great load had been lifted from his shoulders. Mama was pleased he had adjusted himself so well to the accident. He would see a lot of this kind of thing, unfortunately, as a doctor.

Mama and Mrs. Davis cleared away the dishes after supper, and Nim and Karin went out for "a breath of air." Doctor Davis made a fire in the fireplace and got out his favorite pipe. He and Papa were back on the subject of fishing when Mama and Mrs. Davis returned to the living room. Presently Nim and Karin came in.

To Mama's surprise, Nim seemed quite nervous—not at all relaxed as he had been at supper. Before she had time to wonder about it, he said abruptly, "Karin and I have something to tell you. That is, I do; Karin agrees."

Doctor Davis put down his pipe and Papa leaned forward attentively. A log broke in the fireplace, the bright blaze sharply outlining the questioning faces turned toward Nim and Karin.

"I don't know quite how to say this, Doctor Davis," Nim began, "but I have to. Would you mind very much if I changed my mind about accepting your offer? I just have to be a surgeon! And Karin has agreed to wait for me until I've finished all my training and interning and . . ." He broke off, confused and embarrassed.

Mama's heart was in her throat, and Papa was staring at Nim as though he couldn't possibly be hearing right. Doctor Davis spoke in a quiet voice.

"Why don't you both sit down and you, Nim—start from the beginning."

"Well, I guess I am muddling this pretty badly," said Nim. He brought a chair for Karin and placed it beside Mama, then sat down opposite Doctor Davis.

"It wasn't just the accident yesterday that made me change my mind, although that had a good deal to do with it. All of you know that I have wanted to be a surgeon since I was ten years old and cut up my first frog." He was completely composed now and continued in a low voice. "Until I met Karin, there wasn't anything in the world that meant so much to me as reaching that goal. But when you find the *one* girl in ten million, you can't let her get away from you. I couldn't ask her to wait seven years until I could marry her and support her as a wife has the right to expect. And *I* didn't want to wait that long either. I thought I could be happy being a very good doctor and working to be good enough to take over your practice, Doctor Davis, when you wanted to retire—just as we planned. At first I *was* happy. Then I began to feel like a quitter—a man who was running out on something because it was too difficult, because it required sacrifices. It bothered me. I've worried about it all summer. Then yesterday when I realized how helpless we both were in the face of the need for surgery, and you said what you did, Doctor, I knew I *had* to go on and complete my work. Yes, even if it meant losing Karin—the biggest sacrifice I could be asked to make."

He got up and crossed the room to put his arm around Karin. "But this most wonderful of all girls loves me enough to wait *seven* years for me. Think of it. A miracle right from the Hand of God."

Although there was only devoutness in his remark, the lightness of his tone and the happiness in his face broke the tension which had held even Mama in silence since his first abrupt announcement.

Now there was a buzz of voices, all speaking at once. Finally Doctor Davis's deep voice rose above the others. "Since I am the loser in this deal, I think I should have the floor," he laughed.

Then he spoke with seriousness. "Nim, I'm proud of you. Today you have found your real strength as a man. You'll make a great surgeon. I couldn't be prouder of you if you were my own son."

He got up and took Karin's hand in his. "And you, Karin. A doctor—*or* a minister—needs a fine wife, and your decision today has proved how fine you are." A smile came into his eyes. "And this young man better prove worthy of *you*, or I'll personally take him over my knees, big as he is, and give him a darned good paddling."

He was drowned out for a moment by laughter. "And now, since this is a very momentous occasion, Agnes, I think there's a gallon of sweet cider in the icebox. A toast to Surgeon Franzon and his beautiful and *patient* bride-to-be."

Much later, when the others had gone to bed, Mama went out onto the porch alone. A gentle wind stirred the great branches of the elms above her. Soft darkness enveloped the distant hills, now dimly outlined against the starry sky. Crickets sang their night song and from the lake came the deep-throated call of the frogs.

She remembered suddenly what Karin had said yesterday about a miracle on *her* mountain. And a miracle had happened. *Two* wondrous miracles. A man's life had been saved, and another man had found peace of mind and heart and the way of life God intended for him.

"Thank you, God," she whispered, her heart ready to burst with gratitude.

CHAPTER 16

❧ Papa Climbs the Mountain

Winter came early that year. The tangy bright days, glorious with color, too soon gave way to leaden skies and somber barren branches, whipped by sharp winter winds. A full week before Thanksgiving, Mama awoke to a white world. The parsonage itself seemed strangely quiet as she slipped into her warm robe and stole softly downstairs. Pontus was still sleeping soundly. She let him sleep. It was Saturday and he needed this extra hour of rest.

She set the coffee to perking and laid the breakfast tray with special care. Lately she had noticed Pontus seemed to tire more easily. How little the church people realized the demands they made upon the strength of their pastor. Yet it was not in his nature to shirk what to him were his duties. Mama wanted to remind him that he wasn't as young as he once was, but she couldn't do that; he might feel she was complaining for her own sake. How could he even think such a thing? He had given her the most wonderful life any woman could ask. Still, she couldn't help worrying a little, and she prayed a silent prayer as she prepared breakfast.

The ticking of the kitchen clock sounded loudly in the room, reminding her again of the silence of the house. Calle and Torkel had gone to the farm for the week end, Greta was spending the day with Button, and Kerstin was at Pelle's for the Thanksgiving holiday.

This is how it will be, she thought, when the children are all married and Pontus and I are alone.

The thought saddened her a little. It wasn't easy to let your children go, even when you knew they were happy in homes of their own. Not that she wouldn't be content with Pontus alone. But she would miss the excitement of the children's coming and going, the sharing of joys and disappointments as a family.

She shook herself out of such morbid thoughts. Here she was borrowing trouble for no reason. It would be a long time before all the children were married. With Nim's decision to postpone his marriage, Mama was sure the others would wait a while. Greta went to parties occasionally with Gunnar Olson, but she was far more interested in taking her master's degree, than in marriage. Calle preferred sports to dates with girls, and Torkel was intent upon following the profession Pelle had abandoned —teaching. Kerstin, of course, was too young even to think of marriage.

Yes, they would be together as a family for many years yet. And while Papa hadn't said so, she was sure he was pleased too. Two weddings in so short a time had made heavy demands upon his bank account.

She picked up the breakfast tray and started upstairs. Then she remembered the mail. She ran through it quickly and stopped at one with a Swedish postmark. From Deacon Lund! She put it on the tray and hurried upstairs.

Papa read the letter through, between sips of black coffee, before he spoke. "We might do it, at that," he said irrelevantly.

"Do what, Pontus?" Mama laughed. "How do you think I know what is in your letter?"

"I'm sorry, Maria. It's from Deacon Lund. He writes— but here; you had better read it yourself."

" 'Dear Pastor Franzon,' " Mama read aloud, then skimmed through the pages until she came to the part Papa was referring to. "'Pastor Engwall is taking two months' vacation next summer to visit relatives in England. We wonder if it would be possible for you to take over your old pulpit during his absence? It has been a long time since you left us for America, and I'm sure a visit to your homeland would bring joy to your heart as it would to all of ours. The parsonage will be at your disposal, and it is our hope that Mrs. Franzon will be able to accompany you. I'm sure I do not need to tell you how much your coming would mean to all of us, and we shall do everything possible to make your stay here both pleasant and restful . . .'"

Mama was too excited to read more. "Oh, Pontus, how wonderful! Do you think we *could* go?"

"Well, after two weddings, it might take some planning. But we still have the 'Home-to-Lapland' fund—remember?"

Until that moment, Mama *had* forgotten it. But it was only five hundred dollars. Traveling was more expensive now than it was when she had planned the surprise for Pontus. He would need that much at least for his own passage and expenses. And it wouldn't be fair to expect him to cut deeper into his bank account when he had spent so much already for weddings. She would love to go with him, but now it was important that Pontus go. Doubly important. He badly needed a long rest. The ocean voyage and seeing his beloved Lapland again would be just the best medicine in the world for him.

"I remember, Pontus," Mama laughed. "It seemed like such a lot of money then. I guess that was because I baked so many thousand cookies to earn it. But it wouldn't take us very far now."

Papa didn't say anything, just went on drinking his coffee, and Mama wondered if he was remembering how unhappy those cookies had made him.

Presently he set down his coffee cup, and when Mama looked up there was a smile behind his eyes trying to break through. Why, even the *hope* of seeing Lapland again, she thought, was like a tonic.

"Maria," he began, "do you remember the night you and the

children presented me with the money for the trip back to Lapland?"

"Why, of course, Pontus."

"And I told you we'd put it in a 'Home-to-Lapland' fund, and maybe it would grow, like the Franzon family?"

Mama nodded.

"Well, I guess I had better tell you that is what has happened. All the money Steve has paid me from the farm, I put into the fund. And by the time we are ready to leave for Sweden, it will be very well nourished indeed."

"Oh, Pontus! Then we *can* go."

"That, Maria, is what I have been trying to tell you."

And so it was that some six months later, on a bright June morning, Mama stood beside Papa on deck of the Swedish-American liner, both straining their eyes for the first glimpse of *Vingc Fyr.*

"Look, Maria," Papa exclaimed. "It's only a little after five and that sun is shining as brightly as noonday in America."

Mama looked, but mostly at Papa. His cheeks glowed and his eyes were alight with excitement. This was the day he had waited for so many years. She had thought she knew how much "coming home" would mean to him, but now she felt a little pang of guilt that she could not completely share his happiness. It was a feeling so deep no one really could share it. Pontus was a true Swede. All those years in America had not dimmed his loyalty to his homeland; whereas she had loved America, almost from her first day in the new country, quite as much as she loved Sweden. For America had given their children a chance at education—the chance to dream dreams and see them fulfilled.

"Today we are landing, Maria," Papa said with subdued excitement. There were tears in his eyes now, and his voice shook with emotion. "Soon we shall stand once more on Swedish soil. How good God has been to us!"

Mama's throat tightened, but the words she wanted to speak

would not come. Now for the first time she fully realized the sacrifice he had made so many years ago. And never a word of complaint from him in all those years.

They had been alone on deck, having come up early to offer a prayer of thanks for the safe and wonderful journey. Now other excited, eager passengers began to line the rail and crowd the deck, each scanning the horizon for the first glimpse of their homeland.

Presently a shout went up and almost simultaneously hundreds of voices broke into the Swedish National Hymn. At first they sang softly, prayerfully, then the music swelled into a mighty chorus, echoing across the bright waters.

> "Du gamla du fria
> Du fjällhöga Nord
> Du tysta du glädjerika sköna. . . ."

Papa stood reverently, hat in hand, but with head held high. A shameless tear rolled down each cheek, while he sang with the vigor of youth. Mama could not help joining in with:

> "Ack jag vill leva
> Jag vill dö i Norden. . . ."

How true were the words—old pilgrims returning home! Mama was wiping her eyes now along with others. This was her homeland too, even if she was happy in America.

When the first exciting, hectic moments of landing were over, Mama finally stood beside Papa, confronted, across their opened trunks and suitcases, by a stern customs officer. She smiled her nicest smile.

"I assure you, Officer, we are not smugglers. My husband is a *minister*. We are very happy to be in Sweden again."

"Minister or not, the law is the law," he said gruffly. "Now let's see what you have here." He picked up one of Pontus's white shirts and started shaking it.

"I don't know what you expect to find hidden in that," Mama said sharply.

"You'd be surprised, lady. The couple ahead of you was a home-loving pair and *so happy* to be back in Sweden. And what do you think I found? Fifty packages of cigarettes wrapped in a nightgown! Now let me see what you have in that shirt."

Mama said no more, but Papa laughed. "You'd better not wrinkle that shirt, Officer. My wife is very particular about my appearance."

The officer glanced suspiciously at Papa before folding the shirt carefully. And then to Mama's surprise, he winked at Papa. Why, he wasn't as cross as he sounded, thought Mama. He must get awfully tired going through so many trunks and bags. Unfortunately, everyone *wasn't* as honest as Pontus.

With their luggage safely on the way to the central railroad station, Papa linked his arm in Mama's. "Let's walk, Maria. Just to get the feel of home soil under our feet."

Göteborg was a busy harbor city, but Mama couldn't help noticing how clean it was; not at all like American harbor towns she had seen. It seemed almost no time before they were comfortably seated in the train for Stockholm, where they would change trains for Lapland.

Mama settled back, watching the beautiful Swedish countryside rush by. She had really forgotten how green the forests were in summer and how blue and placid were the lakes. And the farms! As neat as pictures with their red-and-white barns surrounded by flower gardens. Cows grazed in the broad meadows and red-cheeked children, flaxen-haired and blue-eyed, hung on the fences, shouting and waving as the train rushed past.

"It hasn't changed at all, Maria," exclaimed Papa. "Praise God for that! It is as though time had been standing still right here in Sweden."

"It's true, Pontus. I guess I had forgotten just how beautiful

it is. But America is beautiful too; and she has been good to us
and our children. We must not forget that either."

Papa laughed. "Always loyal to America, aren't you, Maria?"

When the train finally reached Stockholm, Papa discovered
it was a few hours before the fast express left for Lapland. Time
enough to visit the ancient capital and stroll along the banks of
Lake Mälaren, lying like a great mirror in the golden light of the
never-ending day.

"Such peace and contentment, Maria. Nowhere in the world
is there so much."

"I know, Pontus. But you must remember we are in a country that has not known war for almost two hundred years. Contented, peaceful *people* live here."

"It could be like this everywhere, Maria, if human beings
would only live by God's law and try to be kind to one another."

"Yes, Pontus. But countries are like children. They have to
grow up. Sweden is old and wise. America is still young and lighthearted—and sometimes like a spoiled child too. But one day
America will be old, like Sweden, and when that day comes, I
think she will be wise also."

Early that afternoon they boarded the train for Lapland,
their journey's end, and reunion with all their old and dear
friends. This was the longest part of the trip. As the train rushed
northward, new and different scenes swept into view. Tall
straight pines and spruce, towering beside broad swift rivers, replaced the dense green forests seen earlier. Noisy waterfalls instead of placid blue lakes. Here was a wild, savage beauty to
challenge the physical strength of any man and woman. Perhaps,
thought Mama, that was why Sweden did not have wars—its people were too busy living and enjoying their own country to want
the countries of others.

The hours seemed to pass with the speed of the train. Presently Mama's attention was pulled away from the landscape by
the sound of soft snoring. Dear Pontus! His tired body had finally

won out over his excitement. His head rested easily against the back of the seat. His cheeks were flushed like a child with fever, but a smile still lingered about his mouth. His white hair, longer than he usually wore it, curled softly about his temples. But for the whiteness of his hair, Mama thought, he would look like a very young man. Sometimes it was difficult for her to believe he was actually seventy-one years old.

Even before the train had come to a full stop, Mama had spotted Tant Renberg in the crowd that waited to greet them.

"Maria, I think the whole church is here to welcome us."

"There's Tant, Pontus. Look how tiny she has become."

"And the Lunds, and the Ericksons, and . . ."

The train screeched to a stop, and in a moment Mama and Papa were surrounded by a happy, laughing crowd of old friends and neighbors, and many new faces.

Presently Deacon Lund clapped his hands for attention. Gradually the happy chatter died, then he lifted his hand, a signal for the singing of a hymn of welcome. What wonderful people they are, thought Mama. It seemed only yesterday that she had stood on this very station platform, with Pontus and the children, listening to speeches and songs of *farewell* and finally the strains of "God Be With You 'Til We Meet Again," fading into the distance as the train gathered speed, taking them away from Lapland.

Now Deacon Lund was speaking, a quiver in his voice which Mama decided was more from emotion than his advancing years.

"This is a happy moment for all of us. We bid you welcome, Pastor and Maria Franzon. Welcome to your homeland! We only hope your visit here will be so pleasant you will not want to return to America."

The applause drowned out his voice for a moment. Then:

"And now we know you must be tired from your long journey. And hungry! The ladies have prepared a delicious picnic-supper for everyone, which will be served on our lawn."

Mama was tired, and she knew how tired Pontus was. But it

was a happy tiredness, and they could not disappoint their wonderful friends. How strange it was. A picnic at nine o'clock at
night, and the sun shining brightly.

It was still shining, two hours later, when they stood on the
parsonage steps, saying good night to Deacon Lund.

Inside the parsonage, time truly rolled back. Except that the
furniture was worn, everything was the same. Silently they
walked from room to room, all so filled with memories. The table
in *salen*, with Button's tooth marks still visible, reminded them
both of the spanking she had received. The footstool on which
Mama had sat every Saturday night to shine the shoes. And
Papa's beautiful mahogany desk with the high-backed chair,
where he had prepared so many inspiring sermons. The *vardags-*
room where they had spent many happy hours with the children.

It was when they reached the bedroom, where the picture
of Mama's model still hung, that she broke down, weeping softly
and smiling through her tears.

"Oh Pontus! It *was* a wonderful model, wasn't it? The children are so fine, so beautiful."

Papa put his arm about her shoulders. "It was indeed, Maria." Then he laughed softly. "But I don't think the boys would
exactly appreciate being called beautiful."

Downstairs again, Papa found his old comfortable rocker,
and for a while, tired as they were, they sat in silence, Mama's
hand in his, while memories poured through their hearts and
minds like a mountain stream flowing backward.

"You know, Maria," Papa finally said, "they were wonderful
years here in the parsonage. But some of those times I'm glad we
shall not have to live over."

"Like the nights you walked the floor with Button?" Mama
laughed. "Or the Sunday Torkel painted his face with ink to look
like a heathen, after he had heard the missionary from India?"

Papa chuckled softly. "Those too. But I was thinking particularly," he said soberly, "of the night Calle's temperature soared

to a hundred and five degrees and we despaired of saving him. But God heard our prayers that night, as He has so many times since."

Mama sighed a happy sigh. "Yes, Pontus. We have so much to be thankful for. God has been very good to us."

She was remembering their conversation the next morning, as she let her eyes feast on the splendid view from the kitchen window. Life was made up of joy and sorrow—balanced measures of each—so that you appreciated the joy more because of the dark hours. Like dark strands woven with threads of gold in a fine tapestry, but to which, at the time of weaving, you were too close to understand its values.

The big homey kitchen was filled now with the aroma of herring sizzling in the frying pan. On the back of the stove, plump brown potatoes were bursting from their jackets.

"Just like old times," Mama said aloud to herself, as she sliced the loaf of fresh *limpa*-bread Tant Renberg had brought her, and spread each slice thickly with butter.

After breakfast, Papa went to the study to prepare his Sunday sermon.

So the days passed—peaceful happy days, bright pages from the past. Mama wondered about the children, how they were managing without her, but she said nothing, for Pontus must not think she was impatient to return to America. Or know how much she missed the children.

Midsummer Eve fell on Sunday that year. The church was beautifully decorated with newly cut tree branches which stood in great clusters about the altar, filling the whole chapel with spicy fragrance. And there wasn't an empty pew! Mama's heartbeat quickened with pride as Pontus took his place behind the high pulpit and slowly opened the big Bible. A shaft of sunlight from the small window behind him, fell over his white hair like a bright crown. The chapel was hushed, waiting.

"I shall read to you this morning from the seventh chapter

of St. Matthew: 'Judge not, that ye be not judged. For with what judgment ye judge, ye shall be judged; and with what measure ye mete, it shall be measured to you again. . . .'"

How full and sure his voice was, Mama thought. Like the music of an organ. It was as though she were hearing him for the first time—that long-ago Sunday morning when she had lost her heart to him completely. For several moments she let her mind drift in treasured memory. Then the sound of her own name brought her back.

". . . . Maria and I, as most of you, will again climb the old mountain to behold the miracle of the never-setting sun, and to praise God for such mighty wonders. But let us remember that life is very much like the climbing of a mountain. We must reach the heights before we can behold the view. And in like manner do we all see the world from different levels, for we have not all come the same journey. How, therefore, can we afford to judge each other? Consider first the distance you have climbed. Has he, whom you would judge, reached the same pinnacle of wisdom and faith? For in the fullness of God's promise, the higher we climb, the smaller become the things of earth—doubts, envy, fear, selfishness. And the nearer your Heaven. . . ."

Later Mama stood beside Papa at the door of the church, her heart filled with thankfulness as she listened to the words of praise from these good people. "A wonderful sermon, Pastor Franzon. . . ." "I needed that sermon. . . ." "It's like old times having you with us, Pastor Franzon. . . ."

And finally all were gone, leaving Mama and Papa alone in the quiet church.

"Come, Maria," Papa said fervently, "let us offer a special prayer of gratitude for this day."

As she knelt beside him at the little altar, Mama was acutely aware of the long procession of weary, truth-hungry souls that had found help and guidance in this small white church;

souls led from darkness into the light of true spiritual love, as God had spoken to them through Pontus's sermons.

Wordlessly they arose and walked down the narrow aisle, closing the door softly, reverently, behind them. Only when they were outside did Papa speak. "I hope no one was hurt because we refused the many dinner invitations."

"I'm sure they understood, Pontus *lilla*, how many memories we have to live over again. How wonderful it is for us to be back in the old parsonage. And, besides, we aren't as young as we once were, remember. We shall need to rest before we climb that mountain tomorrow."

Papa brightened at the mention of the excursion. "I still can't believe it, Maria. That we shall once again see the midnight sun from the top of old Gellivara mountain!"

The morning of Midsummer Day was as perfect as a dream. The sun shone from a forget-me-not sky, with not a cloud in sight. Papa was in high spirits as they began the ascent along the mountain trail.

"Have I ever told you how beautiful you are, Mrs. Franzon?" he teased.

Mama looked up at him, the old mischievous twinkle in her eyes. "I think you might have, Pontus *lilla*—once or twice in about thirty years!"

But Papa did not laugh. "The worst of it is, Maria, it's true. I wish now I had told you every time I thought it."

Mama blushed in embarrassment. "Why, Pontus, darling, you know you did not have to tell me; I always knew." But she was remembering the early days of their marriage, before Papa got used to love, and how many times she had woven fanciful dreams, imagining that he spoke to her as he was speaking now.

"You have made my life so rich and happy, Maria. On this perfect day I think I should tell you how much I love you. Have you never wished you were not married to an old gray man?"

The tightness in Mama's throat lessened with laughter. "Oh,

Pontus! How can you ever think such a thing? Love does not die when the body grows older."

As the path became steeper, Mama noticed how heavily Papa was breathing. But his step was firm, and his cheeks pink as a young boy's. He had taken off his cap, and the wind, more noticeable at this height, ruffled his white hair. He might have been a patriarch, stepped from the Bible.

"When we reach that rock," Papa panted, pointing upward, "we had better have some of that coffee. I guess I'm not used to mountain climbing any more. I feel a bit winded."

Coffee and *Vienerbröd* always seemed to taste better in the open, Mama imagined, filling Pontus's cup the second time. And it was good to rest a while. She hadn't realized how tired she was until she sat down. Pontus finished his cup of coffee, then leaned against the back-rock and closed his eyes. It was then she noticed the perspiration beading his forehead and how pale he had suddenly become.

"Why don't you take a little nap, darling? We'll still be able to reach the top in time."

"I think I will, Maria. I *am* tired. And a little dizzy. I guess the altitude—"

He stopped suddenly. Mama regarded him with alarm.

"Just rest, darling," she urged.

She should never have permitted him to attempt this climb. She should have pretended it would be too much for *her*. But he had so wanted to see the midnight sun from the top of the mountain; and she had forgotten he wasn't used to such strenuous exercise. She was deeply worried.

"Maria," Papa said weakly, "we cannot go on to the top. I'm sorry. I hope you won't be too disappointed." He paused, breathing with difficulty. "I think we had better start down again . . . slowly. . . ."

For a moment panic seized her. He would never make it back to the parsonage. She had to find help. But where? With an effort she controlled the fear that was smothering her reason. "Wait here, Pontus *lilla*. There will be others on the trail. I will bring help as quickly as I can."

She ran down the trail as fast as she could, praying that soon she would meet someone. An endless time later she heard voices, and rounded the bend to come face to face with two young men. Quickly, breathlessly, she told them what had happened and urged them to hurry.

Time stopped for her after that. But it must have been many hours later that she sat beside Pontus, lying pale and still in the big parsonage bed. He had not spoken since she had left him on the mountain trail to find help. Her own throat was choked with tears, but she could not cry. She must not. Through the long night hours she sat beside him, listening to his labored breathing. Dimly she was aware of Tant Renberg and Deacon Lund moving about downstairs. How good they were to wait with her— ready to help in any way they could.

Toward morning, Papa stirred and opened his eyes. He smiled weakly and lifted his hand. Mama took it, pressing it tightly in her own as though she could hold back the curtain of darkness she now knew was closing about him.

"Thank you, Maria," he whispered, ". . . for bringing me home."

It was her stifled cry of grief which brought Tant and Deacon Lund to the bedside. Gently Deacon Lund drew the sheet over Papa's face, now so white and peaceful. Tant Renberg's sobbing mingled with her own.

"Oh, why, Maria, *why?* How could God let this happen?"

Deacon Lund placed a comforting hand on their shoulders. "God never makes a mistake. Pastor Franzon taught us that. He will sleep now, where he would have wanted to sleep his last sleep—in Swedish soil."

Later, when they had taken him away, Mama asked to be left alone in the room for a while. And when they had gone, she dropped to her knees beside the bed and buried her face in her hands. "Dear God," she prayed from the very depth of her soul, "help me not to grieve—to willingly let him return to You and the Heaven he so well deserves."

In those moments, alone with her God, it seemed to Mama that a new strength and a deeper understanding poured into her mind and soul; as though God spoke to her with infinite compassion: *He could not climb the mountain with his tired earthly body. I have given him new life—life everlasting—that he may climb ever higher—upward—upward*. . . .

Without Pontus, Mama had no wish to remain in Lapland. Wonderfully kind and thoughtful as everyone had been to her, she was eager to return to the children. For now that the cable had reached them, bearing its saddening message, her place she felt was with them; to comfort them with the knowledge that Papa had said farewell to life as he would have wished to; that his last days had been gloriously happy.

She had spent the past week in Tant Renberg's neat little home. Deacon Lund had taken care of arranging an earlier passage back to America than she and Papa had originally planned. Then, alone, she had gone to the parsonage to bid farewell to the rich, dear memories it would always hold for her. Slowly she walked about each room, living over again every moment from that first day, as a young girl barely sixteen, when she had sat on the rose-colored sofa and convinced Papa he should hire her as a maid, to the last evening they had enjoyed together.

Now she stood alone on the deck of the big ship, waving a final farewell to *Vinga Fyr*. The wind, blowing in from the North Sea, whipped the great waves into emerald foam. Mama tied the scarf closer about her hair and lifted her face to the wind. An unconscious gesture with which she would face the future without Papa. But no! Papa would never *leave* her. It was true that his body slept in the little cemetery beside the big State Church; that loving hands would plant flowers and the grass would grow green each summer over his resting place; and the birds would sing above him in the day-long sunshine. Snow would cover him with a soft white blanket, and the years would come and go. But always his spirit would walk beside her—close—so very close. Until one day she too would walk into the golden sunset and find him waiting to greet her.

Mama brushed the tears from her eyes—tears not of sorrow, but for renewed faith. Presently she went below to her cabin for the long journey home.

Mama had been back in America a little more than a month when Vickey brought her the news.

It had been a busy time, moving from the parsonage into her own little home on the same tree-shaded street, to make way for the new pastor who would arrive in September. A time of stirring old memories again and of finding new happiness. It seemed to Mama that suddenly all her children were grown-up, each of them wanting to take care of her, concealing their own deep feeling of loss so that her own might be lessened. But it was Nim who had taken Papa's place in material things—the way Papa himself had planned—and revealed to her for the first time how thoughtfully and well Papa had provided for her and the children when he no longer would be with them. He had even arranged, before they left for Sweden, for Steve to buy the farm. Could Papa have sensed, Mama wondered, that his time on earth was almost ended? Had he known his heart was weakening, but kept the knowledge from her, lest she worry about him? Dear Pontus!

Mama sighed deeply. A thankful, comforting sigh, feeling Papa's nearness as she had every moment since her return to America.

After a while she picked up her sewing again—a new dress for Kerstin to wear to the concert on Saturday. It would be her very first date with a boy; a nice, tall well-mannered boy, whom Kerstin explained she had met at the Fourth-of-July picnic.

"Oh, Kerstin," Mama had exclaimed when she learned of it, "you're too young. You're my *baby!*"

Kerstin had drawn herself up to her full five-feet-two, in utter disdain. "I'm *not* a baby, Mama. I'm almost sixteen. And besides, it's *just* a concert. Konrad loves music as much as I do."

There was nothing more Mama could say. It was true. Kerstin had somehow passed out of childhood in those few weeks Mama had been in Sweden.

So as soon as the family was settled in their new home, she had asked Kerstin to bring her friend to tea. He was a quiet, serious-faced boy, whose father was an engineer with the Telephone Company. Mama was sure Papa would have approved of the boy, but she wasn't sure how he would have regarded little Kerstin having dates. . . .

The music of chimes sounded through the house. It was a second before Mama realized it was that newfangled doorbell Pelle and Felicia had given her. She put aside her sewing and hurried to the door.

"Vickey," she greeted her daughter. "What a lovely surprise."

"*I'm* not the surprise, Mama." Vickey was so excited she could hardly talk. "But I have a surprise for you. A glorious surprise."

"Well, take off your hat and sit down and tell me about it. Before you explode."

Suddenly Vickey threw her arms around Mama and started to cry. "Oh, Mama, I can't wait to tell you. It's a baby—my very own baby at last."

"*Your* baby? What about John?" Mama chuckled. "And why are you crying?"

Vickey was laughing now through her tears. "You know I always cry when I'm happy. Isn't it wonderful, Mama?"

"The most wonderful thing in the whole world, darling." Mama held her in her arms for a moment while she got control of her own emotions. "Now sit down and I'll bring you a cup of coffee, and then you can tell me all about it."

Mama was almost as excited as Vickey. Her hand shook visibly as she poured the coffee. Her first grandchild! And she was especially glad that it was to be Vickey and John's child. Now their dream was to come true.

Long after Vickey had left to tell Button the happy news, Mama still sat in the quiet room, her sewing forgotten in her lap, her head bowed in silent prayer. God in His infinite wisdom—His perfect planning—was sending a new little life for her to love and cherish. Soon the house would echo again with children's laughter. A new generation would be growing up to replace the old. God's glorious plan of creation—an endless cycle of lives coming and going—timeless, eternal.

Suddenly Mama sat up, her eyes wide. Then she began to laugh.

"Oh, Pontus *lilla*," she said aloud. "I'll no longer be just Papa's wife. I'll be Grandma Franzon!"

But was there anything in the whole wide world more beautiful than a baby—your very own little grandchild?

~

Papa's
Daughter

~ ~ ~

THYRA FERRÉ BJORN

~

BOOK I

CHAPTER 1

❧ The Sinner

Button was a sinner, a terrible sinner, but right now, as she lay in her bed under the gay patch-quilt, she chose to ignore the fact. It was much more pleasant to relive the joyous happenings of a very eventful Saturday. Although she had been in bed an hour, sleep would not come to her tonight. Her eyes were bright and wide as they peeked once in a while from under the quilt and fastened upon the tiny stream of light, reflected on the ceiling from the night lamp burning in the hallway. All at once, however, the room was too still; so much so that the silence became almost frightening, making it seem as if all the inhabitants of the parsonage were dead. Now the only sound that Button could hear was the beating of her own heart, which was suddenly pounding louder and louder, faster and faster, as she remembered Papa's sermon of last Sunday. She could even hear his voice and see him as he stood in the pulpit of the church with his right hand stretched out as if for a warning to his congregation, then his fist suddenly banging down on the Bible as he shouted, "As I have admonished you before, I admonish you again, anyone that dies with unforgiven sins is a child of the devil!"

Papa never minced his words, strong as they were. Button shivered a little. Sometimes Papa made terrible statements about the devil. How terrifying the thought that one might die without warning and be carried off by that wicked creature! Button's throat felt hot and dry. She thought that she must be suffocating and perhaps about to die. She sat up in bed. Why, she, Button Franzon, had unforgiven sins! Her heart beat so wildly she was certain her small body could not contain it. She was terribly afraid. Maybe at times she had flippantly thought that if some of those stuffy, self-righteous members of Papa's church went to heaven, she certainly wouldn't want to go there, but it would be better than to be carried off by the devil.

Button could no longer breathe; surely she was about to die. Perhaps the devil was lurking somewhere in this room ready to fetch her right now. Her heart hammered louder and louder. She knew the devil couldn't be seen until after death but she knew, just the same, exactly how he looked. No one had actually described him to her, but she had formed her own picture from listening to Papa's sermons. The devil was about four feet tall with a dark slimy body and horns that looked like two sawed-off swords. But it was the tail that conjured up the worst picture of all, for it was long, narrow as a rope, with a sharp pointed end, burning with a fire from the very pit of hell. The claws were sharp and reached out to fetch, and grab and hurt. . . . Perspiration formed on Button's forehead. To be captured by the devil would be the worst thing that could ever happen to anyone. She must get Papa quickly so she could confess her sins. She opened her mouth to cry out to him but not a sound would come; her voice was lost in her fears; she couldn't make it work.

Button knew that of the eight children in the parsonage she had the gift of yelling the loudest. There had been times when Papa even had to take special precautions when he administered his laying on of hands so that the neighbors would not hear the screaming or they would have accused the pastor of torturing his own flesh and blood. Yes, she had the ability to scream so loud that Papa could never punish her very long, so her gift had after all worked out to her advantage. But now Button was lying there soundless and unable to move from fright. Presently the Sabbath stillness of the parsonage was broken by a long eerie scream, for with a final desperate effort Button had at last found her voice. A few seconds later she could hear the footfalls of Mama hurrying to her side.

"What in the world, darling," cried Mama, looking down at her daughter with anxious eyes. "Did you have a nightmare? Are you ill? Does it hurt somewhere?"

Button sobbed loudly. "Yes, Mama, I am sick in here." She pointed to her heart. "I am wicked for I have sinned, and I thought for sure I was going to die, and the devil was right here in the room ready to grab me."

"Hush, child, such foolish talk. How could there be a devil in the parsonage! Turn over now and go to sleep like a good girl."

"No, no, Mama. I want Papa. I want to confess. . . . I . . . I . . ."

Before Mama had time to answer, there stood Papa beside the bed, tall and straight and severe, looking through her as though he wanted to uncover all her sins in one sweeping glance.

"What is all this disturbance, Button?" stormed Papa.

Button gave Mama one last desperate look, but Mama,

knowing very well what the outcome would be, smiled tenderly down on her and then softly left the room.

"Oh, Papa, Papa," sobbed Button, "I have sinned and I want to confess so the devil won't get me if I should die."

Papa came nearer the bed. "What have you done, Button?" he asked in a stern voice.

"I stole."

"You what?"

"Yes, it is true, Papa. I stole pennies from Mrs. Lindberg's purse."

For a long moment Papa just stared at Button incredulously. "I can't believe that I'm hearing right," he moaned.

The tears that rolled down Button's face became a torrent.

"I'm confessing the whole truth, Papa. When Mama took me with her to visit the sick this afternoon, she left me in Mrs. Lindberg's room while she and Mrs. Lindberg went in to pray with Lovisa, who is soon to be breathing her last breath. You know Lovisa is almost stone deaf and Mama had to pray very loud to make her hear, and as she did I just happened to see Mrs. Lindberg's purse lying on the bed half open and without intending to I opened it a little more and, Papa, five pennies just rolled into my hand. I wanted the pennies to buy a chocolate fish—one of the ones in Rydberg's store window—the one with cream filling—I think it is French cream filling, Papa. I only wanted *one* chocolate fish."

Papa started walking back and forth in the small room.

"And to think," he said, "that there I stand, Sunday after Sunday. I, the village pastor—I stand there and preach, asking people to live godly lives and my own daughter who is not yet ten years old steals money. Yes, to make it worse, she steals from very poor people who live in the poorhouse so she can eat chocolate fishes with cream filling . . . my own daughter a common thief."

"Don't say those awful words, Papa. Don't you even think that I can be forgiven? Do I have to go to hell like Mr. Anderson who murdered his housekeeper?"

"Have you prayed?" snapped Papa.

"Yes . . . no . . . I mean I prayed when I took those pennies . . . I prayed I would not take them. . . . But I did anyway. . . . Prayers just don't seem to work for me."

"Get up and pray," commanded Papa.

Button obeyed. She felt very small as she stood on the cold floor in her long nightie. Papa pointed down and Button knelt. Papa knelt beside her and prayed first, a short prayer but to the point. Button's voice was very small and her prayer came between heartbreaking sobs. . . .

It seemed to her as if the two of them had been kneeling for hours. Her knees were sore, her back ached and she was shivering from head to toe. Finally, everything was very still within her. Her heart was beating normally again and felt clean once more.

"Papa," she whispered, "I think I am forgiven."

"I am sure you are, Button," said Papa kindly. They rose from their knees. "It is now as if it had never been. You are white and clean. Promise me you will never do a thing like that again."

"I promise, Papa. Never, never, as long as I live!"

"That is very fine, my child."

Button crept back into her bed and Papa tucked her in. He wiped her tears with his big handkerchief. "And now, my dear," he said firmly, "you realize what as a godly parent I am compelled to do."

Button stared wildly at Papa. "Oh, no," she cried. "Not this time, Papa. I thought I was all forgiven. You said I was clean and all white inside. . . ."

But Papa had already departed for the kitchen and right there on the *kåpa* sat the twig he used for dark offenses.

If Button had taken hope, thinking Papa's kindness would interfere with his strictness, she had been mistaken, for he carried out his mission of punishment with just one thought in mind—that his daughter should know "sin does not pay."

"If I had neglected to do this, Button," he said before he kissed her good night, "I'm sure you would very soon have been thinking of those chocolate fishes in Rydberg's window again."

Then Button was alone in the dark once more, but she felt neither anger nor resentment as her tears flowed freely and she rubbed a very sore spot where the twig had hit the hardest. She was thoroughly chastened, but she knew, too, that she had been forgiven. Papa certainly knew how to handle a sinner, and there was no more fear of the devil in her thoughts that night.

Button Franzon kept her promise to her Papa, for even chocolate fishes did not seem so tempting when she remembered what she had had to suffer for them. She sincerely hoped that she would never be tempted to borrow money from anyone's purse again, with God's help, of course. But it did not take Button long to forget that she had chosen to tread the straight and narrow path, and soon she was entangled in a different type of sinning. It had started out to be only a hilariously funny joke she chose to play on Papa, but she realized, alas, too late that the ladies to whom she told her tale believed it to be the gospel truth.

It was the night of the church family-party and Button had been privileged to sit with Miss Lilja, her school-teacher, and Mrs. Lund, the head deacon's wife. The conversation had been scintillating and gay. There had been much fooling and laughter until the two ladies began to discuss Pastor Franzon.

"We have, beyond a doubt, the most handsome pastor for miles around," said Miss Lilja, looking across the room to where Papa was sitting.

Button beamed. It was pleasant to have her Papa the topic of discussion. "Yes, Papa is very good-looking," she admitted, blushing a little.

"And, do you know, I believe that if he didn't have that thick mustache, he would look younger than his years," chimed in Mrs. Lund.

Button swallowed hard a couple of times, and then that awful lie came rushing out without any warning. Tears even gathered in her eyes. "Papa *has* to have that mustache to cover his lip, Miss Lilja and Mrs. Lund. . . . Oh, I shouldn't have told you perhaps—no one outside the family knows about it."

"His lip?" asked both the ladies at the same time.

Button with her eyes of summer-sky blue looked very innocent. "Yes, it is deformed—very deformed. He could never have been a preacher if it hadn't been for his mustache. No one would be able to look at him as he preached."

Miss Lilja's mouth opened wide. "Well, of all things! Who would ever believe that our pastor is so skillfully hiding some thing so hideous under a beautiful mustache."

Mrs. Lund looked disturbed. "Child," she said seriously as she looked into Button's eyes, "don't you ever tell anyone else. I'm sure your Papa would be very angry. Do you realize what would happen if the congregation ever got hold of that information? Miss Lilja and I, of course, you can depend upon not to tell a soul."

Button shook her head. Now what had she done! Certainly she had not intended to hurt Papa in any way. For a moment she felt contrite and thought perhaps she ought to tell them she had manufactured the whole thing out of a very imaginative mind, but the two ladies were walking away, looking as if they had inherited a gold mine, so why should she lose her status of importance? After all, there was little chance that Papa would ever know, and he would never shave off his mustache . . . she hoped. And wasn't the important thing that his upper lip *was* as normal as anyone's?

If Button had stopped with that experience, she would have saved herself and others a lot of grief. Unfortunately, she loved excitement and did not always wait to reason whether a thing was good or bad. When the story about Papa's lip had died down, she again took a step in the wrong direction, and as before the two prominent ladies helped feed fuel to the fire.

This time it was Miss Larson they had chosen for a subject. Stina Larson was a shy, lonesome-looking lady, but she managed to do more hard work in the Lord's Vineyard than all the others put together.

"We must do something very special for her, Ingrid," said Mrs. Lund to Miss Lilja, just as Button happened to pass them in church.

"A splendid idea, Mia *lilla*," smiled Miss Lilja. "Wouldn't it be nice to give her a party at an appropriate time?"

"Miss Larson is my Sunday-school teacher," Button informed them proudly, "and I heard what you were just saying about a party." Then, before she had time to stop herself, words out of nowhere came rushing to her tongue again. "She has a birthday next week—a real big one—she will be fifty!"

"Fifty!" exclaimed Mrs. Lund. "Who ever would have believed that a little mouse like that would hide fifty years behind that calm face of hers. But what a chance! I'll talk to Pastor Franzon and the other ladies and we'll make plans for a big celebration. . . . You just wait and see! And thanks a lot to you, Button *lilla*."

A few days later a committee of ladies were busy making plans. According to Swedish custom, special birthdays called for special doings and, since the fiftieth birthday was the greatest of them all, it called for singing outside the lucky person's window early in the morning. Afterwards, of course, there was the usual coffee in bed, the gifts and speeches. It seemed that everyone wanted to remember Miss Larson and fifty *kronor* were collected and placed in a large envelope for Papa to present to her. As far as the church people knew, Miss Larson had no relatives and no one, not even Papa, who had the birthdays of all his members recorded, had thought of checking up on Button's statement. Since Mrs. Lund had been the one to approach Papa concerning the affair, Papa naturally took it for granted that she had correct facts.

On the eventful morning Button was surprised to be

awakened at four thirty. She had not counted on being invited to this party of grownups. Miss Lilja, however, had called late the previous evening and suggested that Button should be permitted to attend the party. "After all," she told Mama, "if Button hadn't been so kind as to tell us it was Stina's birthday, we never would have known."

Mama touched Button's cheek lightly and whispered in her ear, "Get up, my dear. Miss Lilja wants you to join us in Miss Larson's singing-party. Hurry now, so we won't be late."

Button rubbed her sleepy eyes and dressed quickly. Something as sharp as a sewing needle was pricking her conscience. How had she ever gotten into this predicament? And how would Miss Larson take it? Would she remain silent and pretend that it was her birthday, or would she be very angry? Button wondered how old she really was. It was too late now to stop the festivities, so she would just keep quiet and hope for the best.

Presently she was standing with the rest of the people below Miss Larson's bedroom window. Her heart beat wildly. If she could only escape, but there was no place to go without being seen. There was Mr. Groth with his violin, Peter Janson with his guitar, and Erik Lund with his flute. Exactly at five o'clock the musicians struck a chord loud enough to awaken the dead, and the whole group started to sing a hymn at the top of their voices from the songbooks Papa had brought in Torkel's wagon. " 'A morning without sin we shall awake,' " rang out the happy chorus.

The song had five verses, and when they came to the second line of the fourth verse, the window flew open and Miss Larson, sleepy-eyed and with curlers in her hair, gazed

down at the singing people as if she were still dreaming.
"Congratulations! . . . Happy birthday! . . . God
bless Stina!" echoed the voices from below. But Stina Larson just stood there staring as if she had frozen into a statue.

"Open the door, Stina *lilla*," cried Mama, "The coffeepot is getting chilly."

Miss Larson unbolted the door, and in trotted the
whole congregation of friends and co-workers. A slightly
dazed Miss Larson was served coffee in bed on a big silver
tray, and cups were passed to all the celebrants. If the party
were to be judged by what the ladies had brought for refreshments, it certainly was a success. There were fancy
cookies and coffee breads galore, and a huge cake on which
was written, STINA LARSON 50 YEARS.

Miss Larson, who had still not said a word, was stirring her coffee nervously and nibbling on a cookie.

After Papa had had his coffee, he made an excellent
speech, telling of Miss Larson's faithfulness and finally
ending with:

"You have reached fifty now and stand on the very top
of the circle of life. From now on, Stina, you will slowly
descend, year by year, step by step . . ." and Papa put in so
many pretty words that it brought tears to some of the
ladies' eyes and Mr. Groth had to blow his nose hard. Others
spoke after this and then the gifts—the flowers and the
money—were presented.

Finally it was Miss Larson's turn. She sat up in bed,
pillows propped at her back, her cheeks flushed as red as
roses, her eyes gleaming strangely, and her mouth held as
if she were trying hard to keep from crying.

Mama leaned over her. "You'd better give us a few
words, Stina," she said, and sat down on the bed beside her.

But Miss Larson could no longer control herself. She threw herself into Mama's arms and sobbed as if her heart would break.

"There, now," soothed Mama gently. "We all get over-excited at a surprise party like this. I remember the last time you surprised me! I thought I'd just fall into a heap and die! You'll feel better in a few minutes . . . just remember we are your friends."

Bravely Stina Larson lifted her head and tried to speak. "*Pastorn* . . . Maria . . . friends . . . all of you kind people. . . . I know you are sweet—and wonderful—and well-meaning. . . . I—I . . ." But a fresh flood of tears stopped her.

"We all understand the depths of your feelings, Stina," Mama whispered. "Go ahead and cry if it will make you feel better."

Miss Larson was soon composed again. She wiped her eyes with the sleeve of her nightgown. "That's the worst of it . . . I can't understand any of this. . . . That's why I'm crying. Since you are all my friends, why are you playing this joke on me? Why are you waking me up early in the morning with song, coffee, speeches, gifts and a birthday cake when it is not my birthday. . . . And why in the world do you make me fifty years old when I am only forty-one!"

It was exceedingly quiet in the bedroom. No one dared to move or speak. All eyes were fixed upon Papa as if he would have the answer to this riddle. Button, who had been sitting unnoticed by the door, decided it was time to disappear, but this act helped her for a moment only. . . .

Later that morning, before she could go to school, she had to face Mama and Papa. That telling lies was as sinful as stealing pennies was a lesson Papa was determined to teach his child. Not even Mama, who was still shocked at her daughter's capacity to make up untrue stories, would interfere, but gave Papa a free hand. As a result, Button lost all desire to tell falsehoods. Even though they gave her a temporary sense of importance, it was not worth while. And both Mama and Papa desperately hoped that this time she had really learned her lesson.

She had not. A few weeks later she was thrown into another situation that was to have a great influence on her life. This time it was because of her fascination for words. Not nice words such as the people in Papa's church and the inhabitants of the parsonage spoke. No, these were words that were taboo among all Button's playmates and that she never heard spoken in her daily life. Button was curious by nature, and her ears seemed to be sharper than those of other children, so that they heard and picked up what they were not supposed to hear.

In the village lived a brewer, Sandquist by name, who, everyone knew, drank like a fish. When he was in his cups, he often chased his wife down the street until she found refuge with some of her friends, who would keep her until he was sober once again.

Button had never witnessed one of these scenes until one night when Papa had written a very important letter to the Conference and had asked Button to mail it for him. As she was walking down the street, a couple suddenly ran past her so swiftly that, if it had not been for the stream of words Mr. Sandquist had let out, she would have thought she had just imagined it. Mr. Sandquist had a stick in one hand and a bottle in the other, and the words he hurled after his wife stuck in Button's mind. She had stood there

staring as if she could not believe either her eyes or ears. If
Sandquist had not been such a prominent political figure,
or had not had such an amount of money, he surely would
have landed in the jail outside the village limit. But everybody excused him because his name was Sandquist and also
because they knew that, when brewer Sandquist was sober
again, he would deeply regret his sins and ask his wife's
forgiveness on bended knee; he would buy her candy and
flowers and be the sorriest man ever, until he fell again.

Button had been awestruck. But when she went to her
room that night, she marked down the strange words she
had heard under the title, WORDS UNKNOWN TO BUTTON
FRANZON. The next day she took them to school and showed
them to her best friend, Karin Lund.

"Button," cried Karin, staring down at Button's paper,
"why, those are nasty swear words! You ought to be
ashamed to carry them with you. . . . What if your Papa
saw them?"

"I'm not saying them, Karin, not even thinking them—
just keeping them. . . . It can't be a sin to do that."

"Although I'm just a deacon's daughter, I'd never dare
to keep them," exclaimed Karin, her eyes almost popping
out of her head as she continued to look over Button's shoulder at the paper. "But I know a man that says even worse
words than those. He is a tramp and lives in an old shack
beside the railroad. That man even swears those words
when he is alone. I bet he even says them in his sleep. Old
man Lot, I have heard my Mama say, is the world's cham-
pion swearer."

"Karin," said Button, "do you think we could go down
and listen to him?"

"What for?"

"I want more words. . . . I'm collecting them."

Karin looked horrified. "Why, may I ask, Button Franzon?"

"I'm going to sell them for pennies, or hair ribbons, or pencils, or I may perhaps even get a rabbit's foot. . . . I'll give you half of everything I get, if you go with me to listen to the old man by the tracks."

"We—ll . . . I'll see," promised Karin. "I'll tell you after school."

That afternoon two little girls with yellow pigtails made their way across the field to the railroad tracks. Each was equipped with paper and pencil and could have passed for a miniature news reporter. They were in luck. The old man sat sleeping with his head against the wall outside the shack. He was dirty and unkempt. An old pipe hung from his bearded mouth. The yard, littered with beer bottles and tin cans, was as dirty as the old man. A few chickens strutted around, trying to scratch in the hard dirt. A pig rolled in a filthy sty. The whole place smelled foul. The girls hid behind a bush. A mosquito landed on the old man's forehead. It woke him up and started a bombardment of strange words. The pipe fell from his mouth and landed in a puddle, and that gave Button more words than she had time to write down. Soon the man slept again and the girls made their getaway.

"Did you ever hear anything like it?" asked Button.

"I wonder if there is *one* naughty word that man doesn't know!" said Karin. Their feet were almost at running speed now, and Karin looked a bit frightened. "Don't you ever, ever tell your Papa I took you there."

"I won't," replied Button. She was wondering how she

would remember all those words she had not had time to write down.

The next day a lot of secret whispers were going around the school, and the two girls had no trouble selling all the word lists they had had time to make up. Those unfortunates that could not buy a list found ways in which they could borrow one and commit the words to memory.

Miss Lilja, who had not been entirely blind to the goings-on in her classroom, started an investigation to find the instigator of these whisperings and note-passings. One boy, who had been unable to purchase a list, supplied her with the needed information, but when Miss Lilja saw a list of the words, she stared at it in utter amazement. Feeling the problem too big for her to cope with herself, she decided to ask the pastor if he would come in and speak to the children concerning the second commandment. The next day Papa came and, when he was through speaking, there wasn't a child whose head was not bowed in shame. Many raised their hands in solemn promise that they would never become involved with swear words again.

"There is only one way, though," concluded Papa, "that the school can be washed clean of the stigma that has been put upon it. Evil always has a beginning. Who started this? I shall return to this school at one o'clock tomorrow afternoon and expect to find the culprit waiting for me in Miss Lilja's office."

Deeply frightened that her Papa would hear about this, Karin went to Miss Lilja and told her the whole story. She begged Miss Lilja not to let Button know that she had informed on her.

The next afternoon Miss Lilja simply called Button's name. "I want you, Charlotta, to go to my office and be waiting there when Pastor Franzon arrives," she told the surprised Button. "He will thereby know that you are the one to whom he is to speak."

Button gasped. She wondered how Miss Lilja had found out that she was the guilty one. There was nothing to do now but to face whatever happened, Button thought, as she walked with slow steps down the long corridor and through a door marked *Office*.

Once inside the office, all the bravery seemed to leave her, and the minutes passed by as slowly as if they were hours before she heard Papa's footsteps coming down the hall. As he opened the door, she fixed her eyes on the worn spot in the gray rug in front of the desk. Papa shut the door and Button realized that by now he knew the worst. She waited for the storm to break loose, but there was nothing save a heavy silence as if thick fog had settled over the world. Minutes ticked away on the big round clock on the wall, but still not a sound from Papa. Then Button lifted her eyes, her legs trembling under her. She looked straight into Papa's blue eyes and at first she could not believe what she saw. There was no anger written there, no condemnation, only sorrow and compassion. Her own eyes grew wide. Was that her Papa who had eyes like that, so filled with tender love? They looked like sorrowing stars lost in the night. A strange light gleamed in them. Presently two big tears spilled over and rolled down his cheek. Without one word to her he turned and walked out, closing the door gently behind him.

Button felt like rushing after him, throwing herself into his arms and telling him she was ashamed and broken-hearted and so sorry. She would do anything in the world to make things right again. Anything! Because she loved him with all her heart. But only her heart went after him; her feet could not move. They felt as if they were made of cast iron. She did not know how long it was before she slowly returned to her classroom.

The sadness would not leave Button's heart, which seemed to swell out and embrace all of her. The lists had been gathered and burned in the wood stove in the classroom. Miss Lilja, with tears running down her cheeks, had prayed the Lord's Prayer with the class. Button spoke the words, too, saying them very sincerely: "and forgive us our trespasses."

She walked home alone and spoke to no one. She was conscious of nothing but that look in Papa's eyes. If she had been punished for a week, she could not have felt more chastened. Papa and Mama were very silent during the evening meal, but Button noticed that her slice of cake was bigger than the others. After dinner her brother Nim volunteered to help with the dishes in her place, so Button studied her lessons, then bade everyone good night. Everything seemed so unreal, as if she were moving in a dream. She had lost all desire to be naughty. She knew she would never deliberately or thoughtlessly hurt Papa again.

She did not go to sleep readily and when she finally did, something prompted her to wake up. She stirred restlessly. Suddenly she made her way to the master bedroom. The snores told her both Papa and Mama were asleep. She stood there looking down at them for a few moments. She was a big girl now, almost ten years old. She had been a problem to Papa, and though he had tried to whip the badness out of her, it had never worked. But what his hands had not been able to accomplish—his eyes had. The love in them and the two tears had cured her.

"Papa," Button whispered, touching him gently on the shoulder.

He opened his eyes and looked up at her.

"Button," he said and opened his arms. "I knew you would come to me."

Button nestled close in his arms. "I wanted to tell you that I am more sorry than I have ever been. I don't know why I do those naughty things, Papa, but I have asked God to help me be good. I think He will."

Papa kissed her tenderly. "He surely will, Button, and when a sinner repents, even though she be but a very young girl, all the bells in heaven ring with joy."

Button could almost hear those bells as she glanced out at the night sky on the way to her room. Surely the whole world was rejoicing in the fact that she wanted to be good.

CHAPTER 2

~ The Call

What a wonderful Monday! Strange! This was contrary to what Mondays were supposed to be in the parsonage, for to Papa and Mama they were "blue" days. Button wondered why Mondays should be different from any other day in the week. Hadn't God made seven days, each one lovely and beautiful, each morning filled with breathless anticipation of what it might bring? But, no, Mama had to explain, this was not so when one lived in the parsonage. Then Mondays were "blue," a letdown from the rush and excitement of Sunday when a pastor had to be at his best, preaching, singing, smiling, shaking hands with all the people, and his wife had to use up her spare energy trying to make the children behave in the manner expected of them by the church people and not in the uninhibited noisy way they would act without a firm hand to guide them. Even just getting through Saturday was a chore for Mama, since then the house had to be kept hushed as if Papa were a bachelor instead of a married man with eight children. Unless it was quiet around him, Papa couldn't receive those divine inspirations that prompted so many good sermons! By Monday both Papa and Mama were nervously exhausted, but it had to be another day of quiet so Papa could rest, which meant another task for Mama to keep her household running smoothly without confusion. Mama's patience having been spent, she was apt to be a little snappy with the children and not her usual gentle self. Thus "blue" Mondays.

For Button this particular Monday was anything but blue. In the morning Mama had taken out a brand-new white apron for her.

"You mean I can really wear this today, Mama?" cried Button, showing by her radiant eyes the gladness that filled her heart.

"Yes, dear, you might as well," agreed Mama, "because if we save it too long, you will just outgrow it! It's a very pretty one, isn't it?"

"Pretty! Oh, Mama, it is heavenly! Look at the lace ruffles and all the tiny pearl buttons. No one but Tant Renberg would put so much work into a mere apron."

"Tant is a darling. Remember, Button, that this was your Christmas present from her, and when you see her, tell her how happy it has made you."

She stood very still so Mama could button all the buttons on the back of the apron all the way down to the hem. How thankful I am, she thought, to have a lovely apron to cover up my brown dress. Button hated brown . . . mousey . . . dirty . . . colorless brown. She hoped this would be the last brown dress she would ever have to wear. Why couldn't she convince Mama that brown was a most unsuitable color for her, exactly matching those horrid little freckles on her nose? Oh, why did she have to have freckles anyway! She might have been pretty if it hadn't been for these, but no one could be beautiful who had even a speck of a freckle.

Button would be very careful not to get this apron dirty and when she came home from school, she would take it off and hang it upon the apron-nail in the kitchen closet. Then she would put on the apron she had been wearing the week before. This new one would be turned inside out in the middle of the week so it would look clean again for the rest of the week. Since the family wash was done only twice a year, even a little girl had to be careful not to get clothes soiled.

Button skipped and danced along the way to school. It was spring and the world was going to look new and alive very soon. The long, long winter was gone at last. At the top of the hill, by the bend in the road, she saw Karin waiting for her.

"Why Button Franzon, I hardly recognized you," she cried. "You look like an eloping bride. What a gorgeous apron!"

"Tant Renberg made it for me and gave it to me for Christmas," replied Button nonchalantly, her head high. "This is the first time I've worn it."

"I wish I were a preacher's child. No one would ever think to make such an apron for a deacon's daughter!"

At school all the girls gathered around Button to admire her new apron. They felt of it, examined the tiny buttons, and agreed that it was a most beautiful gift. When class began, Button noticed that Miss Lilja looked her way over and over again. Button was sure that she, too, was fascinated by the lovely white apron. But it wasn't until mid-morning that the teacher said, "Charlotta Franzon, you look so pretty today. Will you come to the front of the room and read to the class?"

Button felt her heart beating fast with joy. It was a wonderful day! In spite of her freckles, the teacher must think that she was beautiful, and therefore was honoring her by letting her be the reader of the day. She walked quickly to the front of the room and stood very poised before Miss Lilja's desk and read from the thick, gray lesson book the story of Fredrika Bremer, who was a great Swedish-Finnish author and had written a book named *Hertha* as well as many other stories.

On the front page there was a picture of Miss Bremer. Button glanced at it. She would have been a pretty woman, she thought, if she hadn't had such a large nose. Perhaps having freckles wasn't so bad after all. It was better than having a large nose. If she ever became famous, she wanted to be very pretty. Button began to read from her lesson book in a strong, clear voice: "What does a little girl mean to this world? Can even she be great and famous? . . ." At those words of Fredrika Bremer's something stirred deeply within Button. She continued reading for the class, sentence after sentence, but she herself did not know what she was reading, for her whole attention was focused on those opening sentences. They echoed over and over again in her mind. Perhaps Miss Bremer, too, had once stood in front of a class and read and perhaps when she did, she knew that when she grew up, she would write words for others to read—words that would make people smile or sigh, or laugh, or cry. The words burned like fire now. . . . Why not? Even a little girl born in a parsonage could grow up and write words that others would read. Yes, Button knew now that she had received a call from deep within her heart to be a writer. She would not just get married and clean and sew and cook and sweep, wash dishes or have children. . . . She would grow up to write books! She would dress in pretty clothes, sit in a lovely room and write stories and be an author just like Fredrika Bremer. And wouldn't Papa be thrilled when she became famous and other children could read about Charlotta Franzon in their lesson books?

"That is all, Charlotta," said Miss Lilja kindly. "That was very well read. Thank you! You may take your seat now."

But Button was so engrossed in her own thoughts that, instead of taking her seat, she had just stood there like a *dumbom*. . . . Slowly she came out of her reverie, flushed, and walked to her seat beside Karin to the accompaniment of giggles from her classmates.

"You looked so queer, Button, standing there so long," whispered Karin. "Did you think we needed more time to notice your apron?"

"Never mind, Karin. I didn't stand there to show off my apron. I wasn't even conscious of it. You sound envious, which isn't becoming to a deacon's daughter, you know. Something much more exciting happened. I know now what I am going to be when I grow up."

"An author?" asked Karin.

Button stared in surprise. "However did you know?"

"Oh, I was just teasing because you read about one. Are you really?"

Button nodded her head, her pigtails bobbing up and down.

"I bet every child in school will read your books," de-

clared Karin, looking at her classmate as if she had been
transformed into a fairy princess.

Button did not answer. She was again lost in deep
thoughts, staring straight ahead at the teacher's desk.

When school was over, Button did not wait for Karin
as was her usual habit, but hurried off alone toward the
mountain road as fast as her legs would go. She must be by
herself to think over all these things that had rushed
through her mind. She would not help Mama this afternoon. Mama would not be worried about her, for she would
surmise that Button had stayed after school to help Miss
Lilja straighten up the room. She often enough did this.

She had walked so fast that she was beginning to gasp,
so she finally sat down under a big tree on the mountain
slope. The leaves were starting to burst their buds, and the
spruce trees spread a heavy, balmy springtime perfume
through the air. Button leaned against the tree and pressed
her cheek against the rough bark. Her eyes felt heavy, and
she wanted to close them and dream the beautiful dreams
that seemed to be floating through the air in her direction,
but she shook off her drowsiness and took a paper and
pencil from her schoolbag. If she was to dedicate herself to
being an author, she must first find out if she could write.

She wrote a sentence in large upright letters and then
stared at it in disgust. "Once upon a time," she had begun.
Why, anybody could write that! It showed no special talent
at all. She would have to do better than that! She would
try again . . . and this time it came!

Button pressed the paper joyfully against her heart,
unable to believe that the words written thereon had come
so wonderfully and mysteriously from her pencil. Who-
ever but a real author could think of words like that? It was

strange, she thought, that locked up within herself there
were words that she did not know she possessed . . .
words that would knock on her brain and beg to be let out.
All her storybooks would begin with pretty words such as
these, so that when people read her books, their sadness
would vanish away, for she would make them laugh and
be gay. Under the title she had written she had signed a
new name, Mary Terrier, which also had come from within
her as if it had always existed there. That would be her
new name—her writer name. For a long time only Mama
and Papa and she would know that Button Franzon was a
writer. How pretty the name looked:

Once upon a Lily Pad
by
Mary Terrier

At first she had not intended to tell Mama so soon, but
the thing that filled her felt like a big balloon and by the
time she reached the parsonage, she was sure that unless
she shared her secret with someone she would burst. Mama
was in the kitchen ready to put an *apple-kaka* in the oven.

"Why, Button, such a beaming face!" exclaimed
Mama. "You must have found at least one hundred *kronor*
on your way home from school."

"Better than that, Mama," sang Button jubilantly,
completely ignoring Mama's cooking art. "Mama, I have
just discovered what I shall become when I grow up. I
shall write books like Fredrika Bremer's! I shall be an
author!" Button stopped her flow of words as the importance of the occasion came to her. "Mama, can we talk for a
while in *salen?*"

Mama looked at her daughter in surprise. It was not like Button to talk this way, but if it meant a turn for the better, she was happy. Instead of a headstrong little girl she seemed like a reformed individual. One of these days she might even be able to say to Papa, "Pontus, I think that Button may turn out as well as the other seven children after all."

Mama took her time placing the *apple-kaka* in the oven. She wiped her hands thoroughly on the towel which hung by the stove, and followed Button into the best room of the parsonage. They sat down on the sofa, and Mama playfully placed her arm around Button's shoulders and smiled down on her.

"Now what is on your heart, darling?" she asked.

Not for one moment did Button hesitate. Her cheeks were flushed and her big blue eyes looked wistfully far, far away, out through the window at the mountains towering against the evening sky.

"I shall be a very famous person, Mama. . . . I shall write books, stories and poems, and everybody in the whole of Sweden will know the name of Franzon someday."

Mama drew a sigh of relief. "Was that all you wanted to tell me, Button? For such a young girl to have such fine dreams is commendable. However, I must admit you had me worried for a moment. I thought you wanted to confess some wrong you had committed."

Button opened her mouth to speak, but no words would come. Surely, this couldn't be all it meant to Mama. It seemed as though all of a sudden the sun had ceased to shine.

"Button," said Mama softly, "don't look as if the world had come to an end. I hope that you can write books someday, but right now you shouldn't live in a dream. You have more important things to think of. First, you must learn to keep house well, for you owe that to the man you will marry someday. There is much to learn about sewing, cleaning and cooking, as well as the art of being a good mother. Do you know, for instance, my little girl, that babies are like tiny, delicate plants on which you have to bestow love and tender care in order for them to grow and be strong? Someday you and I will wander deep into the woods and I'll show you and tell you of the mystery of life. These are the things with which you should be filling your little heart. And as for books, you know that Papa is the book-man in this house. So later, when you feel you are ready to write, you talk it over with him."

"Thank you, Mama." Button's voice shook a trifle. "I just wanted to share my secret."

"Button!" Horror was written on Mama's face. "Oh, Button, my *apple-kaka!* I must have forgotten to turn the oven down. . . . It smells like burning . . . out of my way." And Mama ran toward the kitchen as fast as her feet could carry her.

For a few minutes Button remained still on the davenport, fighting hard to control her tears. Something deep within her was very bruised. Mama did not understand about "the call," thinking her just a little silly girl. If the *apple-kaka* was burned, she would understand about that and would blame Button for taking up her time when she was busy. Little Mama cared that Button had opened the secretmost place of her heart. She would go to Papa. Papa would understand about a little girl's dreams. Didn't Papa understand just about everybody in the whole world?

Since it was Monday, Papa would be in his study resting. Button hesitated a bit outside the heavy door, then with her head held high she pushed it open and stepped inside. "Papa," she said softly, "I have something very important to tell you."

But Papa was not resting! He put down his pencil and closed the big Bible after placing an envelope between its pages. "Button Franzon, what have I told you about walking into my study without knocking on the door first and waiting for an answer? Don't you realize that I could have been praying for a sinner? As it is, I was working on my next Sunday's sermon, and your interruption has made me lose my trend of thought completely. It may never come back to me, and it was one of the best thoughts I have ever had concerning Andrew and the loaves and fishes. Now it is lost not only to me but to the whole congregation as well. Who knows but that that sentence may have saved a soul who will now perish? When you came bursting in like that, I thought that at least the house was on fire or that Mama had fallen down the stairs or some other such calamity. Let me caution you never to repeat this offense or I'll have my own way of dealing with you."

Button backed away from Papa's study. She felt as if her heart would break with the immensity of the hurt, and running to the garden, she put her arms around a tree and cried. Blue Monday! Yes, indeed, it was. But Papa and Mamma had no right to let their emotions affect her life. This had started out to be the most wonderful day she had ever lived and no one had a right to ruin it. She would never share her secrets with her parents again, but would hug them to her heart and keep them to herself. But someday they would see. . . . Button forced a smile and dabbed at her eyes with the corner of her new apron which in her ex-

citement she had forgotten to change. . . . Someday they
would know that she had received a real call, and then she
would never again need to cry because she was hurt. As for
now, she would create within herself a new world where
she would dwell and be happy and tomorrow she would
begin her first story.

"After all," Button said aloud, "there will always be
apple-kaka to bake and sinners to pray for, but to receive a
call to be an author can only happen once to a little girl
not quite ten years old."

The following day, however, Button did not write her
story. Karin prevented it. She was waiting for Button at
their accustomary meeting place on the way to school. As
Button approached, she waved her hand gaily. "Hi there,
author!" she called loudly.

Button looked annoyed. "Hush, Karin, don't let anyone hear my secret," she whispered, taking hold of Karin's
arm.

"Oh, I didn't think it was a secret. Doesn't anyone else
know, really?"

"Well, Mary Terrier, of course."

Karin's eyes grew wide. "Who in the world is Mary
Terrier?"

"I am talking about me, it's my pen name. Lots of
authors use a different name from their own in order to
have privacy until they become famous."

"Gosh, Button, you certainly know an awful lot of
things. I promise not to tell a soul, because I'm so proud to
share your secret."

With their arms around each other, the two girls wandered on toward the schoolhouse.

"Are you a really, truly author now?" asked Karin unbelievingly.

Button nodded importantly. "I am starting my first story today."

"Please tell me what it's all about?" Karin pressed Button's arm hard and looked pleadingly into her face. "After all, I am your very closest and best friend."

"I know that," laughed Button, feeling herself grow several inches taller. She looked wistfully up at the blue sky. "But I don't know myself yet what I am going to write. You see, when you've been given the talent to write, stories just flow out of your mind easily as soon as you sit down with a paper and pencil. You just couldn't be an author without this special talent."

"Oh, my," responded Karin humbly. "I didn't know all those things, and here I was just about to ask you if I could help you write your stories, but if it's only that talent thing you need, then I guess I'd be useless."

"Whatever gave you the idea that *you* could help?" wondered Button, aloud.

Karin blushed. "Well, you see, there is to be a deacons' meeting at our house tonight and since they discuss all the sins of the church people, I thought perhaps you and I would listen in the big closet in *lille-salen*. . . . and you could get an honest-to-goodness true story to write."

"You are mixing up reporters with authors, Karin. If you work on a newspaper, you take down what people say at a meeting. You don't know anything about writing, do you?"

"I guess not. I just thought, since we were such good friends, that perhaps I could help a little, but I know now that it was just a foolish notion."

But Button had been thinking, and there was subdued excitement in her voice as she said, "Wait a minute, Karin. Maybe you do have a good idea. I can always use my talent on the next story. It might be fun to listen." Button's eyes twinkled at the thought of being an unseen listener at a deacons' meeting. "We will do it, Karin! Thanks for telling me."

"You come along with your Papa, or better yet, come earlier, then my folks will think we are doing lessons in my room. . . ." Karin was warm with excitement as she planned each detail of how they would hide inside the closet and get out unseen after the meeting was over. It was only eight in the morning now, and it seemed like an eternity to have to wait until seven at night. It was even harder to concentrate on schoolwork and now and then the two girls would look at each other and giggle behind their hands as they thought of the things their ears would hear before the day was done.

At six thirty that evening the girls stood hidden behind a thick fur coat in the big closet in Deacon Lund's home. It was warm and stuffy in there and the moth-ball smell made Button want to sneeze so much that she almost pinched her nose off trying to suppress the desire.

"Don't you dare to sneeze, Button. . . . If my Papa caught us in here, you would never live to write the story."

Button wiped her eyes. "I'll do my best, but I do hope the meeting begins soon."

And it did not take long before all the deacons had assembled. Button heard Papa's voice saying that *polkagrisar* was his favorite candy. The girls' mouths were drooling at the thought of Mr. Lund passing around candy, but they could do nothing but keep as still as two little mice so as not to give away the show.

Suddenly Mr. Lund called out, "Have coffee ready for us in an hour, Mia dear!" And a door was shut. It was very still in the room for a moment. Button and Karin pressed their ears against the thin wall and the excitement of it all made Button forget her urge to sneeze. This was the most daring thing she had ever undertaken.

"Brethren"—the meeting had started and Papa's voice came deep and clear—"we shall begin this important meeting by asking the Lord to bless us in all that we say and do that it may be for the good of His church here on earth. Brother Lindgren, will you lead us in prayer?"

"I bet he'll pray for ten minutes, at least. He's the longest pray-er in the church with the exception of Mr. Olauson," whispered Karin.

And she was right. Mr. Lindgren prayed very slowly, repeating his words over and over as if the Lord was slow to understand. Finally he said amen and several other amens testified to the fact that the prayer was ended.

"Brother deacons"—it was Papa's voice again—"I know you are just as sorrowful as I am to find that Deacon Petter Anderson is missing from our midst tonight. It puts me in mind of the Last Supper when Judas Iscariot left the disciples to betray his Lord. Our brother Anderson has fallen again!"

"Is he a painter?" whispered Button.

"Of course not, silly," said Karin in a hushed voice. "Anderson hasn't fallen from a ladder. He has fallen into sin!"

"Oh," said Button, surprised. A deacon's daughter certainly had the advantage of knowing the shortcomings of the church members.

"Pastor Franzon," said Deacon Lund. "We all know of Petter's fall. The temptation has been too much for him. My wife with several of the other ladies saw him staggering down the street last Saturday night."

"See, I told you! He was drunk!" exclaimed Karin triumphantly.

For a while all was quiet outside the closet door. Then the squeaky voice of Aron Kvist was heard to say, "He certainly has no right to be a deacon if he can't let the devil's drink alone."

"I move we strike his name from the church roll," said Lindgren.

"Wait a moment," said Papa. "We must never be too hasty in passing judgment on others. It is said that God does not count sins, He weighs them. Let us examine our own hearts. Have we always behaved as it behooves servants of the Lord?"

Button knew that right now Papa would be looking at each man in the room, and his eyes would pierce through all of them until they feared that he could see all their hidden sins. Button felt sure no one would dare to accuse Anderson again.

Papa was speaking again. "I want to talk to this fallen brother and ask him to join us at our next meeting. Perhaps we can be of help to him. He may be sorry and ask our forgiveness as well as that of God. If that should happen, we must not be a hindrance to him, for with kindness and understanding we may place his feet on the narrow way again."

"I still believe his name should be removed," retorted Lindgren, "for as long as he remains on the board, it will be like having one soiled spot on a clean cloth. What will those outside the church think of us if one of our number is a drunkard? You can't hide this sort of thing. I'm sure that the ladies from our church were not the only ones who saw him stagger."

A long discussion followed, but in the end Papa won out, and the girls were glad because they both liked kind Mr. Anderson but disliked Lindgren. Next came the glad news that Miss Sofia Ringstrom had bequeathed eight hundred *kronor* to the deacon treasury to do with as the deacons saw fit for the growth and furtherance of God's work.

"And now," said Papa, "unfortunately we have some more heartbreaking business. What shall we do with Edith Strom?"

"Is the talk about her true?" asked Deacon Svenson.

"It is," answered Papa in a low voice. "I visited Edith yesterday."

"And your eyes confirmed that the gossip about her is true?" This from Mr. Lund.

"Sadly yes," said Papa. "Whenever she sees her father coming home from work, she escapes into the attic and she stays there whenever he is at the house. She is terrified lest he find her and discover her condition. He thinks she is out of town visiting her sister. She is the most pitiable sight I have ever seen. Her eyes are red from constant weeping. She looks like a very sick girl, but she insists that, if her father finds out, he will kill her. I don't see how she can hide indefinitely. He'll have to know sometime."

Everyone was talking now, and words were coming so

close together that it was hard for the girls to get the meaning of what was being said.

"Mrs. Lindgren saw her, too," said Lindgren. "She told me that at this point she looks like a haystack."

"What is wrong with looking like a haystack, Button?" whispered Karin.

"Poor girl," agreed Button, "imagine having a father that wants to kill you just because you look like a haystack!"

And as Button began pondering this situation of one so scared she had to hide from her own father, she was caught off guard, and the sneeze she had so successfully suppressed could be contained no longer. The noise from it came like an explosion, cutting the momentary stillness of the meeting room. She felt Karin's hand on her face, but it was too late. Deacon Lund opened the closet door and dragged out two shamefaced sinners to the surprise of the pastor and the other deacons.

"How did you happen to be in that closet?" he demanded angrily.

"We were playing a game about writing books," sobbed Karin. "We were going to get a story."

"I believe my daughter had something to do with this, too," said Papa.

Button avoided Papa's eyes. She wished the floor would open and swallow her up. Karin was sobbing wildly now, but Button felt no need of tears. She was thinking of Edith. At least she and Karin would not be killed because they had been discovered hiding.

"Did you hear all we said?" asked Deacon Lindgren.

"Never mind answering that," snapped Papa. "Can't you see the girls are nearly scared to death? I'm sure they were just playing a game. Button, you run on home to bed now. No coffee and cookies for you, young lady. And Lund, if I were you, I'd be lenient with Karin. I believe the girls have learned a good lesson and I'm sure they intended no harm but were merely playing a game not realizing that we had an important meeting."

Button did not tell Mama. She hurried to bed so she could be alone with her thoughts. The sorrow in her heart would not go away. It felt as if someone had placed a heavy stone there. She was sorry for kindhearted Mr. Anderson, who occasionally was tempted to drink, and even sorrier for Edith Strom, whose sin she did not know. She realized how fortunate she was to be a little girl with a good mama and papa. There seemed to be many things in life that were truly sad, and perhaps many people were weeping in darkness because they were frightened and lonely. If only she could help all these people. Perhaps someday she could, for she would write a happy book, one filled with joy and laughter. She might even write about a girl named Edith, but this girl would have a wealthy father who was good to her; she would fall in love with a wonderful young man; they would marry and live happily forever. But first she would begin by writing her thoughts in a diary, for then she could capture the mood of the minute. She would write down all the things she felt and not just the things she did, so her diary would be her very own and different from any other. And at the close of each page, she would write a brief letter to God. That was a beautiful idea! Instead of praying words to toss into empty air, she would write them in her book, and God could read them, lovely beautiful words that would never be lost, preserved for eternity!

It had been a terrible but eventful day, and perhaps all this would help her when she was ready to write her story. She knew that, after a night's sleep, she would lose her sadness and that tomorrow's sun would shine from the sky, warming her heart, but never again would she be tempted to listen in at a deacon meeting.

CHAPTER 3

❧ The Diary

In spite of her "special" talent, Button found it was not easy to write a book. Three years had passed since she had received her call, and in that space of time she had filled hundreds of pages in her writing tablet with words, but after reading what she had written, she knew that she had not expressed what she felt and had torn out the pages. Disappointed and frustrated after each writing experience, she would run out to the garden or up the mountain slope and find a faithful tree she could throw her arms around while she cried her heart out. It wasn't really that the words weren't good . . . she knew that if she showed them to Karin, there would be great admiration in her friend's eyes and Karin would think that Button had a great talent, indeed. . . . But there was a discrepancy between the words Button dreamed in her mind and the way they came out on paper. The words on the paper weren't right; somehow they were not really Button's. Oh, some of them were strange and pretty, but they were fake, as if she hadn't held the pencil that jotted them down. It was not like her to give up, however, so she tried over and over again in the hope that someday she would be writing the words she felt in her heart.

She was thirteen years old when the miracle happened on a beautiful moonlit night. Button was leaning out the window of her room, drinking in the gentle beauty of the white summer night that surrounded the parsonage garden, when deep within her she felt something stirring and crying like the sound of music from a violin softly played. How glad she was that she was alone! She felt a wild desire to cry but did not know why, unless it was to ease the tension that had mounted within her and lodged itself like a big lump within her heart.

"I believe I can write tonight!" she whispered, stretching her arms toward the moon. "I am sure, Mr. Moon, that you will help me."

Going to her bureau drawer, Button took paper and pencil and sat very still for a few moments to enable herself to change from Button Franzon to Marry Terrier. She closed her eyes to blink back the stubborn tears. Then leaning over her paper, she began to write:

EDITH
by
Mary Terrier

The night was white with moonlight as a young girl named Edith walked alone along the lonely path beside a beautiful little lake. She had a rendezvous with a young man she had seen only once before. Harold was tall, dark and handsome but came from a very poor family, whereas Edith's father was a wealthy bank director. With Edith it was love at first sight as she recognized that this was the man of her dreams and even though he was poor in material possessions, he was rich in soul. Edith fervently hoped that the two of them were destined to dream many dreams together. . . .

Button wrote on and on and, as she wrote, the crying within her ceased and she began to feel light and gay. Her hand flew so swiftly over the pages she hardly had time to spell the words. The moon poured down its silver on her golden hair and the stars twinkled brightly and mysteriously in the dark night sky. It was exhilarating to be a writer, creating stories about people that existed only in her mind. When she read through the pages she had written, she knew that now, at last, the words she had felt so deeply had been transferred to the paper. It was the same sweet sorrowing sound of the violin, now playing a plaintive love song.

"I have actually started my very first book!" she cried jubilantly to herself. "I have really begun!"

Later that night, as she tenderly folded the written pages and placed them in her bureau drawer, she knew it to be the happiest moment of her life. Before she slipped into bed, she wrote in her diary:

Dear Diary,

Today I have started my book, EDITH, and someday I'll finish it. I know that it is going to be a delightful book and since you, my dear diary, are my closest friend, I shall share with you all the secrets of my heart. You will neither laugh at me when I do foolish things nor tell on me. I now in all secrecy confess to you that I am sorry that my Papa is a preacher. If he only could have been a doctor, or a lawyer, or even an ore-miner!

You see, because my Papa is in God's service, there are a lot of things I can't do. I can't become an actress or a dancer, and perhaps it is also a sin to become a circus performer! Eternally I am supposed to keep in mind what my Papa is and be a good example for others. I am sick and tired of being good. I want to have FUN and everything that is fun is sinful! What an awful state to be in!

P.S.
Dear God,

You know that I love my Papa very much. Please forgive me for not wanting him to work for you. But, why, God, have you made so many things that are forbidden? Can't you laugh at all? Why, then, did you create laughter? When I behold the beauty of your sky, I almost forget that you don't want me to have fun. Tonight your moon is particularly lovely and helped me start my book. Thank you, God, for creating the moon. Amen.

One of the forbidden things that Button loved was to watch young people dance. According to Papa's preaching, dancing was a grievous sin. People who danced certainly ended up in hell. Papa had used such strong words against dancing that Button didn't dare to perform the steps her feet were continually urging her to try. Sometimes the temptation was so strong it was hard for her feet to remain quiet, and then Button would inwardly rebel against Papa's preaching and promise herself that she would learn to dance as soon as someone would teach her. But when dark night descended and Button was alone with her thoughts, she would become frightened at having had such worldly notions and on bended knees would promise God never again to think so sinfully. She humbly sought God's forgiveness, only later to lash out at the Almighty in her diary:

Dear God,

I can't understand it. The wind sways the trees in graceful rhythm and all the little buttercups dance in the sunshine. On the river the ripples shimmering in the moonlight look like a thousand "lille-put people" dancing. Why should a young girl have to feel like an ungraceful, clumsy and stiff lumber log, bobbing up and down in the stream, because it is a sin to sway your body and skip with your feet? If I am not supposed to dance, why did you put a desire and a longing in my heart to do so? Forgive me, God, for talking to you so frankly, but I am tired of thinking of you sitting up there in the sky pointing your long finger at me in condemnation and saying, "Look at her. There she goes now." You know I am unhappy when I do bad things and I admit I frequently do. Just now I feel like crying for ten years without stopping. Amen.

On a Saturday night when Button was almost fourteen years old, she took a long walk up the mountain road. Suddenly she stopped as she heard coming through the air beautiful music, laughter and singing. Button knew where it came from. There was a dance in Larson's red barn. Oh, how she longed to join those happy young people, but Papa had forbidden her to go near any such place. She hardly realized what was happening as her feet left the road and went hurrying across the field in the direction of the red barn. She walked as close to the scene of merry-

making as she dared and, finding a big tree, she stood behind it, making herself as small as possible lest she be
discovered. She need have had no fear, for everyone was
having too much fun to notice her. She embraced the tree
trunk, standing very, very still. A deep throbbing arose in
her heart, but she bravely fought the tears back. Look at
the good time everyone was having, so much fun, everyone
except her. A young couple who were dancing a waltz
caught her attention. As they danced, they were smiling into each other's eyes. They were the most beautiful young
couple Button had ever seen.

"Someday," she said aloud to herself and the tree,
"someday, I shall marry a boy that looks like that and he
will look at me as lovingly as this boy looks at his girl and
he will say, 'Darling, you are adorable, and sweet as a rosebud. As your petals unfold I want to be near to behold you
in all your beauty.'"

Still in a trance, she walked home slowly. The music,
the dancers, the moon, the warm summer night were almost more than she could take. She could not forget the
picture of the young man dancing. He couldn't be more
than eighteen and must either be a visitor or new in the
village, for she had never seen him before. She knew the
girl—Patron Lind's daughter. Those people never went
to Papa's church and right now Button didn't blame them,
for if they did, they never could have had the fun they were
having tonight. It was sinful not to go to church, but just
for tonight she would not let herself think of that. Instead
she would dream of that handsome boy who looked just like
the Harold of whom she had written in her book.

As Button sat down to write in her diary that night,

she pretended that she had come home from the party where she had been dancing with the new boy.

Dear Diary,
Tonight I danced with my dream boy in Larson's red barn. He held me very close as if I were grown up. And do you know what? God wasn't mad at all. When I looked around, He had sent down four little angels who were dancing, too, in their little white robes. As I saw their radiant faces, I knew they were as happy as I.

P.S.
Dear God,
Is making believe a sin? I hope not, for in my heart I feel that you are not cross with me. I see a lovely star that you tossed into the air millions of years ago when the world was new and without sin. It is winking at me. Please, please forgive me for having such a good time tonight. Amen.

It was fun doing things in her diary that she was not permitted to do in real life . . . almost as much fun as really doing them. When she fell asleep that night, she dreamed that she was grown up and that all the world was there for her to have fun in.

When Button reached her fourteenth birthday, she celebrated by having a party for her friends. Mama made a delicious cake and told her that she was almost an adult now, and Papa tickled her under the chin and said she was almost as pretty as Mama was when he first saw her. Button had grown very tall and slim, and she had a graceful way of walking that made her look more like sixteen than her actual age. Her eyes possessed unusual depths for a girl so young, and their color changed with the clothes she was wearing or the mood she was in. Sometimes they looked as angry as the turbulent river after a violent storm, but on Sunday morning as she walked to church with the family, her eyes were calm and blue as the summer sky.

At times during her fifteenth year Button became very irate with her family, especially Mama. Button had not altogether forgiven Mama for not having understood about her "calling" and treating the matter so lightly. Mama was the queen of her household and as the children swarmed around her, like bees around their queen, Button stood silently by, feeling strange and hollow inside, wanting to be close but hindered by an emotion that prevented a feeling of oneness with them. It pained her when Mama romped and laughed and sang with the other children. On rainy evenings Mama would sit down on the floor of the *vardagsroom* and gather her children in a circle around her to tell them stories, but Button would withdraw from the group, escaping to her room with the excuse of having homework to do.

"I can never get that *apple-kaka* out of my mind," sighed Button when alone. "It was so much more important than her own daughter that day long ago." She stood by the window, watching the wind in all its fury whipping the trees and flowers in the garden, bending them almost to the ground. But tomorrow, when the sun shone, they would rise again with a new beauty. Button lifted her head. Her big eyes, staring into the darkness, looked almost green. "If they don't break when they are bent low, neither will I . . . never . . . never . . . " she promised herself "I may have to bend, yes, at the blows of life, but no matter how hard I am hit, I shall never break." She realized that the strength she possessed deep, deep within her, no one could take away. Nor could anyone pry into her thoughts or laugh at her imagination. She lived in a world of her own, a world within a world. She loved this new kingdom she had discovered, a place to which she could escape and be at peace from the turmoil surrounding her, a place of joy and laughter. These quiet times, the book she was writing and her diary were her closest companions.

Karin missed her gay company, for they did not see each other often, since they did not go to school together any more. But one afternoon they met accidentally and decided to go berrypicking along the ditches by the roadside. A little of the old closeness sprang up as they talked and laughed about schooldays. Then the mood changed and Karin complained as she faced Button, the *smulton*-berry-laden straw in her hand.

"What has happened to us, Button? You and I were the closest of friends, sharing everything, good or bad, and now we hardly know what to talk about."

"It isn't your fault, Karin," replied Button, trying to force a smile. "You see, I've discovered that I am different from other girls. Perhaps a writer is like that, wanting to be alone and acting as if she was crazy. I don't even get along with my own family. . . . I am different from all of them. . . . Sometimes I feel as if I don't belong in the parsonage—as if Mama and Papa were not my real parents."

"Perhaps you were adopted?" suggested Karin, trying to be of help. "Some children don't know they are adopted until the time of their marriage when it has to be revealed in the marriage papers. By then they don't care because they have a husband to love."

"How silly," laughed Button. "Why should my parents want to adopt a child when they have so many themselves?"

"Don't forget, Button, you were the second child—and —well—perhaps they wanted to be sure to have a girl after having had a boy."

This was a new idea to Button and one which gave food to thought. She worried about it as she went home to the parsonage, scanning the well-known surroundings in an unrealistic way. Perhaps this was the answer to why she was so different, so restless . . . and had been so naughty as a little girl. This would explain, too, why Mama was so impatient with her and why she hadn't taken an interest in her "calling." She studied her brothers and sisters and found they all resembled one another, but not one of them looked like her. The rest had a snug feeling of belonging and being wanted, whereas she was the odd, lonely one. Perhaps Karin was right after all. Papa hated red hair and Nim had been born with it. Perhaps Mama wanted to be sure that she would have a blonde baby and wasn't taking any chances. Somehow Button must learn the answer.

She thought she had done so when, on a Saturday afternoon after she had cleaned the parsonage kitchen, Mama came in to inspect her work. Usually Mama took it for granted that if Button had cleaned the kitchen it was clean, but not on this Saturday. She did something Button had never seen her do before. She ran a finger along the panels of the doors, frowning at the results. She opened the closet door, hung up an apron that was on the floor, placed a clean newspaper in the wastebasket, took a broom handle and poked under the sofa. Mama was rewarded for this effort by having toys of all descriptions come tumbling out as well as a soiled apron, a bib and even a stale crust of bread. Button was terribly ashamed, but her pride would not unseal her tight-closed lips as Mama's words showered down upon her.

"Button Franzon, I have never been so horrified in all my life! Just look at this mess! Do you call this cleaning? You know as well as I do that dirty clothes belong in the washbin in the hall closet and not under the sofa. And the toys! Since when have you decided that under the sofa is a better receptacle than the big box provided for them? I have a good mind to show Papa just what you have done. He'll switch you, big as you are! However, just this once, I am going to give you a second chance, but as a punishment you are to clean every bit of this kitchen over again. Even the parts that are clean you are to scrub, and it all must be accomplished before your bedtime." Mama gave Button a scorching look and marched out of the kitchen, her heels clicking.

Silent as she had been, Button was raging inside. It would be late when she finished, and her arms and back would ache from all that unnecessary scrubbing. Karin was right! There was no doubt now in Button's mind that she had been adopted. A real mama just wouldn't be so cruel to her own flesh and blood. Her eyes burned from having to hold back the tears so long and if she ever got to her room, she would let the flood loose. After that she would talk it over with her dear diary.

But later that night, when her work had been completed and she was once more in her room, the tears did not come for by that time her imagination was intrigued by the wonderful story this would make. She had no time for tears as she wrote in her diary:

Dear, dear Diary,

You are still my best and very dearest friend and I have shared many secrets with you. Now I know that there is a great mystery concerning my birth. Karin gave me the idea that I was adopted, but I believe now that this is not quite true. Instead of being adopted I am a changeling ... even Mama doesn't know this, but it explains why I am so much trouble and why I love to go wandering at nighttime, forever restless. I really belong to a gypsy family that visited Lapland with their big wagon the year of my birth. My Mama was a beautiful gypsy, hated by her mother-in-law because she had wanted her son to marry another. The night I was born and Mama in her weakness slept, her mother-in-law stole me and ran to the parsonage where a baby girl had just been born. In the darkness of the night she exchanged me for the parsonage baby. I screamed and screamed because I wanted my own Mama . . . that is why I am restless for there is hot gypsy blood in my veins. Mama says she feels sorry for my future husband, for I will not be a good housekeeper, having a house that looks clean on the outside but is filled with trash in places, like under the sofa, where the casual observer does not look. She does not realize how much work it is for a young girl to clean a big kitchen and thinks I sweep things under the sofa just for the fun of it!

Dear God,

You are the only one that knows whether or not I have written the truth. I hope that I am wrong, for I don't really want to be a changeling. I do want more than anything else to feel that I really belong to someone, so if you don't give me an answer soon I may run off to join the gypsies. Amen.

Soon Button was faced with another worry. This time it was Papa. It struck her one night as suddenly as lightning will strike from a clear sky. During the evening meal it had seemed to Button that Papa had been too extra nice to her, passing the dishes of food to her twice and taking an interest in the little things, which was unusual for Papa, strictly out of character. Later he had sought her out alone and the words he had spoken had stunned her.

"Button dear, where did you ever get the feeling that you don't belong to our happy family? I hope it's a notion that will pass from you soon. All young people go through emotional conflicts before they adjust to being grown up, and you are no exception. Life is sometimes very hard for little girls who think they are big before their time. If ever you want to talk to your Papa about some of these problems, I'll be very happy to help you in any way I can."

"Thank you, Papa," said Button, "but I need no help. I am fine."

How could Papa so perfectly read her thoughts? She should have asked him, for a very disturbing thought was entering her mind, a thought she didn't dare to think. Where could Papa have received his information? Surely he who stood in the pulpit every Sunday morning and taught people how to live godly lives, surely he wouldn't go into her bedroom, open her third bureau drawer, look under her whole pile of underwear, and pull out her diary and read it . . . day after day, for how long? Oh, no, she

just mustn't think such evil of Papa. The thought must
have occurred to him because she looked so sad and never
listened to Mama's stories any more. Yes, that must be it.
But how could she be sure? She couldn't very well ask
him! She would have to put him through a test that would
determine once and for all whether or not he was guilty.

That night, when Button had finished writing in her
diary, being very guarded about what she revealed, she
placed a tiny white thread between the pages. This thread
would be the determining factor in condemning or acquit-
ting Papa.

For some unknown reason it seemed to Button that all
the household went out of their way to be extra nice to her
the next day. Nim gave her a picture of a movie actress he
had cut out from an advertisement that had blown down.
This was sweet of Nim as anything connected with the
theatre was taboo in the parsonage. Nim knew how she
admired those beautiful film stars. Pelle smiled his sunniest smile each time she passed him by, and Vickey asked
her what apron she should choose for the next week of
school, while Greta gave her the bigger part of the cookie
she had received for going on an errand. Yes, everyone
seemed to have been instructed to make her feel a part of
the family. Even the little boys invited her to play a game
with them, and Kerstin asked for help in tying her big red
hair ribbon. What had happened? Had Papa told them
about the talk he had had with his oldest daughter? There
was no way of knowing, since she would not ask . . . not
even if her life depended upon it. But it was so pleasant to
be surrounded by love that she almost forgot about the
adoption until Mama asked for her company on a short
house call.

"It will only take a few minutes, and we'll have a nice walk home talking together," said Mama sweetly. "Somehow, Button, you and I seem to have grown apart!"

It was fun walking with Mama. All the old bitterness seemed to dissolve, and she even forgave Mama for not understanding about her being an author. Mama's sweetness was making up for it. They talked and laughed about many things that had happened at home or in the church.

"My," said Mama, placing her arm around Button's shoulders, "you are as tall as I am. And what a pretty girl you are! Please, dear, don't grow away from me. I want to be your very closest friend."

"Thank you, Mama. I know I'll need you. At times I do feel almost grown up, but there's still a lot of the little girl left."

"I hope that there'll always be a little girl for me to hug," smiled Mama, "and a big girl, too. How well I remember the day you were born, Button. You gave me the least pain of all the children, and you were the prettiest of all my babies, so tiny and delicate-looking except for those great big blue eyes. Even that first day they looked around as if to say, 'My, this is a funny old world I have come to live in!' And I hugged you to my heart. Believe me, Button, although I do have to scold you at times, you are still very precious to me."

Button laughed gaily, a big burden having rolled away. "I will not sweep things under the kitchen sofa again, Mama," she promised, mischief dancing in her eyes.

"I am glad, Button, for when you do things like that it reflects back on me, for I am the one who taught you to keep house. People who only keep a clean house on the surface are apt to be deceivers, hiding things in their own lives that they don't want others to discover. You see now why I was so cross finding you doing this very thing?"

"Oh, yes, Mama," answered Button mechanically, for she could hardly hear Mama's words above the tumult of her own feelings . . . her heart was singing with joy and the new happiness that filled her small frame was almost more than she could contain. Mama had proved by her words that she was not an adopted or exchanged baby at all. She was really Button Franzon and belonged to the family as much as any of the other children. How could she have had such foolish thoughts? Oh, to be alone in her room so that she could tell her diary the truth. Life was tremendously sweet and now she would go to work on her book and surprise them all.

When the supper dishes were done and put away and the kitchen as tidy as Mama would leave it, Button kissed Mama and Papa good night and hurried to her room. She was so excited that she took two steps at a time up the stairs. The door to her room was slightly open. She stepped inside and the smile left her face, her spirit sinking down almost to the tip of her toes. There on the rug lay the evidence, a tiny white thread. Papa was guilty! He had shared her every secret. She felt as if she were naked before a crowd of people and wanted to run and hide. Papa was reading her diary! Slowly she sank down on her bed, but the tears would not come. What a blessed relief it would be if she could cry, for now she felt all dead inside. Her new kingdom had been smashed to pieces. "I will never—never —never write in my diary again," she whispered. She pressed the book to her heart and then very slowly she tore out the pages one by one and threw them in the wastebasket. Then she crumbled the black cover. It had been so much fun to talk to her diary, but nothing that had fun in it seemed to last for her. There was still EDITH, the book. She rose from the bed and took it from the drawer. Tenderly she looked at it. Then she folded the manuscript and placed it in an envelope and sealed it.

"Never shall I finish it!" She spoke aloud. "Never, never, never! Edith shall never marry her lover. . . . Sometimes, when I am old and gray, I shall take it out and read it again, but tonight is the end of Mary Terrier. Perhaps I shall still be an author someday, but it won't be until I have moved from home and will have some privacy. Perhaps I shall never write, I don't know. I may be a complete failure."

Button knelt a long time by her bed. It was so much more difficult to speak to God than to write to him.

"Dear God," she uttered so softly that she could hardly hear her own voice. "You are all I have now. My kingdom has been lost, but please help me not to feel resentful with my Papa. I still love him so. Help me to understand and believe that you are my friend. Let me feel close to you, because right now I hardly want to live. I don't think I shall ever smile again. Amen."

When sleep finally came that night, Button had changed from girlhood to womanhood. She realized that childhood was past and that life was not easy to live when one was sad, but she closed her eyes with the thought: There is always a tomorrow, and the morrow could be better than the day before. She would not break . . . just bend—and this was surely bending very low.

CHAPTER 4

❧ Button and Beaus

Along the winding path up the mountainside young lovers walked arm in arm. Unspoken words of tenderness hung in the air. Down in the village the clock in the tower chimed nine times. As Button hurried up the path, she smiled to herself and there was mischief sparkling in her eyes. Here she was acting like an adult and she was only fourteen years and three months old! Yet romance had entered into her life and had completely filled every part of her being. Love had come in the form of Gunnar Borgeson, driving away the sorrow of having to give up her talent, a sorrow that had been so deep that she had been certain that all life's joys had come to an end. How wonderfully mistaken she had been! Papa, of course, knew nothing of this new stage she was approaching. If he had, Button was sure he would have unmercifully squashed it under his large foot as if it had been a bug come to plague the household. No, this secret she must guard as carefully as she would tread on sacred ground. She had tried to share some of her feelings with Mama, who had taken it for granted that the love she was asking about existed for Button only in storybooks.

"Are you reading books that Papa has censored, Button?" asked Mama. "You talk so strangely for one your age, and your eyes are full of dancing stars."

"Am I too young to ask about love?" returned Button. And seeing the laugh Mama was trying to suppress, Button decided to tell her nothing of Gunnar. But she would have to find a way to go on dates, and a way always opened for her when she desired something hard enough.

Button had found the way. Love, she thought, could come at any age, for there were certain things that slumbered in your soul until you yourself awakened them to life. Yes, she had found love bursting forth in full bloom the night she first met Gunnar.

"Of course, Papa must have forgotten how it felt to be young and romantic . . . it was so long ago," Button reasoned as she gazed at the round yellow moon, hanging low over the treetops.

What a divine feeling it was, this very first romance! But how would Papa feel if he knew about her and Gunnar? What a night this would be! Saturday night was made for lovers. All day long she had worked to help Mama ready the parsonage for Sunday. She had worked so hard and well that Mama had been really pleased, not knowing that Button only did it to make the time pass swiftly so nighttime would come sooner.

Now the lamps in the parsonage would be burning low. All would be still and peaceful. Button could picture it all in her mind. In the kitchen Mama would be finishing her last task of the day, that of shining the children's shoes. And in the study Papa would be going over his Sunday-morning sermon for the last time. He would be walking back and forth, sermon in hand, written in his big hand on

lined yellow paper. Then he would stop, place the sermon
on his desk and draw a circle around a certain sentence.
That meant that at this point a good joke would be appropriate. Perhaps he would first tell it to Mama that night, for
Mama was very critical of Papa's jokes. Button remembered hearing Mama tell him once:

"Pontus, your jokes must be so good that you yourself
can laugh at them without effort. An ill-fitting joke will
ruin the purpose of a perfectly good sermon. The people
will remember the joke and not the gospel you are preaching to save their souls."

Papa believed in Mama's judgment, for in most things
she was right.

Upstairs the children, with the exception of her oldest
brother, Nim, would be in bed and asleep. But soon now
Mama would be calling, "Good night, son! God protect
and keep you!" And Nim would blow out his lamp and go
to sleep. In her own room there would be a strange stillness. Button laughed, thinking of the form she had substituted for herself, which was now lying in her bed. It
most certainly had the shape of a girl, and she had carefully pulled the quilt over most of the head. If Mama and
Papa peeked in, they would never suspect that it was her
dummy friend, Flora, reclining there, while their own
daughter was scurrying up the mountain path.

Flora was a strange combination of a pillow, a cabbagehead and some hair from the roll Mama used to pin
over her forehead when she was especially dressed up. Un-
beknownst to Mama, Button had pulled a few strands a
day and had then glued them to the cabbage. The blonde
hair peeking out from under the bedclothes made a perfect disguise. Yes, Button had climbed into bed at the usual

time but, instead of her nightie, she had been dressed in her Sunday dress and had to lie very still so as not to get it wrinkled. At eight thirty she had slipped from her bed, tucked her nightie under her arm, and laid Flora in her place. She had patted the hard head and whispered, "Be a good girl; don't you dare move and give me away," and she had pressed a quick kiss on the leafy cheek.

The front door had squeaked as she pushed it open, and for one fearful second she had held her breath. But Mama had been humming a hymn in the kitchen and Papa was reading aloud, so they had not noticed.

When Button was safely in the woodshed, she had hidden her nightie under a log and had flown free as a bird toward the mountain. To hide the nightie in the woodshed had been a brilliant idea, for if anyone awakened and saw her creeping into the house in her gown, nothing would be suspected as nocturnal trips sometimes had to be made to the outhouse.

Anyway, the happiness in Button's heart crowded out all fear of being discovered. For just a moment she had struggled with the thought that this might be a sin! Quickly she had dismissed this unwelcome idea, for even if it was, wasn't it worth sinning to meet Gunnar and be considered almost grown up? She tossed her pretty head and thought how silly it was of people to sleep away the beauty of the night. The wonderment of love, the gentleness and beauty of the night, the mystery of nature, stirred her so it almost hurt. Button had resolved to live life to its fullest, and no one would have the power to stop her. She would always seek until she found a way to fulfill herself. Right now, for instance, why should she sleep if she could be with Gunnar?

And then, through the shadows of the night, she saw him pass the bench by the lone pine and he was running to meet her. How handsome he looked with his green felt hat tipped back on his dark wavy hair. Although she couldn't see his eyes, Button knew that their dark brown depths sparkled with happiness. They clasped their hands and stood very still for a moment.

"You made it, Button!"

"Of course. Didn't you think I would? I promised you I would find a way!"

Their laughter echoed against the mountain as, arms entwined, they started to climb even higher. Gunnar held her tighter and whispered, "Sometimes, my little one, your bravery frightens me. What a child you are in years and still to me you seem as old as——"

"As you, Gunnar?" interrupted Button eagerly.

He looked down at the flushed face. "Yes, Button. You don't seem a day under eighteen to me."

"Good, then I won't have to feel that your going with me is as if you had robbed the cradle!"

He drew her closer and their steps sounded together as they climbed higher and higher in the stillness of the night. Presently they stopped and looked down at the village below them. Like twinkling stars that had lost their way, the small houses looked . . . stars lost from the sky.

Button placed her hand over Gunnar's mouth. "Let us not talk for a while, Gunnar, just stand here and be thankful that we can be together."

"Are you afraid our talking would break the enchantment, Button?"

"You mean all this happiness that makes us feel as we would burst?"

Gunnar nodded. They walked on in silence.

After a while Gunnar stopped.

"What if they should miss you, Button?" he asked anxiously.

She tossed her head indifferently. "Nothing much . . . a good thrashing and being forbidden to go out nights for a few weeks, perhaps. But nothing *can* happen! Nothing in the whole world! But even if it did, this night is worth it a thousand times."

They had stopped in front of a clump of trees.

"Oh, Gunnar, here it is!" Button held her breath. "I knew that sometime I would find it, just as in my dream. Can you see it?"

"See what, silly?"

"The house, Gunnar! *Our* house! If you dream with me, you will see it, too. See how peaceful it is in this spot so far away from the noise of the world and so near the sky. Our cottage is red and white and just big enough for you and me and our three children. I can see them pressing their noses against the windowpane, waiting for us. How beautiful they are—two boys and a girl!"

Gunnar laughed. "I am afraid your imagination is contagious, for I've been infected. I can see it, too, Button, through your eyes . . . and I like it. . . . It's fun seeing things that aren't there."

"It's called a second sight, Gunnar. I can always see things I want badly enough, and I can always make my dreams come true."

"I hope our house comes true!"

"It will, it will, Gunnar, if we dare to dream it long enough." Button took a step forward. "How low it is with the tall spruces standing watch over it. The two boys look just like their dad."

"And the little girl has a funny little nose like her mother's . . . and big blue eyes and golden curls . . . and when she smiles her teeth are as white as pearls."

"You have caught on, Gunnar; you're doing fine! Our curtains are real lace. We are rich, for you are the busiest doctor in town because everybody likes you . . . but I like you best of all."

"You crazy, precious girl . . . keep on talking like that."

"Our house looks homey, and see, there in the corner is your office with the sign on the door: Gunnar G. Borgeson, M.D. You are so friendly to all the little children the mothers bring to you, bouncing them on your knee and putting your finger under the girls' chins, pulling their curls and telling them how pretty they are. And the old people come, too, for you listen sympathetically to their troubles and try to make them well again . . . only—oh, dear—it will take so long before you are a doctor and we can get married!"

"Perhaps we shouldn't wait. We could run away to Italy and by lying about our ages we could be married right away."

"Our happiness wouldn't last long in the loneliness of a strange land. Imagine Christmas when we would decorate our little spruce tree with roses, and I would be missing Mama and Papa and the rest of the family. I would soon grow sorry that I married you. I am always sorry when I do something wrong."

"I would kiss your loneliness away and call you my little dream girl!"

Button lifted wide eyes toward the star-studded sky. "Yes, it would be all right for you to kiss me then because we would be married."

Gunnar drew her close to his heart. "Button, may I kiss you now?" he whispered.

Button stared at him with unbelieving eyes. Then she laughed. "Of course not, silly! We aren't even engaged yet."

They ran down the mountainside. Strange sounds came from the woods, and the path was deserted. It was very late. Once on the parsonage road, they slowed their pace.

Button said good night to Gunnar outside the woodshed. "You must go quickly now," she whispered. "Papa might come out."

"Until next Saturday night then, precious. . . . I shall count the minutes."

She watched him walk away swiftly into the night. Then with haste she slipped out of her best clothes and placed them in a box she had behind the woodpile. Once in her nightie, she stepped out on the lawn to drink in again the mysterious beauty of the night that held so many promises of a joyful future to a young girl's heart. An eerie sound came from the mountain. Button shivered. The moon was high in the sky now. The stars were fading. Soon the sun would be lighting the eastern horizon. Alone up there on the mountain stood their dream house, unseen by human eyes.

Button breathed a prayer, eyes upraised:

"Please God, dear God, don't be angry with me tonight. Gunnar and I had such a good time. I love your beautiful world, but I love your nights best of all. Good night, Father God! I think I love you too, if you are not cross with me. Amen."

Late as it was, it still took Button a long time to fall asleep. Having put Flora safely away, her thoughts dwelt on the evening. If only she could share her feelings with her diary, but she just had to relive them in her mind instead. Once, she crept out of bed and knelt by the window sill still fascinated by the splendor of the night. So much she had wanted Gunnar to kiss her, but it would have been very, very wrong. The time would come when she would be old enough to act like other lovers, but at her age it would be a sin and God would be angry. Button felt happy knowing she had done the right thing and that even Papa would have been pleased had he known.

Back in bed again, she let her thoughts drift to the night she had first met Gunnar. If only she could have shared this experience with her diary . . . but her diary was no more. Thinking would be safer, since no one could read her thoughts; they would be all her own.

The meeting had happened the night she had discovered that Papa was reading her beloved diary. She had felt desolate, believing that never again would life hold any joys for her. After the parsonage had been stilled for the night, she had gone walking, as if that could relieve the terrible pain that kept mounting within her. She had taken the path that led to the lake, which was not too distant from the parsonage. It had been very early in the spring and patches of snow remained here and there in the shadows where the sun's rays had not yet reached them. The blowing wind had rippled the lake into small waves that made a soothing sound as they were tossed up on shore.

Suddenly Button's eyes had fallen on Gunnar, sitting on a rock not a stone's throw away. His head had been buried in his hands as if he were sorrowing, so she could not tell if he were young or old. She had stepped toward him and as he lifted his head she saw that he was quite young and very nice-looking and someone she had never seen before.

He seemed annoyed that someone had intruded upon his privacy. "Where did you come from?" he blurted out.

"Hi," answered Button. "I was just walking . . . but perhaps I'm not real . . . just a figment of your imagination, or a dream!"

"You could be, indeed." He relaxed. "There was no one here just a moment ago."

"I came like an angel to minister to your sadness or, if I won't do, you could try my Papa. He is the preacher in the village. But probably you are one of those people who never go to church."

"You are right. I don't go to church, and I don't need a preacher. In fact, I don't like them."

Button laughed. "At times I don't like them either."

"You are a strange girl." He laughed, too. "I came here to be alone in order to solve my problems and was angry with your interference, but I find that I like you and I'm glad you came. My father isn't a preacher, but there are times when I don't like him either."

Then he had told her his story. His father was the new director of the ore-mines and wanted his son to learn the business, but Gunnar had set his heart upon becoming a doctor.

"I hate the mines. It's like attending your own funeral to go down into the deep, dark ground with only a small light on your forehead. Each day I feel that I can't possibly descend another time, but my father refuses to listen to me. He says that at eighteen I'm not old enough to know my own mind!"

They talked at length that night and afterwards met whenever they could, and now each Saturday night there were the mountain walks. They both felt that they were deeply in love and though Button had told him she was only fourteen, to him it did not matter in the least, for she seemed so much older. She had told him that he must learn to dare to dream dreams.

"Gunnar, you must believe that you can be a doctor. You must dream it a long, long time, and then it will happen. Dreams are very much like stars——"

"Like stars? What do you mean?"

"Well, at times when you look up, the sky is bright with them, and then again you see no stars . . . but if you take the time to gaze long enough, you'll see that they're really there by the millions. Then you wonder why you didn't see them before. It's the same with becoming a doctor. You must see yourself with the black bag in your hand . . . and don't ever see the light on your forehead or the black pit again . . . blot them out from your mind. Gunnar, I can teach you to dream beautiful dreams!"

And she had, until now they were dreaming together, and tonight he had asked to kiss her. Button had wanted him to do so very, very much, more than anything in the whole wide world. But she couldn't spoil her happiness by sinning, for then the spell might be broken. "Oh, Gunnar," she whispered, "I love you even more than my diary!"

Slowly the picture of him faded from her mind . . . her eyes closed, the long lashes lying like half-moons on her flushed cheeks. Now and then they fluttered a little as if they objected to closing out the new day that peacefully embraced the parsonage in its gentle arms.

If Button could have seen Gunnar, she would have known that he, too, had tossed restlessly, thinking of her, of the night he had met her, of each meeting since, and wondering how life had ever existed without her. Yes, he was in love with a little girl of fourteen who was in both mind and body too mature for her years. What a strange combination this daughter of a preacher was! She could speak of love and marriage as easily as breathing but refused to be kissed. Her hand was warm and responsive and her eyes as bright as the stars of which she had spoken. She could actually make him believe that his dreams would come true. Already he was seeing himself as a great doctor, living in a cozy cottage up the mountain road with a beautiful wife and three lovely children. He could reach his goal with Button beside him. She was foolish and brave and with her sweetness drew him to her and then unmercifully pushed him away. His blood pounded in his veins at the thought of his lips pressed against hers. Like honey they would feel . . . fresh and pure. . . .

CHAPTER 5

❧ Tender Roots

Dummy Flora was no more! She had come to as inevitable an end as had everything else of value and importance in Button's young life. Almost like a funeral her going had been, with a stern preacher officiating, but minus the flowers and tears. For Button had not shed even one tear when she saw that her faithful friend had been shattered into her original elements—one cabbagehead, one pillow with a rope tied around its middle and a tuft of fine blonde hair.

Poor, poor Flora! She had been lying there innocently in Button's bed on her usual stint of Saturday-night duty when, without warning, the door had been pushed open and Papa had entered. . . . Now that it was over and Papa had left (How funny he had looked in his short nightshirt and bare feet!), Button was able to reconstruct what must have happened. A few minutes ago, Papa and she had had a long, long talk, for he had not spared the words. . . .

At nine o'clock last evening he had come to her room with very important news. Thinking she was asleep, he had tiptoed to her bed and remained there motionless for a few moments while he had decided whether or not he

should waken her. Button could picture him standing
there, and then making up his mind, suddenly touching
what he thought was a soft shoulder and bending low to
whisper into what should have been a pink ear.

"Button," he had murmured, but all that greeted him
was a strong whiff of wilted cabbage. It had not taken
Papa long to discover that the smelly object substituting
for his daughter actually was that—a cabbage! His unpredictable daughter must be out in the night, wandering
about in her nightgown, gazing at the starlit sky. Yes, Button was sure that must have been what he had been thinking. He must also have conjectured that he was wrong in
believing that Button had become a good girl. She was
still a problem! There simply was no accounting for the
strange things she did. My, but Papa must have been angry, for he had flung Flora from the bed with such force
that she landed in the corner by the dresser, completely
dismembered. After that he had calmed down a bit and
crept into Flora's place under the gay patch-quilt to await
his erring child's return. During the long wait Papa had
napped now and then, and the brief snatches of sleep had
served to better his mood somewhat, although he was
deeply disturbed by the lateness of the hour. Then he had
heard the unsuspecting Button creeping into the room. Her
face had been flushed and her eyes dancing like stars after
an enchanted night on the mountaintop with Gunnar. She
had reached out her arms as if to embrace the whole world,
and taken a couple of dancing steps toward the bed and
jubilantly bent down to hug her friend.

"Flora, darling," she had whispered dreamily, "You
are an angel to take my place . . ." and as suddenly as a
flow of water is stopped by turning off a faucet, her words

ceased. Flora felt so strange and soft. Presently Button realized that, instead of a cabbagehead, she had grabbed a human one fastened to her Papa, who was gasping for breath.

Button blinked and stammered in surprise, grasping for words that were not there. She felt like laughing and crying, like shouting and whispering, while all the time she was trying to think up an excuse that would save her from this dire predicament. She stared into Papa's eyes, penetrating eyes that pierced through her as they stared back at her unmercifully.

Finally she spoke in a quavering, raspy voice, pretending to be gay. "But, Papa, what in the world are *you* doing in my bed—and at this time of the night?"

"What do you think I'm doing?" snapped Papa bitterly, his eyes shooting flames. "I've been waiting for hours for you, young lady!"

Button made a great effort to look small and demure as she stepped out of her slippers and crawled up on the foot of the bed.

"I was wandering around, Papa. I wasn't at all sleepy, and I felt a wild desire to go into the night. Why did God make the nights so mysteriously lovely if we must sleep them all away?"

Papa was caught off guard by this unexpected question, so he did not respond immediately. In the interval of silence Button shook with fear, thinking that Papa was trying to figure out a punishment that would be great enough for this, the latest of her crimes. After what seemed to be an eternity of waiting Papa spoke:

"Button, I came here to talk to you. It was only nine o'clock then." He paused for a moment. "Mama and I will give you permission to wander, as you call it, out into the night whenever you like. You will have no need to use a dummy or any other invention you might dream up. Just let us know that you are going, bid us good night and for goodness' sake go out with your clothes on. Walk out through the door in a proper fashion, then there will be no law to break."

Button couldn't believe that she had heard Papa's words correctly. If she had, he must have lost his mind! Perhaps studying too hard for his sermons had made Papa sick. Was that why she had found him sleeping in her bed instead of being with Mama where be belonged? What other reason could there be for his giving her permission to run out in the night as she pleased, not even caring if she ever slept? Something was very, very wrong, for Papa was acting entirely out of character. Perhaps she had better run and fetch Mama and tell her that Papa was sick, indeed.

But Papa had sat up in bed, pushed the pillows against the wall and leaned against them as if his last words had taken all his strength. Then he spoke again, this time with a calm, preaching-a-sermon-at-prayer-meeting type voice:

"This evening Postmaster Olauson delivered a very important letter for which I had been waiting a long time. In six weeks we are moving to America. That is why I am granting you permission to roam around. Enjoy all of nature, night and day, in your dear homeland, for you will soon bid it farewell. I trust you will not misuse your freedom."

"Oh no, Papa," promised Button, too stunned to believe that what he was saying could be true.

"Button," said Papa more kindly, "I wanted you to be the first one to hear this news. It shouldn't surprise you too much, for you know Mama has talked America for years, and you also know that recently there has been a strong possibility that I would receive a call from over there. All you children wanted to go, so what could I do but acquiesce? Well, now the time has come, and the day and the hour will come fast."

Button swallowed hard. Papa didn't sound as if this was good news. He looked very sad. How thoughtful he had been to come and share the news with her first. She was sorry that again she had disappointed him. But how could she tell him that she had changed her mind about wanting to go? She couldn't tell him about Gunnar and risk losing the freedom just granted her. She must act happy despite the hurt in her heart.

"Perhaps we shall all like America," she said. "Perhaps Mama's dream of having us all educated will come true. Perhaps even you will like it, Papa."

"Leaving Lapland, Button, will be hard for us all. To pull up our roots from the homeland soil is not easy, and yours are very young and tender. It will be the hardest for you because you love your country with a true heart, but your roots will also transplant easier in the new soil. Don't worry about it, Button. Mama has the best in mind for all of us, and she is always very wise and right in most things."

How kind Papa was and how touching his concern for her. Papa had needed her tonight. He had felt that they belonged together in this parting. Her strong Papa had needed to be comforted! This was a new side of him that Button hadn't known existed. He was human and became bewildered and confused at times just like the rest of the family.

Her arms crept around his neck. "It will be all right,

Papa, and I thank you for the freedom to wander. I'll try hard to be a good girl."

She did not know how many times she had given him this promise, and she had always meant it. Perhaps this time she would keep it.

When Papa left, Button stretched out in bed. It had been a very eventful night, indeed.

Presently her door opened and Papa stuck his head inside.

"I just happened to think, Button," he whispered, putting his finger to his mouth, "that you better not tell Mama about the dummy. There are some things that are just as well for your Mama not to know."

"I promise, Papa. You and I alone will know about Flora."

Papa smiled happily, as the door closed, and a silvery string of laughter rolled from Button's lips. Quickly she covered her mouth with her pillow. It would be a sin to laugh aloud this time of the early Sabbath morning in the parsonage, but the scene with Flora had been so funny. Papa is afraid Mama will laugh at him, Button thought, but sharing a secret with Papa really made her feel close to him.

Although the night was mostly spent, it was hard to go to sleep. The time was so short before she would be moving away. What would America be like? When Button finally slept, she dreamed of houses so tall and straight they reached into the clouds, of wide stone streets where richly dressed people strolled, and of dollar bills raining from heaven.

When she awoke, she was in a happy, excited mood.

After all, if she did not like America, she could always return to Sweden, and Gunnar would be waiting for her . . .
Gunnar and their dream house up on the mountaintop.
She would not worry about the future because all the new
tomorrows could be better than all the yesterdays . . . she
could make them that way.

How fast those six weeks flew by and what a conglomeration of emotions they contained: excitement, anticipation, sorrow, joy. It was bitter-sweet, this leaving of
one's country, and it was hard to believe that the whole
thing was not just one fantastic dream. Every day there
were farewell parties and speeches, and gifts of every de-
scription poured into the parsonage. People were constantly coming and going, and Mama was as happy as a
young bride, singing and laughing the days away. Papa
tried bravely to look happy, but Button knew the sadness
that lurked beneath his smile and saw how heavy his steps
had become. Pulling up those roots is hard for him, she
thought tenderly as she watched him going down the path.
Papa did not like to move away! And her heart ached for
him. She had been unable to analyze her own feelings.
There was a numbness in her heart—or was she refusing to
face the issue? If she looked deep, deep within herself,
would her heart be crying?

Button was in a gay mood when she told Gunnar the
news. It was hard to see the light disappear from his eyes
as if she had struck him.

"Don't take it so hard, Gunnar," she begged, smiling
so her mouth hurt. "Just think of how many new things I
will see. Lapland here in Sweden is not such a big place,
after all. And you can come after me. You can get rich quick

in America, and then you will have all the money you need to study and be a great doctor. People over there have so much money they don't know what to do with it. Some of them throw it away just for a lark. Why, all you have to do is to stand on a street corner and a man driving a big automobile is liable to come up to you and say, 'Young man, you need this so you can take that pretty young girl for a ride. Will you do me the honor of accepting it as a gift?' What could you do but accept? And then I could smile my prettiest smile and say, 'Thank you kindly, sir.' Oh, Gunnar, can't you see how wonderful it all will be! And each summer we could come back to Lapland for our vacation. Please, please don't look so sad. If you like, I will give you my promise before I leave."

"You are still a crazy girl, Button," laughed Gunnar. "What in the world will I do without you! But, little one, I will not extract any promise from you. You are so young and bubbling over with life, everybody will love you."

Gunnar looked past Button as though he was trying to see the unknown years ahead, long empty years without this precious girl.

"I want you to be free, Button," he said slowly, "when you go out into that big, wide, unknown world. If you really love me, space cannot separate us, and you will come back to Lapland someday and we will marry here. But you may meet someone over there who will claim you and your love, so the greatest gift I can give to you is not to tie you down with words . . . only your heart shall belong to me until it makes its choice."

"Oh, Gunnar, Gunnar! You talk as beautiful as my Papa when he's preaching. I'll never forget you. Never, never! I shall give you a gift, too." Button hesitated a mo-

ment as though she was wording very carefully what she
was to say. "Gunnar, I shall give you Karin Lund, my best
friend, for a pal . . . only . . . just be friends. She is a
deacon's daughter, and she will talk you out of your blue
moods. Karin will be very good for you, Gunnar."

Gunnar smiled sadly. "Thank you, Button. I know you
mean well, so I'll be a good friend to Karin because of
you, but I assure you, we will be friends and nothing
more."

Something hurt deep within Button's heart as though
a needle was being pressed into her tender skin. Into her
mind had come the picture of Karin and Gunnar strolling
up the mountain path alone . . . and she—Button—
would be far, far away . . . and who could tell? . . .
Karin was so lovely that before long she and Gunnar could
be more than just friends. Perhaps it would be that Karin
would live in the dream house with Gunnar. . . . But,
then, there could be a new love waiting for Button, too.
Life was full of surprises.

That night, as Gunnar and Button stood on the mountain by their clump of trees, Button could no longer see
their dream house. It had completely disappeared from
her vision. She said nothing to Gunnar, for she knew the
secret of dreaming. If once you let a dream go, you can't
recapture it, no matter how hard you try. Even if you only
subtract a bit from its substance, it dissolves and is no more.
She tried not to be sad, for she had brought it on herself by
her gift of Karin to Gunnar, and now she must determine
to be happy because those two, having each other, would
be less lonely without her. Papa had said it would hurt to
pull up her roots but now one, at least, was pulled, and
though she would see Gunnar again, the agony of the pull-

ing would be over. However, there were two more to go: one for Karin, and the biggest and deepest of them all, the one for Sweden, her dear homeland.

Karin had taken the news very hard. Ever since that Sunday when Papa had read his resignation in church, she had followed Button around like a shadow, even spending most of her time in the parsonage.

They were sitting talking in the parsonage garden. Karin's enormous eyes never left Button for a moment.

"You're just born lucky, Button," she said in a high-pitched voice. "First you are going to become an author, and then you become the special friend of the handsomest boy in town, and now you are going to America where you are sure to marry a millionaire and won't have to lift even your little finger in work."

"Oh, Karin, don't talk so silly. If a millionaire comes along and wants to marry me, I'll simply say, 'No sir, don't marry me. Go over to Lapland and find my best friend. She is prettier than I!' "

They both laughed, sounding as though they were still schoolgirls together. There was so much to talk about, so much to remember. Button told Karin of her gift to Gunnar.

Karin blushed. "Oh, I can't ever fill your place, Button, but I'll do my best if it will make him less lonely for you."

"Thank you, Karin," said Button in a sad voice. Karin's eyes were as big as saucers and they sparkled with a strange gleam. Perhaps it had been foolish to ask Karin and Gunnar to be friends, but it was too late now.

The next night the two girls walked up to the little

red schoolhouse on the hill for the last time. They sat on the broad stone step reminiscing.

Karin took a small package from her pocket. "I brought you a little gift, Button."

"Why, Karin, how sweet!" Button admired the wrapping. "How pretty! Shall I open it now?"

Karin nodded her head vigorously.

Button took her time in undoing the ribbon. The box was white, the ribbon blue, and the paper red.

"I hope you notice that I chose the colors of the American flag," said Karin anxiously, "red, white and blue."

"Thank you, Karin. You think of everything." Button had tears in her eyes and Karin was sobbing aloud by now.

Then the box was open and Button stared at its contents, trying to hide her great disappointment. "I—don't know what it is, Karin. . . . It looks like garden dirt!"

"It is, Button . . . just plain, pure garden dirt, the greatest gift I could bring you. Someday, over there in your new country, you will be terribly lonesome for your old country and you can take a little dirt between your fingers and say, 'This is Sweden! I am home again!' "

"Oh, Karin. . . ." and they were in each other's arms clinging as if they could never part, "you think of the dearest things. I love the dirt and I'll always keep it, and each time I see it I'll think of you."

"And then someday give half of it to your minister— and when you die over there"—Karin was crying so hard she could hardly talk—"when they bury you in foreign soil —he can sprinkle some dirt from your homeland on your casket. . . . Oh, won't that be wonderful! . . . the soil of Sweden sprinkled on you—its own daughter."

"Please, Karin—don't. . . . You make me cry away

all my tears. . . . I—don't want to die—not until I get so old I can't walk—but it was sweet of you to think of my funeral."

"I don't want you to go, Button. Please stay here. . . ."

And Karin carried on so that Button was almost unable to control her. Never had she realized that she meant so much to Karin.

But later Button and Karin dried their tears and were happy again. It is hard to be sad for long when you are young and the excitement of life is before you. So they walked arm in arm down the road just like old times. But Button slept with Karin's gift under her pillow—a strange gift, indeed, but very precious. She would always treasure it.

On the last day in Lapland, Button was excused from all work.

"Let her go, Maria," Papa told Mama. "I will help with the children. Let her wander to her heart's content. This will be the last time, because the freedom of walking in the woods might never come again."

Mama laughed. "Pontus, you talk so strange. There will be mountains and woods over there, too, and lakes and flowers and song and laughter. You talk as if we were moving to a desert island."

And we might as well be moving to the desert, thought Button as the last farewells were being said. Alone, late at night, a gentle spring night that she would long remember, she strolled through the parsonage garden bidding each bush and tree good-bye. Removing her shoes and stockings, she padded across the soft green grass, reliving the thrill she used to get as a child at having the grass tickle her bare feet. It couldn't be possible that all the things in the garden would keep on growing after the Franzons moved away from here. In years to come, if they ever returned to this garden, all would look different, she reflected, as she took one last ride in the swing in the spruce tree, feeling as she had so many times before that it took her over the treetops and the blue mountains to the top of the world.

"I am not going to be sad." She talked to herself. "I must believe in my heart that in my new country I'll find trees and bushes and mountains and new friends." But her heart felt heavy within her, and the smile that she wanted to bring forth froze on her lips. In the stillness of the night she thought she heard a heart beating loud and hard way deep down in the dark dirt of the earth.

"It is the heart of my homeland," she said to the lilac bush, thinking sadly that it was budding and she would never see it bloom. "Mother Sweden is sorry when one of her daughters is about to desert her."

Suddenly she remembered what Papa had said about her roots being tender. He had forewarned her of the sadness she might feel when she took her farewell. She simply would not let herself be sad. She would force herself to feel gay and not to cry. Feeling the tears in her eyes, she started to sing a gay little folk tune to drive them away

> *"Jänta o ja*
> *Jänta o ja*
> *allt upp pa lantavägen o ja*
> *Jänta o ja*
> *Jänta o ja*
> *allt upp pa lantavägen. . . ."*

She sang it very softly so as not to awaken the rest of the inhabitants of the parsonage. She was lucky that Papa and Mama had let her be free to wander. They had been very good to her. Her heart was light again and her feet danced a little on the lawn. Then she picked up her shoes and stockings and, without another look at the garden, she ran up the steps to the parsonage.

Button had never imagined that the ocean could be so big. Gazing at it from the deck after four days at sea, she felt as if it had no beginning and no end, that it was only an endless span of water. Papa had said that in some places it was as deep as it was wide. This she could not fathom, the thought was so tremendous. Today Papa was standing beside her, the two of them alone, and he had thrown his arm across her shoulders. It felt safe and good to stand there with Papa.

"Isn't the ocean one of the most wonderful of God's creations! There's no end to it," exclaimed Button, trying to strike up a conversation that would accord with Papa's thinking.

"It is, indeed," smiled Papa. "I'm so happy that you notice things, Button, and that you respond to things in nature. Some people go through life with eyes which see not and with ears which hear not. This always makes a void, empty place within the soul."

"There are lots of people like that, Papa. You can almost single them out from a crowd. Their faces are always restless and unhappy-looking."

Papa's eyes scanned the mighty waters.

"The ocean to me is a true picture of life, and we are like the ship. To travel safely across the water we must have an able captain. Button, my girl, if you make God the captain of your ship, you will never have to fear the storms of life which are bound to come, and though you may be tossed about on the angry waves, you will be safe. Your ship may creak and groan, but it will never lose its course. And at times the ocean will be calm and gentle as a mother's love; it becomes like a mirror with the moon showering silver upon it and millions of stars glistening over it. But the ship sails on in sunshine and shadow, in storm or in calm, never losing sight of its destination, and our captain sees that we reach the goal."

"I'll treasure your words always, Papa. I like you to talk to me like that, especially now when we're moving to a new country and it may not be easy to be replanted."

They stood in silence while the wind blew the ocean spray in their faces. How far they were from Sweden now!

"Button, was it hard?" asked Papa tenderly. "Did it hurt to pull your roots from the homeland soil?"

She nodded, smiling up at him with bright tears in her eyes. He wiped them off with his big handkerchief. "There now," he soothed, "no use crying."

Button took a deep breath. "Last night I was homesick for Sweden, but it's all over now. I don't like to hurt very long. Will it also be painful to be replanted?"

"No," answered Papa. "There is no pain in that process, just loneliness. It will take patience, of course, but your roots will soon start growing again in the new land. You are young and strong. As for me, I was too old to pull up mine; perhaps they will wither and die."

As they watched the great waves rolling against the ship, they held on to the railing so as not to be knocked down by the wind. Here were father and daughter, so far separated by the years and yet so close in spirit. Perhaps the green-capped waves knew what the future would hold for these immigrants to a strange land?

Button patted Papa's hand. "Your roots will grow, Papa," she said sweetly. "God will see to that."

After Papa had left her to join Pelle and Nim for a walk around the deck, Button continued to stand by the rail, for she never tired of watching the waves or thinking upon the mystery of the sea. Her thoughts sped swiftly across the green water to Lapland, to the little white church, the dear parsonage, and to her wonderful friend, Karin, with whom she had shared so much of her life. And then Gunnar—dear, dear Gunnar, so fine and lonely—now left to dream his dreams alone, for no matter how sweet and funny Karin was, she did not know how to contrive dreams.

Button smiled as she remembered that last date with Gunnar when she had brought Karin along to introduce them to each other. At first Gunnar had looked surprised and disappointed, but Karin had been sweet and tactful.

"I know that two is company and three is a crowd," she laughed, showing even white teeth, "but Button insisted that I should come along." She put her finger against her short nose. "It won't be long though, just walk me home, and we can talk on the way. I wouldn't think of spoiling your last night together."

"Of course you are not spoiling our night, Karin. How silly! We're glad you are with us. Aren't we, Gunnar?"

Gunnar nodded his head.

"Gunnar, this is Karin, my very best friend. . . . Karin, this is Gunnar whom I hope you will soon know real well."

Karin smiled. There were deep dimples in her rosy

cheeks. Her eyes sparkled, and Button thought she had never seen them look so enormous. Karin was tiny and cute, and the smile never left her lips. She held out her hand to Gunnar.

"I know we will be good friends, Gunnar. I'm so glad to meet you. I hope you'll come to my house sometime and taste my Mama's cookies."

Gunnar laughed. "I'll never refuse an invitation to sample cookies. When may I come?"

"Oh, any night as soon as Button leaves."

"Now listen, you two," protested Button, already feeling left out, "it seems you can't get me off fast enough."

"Well, there's nothing we can do to stop you from leaving us, Button," said Gunnar lightly.

"I wish you wouldn't go, Button," sighed Karin. "You know that! But I am glad to meet Gunnar. . . . Gunnar, you are the most handsome boy around town."

Gunnar bowed deeply. "Thank you, Karin. Already I know we'll be good friends."

Button remembered how she wished Karin would not spread compliments quite so thickly. But that was Karin, always diving into things head-on.

"We'd better start walking," she had said, putting one arm in Gunnar's and the other in Karin's.

All the way to her house Karin had Gunnar laughing, and Button felt relieved when they finally left Karin on her doorstep.

"I'll see you before the train goes, Button," said Karin, "and you, Gunnar, whenever you come to call on me."

They had talked about Karin most of that night.

"You didn't tell me how pretty your little friend was,"

said Gunnar, "and she really has a wonderful personality, in a different way from anyone I know."

"Karin is wonderful, Gunnar. Perhaps you won't even miss me when you two get together."

He held her hand tightly.

"There's only one Button in the whole world!" he said, "You know, little one, that I'll never stop missing you, Karin or no Karin."

That had made her feel a little more at ease, but as they were about to part that night she had impulsively given him her lips.

"You may kiss me, Gunnar," she had whispered, surprised and embarrassed by her own boldness. "I know we're not engaged, but I don't think a farewell kiss would be wrong when I'm going so far away."

Gunnar had stared at her, then his lips had touched hers for a mystic moment.

"Thanks, Button," he said in a husky voice, "thanks a lot. I'll never forget you, never."

He was gone and she had stood on the lawn for a while shivering a little inside. She did not know if she had committed a sin or not. God might be very angry with her, and Papa would be furious if he knew, but she had had to do something so Gunnar would never forget her. It was all Karin's fault, she thought. She had made Gunnar think she was very special. . . .

As Button stood there on the ship's deck she wondered if, before God, she was really engaged now. She didn't know if that would make her happy, because already Gunnar seemed far away and perhaps in the new land she might meet someone even more wonderful than Gunnar . . . perhaps. . . .

"Good evening to you, young lady," said a masculine voice behind her.

Button turned quickly and faced a young ship's officer, tall and dark, with a winning smile.

"Oh, you frightened me so I could have dropped right into the deep blue ocean," laughed Button, "but good evening to you anyway. It's a very lovely evening!"

"What's lovely about this one?" he teased, stepping beside her.

"The wind!" exclaimed Button, looking far across the sea. "The wind that blows greetings and memories from Sweden."

"You are homesick already?"

She nodded.

"I'm sorry that I'm part of the crew of this ship where we are forbidden to mingle with the passengers. If I were free, I assure you it would be a privilege to help you get rid of your loneliness!"

Button's eyes twinkled. "Already I've lost a bit of it!"

"What can I do for you?" he asked eagerly.

"Take a greeting back to my homeland."

"What shall I say?"

"Say that Button is doing fine and that she will dream a certain dream to a finish."

"I'll be glad to carry that message. You're an unusual girl and that's an unusual message. I like you, but talking to you longer might cost me my job . . . though perhaps it would be worth it. Good night, Miss Dreamer." He touched two fingers to his cap and, bowing lightly, walked away, straight and tall, without a backward glance.

Later, as Button entered her cabin, she could hear from the happy uproar that her family was waiting for her.

"There's something in your bunk, just for you, Button," cried her sister Greta, rubbing her hands in excitement. "And nobody knows who brought it!"

Papa looked very stern, but Mama was smiling, and everyone watched as Button pulled back the curtain . . . and there it stood—a large basket of the most delicious-looking fruit. Her eyes almost popped from their sockets. She found the note and stuck it in her pocket.

After the fruit had been divided and everyone had left happy, she read the note:

> See what the wind blew in! And
> all of it for the girl who likes to dream.

She slept with the note under her pillow and dreamed of the young man who had sent it. Only in her dream she was not sleeping on a hard bunk, but in a bed made of beautiful thorn-free roses. In the morning she woke up with a smile, and her heart felt light and gay. It was as though her roots were being planted before she reached the new shore, and all because a good-looking young officer had smiled at her and evidently thought her older than her years. Perhaps she would see him again? For after all, he had left her a most delightful gift.

CHAPTER 6

∿ Mama's Way

This is America!" said Papa one morning about three weeks after they had moved into the parsonage in Berkley Hills. "It is called the land of opportunity, but before we find out what it will give to us, we must learn to speak English."

"You and Mama can talk good already," said Pelle.

"Not well enough, my boy. We can speak enough to make ourselves understood, and the only way we can learn is by trying."

Button had never seen Papa in such a gay mood, but then the whole family had entered the United States with hearts beating with excitement and Papa, like the rest, was engulfed in the newness that was all about them. For days now the members of the household had shuffled furniture around and moved drapes and curtains. The parsonage had been partly furnished with pieces of furniture from the church members' attics, discarded things which they had thought would help the pastor's family until they could pick out what was needed. It had been a gracious, kind deed, and Papa and Mama had both been very grateful.

"Button," said Papa, "how about trying your first lesson in English this morning? I want you to take Vickey and go downtown and buy her a new dress. What color do you want, Vickey?"

"Blue," smiled Vickey happily. "Heavenly blue like the sky! But how can Button buy me a dress when she can't speak English?"

"That's the best way to learn, dear, by trying to make yourself understood."

"We can take the Swedish-American dictionary along," suggested Button, sliding the little book into her purse.

"Here," said Papa, "take this," and he handed Button a five-dollar bill. "You do a good job, now. You know I promised Vickey she would get a new dress when we came to our new country. Remember?"

"Perhaps I should go along," said Mama, looking a bit anxious.

"No, Maria, you would do all the talking. Let the girls try for themselves."

Mama walked with them to the bus at the corner, giving all sorts of advice. She handed them a piece of paper on which was written the place where the driver should deposit them.

Tremblingly the girls boarded the bus. They waved at Mama and sat very close together. This was a tremendous experience. What would happen?

Vickey looked up at Button with wide, fearful eyes. "Do you think you can do it, Button?" she asked in a low voice. "I'd love a new dress, but how can we buy it when you can't speak the language and don't even understand what is said to you?"

"I'll find a way," laughed Button. "I'll talk with my

hands." She opened her dictionary to the letter K, looking for the Swedish word, *klädning*, meaning dress in English. "Dress," she whispered to Vickey, "remember that word because we shall need it. Papa is challenging me . . . he doesn't think I can do it . . . but I will buy a dress . . . You wait and see."

Button and Vickey stood in front of the dress rack in Landen's Department Store. A saleslady came smilingly toward them, rattling off a long stream of words which made Button feel very stupid.

"Dress," said Button slowly to the salesclerk, pointing to Vickey. "Hurry," she said to her sister, "find *blå* in the dictionary."

Vickey put her finger on the letter B, and turned the pages. Button smiled her prettiest at the lady, showing her the money. The clerk spoke more slowly now, but it meant nothing to the girls.

"I can't find that word," sighed Vickey sorrowfully.

"Never mind," soothed Button. "See there on one of the dummies is a blue dress."

"Dress, dress," repeated Button, pointing to the dummy.

A light seemed to dawn in the clerk's eyes. She undressed the dummy and held the dress in front of Button. She asked a question. Button nodded, hoping it was the right answer. The lady smiled and ushered Button into the dressing room. She helped Button remove her own dress and slipped the soft blue one over her shoulders. Button tried to protest, but to no avail. A moment later she stood in front of a three-way mirror and gasped as she looked at herself in the glass. Could this beautiful elf be Button

Franzon? The dress was a dream, and the prettiest Button had ever seen.

Vickey's eyes were wide with wonder. "Oh, Button, you are simply beautiful! Just—just like a real princess! You must have that dress. It looks as if it were made for you. I'll wait awhile . . . but you must take the money and buy it . . . please, Button, do."

"But Papa! What would he say, Vickey? It is you who need the dress—but—but it's so beautiful!"

"Just buy it, Button. If Papa saw you now, he couldn't resist buying it for you. . . . We'll make him understand."

Button made no further attempt to make the saleslady understand. She paid for the dress with a trembling heart, and she and Vickey walked from the store carrying a big box between them.

"Are you scared, Button?" asked Vickey.

"Of course not," said Button. "It's done now! If necessary, I'll work and earn the money to pay for it myself."

They walked on to the bus in silence.

Both Mama and Papa met them on the parsonage steps.

"You really did it, Button! You bought the dress for Vickey!" cried Papa happily.

Button avoided Papa's eyes. "Almost," she answered.

"But you have the dress in the box," ventured Mama.

"But not for Vickey. . . . Oh, Papa, Papa! I got the darlingest, sweetest, bluest dress you've ever seen . . . but it's for myself. The lady could not understand that I wanted one for Vickey—and—and—I'll get a job and work for it. . . . I'll pay every penny of it. . . . Please don't be cross with me."

Papa smiled. He winked at Mama.

"Well, Button, I guess you tried your best even if the evidence is against you. Poor Vickey! As usual she gave in to make someone else happy. Mama and I will forgive you this time, and next week we'll take Vickey downtown ourselves, you can be sure, and that little girl shall have a blue dress, too."

Button smiled happily. She put on her new dress for the whole family to see and admire. It was a great day and America was a wonderful country. She just wished that Karin could see her now.

There was a freedom in America not present in Sweden. People walked with ease as if they needed not to take thought for the morrow, and they all laughed and played as if life was a wonderful playground and not a place in which to prepare for old age or eternity. It was fun living in this great big land, and little by little the memories of Sweden faded until it was hard for Button's mind to picture the old familiar places.

Of course succeeding weeks and months brought occasional times of adjustment to all of them, with many a wistful backward look to the peaceful days left behind in Lapland. However, the months and the years moved on as swiftly as a weaver's shuttle. When three years had passed since the Reverend Franzon and his family had landed in America, all of them seemed happy and contented in the new surroundings, though Button often wondered about Papa. Tenderly she watched him trying to embrace all the newness, but she feared that he still longed for his homeland and that he would never really take root in this new land. Although he never uttered one complaint, she noticed that his hair was almost white now and often there was a sad, longing look in his blue eyes.

Button was sure it was this feeling of restlessness that had caused Papa to ask his church for a leave of absence and to purchase a small farm out in the country by a lovely lake. He told the church board that he needed a rest for his tired mind and, kind as they were, they let him go when he gave his promise that he would return in a year or two if they still wanted him.

The farm was a new experience for them all, and Button found she had time to dream again. Anew and more urgently than ever the old call came as it had in the little red schoolhouse when she was a very young girl, the call that had lifted her to the highest pinnacle of joy and then thrown her down into the blackness of her own confusion. Now it knocked at her heart's door and begged to be recognized. She had done a bit of writing, a short story and a small volume of poems, but had not started a book. How could she write in a strange country? How could she express her thoughts in an unfamiliar tongue?

Thinking back upon the years that had gone by, there was much for which to be thankful. Button had learned many a lesson the hard way. She understood now that friendship, no matter how deep, and love, no matter how sincere, can burn out for lack of fuel to sustain them.

In the beginning, full of anticipation, she had awaited each letter from Gunnar and Karin. This was her tie between the new and the old world, and every letter had been full of love and longing. But as the time went by the intervals between letters became longer and longer, and the letters themselves alarmingly shorter until they contained nothing but a record of the good times her friends were having together. She had been hurt when Gunnar wrote about the weekend trip he and Karin had taken to go mountain climbing on Kebnekaise, especially since he had elaborated on how much fun it had been. Then came a letter in which he told Button he had given up his dreams of becoming a doctor.

> Button [he wrote] I believe that my father may have been right the whole time. Now that I am an executive in his office with a fine future ahead of me, the light on the forehead and the dark pit are only unpleasant memories. They will never influence my life again. Thank you for helping me to dream that noble dream of someday becoming a doctor. I have given that dream up, but it was fun dreaming it with you. . . .

It angered Button to think that Gunnar could let go of his dream so easily. But she did not let it trouble her for long, for he was too far away to affect her life and each day he seemed to get farther and farther away now that they could no longer dream together.

Then one day Button received from him a thick, heavy letter. She took it out to the garden, holding it in her hand a long time before she opened it, for her heart sensed its contents and she wanted to brace herself against being hurt. And, of course, she was right. Gunnar had fallen in love with Karin Lund, and he planned to marry her in the near future. He thanked Button with all his heart for the years that had been, calling them beautiful and sweet, but most of all he thanked her for the gift of Karin.

I know [he wrote] that this is not causing you pain or sorrow. When you left, I knew our dreams were over, but I doubted that anyone could ever fill your place. Karin did! She is adorable and likes to spring surprises on me as you did . . . but in a different way. I am sure you don't love me as much as she does and that you would be most unhappy to leave America and settle down in this godforsaken corner of the world. . . .

If she had imagined that this news would hurt, she had been mistaken. Her love for Gunnar was gone. It had either worn out or just faded away, and she was glad that it would be Karin and Gunnar who would find happiness in each other.

Karin was more concerned about Button in her letter and fear crept between the lines as she wrote:

Button dear, if for some reason, you still have any feeling for Gunnar, let me know. I will walk out of his life faster than a lamb can shake its tail, if you ask me. I am afraid that our being always together led to this. We both know that, if you had remained in Lapland, it would never have happened. Although I miss you, I can't help blessing the day you left for America. I will be honest, Button, these years with Gunnar have been the most precious gift I could ever have received. . . .

Button crumpled the letter in her hand and tossed it into the wastebasket. She lifted her head nonchalantly.

"And all she gave me was some dirt for my funeral," she smiled. And she sat down and wrote her friend a reassuring letter, wishing her happiness and telling her that

"after all, Gunnar had just been a passing fancy of youth."
She also wrote Gunnar a letter sparkling with fun. It
would be her very last letter to him.

> You know, Gunnar, life has a way of straightening
> us all out. I am glad that you never followed me to
> America for I have discovered that they don't give
> away expensive autos on street corners and that people
> really have to work to get their dollars. . . . I am glad
> for you and Karin! Love her a lot! She is a darling
> and dear as can be. . . .

So that part of her life was over. It left an empty
space in her heart for a while, but a date with a handsome
young man soon filled it. It was hard, however, to find a
young man that measured up to Gunnar, hard to find one
that measured up to her own ideals. Perhaps she never
would? She had been admired by more boys than many
a girl in her community, and by the time she was eighteen
she had had two proposals, but she had no wish to settle
down. Maybe she would be true to her calling and marry
her dream?

Button had had great difficulty in learning the new
language. Now she could laugh over it, but it had not been
so funny when she had made embarrassing mistakes because she did not understand. The only way was to laugh
at a mistake and learn a lesson from each one. All the rest
of the children had progressed well in speaking English,
but they had continued in school in the new land. There
had been quite a session that day in the parsonage when
Button had defied both Papa and Mama.

"I don't care how important it is to get a good basic
foundation in the new language. I shall not keep on study-

ing. Never! Never! I'm through forever with teachers. I think you are both cruel even to suggest it."

Mama was very provoked.

"There is no shame in learning at any age and it doesn't matter how old you are when you learn a language," she stormed. "You, Button, are a very stubborn and foolish girl."

Button yielded not an inch when Papa put his foot down and said that education was a necessity for *all* his children. She was determined to win this battle and to show Papa that, when it came to principles concerning her own life, she could be as strong and unbending as he was. She was made of the same stuff!

"All I'm going to do of importance," she said, tossing her head, "is to write a book, and I certainly don't need years in school to do that."

Button tried to ignore the pleading in Papa's eyes, but it softened her a little.

"Don't worry about me, Papa," she laughed. "When I write my book, words will pour from me like sugar from a bag. I am going to write humorous things that will make people laugh, you see; not textbooks."

Papa and Mama said no more. They knew they would get nowhere with Button, for it was impossible to talk sense to her. Someday she would pay the price for having refused an education. Papa found Button a job doing housework for an American family where nothing but English could be spoken. He was very upset at his oldest daughter's behavior and decided she would have to learn the hard way. But now those years had gone by and Button spoke English quite well, and she was back with her family on this lovely farm. Several times she tried to start her book, but no words would come. Perhaps she had boasted too much when she had said that writing would pour out from her effortlessly. She had spoken out of ignorance, using words that had no meaning.

Button sat by the blue water of the lake below the farm. The lonely, driving restlessness of her spirit had prompted her to leave the family group gathered around the organ to sing their evening hymn. When the long days had ended, and the chores had been done, Papa again looked like the preacher he had been for so many years. Button had stayed until the prayers had been said and a chapter read from the big family Bible that had been so carefully packed and lovingly carried from Sweden. A lump had formed in her throat and a wild knocking on her heart had made her want to cry or run out and throw her arms around a faithful old tree as she had done when she was a little girl.

Perhaps I miss Gunnar, after all, she thought. Perhaps I don't want him to marry Karin.

The music from the song floated over the water. There was something so homey about a family singing together around the organ, the voices from the youngest to the oldest mingling in harmony. If only that wild desire to cry had not come, she could have been there, too! It always thrilled her to see Papa seated at the organ, his gray locks curling around his ears and forming a curl in the nape of his neck when his hair was as long as it now was. And Mama's face always beamed as she sang, her eyes twinkled like stars, and the smile on her lips was like a heavenly benediction over those she loved. Nim would lean hard on the organ and Pelle always stood close to him. Vickey and Greta shared the same hymnal, their faces intent and serious-looking. Calle and Torkel, the other two boys, would have their arms around each other's shoulders and little Kerstin, her eyes big and blue as blueberries, would nestle close to Mama. What a group they made! . . . It was only Button who was missing, and if they had noticed her absence by now, they would think nothing of it, for wasn't Button like that—unpredictable, always running off at the strangest times? One moment her voice would ring with laughter and the next she would be crying. Why? No one knew. She would be sweet and cross to suit her fancy, so they all had stopped trying to understand her. Well, how could she expect her family to understand her when she couldn't even understand herself?

The gentle beauty of the night brought tears to Button's eyes and a longing crept into her heart. It was a longing for Lapland—for the mountain road—for Gunnar running to meet her, as he had so long ago, his brown eyes sparkling with happiness. She longed to hear Karin's silvery laughter and to hear the bells chime in Papa's little church on a Sabbath as the white summer night spread its wide wings over her homeland.

Perhaps, coming to America had been a mistake! Could it be that dreams remained in the land that brought them forth and that she never would be able to write her book in a strange land?

Button longed most of all for her diary! If she only could forget the tragedy of the first one, she might start another.

Then in the midst of her thoughts there seemed to come a voice from within that spoke to her." "Button," it whispered, "you're doing all right. When tomorrow comes you will smile again."

Over the waters was reflected the flame-tinted sunset sky. She raised her eyes heavenward. What a strange combination of clouds! Surely no artist's brush could capture their wild beauty. And up there in the clouds there was a door, partly open, right into God's heaven! A smile played on her lips, as she was thinking: Mama would say that a soul had just entered heaven and God had not had time to close the door. Mama said such strange things. She had such a childlike belief in the unseen. She literally talked to God, and He always answered her in a voiceless voice—at least so she claimed.

Button's head fell into her hands. She remained sitting in that position for a long while as she reached deep, deep down into her soul to try to find the great answer that she knew must be found somewhere. How did Mama get her answers from God? God did not speak in a human voice. Or did He?

Gently a hand touched Button's shoulder.

"Button"—came Papa's voice out of the night—"I wish you wouldn't follow your impulses and run away. This is the first time it's happened during our family worship. I don't like it at all, and believe me, my dear, you are the loser."

Button didn't mind Papa's mild scolding. Her heart beat fast with joy. Papa had missed her and had come to find her. Just to have him beside her took that awful loneliness away. She would talk to Papa. She would ask him things. Papa must know all about Mama and God.

She sat up and faced him as he seated himself on the large stone beside her.

"Papa, I am sorry. I don't know why I run away like that. There—there is something inside me that seems bigger than I. . . . It drives me and makes we want to run off. But I'm glad you came to me, very glad."

Papa placed his hand on hers, and they sat in silence for a while. Button was first to break it.

"Tell me," she said, "about Mama. How can she talk to God? I have heard her say words into the air as if God was a real person, walking and standing right beside her. And she seems to get an answer, Papa. She just waits until she knows God has answered."

"Mama has always done things in a unique way, Button. If I were you, I'd concentrate on being myself and not on trying to imitate Mama. Her talking is really praying. She just does it in an easy way, as naturally as breathing."

"If I did that, my voice wouldn't carry a prayer. It would just find its way over the lake and be lost . . . lost in nothingness."

"Button," said Papa in a kind voice, "God does speak to men. He always has and He always will. In the Old Testament He spoke to Moses in a burning bush and to Elijah in a still, small inner voice; and later in the Bible, to Paul, in a great shining light. All these men claimed that they heard a voice speaking, but others beside them heard none. God spoke, and they heard His voice in their souls. If you, dear, have something special on your heart to talk to God about, just talk to Him as you talk to me, and I know that when the answer comes you'll understand it. It is God's voice within your soul."

Papa stood up.

"I'll leave you now, leave you by yourself with your God. If you need me, I'll be in my study."

Papa placed a light kiss on her cheek and walked up the hill toward the house. Button walked along the road by the lake toward the woodland. She walked slowly.

Would she know the answer as Papa had said she would if she also prayed the way Mama did? Would God really answer if she prayed without kneeling and with her eyes open?

"Dear Father God," she heard herself say. "You know all the things I'm thinking and even the things I have hidden carefully deep down in my heart. Long ago, when I was a little girl, I had a dream of becoming an author and writing a book that would make people laugh and be happy. Please, God, make my dream come true. Help me to become a writer, God, please, please."

The night was quiet around her and slowly that tranquil stillness of peace floated into her soul. Her heart did not beat wildly as before. And so thoughts came to her mind—wonderful, beautiful thoughts that had not been there a moment ago. They came clear and fast . . . as fast as she could grasp them and she put them into words, speaking them slowly and softly as she walked along.

"I will write a book someday. Nothing will stop me now because God will help me. I shall dream my dream so high and it will be so lofty that it will reach a golden hill where God will keep it until I am ready to have it returned to me. I will eat it . . . I will sleep with it. . . . it will be so much a part of me that someday it will be fulfilled. God will fulfill it through me. . . . Thank you . . . thank you . . . for answering my prayer. My dream is like a delicate flower which will blossom and give me joy . . . in God's fullness of time."

Button's feet had wings as they flew back to the farmhouse. She began remembering the times she had heard Mama talk to God, and now she understood it. She had been very small the first time she had heard it. Mama had gone upstairs to make the beds and Button was playing in the big kitchen, in the Lapland parsonage. She knew Mama was alone upstairs and yet she heard her speaking as though someone was with her. Perhaps, she thought, Mama is talking to me. She ran to the foot of the stairs and called, "Mama, did you talk to me?"

And Button could still remember how surprised Mama had looked as she came to the landing and looked down at her with that warm smile on her lips, saying, "No, little one. I didn't talk to you. I was talking with God."

Yes, she had wondered then how Mama did it, for she was so strict when her children prayed. They had to kneel and close their eyes and approach God in holiness and reverence. And here Mama herself had been walking around making beds, so she couldn't even have closed her eyes. Button could not understand it.

Once Mama had been standing alone out on the lawn gazing upward while a fine rain came down on her blonde hair. But Mama did not seem conscious of the rain; her whole face was beaming as Button heard her say, "God"— and Mama had raised her voice a little as if it took more volume to penetrate the clouds—"You saw the lawn needed water. Thank you for sending the rain to do my watering for me as I was much too busy baking. A great big thank you, God."

She had heard Mama ask God to bless the dough when she made bread, bless it so the yield would be large enough to feed so many mouths; and she had asked Him to keep the milk from souring in the hot summertime.

"Father God, You know that my children don't like sour milk, but if it does sour, You know they would have to drink it, because we can't afford to waste it."

Once, while Mama was holding Pelle's shoes in her hands, Button had overheard her talking to God as if she were scolding Him. "God, you forgot to answer my prayer of last week concerning Pelle's shoes. They are wearing out much too fast. Now I am asking You again, bless his shoes; he has such busy feet."

Button remembered all these things, but she also remembered that Mama believed in her prayers with a childlike simple faith. Never would she forget the school morning she had awakened with a sore throat and her body wet with perspiration. She tried to swallow but felt as if her throat was full of mashed potatoes mixed with gravel. She had sent Greta to fetch Mama so Mama could see she was in no condition to go to school. And Mama had come and placed her cool hand on Button's hot forehead.

"You are real sick, Button *lilla*," said Mama, "poor girl."

Button was thankful for Mama's sympathetic words.

"I am too sick to go to school, Mama, and we're having a very important lesson. Now the teacher will never know how well I learned it."

Mama asked all about her sickness. She shook her head as she looked at Button's throat.

"Yes, you have a good dose of whatever it is, but we'll take care of it. You believe that God does not want little girls to be sick, don't you?"

Button nodded. God cared about everybody. Papa said so. Mama placed her hand on Button's forehead and knelt down by the bed. Her prayer came hurriedly as if she did not have too much time to spare on a busy morning with seven children to feed and most of them to get ready for school.

"Dear God," she prayed, "You see little Button here in bed, too sick to go to school where she has an important lesson. I think she has a little fever and a sore throat, but those things are nothing for You, God, so I ask You please to make her well immediately. Thank you for being so good to us. Amen."

Mama gave Button a big smile, then left the room, closing the door softly behind her. Button snuggled down under the quilt. Despite the sore throat, it would be good to lie here under the covers and smell Mama's baking and listen to her singing as she went about her day's work. Perhaps she would make something especially good for Button since she was a sick girl. If she did, Button would try to swallow no matter how much it hurt. And Papa might play on the organ for her. He knew how much she enjoyed hearing him play and sing . . . and. . . . The door pushed open and there stood Mama.

"Button, what in the world are you doing in bed?" she asked the bewildered child, who now sat up and stared at her.

"I am sick, Mama, remember? I have a sore throat and a fever. . . . You couldn't have forgotten already. . . . I told you about it just a few minutes ago."

Mama took one step nearer Button's bed and pointed her finger at her daughter.

"You *were* sick, Button," she corrected. "You *did* have a sore throat and a fever, but no more! I prayed for you, didn't I? Get up this minute and go to school!"

Mama marched out from the room without a backward glance, and Button crawled slowly out of bed and dressed in her school clothes. She thought of her sore throat and how cold the Lapland air was. . . .

She felt sick most of the day, but she hardly dared to think about it, for that surely would be a sin after Mama had prayed for her. She shivered a little as she sat on her bench, but by the time she started home that afternoon, her sickness had left her. She simply could not return sick to the parsonage when Mama had prayed her well.

Button smiled happily as she entered the farmhouse. What a wonderful night this had turned out to be! A heavy burden had been rolled from her shoulders. God had taken her dream to keep for her until she was ready to write. No longer need she worry. It might take weeks, or months, or years . . . but in God's time her dream would be fulfilled, and she would wait even if it took a hundred years.

BOOK II

CHAPTER 7

❧ For Better or Worse

Years, thought Button, were like a broad road. Sometimes there were long stretches of straightness; again there would be twists and turns, and one could not see very far ahead. Then sometimes around a bend would be waiting a fine surprise—a golden sunset or a lovely lake.

The first years in America had been like that, so different one from another. As Button had gone through the process of growing up, Mama had looked worriedly at her because there seemed to be no thoughts of marriage in Button's mind. Mama could not understand that Button was having a good time being beaued about by many a young man, but that as yet she had not met one who in any way resembled Gunnar. Not that her heart any longer beat with rapture at the thought of him—the years had seen to that—but rather that she could not recapture the glow and sincerity and sweetness that had surrounded that first love.

And then she met Eric Bjork! Eric had been as different from Gunnar as anyone could be, but for the first time a spark of the old romance had been kindled, and her

111

heart had been warmed with a gentle yearning. That had been the beginning of a new era in her life.

At the open window white ruffled curtains fluttered in the warm summer breeze. Out in the huge oak trees birds were singing their morning songs. There must be at least a hundred of them, thought Button, as she let her head sink deeper into the soft white pillow. She lay very still so she would not awaken Eric, who slept close beside her. As she listened to his even breathing, her heart almost turned a somersault in sheer delight; she was deliriously happy in her role as wife! She could hear the lazy lapping of the tiny waves along the shore. Across the lake the White Mountains towered against the sky.

Last night she and Eric had come upon the cabin bathed in moonlight. Never would she forget the thrill she felt, as leaning over her husband's shoulder, she saw him sign their names together for the first time. *Mr. and Mrs. Eric Bjork,* he had written, then turned and grinned at her as contentedly as though he owned the whole world. Button had returned a smile so radiant it proclaimed beyond a doubt that she was the world's happiest bride. She had married the man she loved, and this was their honeymoon.

"Let's not make any plans, Eric," Button had suggested when they had discussed where they would go on their honeymoon. "We'll just get in your car and drive until we want to stop. Then we'll stay at the first tourist place we find. I bet when the people there see the happiness in our faces, they'll know we're honeymooners and offer us the very best accommodations."

"That will suit me, Button," Eric had assured her and

produced one of his rare, warm smiles that penetrated right down to her toes.

Eric was not a man of fancy words. Nor was he the tall, dark man Button had dreamed her husband would be. If anyone had told her a year ago that she would marry Eric, she would have flatly denied it. She would have said, "Eric Bjork is a fine person, kind, good-looking and perhaps a little well-to-do, but wonderful as he is, he is not the one for me!"

They had few things in common, and Eric was not one who wanted to become entangled in Button's dreams. But from the first she had enjoyed his company, feeling secure in his presence, so she saw him frequently. Soon she found she was going out only with him.

"I can't understand it," she had confided to Vickey, who at seventeen was already married. "I don't know whether or not I love him. This feeling is so different from the one I had for Gunnar in Lapland."

Vickey had patted her on the shoulder.

"Don't worry, Sister, one of these days you'll know if you love him enough to marry him, just as I did with John."

And Button did know in her heart the night he had proposed to her. They were out riding.

"Button," Eric had said as he stopped the car beside a shimmering lake, "I want to tell you something strange. Although I've been taking girls out since I was old enough, there has never been a thought of marriage in my mind. I always wanted to be a bachelor. You're the first girl I ever wanted to marry. Will you marry me?"

Button had laughed. "Why, Eric," she said, "if that is supposed to be a proposal, it certainly isn't a very romantic one. Don't you know you are supposed to sweep a girl off her feet or at least take her in your arms to demonstrate your words?"

He had looked at her for a long while and then had started the car and driven on.

"You are like all the rest," he had said finally. "In your heart, you are laughing at me. Well, I won't ask you again, Miss Franzon. If you love me, you'll have to come to me."

Without another word he had driven her to the parsonage, escorted her to the door, and driven off with such speed that Mama had called out, "What in the world, Button? Did you and Eric have a fight?"

"Oh, no, Mama . . . not at all. We're the best of friends. . . . We might even get married."

And Button had left Mama standing there just as perplexed as she herself felt. Inside she had been fuming. Why, he could not treat her like that! She would never go to him—never—never. Who did he think he was anyway?

But she found that she was thinking of him day and night and hoping that he would call again. But two weeks passed and not a sign of him. Eric was a tool designer and an exceptionally fine one, with an excellent income. He must have money in the bank, and he was rather handsome in an intent, serious way. Very rarely did his face break into a happy smile. He was of medium height with blond hair. He, too, had been born in Sweden. That was one thing they did have in common, speaking their own country's language and talking about the old country they had left behind.

"He needs me to make him happy," Button reasoned, "and I need him to keep me balanced." It would be good to find him waiting when she came back from her dream tours. Resting in his strong arms, she'd feel safe. So she waited and waited for his call, refusing to go out with other boys. And one night it came.

"Button," said his voice on the telephone, "I couldn't hold out any longer! Will you come out with me tonight and look at the house I'd like to buy for our future home?"

Eric is pretty sure of himself, she thought, but she felt very happy, so she went with him to see the little white bungalow with green shutters. To Button it was almost like seeing her dream house in Lapland. Eric was kind, but he did not speak of marriage, although his strong arms around her and his kisses told her more than words.

"Eric," Button had said that night, "you'll have to ask Papa for my hand if we are to get married. Also you'll have to join the church, for it's understood in our household that we will marry only church people, and you——"

He stopped her with a kiss. "I'll do both those things, dear. I want you, Button. Oh, I know it may be hard for me to fit into your large family or into your dreams, but somehow I must manage it. You know, Button, sometimes you seem to me like a lost bird flying around trying to find a warm nest. That's why I want to buy you a home, so you will always know where you belong."

But Eric found he could not ask Papa for Button's hand.

"I am scared!" he confessed. "And anyway, that's old-fashioned. People don't do that any more. We, you and I, are the ones who want to get married. What has Papa to do with it?"

"You'd be surprised!" laughed Button. "One thing I surely know, you don't know my Papa!"

At Eastertime Eric joined Papa's church. (Farm days

were over and Papa had gone back to his lifework.) Papa was most happy to receive Eric into the fellowship of the church, for he was convinced that Eric was sincere in joining. Eric still refused, however, to ask Papa for Button's hand, so she finally had to help him.

"Why don't you write Papa a letter, Eric?" she asked, the idea just having popped into her mind, "and if you don't know what to say, I can help you."

"That's a good idea, Button," said Eric in a relieved voice. "Write it soon, will you?"

After Button had finished the letter, she showed it to Eric:

Dear Pastor Franzon,
      I am writing to ask you a great favor, the greatest I have ever asked of a human being. Button and I love each other and I would consider it the most wonderful thing in the world if I could make her my wife. I promise to be a good husband and with God's help to provide well for her. I shall count the moments until I receive your reply, which I hope will be favorable.

                                        With deepest respect,
                                        Eric Bjork

"Why, Button, that's a good job. I couldn't have expressed it better myself. How in the world could you do it?"

"Two things," smiled Button, "a mind and a heart. Now you must copy it in your handwriting and mail it to Papa."

It did not take Papa long to have a talk with Button and to return a favorable reply to the overjoyed Eric and by Christmas time Button wore a sparkling diamond on her finger. Eric purchased the white bungalow and the two of them spent every spare moment picking out furniture and getting ready for a June wedding. What wonderful memories these happy, happy days made.

Now Button looked over at Eric, noting his strong fine features. He was her dear husband and, happy as she was, of that she was certain. Of course, he had been pretty nervous on the wedding day, and they were both relieved when it was over. Eric was not a man who sought out the limelight, so different from her own family where each person seemed destined to be in some position that dealt with the public. Well, she would get accustomed to this new life and learn to love it. The wedding had been so beautiful! Poor Papa! Having two weddings so close, Vickey's and hers, had been hard on his purse strings, but he had not complained when he had seen the light in Button's eyes.

"After all," he had said to Button, "our family can use a man who knows how to work with his hands."

Mama, of course, had cried all through the ceremony and the tears had been streaming down her cheeks when she had kissed them good-bye.

"Be good to her, Eric," she had whispered. "I declare, she can sometimes be a pack of trouble."

Papa had shaken Eric's hand so hard Button was afraid it would fall right off.

"Eric, my son," Papa had said in his preaching voice, "you are getting one of the nicest girls that ever was born. Oh, she might be up to mischief, she always was, but your life will never be dull with Button beside you."

Dear Papa, how good he had been. Button knew that

both Papa and Mama had been a bit disappointed that she had not married a minister. Perhaps they wondered how she would get along in such a complete change of environment, but Eric was smart and they felt he would go a long way in his line, and as far as worldly goods were concerned, Button would have much more than Vickey, who had married a preacher. So Papa and Mama had given Eric and Button their blessings with hearts overflowing.

At the close of the wedding reception Eric and Button had slipped away to begin their honeymoon journey. Eric was proud of his shiny new car, but they had not gone very far when Button sitting close beside him said in a wistful voice:

"Oh, Eric, I can't bear to think of our little dream house being alone on our wedding night. It will have its arms stretched out in a warm welcome, but no one will come up that walk unless—do you think we can turn back? I'd so much rather stay in our own home tonight and start our trip tomorrow. Am I being foolish, Eric, when we are already on our way? But darling, being in our own place would be heavenly."

Eric had turned the car around and headed for home. He was as glad as Button was to spend the first night of his married life in his own home. Thus in the evening dusk they had stood outside their bungalow, gazing at the red geraniums blossoming in the window-boxes beneath the front windows, and at the roses, which Eric had planted that spring, climbing up the porch trellis.

Eric, full of pride, took out the new key, but Button held him back.

"Wait, darling," she whispered. "Let's just stand here

and take it all in for a few minutes and then, as we walk toward the door, hold me very, very close."

She needed his comforting arms around her as she started this new life. What would it be like? Would she always be as happy as this? Would they have little ones running around in this house, pressing their noses against the windowpanes? Would Eric learn to smile more, and would she be the good wife she wanted to be? As Eric opened the door, they stopped.

"Would you think me queer, if I asked that we kneel, Eric?" Button asked.

"Not at all, honey! I'll do anything to make you happy," answered Eric, holding her hand tightly in his.

Button remembered Mama telling how she and Papa had knelt at the threshhold before entering their home in Lapland when they had returned as newlyweds. She had always wanted to do the same. They knelt and prayed silently that God would bless them and everyone who entered their door. Then Eric carried her across the threshold and kissed her tenderly.

"Welcome home, Mrs. Bjork!" he said with a strange catch in his husky voice.

Certainly everything had been perfect, blessings unnumbered were pouring down upon them. She was sure Eric would be the kindest and most thoughtful husband in the whole world.

Now, lying here in the big bed in the log cabin, she remembered how Eric and she had wandered through their home that night before last, and she had touched each new thing caressingly. They had planned where to place the numerous wedding presents that would add so much to their new home. How spotlessly clean their house was!

They must always keep it so—no discord, no ugly words, no complaints, no criticism . . . just joy and love and laughter for years and years until eternity began.

So they crept into their new mahogany bed whispering lovers' sweet nothings to each other. Button had bubbled over with words.

"Darling," she murmured with her check pressed close against her husband's, "promise me you'll live to be a hundred and eleven years old, because I could never think of life without you, Eric."

He laughed heartily.

"Why do you laugh?" Button asked, a tiny bit annoyed.

"Oh, I was thinking that you would be a hundred and three that fall—and a picture flashed through my mind of how you would look."

"Now that wasn't even kind of you, Eric," she scolded, "and surely not a bit romantic. Don't you know that to you I shall always be beautiful because love is ageless? Oh, Eric, Eric, you must learn to say pretty things to me. And do you know what? I would simply fold up and die if you stopped loving me!"

Eric kissed the frown from her forehead and held her so close she could hear his heart beating wildly.

"Honey," he said seriously, "you'll have to learn to accept me as I am, and I am not a man of flowery words. I am not capable of feeding you those pretty phrases you seem to crave. It's too hard for me to get them out, Button. I want you to understand this about me from the beginning. But, dear, you will learn that there are other ways beside words in which a man shows his beloved that he loves her. Love is also measured by the way he acts and what he does for her."

"Thank you for telling me, Eric, the first night. That was very wise of you. Now I will understand you, so please, don't worry about it."

In the morning they had driven toward the White Mountains in beautiful, picturesque New Hampshire, and that night in the moonlight they had seen the vacancy sign on the log cabin by the big lake. They both felt they must have been divinely led to this spot, for they couldn't have found a prettier place to spend their honeymoon.

Yes, life was wonderful and Eric would make a fine husband and father. God would bless them as He had blessed Papa and Mama. Button touched Eric lightly on the cheek.

"Wake up sleepyhead," she whispered. "It's morning! Even a hundred and eleven years are too short to live if we're going to waste them sleeping."

Eric reached out his arms and drew her close. "Already you have become a very disturbing wife. But you are as adorable as you are crazy. I know now what your Papa meant when he said my life would never be dull living with his daughter!"

That first year was heavenly, and there certainly wasn't one dull moment. To Button marriage was far more than she had ever dreamed it could be. Every day Eric became dearer, and she learned that underneath his reserved manner he hid much goodness. It shone out in so many little ways, but most of all Button felt secure in his strength. Yes, Eric and she belonged together. God had made them for each other. He was a perfect husband, and they would

sail through life on a calm sea and someday there would
be children to share their happiness. Button needed only to
close her eyes and she could hear the sound of children's
voices. In her mind she had already turned one of the rooms
into a dainty nursery. Tired as he was, Eric would come
home with a glow on his face and stop in the kitchen doorway while she flew into his outstretched arms. Life would
always be like this for them even when they were both old.
She would keep it this way and would never lose the thrill
of feeling that pressure of his fingers which he had told her
meant, "I love you, darling." No, they would always treasure this perfect happiness which hovered over their home
like a thousand angel wings.

In those first few months, with Mama as her teacher,
Button learned to be a good housekeeper. And Mama also
told her how to handle a husband the right way.

"One of the most important things," Mama had advised as they sat in the sunshine on Button's front step one
clear October afternoon when Mama had come for lunch,
"is always to have the dinner ready when your man comes
home from work. Have the table set as perfectly as though
you expected company, the silver straight, and a centerpiece of flowers or something green. This adds so much to
the meal. You see, Button dear, it's the small things that
make a house into a home. Eric should smell rolls baking
and coffee percolating as he comes up the walk at night. He
should know that loving arms will greet him and that busy
hands have prepared everything for his comfort. Thus he
can leave his burdens outside the door and forget his weari-
ness from the strain of work. He should feel that here he is
king and this his castle."

"I love to hear you tell me these things, Mama. I guess

a woman who does all those things will never lose her husband's love."

"No, of that I am sure," continued Mama happily, "and don't forget, my dear, that the nicest music to a hungry man's ears is the clatter of pots and pans in the kitchen. It makes a man feel important. God made him that way so never blame him for it. When you promised in your marriage vow to reverence your husband, it did not mean that you would gaze at him adoringly night and day as some people do at a preacher in the pulpit. No, it meant that you would darn his socks, wash and starch his shirts, have his meals ready and give him plenty to eat. Also it meant that you would keep yourself clean and pleasant-smelling, using a little touch of perfume behind the ear on the side of the face you turn toward him to kiss."

"Oh, Mama, you are so clever. I'll never forget your advice."

Button was especially glad she had not married a minister so she would have had to live in a parsonage the way Vickey did . . . even if Vickey thought that was part of heaven.

"It takes a lot of living to make a house a homey place, Button," insisted Vickey. "Just think of the generations of people who must have lived in this old parsonage. Here people have laughed and cried for almost a hundred years. Its wooden arms have sheltered them in joy and through sorrow. It possesses character, style, memories. I'm not a bit envious of your new bungalow."

"But our house belongs to us, Vickey! Someday it too will be old, but we are the ones to begin its story. Here we came on our wedding night. We were the first to ask God's blessing upon it. Here I cooked our first meal and in time, here I'll hold our first baby in my arms. And it is small—so small that when we're away from it, we can hold it in the palm of one hand. We will have years and years to pour our love into it."

Well, they were both contented and satisfied with what they had, and that was the important thing. Every object in their homes was hallowed, and how could it be otherwise when in each all was peace and joy and love?

There was something Button had carried with her from Sweden that she wished she could have left behind. It was a sense of fear about America. People there had told her hair-raising stories of murders, kidnapings and burglaries which happened all the time. She had tried to drive these stories from her mind, but on nights when Eric worked very late, they came back to haunt her. One day she read about an axe murder which had taken place in their community, and although she did not mention it to Eric, she was almost overcome with fear. What would stop a man like that from coming into their little home in the silence of the night and murdering them both? She knew it was a horrid thought, and that Eric would be very cross if he knew that she let things like that take possession of her mind. She tried to think of happy things, but when she was alone, her mind would wander back to the murder and she would shake like a leaf. Her imagination built the fear up more and more. It was best to be on guard at all times. But how? So the idea came to her. No one would be able to sneak up on Eric and her as they were peacefully sleeping in their bed if she secured the door. The next day Button purchased a large brass hook and ring from the hardware store and fastened them in their proper places.

She wondered what Eric would say about it. She wouldn't tell him, but would hook the door after he was in bed. If he happened to catch her, she'd just have to explain that she hadn't been able to sleep because of the fear that possessed her. Eric would surely pamper her about the hook . . . he had to.

Eric did not see Button slipping the hook on the door that night, but in the morning they were awakened by a severe thunder storm. She had awakened before Eric, having enjoyed undisturbed sleep for the first time in weeks. She was lying in bed thinking that the hook really did not detract too much from the look of the door when Eric opened his eyes and spotted it.

"Button," he cried, "how did that hook get on the door?"

"I put it there," said Button meekly.

"Do you mean to tell me that you hammered a huge hook into our expensive woodwork? How could you do a thing like that and what in the world for?"

Never before had Button heard Eric speak to her in that tone of voice. Her heart sank. Perhaps he would not understand after all. Better tell him the truth.

"I put it there so we wouldn't be murdered at night when we were sleeping. I've been terribly frightened ever since the axe murder. I had to do something!"

Eric sat up in bed. He was furious.

"Are you implying that I am not capable of protecting you? Do you think I am a mouse? And there you are sleeping right beside me! What do you think people will think when they see that hook? They'll think I am as frightened as you! It's ridiculous. I shall remove it at once."

"You will do nothing of that kind, Mr. Bjork. When

other couples get murdered in their beds, you'll thank God you had a wife smart enough to take precautions against it. If you touch that hook, I'll walk out of this house and never come back!"

"O. K. I suppose that hook will have to stay. It will remain as a symbol of the disgrace of my manhood and the foolishness of your womanhood. It has been like that since Adam and Eve. A woman loves to make a fool of a man."

Button stared at her husband. The stinging tears were hard to keep back, but she wouldn't allow herself to cry. She looked at him with eyes full of hurt pride and contempt. "I think you are horrid!" she blurted out.

Eric neither answered nor looked her way. He dressed quickly, walked through the hall and kitchen, and, without eating breakfast, he opened the door and slammed it hard behind him. Not a word of good-bye had come from him.

Button dressed slowly. She let the tears fall now. Her whole beautiful dream world had tumbled down. Everything was spoiled. The ugly words had come, their house was not the same . . . would never be the same. Eric was not perfect! He was very human and had a terrible temper. No one in the parsonage would ever have walked out like that, or if he did, a few minutes later he would have been on his knees, asking God's and the injured one's forgiveness. Now everything she considered sacred in their home had been desecrated by Eric's act. What should she do?

Button searched her own heart carefully and honestly. Could she help it if she was frightened by the gruesome things she read in the newspaper? Wasn't it Eric's duty to love and understand . . . for better or worse?

Then suddenly a wild desire to write came over her. Soon her pen was flying over the paper at a furious rate, the words coming so fast she had a hard time holding them back. The story she wrote was about a young girl who thought she had married a perfect man but after a year of married life discovered his imperfections. There had been a big quarrel about a minor thing, and the husband had left the house without eating his breakfast or kissing the wife good-bye, and he had slammed the door behind him. The young wife was sitting in her living room thinking of what an ill-tempered, inconsiderate, selfish brute of a male she had married when the door bell rang twice. Carefully wiping the tears from her eyes, she had opened the door and there on the steps stood a boy with a big box, which he handed her. Upon opening it, she found it contained two dozen beautiful red roses.

"Oh, my husband is sorry he hurt me this morning," the wife said to herself while all the bitterness she had felt completely vanished away. "This is his way of saying that he wants me to forgive him. Now I must go him one better. I'm not going to let him know that the flowers have come, but I'll telephone him to say how sorry I am for my part in the argument . . . I'll admit I was wrong . . . I'll forgive him and he'll be happy again—thanks to the red roses."

The husband seemed very surprised when she called him, but they made up and all was well. In a few minutes she would call him back and thank him for the roses. As she put back the receiver, the bell rang again, and there stood the same boy looking flushed and embarrassed.

"L-l-lady," he stammered, "will you forgive the awful mistake I made in delivering the roses to you? I lost the card and thought I remembered the correct house number, but I just found the card and I should have given them to the lady next door."

As Button wrote, time and space were forgotten and even the unhappiness Eric had caused her dissolved into thin air. All her clouds had vanished and once again she was basking beneath a blue heaven. After the story was finished (and she had given it a happy ending), she placed it in an envelope and mailed it to a magazine. Perhaps, after all, this was a day of good luck, and she had needed a jolt to make her write a story.

After the envelope was mailed, she took courage and called Eric.

"Eric," she said sweetly, "this is the naughty girl you married a year ago. . . . I got lonesome for my husband."

"Is that because there is a bad man in the house?" he asked teasingly, but he was laughing, and Button knew his anger had gone.

"I've removed the hook, Eric, and filled in the holes with plastic wood. Then I rubbed some polish over the spots and they are hardly noticeable. Am I forgiven?"

"Of course! After all, since this was my wife's first offense, I'll have to be lenient. But you'll have to promise not to tear down my manly pride again!"

"I promise, Eric, and there'll be steak waiting tonight. Why don't you ask your boss to come for dinner? Don't tell him I suggested it, and will he be surprised when he sees what a delicious meal I've prepared. He'll wish he wasn't a bachelor and will propose to the first girl he sees just to get a wife—after having had a sample of your wife's cooking!"

"Perhaps I will ask Mr. Nord, Button. He may think that we have steaks every meal! But let me tell you some-

thing, Mrs. Bjork, you are the world's biggest schemer. . . .
But I don't mind as long as your schemes include a steak."

Button hung up the receiver The world was fine again.
She was sure her story would sell. She would, indeed, cook
the biggest steak her money would buy for Mr. Nord and
her husband.

CHAPTER 8

❧ The Angel

Button's story was accepted by the small magazine to which she had sent it, and she received a check for five dollars with the request for further stories of a similar type. This made her so happy she felt as if she were dancing on clouds. With the money she bought a heavy doorstop which she told Eric would always stand by their bedroom door as a reminder to her not to fasten any more hooks on it.

The first year of their marriage had flown by as swiftly as if it had wings, and again it was summer. Eric and Button, with Vickey and John, had rented a summer cottage for two weeks. The White Mountains had been the choice of Eric and Button, since there they could relive their honeymoon days. The two weeks were much too short, and Button found it unbearable to think of going back to the city heat.

"I still have two more weeks' vacation," said John a couple of days before their time was up. "If this place hasn't been rented, why don't we stay another two weeks and you, Eric, could drive up for weekends? It may be hard on you, but at least it would give you two long weekends here."

"Poor Eric," sighed Button. "That's the only time I wish you were a preacher, when vacation comes around."

"I'll live through it," laughed Eric, who looked brown and rested, "and it will be wonderful for you, Button. Let's go and ask if we can have it for two more weeks!"

They returned with good news and settled down for another two weeks of stimulating mountain air.

Without Eric the week seemed endless to Button and when Friday night finally came, she announced that she would walk up the road to meet her husband. She couldn't wait to be in his arms again. She tied a bandana tightly around her hair. A fine rain was falling, but the clouds were breaking and it looked as if the rain might cease at any moment. Darkness was beginning to fall like a dark veil over the woodland, so Button walked fast. Now and then a bird chirped, and far in the distance a dog was barking. From the lake came the gay voices of young people who were swimming despite the rain and darkness. Oh, how Button longed for the sound of Eric's car! He simply must come before it got too dark or how would she find her way back without a flashlight? How foolish of her to have forgotten to take one along. But she walked bravely on, for surely Eric would come at any moment, and he would be proud to see that she had walked all this way by herself just to meet him. She must have walked at least a full mile.

This was a very special night! So special that only God in heaven and she knew the importance of it. She sat down by the edge of the road to rest awhile, drinking in the scent of fresh pine. Would Eric be glad to hear the news? And how was she to break it to him? She could say, "Eric, the most wonderful thing in the world has happened to us—the miracle of the ages from the beginning of time. . . .

We—you and I are going to be parents—and do you know what? . . . It's going to be a Christmas present or a New Year's one anyway. Isn't it wonderful?"

Or perhaps she should just put her arms around his neck and kiss him and whisper, "I am about to become the mother of your first-born, Mr. Bjork!"

Or better yet, she could just look deep into his eyes and let him read the secret in hers, for by now she was sure it was written all over her face. A joy like hers could not be concealed.

It had been a strain to wait all these weeks to tell him, but she had wanted to be absolutely sure first, and Mama had said, "When you feel life, then you are sure, Button." She had shared her news with Mama, Vickey and Greta—but Eric—well—she had wanted to be without a doubt before she told him.

And now, just today, it had happened. Button had been having a good swim in the cool, clear water and had sat down on the dock to dry off. A beautiful bluebird had flown to a branch not far from where she was sitting. It sat there looking down upon her, and then, for the first time, she felt something stir within her, like the lifting of a tiny finger—then it felt more pronounced like a tiny ball rolling over. Oh, it had brought tears to Button's eyes and she had offered a prayer of thanksgiving for her happiness. Then she had gone up to the cottage to tell Vickey. Button had stood there gazing into Vickey's blue eyes and then embraced her sister.

"Vickey," she cried, "I felt it! It is real! So tiny—but it let me know it really is there. I'm so happy I could die!"

And Vickey had kissed her. "God bless you!" she had whispered.

It had seemed to Button that night would never come. With night would come Eric and she would tell him her secret and need no longer keep it locked in her heart.

The rain had stopped. A lone bird twittered in the tall treetop. The air felt fresh and pure. She took a deep breath and filled her lungs with mountain air. "For my little one," she smiled.

From now on she would always think of that new little life first. How much she loved it already! And now Eric, too, could share this new love. She could hear a car coming down the twisting road. Her heart almost stopped with joy! It was he! It was Eric! She tore off her bandana and waved it. Eric stopped the car and opened the door.

"Hi! How about a lift for a tired hiker?" she laughed.

"Why, Button, how did you dare to venture this far into the woods by yourself? But it's a very pleasant surprise, indeed."

She seated herself close beside him and he kissed her hungrily.

"I had to meet you, Eric. I was terribly lonesome!"

"That's fine, honey. I like to have you get lonesome for your husband."

They drove in silence thankful to be together again.

Then, "Eric, don't you think it would be nice for me to have a little son to walk with me?"

Eric laughed. "No," he said teasingly, "positively not. I don't want any competition—at least not for many years."

Button's heart stood still with fear. Eric did not want a baby! How could she tell him now? Why had he spoiled it all? Her sensitive, foolish heart ached and her throat was full of crying. She pulled herself away from him, almost hugging the door.

"I don't care what you want, Eric," she blurted out. "You are going to have a baby whether you want one or not—because—because—there isn't a thing we can do about it now."

Eric slammed on the brakes. "Button, you silly little girl! Do you realize we almost had an accident? Do you think that's a kind way to break such news to an expectant father? Do you really mean it, dearest? Are you sure? I couldn't take it if you were fooling me!"

There were tears in Eric's eyes—real tears—and Button felt that she had reached a joy so divine it could not belong to this earth alone.

The world became topsy-turvy. Everything was centered around one thing, the baby . . . December . . . Christmas! Eric was the most tender expectant father Button had ever seen. It was as if he had been transformed, all the mirth that had been held back by his reserved nature suddenly exploded. He was a happy man!

Button forgot about her writing. This new experience so completely dominated her that she poured every ounce of her strength into creating a nursery so beautiful and sweet that it would have been fit for a prince. For the little white crib she embroidered a bedspread, showing diminutive angels showering roses down from a blue sky. Weeks of work went into the scarf that covered the small bureau and into the white ruffled curtains which were tied back with wide pink satin ribbons.

Eric bought a daybed for the nursery, saying to Button, "For you, darling. I know you'll want to be near the baby when you first come home from the hospital; it will be so helpless then, you won't want to leave it alone."

Button made some fluffy pillows to throw upon the bed so it would not look so large amid the baby things. Three months before she was due to have the baby all was in readiness and the nursery became to her almost as sacred as a shrine. Each day she knelt and prayed by the little crib, asking that the new life might be healthy and happy and good.

Then Button had to face her first disappointment in connection with the nursery. There was to be a big convention held in Papa's church and delegates would be coming from near and far. Thus Mama came on a special errand to see Button on a sunny November morning.

"Button," said Mama, as she sat drinking coffee in her daughter's spotless kitchen, "I informed the convention committee yesterday that I knew that you and Eric would be glad to take one of the delegates for a couple of nights. We have so many people coming that we have to make use of every available place. Everyone who has a space at all has volunteered to take at least one guest. We are having seven in the parsonage for four days. Your guest will be an elderly farm lady, and I'm sure she will just love to sleep in your little nursery."

Button, her eyes getting bigger and bigger, stared at Mama. "Mama, you can't mean that! Not that we shall ask an old lady to sleep in our baby's nursery."

"Oh, she won't mind that it is a nursery, Button. She'll be grateful to have so nice a place to stay."

"Well, I should say SHE won't mind." Button was so upset she could hardly speak. "I should say SHE would be very comfortable, indeed, only she's not going to be; no one is going to sleep in the nursery until the baby has slept in it first."

Mama looked at Button a long time without answering, but under her steady gaze Button lived through the years of her childhood. She saw the endless line of people who had been guests in the parsonage. A strange crowd of crippled and sick ones, but also those happy and well. She knew that Mama never closed the door to anyone as long as there was one place left to crowd someone in, and she always served her guests the best the house could afford. That was Mama's way of serving God.

Finally Mama smiled. "Button," she said kindly, "I'm sure you're not a foolish, selfish girl. You certainly are not going to keep an old lady from realizing her dreams of coming to the convention because of your emotionalism over an unborn baby. Think upon this seriously before you reply. But, little one, let me tell you that there will be a special blessing coming to you if you open your home to Mrs. Frankenberg."

Button lived through agony until Eric came home from work. He found her snuggled up on the daybed in the nursery, her eyes red with weeping, and no supper prepared. Sobbing, she threw herself into his arms and told him the whole story. The lines on Eric's forehead deepened as he tried to solve this new problem.

"Never mind, Button," he finally said. "Dry your tears and let old Mrs. Frankenberg come. That is better than to have trouble with Mama. You know very well that if Mama has made up her mind that we are going to have that old woman in our nursery, no power on earth can stop her."

"But, Eric, it is so unfair! This is OUR house and OUR baby and OUR nursery. Mama has no right to interfere."

Eric took his handkerchief and wiped away the falling tears and in no time he had convinced her that there was no other way out of this situation but to cater to Mama's wishes.

Mrs. Frankenberg proved to be a very happy, talkative old lady and because she lived in the country she was delighted with all the things of the city.

"I'm going to spend as much time at the meetings as I need to bring back a report to our church," she informed Button, "but I'm also going to do all my Christmas shopping. I was pretty lucky to have been chosen delegate from our group. It has never happened before."

"I'm glad you could come," replied Button, wondering if she was telling a lie, though she really felt better about the whole affair now that she saw how truly delighted the old lady was.

Mrs. Frankenberg was thrilled with all the wonderful things she could buy in the Berkley Hills stores, and she came home with bundle after bundle. Button wondered if she got to church at all.

One afternoon Mrs. Frankenberg unwrapped a package that contained the softest white flannel cloth Button had ever seen and yards and yards of delicate, rare lace.

"This is for nightgowns for my two sisters," the old lady confided to Button. "They're both large women, so I bought plenty. Did you ever see flannel so soft as this? I simply couldn't resist it."

Button admitted she hadn't.

"I'll have plenty of time to sew it before the holidays, and can't you just see the gowns with this lovely lace? I know two women who are going to be very lucky this Christmas Day. By the way, do you mind if I don't wrap it

up for a while? I get pleasure just looking at it from my
bed. May I leave it in the crib on top of all those angels?
. . . See, I bought scissors, pins and thread and I'm all
set to go."

What could Button do but say that was all right? She
had never met a person who could get so enthused over
little things. Well, the nursery was lived in now, so what
difference would it make if Mrs. Frankenberg placed the
cloth in the crib?

Mama had more requests. The hard-working church
women needed a bit of extra help for their luncheon the
next day. They would not let Mama help because she had
her hands full with so many guests, but would Button go
down and help with a sit-down job, like buttering rolls? It
would take some of the burden off the few who were working.

Button left her house at nine the next morning. Mama
had been so happy that she had said yes. Mrs. Frankenberg decided to do a bit more shopping before the last
meeting.

With Button's house empty, Mama had her own plans.
Last night she had obtained a key from Eric, remembering
the special blessing she had promised Button. God was a
little slow at times in bestowing His blessings, and Mama
wanted Button to see that her words were true. She would
help God out today, and since she didn't have to be at
church until afternoon, she had time to go to Button's house
and make her a nice daffodil cake and frost it with fluffy
cream icing. Button would love that and she could put in a
brun peparkaka, too, just for good measure.

It was fun to be in Eric's and Button's immaculate
home and to putter around in the kitchen. Before Mama

started her baking, she tiptoed into the nursery. Poor Button, it had been hard for her to give in, but it was good for her. Young people of today were apt to think only of themselves, and when it came to her own, she had better nip that trait in the bud. Her eyes rested upon the little white crib and its bundle of soft white flannel.

"Why," she said aloud to herself, "think of that, Button is going to attempt to sew baby clothes! The way she sews this lovely flannel will be ruined in no time at all. . . . Such beautiful lace, too."

An idea popped into Mama's head. Instead of making a cake, why not make the baby clothes? She could do it in no time at all on Button's sewing machine, whereas it would take Button forever. Mama was an excellent sewer, and wouldn't Button be happy when she saw a pile of baby clothes all finished! Button would know she really had received a blessing for accepting Mrs. Frankenberg.

In a few hours the task was completed. Mama smiled impishly as she folded the little nighties, shirts and diapers, three piles of them. If Button had spent months at it, they wouldn't have looked as well. There was one yard of material left, and Mama spread it over the clothes and placed on top the scissors and thread and the strip of lace that was left over. It looked as before. She would not tell Button until tomorrow when Mrs. Frankenberg had gone home. What a surprise!

Mr. Frankenberg came home late in the afternoon, tired from attending meetings and Christmas shopping.

"I got it done! I got it done! Every last bit of it. Not one Christmas present left to buy. But"—she looked pleadingly at Button—"would you mind if I stayed one more night and left in the morning. I would have to rush so to catch that bus now."

"Of course, you may stay, Mrs. Frankenberg. Have a good night's rest, and I'll wake you early in the morning. That will be so much better."

What else could she say, even though the old lady had worn out her welcome a long time ago? Tomorrow it would be all over, and she could clean the nursery and put her home in order the way it had been before the guest arrived. Her stay had not been too bad after all.

The next morning she woke Mrs. Frankenberg as soon as Eric had left for work. She cooked her a nice, big breakfast, to send her off with pleasant memories since she was their first overnight guest and was not responsible for Button's own attitude toward the nursery.

Mrs. Frankenberg was all sunshine. She appeared in a red robe she had bought. "If you excuse me, this robe is so warm and pretty-looking, I thought I would eat first and pack afterwards," she said, her eyes feasting on the delicious-looking ham omelet Button was placing on the table.

"Have a good breakfast now," Button smiled. "You'll have plenty of time to pack and get ready. The bus is just down the hill, you know."

"I don't know how I'm ever going to thank you. I've been so comfortable in that darling nursery. I wish you lots of luck with your first one. The child will be very lucky having you for a mother. How can I ever repay you for your kindness to an old lady?"

"Oh, don't even think about it, Mrs. Frankenberg," assured Button. "It has already been paid for."

Mrs. Frankenberg took another piece of coffee bread.

"You mean the church will pay for me?" she asked bluntly.

"Oh, no, I didn't mean that kind of payment. There are other ways you get repaid for the little things you do for others. Mama calls it a special blessing."

"Well, I'm glad to hear that," laughed the old lady. "You see, I had intended to buy some little thing for you and Eric, something to remember me by, but with all the Christmas buying I did, my money just melted like snow in hot water. But you'll be glad to know that all my shopping is done, every bit of it, and on top of that I have a lot of good preaching tucked away in my heart. I've had a great time."

Button washed the breakfast dishes. She was glad that Mrs. Frankenberg was so pleased with her first conference and her visit. It left a rather special glow on the nursery. She felt a bit ashamed now to think that it had taken both Mama and Eric to persuade her to accept the old lady.

It was strangely quiet in the nursery, so quiet that Button wondered if Mrs. Frankenberg had gone back to bed and would ask to remain another day. Heaven forbid! If she did, Button would just have to tell her, in a nice way that this would have to be all, at least for this time.

Presently the door to the nursery opened and out stepped Mrs. Frankenberg with a suitcase in one hand and an umbrella in the other. Her hat was pushed down over her eyes and her mouth was set in a hard thin line. She marched right by Button without looking at her, and her heels made a clicking sound as she walked through the hall. At the front door she stopped and drew a deep breath. She placed her suitcase on the floor and put her free hand on her hip. Her eyes bored through Button's with a murderous look. Then without one word of explanation she opened the door, walked out, and closed it with a bang.

For a minute Button stood as if transfixed, staring at the closed door. She searched her mind to see if she had said or done something that could have offended her guest to such a degree that she had become like a thundercloud. Button could recall nothing, but she couldn't let her guest go off like that. Something was wrong, desperately wrong. She put on her coat and hurried after Mrs. Frankenberg and soon she caught up with her.

"Mrs. Frankenberg," she called, and puffed from running in her heavy condition. "Please, Mrs. Frankenberg, I'd like to walk with you to the bus and carry your suitcase. What has happened! Is something wrong?"

The old lady stopped and put down her suitcase. She pushed her hat away from her eyes, which were red from crying, and again she gave Button one of those looks that made her cringe. In a voice loaded with contempt, she said, "I owe you neither a good-bye nor a thank you, my dear Mrs. Bjork. As you told me, you have your own way of abstracting payment from a poor woman who was invited to stay at your house as a member of the church of God. A very lovely minister's daughter you are! I want neither your help nor your company for that might cost me my new red bathrobe. Who knows? And now may I bid you farewell and a very merry Christmas?"

Button went back to the house. The old lady was a lunatic. She was crazy as a loon, and here she had been staying right in their home. All sorts of things could have happened. Well, what a relief to have her gone. Now to open all the windows and let in some fresh air! Wait until she told Eric! He would be furious. She herself felt as if someone had thrown a pail of cold water over her.

The telephone rang and Button was relieved to hear Mama's happy voice.

"Are you tired, Button?" asked Mama sweetly.

"A little," confessed Button. "And happy that Mrs. Frankenberg has gone. Mama, something is wrong with that woman's mind."

"Mrs. Frankenberg's? Oh, no, she's a bit eccentric, but she has a heart of gold and is harmless. Living alone in the country may make a person a bit queer at times."

"Not just a little queer! I am at my wits' end trying to understand her actions."

"Let's forget her, darling. I called to see if you found the surprise—the special blessing that was coming your way."

"I'm afraid not, Mama. Mrs. Frankenberg just left."

"Well, look in the crib, dear."

Mama remained on the phone while Button looked. The first thing she saw was that Mrs. Frankenberg had forgotten her beautiful, soft flannel. She went to the crib and lifted it . . . and then stood with her mouth open staring at the three piles of the loveliest, darlingest baby things. For a moment she was going to hug them to her heart when she suddenly realized what Mama was about to tell her.

She dashed back to the phone. "Mama," she cried, "oh, Mama, you sewed up all the flannel!"

"Yes, Button, that is your blessing for being good. I went over to your house yesterday while you were working at the church. I intended to make you a daffodil cake, but I discovered the flannel and knew you were about to make baby clothes, so I made them up for you, little one, with lots of love tucked into every stitch. I hope you are pleased."

"Mama, Mama! Oh, dear! Poor Mrs. Frankenberg!" And Button started to laugh uncontrollably.

Mama could not stop her, no matter how she tried, so she put down the receiver and had Papa drive with her to Button's house where she learned the whole story. Mama and Papa both laughed at the strange twist Mama's blessing had taken.

"No wonder the poor dear was as mad as a hornet," said Button seriously. "She believes *I* took that flannel in payment for her lodging. And she was so delighted with that material she had bought to make nightgowns for her sisters. Now I can forgive her with all my heart."

The very next day Mama bought new material for Mrs. Frankenberg and Papa drove the thirty-five miles to her farm so Mama and Button could explain the error. Even Mrs. Frankenberg had to see the humor in the situation, and she, too, had a hearty laugh so everything turned out well with the blessing.

Early December was extremely cold that year. But in the middle of the month Button awoke one night to hear the rain beating against the windowpanes. At last the cold weather must be easing up, she thought, only to awake the following morning to a world coated with ice. Silvery icicles hung from every tree and bush, and the street and sidewalks looked like a polished dance floor. It was a fairyland sight unbelievable in its beauty, but Button's heart sank as she beheld the splendor. She had been invited to Vickey's for lunch, but how could she get there in her condition? This was the fifteenth day of the eighth month of her pregnancy, and it was hard enough to walk across the floor, let alone on the ice!

Eric must have read her thoughts, for as they were dressing he said, "Button, one promise for today. Stay inside like a bird in its nest, for it's very slippery out. If you step out, you might fall, and you mustn't do anything that might injure either the baby or yourself."

Cleverly Button avoided giving a direct answer.

"My husband is very, very wise," she recited, "and very strict. How would I dare to disobey him?"

Eric was satisfied with her answer, not knowing what was going on in his wife's mind. I did not actually say I wouldn't go out, she was thinking, but I made him think I wouldn't. He doesn't understand how important it is that I see Vickey's new baby and finish the last stitches on the carriage robe. Nothing can happen to me. I won't let it. I'll be very careful when I walk."

As Eric was ready to leave for work, he repeated his words. "Remember, no going out, Button. Have you everything you need for the day in the house?"

Button nodded her head. "Our baby is very happy this morning," she smiled, "and so excited, knowing it will be only a short while before it meets Father and Mother in person. Oh, Eric, we can count the days now!"

She blew him a kiss as the car backed out of the driveway. It skidded back and forth. How slippery it must be! thought Button, remembering Eric's words of warning to her.

Button hurried through her work. She must leave early so she would be home in plenty of time before Eric returned from work. The bus was only down the hill. It would be cozy to spend the day in Vickey's homey parsonage, and Littlemont was only half an hour away by bus. A big fire would be burning in the fireplace, and Vickey's calm personality and sweet charm would be soothing on a wintry day such as this. They would talk of the latest things that had been going on in the family, go on to little happenings in John's church, and end up comparing husbands as they always did, each claiming she had the better one. Of course, it would only be in fun. There were never two sisters closer to each other's hearts.

As Button dressed, she stood a moment before the mirror. She was round as a ball now, but soon her body would yield up its fruit and she would look normal again and have a sweet little baby sleeping in the nursery. Only a short time now—two more weeks, and they would pass swiftly.

"You little rascal," she whispered to the child within her. "You dear, darling, little rascal. I love you as much as a mother can love a baby, and I can hardly wait to see you and say 'hello.' What do you look like? Are you a husky boy or a tiny, cute little girl? Whatever you are, please hurry and come to us."

It was very icy, and Button walked slowly, using special care with each step. As she came to the hill, she stopped. Again she could hear Eric's voice. His words rang in her ears pleadingly. She never knew Eric could be so concerned over her welfare. Should she turn back and telephone Vickey? But the day would be so long! Slowly she started down the hill. She was over halfway down when her feet went out from under her and she tumbled over and over until she came to rest against a telephone pole. She tried to ignore the fall. She tried to laugh. How comical a sight she must be lying there like a huge snowball! But instead of laughter, crying came and the tears ran uncontrollably down her cheeks. She was very, very frightened. She couldn't get up, the sidewalk was too icy and she too heavy. Friendly people came and saw her predicament. She was carried into the home of a neighbor, who, at Button's request, called Doctor Davis.

He came immediately and shook his gray head. "You've had a bad fall, Button. I must call the ambulance and get you to the hospital. I'll call Eric at once."

"Oh, no, Doctor Davis, don't call Eric. Call Mama."

"Suppose you leave this to me," responded Doctor Davis. "We're not playing a game, and I think I know what I am doing. I know what is best in this case."

Button insisted no more. "I'm sorry, Doctor Davis," she said humbly, trying not to cry . . . trying not to think that something could have happened to the baby.

Eric came to the hospital in his working clothes. His face was drawn and his eyes sad. His hands were black, but he did not apologize, nor did he tell her, "I asked you not to go out."

It would have been so much better if he had scolded her or asked questions. He just sat there in silence, holding her hand and stroking it softly now and then.

Button stayed in the hospital a week before the baby was born. All was so strangely quiet within her. She prayed in desperation, "Please God, don't let anything be wrong with the baby. . . . I was foolish as I have been so many times . . . but Eric is so good. . . . Please, God . . . don't punish Eric." But she felt as if her prayers were not reaching God. They only went as far as the ceiling and then fell flat on the floor. How could she pray, when she had deliberately gone out on the icy street and fallen with the baby that had been entrusted to her?

On the eighth day the pains began, and shortly after that Button lost consciousness. She did not know what was going on or whether it took hours, days or weeks. Once it seemed as though she heard Papa's voice and Mama whispering her name. . . . Someone was crying, and she longed to reach out her hand to tell them not to cry over a fate she deserved . . . but she couldn't move . . . she couldn't see. She thought Eric had touched her nose—he had a certain little way of doing it—but she wasn't sure. . . . All was darkness, fear and pain.

When Button finally awoke, Eric was sitting beside her. He looked thin and worn, but he smiled and caressed her cheek. She wanted to ask about the baby, but there was something in Eric's face that made her afraid to. She smiled and, holding his hand, drifted off to the silent world again.

A month had gone by and Button was home in her bungalow again. A strange, empty house without the nursery. There was a desk where the crib had been and on it stood a shiny new typewriter. The spread with the angels and roses was gone, too, and the daybed had a bright blue slipcover. Greta had moved in to help around the house. There were flowers and candy and books—everything that anyone could think of—but no baby. And no one spoke about it. Her baby girl had died, died because of a careless mother.

Button had lost her smile. Day after day she sat in the big chair by the living-room window doing nothing but

looking wistfully far away until late afternoon when, following the doctor's orders, she would walk down to the
corner of the street and back again. She ate whatever was
placed before her, but she could taste nothing because of a
dryness that left her throat hot and sore. She talked very
little and asked no questions, but inside her heart there
were burning questions. How had her baby looked? Had it
been deformed because of the fall?

Tenderly and lovingly her family sorrowed with her.
She was surrounded by their love and kindness; their sweet
concern made her feel as if her heart would break. She
tried to eat dinner with Eric, and one day she decided to try
to prepare his meals the next day. Somehow she had to
fight her way back to life for Eric's sake. Time went faster
if she was busy, so she thanked Greta for her kindness and
asked her to go back to the parsonage. Greta gave her big
sister a hug and an understanding smile—Button was alone
again.

Then one day Button walked into what had been the
nursery. The only things left to remind her of it were the
wide satin ribbons around the curtains. Where had the
nursery things been placed—the crib, the bureau, the bedspread with all the angels . . . tiny darling angels, waving
and smiling, showering roses down from their pure white
wings? Angels! thought Button. My baby is an angel now!
It had never entered this sorrowful, disappointment-filled
world but had lived safe within her body, loved and cherished, and then flown straight into God's heaven. Her face
broke into a smile. Why, she, Button Bjork, was the mother
of a real angel. Perhaps at night it winged its way down to
sit on her bed and whisper words of comfort in her ear.
Perhaps it said, "I love you, Mommie; don't be sad."

And for the first time the tears poured forth, cleansing her of all bitterness and spreading a balm over her bruised heart. After that she could laugh again. When Eric came home that night, she met him with a smile. The deep lines on his forehead disappeared as he smiled and took her in his arms.

"Eric," she whispered softly, "come with me into the nursery."

Silently he followed, holding her slender hand tightly in his strong one. In the doorway she stopped.

"Darling," she said, "do you know what? You and I are the parents of an angel, a tiny white-robed angel that can fly up and down between heaven and earth, and she will always love us, Eric, always. And someday this nursery will have other cribs and other babies will coo and smile and reach out little chubby arms toward us. But, dearest, no matter how many children God grants us, we'll never forget our first baby because she made a bridge for us to walk upon, a bridge covered with roses, that reaches all the way from earth to God's heaven."

CHAPTER 9

~ Two Tiny Plants

Eric and Button waited four years for Charlene to join them and when she came, looking as beautiful as a tiny doll, their happiness knew no bounds. In another four years little Lynn arrived. Now they were really blessed.

"I am so glad there are four years between the girls," Button informed Vickey. "That way I was given enough time to get one little plant growing before I had to devote myself to the next one."

"Well, that's one way to look at it," laughed Vickey. "To tell you the truth, since I had to wait so many years for my first one, I was happy the other two followed closely."

"Probably I'm just finding an excuse for having had to wait so long between mine," confessed Button. "I felt it wasn't fair for me to have to wait so long when your three came one right after the other."

By now the nursery showed signs of having been well used, and the house echoed with laughter and singing. Button knew that God had been good to her. At times, she thought the wound in her heart had healed and that the memory of the angel had faded, but it was not so. When

151

she was alone, or when she awoke in the still of the night and couldn't go to sleep, the memories haunted her. Would God pass judgment on her for having carelessly killed her baby? Even if she hadn't meant to. . . . She should have listened to Eric begging her not to go out. In her mind she would again walk down that icy hill and feel herself falling, falling. . . . This introspection would leave her in a restless frame of mind and she would wonder if life could ever be the way it was before the accident?

Whenever this occurred, Button would seek out the girls wherever they were. If at night, she would tiptoe into their bedroom and stand beside their beds, listening to their even breathing and touching their golden curls. She would thank God over and over again that she had them. If during the day, she would leave her household tasks and walk with them to the park where they would feed the ducks and the long, shimmering goldfish. Engulfed in their childish chatter and happy laughter, her heart would find peace once again. Sometimes they would return late from these excursions, so after having fed and bathed the girls she would tuck them in their beds and listen to their prayers:

"Bless our Daddy so kind and good
And our Mommie who cooks our food.
Bless the whole world that goes round and round
And the birds that make such pretty sounds.
Bless our mind, our soul, our heart,
And let us not from Thee depart."

Button had written that prayer especially for her little girls. Often she occupied her mind by writing poems and prayers and sometimes an animal story to tell her daughters when they were good.

Early in the morning, right after Eric had left for work and while the girls were still in dreamland, Button would go out to work in her garden. She would kneel down on the soft grass and weed the flower beds. The world was beautiful in the early morning, so fresh and pure. The birds busy singing and building their nests and the sun shining lavishly down upon the earth would make Button's heart glad. How soft the dirt and how moist in her hands! The flowers bloomed these summers as never before, as if they wanted to show their thankfulness for the loving care they received. While she worked in the garden, no evil thoughts could penetrate her mind, but all was good and right and fine.

It had not taken Button long to discover that Charlene had inherited her mother's childish restlessness and naughtiness. At times she worried about her first-born daughter. She was too bright for her years, and her active mind could always find something to do—usually something she wasn't supposed to be doing. Many times the telephone would ring and there would be an irate voice at the other end of the line saying, "Mrs. Bjork, this is Mrs. Murphy, your neighbor three doors up the street. I want to inform you that the little girl of yours who looks like an angel with her blue eyes and golden curls—well, that little girl has just snipped off all my tulip blossoms—every single one of them and I had planned on using some of them for my centerpiece when I entertain the bridge club tomorrow night—and—and——"

"Mrs. Murphy," Button would hurry to say in order to stop the new complaint which she was certain would follow the first. "I'm so very sorry, but please forgive the little one. We often let her snip flowers in our garden, and she must have thought she could do it elsewhere. I'll have a bouquet sent to you from the florist; that is the only way I can compensate for her mistake."

And the next day:

"Is this you, Mrs. Bjork? Your little girl emptied my cream into the sandbox to make mudpies—my heavy cream, and I was having company today."

"Mrs. Jones! Thank you for calling me. I'm so sorry! I'm just on my way to the store, and I'll buy you another half-pint. I usually give Charlene the water for her mudpies in a cream bottle so she must have been all mixed up. Please forgive her."

Button was at her wits' end with Charlene. And one day she had done far more than her share of mischief. There had been call after call complaining about her and several times she had ignored completely the things Button had asked her to do. Button decided that she was too lenient with this child, that was the whole story. Because she had lost her first baby, she was loving these two too much. But she would change her tactics. What Charlene needed was a good dose of the hairbrush, and this very night she would inflict a bit of Papa's discipline on the child.

"I must punish her," Button repeatedly told herself, paining at the thought.

The hairbrush might just be the thing to dispel Charlene's naughtiness. She'd try it anyway, and she wouldn't spare that brush. Charlene would know that she had been punished.

Charlene had been bathed and powdered. Since she was a big girl now, she put herself to bed. It was time for

Button to tuck her in and read her a bedtime story. Lynn, a sweet baby who never fussed, had been asleep a long time.

She takes after her daddy, thought Button. She's as tranquil as a calm summer sea and loves harmonious and peaceful surroundings.

How thankful Button was for chubby, dimpled little Lynn and how she prayed that Charlene would outgrow her restlessness!

Button walked quickly up the stairs. The door was wide open. And surely the figure on the bed could be an angel, lying there so pink and soft in her dainty nightie. She stepped inside the door, hiding the instrument of punishment behind her back, but she had hardly got a foot inside the room when something flew at her as swiftly as an arrow and two soft arms wrapped themselves around her neck. A rosy cheek pressed against hers.

"Mommie," said a little voice in her ear, "Mommie, have I been a good girl today? I've tried so hard!"

The brush slipped to the floor. Button kissed Charlene tenderly, brushing her hand over the blonde curls.

"The best we can do is to try hard, darling," she whispered, a tear stealing down her cheek. "But tomorrow let's try a little harder."

She sat down on Charlene's bed and sang softly to her until her child's eyes were hidden behind the long dark lashes as if a priceless pair of drapes had been drawn closed. But Button remained seated on the bed for a long time, thinking and watching as sleep descended upon Charlene like a gentle benediction.

How could she have punished her? She was sure she had done the right thing, for when God looked into her own heart at night, perhaps He, too, had to smile as Button asked Him how well she had done. Could it be that she, too, deserved to be punished but that God, in His wisdom, judged her by how hard she had tried to do her best . . . how hard she had tried to be a good mother!

If ever there was a proud father, it was Eric! He played endlessly with the girls, bouncing them on his knees and spoiling them by bestowing upon them anything their hearts desired if it was within his means to do so. Never did he raise his voice to correct, nor his hand to punish them.

"It's all up to me," said Button grumpily, "all the unpleasant tasks of parenthood."

Very often quarrelsome words were exchanged between Eric and Button because of Charlene.

"You don't have to hit them to be a good parent," Eric protested. And always at times like that he would hide behind his newspaper and say no more, afraid that any further comments from him would throw his house into a state of confusion.

One day he came in unexpectedly and found Button whipping Charlene with a stick. She held the screaming child over her knee and energetically inflicted the paddling. Eric stood as if paralyzed.

"Button," he cried when he found his voice, "you that are so big ought to be ashamed to hit her that is so little!"

Button released Charlene and stared with hurt eyes at her husband. But the sharp remark she was about to make never left her lips. There was no use. Eric understood nothing when it came to rearing children. She gave him a desperate look which she hoped would penetrate deeper than words. What he needed to teach him a lesson was to stay home one whole day and watch Charlene. After that he, too, might be willing to use a stick on his offspring.

But later that night when, as always, Eric and Button discussed the issue, Eric had been considerate, kind and gentle.

"Button, perhaps you think I'm shirking my duty when it comes to disciplining the girls, but I have my own ideas of what is right. I was so often spanked as a small boy, I decided that, if I ever became a father, I'd never spank my children. You see, I want them always to keep the memory in their hearts that I was good to them."

Button drew a deep sigh.

"Well, dear, then I'm afraid they'll always remember me as an ogress of a mother, for someone has to punish them when they're naughty so that later in life they'll know how to discipline themselves . . . and with Charlene——"

"Quit being so critical of the child. She resents it, and it isn't good for you, either. Someday you'll end up a nervous wreck the way you carry on."

The sad thing was that Button had to admit that Eric was right. Charlene reminded her more and more of her own childhood and the naughty things she had done. Perhaps she resented this constant reminder and vented her feelings on her child. She didn't wish to recall the hurts she had inflicted upon Papa, for since Papa's death she wanted only the memory of their happy times together to remain in her mind.

So Button reverted to the way she had behaved in the parsonage . . . she withdrew from her dear ones. When they asked her to join their fun, she claimed a headache.

"What's wrong, dear?" Eric asked one night after the girls were tucked into bed. "You always complain of a headache these days and you're always tired. Don't you think you should see the new man who took Doctor Davis's place when he gave up his practice?"

"Oh, Eric, there's nothing wrong with me," Button assured him, forcing a laugh. "All mothers of young children get tired when night comes around."

Button knew that was not the truth. There was something vitally wrong. Sleep did not come quickly any more and she awoke unhappy in the morning.

Instead of a new doctor, I need Eric's arm around me, she thought, assuring me that I'm being a good mother. He makes me feel that I'm a failure and I want to be my very best!

Another thing that troubled Button was that she felt Eric had transferred all his affection to the girls. Before their arrival she had been the center of Eric's life, and now she had been pushed into a corner. Stronger and stronger this feeling grew within her—that lost, lonely feeling of not belonging to anyone.

Every Sunday afternoon Eric took the girls for a long walk. Button knew the little ones looked forward to this event all week. Lynn would ride in the stroller and Charlene would skip beside her. How dear they looked as they walked away! She longed to be part of that picture, but she had refused to accompany them so many times that they never invited her any more. All three seemed to be perfectly content to kiss her good-bye and be on their way.

They have a much better time without me, she thought sadly. Eric never gets cross with them. No wonder they love him so.

Perhaps she was too strict to compensate for his leniency; but who would discipline them if she didn't? Being parents carried certain responsibilities. Even that thought did not stop the pain in her heart.

Although she had consistently refused to join her little family in their outings, she dreaded being alone at home. Time and time again her thoughts went to the tiny baby she had never seen.

She would have been twelve this Christmas, she thought, and wondered what this child would have been like. Would she have had a restless nature such as Charlene's or would she had been serene and dimply like Lynn? Perhaps she would have differed from both of them. . . . Her heart longed for her dead baby until she shifted her thoughts to Papa, who never had seen her girls. Papa had passed away in Sweden the summer he and Mama had made a visit there. Mama had left him to sleep in Swedish soil, for she knew he had always wanted to rest in his homeland. It had been a dark day when the telegram from Sweden had reached America.

Mama had returned to America alone, and how beautifully Mama had mastered her sorrow! Button had been ashamed to manifest her grief for Mama's sake, so she pushed her great sorrow deep within her soul. It was only at times like this—although many years had passed—that she let herself grieve in loneliness for him.

"Papa, Papa, I miss you so," she whispered, her cheeks wet with tears. Life had never been the same without him. If only she could live those years with Papa over again, how differently she would live them.

Button knew that Papa had not been afraid to face death. She remembered that once, when they first had come to America, the whole family had taken a trip to Niagara Falls. She had been young then, but she had never forgotten Papa's words. He had held her arm as they had walked along in admiration and wonder over the mystery of God's creation, the magnificent beauty of the falls.

"Button," Papa had said as they stopped and listened to the mighty roar, "to me it seems that death must be like these falls. It comes roaring upon you with a tremendous force that nothing can stop. You are thrown and tossed and bruised and beaten upon the rocks, but suddenly you are swept into the stillness of the lake below and carried off into green pastures. Death is a tunnel between heaven and earth."

However, there were also days of sunshine and laughter. Button was her old self whenever the big Franzon family gathered on a Sunday night in one or another of the married children's homes. There were four of them married now. Vickey had been the first one. (It was she who had announced the glad news of the coming of the first grandchild when Mama returned from Sweden without Papa. Button had waited to tell her own news so as not to detract from Vickey's glowing pleasure.) Vickey had had her son before Button had had the "angel," and now Nim's Karin also was awaiting her first. Pelle and his wife, Felicia, were still studying, so for a while had postponed having a family. There were so many around the dinner table now that it was hard to find room for them all, but the place where Papa had sat remained empty, and it seemed odd they could be so gay without him.

Because of Eric's wish, Button refrained from using corporal punishment on Charlene again, but she had to find substitute ways by which to punish her when she had been extremely naughty. One trying day Button left her in the kitchen while she and Lynn went down the street to do some shopping. Her little human plants were growing up! And Charlene had to learn that being naughty did not pay. This particular day Charlene had gone to the extreme limit of naughtiness in whatever she had undertaken to do, so Button was going to teach her a lesson that she would not soon forget. It was a blazing hot July day and Button feared that perhaps she was punishing herself more by going than she was her daughter, but Charlene loved to go shopping and to deprive her of doing so might serve to make her more obedient in the future. Button put on a clean, crisp white summer dress and on Lynn she put a frilly pink one. Just the sight of the two of them all dressed up would set Charlene to thinking, she hoped.

"Charlene," she said, taking her daughter's small tanned hand in hers, "I'm doing this to teach you a lesson. I hope Lynn and I will never need to go without you again. Do you understand this?"

Charlene nodded her head, looking up at Button with large innocent blue eyes that always tempted Button to take her in her arms and hug her to her heart, but she refrained.

"Mommie, why am I naughty?" she asked.

"I wish I knew, Charlene. You really have a heart of gold, but you do all the wrong things that make the neighbors complain about you. For instance, why did you cut the rope by which Duberry's new pup was tied? It allowed him to run away, and they spent hours looking for him."

"But God sent him back when I prayed that I was sorry."

"Yes, but see what extra work you made for God!"

"I never thought of that. Next time I won't bother Him."

"Oh, Charlene, Charlene darling, perhaps Mommie said the wrong thing. I don't think God minded. He is so good and He loves you so. But now, I want you to stay in the kitchen and not leave it until we get back. You may sit by the table and draw pictures. And while you're sitting there, you might think of one good deed you can do—a very unusual deed—something no one else would bother to do. This will show Mommie that you want to be a good girl."

"I will, Mommie! I know I'll think of something and next time I'll go with you and Lynn when you shop. Won't I?"

"I hope so, darling!"

But even while shopping, Button couldn't help but long for Charlene. How she missed that child. Perhaps she had punished her foolishly this time. She might not even stay in the kitchen but go out into the neighborhood and devise more mischief. The thought was alarming and caused Button to stop shopping sooner than she had anticipated. She hurried home but found Charlene seated at the table drawing pictures and being as good as could be. This, then, must have been the right punishment in spite of her qualms. Button clasped Charlene in her arms, relieved that the episode was over. Charlene wasn't mean, just naughty, and she would outgrow it. Some plants needed special care and Charlene was one of those rare stubborn ones, but once they started to grow they proved to be the most beautiful flowers of all.

It wasn't until suppertime that Button noticed the spots on the ceiling. She called Eric's attention to them.

"Look, Eric, there must be a leak in the upstairs bathroom. You'd better look into it right away."

"I can't see a thing wrong," said the puzzled Eric after he had checked the bathroom. "The floor, however, looks as if it had been all wet and then wiped up. . . . Charlene," he said, "do you happen to know anything of water running in the bathroom?"

Charlene nodded. "It did overflow, but he wiped it all up. The rags are down the cellar."

"He?" asked Eric and Button simultaneously. "Who is he?"

"Oh, the garbage man, of course!"

"The garbage man! Please, please, Charlene, tell us quickly what the garbage man was doing in our bathroom?"

"That's a secret," smiled Charlene, "a great big secret between God and me!"

"But Mommie and I want to know, honey," said Eric and took the child in his lap. "You'll tell Daddy, won't you?"

"Is the deed just as good if I talk about it? Will it make me just as un-naughty?"

"Yes, yes, darling!" Button's heart was beating like a sledge hammer by now.

"I saw Mr. Garbage Man sitting in the yard eating a sandwich. He looked terribly hot and dirty and, Mommie, you asked me to think of a deed that no one else would do— so I called to him and asked if he wanted to take a shower to cool off and get all clean. He was up there a long time and after he was gone the ceiling was wet, so when I saw the water, I made him come back and wipe it all up. He was a very nice garbage man and so good. He even said thank you and patted me on the head. He said I was the nicest girl he had ever seen and that my folks should thank God for having me. Wasn't that a real honest-to-goodness good deed, Mommie?"

Button and Eric looked at each other, his look accusing her, and hers pleading with him to understand why she had punished Charlene by leaving her alone. With each other they only conversed with their eyes, but to Charlene they reached out their arms.

"We'll talk about it some other time, honey, but you did a very unusual deed, indeed, and we know you meant it from your heart," smiled Button. "I don't believe that man will ever forget you."

Those years the Bjorks spent their summer vacations in the White Mountains since now they could rent the whole cabin where they had spent their honeymoon. What fun and enjoyment they had during these two weeks. They took advantage of every moment, spending their time boating, swimming, fishing and hiking through the woods.

One evening Eric had gone fishing, and Button and the two girls had sat on the dock and watched him row away. The gentle night was creeping in upon them. The stars would soon twinkle over the woodland. A whippoorwill called from a tall treetop, and a big round moon was beginning to peek from behind the mountains. To think that here it was they had spent their honeymoon. Isn't life wonderful, thought Button, holding an arm around each of the girls. God was good to have given her these tender plants to nurture, and it seemed as if Charlene was at last overcoming her bad traits; she had been as good as gold for a long time.

Their nearest neighbors, the Goldbergs, were packing their station wagon in order to leave in the early morning hours. They had just been over to say good-bye. They were from Philadelphia and the two families had become good friends. Button was happy that her own vacation still had a week to go, for, although she would miss their neighbors, to be completely alone with Eric and the girls would be like a little bit of heaven—a whole long week.

"Mommie, what is a honeymoon?" asked Lynn. "Is that one coming up behind the mountains?"

"No, darling, a honeymoon is when two people go away someplace and no one knows where they are. They just whisper sweet words to each other and are so nice that the whole world seems sweet like golden honey."

"Is that why Daddy and you are always nice?" asked Charlene.

"Perhaps so, dear. Daddy and I had a wonderful honeymoon, as you know, right here in this log cabin, and no one in the whole world knew we were here."

Button put the girls to bed, hoping that her definition of a honeymoon would suffice. After all, how could she explain the meaning of honeymoon to two little girls?

The children slept in the back room in a big double bed, pleased and proud to be bunking together. Now that Lynn was getting older, Charlene and she had more things in common and they seemed content in each other's company. That might be the reason for Charlene's better behavior.

The following morning Eric and Button slept later than usual. That was one of the satisfying things about a vacation, that there were no time schedules to keep, no rushing about, just complete relaxation. Button awoke in a happy mood. She would surprise her family and make *plättar* for breakfast. They all loved these tiny, flat Swedish pancakes, and she had real lingonberries to serve with them. She worked quietly so as not to awaken the others until everything was ready. She set the table on the porch, overlooking the lake and flooded with bright sunshine. All being done to perfection, she went to call the girls. It was most unusual to have them sleep so late, yet she had not heard a sound from their room.

Button pushed the door open quietly and then her heart stopped.

"Eric," she screamed, "they are gone—the girls are not in their beds!"

She had never seen Eric fly so fast. He searched every nook and cranny, inside and out.

"They must be playing a game and hiding somewhere." He tried to sooth Button, but she could sense that he, too, believed that something more serious had happened.

After a long, futile search the village police were called, and they combed the woods and searched in all the empty cottages. With nothing to do but wait, the endless hours seeming long as weeks. Could the children have been kidnaped? Button refused to believe so, for who would take two little girls whose parents were not wealthy?

At three o'clock in the afternoon, emotionally exhausted, Eric and Button were sitting on the porch, trying to comfort each other when the Goldbergs' station wagon drove into the yard.

"Look, Eric," exclaimed Button, "the Goldbergs must have heard about the girls and they have come back to help us. . . . How can we ever be thankful enough to God for friends like that . . . ?" But she had time to say no more before the two girls flew out of the car and into their arms. They were hugged and kissed and squeezed while tears ran down both Eric's and Button's cheeks. Mr. Goldberg stood beside them, but his face was not radiant. His wife remained in the car. Finally Eric found his voice.

"But—but—how does it happen you are with the Goldbergs?"

"Yes—how? I may be fired from my job for not showing up on time," fretted Mr. Goldberg. "And my wife gets motion sick, and now we have all this extra distance to go. We had gone many miles before we discovered them. They had crawled under the seats in the back and had fallen asleep on an old blanket. With the suitcases piled high on the seats, we never knew they were there until we heard Lynn whimper that she wanted to go home."

"But why—why did you get into the wagon?"

"We went on a honeymoon to be good," sobbed Lynn. "Charlene said to."

"Mommie, you said if two went away alone and no one knew about it, the whole world would be sweet like honey. Lynn and I wanted to try it. Was it naughty?" asked Charlene.

Even the Goldbergs couldn't help joining in the laughter.

"Let that be a lesson to you," said Mr. Goldberg. "Next time you talk about your honeymoon, be sure the girls aren't around. You never know what ideas pop into children's heads. It was lucky they just went into our station wagon."

That night Eric and Button thanked God that their family was together again. Those had been anxious hours without Charlene and Lynn, but they had not been scolded for their impromptu trip. This was all part of growing up. Soon they would be tiny plants no longer but would have to guide their own lives . . . and those few hours they had been lost had been like death itself.

"Oh," said Eric, "in the excitement I forgot to notify the police. Everyone has been so kind to us, but this will be the happiest news I've ever carried."

And never had two parents been so thankful.

BOOK III

CHAPTER 10

❧ Years That Trembled

I am going for a walk, Eric," called Button from the front hall, as she put on her jacket and tied a bandana around her hair.

"I wish I could go with you," answered Eric from upstairs. He was reading a bedtime story to Lynn. "But someone has to stay with the girls."

Button walked out into the dusk of an autumn evening which was permeated with the pungent smell of burning leaves. She chose the road leading through the park. A bit of blushing sky was still visible where the sun had descended to the horizon, but Button was blind to the beauty around her. Nor did she smell the smoking leaves. She was hardly aware of the season of the year, having but one purpose in mind, to walk as fast as her feet would carry her. If she had been much younger, she would have run swiftly down the street, through the park, up the hill and down again. A woman in her forties, however, does not run, nor does she cry or laugh or scream or give vent to any emotion in public as she walks along. She simply places one foot before the other and holds her head high. If she meets an acquaintance, she nods and forces a smile to her lips, even though her heart may be breaking.

As Button walked along, she tried not to think of the past years, and she tried not to think of the years ahead. She had to live in the present, a fact which she had never faced before. She had to put an end to her dreaming and learn to be like other people because she was sure that was the way Eric wanted her to be.

"No one can say that I haven't been a good mother," she told herself. "No one can say that I haven't tried to make my marriage a success. And Eric and I have been as happy as two people can be . . . we've shared whatever life has brought our way . . . we've loved our home and planted and cared for our garden . . . we've loved our girls and have given them not only material things but lofty thoughts, as well, that would feed their souls. Long ago we sorrowed over our first-born, whom we never held in our arms. When Papa left this earthly life, and I grieved for his going, Eric stood close beside me, a bulwark of strength and comfort. We have done all we could to create happiness, but inside my heart there's a vast emptiness, a crying, a knocking. I hear it at night when I sleep; I feel it the first thing in the morning when I open my eyes. I can't get away from it. I can't tell Eric about it, for he wouldn't understand. I don't know what to do . . . I just don't know."

She walked fast as she thought. Walking helped a little when she could walk alone. It was as though she wanted to escape from the gloom that entrapped her, but it was always waiting for her inside the door of her own home when she returned. She had felt like this for the past few years and she was not getting better. Where she was heading she did not know and she was afraid to face the future. What had happened to her? Somewhere, back in the years, she had lost herself. Part of her was still crying and calling her back. But life's highway is a one-way street and one cannot turn back. Once she had been gay and full of laughter. Now there was only sadness. Once she had dreamed beautiful dreams. Now she had lost the magic and the daring of dreaming. How does one who is broken to pieces become whole again? Once she had walked and talked with God, and she had given Him her special dream to keep in His care, believing that someday He would give it back to her, but He had not. How noble had been her dreams of becoming an author and writing a book that would make people laugh! She knew now that she would never write. Her head ached constantly from too much thinking, and the tension within her increased with each new day. She somehow had lost the real Button . . . but worse than that, she had lost her God, and there was no tragedy worse than that. And there was no Papa to talk to or to advise her.

For years after she was married she talked about dreams. She told Eric, "You must learn to dream," but Eric had been cross with her.

"That's the trouble with you, Button. You don't live in a real world. You're always up in the clouds. Fantasy is forgivable in one who is young, but you're not a child, you're a mature woman. Now you must act like one. What will the girls think? Don't you suppose they want a mother who acts like other mothers? The mothers of the children they know talk about how to make dresses and how to fix their hair and of the latest party and who is invited and who is not. They talk of school doings and the P.T.A. and many other everyday things. But our children's mother talks about writing books and flying to the moon and picking money from the street."

That was the longest speech Button had ever heard Eric make. She had stood there hurt and ashamed. She had had no idea that those were his sentiments.

"I'll try hard, Eric, to be different," she said meekly. "I'll do my best not to dream, but you knew I was like that when you married me. If you had just wanted an ordinary, sane woman, you should never have married me."

"Now dear," uttered Eric apologetically as he placed his arm around her, "I didn't mean to hurt you. You were all right for me and I didn't mind that talk, though I never understood it, but we have two daughters now. Please, Button, try to understand what I am trying to tell you without getting your feelings hurt."

She honestly tried, but the hurt grew deeper each day and her head ached more and more. One day Eric suggested taking her to the doctor. Button hesitated about going, for she felt that no new doctor could ever take kind old Dr. Davis's place, but reluctantly she went and found that Dr. Hasselton was very pleasant and just as kind as their old doctor had been. He gave her a very thorough physical examination and then spoke to Eric, who was waiting in the outer office.

"Mr. Bjork, there seems to be no physical cause for your wife's troubles. I would say the trouble lay more in an emotional conflict. Her nerves are not very steady. There seems to be something depressing her, making her moody like a person without hope. Can you give any reason for this?"

But Eric knew none.

The doctor shook his head. "It's hard to prescribe a

remedy when one doesn't know the cause of a condition. All I can suggest for the time being is that you give your wife a good time, make her laugh, have fun so she will find life enjoyable. This is very important, so do your best, for if she remains in this state, I'm afraid that she is headed for a serious nervous breakdown."

After that visit, Eric became so considerate and thoughtful that it was almost unbearable to Button. He endeavored to anticipate her every wish and kept the girls from tiring her whenever he was near.

"Remember, Charlene, Mommie isn't well; no noise, please."

And to Lynn, "Don't bother Mommie when Daddy is here. We must be very careful with her, remember?"

Thus, whenever she entered a room where the girls were, they dropped whatever they were doing and walked on tiptoe, looking at her wistfully as if she were a person from another planet. This was the last thing Button wanted, to be estranged from her daughters, but how could they understand what was even beyond her own knowledge?

Button missed Mama, too. She had moved to sunny Florida where, Nim had informed her, her life span would be increased immeasurably. Nim and Karin lived in Florida also. Nim was a surgeon now, "and a very busy one," Mama wrote. Mama did not live with her son and his wife. She had sold her Northern home and had bought a brand-new cottage in Miami. She was very happy there, and she still had Kerstin with her. Both Torkel and Calle were in theological school studying for the ministry, following in Papa's footsteps. Pelle and Felicia were still in the East, as was Greta, who was teaching school. It was strange to think that the large Franzon family were all scattered now, close as they had been while Papa was still with them and they lived in the parsonage. Button remembered that once long ago in Lapland, Papa had told them that this was bound to happen.

"We must be thankful as long as we can all be together," he had said one day after the morning prayer. "Life will part us soon enough when you all grow up and get married and have your own homes. It's wonderful to be as close to each other as we now are, but the years will change that and we will grow apart. Life has a way of running out of time very quickly."

The next day, when it was Nim's turn to pray, he had ended with these words, "Thank you, God, that we can all be so happy together in our parsonage. Please don't let us part from each other, but let us all die together."

Button missed Mama's daily telephone calls most of all. Each morning Mama used to call her and she always sounded happy as a lark. Those calls had made each day begin a little brighter for Button.

"Hello, Button," she would say. "What a wonderful new day God has given us to be glad in."

And then they had talked of everyday things, and Mama in her sunny way had solved any problems that troubled Button. Now Mama was hundreds of miles away and Papa still farther.

That night, when Button returned from her walk, Eric was waiting by the door. He took her jacket and hung it in the closet.

"You were gone a long, long time. I was worried about you," he said kindly.

"Oh, I'm sorry, Eric. I was just walking. Somehow, I

feel better when I walk, but now I'm very tired and, if you don't mind, I'll go right to bed."

She was undressed and in bed in a few moments. Eric brought her a cup of hot milk.

"Drink this and you'll feel much better. I hope you'll sleep through the whole night," he said as he sat down on the edge of the bed.

Exhausted as she was, sleep would not come. Hours later when Eric came to bed, she pretended to be asleep, lying very still with her eyes closed. It wasn't long before Eric's heavy breathing told her he was asleep. She opened her eyes wide then and stared at a small patch of light reflected on the ceiling from the streetlight. She knew she would lie awake for hours and hours, and the night would be dreadfully long. Toward morning she might doze for a short while but awaken at the slightest noise, exhausted from the lack of sleep. It had been like that night after night for a long time; for how long, she had stopped trying to recall.

There were sleeping tablets in the medicine cabinet and, if the night became too unbearable, she would take one. . . . Sleep finally came but not a restful sleep.

The next day her nerves were even more tense and her gloom thicker. Somehow she must get hold of herself, recapture the gay spirit of her former years. There must be something that could mend those nerves!

One day when she came home from her walk, Mama was there. What a happy surprise! Eric had written asking Mama to come, and she planned to spend a whole month with them. Button could relax from all responsibility, for Mama took over the household. Happiness reigned for a short while, but soon Button drifted back to her moodiness, and there was nothing Mama could do to help her.

"Well, I've done all I can," exclaimed Eric, throwing up his hands in despair. "I don't know what more I can do."

"We have to wait—and pray, Eric," soothed Mama. "Pray that God will make her well. And don't despair or lose courage. It's all for a purpose, for in God's plan He takes even the bad and turns it to the good. Only, we must have patience."

"But it has been such a long time since she was well. Perhaps she never will be cured at home. A rest home might be the answer, Mama? If she got away from us all, she might get well much faster."

"Well, let's wait a little longer," said Mama. "Nerves take a long time to heal; we all know that."

And Eric waited. Mama went back to her sunshine, and Button escaped further and further from them all into a world of her own—a strange, dark, fearful world.

One sleepless night while Button lay staring at the ceiling, a wild desire came over her to go for a drive. She slipped softly from the bed so as not to awaken Eric and made her way to the garage. Soon she was driving along the highway with the dark night enveloping her. It had been a daring thing to do, and Eric certainly would not have approved if he knew about it. Yet, if she drove fast, she left that gnawing feeling at the pit of her stomach behind her. She drove thus for two hours and then returned to the house. All was still. Eric was a sound sleeper and did not waken when she crept into bed beside him. She felt better than she had felt in months and soon fell into a deep untroubled sleep.

This drive in the dead of night gave her something to

hold on to. Faster and faster she had driven on the highway, farther and farther from the city, until at last calmness descended on her disturbed spirit. Then she had turned toward home. As she drove along, she had tried to find an anchor that would hold her fast. She reached out desperately for whatever she thought would help. The thought of God came first, the friendly God she had known in her youth, the God who had lived with the Franzons in the parsonage. Button remembered how secure they all felt when Papa and Mama went calling and left them alone because the last thing Mama would say was, "You be good children now. Know that God is right here with you while we're away. He will watch over you carefully, but remember, you can't put anything over on Him. If you're good, we might bring something nice home with us. Who knows?"

After Mama and Papa had left, Button recalled, they had wondered where God was sitting.

"Perhaps on the sofa," Calle had suggested. "There's no other place big enough."

They all had agreed that Calle was right and they had walked around the sofa very carefully, wondering what God would look like if they could see Him. When, by chance, a storm came up while Papa and Mama were gone, and the thunder rolled ominously and the lightning flashed threateningly, they had not been afraid, for who could fear with God himself keeping guard over them!

"I believe that is God out riding," Greta had said, as she pressed her face against the window and watched the rain pouring down in torrents. "And when we see the lightning, it's the fire from the wheels of God's chariot, for His horses run so fast that, when the wheels go over the stars, it looks like fire."

Yes, although their parsonage God had been very strict and despised sin, He had also been very good and watchful; it was comforting to have a God such as that. Now she had almost completely lost Him. But she must and she would hold on to herself so she would overcome her inner disturbances and once more be well again. She recalled a story from the Bible of Jacob's wrestling with God; maybe she, too, would have to wrestle with God before she could again find peace and be cured of every ill.

The third time Button took the car at night, Eric was waiting for her when she came home. He had a light on in the living room, and she could see him pacing back and forth. She stood in the doorway, her eyes looking pleadingly into his. He must understand that this driving was something she was compelled to do by a force within her that was stronger than herself.

"Button," said Eric kindly, "sit down on the sofa and we'll have a little talk."

Automatically she sat down.

"You know," he said, taking her hand in his, "this can't go on any longer. Can't you imagine how worried I was to know that you were out in the middle of the night, driving who knows where in your tired state of mind? Please, promise me that you won't take the car out any more at night."

"No, Eric, please don't make me promise that because driving at night has really helped me. After I come back, I can sleep."

"For my sake, dear, please!"

"No, I can't. It helps me, and I'll get well soon."

"Then there is no other course that I can take. . . . I'll take you to Doctor Hasselton tomorrow afternoon, and he'll have to make arrangements to place you in a rest home. It will be a private place, my dear, but a place where you can get well."

Button stared at Eric for a long time. Then her eyes filled with tears.

"Eric, I haven't lost my mind, if that's what you're thinking. But if you send me away, I am sure I will. Driving the car at night has helped me. I can sleep when I come home, and my heart does not beat so rapidly. Please, Eric, just let me drive, and I promise I'll soon be well."

But Eric would not. After that the door to the garage was locked, and Eric kept the key on his key ring. Button had never been so frightened. Wasn't there anyone who could help her? She hadn't lost her reason; she was only sick. . . . What would she do if Eric put her in—in that place?

One day Eric took her again to Doctor Hasselton. While she was dressing in the examination room, Eric and the doctor conferred in the adjoining office. She pressed close against the wall and tried to listen to their conversation.

"I can't take it any longer, Doctor," Eric pleaded. "You'll have to help us."

Doctor Hasselton answered very softly. Button strained her ears to hear him but could not, so she dressed very quickly and joined them in the office, looking anxiously from one to the other.

The doctor shook Eric's hand and, patting Button on the shoulder, said, "Be a good girl now, Button. We'll soon have you sitting on top of the world. I'll see you in a week, and I hope to have a very good report from Eric concerning you."

She wondered about that as they drove home. Did Doctor Hasselton mean that she would get better in a private rest home where people were confined who had lost their minds, or did he mean that he had persuaded Eric that she was better off at home? One thing she knew, that Eric could not confine her without a doctor's signature. The next time she saw him, she would ask him, but not Eric. She would try to act well . . . she would pretend to sleep . . . she would pretend that she was happy . . . she would be a good actress. Perhaps if she earnestly tried, God would help her . . . at least she would ask Him.

Button tried very hard to act as if she felt well, but it didn't fool Eric. Some people claim love is blind, but that certainly wasn't true with Eric, whose love made him see more sharply. He couldn't read Button's thoughts, so he believed this behavior to be a new phase of her illness. The lines in his face deepened, and his eyes looked sadder each day. There seemed to be nothing Button could do to help him, for her heart couldn't ache any longer . . . it felt dull and heavy, and she didn't care what either Eric or the girls were thinking. She felt as though she lived in another world. The years were trembling beneath her feet; there was nothing she could hold on to. If only Papa had been with her. Papa would have understood, for he knew everything; he would have found a way for her to get well. He would have said, "You're not giving up, are you, Button?" She could hear his voice, so full of strength and assurance. "Our life is like a ship. If we have an able captain, we will never lose our course."

Those words he had spoken long ago, and she wished she could hear him say them again. Then she remembered herself—the former Button—the one she had lost back in the years . . . the Button she had been before she lost her angel and before Papa left this earth. . . . That Button had been strong. Then she heard a voice within her, reminding her of the promise she had made to herself that, even though life's storms made her bend very low, she would never, never break. Something stirred within her— a longing—a caring for life that had been absent for too long a time. She heard herself speak:

"I must will myself to be better. I must believe that tomorrow is better than yesterday . . . I must will to will . . . will to will . . ." And somehow, from that moment, she found the incentive to try to get well.

"Father God," she prayed that night, "give me back my faith in life, in my loved ones, in my dream—and in You."

As night closed around her, there was hope in her for the first time since her illness, as though a star had pierced her darkness to let God's light shine through to her soul.

CHAPTER 11

❧ Dear Doctor

Button had an appointment with Doctor Hasselton. She had come to his office half an hour early. It was pleasant to sit in his lovely waiting room and somehow, here, it didn't hurt her to think. It was strange how close she had grown to feel toward this new doctor. It was almost as if Doctor Davis had never been, and yet he had been the Franzon family doctor and friend from the time they had come from Sweden until his retirement. He and his gentle wife had moved to California, and at first the world had seemed empty without him. Not that there had been much sickness in the parsonage, for Mama had prayed most of it away! But there had been many talks over the telephone and an endless amount of advice from the kind doctor, who felt that for the best welfare of the community a doctor and minister should work closely together. Button wished Doctor and Mrs. Davis a most enjoyable sunset of life as they lived its last chapter.

It was Doctor Davis who had recommended Doctor Hasselton to Eric when he had written him, asking his advice concerning Button's illness. Doctor Davis had given his successor the finest recommendation:

184

Doctor Hasselton is a fine medical doctor, advisor and surgeon. He is also very cognizant of the fact that emotional disturbances can cause physical suffering. He is a fine church member, which would be important to Button. I have complete confidence in his ability and believe that he can cope with any situation. If anyone can help our Button, Doctor Hasselton can.

That had been five years ago . . . a long five years during which Button had been ill, not with a disease that could be easily diagnosed, such as of the liver or heart, but one that couldn't be pinpointed. That it was nerves, both the doctor and family agreed, but what caused them to act in this behavior pattern was something not easily answered.

Well, Button thought, if everything could be just black or white or rosy colored . . . but into the tapestry of life must also be woven the grays and they were the nonunderstandable ones. Beautiful blues and greens were fine, blended with golden colors from blushing sunsets and majestic sunrises, for they signified life at its best. White stood for a heart right with God, black for life's sorrow, but gray represented turmoil and confusion—dull, dreary, monotonous gray being painfully woven into the fabric of her life.

Button was glad that Doctor Hasselton was such a fine man, easy to talk to and easy to look at. He must be about her own age, she reflected, with dark hair and brown eyes that penetrated deeply as he consulted with his patients. Button liked his hands best—strong and firm but gentle hands from which strength seemed to flow as he placed them on hers when she was troubled. Sometimes with his hand on hers, she felt as if she had been given a transfusion of new life. No matter how dark the shadows were around her, after a talk with the doctor, they lightened.

Today she had an important question to ask the doctor.

He came into the office earlier than usual and his kind nurse opened the door of the waiting room.

"Doctor Hasselton is ready for you now, Mrs. Bjork," she beckoned smilingly.

A few minutes later Button was sitting in a comfortable chair opposite his desk. He smiled across at her and she returned his smile timidly. Strange how much easier it was to smile at the doctor than at Eric.

He began the conversation. "You're looking very well today, Button. I hope you'll tell me that you feel as well as you look?"

"I wish I could, Doctor. Whenever I'm here with you, I feel fine. All my fears and troubles disappear. I think each time I leave your office that the coming week will be a good one in which I'll make great progress, but the minute I close your door all my fears return."

"There's no need to give you a physical exam each time you come in, Button, nor to take your blood pressure, so we'll spend our time just talking. In spite of everything you say, I'm going to make believe that you really are better. Will you co-operate and help me in my game?"

"I'll try!"

"Eric phoned me last night. We had a long talk, and he expects much from your visit with me today."

"Too much, perhaps! Please tell me, is he planning to send me to an asylum?"

"What a terrible way to put it, Button. Certainly not an asylum. Eric has a rest home in mind, a place where a person like you can get the care and rest that you need and come out cured. Those places are very expensive, and it will take all your savings if you go. Don't think that Eric would even consider a place like that except in your best interest. Believe me, Button, he's tried his best all these years to help you, but you don't respond very well."

"I know. I'm sorry for him, for me, for the girls. I know Eric has the best in mind, but I will not go—not even to a home like that. . . . Please, Doctor Hasselton, help me." And Button gazed at the doctor with wide imploring eyes, full of helplessness and despair.

The office was very still. The telephone rang and the doctor talked with another patient. Button's eyes wandered around the room and suddenly the odor of antiseptics and the sight of the prescription pad made her feel fenced in. She had a wild impulse to run, just to get away, but the next moment she was composed again.

"Button," said Doctor Hasselton very gently, "I want to help you! But if I persuade Eric not to send you to a home, you must work with me. You see, neither I nor anyone else can mend your frayed nerves. You're the only one who can do it. It's up to you, so let's try a little longer and harder to get at the root of your trouble. There's something buried, deep, deep within you, that is the cause of your illness. It's bottled up there and if we don't release it, you'll be blown to pieces as if by an explosion. Will you search deep and try to tell me what it is?"

"I'll try. You know, I lost my first baby. I fell on the ice and it died. I killed it."

"You know better. You loved that baby and wanted it more than life itself. You did *not* kill it any more than I kill a person upon whom I am called to operate too late."

"Thank you. I'll try to think of it in that light. I don't dwell on it too often now. I'm too tired."

"That could have been the beginning of your trouble, the shock to your nerves, but you're much too intelligent to let that incident alone ruin your health."

"It's missing Papa, too! Sometimes I think I can't stand to live without Papa. I grieve over the heartaches I caused him when I was little. . . . I—I . . ."

Button placed her head on the desk and let her tears flow. Doctor Hasselton lifted up her face and shook his head. He wiped the tears from her eyes.

"You're not a little girl any more, Button, but a grown woman. You know that we all have to part with our loved ones. Your father was an old man and ready to enter into the larger life. Would you be selfish enough to hold him back from what God had prepared for him? We who have hope in this mystery called immortality do not sorrow as do those without hope of eternal life. You still have your mother. I lost both my parents when I was young, and believe me, my dear, I loved them dearly and life was hard to face without them. But do you think I should have given up my talent and sacrificed my career to devote my time to grieving? Would that have brought them back?"

"Oh, no, I can see how selfish I've been. I was only thinking of my own loss!"

Button tried to force a smile, but it soon died on her lips.

"Doctor, do you think I could have married the wrong man? Perhaps I don't love Eric the way I should?"

Doctor Hasselton laughed a hearty laugh.

"Forgive me, Button, but your question struck me funny. You see, in my profession I see so much of the inside of people's marriages. I recognize an unhappy marriage when I see one, but from what I have seen of you and Eric, I'd say you were made for each other. Think of how he has stood by you and loved you and been concerned over you through all these years of your sickness. That takes real love, believe me, for he's had to live through many dark hours. Yet all he wants is for you to get well . . . not only for his sake but more for your own. He wants you to live again in your world of joy that was such an integral part of you. He told me that you used to be so gay no one could come near you without catching a good share of it."

"I know you must be right, but being so confused that question just popped into my head. I know if I were well, Eric and I would be very happy together. Perhaps it is Charlene. I may get too upset with worry over that child. She's constantly doing things she shouldn't do."

"Now you are looking for a needle in a haystack. If all parents of naughty children became as ill as you are, we would have a pretty sick world! Often, you know, the naughtiest children grow up to be the smartest people. The alertness and inventiveness that cause so much mischief when they're young become their most admirable traits when they mature. You have two lovely daughters, Button, and neither one of them could be the cause for your breakdown."

There was one more thing. It flickered like a light within her heart. It was her dream—her writing—but somehow she couldn't talk about it. . . . There was no use to try. . . . He might laugh at her, thinking she was just trying to find things for him to analyze.

"I suppose, I should be ashamed of myself," she said, "for when it comes right down to it, I don't have any reason for my trouble. But it's there. . . . I can't get rid of it . . . it grows and grows. . . . I don't know what to do."

Doctor Hasselton stood up. "Well, my dear," he smiled, "you've done your best for today. We'll find this thing that troubles you. Now promise me that you won't worry over the cause of your illness. From now on you let me worry about that! And you can feel assured that no one, not even Eric, can send you away without my consent. I am your doctor, Button, and you must trust me. I'll do everything in my power to help you. I won't let you down, I promise."

She shook his hand. "I don't know how to express what I feel, but I am so very grateful. I feel as if a heavy burden had been lifted from me. I feel confident that, as long as you stand by me, we can lick this thing together. I, too, promise not to let you down."

He put his arm around her shoulder and smiled down on her. "I like to hear you say that, Button. You wait and see; this may be the end of all your confusion. I feel that today we have really accomplished something worth while."

Button walked home feeling happier than she had in years. Oh, Doctor Hasselton was the most wonderful man she had ever known. He would never, never let anyone send her away from her home—not even Eric!

That night, when she returned from her long walk, she felt happy. Eric was working in the cellar, fixing a bicycle for Lynn. The girls were asleep. The house was still and peaceful. Button sat down at her Governor Winthrop desk in the cozy living room and almost before she realized it, she had started a letter:

Dear Doctor,

I must write to you tonight. During every minute of my long walk, my thoughts were with you in your office. I could see your face as kindly and patiently you minister to those who come to seek your help. You are so wonderfully kind, and I want you to know that my heart is so full of gratitude that I can hardly express it. You are the most wonderful person I have ever met. Thank you for giving life back to me anew. I can live it now without fear. I shall get well because of you. Nothing in the whole world can harm me. I shall go to bed after I have mailed this letter, and I believe that I will fall asleep quickly. I hope that you understand what I am trying to say. Words seem so inadequate to express what is in my heart. Please realize that those long hours you give to mankind are worth while . . . so very worth while.

Good night,
Button

She hurried to the corner to mail her letter before Eric came up from the cellar. When he did, Button was sitting in her favorite blue chair, reading a magazine.

"Button," he said, with beaming face, "how well you look tonight and so happy. It's good to see you sitting there just like old times."

"I feel better, Eric, a lot better. I hope it continues."

That night she was awakened only once by her own thoughts, which were again with Doctor Hasselton. She hoped that he had a kind and understanding wife, for tomorrow he might have to mend another broken heart. Soon she drifted back to sleep, a happy smile playing on her lips.

Button did not walk alone any more. Doctor Hasselton

walked beside her. They did not speak to each other, but he was there; a dream figure, of course, but more real than flesh and blood to Button. She felt secure now. Life had meaning once more. At last she had found something to hold on to, and the old sparkle began to return to her eyes.

It was time for another visit. Wouldn't Doctor Hasselton be surprised! He wouldn't recognize her as the same person. Going to his office was as much fun as going on a trip.

As she sat in the waiting room, an unexpected fear came over her. She hadn't given it a thought before, but had she been foolish to write him, busy as he was? She could not even remember what she had written. She should not have mailed her letter so soon before thinking over what she had said. Anxiety filled her. Perhaps Doctor Hasselton would scold her in a polite way and tell her he was a very busy man . . . that he had to limit his time with each patient to the office visit . . . that reading letters was not expected of him as a medical doctor. . . . Oh, why had she done such a foolish thing! She always rushed into things impulsively, without thinking, and now this last might be worse than the first. Button almost decided to walk out of the waiting room, make an excuse to the nurse, when . . .

"Your turn, Mrs. Bjork!" said the nurse from the doorway, and there, inside the other door, she could see Doctor Hasselton's smiling face.

"Why, Button!" he exclaimed. "You look wonderful today. I was so happy your shared your thoughts with me. Do you still sleep well?"

"Doctor Hasselton, I want to apologize for bothering you with my letter. . . . I'm so ashamed of myself. I just didn't stop to think. You see, the minute I sat down to write, the whole world straightened out for me. I forgot that you are a busy doctor and can't be expected to spend your valuable time reading silly letters——"

"Button, what are you saying? Now stop that kind of talk this moment. Anything that helps to soothe your nerves is a tonic for you and all right with me. My time is consecrated to helping my patients, and it doesn't matter to me whether it is through office visits or reading letters. My only concern is to cure my patients."

"Thank you, that is a great relief. . . . I was so worried!"

After the examination and the usual preliminaries were over, Doctor Hasselton handed Button a prescription.

"Button," he said, "don't take this to the druggist. Because of its importance, I have written it out for you. It is not a prescription for a new tonic or stronger sleeping pills, but I believe it will work better."

Button glanced down at the paper, then a happy, silvery laugh came from her lips.

"Read it to me," said the doctor.

Button read: " 'I, Doctor Hasselton, do hereby prescribe that Mrs. Eric Bjork write me a letter at least once, but better yet, twice a day, until further notice. Doctor Hasselton.'

"Oh, I like that prescription! You can be sure I'll take it as directed. You've made me the happiest person on earth, Doctor."

And it worked! Button couldn't wait for each new day to come so she could write more letters. She wrote one in the afternoon after her walk and very often she wrote a shorter one before retiring. The afternoon letters were more in the form of a report, but the evening ones were of a more dreamy nature.

Afternoon January 10, 19——

Dear Doctor,

I walked today in the snow while the wind whipped my face and the world looked like a huge bowl of whipped cream. (I love whipped cream!) But in spite of the beauty of this winter wonderland, I did not see the snow. No, in my heart it was spring. The first tulips were lifting up their little heads from the dark earth, the lawn had a fine shadow of soft green grass, the leaves were bursting forth on the branches of tree and bush and, of course, hundreds of birds were singing their joyous melodies as they were building their nests! Yes, in my heart spring has come even though the calendar says January, and all because I am getting well. I feel like laughing and singing and having fun. To me this all seems so new that it is almost strange . . . and yet, this is the way I used to feel a long, long time ago . . . and all because of you.

Button

Evening, January 10, 19——

Dear Doctor,

This is just to say good night! I have had such a fine day. I am tired tonight . . . a real honest-to-goodness tiredness and I know that I can go right to sleep. Having been without peaceful sleep for so long, I can really appreciate it now. There is a big silly moon tonight peeking down at me. I wonder, can you see it from your office window and, if you can, does it make you wish you were very young again? (Now that was foolish and perhaps I shouldn't have written it, but I wanted to, so I did. I hope it is included in your prescription!) I will stop now before I say something worse!

Good night,
Button

And the next day:

Dear Doctor,

This is a new day! I am happy because each new day presents a challenge for me to do better, be happier, and send you a better report. It is like climbing a mountain . . . way, way up there is the top for which I am aiming. Sometimes I have almost reached it . . . just a few more steps, and then I tumble down . . . down . . . until the top seems farther away than before. But I shall reach it. One day I shall stand on the summit and shout, 'I made it! I made it!' I know that each tomorrow I shall be better than I was on the yesterday. That assurance I have in my heart, so why should I fear?

Button

Because life commenced to be good again, Button very soon began to feel at home with her family. Sometimes the four of them walked together now, and very often Button would be in a storytelling mood and relate things for the girls from her own childhood. At night, when the girls were in bed, Eric and she often took long rides out through the countryside. She sat close to him and slipped her arm through his and they talked small talk that was gentle and soothing to her spirit and brought them closer together. They spoke of the girls' futures and the things they would plant in their garden the following spring, where they would spend their next vacation, anything connected with the daily routine of their homelife. They never mentioned the past or Button's sickness, and Button never told of her letters to Doctor Hasselton. A year had gone by and she still abided by that prescription. To write her letters had become the pattern of her day, a gay pattern, making bright colors in the tapestry of gray.

One day as she was writing her letter, a thought came to her. She was well now. She really had no need of writing. Then why did she still keep on? But just the thought of stopping made her feel as though the sun would stop shining. She hadn't the strength yet to stand alone, she told herself.

It was marvelous to be well. Her letters were happy ones now, full of humor and laughter. She did not go to the doctor's office so often any more; the period between visits was lengthening.

One beautiful spring night, when she had just mailed her good-night note to Doctor Hasselton, the question as to why she was still writing him came to her with an overwhelming force. Over and over again she asked herself that question. Did Doctor Hasselton mean more to her than her own husband? It was a frightening thought and one Button did not like to face. But she did, for honesty had always been a sacred part of her marriage to Eric. If she was doing something wrong, she must analyze the situation carefully. She tossed on her bed that night, thinking of Eric . . . how dear and fine he was and how hard he had struggled through those unhappy years. He certainly was entitled to something better than a wife who lived only for the letters she could write to her doctor. However, she wasn't unhappy with Eric, nor was she jealous of Doctor Hasselton's family. What then, had happened to her?

Miraculously the fog around her lifted, and she was out in the clear. She could see distinctly, and she had her answer. . . . Her dream! Her calling! How blind she had been! Writing those letters had fulfilled the dearest desire of her life—to write! Her heart beat wildly with joy. "I have found it!" her heart sang. The doctor had told her there was a reason for her emotional disturbance, and she had found it. It was the neglecting of her talent that had made her ill; it had been dormant for too many years . . . it had ached and cried and sobbed within her and she had not known. She did not need to write letters any more. Her heart was clean. All was well. She would write the final letter to her doctor and give him the glad news.

The morning was utterly beautiful! Eric had gone to work and Charlene and Lynn to school. Button sat a long time at her desk, staring down at the white paper that would soon be filled with words—the last letter to her doctor. The paper was so still, so white, and it drew her like a magnet and slowly her heart followed:

Dear Doctor,

This is the last letter that I shall write to you. For a long time I have known that it was not necessary for me to write, and yet I couldn't bear the thought of not writing you. Why? I kept asking myself. Today I know the answer. Can you understand that I wanted to write to you more than I wanted to eat, or sleep, or live? When I acknowledged that thought, it frightened me. I wondered if it was wrong. Did I like you too much?

It was as if my writing to you was a crutch which I no longer needed but refused to discard. Then, as brilliantly as the sun breaks through the clouds, the answer came to me. Not you, but my love of writing was the object of my affection. As a little girl I received a call to write and I gave my dream into God's keeping that He might give it back to me. But for years I have neglected my talent; it has lain dormant in my heart, receiving no consideration, no nourishment, no love, and it made my body ill. That was the cry I heard at night, the gloom that was my companion during those long dark years. Can't you understand it now? You said we would find it and we have, we have! I shall never get sick again for I shall write, not letters, but stories and poems and anecdotes. I can hardly wait to get started, and I know how happy you are for me. I still think that you are the most wonderful person that I have ever known. You did it! Perhaps it is more tangible to see a person get well from a sick stomach, or to set a broken rib, but to lead a person out of darkness into light, to heal one's blindness so one can see, that is more than a cure; it is a miracle. It worried me that I might be in love with you, but I did not understand. I never loved anyone but my Eric, and now that I know this, I can be a better wife to him. I wonder, are there others who are sick to their souls because they have lost their dreams, because great talents are slumbering deep, deep within their hearts? That is your field, Doctor, but I pray my foolish letters may become an instrument for you, a tool by which to dig deep beneath the surface of something called nerves into the center that needs healing. I am the fruit of your labor for all the world to see, and when my first book is written, you will have had more to do with its production than anyone will ever know. So here I am, Doctor, happy, gay and fully recovered!

In deep gratitude,
Button

"Eric," said Button a few nights later as they were sitting hand in hand before the open fire in the living room, "I'll never be sick again. I've found the cause. It was not the angel we lost, or Papa's passing away, or the trouble with Charlene. It was my calling which I pressed down deeper and deeper. Perhaps you will never fully understand what I'm trying to tell you, but watch me and see that from now on I shall be the happiest person on earth. Doctor Hasselton helped me with my problem; it was like a picture puzzle not yet put together, but now all the pieces fit and the picture is whole."

"Then we owe Doctor Hasselton more than we can ever pay him."

"Yes, darling! We owe him our very happiness. You see, Eric, life is a trust given to us by God, and we are like a garden where seed is planted. A seed must either grow or die. My seed was meant to grow into writing, and it almost died, but fortunately I recognized it with the doctor's help."

Eric gave Button a puzzled look. "I can't follow you, dear, but I feel I should sit down and write our doctor a letter of thanks . . . for getting you back . . . and the way you are talking, I know you are really back."

Button laughed. "No, Eric, don't write him. Just give him a ring on the phone. He's a very busy man."

Eric drew her close. "I don't think I'll ever be able to understand this woman I married. I discover new traits each day . . . but they don't worry me . . . I like you just the way you are."

That night Button was too excited to go right to sleep; she could feel something stirring and knocking within her and she spoke to it as a mother would to a child.

"Be still, my soul, for out of you shall come, very soon now, a beautiful dream that God has given back to me."

She slept that night with a joyous smile on her lips and with a heart that was happy and content.

CHAPTER 12

❧ The Awaking

It was as though Button had suddenly emerged from the mist into the sunshine. The world was new! Its beauty was breath-taking! Every dewdrop was a miracle as it glittered like a diamond on the roses in the garden. To think that for those many years when she had lived among the shadows she had been blind to the beauty of Eric's roses. Now she waited anxiously for rising time to come each morning so she could stroll through the garden with him before he went to work.

One morning as they stood by the rose bed, Eric cut a red rosebud that was just opening, so exquisite in its beauty that Button thought it must be one of the loveliest of God's creation.

"For you, my dear, from all the flowers in the garden, welcoming you back," he smiled.

"Eric," Button whispered, "Eric, you've learned to say pretty words. That was so lovely I could cry! I feel as if all the flowers, bushes and trees are lifting up their heads and looking wide-eyed, saying, 'Look, our Button is back!' I know they are as happy as you and I. Now we shall live and enjoy every moment of time. By the way, Eric, how many years are left until you are one hundred and eleven?"

Eric laughed. "The same old gal, talking silly as she used to do. But now I like it. Your illness taught me a good lesson, for I never could get used to that other Button, gloomy and cross and without the magic power of dreaming lovely dreams."

"And now, Eric, I shall write. . . . I'll write because I know it is part of God's plan for me. I'll write a book, Eric, but first I'll create a story for our girls, a story of Mama and Papa and our life in the parsonage in Lapland. I'll tell of our coming here, to Berkley Hills, and the new experiences we had in this country. It will be a gay story, full of life, and they will treasure it always and hand it down to their children and their children's children. It could be that years and years from now, Eric, someone will hold up an old manuscript, yellow with age, and say, 'My great-great-grandmother wrote this story way back in the nineteen hundred fifties.' Can't you picture that?"

He drew her close. "I can picture almost anything while you are telling me, but the most important thing is that you are happy. That makes me glad, too. And now may I tell you something about me?"

"About you, Eric?"

"Yes, me. You're not the only one who has dreamed dreams. Believe it or not, I've had a dream for many years. It's not as lofty a dream as yours, for I could never 'hitch my wagon to a star,' but it's a dream just the same. Button, I'm starting my own shop."

Button stared wide-eyed at her husband.

"Eric, oh, Eric, how wonderful! When? . . . How? . . . What? I'm unable to think for a moment. You mean

that you'll have your own machines . . . your own men
. . . not work for anyone else . . . your own place?"

"Something like that, dear. The machines are ordered.
I'm resigning from my job next week, and tonight I want
you to go with me and look over a couple of places I can
rent."

After a happy Eric had driven off and she had blown
him a kiss, Button poured herself another cup of coffee and
sat down on the bench in the garden. The bees were flit-
tering among the flowers, the birds were chirping their
morning songs, and the sun was shining with a new brilliance. Her eyes opened wide to drink in all this beauty
and her heart beat fast. To think that she could have been
so unperceptive as to have lived with Eric all these years
and not know that he, too, sheltered a dream. During her
long illness, all through those dark, trembling years, he had
held fast to his dream. And she had thought him incapable
of dreaming! His dream had been different from hers, and
his was on the brink of fulfillment. She was glad! God had
been good to them! As Mama had said, "He does more than
we ask Him to, for he just loves to make us glad!"

These mornings she delighted in getting breakfast for
the girls and watching them go off to school. They were
both blue-eyed blondes, real Scandinavian types. Charlene
was in the last year of high school and would be leaving
home in another year to attend college. How swiftly the
years had flown by! Imagine, little Lynn in junior high.
Soon both the girls would be married and have their own
children. She and Eric would be grandparents! Life offered so many joys, each year a new joy and a new miracle.

Button did not fear the future any more, for in her
heart she knew that she was ready for the dream God was

giving back to her. All she had to do was to commence to write and see her work take shape and form. Now she understood that she had profited from those years of darkness, for she had learned what it was to suffer and to feel lost and bewildered and separated from God. She had gone through life's hard school. Because of this experience her writing would be richer, for she now knew how it felt to walk in the shadows! Once she had heard a voice in her heart saying, "If you can live your dream," and wasn't that living it—to go through joy and sorrow, light and darkness? So in His great plan God can take all the dark yesterdays and turn them into bright tomorrows. She was thankful her suffering was over but glad that she had gone through it, for she had grown stronger because of it, and more mellow in her judgment of others.

Button arose from the garden bench. Today she would start her book for the girls, her Mama and Papa stories. She would use all the talent she possessed, for this would be a trial book out of which her real book would come later. She felt that the words were already in her mind and heart, planted there by God.

There on the kitchen table were the paper and pencil. They drew her like a magnet. She wished Doctor Hasselton could see her now, for she was as happy as when, at this very table, she had written many letters to him. Her gaze wandered out through the kitchen window to the light blue, cloudless sky. . . .

Doctor Hasselton was pleased with her recovery.

"We did it, Button," he beamed, "together we found it! You are cured now for good and need never go backward, just forward to new health and joy and happiness, and someday I shall read that book. Your dream is to create stories. I, too, have a dream, a desire to create whole people. Every doctor has a dream in his heart. Mine has just begun. As you said in your last letter, your illness will serve to help others. I'll always wonder as I deal with people whose nerves are afflicted, if deep, deep down within that person there slumbers another Button . . . someone who has lost a buried dream. I've seen a bit of the mystery of the soul. I know much more now about how to help others."

"I am so very happy," Button smiled. "We all have dreams . . . even Eric. His was strong and practical and tangible, but it followed the same pattern as mine. We call it by different names, perhaps, such as faith or hope or longing, but the foundation of all those yearnings and moods are dreams that knock on the heart and beg to be recognized."

They talked about Eric, and how he had surprised them both.

"Yes, Eric will be a strong dreamer," the doctor said. "I marvel at the courage and strength and fortitude he displayed all through those long dark years. He never lost his sense of balance. You have a man, Button, that many a woman would envy you, for he is kind and has strength of character and will not easily be upset as he sails over life's troubled seas."

"He's like a ship which has an able captain," Button had answered, remembering Papa's words of long ago.

"Yes," confirmed the doctor, "what better definition than that could be given. Eric is a firm, staunch ship that can traverse any ocean."

It had been good to talk to Doctor Hasselton that day.

What a dear friend he had become! How could they ever have succeeded without him?

What an ideal day to begin her story. The girls had left early for a weekend trip with their church group. She and Eric would be alone in their house for the first time in years. As this was Saturday, Eric would be home at noon, but she had the whole morning free and she would use every second of it. There was also the possibility that Eric might telephone her that he wouldn't be home until later in the afternoon, for that happened often these days when he was winding up his work at his place of employment. Now that she knew his secret, she realized why he had spent so much time away from her. Soon now, very soon, he would be his own boss. She also understood now why he had been so happy and relaxed even when very tired, for his dream was coming true. He could visualize it in his mind now and because of this, he was growing in greatness. All was well with his soul, and he would give his time to building stronger and more noble dreams.

Button took one longing look at the paper and pencil, but decided she better put the house in order first. In Charlene's room the bed was made and everything in perfect order. Her older daughter had inherited her grandmother's perfect housekeeping ability. It was different in Lynn's room. Button smiled as she thought of her younger daughter. As much joy and happiness as she created with her sunny disposition, she certainly wasn't tidy. Her room looked as if a cyclone had struck it. Always there was plenty of work to do after her. Charlene never would walk off without helping with the dishes, but Lynn sought for every opportunity to escape from labor. "She will straighten out,"

Button assured herself. Hadn't the many hours of worry over Charlene as a child turned out to be needless? She was a fine girl now. Who could say what slumbered in her two girls' hearts? They too might be dreaming great dreams for the future. The greatest gift she could give them was to allow them the freedom to grow up to be themselves. Their pattern might be very different from Eric's or hers, for didn't God stamp His own peculiar design on each heart?

After finishing her work, she wandered once more through the rooms. It was such a dear house . . . old now and not sparkling new as in the beginning . . . it had been lived in with laughter and tears, with songs and sighings. What precious memories, what many heartaches were hidden within its walls, serving to endear it to their hearts more and more with each passing year. The fresh garden flowers she had picked this morning wafted their fragrance through the rooms. She would not exchange this home for a mansion.

The kitchen with its big window overlooking the garden was the nicest room of them all. Now it was summer, but the view in the fall, when the autumn leaves flaunted their rainbow colors, would be just as beautiful. In fact, it was hard to decide which season was the prettiest. Button loved the spring when the tulips poked up their curious little funny faces to look at the green world, and the early summer when Eric's roses burst into bloom. But perhaps she loved winter best of all, for the snowclad trees and bushes transformed the yard into a fairy wonderland, reminding her of her own childhood days in Lapland where winter cold froze all nature into a crisp, magic white world. Every season had its unique beauty, and she would never stop being grateful to God for giving them a home such as this. The kitchen was painted yellow and blue, the colors of her homeland flag. The true blue color was that of the Swedish sky mirrored in the hundreds of lakes, and the yellow, she had told the girls, was the exact shade of the ripe grain, ready for harvest, blowing in the wind in the Swedish fields.

Someday, she hoped Eric and she could take the girls to Sweden that they might see and get the feel of their parents' birth land . . . someday when she was an author and Eric a successful businessman! So new dreams were being spun and would be dreamed high until fulfilled.

At last she was ready to start her task. This would have to be a fine story. She must relive it again and again so she could really put Papa and Mama and the parsonage down on paper. Since this book would be her first attempt at real writing, she must open her heart and mind so that everything that was hidden there could pour forth freely.

She let her thoughts wander back. It was spring in Lapland. No place on earth was more beautiful! The leaves on the trees were so fresh and delicate, and in no other place in the world could they be so green, green. The twilight lingered for hours over the mountain until, by the time summer came, there was no darkness at all, just an everlasting day. Oh, she had almost forgotten the beauty of her homeland! The cuckoo bird that called in the treetop, the dark forest, the fields with hundreds of different wild flowers, the little children picking huge bouquets to take home to their mothers. Barefooted they tramped up the road, flaxen-haired and red-cheeked, with laughing blue eyes and chubby brown hands! She had been like that, running barefooted, picking flowers and *smultron*-berries in the ditches. Karin and she had strung those miniature red strawberries on straws and what fun to carry them around to tempt others and finally to sit down on a large boulder and eat them one by one! And the lingonberries! The woods were full of them, and each fall Papa would take them all to pick pails full of them. Button could still smell the sauce as Mama cooked kettles full to store for the long winter and eat with potatoes instead of meat. And the preserve she made to eat especially with *plättar*. . . . Button must recapture all these memories so her girls, too, could live in Sweden while they read the story of her childhood's land.

And so Papa . . . dear, dear Papa! She was in her early teens . . . perhaps it was only thirteen, when they had walked up the mountain on a lovely spring night. What a night! The stars, the moon, and the blue mountains that had looked black that night in the moonlight, the smell of new green leaves, lovers walking arm in arm, soft whispers and silvery laughter all mingled together to make this magic night. The mountains were full of love words . . . and she was walking with Papa. . . . She had had other plans but Papa had said, "Button, I want you to take a walk with me up the mountain road tonight."

When Papa said that, you walked with Papa. He had been very quiet, obviously unaware of the beauty of the night . . . most likely pondering upon his sermon for the following Sunday. Papa received inspiration for his good Sunday sermons by taking long walks. Well, Button was not in the mood to walk quietly. She wanted to talk! She wanted to laugh! She wanted to have fun! She would make Papa talk to her as never before; she would have to or she would scream. So she placed her arm in his and snuggled close. She measured her stride and tried to make it coincide with Papa's long steps.

"It's fun walking!" she said laughingly.

Papa did not answer. He seemed to be totally unaware of her presence.

"Papa," she ventured again. "I've often wondered about you and Mama. How did you happen to marry her when she is so much younger than you?"

Still silence from Papa. He walked fast, looking straight ahead not even glancing at Button. He was quiet for so long that Button thought she must have offended him by mentioning his age. Perhaps he would just ignore her question, for she had been foolish to ask him. Papa was very sensitive and she had wounded his pride.

Then . . . first a chuckle from Papa . . . then he laughed out loud . . . and his arm went around her shoulder.

"Button, my dear," he said, "how I married your Mama . . . that is still a mystery to me. But if you want a story I'll tell it to you."

A story! Papa had been in a storytelling mood and she would never forget the one he had told her. She never knew Papa could be so comical. She laughed more in that one night than she had in a year. And she would write it just as Papa had told it. She would call her story: THERETO I PLIGHT THEE MY TROTH.

Button wrote with joy! Her pencil flew over the paper. She forgot time and place, and when Eric came home at noon there was no lunch ready for him.

"Oh, darling," she cried, "forgive me . . . I had completely forgotten that I had a hungry husband. I'm having so much fun writing this Papa and Mama story. Oh,

Eric, the girls will love it. They will never have heard of a stranger romance."

Eric frowned, but Button knew it was only to tease her, for behind that frown lurked a happy smile.

"If this is an example of what it is like to have my wife an author, then I will have nothing of it. I shall put my foot down right from the beginning—no lunch—no coffee percolating—just a starry-eyed wife with roses in her cheeks."

"Oh, Eric"—her arms went around his neck—"I am sorry! But as for putting your foot down, you're much too late, Mr. Bjork . . . that foot of yours wouldn't even leave an imprint!"

Soon she had lunch on the table and they discussed the story she was writing.

"Will it be ready for Christmas?" asked Eric.

"I think it will. If I write every chapter as fast as I wrote this first one, it will be ready in a week!"

Day after day Button continued writing until she had four chapters completed. Then she showed them to her friend, Vera Sallin, who was known as a literary critic. Vera read the story with genuine interest.

"This is excellent," she assured Button when she had finished reading it. "Of course there are errors of spelling and construction, but those are not too important and can easily be corrected. I'd be happy to do it for you and at the same time type it for easier reading."

"Oh, thank you, Vera," responded Button with a jubilant face. "I'm so glad you like it! And now I understand what Papa meant about my need for studying. What a fool I was not to continue my schooling in America. How I wish I could undo that big mistake. But it's too late now. You're

a dear to help me get the book written correctly so I will
not need to feel shame before my girls. Having it typed will
make it look like a real book."

Vera finished the work in a week and telephoned Button.

"Come on over, Button. I've something I would like
to suggest to you."

Vera had coffee ready when Button arrived breathless
with excitement.

"I can't wait to see it, Vera. Does it look like a book?"

They drank coffee in Vera's cozy living room. A heavy
rain was beating against the windowpanes, but Vera had a
sparkling fire lit in her huge fire place to take the chill
from this damp, late-summer day. Button watched the brilliant tongues of fire leap up and down on the big log.

"Button," asked Vera when their coffee was drunk,
"have you ever considered what a good book this story
would make?"

Button laughed. "You mean that all that foolishness
I've written about Papa and Mama should be put into a
book for people outside the family to read?"

"Yes, my dear! They would love it! Button, you have
a rare gift of making words live on paper. You say things in
a simple, natural, home-spun fashion that will fascinate
people."

"But if I sold it, I couldn't give it as a gift to the girls
at Christmas," protested Button, her heart beating madly.

Vera looked seriously into Button's eyes. "Don't you
think the girls would like a real book better?"

Button had never thought of that. It would be wonderful . . . too wonderful for her to grasp.

"Why don't we try to sell it to a magazine first?" Vera

suggested, and she mentioned the name of a prominent magazine.

Button followed Vera's advice. Gently she folded the manuscript and placed it in a large Manila envelope. She enclosed another envelope, self-addressed and stamped just in case . . . if . . . but she would refuse to consider an *if*. She took it to the big mailbox on the corner and deposited it with a prayer.

"Please God," she whispered as she watched it slide down the chute, "please God, don't let them return it to me. Make them accept it . . . please . . . please. If you ever answered a prayer, let it be this one."

Then came the longest wait that Button had ever known. She waited two endless months and three days. Each time she saw the mailman walk up the street she became sick with fear, hoping that he would not produce a large Manila envelope.

Vera was hopeful. "I'm almost certain they'll keep it. If not, you would have heard by now."

"Oh, I do hope they will," sighed Button. "I must learn how to wait patiently, but it is so hard."

One afternoon when she came home from shopping, there it was! It struck her without warning. Right in the door it was, staring at her big as life. Her heart sank and her eyes filled with tears. . . . It couldn't be—but it was. They had sent it back—they didn't want her beautiful story.

It was a hard blow to take. At first it seemed unbearable. She felt as though her dream was lying at her feet bruised and trampled upon, screaming at her for mercy. Mechanically she opened the envelope. Enclosed was a letter from the editor-in-chief—a super-duper rejection letter.

Button's humor, the hominess of her story, her gift of making the characters live were all very fine—*but*. . . . That *but* was such a little word, yet it had the power to upset her whole life. . . . She would just have to do what she had planned from the beginning, give it to her girls. They would love it. Of that she was sure.

Eric found her sitting by the kitchen table her head in her hands and the manuscript before her. He placed his arms around her.

"Oh, Eric," she sobbed while her tears fell freely. "I wish I'd never sent it! I'm crushed now. My heart is broken."

Button wept, clinging to Eric as a drowning person clings to a lifeline. Slowly he released her stranglehold.

"Little one," he comforted as though she was a child, "listen to me. Put that smile back on your lips and that gleam in your eyes. Life hasn't ended because you've met with a disappointment. Don't give up so easily. Some other magazine might accept it. Don't lose heart at the first blow."

Eric was right. She had to go on living. She had to brace herself and try harder. She must start dreaming anew, the same dream.

"I shall never give up, Eric, never, never! Someday your wife will be an author so you had better prepare yourself, Mr. Bjork. I might even become famous! I've just begun, but from now on I shall dream higher and higher ever higher."

He kissed away her tears.

"Fine, Button. I'm proud of you . . . and whatever will be, will be. . . . Let's leave it that way, my dear. I'm sure that any girl who dares to dream the way my wife does will someday see her dream fulfilled."

BOOK IV

CHAPTER 13

❧ With Mounting Wings

Five years might seem long, at times, as they pass down into the history of a human life, but to Button they had been like a golden summer of sunshine and joy. Now as she looked back upon them, she knew that she would love to relive them over and over again. Such unlimited happiness she had never experienced before! Eric's shop was progressing well, causing him to grow younger-looking instead of older. How well she understood the mystery of that, for Eric, too, had a heart overflowing with joy because his dream had been realized.

Yes, many changes had taken place during this span of years. Charlene had married while in her second year of college and Dick, her husband, had become a dear son and had entered into business with Eric. Charlene and Dick had two little boys, so Eric and Button were grandparents at last! She had found that holding two little wiggling fellows in her arms made heaven come upon earth. New dreams were, perhaps, being shaped in Eric's mind. Could it be that his shop would be passed down to the next generation? There was something challenging in those thoughts that Button knew he had each time he gazed into a pair of dark brown eyes sparkling with life and mischief. Being grandparents, both Eric and Button had decided, was a wonderful way, planned by God, to keep you feeling young.

Lynn was still in college with the world open for any field of work that she might choose. Button hoped it would be in the field of religious or social work, something in Papa's line, serving humanity. However, her popularity and the number of boys who were weekend visitors made Button wonder if wedding bells wouldn't end the thought of a career. Eric shook his head and said that Lynn had promised him she would finish college before she settled down with a husband, and he was confident that she would keep her word.

Mama still lived in her little white bungalow in sunny Miami. She was getting on in age but lived all alone since Kerstin, too, was married. She claimed that she liked the peace and the quiet surrounding her and would live this part of her life's story in anticipation of the day when she would be called into the golden sunset and be reunited with Papa. All her children were married with the exception of Greta, who still preferred the call of a higher education to what she called the drudgery of marriage.

"You see, I shall be like Papa," she laughed when the family teased her about being an old maid. "After all, he was forty-three when he married Mama, and she really had to work awfully hard to catch him at that. I'm going to have a doctor's degree in education before I even consider settling down. Also, I'd like to have a trip around the world, and what man could give me that? I'm going to rent an exclusive apartment where I can just close the door when I want privacy and come and go as I please. Someday I may even buy myself a long sleeky car to hop into when I want to see you all. So, don't feel sorry for me. I'm living the life I want—independent and free."

Well, thought Button, if that is Greta's dream, good luck to her . . . everyone after her own heart's desire! Mama felt that whatever the children did was in God's plan for them and that thought made her very happy. Nim was still a surgeon in Florida and the other three boys had followed in Papa's shoes and were in religious work. Then there was John, Vickey's husband, a minister too. Button knew that Mama must be weaving new dreams into her tapestry of life as she surveyed her great-grandsons, that her highest wish and prayer for them was that they might become ministers as had been their great-grandfather. There was no higher calling unless it was that of being a mother of ministers.

Yes, so very much had happened these past five years, but the greatest of all to Button was the fulfillment of her childhood dream. At this very minute, as she was sitting in her living room, she held the fruit of that dream clasped close to her heart. God had worked in mysterious ways since that Saturday when she had begun her story for the girls, to the present when that story had emerged as a full-fledged book. Button had not recognized that that day had been God's chosen time to give her back her dream . . . that she was ready for it . . . that had been the day of the fullness of time in God's sight.

Her friend Vera had been the instigator of her attempt to write the story not just for her girls but for the whole world to read in a book. Button had been filled with tremendous hope that the first chapter would be sold to a magazine as a story, but she had reckoned without God. The picture was clear now, for that first chapter should not have been printed that way, separated from the rest of the story. Although she had shed many a tear with each subsequent rejection slip from various magazine editors, now she was thankful for them. How shortsighted humans are, she was thinking. God sees clearly far into eternity and He had known it was for Button's best interest not to succeed with those magazines, for if she had, she wouldn't today be hugging this book to her heart.

After many rejection slips, Button had ventured out to give talks on her story—just to small groups at first. If a speaker had at the last minute canceled an engagement, she had willingly filled it. She found that it was almost as much fun to tell stories as it was to write them. That was a gift she also had received from God, a special talent that she had always known she possessed. She recalled that, while she was living in Sweden and was left in charge of the parsonage and the younger children when Papa and Mama were calling on the sick people of the church, she had entertained them and kept them spellbound by her storytelling. In her mind she could see them now sitting, according to size, on the wooden sofa in the parsonage kitchen while she sat on a chair in front of them. She could make up stories quick as a wink. They just came without effort, just the way her writing did. It was, indeed, a precious gift. As she spoke to her groups of people, she would imagine that they were all children sitting on a wooden sofa . . . and she would talk herself right into their hearts.

Often after she had made a speech, people would say

to her, "Have you ever considered what a wonderful book that story would make? Why don't you have it published in book form so we can purchase it?"

Button had smiled her sunny smile. "Perhaps I will someday. If you'll give me your name and address, I'll notify you when that book is ready, and you can buy it from your favorite bookstore."

And she had meant it. She must write that book for all those who wanted her simple PAPA AND MAMA STORIES. The more she spoke before groups, the longer became the list of names until she had so many she hardly knew where to keep them.

Two years had passed since she had begun to write her story. Eric and she again went to beautiful, mountainous New Hampshire for their vacation. As they drove along, Button noticed a sign saying, CAMP FOR THE SOUL.

"Eric," she said, "I like that. Let's stop for a while. Our souls need as much refreshing as our bodies. We've had such a fine time staying in hotels, swimming and climbing mountains, let's make this last part of our vacation different and attend something we know nothing about."

Eric laughed. "My still so unpredictable Button. Where do you get all those crazy ideas that pop into your head? You see a sign and you want to stop. You have no idea what it's all about. A rest for the soul sounds very good, but not to me. I feel cramped and fenced in sitting with crowds of people. Do you know the way I like to worship and get rest for the soul? I like to sit in a rowboat in the middle of a lake, where the hymns are sung by the tiny waves that play upon the keel of my boat. To sit and let the sunshine beat down upon my bare back . . . to watch the float . . . I tell you, that is tonic for my soul. . . . When I pull up my big shiny fish . . . then I feel refreshed."

Button sat still for a moment, trying to find a solution.

"Eric, a voice within me calls me to that camp. I feel I must go there. I don't like to have us separate . . . but I can't stand your type of vacation worship. My heart aches for that poor fish. I think it may be a mother or a father fish and the children will be orphans . . . and I can't bear to watch a fish lying in the bottom of a boat gasping for breath. But if that's what you want, let me go my way for a couple of days and you go yours, and then we'll both be happy."

Thus they parted. Eric drove her into the pine grove where people with shining, happy faces had gathered for a couple of weeks of spiritual strengthening of their souls. She found that there was a room she could have so she kissed Eric good-bye, feeling a little sting in her heart because they so seldom liked the same things.

Button enjoyed the beauty of the lovely spot where the camp was located; she mingled with kind, gracious people and gazed at the majestic mountains which stood guard around the camp. This new experience delighted her heart. On the second day of her stay, however, news came over the radio that a hurricane was on the way and might strike in that vicinity late in the afternoon. Button did not worry over Eric, for he was very capable of taking care of himself and would probably seek refuge in the nearest hotel. All the campers gathered in the large Inn of the camp where they would stay until they heard that it was safe to go out again. The leader, a fine young man, suggested that different people entertain the crowd in order to make the time pass faster. He asked for volunteers. When no one responded, Button, remembering how happy she had made the children at home when she had told them stories, offered her services.

"I can tell a story of How My Mama Got My Papa," she laughed.

Never had she told a story better. She could see her audience relax and forget about the danger that was threatening. Soon they were laughing heartily. By the time she finished, the sun was shining and the hurricane had missed the camp by several miles.

This episode added two hundred names to Button's list of people who wanted her book, if it ever came into being!

Eric picked her up and, their vacation being over, they drove back to Berkley Hills. Life settled down to a regular routine until one afternoon when a very distinguished gentleman rang the door-chime. He introduced himself as a Mr. Warren, and asked Button if she would mind repeating for him the story she had told at a religious retreat in the New Hampshire mountains a few weeks before.

Button bubbled with delight. She was becoming famous for her storytelling! She offered Mr. Warren a cup of coffee and a piece of her delicious cake to eat while he listened to her. Once again she assumed the role of an entertainer and, as she began to speak, she forgot that she had an audience of only one. In her mind she could see the faces of the people at the camp become relaxed and carefree even in the midst of a severe storm, and she fancied she was speaking to them again. As a result, she told her story to Mr. Warren as well as she had told it to them.

"Mrs. Bjork, I hardly know how to thank you. That was a fine performance. I am the manager of one of America's finest and oldest speaking bureaus. Would you consider signing a contract and becoming one of our artists?"

Button couldn't believe her ears! Her eyes twinkled as brightly as stars.

"I would love to," she whispered, wondering in her heart if Eric would mind having her traveling around the country as a lecturer. She hoped that he would understand that this, too, was part of the plan for her life. She must take advantage of this opportunity.

Mr. Warren continued:

"One of our representatives was caught in the hurricane in New Hampshire and drove into that religious camp for shelter. She saw how efficiently you calmed the spirits of those worried people and how expertly you told your story, so as soon as she came back home she called me and said, 'Another star is born!' You will do well with us. Have you ever considered putting that story in a book? Being an author would add to your prestige, Mrs. Bjork."

Button had signed the lecture contract that day and although Eric was a bit disturbed, he would in no way hamper this new Button who had emerged from the shadows into the bright light of day.

"Go ahead," he said. "Someday you'll tire of that hurried, strenuous life, and you'll be very content to stay in your own nest. In the meantime have fun, dear!"

Mama had been surprised, too, and she had written:

All I can say, Button, is, what in the world will you think of doing next! But, of course, I give you my blessing. And remember your Papa was a fine speaker.

He would be proud to know his daughter had the courage to speak to large clubs. God bless you, darling.

And Button had the courage! She spoke to Women's Clubs of all sizes. She traveled far and wide with but one purpose in mind, to make people laugh and be happy. Their laughter was her great reward. People forgot the dangers of atomic bombs and the worry over their children. Button made them believe that God was good and that this world was not such a bad place to live in after all. Each time she returned home she flew into Eric's waiting arms and wondered how she could leave him and her precious home alone for so many days. In the late hours of the night they would sit close together and she would tell him about her trips, and Eric would tell her of the happenings in his business world, of new orders and fine contacts, of a larger demand for products going out. She would bring out her large box of book-order slips and play with them.

"Look, Eric," she would say. "There has to be a book. I can't disappoint this many people."

Step by step she came closer to the realization of her dream. The right people came into her life to help her at the right time. Finally she found an expert literary agent who took over the correcting and selling of her manuscript, and Button devoted her time to her lectures. She lived for the day when she could announce to an audience that her book had been accepted by a publisher. One day the news came . . . the great, great news! Her agent telephoned her to say that one of the country's leading publishers had accepted her story with great enthusiasm. Button thought she would faint with excitement. That moment was so sa-

cred she could hardly bear it. Her heart kept whispering,
"Thank you, oh thank you, dear, dear God." After she had
been interviewed and photographed by the local newspaper, and friends and strangers alike had called to congratu-
late her, she wondered if it were all true or if she were
dreaming a beautiful dream. There had been a long wait,
but now it was a reality . . . it had come to pass . . . her
dream had been fulfilled.

She had to laugh at herself when she realized how
naïve she had often been, doing foolish things, but wasn't
it characteristic of Button to go her own way, ignoring the
advice of those who were standing by to help her? She remembered particularly that time in the early spring, when
she was walking down Main Street, reflecting upon her own
future. Suddenly the thought came to her that she had not
informed the local bookstore that she had a book being
published. There were only a few months left now before
the publication date. She ought to introduce herself to the
owner of the store and inquire about an autographing
party. Button had no idea that books were sold by the publisher's salesmen but took for granted that each new author would have to promote the sale of her own books. Certainly an autographing party would help, and the local
bookstore should be willing to give her one. She decided to
visit Mr. Logan and tell him the good news. So she stepped
inside the door and inquired for him from the first clerk
she met.

"And who may I say is calling?" asked the clerk. "Mr.
Logan is a very busy man."

"He probably doesn't know about me yet," confessed
Button. "But he will, for I am a new author and have my
first book coming out in the fall. Isn't it wonderful?"

The unimpressed clerk had already departed up the stairs in search of the chief executive. In a few minutes she was back, followed by Mr. Logan.

Button smiled her prettiest.

"May I introduce myself? I am Charlotta Bjork of this town, and I have written a book that is coming out this fall. It's my first book, you know. I was wondering . . . you will be selling it in the store, won't you?"

Mr. Logan gave her a curious glare.

"And who is your publisher?" he asked dryly.

Button mentioned the name with pride. It had a transforming effect on Mr. Logan's face, which broke into a smile.

"A very fine publisher, indeed, Mrs. Bjork. You are very fortunate and can feel assured that they will push your book . . . a fine publisher. . . . I wish you much success!"

Mr. Logan grasped her hand warmly. "Very pleased to have made your acquaintance. I presume their salesmen will be around any time now. We surely will order a supply of your books. Thank you for coming in."

Button stared dumbfoundedly at Mr. Logan. This couldn't possibly be all he had to say! Why, he hadn't even invited her into his personal office where he naturally would meet with prominent people. Button hurt with disappointment. She was afraid that at any moment the tears might gather in her eyes, but she took courage and said as she pulled herself up to her full height, "Mr. Logan, I was wondering about the autographing party. Do you have the time now to discuss the matter with me?"

It was Mr. Logan's turn to stare. "The autographing p-party?" he stammered.

"Yes," said Button boldly. Never had she felt more like Mama than at that moment. "Don't you think you ought to give that kind of a party for a local author? It isn't every day that a book is written by someone in your own community."

Mr. Logan smiled kindly, a sad, wistful smile.

"Mrs. Bjork, I can see that you are very new, indeed, as an author, for you have as yet not experienced the suffering of being 'an unknown.' It takes a long time for a new name to become established. We wouldn't dare to buy as many of your books as we would those of a well-known writer . . . but don't despair . . . the time will come . . . but as far as an autographing party is concerned . . . I wish that I could say this kindly or that you would try to understand . . . the last time we had such a party was twenty years ago and that was for a well-known author who had written a fine book. . . . It became a best seller, as I recall it. Only about a dozen of his closest friends came in. . . . Seeing the hurt in his eyes, we disguised our own salesladies as prospective buyers and had them leave the store and then come back in to buy four or five copies of his book . . . just to ease the strain. . . . Autographing parties . . . they are a risky business even for well-known authors."

Button could not believe what she heard. She had counted on a fine time planning the party with Mr. Logan. She had even thought to surprise him by telling about the lists of names she had and offering to turn them over to him for a good start on the sales. His words had spoiled all that. She felt hurt inside and giving him those names might be "risky business."

"Mrs. Bjork," said the bookstore owner, again smiling down upon her and patting her shoulder as if she were a

child, "don't look so sad. I wish I could be more encouraging at such a time as this, but I have been in the bookstore
business for many years. . . ."

Deeply disappointed she had left the store quickly
without a backward glance. She had pictured this meeting
so differently. Being an author wasn't as important as she
had thought it would be. Button took her time going home.
A thought troubled her. How was she to sell hundreds of
books if booksellers were not enthusiastic about stocking
books from unknown authors? Then characteristically she
changed her thoughts. What had she expected! Mr. Logan
really had been more than kind and gracious. After all, he
didn't know this Charlotta Bjork from Eve. It had been
considerate of him to leave his busy desk and talk to her.
She must learn not to be ungrateful when a person did his
best. Besides, wasn't she forgetting that she had promised
to leave everything in God's hands? Hadn't He proved over
and over again that He knew what was best for her life? A
book was coming out! Her dream had come true! Soon she
would hold a book with a jacket on which her name was
printed and with pages and pages containing thousands of
printed words that she had created. It would sell! It would
sell if she was thankful and asked God to bless it.

As she reached her front door, she heard the demanding ringing of her telephone. She hurried to answer it.

"Mrs. Bjork," said a pleasant, slightly familiar voice,
"this is Mr. Logan from the bookstore. I've been doing a
little thinking. I like your courage and spirited enthusiasm.
I believe we'll take the chance and give you a fine autographing party. We'll hope for the best. Drop into the store
next time you come downtown and we'll make some plans."

Button was breathless with excitement and the party

had turned out to be a huge success . . . much more so than either she or Mr. Logan ever had anticipated. The bookstore had gone to great lengths to prepare for the event. The store itself had been converted into a lovely parlor with soft rugs on the floor and lounging chairs and flowers everywhere. On the beautifully decorated punch table were large plates of Swedish coffeebread and *peppar-kakor*. Seated at the table, one at each end, were her own girls, pouring the coffee. Dressed in their sweet gowns they rivaled the roses on the table in prettiness. Button was sitting behind a long narrow table piled high with books. When she first sat down to autograph the copies, they resembled a high mountain, but they soon dwindled down as the endless line moved quickly before her. Button signed her name hundreds of times and was hugged and kissed and congratulated. Her cup overflowed with happiness and contentment. Representatives were there from the publisher's, and Mama had made the trip all the way from Florida. Pelle, Vickey and John were there and, of course, Eric, looking proud and handsome as he walked around shaking hands with the many people. Button believed he actually enjoyed it!

If Mr. Logan had been worried about not having customers, his worries were needless, for it seemed as if the total population of Berkley Hills had turned out to recognize the new author. The people waited patiently in line to reach the book table. Surely this was the crowning moment of Button's life! Looking at Mama, beaming in the soft chair placed there especially for her, caused Button's heart to beat with joy. Mama was dressed in pink lace and her hair was waved back from her forehead, her eyes could have outshone the stars in the sky, and her smile was as radiant as a summer day. Was it all a dream? If it were, Button prayed that she would dream forever. She felt as if her soul had been lifted with mounting wings above the earth to a golden hill where her heart told her dreams were fulfilled.

Yes, precious memories to be stored in her heart forever! One tender, sacred memory which was already planted there was the memory of Papa, which would blossom as a rare flower to keep her sweet and humble always, for that had been her promise to him.

The week after the autographing party Button and Eric were sitting in the living room talking over the things that had happened to them both—the shop . . . the book . . . the girls—and the future, which now looked bright and promising.

"Eric," said Button, moving close to him on the davenport, "one by one my dreams are coming true. My heart is overflowing with joy and thankfulness . . . burdens and cares seem far away . . . certainly I should be full of sunshine. In spite of all this there is one desire left . . . a yearning deep, deep down in my soul . . . a yearning to go home . . . back to Sweden."

"Well," answered Eric, taking her hand in his, "I see no reason why you shouldn't go back if that is what you want. You have the money for the fare. How does it feel, Mrs. Bjork, to be financially independent of your husband?"

"Oh, Eric," she whispered, disturbed. "Eric, Eric, don't you ever talk like that! I want to be dependent upon you always . . . until the day I die. You have always been overgenerous with me—my own checking account, my own car! I've had so much! I never lacked anything . . . except for that longing in my heart to write . . . and now even that has been filled. We'll pool our money, darling, and do all our planning together. Even if we're fortunate enough to make much money, let's always stay dependent upon each other."

"That was a fine speech, Button, and I quite agree. There's always that fear that you will become so famous you will grow away from me, get beyond my reach. . . . All I ask is that you stay yourself, Button, full of your crazy talk."

"Oh, Eric, Eric, I promise! Is it crazy enough for me to ask that come spring I may board an airplane and fly home to Lapland for a couple of weeks? I want to—to—to . . ." Button's eyes filled with tears and unashamed she let them roll down her cheeks. "Eric, I want to go home and tell Papa."

She reached Lapland at Eastertime on a cold, bleak day. By late morning, while darkness still lingered over the land, Button stood by the big gate, outside the State Church, that lead to the well-kept cemetery. Ever since Mama had come back to America alone, Button had wanted to make this trip. As much as she had ever wanted anything of life, she had wanted to come home to Papa's last resting place . . . to keep a tryst and to make a promise.

Button had flown over the seemingly endless ocean, but the trip had been completed in no more hours than it had taken days when the family crossed from Sweden. The world certainly changes and progresses, thought Button. She had, of course, written to her childhood friend, Karin, and had received an invitation to visit there. Gunnar and

Karin had met her at an airport and they had traveled in Gunnar's comfortable automobile to the Borgesons' lovely villa on the mountainside, a big elegant home that showed every sign of wealth and comfort. They were the parents of five boys, all grown, with the exception of the youngest, who looked at Button with a pair of dark brown eyes that looked exactly like Gunnar's, the way she remembered them. It had been wonderful to see her friends and, of course, she had brought them a copy of her book.

"Button," said Gunnar as they sat at the dining table that first night while a trim little maid served the meal, "you made it! Your dream did come true!"

"Didn't you think it would, Gunnar? Dreams always come true if you dream them high and are persistent enough to dream them until they grow, mature, take shape and form. If you give your dreams to God to keep, they won't get lost in the humdrum of life and at the appointed time they will be given back to you."

Gunnar shook his head. "You still speak in riddles!" He flashed her a sparkling smile. "We're very happy for you, Button."

"Oh, yes, happy and proud," added Karin. "I think this is the most exciting thing I ever heard, and remember, I was with you the day it began . . . right when the dream started. Remember the day you wore that pretty apron?"

"Yes, Karin, and you thought I remained so long in front of the class because I wanted to show it off . . . and have you forgotten that deacons' meeting?"

"Hey, girls," protested Gunnar laughingly, "you're leaving me behind. . . . I can't follow you . . . I never heard of those episodes . . . if I had, perhaps I never would have dared to marry Karin."

Button joined in the laughter, but she couldn't help feeling that there also were many things that she and Gunnar could speak of, that only they two knew. Never, now, would they mention these things to each other. Nevertheless, they were spun into the fabric of their lives.

How pleasant the visit was and how enchanting to wander back to the old familiar scenes! Yet many changes had taken place as this small mining town had prospered and progressed. Button had only a few days to stay here before returning home and she was not sorry because she knew that her heart belonged with her loved ones in her wonderful America.

"I'll drive you to the cemetery tomorrow morning," said Gunnar the night before Easter. "I don't know why you insist upon going at daybreak, but I do know it is too far for you to walk."

"Thanks, Gunnar, but would I be presuming too much, if I asked to borrow your car and drive myself there? Please forgive me . . . but when I enter that cemetery, 'd like to be alone."

And Gunnar had understood.

Now she stood in the cemetery as the first rays of the sun touched the cold tombstones. Slowly Button began her walk between the graves. Mama had given her explicit directions so she had an idea where that certain stone for which she was looking stood. As she walked, she thought of the first Easter morning and of the woman who had also walked to a grave. The mystery of the morning captured her imagination. The birds were singing now and she breathed deeply of the fresh mountain air. Around her was a heavy, dewy fragrance. . . . All was quiet and peaceful here among the dead. Here in this little cemetery so far away from the noisy world people slept their final sleep. These people had lived and dreamt and watched the sun rise as she was doing, and now their bodies rested in the peaceful soil of their homeland while their spirits were home with God. Here she was searching for Papa, but she knew he was not here . . . only a stone to mark the place where his body had been laid to rest. Papa was far beyond the cemetery in the safekeeping of God's golden eternity. He lives forever! That message he had preached all those many years.

Now she had reached her destination. Reverently she approached the grave and stood there for a moment, her head bowed in prayer and her hand resting on the stone. A sunbeam gleamed upon a name. She read the inscription carved upon the stone:

HÄR VILAR PASTOR PONTUS FRANZON
Född 1867
Död 1938
(sov gott Papa lilla)

How like Mama to have added that extra sentence. Translated it read, "Sleep well, Papa dear."

How long she remained in the cemetery, Button did not know, but she spent a long time talking with God, thanking Him for a father like Papa, for the wisdom and love he had planted in her heart, and even for the discipline he had enforced to mold into her a strong character. Before she left, she knelt down on the cold ground and lifted her face toward the sky.

"Papa," she whispered as the bright tears shimmered in her eyes, "I know that you're not here, but this is the place where your dear body was laid to rest. This Easter morning I want to make a pledge to you and a promise that I will follow in the faith that you gave me . . . that I will live as you taught me . . . and that the memory of you will always keep me humble, realizing that all good things are gifts from God. Papa, many a promise to you I broke in my childhood. I caused you much trouble and heartache, but, Papa, I've come all the way from America back here to tell you that Button has turned out all right and you can be proud of her now."

So she left him there and part of her heart with him, and flew back home again to Eric, Lynn, Charlene and Dick and their boys. She was richly blessed to have all these to hold and love forevermore.

Charlene had met her at the airport in New York.

"I had to come all the way, Mommie, to be the first one to greet you. I wouldn't even let Daddy come with me for I have such good news, Mommie. There's going to be another baby . . . in September . . . your month . . . perhaps another author . . . who knows?"

Button drew her close.

"I'm so happy, darling, so happy! But how many children are you going to have? Three is quite a handful!"

Charlene laughed. "I just love having babies, Mommie! I sometimes think that I may have as many as Grandma Franzon. Perhaps they'll say it's inherited! I just can't imagine not having a little baby in the house."

Yes, Charlene indeed resembled Mama and life seemed to follow a pattern. Hadn't Mama received the news when she returned from Sweden that she was to have a grandchild? . . . Only this was Button's third. Yes, indeed, she was blessed!

It was another morning and the world was fresh and new. Button's eyes were wide as she beheld the wonders in her garden and listened again to the happy chirping of the birds as they built their little nests. She had just waved good-bye to Eric and the smile was still on her lips for Eric had asked, "What is that that you hold so tightly to your heart?"

And she had responded, "Dirt, Eric, just plain garden dirt."

"And why the box, Button?"

"That's such a long story that, if I were to tell you, you'd never finish that gauge today . . . so good-bye, dear."

Eric had laughed. He probably thought that this was just some new crazy thing Button had thought up . . . to carry around with her a bit of dirt in a box.

Button walked to the tulip bed and gazed down upon the profusion of colors. Soon the lilies of the valley would be in bloom and the lilac was budding. She almost worshiped this plot of land Eric and she had made into a beautiful garden. The love of one's land! she thought. There is where your heart takes root and that was why she wanted to share with it a most precious gift, the gift Karin had given her when she left Sweden.

"It is Sweden!" Karin had said. "You can hold it between your fingers and say, 'I am home!'"

Slowly Button emptied her box among the flowers. She saw the dirt spill over the leaves of the tulips, gray dark dirt that once had contained seeds in her homeland.

She had known she would do this ever since she had said good-bye to her friends after leaving Papa's grave. When she had first come to America, she believed that no matter how carefully she tried to pull up her roots, a few would remain in the land of her birth. . . . Those few roots had called her back . . . but now that she had kept her tryst with Papa, those last roots had been severed.

Over to this great land in the west people had come. Immigrants they were called, whose hearts were weeping with loneliness for the land they had left. But they pressed onward until they knew they were claimed by the new land. They learned that they belonged, not back in the yesteryears or in the land that gave them birth, but in the adopted country whose arms had been open wide to give them a mother's sheltering love.

Button could visualize the long procession of wanderers who had found their homes here. And wasn't this nation's greatness built upon this love the wanderers carried with them from their home soil and planted over here? She was proud to be one of these people, for she loved this land which had fulfilled her heart's desire.

Gently her fingers touched the dirt and together with a tear that rolled from her eye, she mixed it with the garden soil.

"To my new beloved country," she heard herself say aloud, "as a gift from Papa's daughter."

As Button's eyes swept over the horizon, a smile came to her lips, for she knew that her heart had found peace and that her roots had dug themselves deep into the rich soil of her new homeland.

Mama's
Way

~ ~ ~

THYRA FERRÉ BJORN

~

~ Chapter One

"I wish you would write a book about what you have told us here tonight," a minister said to me some months ago when, as a guest in their lovely home, I was about to bid him and his wife good night and retire.

"Yes, you really should," chimed in his charming young wife. "I wish we could have shared this evening with the whole world."

I was a bit perplexed as I looked at them.

"You mean a book mixing all the things we have talked about since we began at ten thirty P.M.? It would be a very religious book. I can't write books like that. My brother is the theologian, I stick to the home-spun family stuff."

The minister put his hand on my shoulder. "You might think I am fooling," he said, "but I am dead serious. And I don't mean you should write a book dealing with theology. I want you to write a book just the way you talk! Believe me, a book like that is very much needed in the world today. I have to confess I don't go all the way with you in your philosophy of life, but your talk has helped me. It has made me stop to think. We ministers so often get into a rut."

When I went to my room, his words kept echoing in my tired mind. This was the second time I had been invited to talk in his big church, and the second time I had been a house guest at the parsonage. I loved coming here. They were a delightful young couple with wonderful youngsters. He was a promising minister who, I predicted, would go far in his calling, with just the right kind of wife to be a good helpmate during those busy long years ahead. And there was a certain hominess and warmth in this parsonage, and a welcome not just in words, but in the spirit that prevailed here. How well I understood why they were so loved and cherished by their congregation!

The first time I had come, I had been a stranger, but now I was a friend. It was one of those friendships that changes an acquaintance in a short space of time. Bedtime had been late that first time, too. There we had been—the minister, his wife and I—talking into the wee hours of the morning. They were not just casual things about which we had talked so long together, but spiritual things concerning God's Kingdom.

This evening, however, the living room had been filled with guests after the lecture. Special friends had been asked in for a social time, but also for another purpose. My new friend had sprung that on me as I was having my second cup of coffee.

"I have invited these friends in tonight, hoping that you could repeat the talk we had the last time you were here. Do you remember how you told my wife and me of the things you have prayed about and received an answer? I want you to tell these folks specifically about the time when you could have had a terrible accident and you let go of the wheel and let God take over."

Now I let my mind wander back. How well I remembered our first visit. We had talked about prayer during those hours. I guess I had done most of the talking. They had been such good listeners. Tonight he had extracted, little by little, all those things he wanted me to repeat. I had never realized what a lasting impression the earlier conversation had made. It was two o'clock in the morning before the guests left and then the three of us had lingered for yet another half hour. . . . I went to bed quickly, but I couldn't go to sleep. Thoughts kept racing through my brain. I was tired, I told myself, too tired. I had driven a hundred miles in one afternoon, spoken to a crowd of three hundred people that night and talked until two thirty in the morning. But I knew it wasn't just being tired. It was the joy that filled my heart. A seed had been planted. A book was going to be born because it had been conceived in my heart. I had never thought I would write a book on religious matters. Not that I hadn't wanted to, but with all of today's great, well-educated theologians and philosophers, who was I to state my simple way of thinking and knowing God? Still, I knew I had much to tell that would be helpful to housewives and other lay people. And writing a book like that would be wonderful. It would be like talking, like telling a story.

I remembered how gloriously happy I had been when, early in my married life, I found that I was going to bear a child. Writing a book affected me the same way. I am never happier than when I have one in the making. It is fascinating to watch the words come out of the typewriter. My way of writing is, perhaps, a bit unique. I never do any research, never make any notes, or gather any materials. I just sit down and let the words flow from my mind, knowing they are already written in my heart.

In God's eternity there is no end and no beginning. So in the God-Mind, this book had already been written. All that was left for me to do was to record it. That wonderful knowledge had come to me when I wrote my first book, PAPA'S WIFE, and I used the same method in writing PAPA'S DAUGHTER. I never worried about words. The most important thing was to be still and cut off all thoughts of material things, to focus my mind on God from whom all talents and thoughts came.

It is exciting to write. There is no labor connected with it, rather a relaxed, happy knowledge that word after word will form sentences, and sentences pages, and pages chapters and so on. When the words stop coming, that is the end of my writing, and a book has been born.

But to be still was the most important part, to let the mind rest. Words are like music. They are only so many notes. A person can play them and one knows that they are just notes put together. Ah, but if an artist takes these notes—the very same notes—they come out as living music that laughs and cries and moves all the listening world. All writers use words, but their effect depends on how they are put together. And words given to me by my Heavenly Father, I knew, would come out in beautiful poesy.

And so instead of sleeping, I basked in the wonder of my new thoughts. I was not a theologian, so I must not be preachy. But I could tell in a simple way some of the things God had done for me here in this earth life.

As I thought about this yet-to-be-written book, I remembered all the letters—almost a trunkful—from people who had written to me regarding my two earlier books. They were from many different countries, and of different faiths. Many said my writing had helped them solve their problems. Reading about Papa and Mama and their happy family life had made them realize that God *was* good and that this old world was not such a bad place to live in after all. There were those who had expressed a desire to catch some of that happy, deep faith in God that Mama possessed. I recalled how many letters I had written in answer to those I had received, trying to share some of my own trust and faith in God and life. I hoped that I had set some people walking in the right direction. A book of the kind suggested by my minister friend might be of help to many. I would pray that it would be the type of book that would speak to the heart.

Yes, I would write a book the way I talked. It would be a simple book, so simple that a child could understand it. It would not be too long and would be spiced here and there with a trifle of humor. I would go back into my childhood and pick up the path of my search for God and I knew that I would find on the way gold nuggets that I had missed when I had hastened over that road many years ago. It would be wonderful to recall it all. . . .

And then, as I was thinking, a plan came to me. The things I would tell in my book would be the things I had learned at my Mama's knee, things she had in her gentle way imprinted on my mind as far back as I could remember. Papa had been the preacher, the pathfinder, my ideal, the one I wanted to try to live up to. But it was Mama's way that I had taken. It was her love for people that I had inherited and her love of serving the Lord God. And now, as I walked back through the long corridors of time, I saw how much like Mama I was in the way I prayed and talked and dreamed. So my book would be about Mama's way as I had followed it.

Wasn't it Mama who had told me stories about God as I sat on her lap, stories that had made me see God in nature, that made God a very part of it all? Yes, in my childish mind I had seen God's cheeks puff out as He blew out the wind; His chariot, cleaving the sky in the thunder and the lightning, become a burning snake winding its way to the earth. And it had seemed to me that in the silvery moonlight God was pouring His blessings down on this world He loved so much. Each blessing glided down on white angel wings to

9

transform everything it touched into peace and joy. In the early mornings, when dewdrops were still on the grass, I could feel God walking beside me. And so often in the cold winter, as I walked through a wood transformed into a white wonderland and stood spellbound at the picture I saw, I felt Him near. Each snow-laden tree and bush looked like a bride kneeling to pray. So it was in the springtime, when the soft fine rain fell on my uplifted face in a gentle caress. Surely the God my Mama had told me about was there. And even autumn did not conceal Him away from my view, for when the leaves had outlived their brilliant color-play and limp and sad singled themselves to the damp ground, it seemed that if I would but listen, I could hear a whisper. God was speaking to His trees, assuring them that this was just for their own good, a time of rest which would enable them to bring forth even more abundant loveliness. And there would be another spring, new life, as soon as the winter was over. And so my heart felt no sadness as the trees disrobed, because His promise was there. God's creation could never die.

How strange life would have been and how empty even now if I didn't believe in Him that way, if I was not assured that He was there beside me. How terrifying would be the thought of bombs and new weapons of destruction if I didn't know, without a single doubt, that the world is in God's hands and He holds the reins and that men can go just so far and no further. Just a whisper from Him and they are gone from this world like a vapor, and they are no more. For life on earth is measured in years and no matter how good or beautiful, how wicked or destructive, people are, there comes an end to their years and only the things that they have done remain.

There came a time in my life when the beautiful, secure picture of God that Mama had given me began to dim. It was in my adolescent years, I remember, that there was doubt and many a question mark as to how God could be. But when the turmoil of those years was over, and that first storm of life had passed, I saw Mama's pathway again and as I began to walk on it, I found that I had mellowed a little because of those confused years. And so, I learned from my own mind things to which my heart agreed, such as, we will our own thoughts through our imagination. In my childhood my imagination and I could travel, taking away the drab and dull, tinting life to any color we wanted it. Even as an adult, this friend has never left me. As a child it was my playmate; as an adult, a mirror of my thought life. Because of it, I came closer to God as I learned to discipline my thought world.

I wanted to live in a happy world, so I willed my

thoughts that way. I put a keeper at the door of my mind and let only good, constructive thoughts enter. I became a sort of mystic, and I still am, for I never lost that childhood friend that transformed living into happiness. We are all mystics in those first enchanting years of life. We play train on the kitchen chairs and travel in five short minutes all over the world. We sit on a magic carpet and whisper, "Lift," and we are raised up into the sky. We sail on fleecy clouds and drop in to have a party with the moon man's children. When we return to earth again, we have stardust in our eyes. Don't you remember how you talked to trees and flowers? They were your closest friends. Perhaps you, too, feasted on bark and leaves, served on broken pieces of glass, and believed you were dining in a king's palace. Ours was truly a magic world, filled with wonderment and make-believe. In a world like that, through the mirror of our imagination, it was easy to see God in all the earth.

Oh, there was a time I had said to Mama, "Mama, explain God to me."

And Mama had smiled, that warm little smile of hers.

"How can I explain God to you, my little one?" She looked far into the distance as though she waited for an answer to come from above. "It is like asking me to describe the function of my heart, or to tell the mys-

tery of my brain cells. I know very little of those things.
I can't explain them. I only know they are there and
that I couldn't live without them. But with God—it's
funny I never thought of explaining God. I guess I
like to believe that everyone accepts Him just as I do.
I know I couldn't exist without His power. Without
Him, everything would crumble into nothingness, because all things have their beginning in God's creation.
You see, there are so many things we have to accept
without having them explained to us."

She sat still for a moment, then continued, with me
hanging on to her every word: "Now if you had asked
me to explain myself, I would find that even harder to
do. Sometimes the questions come to me—Who am I?
Where do my thoughts come from? What creates
within me such emotions that sometimes I feel as
though they would tear me apart and sometimes that
they would lift me to the pinnacle of heaven? What
creates this joy and sorrow, tears and laughter? The
texture of my hair? The way my eyes see and my ears
hear? The way I walk with balance and know what
to do or not to do? Where was this life in me before I
was born? Where do I go when the gates of death
swing open for me to enter in? There are more than
a million questions that I can't answer even for myself. But this I can say with confidence—I am because
God created me. He made me this wonderful way.

That is how I exist. That is why I laugh and cry and think and dream dreams. I accept myself because I am—but all because of God. . . ."

So my book would be a book of stories of the way I had walked and of the people I had met, troubled people seeking some lasting values for this life on earth. Perhaps by the telling of those stories, others would be helped. Much of my book would be devoted to writing about the power of prayer. That would be my theme: how God's answers to prayer are beyond what we can ever comprehend. I would share things that had taken place in my own home among members of my own dear family. And so, I thought, I would be able to fulfill my friends' wishes and write a book the way I talked. And it would be born in due time and would carry a message to those who were too busy or too tired to read deeper books on religion. This book would be relaxing and at the same time it would give food to the soul.

For to become balanced persons, three things within us must be fed, the body, the mind and the soul. . . . The body always seems to be taken care of first. It is very demanding. It will not let us forget. If we do, it causes us much pain and discomfort. The mind, too, demands feeding, because it is restless when left inactive. People hunger for fine literature and most homes have books and magazines galore. And it also feasts on plays and radio and television programs and lectures. But the soul is often neglected. It is shy and patient and makes no outstanding demands. If neglected, it cries softly within the heart and we are filled with an anxiety and despair which at times we do not understand. There's that uneasy and lost feeling. If the soul is never fed, it will just wither and crumble into a small unnoticed something. It is a sad thing when a soul that should glow and sparkle is slowly starved into nothingness.

To feed it properly, we must read the Bible and spiritual books, listen to good sermons and go to places of worship. And most of all, we must not neglect prayer. Our prayers should go up all day long, happy prayers full of joy and thankfulness for all the wonderful things God has poured down upon us. If a soul is fed, it is happy, but it has no rest until it rests in God.

How sad that some people think prayer is only to be used when we are in danger or in desperate need of something for ourselves. Prayer is really as necessary as breathing. It is our contact with our Father God, for in Him we live and move and have our being. When we know that we can breathe a prayer many times during an hour, just talking things over with God, and not always asking for something, then we have found the secret that our Master spoke of to His disciples. It is the pearl for which we would sell all in order to possess it. People who have found the secret of praying are happy, smiling people. There is a light in their eyes that reflects the glow that is in their souls. Happiness cannot be hidden. It is a light that shines in the darkness.

The world may seem dark to many people, but it is only one step away from the light. That light, God's love to mankind, is so magnificent that I stand amazed when I think of it. And God sent Jesus into the world to show us His Father's heart. When we read the story of his life, then we have seen God.

My prayer is that MAMA's WAY will be the road many people will want to walk on, because Mama followed the words of the Christ, who proclaimed to our world almost two thousand years ago:

"I AM THE WAY—THE TRUTH—AND THE LIFE. . . ."

❧ Chapter Two

My training to serve God began in the school of prayer, which is the strongest power on earth. As my mind wanders back into my childhood days, and memories unfold as pages in a book, I remember how Mama brought us eight children up on prayer. She served it both as a full-course meal and as snacks in between. There was no escaping from this order. It was the only contact between heaven and earth, so when one wanted to commune with God, one must pray. But some confusing thoughts entered into my childish mind when I discovered the difference between my parents' prayers. Often I wondered which one of them was right and who used the true method to approach God the prayer way.

Mama was impatient in her praying. She was never willing to wait for things, but expected an immediate answer. Papa seemed to leave the outcome up to God. If he could not see an answer, he accepted that as

God's wisdom, and no doubt clouded his faith in God's power. Perhaps, I reasoned within myself, it was the things they prayed about that made the difference. To Mama, prayer came as easy as breathing. Even if she knew people termed her prayer method strange and naïve, it never seemed to bother her. She kept on praying that the cake she had placed in the oven would not fall and that the food would stretch a long way because there were so many to feed at one table. And there was the long line of people who depended on her help and came to ask her to take their problems to God for them. Those people surely believed that God would answer them through Mama. They felt that in some strange way she was "in" with God and that He would grant her what He would refuse them. So prayers would be sent out for a quick sale of their house, for a husband to be kinder to his wife, and children to recover from their colds. I often heard her prayers and saw the people coming, and I never remember one who went away disappointed. Things did change when Mama talked with God.

Of course, Papa, as a minister, had certain prayer projects. His prayers were always sincere as he was himself, and many people came to his study with their prayer problems. Then there were the sickbed prayers where he made his daily calls. Papa's prayers seemed to me loftier than Mama's. They were bigger prayers! Still, when Papa prayed for the man who had a bad case of lumbago and was in pain day and night, he seemed to get worse instead of better. He wasn't healed. And how can I ever forget that lovely wife with a devoted husband and their family of five small children? Knowing she was at death's door, Papa prayed for her all night long. All hope was gone, but my Papa prayed on, torn by fatigue and compassion. But the wife died. Could God answer only small prayers? I wondered. I felt sorry for Papa. I decided I must help restore him to those church members who trusted him. I would tackle something really hard. I would help Papa to pray and give him the credit in the church when the answer came. I chose for my project a man with one leg two inches shorter than the other. Day after day and night after night I knelt and prayed that God would make his short leg grow as long as the normal leg. For a year I believed and watched the man with great expectation and eagerness. But the answer never came; he limped as badly as before. It was so discouraging it pained me. There was something wrong with the way Papa and I prayed. But what?

Then came another discouraging experience. This time it was one of my sisters, who had a panicky fear of the dentist. Having observed Mama's way of talking to God, she hit upon a bright idea. There was no need to tell Mama and Papa that she had a big cavity in her tooth. She would go directly to God and tell Him about it and ask Him to do the work on it. It would be wonderful! There would be no more suffering in that dentist's chair. Mama had always said that nothing was impossible for God to do. My sister decided to try it that very night; she would set forth alone on this prayer adventure.

"Please, please, God," she prayed as she knelt by her bed, "fill my tooth. Fill it good and hard . . . and do the work while I sleep. I want it all filled when I wake up in the morning. Thank you for being so good to me . . . and I shall always try to be a good girl. Amen."

The next morning when she awoke, she slid her tongue over the spot where the cavity had been. It wasn't there—the tooth was filled. She was healed! Breathless with excitement, she rushed out to Mama in the kitchen.

"Mama, Mama," she cried, "God has done it again!"

Mama stopped beating the eggs and gazed with surprise at her young daughter. "He has done what?" she asked.

"He filled my tooth last night, Mama, when I asked Him to. I didn't want to tell you I had a big cavity and that I was afraid to go to the dentist. So I asked God to fill it. Isn't it just wonderful? Now we'll never need to pay money to the dentist again, even if he does only charge us half price."

Mama patted the excited girl on her blonde head. She asked to be shown the miracle and, equipped with a toothpick, she poked at the tooth. It didn't take her long to come to a verdict. She looked tenderly down at her offspring as she held the toothpick in front of her eyes. "It wasn't God this time, darling." She smiled. "Your tooth was filled with a piece of bread."

I surely felt as though God and Mama had both let my little sister down, but Papa explained some things to us that morning around the breakfast table. And he gave us a clear understanding of how God works through prayer. God was a wise God, he said, and everything in His world was made in order. Dentists had been given their skill by God to help people, and children should be thankful they could go to them when they had a bad toothache. It wasn't that God couldn't . . . it was that He didn't choose to. My sister's prayer had been a foolish, selfish prayer and not one to honor God.

That made me understand another of my child prayers that I had wondered about before. Every Christmas season our church had an auction where things were sold to benefit the poor and needy. Strange as it might seem now, looking back on our strict church discipline, chances were sold to make money. A certain big item was chanced out and, of course, that would be the thing that made the most money. That year it had been a doll. No, not just an ordinary doll. It was a creation! I, who only owned one little rag doll, stood in awe before it. To call a doll like that mine would be like living in heaven. I can't remember anything I ever wanted more than that doll. Jubilantly I watched Papa buy a chance. It was number 8. Then I went aside from the crowd and prayed the most sincere, heartbreaking prayer ever prayed. I promised God everything if He would see that I got that doll, and there was no doubt in my mind as I went back and watched the drawing. Already I felt as though I held the doll in my arms. My heart was broken when number 15 won. And, lo and behold, the prize went to a well-to-do family with a girl my age who already had five beautiful dolls. It was unfair of God, I had been thinking, and I was bitter toward Mary who had so many things. But I had never dared tell Papa that God was not fair. Now Papa's words set me straight. My prayer had been a selfish, foolish prayer. I had wanted something for myself which was not to the honor and glory of God. And so the Lord God again rose to His former height and majesty in my mind. My faith was restored because of my sister's prayer.

Little by little I seemed to grasp more of this strange power that we earth people use to contact God for the good of the world we live in. But still I didn't really know what prayer was until one day I accompanied Papa on a call to an old man's shack on a cold fall afternoon. It was three long miles to his dwelling and Papa and I walked it through the forest. I must have been about nine years old at the time, but how well I remember that walk! It was fun to walk with Papa. He was so big and strong, it gave me an air of importance. I felt very secure having him hold my hand. In my mind Papa was the greatest person on earth. He came next in line to God. Nothing bad could come to me when Papa held my hand.

The man was bedridden, crippled up with aches and pains. His shack was very primitive. He insisted that Papa make coffee for us. So Papa put on the muddy-looking coffeepot and found some cookies, and although they were musty-looking and smelled funny, he ate two. I didn't want any, but one look from Papa made me understand it would be very rude not to eat one. It might hurt the man's feeling. After we had had our coffee and had served the old man some, too, we sat down by his bed and Papa read from the Bible about the lame man that the Master healed. After the reading, we knelt to pray.

Papa prayed first. It was a long prayer. I soon lost

track of it and escaped to my own imaginative world. Then, suddenly, Papa nudged me to indicate that I was to pray, too. I meant it from my heart when I asked God to make the man well, and I even thanked God for the musty cooky. After my "amen" there was a short silence and then the man prayed. He clasped his disfigured hands and lifted his face heavenward. Something very special came into his voice, and although it was against the rule, I opened my eyes to peek just a wee bit at him. I couldn't figure it out, but his face changed as he prayed. It was radiant with joy, almost shiny, and my eyes opened wider and wider. That man never asked to be healed. He didn't ask God for anything. He just thanked Him as though he had been given everything in the whole world. He thanked God for the poor little shack in which he lived, for his warm bed, and for the kind people who dropped in to care for him. He prayed for his pastor and the blessing he had brought in coming out to read and pray with him, and even for his little girl who prayed so sweetly. He went on thanking God for the birds in the branches of the big tree outside his window and the snow that soon would come and make the world white; for summer and its beauty and this windy fall day that made him feel snug and sheltered in this room where he was sure of God's protection day and night. I never closed my eyes again during his prayer because I loved to see how quickly he kept changing as he talked with God. When we bade him good-bye, he looked as happy and contented as though he had no discomfort at all. And where before his face had been twisted with pain, it now looked relaxed and joyous.

How could it have happened? I wondered, perplexed. How could words tossed into the air make such a difference? The man was still sick, but that prayer had taken the sadness out of him. I realized that the change must have been within his heart—it was the joy from a happy inside that shone through. On the way home I asked Papa to explain prayer to me. And Papa did his best to try to come down to my level.

"My girl," he said, "prayers are the thoughts that come forth from our inner being. Prayer is our highest self, the very best within us that comes out in words from our lips. For once we are absolutely honest, knowing that we can hide nothing from God. As we pray, we become humble and sincere and there is a desire deep within us to be good. Forming prayer into words makes it more tangible. The words form a contact with God, so that our eyes reflect a glimpse of His glory. The heart beats with joy, for we know in God there is help for all our problems."

I walked silently beside my Papa for a long time.

He had talked to me as though I were a grownup, and I was proud and happy. The wind blew in the treetops. It was bitter cold. My feet ached now and I felt as if there were little stones in my shoes. It was getting dark. Papa still held my hand in his. His words are true, I was thinking; prayer must be like that. I had seen it in the old man's face. When he had made the contact with his God, he had forgotten his pain and loneliness. His aches were still there, but he could bear them with courage. Perhaps, I thought, that was a greater answer than to be made well.

"Look, dear," said Papa. "See the lights over there in the village. See, there is the parsonage—Mama just lit the lamp. Soon we will be home!"

It's like prayer, I was thinking, as my heart beat fast in the gladness of this new thought. Prayer is like walking in the dark and suddenly seeing a lamp being lit to tell you home is there. In prayer God is waiting for us, just as in the parsonage Mama was waiting for Papa and me. She knew we would be cold and hungry and tired, and she would meet us with open arms to welcome us home. It would be warm inside those walls, and clean and homey. Good food would be cooking on the stove. Mama would take my shoes off and warm my feet, placing soft slippers on them. I could see it all in my mind as I walked with Papa toward the light.

And so it was with prayer. The sick old man had seen the light of God's world; he had seen his Father's house and knew that he soon would be home. There would be no more sickness or pain or loneliness there, and no more sorrow. And the light of prayer would lead him home.

For the first time I seemed to understand what prayer was good for and why it was the only pathway that leads us from our earth mind to God's Kingdom where all is well. And it wasn't so far to reach; one had only to walk toward that light.

It was as though a big star had appeared in the sky of my limited thought world. God was real! Prayer was not asking selfishly for what one wanted from God. Prayer was contact with a power so great that just one spark from that source would transform things into good.

A little later in life, when I was just about to leave my childhood and step up onto higher ground, I heard from Papa about prayer again. It was when I felt my mind stretching and my thoughts widening and I understood that what counted most in life was the value we set on things and how much we were willing to pay to keep that value.

Papa was sitting at his big desk in his study and I was standing beside him. I was thrilled to be a part of that room, even if I was only a part like the desk, or the Bible, or the picture of The Rich Young Ruler approaching the Master. I was a small part, indeed, but I was there, and Papa put his pen away and leaned back in his chair.

"What am I writing?" He repeated the question I had asked him. "I am trying to explain prayer for the prayer session this week."

"And what did you write, Papa?"

He lifted the white paper from the desk and began to read:

> "Prayer is the best in us approaching a Holy God. It is as if we were disrobed of our vanity—our pride—our selfishness. It is the highest honesty in our hearts that truly seeks to adjust to a higher will. It is when we lose self that we find the Christ within and there is the contact made. Prayers have an answer. We are at home in our Father's House. Oh, that we would dwell there forever. . . .

They were like the words he had said before, and I understood what he read. Prayer would be my light to lead me through the unknown years ahead. I would always believe in it because I had seen prayer's answer in the face of the sick old man a long time ago. There was a man who had contacted God and found peace.

As the years went by I understood more and more. It became clear to me that prayer was never an individual thing; it was universal. What we ask for one affects all, because prayer is always answered. It is like a missile shooting through the air into space. It is never lost, but will keep on doing the good it is sent out to accomplish. It belongs to eternity. Somewhere a heavy burden will be lifted, because someone knelt in prayer. A pain too torturing to bear will lose its grip and a heart caught in agony and despair will find sudden rest. Because of prayer, God comes to men. Prayer will find its goal. Our sight is short and we see only so far . . . but far, far beyond the horizon prayer finds its answer through the channel God has directed. What a loss to the world and heaven, too, that so many neglect to pray.

The prayers of those who have chosen to serve God here on earth go before them, as a preparation. And so when contact is made, help comes swiftly and it is as strong as eagle wings. Prayer is the strong, silent partner to those who believe.

❧ Chapter Three

What a difference it makes to know all about prayer, to understand its mystery, and then to try to reach out and touch it. I do sincerely hope that sharing my reaching out will help others to begin to measure the strength of their faith and see how high it stretches into the unknown. I realize now if we know deep within our hearts only a speck of the greatness of our God and can also comprehend this with our mind, we have found the contact. One has to believe in his heart and think with his mind and find that the two will melt into one great and glorious experience, before one can pull the lever that releases the power in prayer.

It took me a long time to realize this in my own mind. Yes, I prayed each day and I believed in my heart that God would and could protect, help and give me strength. But when it came to reaching out and trying it, I was still a babe in understanding.

It was once when Mama came up from Florida to spend a few weeks at our home in Longmeadow that I made my search more intense and, as I really believe, made myself dare to launch out. I was a mother of two grown daughters and I had even held my first grandson in my arms when this came to pass.

Mama was sitting out in the garden reading an article about prayer in a magazine. Sitting in another chair beside her, I had watched her expression as she read. Presently, she threw the magazine aside.

"I can't understand why they make it so complicated, when it is so simple," she burst out impatiently.

"What is so complicated, Mama?" I asked.

"Those things they write about prayer. . . . Why must people feel that they need to go to school to learn to pray, and still hardly dare to believe that they should expect an answer?"

I smiled as I watched the frown on her forehead. If the world only knew that my Mama was an expert in prayer, I was thinking. If they could only know that her prayers always seemed to get an answer with unbelievable speed. Oh, surely the world of today would find her naïve. But did not the Master place a child in the midst of His disciples and tell them that that was the pattern they were to follow in their faith?

"You know, dear," said Mama, "prayer is too simple. That is why some people don't use it more. It is simple enough for a little child to understand. You just ask God . . . or tell Him the problem and *leave it there*. God is ready and willing to take care of all his earth people's needs."

Those three words stuck in my mind: "Leave it there." That was one of our troubles in praying. We carried our heavy burdens to the Lord, sometimes with the help of others, and after placing them humbly at His feet, we picked them up again and continued to carry the load. That was what made Mama so happy after she had prayed. She had left whatever it was she carried—for herself or for others—left it right there with God—sure that it was in His hands now. She could relax and rest, knowing that the answer was on its way.

We did not talk about the subject any more. There were busy days as always in a happy household. I meant to read the article Mama had fretted so about, but I never got around to it. The weeks went by and Mama went back to her Florida and as fall came on, I started to lecture on my yet unpublished first book. Driving and speaking kept me busy. There was a glow within me, as I waited for some publisher to accept the book. I felt this newborn babe was a gift from God. My childhood dreams had finally been fulfilled, and my heart held great hopes. And so came a night when I, for the first time, took Mama's advice to pray and leave it with the Lord God.

It might seem like a silly prayer, but I offered it on the spur of the moment, and with as much sincerity as if I prayed for the greatest cause in the world. And it wasn't just the small thing I asked protection for that mattered. The thing that counted was that the answer did come.

I was returning home from a two-hundred-mile speaking trip. It was a cold November day. The trees were disrobed and the glory and beauty of autumn were all in the past. It was that time of year when the earth seems a little dreary and when you long for the soft white blanket of snow to fall and cover it up until spring comes again. I was tired! I had spoken to a large woman's club group and, as always, I had been asked when my book was to be published. I still had no answer. If I had but known that Rinehart & Company would take it a month later, in December, I perhaps would not have noticed the bare, bleak world. But I was a bit depressed. In Springfield I stopped on a busy street to go into a drugstore. I slid out on the right side of the car to avoid holding up the stream of traffic. It was only when I reached home that I noticed my little blue velvet hat was missing. It began to come clear to me how it must have happened. The hat had been beside me in the front seat of the car, and I had evidently pushed it off the seat into the street when I went into the drugstore. It was a good hat and one of my favorites. Furthermore, it had been bought to go with my lecturing dress and I just couldn't lose it. My first impulse was to drive back and see if it was still there, crushed, of course, with all that traffic. Nevertheless I wanted it, and perhaps it could be restored.

But I was very tired and weary. I had had a long ride and home seemed so good with its light and its happy voices. Outside it was dark and cold and I had already put the car in the garage. And so, the thought came to me . . . perhaps it wasn't even right to ask God about it, but I would. I would do what Mama had told me; I would pray to God to protect my hat until morning and just "leave it there" with Him. I can't remember if I spoke the words out loud, or if they just came from my heart, but this is what I felt:

Father God, I don't know if this is an orderly prayer; if it isn't, forgive my foolishness. But I think of you as my wonderful heavenly Father, and I want to talk to you as a child would talk to his parent. Tonight I am like a little child holding up a broken toy, asking you to fix it. You know all about my little hat lying there on the busy street. It is a good hat and I should be concerned about it. Please, Father, protect it for me until morning. I thank you with all my heart.

Amen

I went to bed early and had a good night's sleep. I forgot about the hat during the night, wanting so to follow Mama's suggestion to "leave it there." About eight A.M. I was ready to drive back and pick it up. My younger daughter wondered where I was heading so early in the morning. And when I told her, she just sat down on a chair and laughed to her heart's content.

"Mommie," she cried, "you do the funniest things! No one but you would ever believe that a thing like that could happen. How in the world can you expect the hat to still be there? And if it is, it surely wouldn't look like a hat by this time."

I assured her that I knew what I was doing, and I expected to be able to show her my hat when she came home from high school that afternoon. When we parted, she still had that funny smile on her face.

"I am sure it will be all right!" I kept saying to myself as I drove along. There was a calmness in my heart and an anticipation that excited all my other emotions.

I parked the car in the same place as I had the night before and slid out just as I had done then. And when

I looked down at the street, there it was—the little blue velvet hat, as nice and fresh as if it had just come out of a hatbox. For a moment I held it in my arms and hugged it gently as though it were a child. Tears rolled down my cheeks.

"Thank you, Father God," I whispered. "You did care and you did hear my prayer. I just don't know how to thank You."

It was a miracle! And it surely was to the Glory of God because I felt my faith grow and vision widen. Cars had been coming and going all night. They had been driving an inch in front of the little blue hat and an inch in back. They had parked beside it and missed it by an eighth of an inch. How many times it must have been in danger of being crushed, but it had been protected. If God could care enough to protect a little hat, how much more would He care to protect me as I traveled on the busy highways. A warm, gentle feeling encompassed my heart. I had touched prayer in a strange way, and it was wonderful!

You might ask me: Do I recommend that people pray for God to take care of things they do not feel like doing themselves? No, I don't! It is important for a prayer like this not to be minimized, or made fun of. I believe that we should pray from our own hearts for whatever need is there. But we must be true to our own selves, and not try to copy others. We are all individuals and we will have to agree to disagree on many things. But we must not take from each other the uniqueness of personal faith. I knew I had done a thing that Mama would have done. Papa would have thought it a silly prayer, although, I know, he never would have doubted God's power to answer it. God sees in our hearts what we are. It is not what we ask, it is the sincerity and the trust that flows out of a trembling heart that our God honors. A lark, could it pray, would not ask to swim under water; and could we picture a perch—if a fish could pray—asking that it be able to sit in the treetops and sing? No, we know that it would only be right for the lark to pray that it could sing more beautiful songs and soar higher and higher in a blue sky, and for the perch that it could swim in deep, clear water. So it is with us. That prayer was true to my nature, and that is why God honored it. And my faith grew, because I was naïve enough to believe in it with both my heart and mind and leave it to God's will. Some people could never pray a prayer like that and feel right about it. And they should be admired and honored for their high ideals. But let us be ourselves. That is the way we can best serve our God here on earth. How clear that became in my mind, and how much I needed that lesson! Praying was just like learning to float. What a time I had until I really felt that if I threw myself on the water and trusted it, it would bear me up. But if I was frightened and didn't dare to let go of myself, I would sink.

The next lesson that I was to learn concerned the prayer of intercession, when someone else prayed to God for my protection.

Again I was on a lecturing trip. My first book had been published and was a great success. I was happy and grateful and my lecturing now stretched far and wide. This time I was returning home from Portland, Maine, where I had spoken to a large club. I had been invited to spend the night with a minister friend and his lovely wife who had a little cottage by the ocean. Those were the high lights of my traveling, the wonderful dear friendships I made and the warmth I felt from being wanted. God was so gracious to me. He knew how I loved people and now I was meeting fine and noble people, adding day by day to my long list of earth friends.

It was February, and the ocean was stormy. I think I shall always hear in my mind those waves rolling in and out against the rocky shore that night. The ocean sang the lullaby that rocked me to sleep, and in the morning I awoke refreshed and rested and ready to start my journey home. First, we had breakfast in a dining room with windows on three sides looking out on the ocean. There was a glow around the table, a glow of love and fellowship. The minister read aloud from the Bible and shared with us some of the deep thoughts from his daily five A.M. meditations. The room was filled with a humble, sweet spirit. As we parted we clasped hands in prayer.

"The radio is forecasting a big snowstorm," said the pastor. "You better get going. Drive carefully and God be with you."

As I kissed my hostess good-bye, she clung to my hand, lifting her face in prayer:

> Dear God—protect her. Don't let anything happen to her. And lead her safely to her loved ones.

Her sweet sincerity was still ringing in my ears as I drove toward home. God was so good to me and the world was full of wonderful people.

I had only gone about thirty miles when the storm began. It started slowly, but became worse and worse. It was sleeting and freezing and it was hard to keep the car on the road. But I drove slowly, trying to remember that each mile brought me a bit closer to home. It was on Route 128 that it happened. A big truck had been in front of me for miles and miles, and the traffic moved fifteen miles per hour. I am impatient by nature and after a while this got the best of me. If only I could get by that truck, the long line in back of me could get going, too. Looking for an opportunity to pass, I came to a place where the road looked fairly smooth. Even if it was slippery, I would try to get by that big thing. So I stepped on the gas and got the speedometer up to thirty miles. I was halfway by the truck, when I realized my foolishness. But others had pulled out in back of me; I had to make it. The car slipped and skidded and when I was almost past the truck, I lost control of the car. I began to spin around and panic seized me. This was it, I thought. This was the way it felt to have an accident. Would I crash into the truck? Would other cars pile up? Would this be the end? "Please, God, let my husband think to cancel my speaking engagements." Would I land in the hospital? Would I die just in my glory with a successful book out? My thoughts were racing at lightning speed through my brain and then the calm. . . . It was only seconds—but again I was back in that cottage by the ocean. I saw my friend lift her face, asking God to protect me. And somehow I knew that that prayer had gone with me and it was here now to do its work.

"I can't drive, Father," I called out. "Take the wheel."

The next thing I knew, I was sitting on an uphill bank by the road, the car facing the opposite direction. The kindly truck driver stood beside me. All traffic had stopped. His truck was zigzagged across the road. Another truck behind him had parked across the road, too, to stop all traffic from trickling through.

"It was a miracle," said the truck driver. "How could you get control of the car and drive it onto the bank just when I was sure we were crashing? You were two inches from me, Lady. You gave me the worst scare I've ever had."

But I couldn't answer. How could I tell him I hadn't driven the car, that I had let go of the wheel and let God take over? Would he understand if I said prayer had protected us? Finally my voice came. "I prayed," I whispered. "I was foolish to try to pass, but I didn't want to hurt you, too."

"You surely did something!" he gasped.

My head was as light as a feather. I felt unreal. Perhaps I was dead after all, I was thinking, and it just felt as if I were alive. But the kind driver and another truck driver took the car down from the bank and made me walk around a little to get some exercise. Then they drove after me, asking me to stop at the next restaurant for a cup of coffee. They didn't leave me until they were sure I felt strong enough to drive on. I shall never cease to wonder about their kindness and concern. Although I never found out their names, I shall bless them forever.

What an experience that was! Now I never start off

on a drive in my car without lifting my face in this prayer:

Father,
Help me to drive so I won't endanger others,
and others to drive so they won't endanger me.
And take the wheel and drive with me, so I can
feel completely protected.

And then I start off. Whether my drive is long or short, I know that prayer will protect me from harm.

As time went on and I grew in faith, I realized more and more how powerful prayer was. If only all people knew that, I was thinking. How we could pray "big" prayers for our world. We could whisper them through the whole day—prayers filled with love and concern— left in God's care. But soon I was really to be tested on my beliefs in a way I had never expected.

Sickness had come to us! My dear husband had collapsed one day and had been rushed to the hospital for an emergency operation on his stomach. His small Tool & Die Company was only a couple of years old, and he had not as yet gotten on his feet financially. But he had been struggling along, trying to meet the bills and working as hard as he could. He had only a few men on the payroll besides himself. But money had to come each week to meet that payroll. When he became ill, there was no income and it would be months and months before he could go back to work again. Besides that there were private nurses around the clock and what money we had was dwindling away at a rapid pace. I had had to let the men go and turn the key in the closed door of the shop. If my husband got well, the shop had to be there waiting for him. I knew that would have everything to do with his recovery. Although I didn't know just how, I knew I must keep up the rent on the shop or ask for credit. One night with tears running down my cheeks, I sat down to write to all the creditors, telling them how things were and why the bills were not paid. People might say that the world is hard when you are in trouble and that business is business, but I have never had such kindness and understanding come to me as from those business firms. Every creditor answered my letter most graciously, telling me not to worry. They would be happy to put the bills aside until my husband was able to open his shop again. I was amazed at such kindness, but not one of them sent us a bill during all those months. Some even wrote and asked if they could help.

It was surely a joy when he was able to open the shop again and get his men back. He could not work, but he could supervise. And if money came in so he could pay those men, we would soon be on the go again. Things went fine for a couple of weeks and then came one week when some money we had counted on wasn't paid on time. We needed three hundred dollars to pay the men their weekly wages, and there was no money to be had. You can't send a man home to tell his family that there just was no pay. What were we to do? I shall never forget that September day when my husband came home for lunch with a strange blank look on his face. I guessed the trouble before he told me.

"The money did not come," I said.

"You are right. Not a penny—what shall I do?"

Well, what should he do? We had borrowed from the bank all that we could. There was no one we could ask for money, when all we had was bills and more bills. Presently a smile came to my husband's face. He placed his finger under my chin and lifted my face toward his.

"I know what we will do," he said. "Remember that faith of yours that you can ask God for anything when you are in trouble and He will look out for you? Now I expect that faith of yours to go to work. If it is real, money should rain down on us from Heaven, shouldn't it?"

I nodded, forcing a smile and trying to look unconcerned. But I was scared. I had said those words many times, tossing my head with assurance when he had kidded me. I knew my faith was real. God would help if we asked Him. But hadn't we prayed right along for money to come in time? Why had not God answered us before this? And now, there were only two hours before the bank closed—only two hours. Would God work that fast?

My husband went and sat down in the garden with his newspaper, while I prepared his sandwich and coffee and carried them out to him. I couldn't eat myself. As yet, I had not prayed. I didn't know just how to pray or what to ask. I stood in the kitchen looking up at the blue sky and the bright sun. It was warm for September, the flowers in the garden were in bloom.

> "God," [I whispered.] "Father God, I don't even need to tell you, but money must come in time to get into the bank. I don't know how you are going to do this, but I am asking you and leaving it with you. Here, take this heavy burden. I shall not take it back. I know my faith is real. Prayer is power. I know you will not fail me."

Presently a name came to my mind. It was the name of an old friend, but she was not a wealthy person. She worked part time as a cook for a rich household. Whatever made me think of her? Time and time again, her name came to my mind. Was I suppose to get in touch with her? If so, how would she get three hundred dollars and would she be willing to let us have it for a while? I went to the phone and called her place of work. It was her day off and she was not there. I called her daughter's home. No, she was not there. Her daughter expected her, but not until four o'clock. She was downtown shopping.

I was about to hang up when the daughter called out, "Wait a moment, I see Mother coming up the walk now. You can talk to her."

Then my friend was on the phone. My heart almost failed me. But I gathered all the courage I had and asked her straight out, could she possibly lend us some money?

"Yes," she answered quickly in a strange voice. "Come over to my house in a half an hour. I'll be waiting for you."

We drove to her house. "Did you tell her how much we needed?" asked my worried husband.

"No," I confessed, "but she said we could borrow some money."

"How could she be carrying that amount of money in her pocketbook?" he ventured, looking at me as though I could solve the problem with some more words.

We drove the rest of the way in silence. "I mustn't worry. That's taking the burden back," I lectured myself. "I must know that this is the answer."

She was sitting on her front porch when I came up the steps. "How much do you need?" she asked simply.

"Three hundred dollars," I said so softly that I could hardly hear my own voice.

She opened her pocketbook and counted out the money. "Go quickly, so you can get to the bank before it closes," she said.

I thanked her with tears in my eyes, but one more word. "How did you happen to have it?" I asked.

"I will tell you that the next time I see you. There is no hurry about returning it," she assured me. "Use it as long as you need it."

I placed the money in my husband's lap. "Money from Heaven," I whispered as I threw myself in his arms.

He never forgot that day, and from then on, he never doubted what prayer could do, or that God surely cares for us and is willing to help when we ask Him.

Later the lady told me herself how she came to have that money in her pocketbook just when we needed it.

"I was walking around downtown shopping," she said, "when suddenly something like a voice speaking within me urged me to go to the bank and draw out some of my savings. Unable to get the thought out of my mind, I drew the three hundred dollars. I was sure one of my children had been in an accident and needed it. So, I left my shopping and drove straight to my daughter's house. When I arrived and heard your voice, I knew that it was God's voice I had heard, and that I was to help you."

This made a lasting impression on all three of us. Nothing like that had ever happened to her before, and she counted it a privilege to be used by God to answer a prayer.

It was so easy for me to pray after that, whether about big things or little things, because I knew God was closer to me than my own heartbeat and nearer to me than my own breath. Why should we fret and worry and be unhappy, when we have a God like that, who is our Father?

Then came one night when I was driving my daughter to her home, which is about twelve miles from mine. It was a foggy night and the fog seemed to get thicker every minute. As we went up a steep hill and reached the summit, it became simply impossible to see where the road went. By inching ourselves forward, we finally made it downhill again where we could see just enough so we didn't drive off the road. When I was to drive back home, I was really frightened. How would I be able to make that hill? But then I remembered prayer. My fear vanished, for I knew God would be with me.

"Thank you, Father, for your protection," I whispered, as I started out. Just as I reached the foot of the hill and began to climb, a big truck came behind me. Its bright lights dented the fog and I was able to get over the hill. Again I knew that if I only remembered that wherever I was, God was, I need not fear. For there was not one situation that my God could not handle.

Yes, I have prayed about almost anything and now I feel very much like my Mama. Things I found strange that she should pray about, I was praying about myself. And I can now understand her assurance and perfect trust in God.

One night I was in Chicago on a speaking trip. It was midnight and I was changing trains for Lincoln, Nebraska. I had two heavy suitcases and my portfolio to carry. There was only five minutes between trains and a long way to go. There were no redcaps or any help that night, just passengers pushing away, trying to get ahead of each other. On top of that it was raining, a cold drizzle. How can I ever make it? I was wondering, as I struggled on through the night, feeling very much alone and tired. I just had to make that train to be in Lincoln in the morning. My arms seemed to give way—when suddenly, like a warm glow from a fire, the thought came to me: How foolish I am. God will help me. Didn't He always help me when I asked

Him? I put down my heavy suitcases. "Father, God," I whispered, "help me to get there in time. I just can't make it myself."

Presently a man came out of nowhere, it seemed, and stood beside me.

"May I help you carry those bags?" he asked. He took my suitcases and I told him which track I had to go to and we made it right on time. He carried them right on the train and before I had time to thank him, he was gone.

I have told these things to the glory of the wonderful God I am serving. Surely He has a plan for me in this earth life. I was trained enough now to begin my work of helping others, ushering them into a new thinking and a stronger faith where they would learn, too, to touch this magnificent power called "prayer."

❧ Chapter Four

There are great men called to preach the word of God from beautiful sanctuaries where there seems to be a holy atmosphere fitting the worship place of God. Others are called to be missionaries in remote countries, far from civilization. And there are some who feel the call to witness to their own families and neighbors in their own home towns. But now and then we find a person who has only the deep desire to try to be a light for his God wherever he is, and to do God's bidding at the right moment, to the right person, whenever the call comes.

It was my desire to listen to God's voice and be of help whenever I felt that call, which I heard so clearly in my heart. Never was it a planned thing. Suddenly and unexpectedly, I found myself talking to people concerning things greater than ourselves. And I knew it was a call because the person I was led to speak with was always trying to fine happiness.

One of the dearest women I know I met in one of our city's big department stores when I was buying a coat. The coat needed a little altering and this lady was the fitter who was called in to do the job. Her hands were nimble and she worked quickly, looking up at me every now and then to make some casual remark about the coat, the weather, or any small talk that had very little meaning, when suddenly she put her pincushion down and stood up beside me.

"You know," she said, "day after day as I've pinned up coats and let them down, I've always hoped that someday I would meet a person who was different from the crowd. This life gets so monotonous sometimes. Lady, you are different! Will you tell me why?" She looked at me with great expectation and I gave her a little smile, having been taken by surprise at her remark.

"If I am different, perhaps it is because I am on the top of the world," I said gaily. "You see, I just had my first book published. Another thing could be that I love life and people. Sometimes I can't wait to live each new day. And when I think how wonderfully special God is, I bubble over with joy. Perhaps it comes out and spills over."

"It surely does," she told me. "You are the happiest person I've ever pinned up a coat on. Tell me, why is God so special to you?"

"Isn't He special to you?" I asked.

She shook her head. "I don't think God even knows that I exist."

Before I left the store that afternoon, she had promised to accompany me to a lecture I was giving that same night. At eight o'clock that evening I picked her up outside her apartment house and we drove off as though we had always known each other. . . .

"I loved your talk on 'Mama and Papa,'" she confided in me on the way home, "but that was not why I went with you tonight. I want you to tell me more about God."

We talked late into the night. She was lonely and was carrying some heavy burdens and thousands of worries about the future. We talked many times after that and when I went to a retreat the next fall for a bit of spiritual growth, she came with me. Here, it seemed, she found what she was seeking and that retreat changed her life. She became radiant with a joy that often rubbed off on those whose coats she pinned up. For she had found her place at the table of the Lord and her hungry heart had found the food it needed. And I had gained a friend so loyal and fine that I shall always be thankful that we met that day I bought a coat.

It is a simple little story, but helping someone lost and bewildered to find the light is such a joyous task that I wouldn't exchange it for all the money in the world.

It was summer with all its sunshine and laughter! Happy church people had gathered at a conference held in beautiful, historic Northfield, Massachusetts. I was one of the group sent as delegates from the church to which I belong. But I had also come for a rest and to strengthen and refresh my own spiritual life. I hoped to bring back with me a fine report as a result of the inspirational truths I was to glean from those ten days.

I named her "The Silent Lady" and I don't think I have ever seen a mature woman so beautiful. But she avoided all of us. And when someone tried to reach out to her in friendship, she would dismiss the person with a polite, but cool smile. As I watched her day after day, my heart ached for her. Why is she so lonely? I wondered. And why doesn't she want friends?

Every day she took long walks. I saw her start off. She walked slowly, but with a certain unusual grace. Her head was held high and she had perfect poise. I felt the call to speak. But how do you approach a person who does not want to be near anyone and who carries the sadness of all the world ingrained in her features? She had soft long golden hair which surrounded her velvety cheeks like a crown of glory. Her eyes were blue and wistful. They were dreaming eyes that seemed to look and still not see, eyes that looked as though she cried into her pillow at night. Although she was physically tall and stately, there was something small and helpless about her personality.

There must be a story behind that face, I was thinking, a sad heartbreaking story. I must see if I can help her. After all, a servant of God is always on call, regardless of whether it is vacation time or not. So one afternoon when I saw her going off for her walk, I waited fifteen minutes and then I took the same road she had taken, knowing that sooner or later we were bound to meet. We did! I saw her coming around the bend toward me and also saw the expression on her face when she knew she would have to meet me. Just as we met, I stopped.

"May I accompany you back to the dining room?" I asked. "I was just about to turn back. What a glorious day! And isn't Northfield one of those unusual places where you feel as though you were stepping on sacred ground?"

I had turned and was now walking beside her. She smiled back at me, but did not answer my flow of words.

We walked silently for a few moments and then I spoke again, at the same time sending up a little prayer that God would give me the wisdom to say the right thing.

"I don't want to be rude," she suddenly burst out, "and I hope I don't seem ungrateful for your kindness, but I came up here to be alone."

"I had a feeling that was the case and believe me I don't want to force my friendship on you, but somehow I can't get you off my mind. You look so sad, as if you were carrying a heavy burden. How I wish that I could help you!"

"I don't think anyone can help me," she answered sadly, "but I am touched by your thoughtfulness. You see, just now I am trying to run away from life."

"Oh, that is too bad. Life can be so beautiful!"

She smiled a bitter little smile. "For some people, yes, but never for me. I lost my mother whom I adored when I was very young, and my sister became like a mother to me. I clung to her because she was all I had. My father never knew what it was to be a parent. But at the age when I needed my sister the most, she died of that dreadful cancer. I, too, died a little inside every day during her long suffering. But there was nothing I could do to help her, or to keep her. I think that was why I married so young. I needed security. But getting married was the worst tragedy of all. You see, I married a man much older than myself. We were different in every way and as the years went by

I became more and more afraid of him. Just recently I left him, but he will not let me go. I thought that at a conference like this, with so many people, I could hide from him. But I learned last night that he is here now and registered at the Inn. He might come anytime and force his attentions on me. Who knows, maybe if I cross him too many times, he might even kill me?"

It was a long speech and she stopped, perplexed.

"I don't know why I told you," she cried. "I never tell anyone my troubles. But somehow, right now I am so overfull with worries and anxiety—it is hard to keep it all inside me. Please forgive me for talking like this. I don't know why you want to bother with me in the first place."

I put my hand on her arm. "I want to be your friend," I said simply. "I am sure that God has sent me to help you."

She stared at me. "God!" she almost sneered. "What does God care about what happens to me?"

"You are wrong, my dear. He does care. There is not one person on this earth He is not concerned about. I am sure He wants you to be happy. You know that eyes have not seen nor have ears heard what glory He has prepared for those who love Him."

"I am afraid I don't love Him very much. Oh, I go to church for my daughter's sake. You see, my husband and I are not of the same religion and I have defied him in bringing our daughter up in my faith. That, of course, is half the trouble between us."

"God loves your husband, too. I am sure he also is very unhappy."

"God wouldn't love him if he knew what a devil he is," she snapped.

"Oh, yes," I insisted. "You see, God sees deeper than his deviltry. He sees deep down into his heart. Something has made him that way, and you have to try to think kindly of him."

We talked every day after that. Soon she asked me to walk with her. We sat together at mealtimes and she even went to church with me.

One night we stood together on the top of a hill. The world below seemed very far away. Presently she came closer to me. "Please," she said, "will you tell me about God. I want to be friendly with God the way you are. But I can never be like you."

"Oh yes, you can," I assured her. "You have to learn to pray, to talk to God as your Father. After you have learned this, you will never feel alone again."

"How can I learn?" she asked eagerly.

"You have to talk to God as though you were a little child, a hurt, bewildered child, longing for His love. Just forget you are grown up, forget all the things that have been. You are a little child again, telling your Father your troubles. I don't need to tell you any more, for after you have talked with God like that, you will feel His love and His guidance and I can guarantee one thing: you will be happier than you have ever been, and everything will work out in the right way."

The next morning when she saw me, she came rushing up to me. She did not look shy any more and her face was lit up by a radiant smile.

"Do you know what?" she burst out, talking so fast she could hardly get her breath. "I tried it and it worked. Last night I became like a little child and I knelt by my bed and talked to God as to a Father. I told Him everything, even the hatefulness that seemed to live in me, and all that bitterness. I asked Him to forgive me and to wash my soul clean from all its hurts and resentments. I stayed on my knees a long time. And for the first time in many, many years, I let my tears flow without holding them back. You know, after that I slept so peacefully that when I awoke this morning, my heart was light. I felt as though I loved the whole world. I was glad to be alive, and I know that happiness will come. I can feel it!"

A few nights after that we were sitting together in the chapel with her husband sitting between us. "I got strength to let him come," she had told me. "I feel sorry for him. God will help me to be kind to him, for I know he is a sick man."

And during the service, she leaned forward and whispered to me. "Did you see it? The bird . . . it was flying over the altar . . . a small white bird flying noiselessly about. I think it was God's sign to me. Do you think I saw the Holy Spirit?"

I knew there had been a bird flying in the chapel. I had seen it, too. It flew absolutely without noise. To me, the bird was gray like a little sparrow. But she had seen it white!

"Whatever it means," I whispered back, "it is beautiful. Believe it is whatever your heart tells you."

Her life was changed after that summer. We became the dearest of friends and looking back now, I can see how wonderfully God fulfilled those words I had spoken of her future happiness. Years have passed by since that summer in Northfield. After a short while her husband passed away. She married again, one of the finest men on earth. Her happiness now is like a warm glow that surrounds her whole being. Together the two of them can take their problems to God and together they can worship Him. And I shall never cease to marvel how God leads those who are willing to serve Him in helping others. And I, through that experience, gained one of the most precious friends a person could ever wish for here on earth.

I went to Northfield other summers and it seemed that I was always called to help at least one person there. Once there was a little minister's wife who couldn't stand the prayer laboratory sessions.

"I am almost sick when I get out of them," she told me. "Something is wrong with the whole thing! I shall not attend again."

"If you feel like that," I said, "it isn't because the prayer laboratory has something wrong with it. It is because you have something wrong within yourself."

I don't know why I said those sharp words to her. It was not at all like me, but they had just come out as though no power on earth could hold them back. And she stood there stunned and hurt and bewildered, as though I had hit her with a whip. But I heard my own voice speaking words more kindly now. "You see," it said, "prayer is like a mirror. In it we see our true selves. If the picture is not a pretty one, it hurts. We have no use for prayer, no need for it. Prayer changes things and we don't want to be changed."

The next moment she was in my arms. "Can I talk to you?" she asked. "You are right. There is something wrong with me."

And it was something very, very wrong. She had been a hypocrite and a faker and she hated the very work of her husband's ministry. But we got it all straightened out and today she is one of the dearest, happiest workers in God's kingdom. And she has her own prayer group to help those who need to learn to pray. I shall never forget the big stone where the two of us knelt and asked God to change her life. And I saw the miracle take place as she said, "I felt as if I took off a dirty old garment and put on a beautiful new white one."

We rejoiced together over her happiness and I am sure in God's heaven all the angels were ringing their bells in gladness over a sinner who had repented.

Oh, when I look back through the album of my memories, there are too many to get them down on paper. I turn the pages reverently, for each person that was sent to me got the help God had already prepared for her. I was just a small tool, who said the right word at the right time.

I see, for instance, a young girl I met in a restaurant. She was a violinist and God had bestowed on her a great talent. But she had one handicap. She had a fear of forgetting her music when she played, a fear that her memory would suddenly go blank and when she felt like that, her fingers would stiffen and she would lose her touch.

After talking together for a while, I had asked her to pray about it, and she had said, "I just don't seem to get through to God. You pray for me! If I can think of you praying for me, I might forget my fear."

I promised her that I would remember her in prayer

every day. And I asked her to start memorizing Bible verses. "They will give you confidence and you will not forget what you have to remember," I told her. "Whenever I want to be sure to remember, I memorize a long Psalm. Psalm One Hundred and Three was the first one I tackled when I was new at speaking and had an hour-long speech to remember."

"You remembered the whole One Hundred and Third Psalm?" She stared at me.

"Sure, that's not much. Just try it and see."

"Oh, if only I could do it!"

"And when your fingers feel as though they are getting stiff, change your thoughts. Don't let fear come in. Think of God. 'He keepeth him in perfect peace whose mind is stayed on HIM.' Think of God as beauty. Think of a beautiful sunset on a lazy summer night, of a lone bird flying across the sky as the clouds are tinted in azure and gold. Think of a supper table with a dear little family sitting around it, all bowing in evening grace; of a kitten stretched out on a bed, or a dimpled baby asleep in his mother's arms. And of all things, know that where you are, God is."

"I will try it!" she promised.

We parted, but one fall night, later that year, I received a telegram from her. She was to play in a big concert hall. She gave the time of her performance and said; "Think with me on God."

It went beautifully. Her fear now has left her. Her fingers never stiffen. And again I stand amazed before the ways the Lord God leads His own. I, who knew nothing of music, had helped a great musician to find herself. But then—all things work together for good for those who love the LORD GOD.

❧ Chapter Five

A lamp once lit cannot be hid. It will shine out into the darkness and because of it, many will be guided along their way. So when God's light is lit in our hearts, we cannot hide it from the world. Wherever we are, we will shine and because of it many fellow travelers here in this earth life will see more clearly.

As I look back now, I know for certain that many people, even those very close to me, often found my conception of God and prayer a bit odd. Perhaps it was because of the lightness in the way I talked about prayer, the assurance I always had, that when we pray, there is always an answer.

Some people made a joke of my words. They were kind jokes, so I didn't mind too much. I knew they did not understand this new philosophy; not really new, it had been since the beginning of time. I heard people saying something like this: "If we were to be like you, there wouldn't be a thing to worry about. We'd just have to smile and be happy each day and God would take care of all our affairs."

As I said, I knew they didn't mean to ridicule me. For underneath I know they felt that there was something solid and worth while in my approach to God. And in some strange way they perhaps felt I was especially favored by the Lord, and that He, in His goodness, tolerated my strange ways.

But there came times in those people's lives when even my philosophy came in handy and they actually took advantage of it.

Once a Director of Religious Education and a Sunday-school worker, having attended a convention far from our home city, developed car trouble on the way home. It was just one of those times when two women drivers alone on the highway were stuck. It was summer and the weather was hot and muggy. Standing by their car at the side of the road, unable to go anywhere, was not a pleasant thing.

Presently the Director of Religious Education spoke up: "It's too bad our friend, Thyra, is not with us. She would just pray and, presto, out of nowhere a mechanic would appear, drive up to us and say, 'Ladies, may I have the pleasure of fixing your car? It will cost you absolutely nothing!'"

Her friend agreed that that was just what would

happen. Thyra wouldn't tolerate being stuck anywhere. God would see that she was taken care of.
They stood there another half an hour. Cars swished
by them, little cars, big cars, trucks, trailers, until
finally they became impatient.

"Let us try praying about it," one of them said. "It's
hard for me to believe that God interferes in things
like this, but it won't hurt just to try. And we certainly
need help!"

They both became serious about it then and reverently bowed their heads in prayer:

> Dear God, our friend would ask You to help us if
> she were here. Now we want to try it. Please God
> help us out of this predicament, so that we can be
> on our way before darkness overtakes us. We
> thank you, God!
>
> Amen

They told me this story themselves. They said that
after their prayer it seemed as if a hush came over
their surroundings. It was broken by the sound of a
car, which, as it approached them, slowed down to a
full stop. The driver, a pleasant young man, asked if
they were in trouble and if he could be of some assistance. He lifted the hood and fixed the car and
they had hardly had time to think before they were
on their way again.

"We were so thrilled," they told me. "We want to believe it was our prayer. But, of course, it could have been just a coincidence. But there by the roadside we assured ourselves that it was an answered prayer."

I still smile when I think about their words and their doubt. If an answer to prayer is just a coincidence, what difference does it make if that is the method God uses? Isn't it wonderful to have a coincidence take place each time you pray? A coincidence that happens for the good? And God is good.

I had almost forgotten that incident when something else happened to me. This time I really got scared and I wondered if it was wrong for me always to bare my heart's thoughts when it made people think all sorts of odd things. At first I felt like laughing the whole thing off. It was crazy! I admitted it to myself. But there came a thought of the seriousness with which the man approached me, and although for a few moments I tried to grasp for straws, I did finally find my Father's hand. And I knew, even in this situation, He would lead me to do His will.

It was exactly nine o'clock on a rainy Saturday morning when the superintendent of a church school telephoned me.

"Thyra," he said in a very humble voice, "Thyra, I have a strange request to make of you. I know God always hears you when you pray and now I want you to pray that He will stop the rain and make the sun shine with all its might so the grass will dry."

I must have been quiet for a long time. Thoughts were racing through my brain. Had I, through my way of praying and talking, dishonored the holy name of God? Anyone should understand that you didn't ask God to interfere with the weather. Why, while this man wanted the sun to shine, some farmer might be praising God for the rain.

"I can't pray a prayer like that," I told him firmly. "I don't think God would want us to ask Him to change the weather to suit our own fancy."

"Believe me, my dear, it is a far cry from suiting my own fancy," he hastened to explain. "This is a real need! You know our Sunday-school picnic is set for one o'clock today. Last night we secured all the food and made everything ready that we could. We worked until midnight packing dishes. The church hall can't hold all that crowd of youngsters, and furthermore, there is not another free Saturday in June that we can get that picnic area. And think of all those children who have counted the days to this picnic. Don't you think God cares about children?"

My heart was heavy and for the first time since I had given myself in God's service I wished that people would take their troubles to their minister. How could I ever pray that God would stop the rain?

"You know," he continued, "this morning when I awoke and saw the clouds gathering in the sky, when I heard the weather report for rain all day, I began pacing the floor of my bedroom, wondering what to do. Then suddenly, I remembered what I had heard you tell a group of your Junior Highers—that you never doubted God's power to do anything, and that a prayer prayed in faith could move mountains. I have never gone in for that sort of thinking, and praying, I'm sorry to say, has not been in my daily routine. But this morning I felt like praying. I knelt down and prayed as I had in my childhood. And I am not ashamed to tell you that tears came to my eyes as I asked God to forgive my thoughtlessness about serving Him. And I begged that He would hear my prayer and let it be a pleasant day. I had a strange feeling He heard me. But because you seem to know Him so well, I want you to add your prayers to mine. It says in the Bible that where two or three ask in His name, it shall be granted."

That did it. I, too, was sure that God had heard his prayer, and I surely could not refuse to add mine to his.

The clouds lifted. The sun came out and it turned out to be the most beautiful day we could have wished for. All the people on that picnic were completely unaware of the prayers that had gone up for the afternoon, and of how gloriously they had been answered.

I couldn't help but wonder how Papa would have regarded that prayer. Perhaps to him it would have sounded like an unorderly one, but God certainly set it in order. And because of it, a man had acquired a new faith in God and joy had filled his heart. He knew now that God was real and that He does listen when His earth people pray, listens and smiles down on them in a glory and power greater than the sun.

That incident touched me deeply. I knew if I told people about it, they would probably say that it just happened, that the weather often changes suddenly and that it would have turned out that way, prayer or no prayer. But that man and I will always know in our hearts that both of us had touched prayer in a tangible way, unseen by human eyes, unbelievable to some people, perhaps, but it had made our faith in God grow to new height.

Yes, this faith is a strange and mysterious thing, but underneath it is a power greater than the atom. If the leaders of the world today would lay aside all their resentments toward each other, and seek the power of prayer, which is God's gift to men, as diligently as they do atomic power, they would find a solution to all their problems. If wardens in prisons, doctors, and ministers all over our world would embrace it, the world would change in the twinkling of an eye and become that paradise God intended in the beginning of time. Perhaps a decade from now the world will wake up! But if that is to happen, I know it will only be if those who have faith pass it to others. That is the only way it can be received. You catch it as you catch the measles and when you have it, you really have it! And what a blessing if believers would radiate this spiritual power so that an epidemic of prayer would spread all over the world.

Sometimes you never have to say a word about it, you just live it. A woman who worked for me in my household told me one day that she had caught it by being in my home.

"I had a great problem," she confided in me. "There was something that had happened and I didn't dare to tell my husband. Watching your way of praying about things, I knew I could do it, too. So one day I knelt on the living-room floor, right beside the vacuum cleaner and prayed that God would take this problem and solve it. And you know, my husband put it off with a smile. I had never known that prayer could be so powerful."

Prayer works for all problems, your own and those of others. I want to tell you about a friend I made, again on a summer vacation in the mountains. She was a darling person in her thirties, with sparkling brown eyes and a winning smile. The management planned many things for the guests to do together, and I enjoyed her company. But gradually, I saw her slipping away from me. A certain man with an ailing wife had attracted her attention. One day when I didn't go on a planned trip, but stayed home to write, this man's wife, who also had remained behind, came to see me. She was in tears.

"Forgive me if I bother you," she sobbed. "I have to talk to someone and you seem so kind and, as a writer, I know you understand people. I hope you can help me."

I left my typewriter and we walked down by the lake.

"I am losing my husband," she blurted out. "Losing him to that friend of yours, the one with the eyes. He has fallen . . . and I know he will leave me. How can I stop him?"

It was a lovely peaceful day and I tried my best to calm her down. There is little one can say in such a case. I had seen it with my own eyes and I was a little afraid of the outcome. Then I remembered my calling and that no problem was too big for God. I promised I would try to convince the young lady how wrong it was to take a husband from his wife. With that she left, still crying as she walked to her cabin.

I spent most of the morning by the lake, meditating. I didn't worry any more. I knew if I could be still in my own heart, knowing that God was God, the right solution would come.

The next day I made it a point to go boating with my friend. After a while I let go of the oars and let the boat glide by itself and I started to talk about prayer. We had talked about it before, so the subject was not new to her. I also told her frankly what I had observed and I asked her if she was interested in this married man. She admitted willingly that she was.

"I'm not in love with my own husband any longer," she said, looking up at me with large wistful eyes. "Our married life is very monotonous. We have grown out of words. There is not even anything to talk about any more. Our children are the only thing that holds us together. Sooner or later we will part. And this man is tired of his ailing wife. He is a wonderful guy! Isn't it better that two are happy than four miserable?"

I knew I was treading on dangerous ground. A home was at stake. No, not one—but two homes. My heart prayed as my mind searched for the right words. But before I had time to say anything she spoke again.

"It was like electricity," she smiled. "When we met and looked into each other's eyes, well, we just knew we belonged together . . . that's all."

"How was it when you met your husband for the first time?" I asked. "Tell me a little bit about the time way back there when you two fell in love."

"Oh, it was very romantic then! I was sure we had enough love to last through eternity. Funny, I never thought then I could ever look at another man."

So she told me their story, a lovely romantic story of how two young people met and fell in love and got married. When she was through, she sat very quietly for a long time. Her eyes were sad. "Oh, those first years we were so happy! Life was wonderful! What do you think happened to us?"

"You didn't keep the fire burning," I answered. "You see love has to be fed. It has to be cared for. It is a precious, delicate thing, which is hurt and bruised so easily that it can lose its beauty. And without attention, understanding and most of all tenderness, it dies."

"Yes," she admitted, "ours did. It died."

"Would you want it back?" I asked softly.

"Oh, if I could have my husband back the way he was when we were first in love—if he could be the same once more—I would be the happiest woman alive. I hate this business of stealing someone else's man. . . . I don't want his wife to suffer. It is just that I want so much to be happy. I have so much to give."

"Then," I said, "before you really give up your own husband and break up a home, couldn't you try to fall in love with him again? I am sure the old feeling is

77

there still. Sometimes love is not dead, it is only covered over with hurts and neglect and bitterness. Why don't you go home and make up your mind to win your own man again? If you have the power to make this man fall for you, I am sure with the same tactics you could win your husband back."

"Do you think I could?" she asked, breathless with excitement.

"I shall pray for you every day, if you will promise me you'll try."

We parted the next day. She packed her suitcase and went home. She was a dear person, a little mixed up, but with an intelligence and ambition found in few.

I didn't hear from her until Christmastime when I had a long letter bubbling over with news. It had worked! She and her husband had found each other again and now their love was deeper than ever. And she was sure it would last because now it was based on the prayer that God would help them to be tender and understanding in the years ahead.

Following one of my lectures, I spent a weekend in a minister's home. It was a typical parsonage with the busy life of church duties: people calling, food to cook, children to attend to. At nighttime a very exhausted minister's wife tried to entertain me in her living room. Her face showed strain and anxiety and I noticed that her words did not come very easily. Suddenly, without warning, she placed her head in her hands and burst into tears.

I tried to comfort her, perplexed at what could have brought this on. She raised her head and tried to smile through her tears.

"Forgive me," she said. "I'm just tired!" She was quiet a moment, fighting to win control of her feelings. "No, it's more than that. I am a hypocrite. I hate being a minister's wife. Most of all, I hate this big old parsonage. We always live in tumble-down old places that are as big as arks. Other young people have nice new homes with shiny kitchens, but you've seen that dump of a kitchen I have to work in. I hate the kitchen most of all."

"Why don't you ask God for a shiny new kitchen?" I asked her.

She stared at me through her tears.

"God doesn't just give away shiny kitchens," she almost snapped. "Oh, no, this is my lot, and I will have to bear it. . . . I'm sorry and ashamed of my outburst, but sometimes I have to explode. There is no one to whom I can tell these things."

"I am glad you told me," I said. "But I still think that God would want you to have a shiny kitchen. You labor hard in His vineyard. Let's pray about it."

I took her by the hand and we walked out into the

kitchen. There we bowed our heads and I prayed a simple prayer, asking God to give her her heart's desire.

Two months later I received this letter from her:

Dear Friend,

Thank you for praying for me and thank you for coming into my life when I was at my lowest ebb. You did more for me than you will ever know. Every day since you left two months ago, I have prayed that God would see that I got a shiny kitchen to work in. It seemed that that was what really would make me happy.

But as I was praying day after day, something seemed to happen to me. I was slowly changing. I began to think about my dear husband and how hard he worked, never asking anything in return for his long hours except to serve God. I saw that I was making his work twice as hard for him with all my complaints. It came to me how I had known when I married him that I could never have things that other young people possessed. I had known it wouldn't always be easy to be a minister's wife. We had been very unhappy of late. With every beautiful new home we were invited to, I had come home full of bitterness and resentment. I was so full of it that I was actually ill. Then you came and spoke to us in our church and later to me alone. You took me in your arms and made me believe that God cared. I know now that God must have sent you. You made me believe in God's abundance and I really began to have faith that I could somehow get a shiny kitchen in this old parsonage.

But as I was praying, a thought came to me. I was not so shiny myself. Perhaps I'd better pray that I was made over first to fit that new kitchen. After that the kitchen did not seem so important. I asked God to take away my self-pity and forgive me my ungraciousness. And He did! I even didn't mind my dull kitchen. But—well, I know this is no surprise to you, but it is a miracle over all miracles to me. I have my shiny kitchen! The trustees of our church decided to modernize our kitchen for a Christmas present. And it is beautiful—fluorescent lights—cabinets—stainless steel sink—new tile floor—everything I had dreamed of. And I had never even hinted I wanted it. But the most important thing is that I am made over, that happiness has returned and that I now believe that nothing is impossible for our God.

Thank you again for coming to help me get my feet on the right path again. God bless you always.

What more is there to say? It's just as Mama proclaimed. God does more than we dare think because He loves us as a Father.

❧ Chapter Six

Many honors have been bestowed on me since I became an author and I have felt unworthy of them, but grateful for the joy they have brought me. I have been a speaker in universities and at various conferences and there was the summer of 1956 when I traveled back to Sweden and had the honor of an audience with Queen Louise. As I sat there in the beautiful blue living room of her summer palace in Skåne, the thought came to me: Can this really be me, that same little girl who dreamed of becoming an author so many, many years ago? Was it I sitting here talking face to face with the Queen of my homeland? Indeed, it was an honor that only God could have made come to pass.

But there was one honor I received that is above all others. It is the one I hug to my heart, and although it pains me a little, I shall keep it there always and be forever thankful that it came to me.

I sat one spring night in a chapel where I had been placed in the first pew. It was decorated with lovely flowers and there was a certain gaiety about it that I felt didn't exactly belong there. But this chapel had to serve two purposes: for worship and for social events. I could visualize it on a Sunday morning with an altar and a cross, but now the velvet curtains were drawn concealing scuffing, whispering figures on the big platform. There was to be a play that night and I was the honored guest.

This could have been the prelude to any gay evening, I was thinking as I sat there, an evening of fun where a group of ladies were meeting to enjoy the artists and the refreshments that awaited them after the performance. Yes, the excitement was there, the flowers, the atmosphere created by the girl appointed to stand guard by the velvet curtains and the distinguished gray-haired lady who skillfully played the organ. It could have been all fun and laughter, with an author flown in from a distant place to see her own creation, a chapter from a book she had written, acted out by amateurs who had a knack for that sort of thing.

It was even hard for me to remember that whatever name had been given the place, it was still a reformatory and these women were serving time for crimes they had committed.

I had arrived early in plenty of time to observe and to think. In my heart there were mixed emotions, but primarily gratitude to those dear women who liked my book, PAPA'S WIFE, so well that they had chosen to dramatize a chapter. And I rejoiced for the friend who had given them the book and her time to help with the work of the play, and who had accompanied me to the chapel. And I had only praise for the lovely warden, a wonderful woman with a vision of transforming this institution into a warm, livable place for those who had erred. Already the walls had been changed from a drab gray to pastels, each cell painted in light, sunny shades. They were orderly, comfortable rooms where a person could think and hope to make restitution if she were willing to seek a higher aim in life. I was more excited than I had ever been before, because this was the first time I would see my own creation through someone else's eyes, real and moving. Despite all this, I could not erase the sadness deep, deep within me. Why did young girls and women have to go wrong, when God had so generously given the same power to all—the strength to endure in time of temptation? But I ought not think of that sad part. I was here to enjoy a play and I would, for if I made up my mind to do it, I could— even if it was in a prison.

Everything went off to perfection! What skill and

talent was wasting away within those walls! I was carried away with the warmth and humor of my own story, which I found really worth listening to.

There were also other talented women who performed. A chorus sang many beautiful selections and a very young girl, with a tiny, childlike, angelic face, sang. At the end of the performance, a gorgeous corsage was presented to me by the chairman of the play with words that warmed my heart. I would commit them to the pages of my memory and in the future years as I looked back, I would turn those pages one by one and relive those memories again and again.

When it came my turn to speak, I arose with a big lump in my throat and eyes burning from unshed tears. My heart pounded fast and hard as I faced my audience, that sea of faces, young and old, different features and expressions, but eyes all the same as though the light had been blown out of them. Although their lips smiled, their eyes didn't change. I had chosen for my topic: To Dare To Dream. I spoke without notes; in fact, I let my mind rest and my heart did the talking. I could see that my words touched them for now and then a tear rolled down a worn cheek or the stony face of a young girl. And as I talked on and on, it seemed as though some of the faces challenged me. It was as though they were saying:

"It's all right for you to talk. You have had a life sheltered with love and happiness. What did we have? If you only could take a peek into our pasts, perhaps you would not have the nerve to stand there, telling us these things. Life was against us from the beginning, but you would not understand. Only we understand why we are here, locked up so as not to hurt the outside world."

It was hard for me to talk. I felt there was so little I could say. I did not want to say another word, but rather to take them all in my arms and make them understand that I cared and, more than I, God cared and loved them all.

During the social hour that followed, I had a chance to talk to some of them. Their curfew had been extended that night to eleven o'clock. Many of the women thanked me for my book and for my talk. There was one young girl who asked me if I would give her a few moments; there was something she wanted to talk over with me. We sat down on a bench away from the rest.

"I'll be out of here in a few days," she said slowly. "I think that God must have sent you to give that talk especially for me. I have always wanted to be a singer. I know I have a good voice, but do you think there would be a chance for me after having served time?"

"I am sure there would!" I answered, hoping with all my heart the world would be kind to her.

"I think now I would dare to dream," she went on, "if only I could forget my bitterness against the woman who took away my happiness. You see, I wanted to kill her, but I didn't get very far. I was in once before and when I was free, I went for her again. Hate does that! You can't help yourself."

"It is like a hurricane," I said. "It tears down and destroys, stopping at nothing until the calm finally comes. And then what a pity to look at all that destruction, done just in a few moments."

"You're right; you can't stop hating once you start."

"Would you care to tell me your story?" I ventured.

"Yes, I want to. I know it will help to talk about it. I need advice. You see, I loved a man, not knowing he was already married. But even if I had known, I don't think it would have made any difference. I came from a broken home. All I can remember is cursing and swearing and parents stumbling around too drunk to walk. I had my dreams when I was a little girl. I used to love to sing my doll to sleep. But I wished my mother wouldn't cry so much and that my stepfather wouldn't hit her. I began to do the wrong thing early. No one seemed to care what I did or with whom I went out, or when I came in. Then I met this man and fell in love, really in love. My whole world changed. I wanted a happy home for him with children who laughed and sang and were not afraid of their father. I was very young when I left the place I had called home. We rented a small room in the dingy part of town. We were never married. He told me that marriage was just a paper, but people who loved each other were married in their hearts before God and that was all that counted. And we were happy. Oh, we had so little and some days he didn't come home to me; sometimes he was gone for a week at a time, but I knew he always would come back and when he returned and I was in his arms, I forgave him whatever it was that had kept him away so long. I was going to have a baby. It was frightening, but he assured me all would be well. But when my time came, he was gone again, I couldn't find him, I didn't know where to turn. I was sent to a home for unmarried mothers. He never came to me. But there was the baby, so little—tiny as a doll. I held her in my arms and I loved her as much as any mother could love her child. But they told me I had to prove I could support her before I could have her and until then she had to be a state child."

She stopped and wiped the tears from her eyes.

"It was too much of a sorrow. I couldn't bear it," she said, and now her voice was under control. "I never have seen my baby since. And now, after being locked up twice, I probably never will. The authorities saw to it that I got a job and I moved home with mother again. I had only one thought in mind and that was to find him. I wanted to hear in his own words why he had left me. I found him all right. I found more than him. I found that he was married and had a family living in the better part of town. I couldn't hate him, but I hated the one that was his wife with all the hate my young heart could hold. One night I went there. She opened the door, and I went for her face. I was pretty rough. He stopped me and called the police. He claimed he didn't know me. They put me away for a while. I couldn't wait to get out so I could finish her. I tried again, but failed completely and I only got a longer sentence. But it is up now. I had planned to . . . well . . . your talk has changed that. For the first time I realize I have only hurt myself and my own future. I'll never come back here again. I want to do what is right. I want to be a great singer! Perhaps someday I can have my child? Oh, do you think I can dream my dream high enough?"

"I know you can! God will help you. I shall pray that you will meet wonderful people who will help you. Someday you will look back on these years as only a bad dream. Just let go of your bitterness and resentment, try to overcome the evil with good."

"Thank you," she whispered, tears gleaming in her eyes and a smile on her lips.

And I have prayed for this young girl and I know

wherever she is my prayers will follow her. Perhaps I shall never know the outcome of her life, but God will know. For doesn't He leave the ninety-and-nine to seek that lost little lamb? She, too, was a lost little lamb. Long after that visit, I could still see her eager face, her eyes filling, her expression becoming bitter and changing again. I prayed that in some way I really had helped her to find herself. Even if it was just to give her courage to dare to dream, it would be worth all my prayers.

It took me a long time to feel peaceful again after that visit. And I long remembered that spring night. God could change that girl's life and other unhappy lives, too, making them shine with joy and beauty from within. All I could do was to leave it with God. For God can make life beautiful!

When I think of beauty, my mind strays to a lovely big home on a mountaintop in the State of Vermont. I was invited to stay there as an overnight guest during one of my trips. There lived a man who had fallen in love with that mountain many years before. He had often taken rides in his car up those hills and a sadness had always filled his heart when he saw the tumbled-down old farmhouse erected there. The people who lived in it seemed to have no eye for beauty. Year after year, the farm looked sadder and sadder. One day he noticed that the people had moved out and there was a "For Sale" sign on it. The farm had become an empty shell—a house with nobody in it.

Most of the man's friends thought he had lost his mind when one day he sold his comfortable modern home in the city and purchased the old house. But they soon discovered they were wrong. He had had a vision of what that farmhouse could become. It took plenty of hard work by his whole family, as things were torn down, new lumber replacing the old. For a long, long time their labor was tedious and they had to wait for things they could not afford until they had money to purchase them. But eventually the transformation had taken place, his vision had come true and there stood a stately mansion with a view so breath-taking that eyes could not feast on it long enough.

He had sold his comfortable modern home and paid a sum of money for this place. But the things he valued most could never have been bought. Those things had been a gift from God, thrown in as extras. There were the hills, the valley and snow-covered mountain peaks as far as the eye could see. He had made this transformation with a house, but I couldn't help thinking how many times God had done the same thing with a human being. The world may put little value on a certain life, but God sees its potential if only He has a chance to make it over.

I went to bed early the night of my visit. The mountain air had made me so sleepy that I couldn't keep my eyes open. My friends graciously excused me and it took me only a moment to fall asleep. It must have been about two o'clock in the morning when I awakened as if a hand had touched my shoulder. I sat up. The room was white with moonlight. I slid out of bed and walked to the big window facing the mountains and stood there spellbound. I don't think in all my life I had ever seen anything so breath-takingly beautiful as the countryside I gazed upon. The mountains and hills were like black silhouettes against the star-studded sky. A round gold moon hung over the highest mountain peak, and below, far below, lay a sleeping village. This world looked so peaceful and contented. My heart, it seemed, couldn't hold such beauty by itself. I wanted so to awaken the household, but one just doesn't do that. Somehow, I had to be content with hugging all that beauty to my own heart, knowing that in the morning I would have to travel on. These lucky people! Because of a man with a vision, they feasted on this view night and day.

I went back to bed, but sleep would not come. My heart was suddenly sad because I thought how ungrateful mankind was to God who had created this beautiful world. It was as though I longed to make amends, as I whispered:

Father God, I don't know just how to thank you in behalf of all the world for all the things You have given us. Forgive us when we forget You so easily. The tenderness with which You have planted trees and bushes and flowers, the magnificance of your mountains and forests, birds and all wild life that lives and moves there, Your bubbling brooks, blue lakes, and great oceans, for these I thank You. And I thank You for the smallest flowers and the softest moon beam and most of all, because You are a loving Father.

And then it came to me what a blessing it was that I could see beauty and feel it in my heart. So many had eyes, but they couldn't see, and their hearts had no room to tuck in little beauties. And I wondered if this night, so significant in its splendor, would always be retained in my mind like the other things that had etched themselves there.

There seemed to be three special occasions that have gone with me always through my life here on earth and that have become guides for my reasoning.

The first memory was from my early childhood. I was in Sweden and only three years old, standing on the deck of the ship. The family must have been on a trip, although I cannot remember anything about it. But I can feel myself standing there on the deck floor, feeling very small. In my hand I held a toy, a little milk pail. It was shiny and new and my heart thrilled that it was mine. I can remember hands lifting me up on to the rail so I could see the ocean. I leaned over and looked far, far down and I saw the big blue-green waves. The sight of those great waves frightened me and I let go of my toy and watched it fall into that wet grave, sink and disappear. With it went my heart. I sorrowed for days over my loss. And strangely enough, to think about it now, still brings pain to my heart. Was the ocean as deep as a sorrowing heart? Was that the lesson I had to learn? Otherwise, why didn't I ever forget it? And even now when sorrow comes, I am still that little girl, seeing that toy disappear from my sight. Perhaps it gave me a better understanding of suffering and helped my heart to know how much there is to bear in the world.

There was a different night that found me, a teenager, waiting for the man to whom I had pledged my heart. It was a crisp fall night, with the scent of burning leaves filling the air. The dark velvety sky was pinpricked with a million glittering stars. And I remember looking up into that firmament and wondering how far it was up to those stars. Even if I could have measured the distance, I thought, it would be too high to count. At that moment I was completely happy because my love was just as great as that unmeasured distance. It could never be measured, it was too great to count. I knew then that many times during the numerous tomorrows we would spend together as husband and wife, when disappointments would come or we would be on the outs with each other, that moment under the stars would come back to me. And it has. I knew then that my love was great enough to get over whatever obstacles might stand in our way and a new wonder at the heights of love filled my heart anew.

Then there was the third time: I had been through a serious operation and for a few days had been wavering between holding on or letting go completely. I had been unconscious for days and had no memory of my family sitting beside my bed. But as my mind began to clear, I seemed to remember one thing from my long siege. I knew my husband had been there beside me. Twice someone had touched my nose lightly, a particular caress which only he used. And in my fight for life, that slight touch had given me the will to live. It was the security of love, as broad as the distance from east to west. Since that time, if ever I question the strength of love, I feel again that touch and a warm wave of security floods my heart.

Those memories, too, are blessings from God. Often we wander away from His love, but there must always be a return home, because His love is inescapable and stronger than any human love. And He, also, has His special ways to make us remember the little things that He has planted in our hearts to keep us from ever separating ourselves from that love.

I would like very much to believe that for one moment this world would change, that for a short space of time everyone in this whole universe would join in a prayer that would envelope the whole earth like a cloak. I would like to visualize each person, from the smallest baby to the most aged oldster, lifting his heart in complete honesty to his Lord. There would be a hush in prisons and institutions as a smile came to the lips of strong men hardened by hate and crime because God's love came into their hearts. There would be a light in the eyes of the mentally ill and a stillness would linger over sickbeds and hospitals as hope and peace replaced the sting of pain in tortured bodies. Little children would laugh, free from fear and hurt, as husbands and wives in that instant renewed their vows to each other. I can see it now, king and peasant, president and general, bishop, minister and priest, and all faiths united. For just one moment there would be no division, no labor problems, no jealousy, no hate. Even in nature, trees, bushes, flowers and plants, animals and birds would offer up their silent tribute of praise to their Creator. And again there would be an Eden, a paradise . . . God's kingdom on earth.

But although a universal prayer offered simultaneously by the whole world cannot be, we who do believe can build our own worlds within our own hearts and, as His servants, we can usher others into that moment of prayer. And because of the good that can shine forth from our world within a world, love can overcome some of the hate. Evil can be covered by the power of good, with peace filling the heart instead of tension. We can plant happiness wherever we go and sorrow can disappear as trust supersedes suspicion. . . . It would take so little on the part of each of us to change so much and make it right.

And I and my friend, the imagination, would still like to believe that we could build a big bonfire of all resentments, mistrust, evil thinking and worries, a fire that would burn high and long, turning them all into ashes. And after the fire had died away, we who desire to serve God would never let anything but good thoughts enter in. What a glorious world for us to live in—God's world! It would be a world ruled by love, a love that could drive away all fear.

How seldom we realize that we are just guests in this world and that our bodies are but the earthly homes of our souls, which we stay in only a number of years called "time." But this I know, that this person within, the real me, when I have moved out of my earthly dwelling, will move into a new world, a new dimension, a higher level. And I will step upward . . . upward until I am once again united with my Creator.

❧ Chapter Seven

Someone asked me one day just recently, "Does God always answer your prayers? Is there such a thing as an unanswered prayer?"

I didn't speak at once. To me, there are no unanswered prayers. Although it might not seem so to many people, God always answers a true prayer, a prayer that comes from a humble heart, seeking for a solution. Perhaps people do not understand that because God answers in His way and sometimes it is not to our liking. A prayer must always be ended, "Thy will, not mine, oh Lord."

I have written in this book about the many, many prayers God has answered in a tangible way, a way that I could see with my eyes and sometimes touch with my hands. They have been wonderful to experience, these answers, because they have made my heart sing and my faith grow in such a way that it has become a "knowing" faith that can now trust without seeing.

When I think of the many seemingly unanswered prayers, I think of a lady I met on one of my long speaking tours. I was far from home and, being a home-loving person, hotels are to me very dismal places in which to stay. When a program chairman realizes this and takes a special interest in seeing that I share a bit of her company, it makes me doubly joyful.

I had sensed that this fine woman was in need of friendship. She told me that she belonged to a small prayer group in her church and that she was a hard worker among the young people. But she had a great problem that was almost breaking her heart. We had had lunch and dinner and spent the evening together and were walking back to my hotel, when she opened up her heart to me.

As she talked, I glanced down at her eager face. She was a tiny person with almost childlike features. It was a lovely face that had succeeded in hiding the tears and heartache that would have shown had she not have been such a clever actress.

"Perhaps you have wondered why I haven't invited you to my home to share this time before your train?" she said. "Well, I will tell you because I have a feeling you can help me. You see, we live on the wrong side of the tracks. My husband could have been a successful businessman with money, position and a happy disposition, but he refuses to progress with his time or his job of the future; and today he is exactly where he was the day I married him. Once I got him, in a weak moment, to buy a lot in one of the better sections of town. The value of that lot has more than doubled during the years. But instead of building our lovely home on it, he is going to sell it. The only thing that has kept him from doing it is the thought that soon the prices will be even higher and he will make more money on it. You know, for years I have been praying and dreaming that I would live on that spot. I have driven up to it at night, stopped and visualized our home standing there. My faith has been so strong and my hope so great that now, when I see it about to crumble to ashes, I can hardly bear it. I know I shall always live where we live now if I stay on with him and that my dreams will fade away one after another."

"I wish I could help you," I said softly. "I wish I knew a way, but all I can say is that I will pray that God will make your dreams come true."

"Thank you." She smiled through her tears. "I shall treasure that thought and I shall know that I am not alone as I pray, but that you will join yours with mine."

"And you must stop fretting about it, my dear. Try not to think hostile thoughts toward this man who is your husband. You must lift him up and see him as the man he ought to be."

"I know the method, the love way, the Christ way. I will try as long as I have strength to go on. But it isn't just the new house. It's also that he hinders me from taking civic positions that I could hold if my address were different."

"Yes, but you can work in your church and hold positions there, high or low."

"That's true. I have my church as my field, but in clubs or any place of importance in the community, I'm licked."

She told me many other things about her husband. They poured forth like liquid from a bottle that has just popped its cork, having been too full too long. And I could see that man so clearly, a man from an old European stock, a stubborn man who refused to budge even one inch, who scoffed at progress and was antisocial. What a life for this darling little lady to live! She should have been sparkling with joy and radiance. She was as brilliant as she was pretty, but she had that longing in her eyes to live life, to give and take like other women, and to follow the pattern indicated by talents God had given her. She really did carry many heavy burdens and I promised I would pray that God would change things for her. We prayed before I left and as I held her small hand, it clutched mine as a drowning person's would. Tears rolled down her cheeks as I heard her pray:

> "Dear God, I want all these things, but I am willing to wait until your time comes. I desire to be a great light shining for you in my community. You have given me so many talents, but if your will for me is to be a small light on a back porch, I shall be just that until you let me shine in a greater way."

She said many more things in her wonderful prayer, which was so humble and sweet that I almost expected God to send an angel down to straighten out her life right then and there. But the answer has still not come, and we have been praying for years now.

You wonder why. I do, too. But I know that God is answering in His own wonderful way and someday we will see that answer. In the meantime she writes me several times a year. And when her letters come, I glance down at the address and my heart sinks a little to see that it is still the same. Why doesn't God answer? But I have learned never to question God. His ways are wise. He knows why, and His love never fails her. Her life has been more radiant since that night we talked. As she writes in one of her dear letters:

I have come very close to God these last years. I can now take this life and make the best of it. I have been working on coming closer to this strange man I married. There is a loneliness in his self-willed heart. I am praying now that he will open it and let me fill it with love.

The material things don't matter as much if only he would place his hand in God's and let Him fill his life with joy. . . .

And I say to myself, "Isn't that an answer? Isn't it like that crippled old man's prayer so long ago?" God is making a beautiful vessel to serve Him. She is serving even now as a great light just where she is and someday she will help her husband to find God's love. But to the world, that is not an answered prayer—only to those who can pray again and again: "Not my will, Lord, but thine."

I have come in contact with many cases like that one, and I haven't seen the closing chapters of them yet. I need only to look back on my own writing career to trace God's way. As I myself waited many years and thought my prayers were lost, God was fulfilling them in the most magnificent way which I would never have dared to dream of.

I have talked to Mama about unanswered prayer and what she thinks about it. And, as always, she makes me see it so clearly.

"It is easy to understand," she says in her soft voice, "if we think of our own children. Can we grant them anything they wish for? Don't we know that sometimes they ask us for things that would harm them? We really answer them the right way—we refuse to give them what they ask."

Yes, God, in His wonderful love and desire to grant us what we ask, gives His angels orders to sort out our prayers. Some prayers are not prayers at all, but only the selfish desire to fulfill a longing in a person's heart to possess certain things. A thing that God, in His wisdom, knows would not be for our own good.

A true prayer should be a giving prayer. Whatever we ask for should help us to grow closer to our Creator, and we should pray, not just for things to be given to us, but also to our fellow men.

But this thought also comes to me often: when we receive, we must also give out in turn to others. Such giving is like an artesian well: the more we give, the more is given to us so that we may give again.

"Give and it shall be given unto you," said the Master. *Giving* is also a form of prayer. Many are the gifts we should ask God for—especially the opportunity to be useful during our earthly journey, and for *the spirit of giving*, which is one of the greatest of the gifts.

Mama has that gift and she uses it in every day

living. It has always amazed me, this love that Mama possesses to give out. And because of it she will never lack things because the Master has said: "As ye measure to others, so shall it be measured unto you."

Mama lives on a very small monthly income, but she gives as though there always was an abundance to take from. First of all, she gave her own life to God, promising to do His will. When she married a minister, she gave to him her very best; nothing was too hard, his work became her work. As the children came, one by one, she gave all eight of us to God.

"They are yours, Father," she said. "You have just loaned them to me. Help me never to stand in the way so that Your will can be done in their lives."

And I remember many times in the days of my childhood, when strangers dropped in at the parsonage as we were about to sit down to a meal. How willingly she shared what there was! And I am sure God stretched the food because there was always enough for all.

One day recently Mama was a little low on funds. She had only two dollars in her billfold and still a half a week to go before more would come. She was on an errand down in Miami, Florida, where she lives, when on impulse she decided to dine in the big ten-cent store around the corner. It would be economical, she decided, as she could eat a bowl of soup for a quarter and so save on her slim budget. As she sat down at the counter, a lady sat down beside her. She looked very gloomy and downhearted and all the warmth of Mama's soul went out to give her some joy.

"I was just about to have dinner," said Mama lightly. "Why don't you be my guest and we can eat together?"

The lady was more than willing to accept the invitation, and Mama thought it would be good for her to have a big bowl of soup, too. But instead of soup her newfound friend ordered a big dinner that cost Mama $1.65. Mama never regretted it.

"She was very hungry," she said. "I was so glad to share with her."

And the next day, when Mama opened her mail, there was a five-dollar bill in a letter. She wasn't a bit surprised.

"My wonderful God is like that," she beamed. "He never lets me do anything for Him but right away He sends it back to me . . . and always, always He gives me more than I gave Him."

And she goes on her mission tours, giving a little plant here and a basket of fruit to someone else, but most of all, in words and prayer, she shares her precious faith in God.

At times I know Mama's giving became a real sacrifice. I am thinking now of one certain time when I know Mama gave so it hurt. After Papa had left us,

Mama drove a little Ford that was somehow a part of her. She loved to take off for long trips and she traveled far and wide. We children never considered Mama a good driver, and we thought perhaps it was because she had been too old when she learned to drive and never really got the knack of it. Or it might be that she had her unique way of living. Mama never liked to be tied down to rules. But despite this fact, Mama never lacked passengers. It is true that people sometimes sat on the edge of the seat when she decided to step on the gas, but they always knew the ride would end well. As one old lady confided to me: "The way she goes about it, sometimes you wonder what is going to happen . . . and you know she just can't make it . . . but, you see, we all know that God drives that car and it is the safest place to ride in."

Many things we still laugh about as we remember the days when Mama drove her Ford. She did not believe in stop signs.

"Why should one stop," she sighed, "when not a soul is coming? Just a waste of gas."

Once she parked her car outside a drugstore, under a big sign that warned: ABSOLUTELY NO PARKING AT ANY TIME. But Mama had looked around and calmly parked right under the sign. She proceeded into the store and when she returned, there was an officer of the law waiting for her.

"Lady, can't you read?" he asked curtly.

"Of course I can read, officer," Mama smiled, looking rather surprised at such an accusation.

"Then why did you park your car here?" the policeman snapped, taking out his pad and pencil. "It warns clearly enough, no parking at any time."

Mama smiled her sunniest smile and she patted him lightly on the shoulder.

"I'll tell you why," she said almost in a whisper. "I was in a hurry and I looked around and there just wasn't another place to park. Now will you please run along so I can get home with this medicine?"

She stepped into the car . . . still smiling and waving as she drove off. The police officer just stood there staring after her. He shook his head slowly and put his unused pad back in his pocket, but there was a smile playing on his lips as he walked off and he looked like a happy man.

When the time came that one of Mama's daughters was going to be married to a minister, her joy knew no bounds. There was a strange twinkle in her eye. She had a surprise wedding gift for them; it was so small, she hinted she could keep it in her pocket. We were all curious as to what it was and tried to pry it out of her, but she would tell no one. It was her big secret. And when the day came that she presented her gift—a small box carefully wrapped with all the frills appropriate for a wedding gift—we hardly could believe it. It was a small key. The key to Mama's Ford. How could she do it? we wondered. That car meant everything to her. But she explained that she really didn't need it. She used it only for her own pleasure, while the young man who was to become her son-in-law had no car and perhaps could not afford one for years. It would be selfish of her to drive around while he might need to reach the sick or the bereaved quickly. . . . So that was the gift she gave.

The car was shined and polished when the newlyweds drove off. Mama's eyes had a strange shine to them, too, but we could not detect whether a tear gleamed in them as she saw her beloved Ford make the turn at the bend of the road.

One day I sat down to note on paper how much Mama had given to others during a month's time. I didn't get very far, for I soon discovered she had given much more than her income, but still she had money left over. Who can understand the mystery of such giving? But that too is part of Mama's way.

I do sincerely pray that someday I will possess her gift. That I also will give, knowing that giving to others, prompted by love, is sometimes a greater prayer than mere uttered words.

Who on this earth can understand the magic of prayer? Volumes of books have been written on it, but the secret of it is still in the souls of men. Many times I have stood perplexed when great Christians have suffered difficulties and gone through deep waters while prayers from scores of people have gone up for them—and still seemingly no answer. We have to learn then to say with Paul:

My grace is sufficient for thee: for my strength is made perfect in weakness.

Many things in the prayer world are happening in silence known only to individuals who hug the mystery and glory of it to their own hearts. But God knows all things and to trust Him in all His ways gives us a strong faith. A faith that is willing to admit the limitations of finite mind, to acknowledge that God is greater than our faith, that in His eternity there are no unsolved problems, and that, by the light of His love, someday we shall understand.

✒ Chapter Eight

To some people a lecturer seems to live a very glamorous life. They picture me as traveling in style from one great city to another, always being honored and surrounded by admiring people. It is true in many ways; meeting people and seeing new places is a pleasure, but it involves a lot more than happy traveling. Sometimes there are lonely days and nights in hotel rooms far from home; there are planes that are grounded when there is a fog, trains that are hours late, or a drive in the car through a storm, along icy roads or in deep snow. But the greatest joy I have found on my many, many miles of traveling is the knowledge that wherever I am God is with me. There is no lonely place when I can pray. There is no place so dangerous that His hand cannot protect me and when I am back safe and sound in my dear home, I am filled with joy and gratitude because I can tell the story again: He was with me in a special way.

At the beginning of 1959 as I glanced through my engagement book and remembered I was to go on a speaking tour in the Middle West in the spring, I had a strange premonition that I should not take this trip. I am a sensitive person and premonitions have very often proved to be a true warning against a catastrophe. So, acting on an impulse, I sat down to cancel these engagements, only to realize that engagements are not canceled that easily as there are such things as contracts involved. I soon concluded that I must take this trip regardless of my feelings.

As the day for my departure drew near and I checked the airlines for passage, I had again that same strong feeling—this time that I should not fly. Free to follow my own judgment, I gave up the thought of flying and checked on train schedules only to find out that every train I would have to take would bring me to a strange city and in the very early morning hours. One thing I detest is arriving as a stranger in a city when it is asleep, so I canceled out the thought of trains and fell back on driving my own car.

My husband objected vigorously. "What about snowstorms?" he asked anxiously. "This is March and sometimes we even have big storms in the month of April."

"Well if I get stuck, I get stuck," I said nonchalantly, but I later agreed it would be a good thing for me to have a companion, such as my secretary, to share that long drive, someone to talk to on the long miles that had to be traveled.

A friend of mine, a pleasant person and a good driver, said she would be happy to travel with me, so my mind was at ease as I began to pack for the trip.

The Middle West experienced one of their worst snowstorms in many decades the week before we left. How happy I was that it had been the week before. Now surely we would have nice weather, because a storm like that does not repeat itself very often. But as it was we started off in a New England snowstorm, one that had blown up after a spell of warm spring weather. As we drove on and the miles accumulated behind us, we found the roads free from snow and it seemed as though driving had after all been the right choice.

We had been on the road two days when we learned from our radio that snow was racing around us on both sides. Toward the south and north, within thirty or forty miles there were big snowstorms, but my heart was light. I had left this trip in God's care and surely we would be protected. The sun would shine and the roads would be good and all would work out even better than we could have expected.

I was thinking how wonderfully I had always been protected on my long automobile travelings. Ever since that time when my car left the icy road, nothing had happened that could be termed dangerous. Oh, there had been that flat tire, but just once. And having a flat tire come your way only once, when you have been going on lecture trips for six years is not too bad. It had been a little frightening when it had happened, of course. It had been in Connecticut late one night, past midnight. I had been traveling through woodland for miles and miles, on my way from a lecture, when suddenly the car swirled and my heart sank. "Oh! no," I said out loud, "it can't be!" But it was a flat tire and I, not knowing how to change it, had to drive along at a snail's pace, hoping that I would come to some house, some place, where light would be shining. After ten miles more of driving with tense nerves and a ruined front tire, I saw a light . . . a bright, shining light. I stopped and discovered that it came from a tavern. I didn't dare to go inside, so I sat by the roadside waiting. After a while a man came out and I called to him:

"What does a gal do when she is stuck with a flat tire in the middle of the night and doesn't know how to change it?"

He didn't even look my way, but he answered in a very indifferent voice, "She is out of luck, I would say, for all the garages are closed."

My heart prayed desperately. I was a little afraid.

Here I was on a lonely country road, in a car I couldn't go on with, talking to a man who was very unsteady on his legs, outside a tavern filled with many souls like him. I had to have help and one thing my mind must be sure of was God would never fail me.

"Listen," I almost shouted, "you don't think there would be a couple of gentlemen who would care to help a lady in distress?"

He started back to the tavern. "I will find out," he called back.

A moment later he came out accompanied by two other men. They were on the glad side, but they were very helpful and kind and changed the tire very quickly. I offered up my thankfulness to my heavenly Father as I handed each one my book "PAPA's WIFE."

"I am an author," I explained, thanking them. "Take my book as a souvenir. I hope you will read about how my Mama always got herself out of trouble. I feel very much like her tonight."

When we reached Joliet, Illinois, we were told the forecast had been for four inches of snow, but the weather had changed its mind and no snow had appeared. Those words sounded good to me and it really seemed as though this trip would be free from trouble after all.

Then in Moline, Illinois, it happened. I had spoken

to a women's club group on a Saturday afternoon and Sunday morning we would have to start for a city three hundred miles away, located in the northern part of Wisconsin. As we were retiring for the night, we listened to the weather forecast for the following day and my heart stood still. There was a prediction that the big snowstorm of the week before would repeat itself. On top of that there would be winds up to tornado force, and if that were not enough, there would also be thunder and lightning.

"What are we to do?" asked my companion. "We certainly cannot start out in weather like that."

"We have to go," I said firmly. "When you are scheduled to speak at a club, it does not matter what the weather is, you have to get there, that's all."

We left it there. I know my friend was not very happy. Evidently she had thought it would be glamorous to travel with a lecturing author and it had been fun until now. But she would know very soon that this kind of life is not always easy.

As I knelt to pray that night, I talked things over with my heavenly Father. He had changed the weather before. Perhaps through His love and care there would be another forecast for better weather in the morning. With that thought in mind I went to sleep, only to be awakened about three by a terrific thunder crash. I rushed from my bed and looked out from the sixth-story hotel window. The wind was blowing with such a might that signs and everything that could be pried loose were blowing about on the streets. It seemed that the wind would crash through the windows any moment, and it was snowing—snowing hard and drifting because of the strong winds. I was glad my friend was sleeping. As it was, I couldn't believe my eyes.

"Oh, God" [I whispered, disappointed and with a terrible let-down feeling] "how could you let it happen? You know I asked you not to let it snow. I have to go! Don't I? I tried so hard to get out of it, but I was so sure You would pave the way for me, that You would answer my prayer as You have done before. Now what shall we do?"

It did not occur to me that I was scolding God as I stood there looking out on the drama the wind and snow played. It was only moments later that I became penitent. Who was I to talk like that to God? Shouldn't His promise to be with me until the end of the world be enough for me? He had not promised that my way would be easy, but He had promised that wherever I was, He would be near. I knelt to pray for forgiveness for my arrogance and my heart was calm once more. I would start out with my hand in God's, trusting Him through the storm.

It was a little hard to convince my friend that start-

121

ing out would be wise. The radio had been blaring about the destruction the snowstorm had brought. Planes were grounded and trains were stuck in mountains of snow. My premonition had been right after all. If I had traveled by either of those means of transportation, I surely would have been stranded. Everything was canceled because of the snow—church services and other activities; even some of the newspapers were not being delivered. Roads were blocked and most of them closed. State police warned that only those facing some emergency should drive as the roads were more than icy—they were hazardous. But with three hundred miles ahead of us, we had at least to start out.

The garage man at the filling station shook his head as he dug out my car. He didn't say anything, but I know he wondered if I was in my right mind even to think of starting out on a day like this. We ate a hearty breakfast before we checked out of the hotel. Who knew when we would eat next? It was nine A.M. as we drove into Davenport, Iowa. It was really tough to drive, but we moved forward anyway, and if we only could keep going, the trip would take time, but we would make it.

The miles do not pile up very fast when you drive fifteen . . . ten . . . five miles an hour. The wind whipped the snow in a wild fury and it surely had a wide playground over those miles and miles of Iowa field land. The world turned into a whirling, crazy merry-go-round. Sometimes we couldn't see the road and then we had to stop because the windows were covered with white, glistening snow. It became almost unbearable, all that whiteness; it affected the eyeballs till they ached like a toothache, there was no end to it. The roads were deserted, no life anywhere. It seemed as though my car was the only thing moving in this whole white world. All eating places were closed so we could not reinforce ourselves with so much as a cup of hot coffee. Once we found a gas station open and although we had plenty of gas, we filled the tank. It was that feeling: one never knows when one will see an open gas station again.

How glad I was that I was not alone. My friend was a good sport. She never complained. She no longer seemed the least bit apprehensive. How many ladies, I was thinking, would have been scared to death riding in a car on this day. I was lucky she was the one who had had enough faith in me to take this long trip. We talked, we sang, we tried to recall amusing incidents to tell each other—anything to make the time go faster.

"My family will be worried about me when they read in the newspapers how bad the storm is out here," she said once.

"Mine never worry about me," I stated calmly. "My husband claims that if I got stranded on top of a high lonely mountain, someone would suddenly appear and bring me down safely."

"But this is a terrific storm," she insisted.

"I know," I answered, thinking longingly of home. "It could be that perhaps even my family are worried this time."

We had gone a little over fifty miles by that time. It was two o'clock in the afternoon. Only fifty miles since nine o'clock that morning!

Presently we saw ahead of us something that looked like cars—a long, long line of them all standing still. Could this be the end of our trip?

We soon learned that there was a snowplow ahead. The road had been cleared on one side only. How fortunate we were that it was our side! We moved slowly behind the plow. Like a funeral procession, evenly, at snail pace. At two thirty P.M. we arrived in the little town of Zwingle, Iowa. Here the plow stopped and we were informed that that was as far as we could go; from now on our destiny depended on a plow from Dubuque County and very likely it would be a long, long time before it came through.

There were thirty cars sitting in a long row like white ducks. It was a closed highway ahead of us and the snow was drifting higher and higher. It was long past lunchtime. We had not eaten since morning. This town had no restaurant open because it was Sunday. There was no place for tourists!

As the plow turned around to plow the other side of the road I, on impulse, pulled out and turned around, too.

"Are you going back?" asked my companion. "What in the world would be the sense of going back?"

"I don't know why I turned back," I confessed. "You must get used to me. I do things . . . I don't know why, sometimes."

The plow had stopped. I passed it and up the road a bit I stopped beside a man who was out shoveling snow.

"Tell me, is there a protestant minister in this town?" I heard myself ask.

"Sure thing," he laughed. "You are parked by the parsonage."

"What do you want the minister for?" asked my friend.

"You wait and see," said I. Suddenly a bright idea had come to my mind.

I went back and asked the plow men to clear a little place beside the road so I could park my car safely. Then, leaving my friend in the car, I stepped knee-deep into the drifts to reach the parsonage door. I made it, looking like a snow-man myself, but I rang the bell and the door opened and I stood face to face with a friendly minister. In a few moments I had told him our predicament and he had invited me and my friend into the cozy living room.

"I am a minister's daughter," I laughed. "That is why I am bold enough to come in like this. You see parsonages to me are the friendliest places in the world."

"Of course," he said warmly. "That is what we are here for. I want you to feel at home and stay as long as you need to."

His wife came into the room having been awakened from her Sunday-afternoon nap. She was as kindly as her husband.

"I believe God had His hand in this," she said. "You see we always have a big Sunday dinner a little after noon on Sundays, but for some strange reason I couldn't seem to get started to cook it today. Now I know why. We were to have guests! We'll love sharing our dinner with you two snowbound travelers."

So we had a tasty chicken dinner in the lovely parsonage while outside the wind blew and the drifting continued. We talked and rested and the time went by. At ten o'clock that night the plow from Dubuque had still not come through. We learned later that it didn't come until much later—in the early morning hours. The cars we had come in with were still sitting there. My heart ached for them, but it was also running over in gratitude to my Heavenly Father. He always looked out for me . . . always. . . . How could I ever love Him enough for all He did for me? Yes, right here on the snowy fields of Iowa, His love surrounded me. . . . He had cared for me in a way that I would never forget and He had given us shelter in the storm.

We spent the night in the parsonage. After a good sleep and a fine breakfast we started off early the next morning. The plow had been through by then. The sun was shining and the wind had died down. It was a beautiful, beautiful world and though the road was icy in spots and plowed only on one side in many places, we reached our destination in plenty of time.

It was spring weather when our fifteen-hundred-mile journey was completed and we started our long trip home, but as we came nearer and nearer our own territory, I still was thinking of that Sunday in Iowa . . . the mountains of snow . . . and the drifting of it . . . and the wind blowing over those miles and miles of Iowa farmland . . . then the lull in the storm . . . the refuge in the warm, friendly parsonage. And I whispered to myself: "Why should I ever fear when the Lord God is my God!"

✿ Chapter Nine

People often ask me about that trip I took abroad in 1956. "Tell us a little about it," they ask. "How could you have time to visit so many countries in only three weeks?"

"Because all I wanted to do was to see a little bit of those countries. I wanted to walk on their streets and mingle with their people, get the feel of them, so to speak. My book was going to be a part of them. I was grateful that I could share my life with so many. The least I could do, when I was flying to Sweden anyway, was to pay them a little visit."

"And did you enjoy it?"

"I surely did! And it gave me many pleasant memories."

After the person has gone and I am alone, I let my thoughts wander back again to that summer when I boarded that big transatlantic plane for Sweden. I was going home to my native land after being away from it twenty-one years. The place where I was born was very dear to me and as a child I had possessed an almost passionate love for it. How often I had dreamed myself back to it in fantasy—the mountains that stood as strong guards around the little village up there in the north, the pleasant green valleys and the swift-flowing rivers. How carefree I had been, playing my games in the stately forests. It was always bitter-sweet to think about it, but now I was going home to hug it again close to my heart.

Sweden was such a tiny speck on the map, but this was the land where I was born and here I had learned to laugh and sing and pray. I had even tasted the pain of sorrow here. On long, white, romantic spring evenings I had first met love. And I had listened to the birds sing in the endless golden summer nights. Going back to see and feel it all filled my heart with such excitement there was room for nothing else.

My husband and younger daughter had come to the airport to see me off. I can still see them standing there waving as the plane lifted and we sailed into a white cloudland.

It was not my first flight . . . far from it . . . but it was my first across an ocean and I have to admit that I who trusted God to protect me on land and on sea and in everyday life, was not so sure if He could protect me while I was crossing a wide, deep ocean. I was ashamed of myself. Why couldn't I trust and be happy as I always was? It took a little while . . . a little meditation . . . and a good dose of Mama's faith before I could put the fearful thoughts away. But when I once did . . . it was for always, and as night came upon us, I could close my eyes and rest in the care of Him who never slumbers. How silly I had been to be anxious. I had acted as though I didn't have a Heavenly Father. But now I knew I should fear no more, because I loved my God so much and love driveth away all fear.

There had been so much to enjoy in Sweden and the time went much too fast. My visit with the Queen in her summer palace at the most southern peak of Sweden was the high light of my stay there, but I had to hasten on. Sweden had not taken my first book then, but Denmark had, and England and Holland, and I would visit all those countries. A very short visit, just to stop in and say hello and good-bye.

The day I left the Queen's palace I took the ferry over *Öresund*, and went right into Copenhagen. Denmark is a quaint, gay country and I fell in love with it the moment I landed. I went to my hotel and called my publisher. They bade me welcome and were most gracious, telling me that they had planned a happy day for me; an editor would pick me up at the hotel in a half an hour and I was to go with him as he was my host for the day.

It was very exciting! I felt almost like a young girl and I hoped that the editor would be a pleasant person. When I answered the house-phone and was told that my caller had arrived and was waiting in the lobby, I hoped in my heart that he would be a very wonderful person. And he was—tall and handsome, with a pleasant smile, and a lot younger than I—but why not? It would be fun spending the day with a person like him. I was so appreciative of that publishing company, the way they had planned everything to let me, a total stranger, see all the noteworthy things in Copenhagen, the deer park where hundreds of tame deer and little fawns were running around.

"Don't pat the fawn," my host warned me, as a tiny brown Bambi-deer came up to us. "You know if you touch him, the mother will have nothing to do with him, because she will smell the touch of human flesh on her baby."

We rode in an old-fashioned wagon behind a couple of fine-looking horses. It was so much fun, laughing and talking about Denmark and its history while he pointed out houses of importance. We walked a great deal and finally took a long boatride on the blue, blue water. We had stopped to see the little mermaid sitting on the big stone, and later, in the open boat, I looked longingly to my right.

"That is Sweden," I said. "So near and still so far."

"Yes," he said. "No one remembers the wars that used to be, how they were always fighting to get land for their people. Denmark is so small, Sweden could have let them have a little chunk more."

"It was the brave Gustave Vasa that saved us from you," I laughed. "If it hadn't been for his brave actions perhaps Denmark would have had all of Sweden, and I really would have been Danish like you."

"That was a long, long time ago, and the two countries are happy and contented. Sweden's princess became our beloved Queen. All is well, there is no feud any more."

It was so pleasant to talk of history and to feel the warmth and friendship that existed. I loved Denmark! I could say it over again, but I perhaps would never have known how wonderfully kind and gracious their people could be if I had not written a book called PAPA's WIFE, which the Danes translated.

We ended our day by going to the famous park, Tivoli, and there, in a beautiful restaurant, we had a farewell dinner.

It had been a lovely summer day but now, as so often in Scandinavia, the heavens opened and without any warning the rain poured down in buckets.

"We have to eat slowly and by the time we are through the sun will shine again," said my friend the editor.

It was cozy to sit there, warm and snug, and watch people scurry to get away from the rain. We were talking fast now; there was still so much to talk about. I told him a little of my husband and girls and he told me about his lovely wife and so our talk came to my writing.

"I always wondered," he said, "as I read your book, if there still could be a person so simple in her way of life and so naïve and uninhibited . . . could it be? Or had you written a book of that type on speculation?"

"And what do you think now?" I asked.

"Now I don't think, I know . . . YOU ARE THE BOOK!"

That was a great compliment. I told him some of my philosophy and beliefs.

"If only more people could have a faith like yours," he said, "we would have a different world today."

As we rode back to my hotel in the taxi he suddenly became very quiet. Presently he began to laugh.

"I never thought I would want to tell you this," he

chuckled, "but feeling now as though we are old friends, I think it would give you a kick."

"What in the world have you held back from me?" I asked curiously.

"It is a confession! You know, when we were told in the office yesterday that one of us had to spend the day with you today, no one wanted to take you out. We didn't like the picture of you and knowing you were Baptist in religion, we thought perhaps you were very pious and there would be no fun. So we flipped a coin —and I lost."

"Poor you," I whispered, a little bit hurt, but more amused.

"Poor nothing," he said and now he looked serious, "honestly I would not have missed this day for anything."

The next morning I left Denmark for Holland. It would always be pleasant to think back to that day. I felt ten years younger; my ego had suffered a little, but that was good for me. I'll have to find a better picture if I need one for another book, I thought. . . .

It was a fine trip: the food good as always on those airlines, people pleasant to talk to, and traveling alone was an adventure, knowing no one, going to a strange land without a friend to meet me. It was all training for the new life I suddenly was living.

Holland was just the way I had pictured it. It could

have stepped out of a story book. There was a big art exhibition going on and almost all hotel rooms were taken, but I managed to get one in a small second-rate hotel. I took a long walk that afternoon. I walked on the streets of Amsterdam and mingled with the people and stood amazed at all the bicycles. Why everybody rode a bicycle! Lovers with their arms around each other, nurses, priests, schoolchildren—all passing in droves on bicycles. It was quaint—the docks and windmills—Holland, the way I had dreamed about it.

In the morning, after a good night's sleep, as I walked down the stairway to the dining room a certain aloneness faced me. I hadn't minded traveling alone and walking alone and being by myself at night, but this morning as I was to eat breakfast I suddenly saw myself sitting all alone at a table. All the people would be speaking Dutch and I would sit there like a dumbbell. Perhaps someone would speak to me in Dutch and I would have to tell them in English that I was sorry I couldn't talk to them.

I was the first one in the dining room. People must be sleeping late, I told myself . . . or were they early and I late? I knew nothing of the customs in this country . . . not even what time they eat breakfast. I sat down at a small table and a maid brought me bread and cheese and butter. Presently another lady entered the room. She was young and pretty, walked with light steps and headed right for my table. Now it comes, I thought. I have to smile and make my voice gentle when I tell her I do not understand. She spoke to me, a long sentence. I waited until she had stopped, then I spoke slowly, pronouncing the words as clearly as I could.

"I don't understand . . . I speak English. . . ."

She stared at me for a moment, then she burst into clear silvery laughter.

"But I was speaking to you in English," she said.

I was very embarrassed. I had been so sure she was going to speak Dutch, I even heard Dutch when she spoke English. Doesn't that prove what your mind can do to you? We had a gay conversation and I learned to my amazement that she came from Longmeadow, Massachusetts, my own home town. Her father was a well-known doctor in our community, her house only a couple of miles from where I lived.

My Dutch publisher entertained me that day. He was as gracious as my Danish one. In his car I had a chance to see a lot of Holland, driving to all the famous little places where the houses are below the water level and have little bridges leading to their doorways. Everybody clomped about in wooden shoes and in native costume, even tiny children dressed like the adults. I was most grateful to hear a little of the history of Holland and of its wonderful Queen and her family. It was a most memorable day, and I never regretted going there.

The next day I flew to London, which was even more magnificent then I had thought possible. It was Saturday and the publishing company office was closed, but one of the editors met me and I had tea with him and we had a chance to talk a bit. I stayed at a lovely small hotel and I went sight-seeing all by myself. I got along very well in England except for a mistake with a taxi. I was very confused about English money, so different from the other countries and especially America. The first time I took a taxi I didn't know what to pay the driver when he told me the fare. I filled my two hands with money and said to him:

"Please help yourself. I have no idea about English money."

He did! Later I discovered that that was the most expensive taxi ride I had ever had, and I blamed it on my own foolishness and a taxi driver's greediness.

After leaving England for Scotland where I spent only a few hours, seeing a little of its moors and millions of flowers, growing just anywhere, I returned to America.

It was a pleasant flight. I was pretty used to flying by that time, but best of all . . . we were flying home.

The sad part was I would have but a day with my family before I'd have to fly to Wisconsin where I was to speak at a Christian Writers' Conference.

It was hard to leave so soon. But I had promised and this was my new life; I must be grateful for the way I was received.

It was at that Conference I met the well-known author Margaret Lee Runbeck. How happy I am that we had time to talk and make friends. She was one of the dearest and sweetest Christians I had ever met. She invited me to visit her home in California . . . but only a month or so later God called her into the larger life. I know heaven is much richer with her there, but oh, how much we could have used her and more of her wonderful books here on earth.

When I was on the plane again for New York, this time home, to be really home for the summer, I relaxed for the first time in months. It seemed I hadn't stopped a moment since my book had come out the fall before. I was homesick, I discovered, because all fame in the world cannot make up for the happiness of a home. I felt almost like a bride! My thoughts went back over the summer that was almost over, thanking God for the blessings I had received. I had never really felt alone though; God had been so close to me. And I repeated to myself again, to confirm my faith: WHERE I AM, GOD IS. With my hands in His I could go anywhere. His protection never failed. Life is such a sweet thing. How happy I was that I was born! Every day I must remember to thank God for life.

It was dark, so I could not see the land below me, but I knew how it looked from the plane. Little farms seemed like toy houses and roads like pencil marks and a tiny speck of blue was a lake. God bless America my dear homeland! The blessing that flowed from it had begun with the pilgrims who came here to have freedom to worship and pray. Their prayers were so great that they still hover over this country of ours. We are still living on those blessings they brought by their faith and love to their God and their new land. It is sad to know that among the good so much evil exists. But we must not be dismayed because the Master said, "This is what shall overcome the world—*our faith.*"

We must dare to walk with courage, knowing that each good thought will overcome one evil . . . our prayers for our Nation must never cease. We must believe in our America. We must choose a godly man to be our President and our love must begin in our own hearts and go out to our Home, our City, our State and our Nation. That is what God desires from us—that we love mercy, and do justly and walk humbly with our Lord. Perhaps the day soon will be here when our people will turn from wrong and walk the Pilgrim way . . . which also was the prayer way.

It was midnight as we flew in over New York City. Is there a more magnificent sight to see, than New York City at night from an airplane? Its miles and miles of lights looks as though the whole firmament had fallen down to earth. We had had a little disturbance on this plane ride. There was a man who had become almost frantic as we flew over Lake Michigan. He had had a vision that we would crash in water, and he demanded life belts for all of us. When he was told there were none, he became very excited. The little sailorboy sitting beside me peered anxiously into my face.

"Do you think we will crash?" he asked, looking very tense and worried.

"Of course not," I smiled. "This is a good trip, God is with us."

"I think you are right," he said in a lighter tone. "I want to go home to my bride."

"And I to my husband. I have been away a long time. God is good to us; He will protect us."

As we landed, the disturber hurried off quickly. I wondered if he was angry that we hadn't crashed; he looked so disappointed.

The sailor shook my hand.

"Thank you he said," almost as though I had been responsible for the safe trip, "I knew you were right. I can see you love God—it shines out from your eyes."

He hurried to the arms of his waiting bride. I looked for my husband. . . . I walked slowly. . . . Everybody seemed to be greeted by someone. . . . I was the last one through the gate. . . . He wasn't there!

I don't remember any other night like that. As the minutes ticked away on the big clock on the wall of the big waiting room, I told myself: He has been delayed. Very soon I will see him rushing toward me, explaining the reason he wasn't on time. Thinking that way made me calmer. I must remember something special . . . something gay . . . something funny. Memory is such a wonderful thing that God had given us. You can turn it back like the pages of a book. It was easy for me to think of an incident and so live it over again in my mind. It was one in the morning now and no sign of my loving husband, but I tried to face it bravely. . . . I would think of that time in greater Boston when I almost became the prey of a big, brusque police officer. I admit now that I was wrong, but the sign had said "Boston" and the pointing arrow had been as big as a billboard, and I had known that I had to follow that sign. I had come about one hundred miles from the New Hampshire way and I had another engagement; my time was short; I dreaded the heavy traffic, but I must make it on time. As I came to an intersection with three double lanes, I somehow got into the wrong one. Seeing the "Boston" sign, I knew I had to follow it despite the traffic, but I saw the policeman standing in the circle directing the cars. He was waving his arms this way and that, and to be sure he would understand my situation I opened my window and pointed to the left. He shook his head and pointed to the right. But I was *not* going to the right. . . . I didn't know where the right-hand lane would take me. . . . I had to go left . . . I had to go to Boston. So, I didn't move. I just sat there. About fifty horns began to blow at me from all directions . . . the cop beckoned even more forcefully than before; his face was red as a beet, but I had still not made up my mind . . . I couldn't go right . . . I had to go to Boston. The policeman's lips were moving as though he was saying words under his breath . . . I knew I had to do something, so I suddenly shot over two lanes, straight to the left . . . to the sign saying Boston.

"Please dear God, glue him down," I prayed desperately. "I have to go this way."

But the Lord God did not hear my foolish prayer. A sharp whistle blew . . . the officer came towards me as I obediently pulled to the curb. I tried to be brave . . . I tried Mama's method. I smiled my prettiest.

"Do you know it is against the law to disobey an officer?" he barked.

"Officer, I did not disobey," I said meekly.

"Then tell me just what did you do? I motioned to you to go right, didn't I? But you just sit there, holding up a mile of traffic at the busiest time of the day . . . and when you finally decide to move you drive across two lanes of traffic and sail off to the left. . . . It is because of people like you that we policemen get gray hair before our time."

"Well," I ventured, feeling my way with every word. I was in trouble. Even God would not help me now. "I was going to Boston . . . and that sign as big as a house says Boston is that way. . . . I am to speak in Boston and I am late now. . . . I couldn't go the other way. I would not know where I was going. I have to follow signs. . . . I thought you would understand. . . . I couldn't talk to you . . . so I did what I knew I had to do."

"I understand perfectly, lady, and this little note will make you remember to obey the law. . . ."

I stared at him unbelievingly. "You are not going to give me a ticket!" I cried in horror.

"Well, what do you think I would be giving you?"

he snapped sarcasticly. "Your license and registration, please."

I didn't move, but I looked pleadingly into his angry face, "I have never had a ticket and I have been driving eighteen years. You are not going to spoil it now, are you?"

He came closer and his voice was almost a whisper. "Do you see that officer standing at the corner. Well, he is the sergeant. If I didn't give you a ticket for the commotion you have caused, he would demote me. He saw the whole thing."

"Good," I said. "I am going over to talk to the sergeant."

"You are going to do what!" he almost screamed at me. "I'm warning you—the sergeant is a hard man."

I had reached the end of my rope. I was tired and I had never had a man talk to me in that tone of voice before. I felt the stinging tears coming into my eyes; there was no holding them back.

"I don't care," I sobbed. "I am going over and make that sergeant understand. I'll explain how I came a stranger into the town's worst traffic jam. I am confused and bewildered. I don't know where to go unless I follow signs . . . and you are not even nice to me I'm not used to having men bark at me. . . . I'll never drive through this town again . . . and now you have made me cry and I am late for my appointment."

He looked confused for a moment. Then he began to wipe the sweat from his forehead. He looked sad and dejected.

"Lady," he said, looking past me. "I've never met a woman like you before. Please drive off . . . to Boston. As for the ticket . . . let's forget it—shall we?"

He walked quickly back to his post to direct his delayed traffic. I felt sorry for him. I was in the wrong . . . but apparently his bark was worse than his bite. . . . and I—well, I had helped myself out of trouble . . . I still had a clear record . . . but I had used a woman's cheapest—and surest—weapon . . . *tears.*

Suddenly I realized I was still sitting on that hard bench in the airport . . . I was still waiting. . . . even reminiscing hadn't seemed to soothe my anxious heart. Where was my husband? Why didn't he come? It was one thirty-seven now! There must have been an accident . . . he would have called and had me paged otherwise. Perhaps he was hurt, lying on the road somewhere . . . perhaps he was in the hospital! He might even be dead. . . . But I mustn't let myself think such thoughts. I must have faith. Something might have happened at home that had delayed him. Why hadn't I thought of it before? I would call my daughter; she would know what time he left for the airport.

I got my daughter out of bed, but she was glad to hear my voice.

"I can't understand it," she exclaimed. "Dad left here at seven P.M. He wanted to be sure to be there when the plane came in."

As I walked back to my bench, my heart was in my toes. There must have been an accident he was involved in, but he would come . . . those things take time. I must be calm, I told myself. I would think of another funny incident, I would try to entertain myself. . . . The airport was almost empty now. Everybody seemed to have closed up their booths and gone home. There seemed to be no more planes coming in. I fought back the tears and made myself remember a certain time in a town in Pennsylvania. I had been speaking in the afternoon and had hours and hours to wait before the train would take me to Buffalo. To kill time I browsed around in a lovely gift shop. A lady I had met and struck up an aquaintance with accompanied me. She was good company and as always I was amazed at how wonderfully well things turned out for me. Suddenly she asked me a simple question.

"When did you say your train was leaving?"

"Eleven thirty, almost midnight," I answered.

"Are you sure?" she insisted. "There is only one train going that way each night. If you missed it, you would not make your next engagement."

"I am sure! But I will look so we don't have to worry."

I opened my pocketbook and took out the ticket and looked . . . I looked again! I stared at it. Finally I gasped . . . it is leaving at eight fifty-five . . . and it is eight forty-five now. . . . What shall I do?"

"It takes twenty minutes in a taxi . . . and it takes time to get one, too. What in the world will you do?"

"Dial the station for me!" I cried, "I am too nervous."

She did the dialing and I got on the phone, gasping for breath in the small phone booth.

A pleasant voice answered, "This is the Union Station. What can I do for you?"

"Has the train come in?" I blurted out, trying to talk fast.

"It is just coming in now, lady."

"Please hold it for me. I will get a taxi right away. . . . I'll be there in twenty minutes . . . I have to get that train."

"Lady," came the astonished voice, "I can't hold a train . . . no one can hold a train for——"

"But you have to," I insisted, "I have paid for a

148

sleeper on it . . . I have a speaking engagement . . . please. . . ."

"Listen," cried the voice on the other end, "the only one who can hold a train is the station master. I'll get him for you and you try to talk him into it. . . . Where did you say you were going?"

"I didn't . . . but I am going to Buffalo."

"Lady *that* train leaves at eleven fifty-five." The telephone clicked. She had hung up on me.

I just stood there; slowly I opened my purse again. I had looked at the wrong ticket . . . the one from Buffalo to home.

About eleven thirty that night I entered the Union Station in that little town. The clerk was just going off duty and her successor had come in. Just as she was leaving, she turned back and faced the other lady.

"I want to have you get a load of this," she said. "Of all the crazy women! You ought to hear the nutty one I had on the line tonight. She called up and demanded I hold that train. 'You've got to hold it,' she screamed at me. . . ."

As I stood there and listened, I heard my story getting bigger and bigger. Was she a good storyteller! Only she put in a lot of extra words that I knew I never had said. I couldn't help it then . . . I walked right up to the window.

"What can I do for you?" asked one of the ladies.

"Oh," said I, "I just wanted to introduce myself. I am that nutty lady!"

It perhaps wasn't very nice of me, but it was worth it to see the look on their faces . . . the situation had been bad enough the way it was without their adding to it. . . .

I looked at the time. It was almost two o'clock now. I couldn't think of any more stories. I was frantic with worry. I was so frantic I couldn't even pray. It looked as if my husband wasn't coming. Perhaps I would have to sit here all night. I took my suitcase and walked out into the air. There I sat down on the suitcase, close to the door. At least here I could see if he drove in. There wasn't a soul in sight. I had held my tears back so long that now I just let them roll down my cheeks. I had never felt so lost and completely alone. I heard footsteps and a nice-looking pilot walked by me. He took a look and stopped.

"Lady," he asked, "are you in trouble?"

"I sure am," I sobbed. "I have lost my husband. He was to meet me at the plane at twelve o'clock tonight and he never came."

"Well, that can happen," he said, smilingly. "You're not the first wife to be stood up."

"But you don't understand," I explained. "My husband is not like that . . . something has happened to him . . . he never would leave me like this. We love each other. He would die for me. I am so upset I can't even pray . . . if I could pray, all would be well."

"You are so upset you don't even know what you are saying," he said. "But let me ask you a very common question . . . one we very often ask in cases like yours. Are you sure you are at the right airport?"

"Of course I am," I answered sadly. "I am at the La Guardia Airport."

He looked at me. "No, lady," he said, "you are not. You are at the Newark Airport!"

Now I stared back at him.

"But how did I get here?" I asked bewildered. "The girl where I bought my ticket told me I would come in to La Guardia and I never looked."

He was just wonderful. He stuck by me and helped me get my husband paged at La Guardia Airport. The poor dear had been waiting there since eleven o'clock frantic with worry because I hadn't been on a plane that came in a half hour later than I had told him. . . . He had met every plane since. But when I suggested that he hurry over to pick me up, he told me in no uncertain terms I deserved to be left to take the train home in the morning. . . . Why in the world hadn't I found out where I was landing? But I know my man pretty well. I got him calmed down and when he picked me up at the Newark Airport and saw my red eyes, he forgot his anger and as we drove home those hundred and fifty miles to our own town and I sat there close beside him, almost forgetting that we had been married twenty-nine years, I felt as though I were eloping and we were off on our honeymoon . . . and I thank God that I can say we lived happily ever after.

❧ Chapter Ten

As a child I often wrote letters to God as prayers. In the parsonage we children were taught to share everything with each other. If one was sad, it effected all of us. If something wonderful happened to make one especially glad, there was joy and laughter in the whole family circle. So I found sharing certain things easy, but I learned that when it comes to sharing those thoughts planted deep, deep down in our hearts, most of us would rather not. They are too sacred. They belong to us alone. Then I discovered that, by writing to God, I shared more of my inner life with Him than if I prayed in words. I still have many of those prayers, not from my early childhood, but from a later time in my life as a housewife, because even as an adult I often felt the need to talk to God the writing way. I never thought I would share these thoughts. I kept them in my desk where I could pick them up easily, and at times when my mind was very tired, I used to read them again as part of my worship for the day. I now want to share some of them with the world. Simple as they are, I want those who read them to remember they were not written as a lesson, or a story, but for me . . . and me alone.

August 29, 19——
Dear God,

This morning I started the first breath of awakening with a prayer of praise. It seemed to set the whole day right! I was almost walking on air when I came into my kitchen to fix breakfast. After we had had our devotion and my Bob had left for his business, I hurried with my housework and when all was in order, I devoted twenty minutes to being still. Father God, I have discovered that to be absolutely still in mind and soul and body, to stop all thoughts and let every cell in my body relax, makes it easy for me to hear Your voice in my heart. I wait and let You talk to me. It has taken me such a long time to be able to be still twenty minutes. I used to begin with five, and they really seemed so long. Now twenty minutes does not seem any longer than five did. I ended my silence by meditating on the Twenty-third Psalm. All through the day I tried to catch glimpses of You, in people's faces, in the birds that sang in the trees in my garden, in the beautiful flowers and the golden sunset. But despite all of that my day was not perfect. I didn't guard it well enough. Negativeness crept in here and there and many times I was impatient with those around me. I am not happy about my progress for today, but I will try to do better tomorrow.

Yes, these letters became a chart of my spiritual life. I could check back and see how much I had progressed in a certain space of time. It was almost like a report card and I wanted to make high grades. And I found that my writing did draw me closer to God and closer to the best of me, although at times I was very discouraged with myself.

September 1, 19——
Dear God,
    Today it seemed as though I failed in all I did! My heart was heavy when I awoke because I carried yesterday's trouble with me into the new tomorrow. Instead of starting with a prayer, my first thought was about myself. I felt tired and distraught and my face showed it at breakfasttime and made the rest of my family gloomy, too. I found the housework a heavy burden and grumbled about the many tasks that were awaiting me. Somehow I could not find a moment to have my quiet time. I was too busy. Now, as I

look back over my day, I can see nothing in it of value for eternity . . . nothing to help the world. I am sorry because it could have been a good day if I had remembered that *prayer changes things.* I am resolved to do better if You give me another day.

September 22, 19——
Dear God,

Being a mother is such a wonderful thing! I marvel to think that You trusted me with two little daughters to mold and fashion in thoughts and deeds. I want so much to do my very, very best. I find it hard to be strict though, especially when two big blue eyes look up at me filled with glittering tears as I am about to administer punishment. When a small girl's voice sobbingly assures me that she is sorry and will never be naughty again, I sometimes can't go through with it. I hear myself saying, "Darling, Mother will give you another chance to be good!" I wipe her tears and her face lights up like a sun peeping through the clouds, and my heart is light once more. I hope she has learned her lesson and really and truly is sorry.

I can see myself as a child of Yours, saying the same words as I sin against Your holy will, and You always give me a second chance. Sometimes, though, You have to lay Your hand on me

and I know then that is the best for me. I know
it is Your love for me that makes You do it. I trust
my little girls will know that when, in later life,
they will look back on their childhood days. I
don't want them to say I was a weak mother. I
want them to know when I had to punish them
my heart broke in little pieces, but I had to do the
things that were necessary to help them grow up
to be wise and strong and to walk with courage.
I will always remember how my own Mama told
me that children are not our own, they are a precious loan from You. With such a loan we must
try to be worthy of our little ones and bring out
the very best in them to Your glory.

They both are sleeping in their little beds right
now. A few minutes ago I went to their room and
softly opened the door. I stood there a long time,
my heart so full with joy I thought it would
burst. I thought: Being a mother is the greatest
thing in life . . . the highest calling . . . the
finest profession. Because today's daughters will
be tomorrow's mothers. They are the flowers that
hold the seed for the new world without end. In
a mother's heart you have planted so much of
Your own goodness. Its love is deep enough and
wide enough to last for a whole lifetime. A mother's love is really the only completely unselfish
thing on earth. Even a husband and wife love to
be loved back. A sister and a brother give back to

us according to what we give to them. Our best friends expect a reward for their friendship and they are true as long as we are true to them. But the real mother asks nothing in return for her love. She prays that her little ones will grow up to be fine and good and true. There are mothers who sacrifice all the comfort of life to give their children an education, and there are other mothers who patiently and silently wait years for a prison gate to swing open so they can hold their crime-sick lost boy in their loving arms. Oh, Father God, just now that story my Papa used to tell in his sermons so long ago comes back to my memory. A story I never can forget and that truly pictures to us a mother's love.

He told of a prisoner who was going to be executed in a small town in a certain country far away. This town had an old tradition that a prisoner would hang when the bell rang from the town's only little church. The execution was about to start. All was set in order. The bell ringer had been told the time, but nothing seemed to happen. Some of the officials rushed to the white stone church; they saw the bell ringer, pulling the bell rope with all his might, but no sound rang out. They sent a man up to the belfry to investigate and there they found the gray, wrinkled little mother. Her hands were clutching the bell clapper; they were bleeding and bruised but they kept it from making the sound. Her heart would not let the bell ring because that would signal the death of her only boy. The legend tells that the warden was so touched by this great mother love that he stayed the execution and the boy's sentence was commuted to life in prison. I have always hoped that perhaps that boy was eventually given his freedom and became a good man for his mother's sake, but the legend does not say . . .

I am glad I was born a woman and that the privilege of becoming a mother was given to me. I have made up my mind always to try to live up to its greatness. My heart almost breaks when I read in the newspaper about mothers who have lost their calling . . . who have fallen from grace . . . oh, that they would wake up to the fact that God's greatest gift was bestowed upon them.

As I lift those letters now, one by one, and lovingly read them again, they stir my heart anew to serve You better, God. I don't write letters to You any more. That stopped when I became an author. Now I pray more in words than I ever did before in all my life, but there is an unwritten prayer in those words . . . there is the same longing to love You more . . . to serve You better . . . and I still try to keep those silent moments. There is a terrific power in silence . . . it surely is better than gold.

October 7, 19——

A wonderful new day! How thankful I am for earth life. Each day I seem to know more and have a better understanding of this journey. We build here on earth for ourselves a house not made by hands. We must live our lives so the world is better because of us. As our thoughts go out on the ether waves of time, they must carry strength and healing on their wings. I like to start each new day with this one thought—GOD —and I want to live each moment for one reason only—You, GOD, I want to end each day with my hand in Yours.

> Lift up your head and smile
> And living is worth while
> Be brave when days are dark
> With springtime comes the lark
> Be still and know . . . my soul
> That God has made thee whole. . . .

November 4, 19——
Dear God,

My Bible verse for today is Psalm 3:3

> But Thou, O God, art a shield about me
> My Glory, and the lifter of my head.

What is a shield? An umbrella is a shield against
the rain. A coat a shield against the cold. An
apron a shield against the dirt. It is so precious to
know that You, Lord God, are a shield for me
against anything that could harm me. The greatest harm that could come to me would be those
things that would crowd out the spirit of truth.
Evil thoughts! My wonderful God, You have
placed Yourself between them and me. You stand
there as a bright, shining light and when I look
at the light long enough, I can't see anything but
the light. You are my guide! When I walk with
You beside me, all is well within me. My soul re-
joices in Your love. The little hurts of life that
come my way I gladly endure because of my
Love for the Lord, I say, "Because the mind of
Christ dwelleth in me I want to bless and not
curse . . . give, and not look for the reward."
It is a big lesson to learn, this lesson of living a
triumphant life in this world. But I know I can
. . . and I will.

My girls are not little girls any more. They have
grown into adults and now should know how to walk
on the road of life. But how I remember the struggles
I had to try to give to them a strong foundation. I saw
them go into the mysterious, confusing years of adoles-
cence. I saw love come and love go in and out in those

tender years. I have seen them hurt when dark shadows had shut off the sun for a time, and I often cried with them as they faced the storms of life. I told them they must set their faces against the storm and walk on to be made strong to meet the next one. I walked miles and miles with them as we talked and they opened the secretmost parts of their hearts and let me look in. Sometimes one of them would say: "Mommie, you understand better than any girl friend and I know it is because you have lived through these things . . . and, you know, you haven't forgotten." And then there came times when I had to make a choice to keep myself on the high pedestal where they had placed me or to step down and let them see me as I really was. There come great temptations to our young people. Their emotional life is not stable and sometimes young love runs away from common sense. Once I talked this over with one of my daughters. She had told me how frightened she suddenly had become of love . . . how it had failed her at a time when she had believed it was life's highest and most beautiful emotion. Her love had turned almost into hatred for a young man she had believed was only fine and good. I knew I must help her. It was my duty to open her eyes so she would see and understand clearly that sometimes a frustrated emotion is like a hurricane; it destroys in a few minutes what has taken a lifetime to build up. But to do this I had to share things buried deep, deep in my soul, things I had thought I would never think of again because they were not a part of my better self. That was the day I wrote only a short letter to God.

May 18, 19——

Sometimes it almost breaks my heart to have to bring up daughters. Why do dark shadows have to descend on young hearts so trusting and brave? Why does evil creep in like a snake to rob their garden of its flowers? Today You know I swung that heart-door of mine wide open as my daughter came to me hurt and bewildered because of the shape a beautiful love had suddenly turned into. Did I do right to tell her my story of the time the same thing happened to me? I hope so. Take my words and bless them that they may become a light . . . a beacon to lead her on . . . and, Father God, don't let her think less of me because of it.

Yes, I did tell her. It was spring! A big full moon peeked in on the porch where we were sitting lazily sipping our coffee. The air had something of expectancy in it, flowers were beginning to bloom and the leaves were still tender on the trees. As young love, I was thinking.

"I don't think I ever want to see him again," my daughter said with so much sadness in her voice my heart almost broke, too.

"Don't make hasty judgment, dear." I tried to make my voice light. "Love has to have its tests! If we love high enough, we try to understand and forgive."

Her mouth opened. "Mom," she cried, "you are taking his part! How can you?"

I patted her arm softly.

"Honey," I said, "I take his part because suddenly I am you. The years are rolling back. I am a young teenager and I have met with such sorrow my heart cannot take it . . . I want to hate, too, but after the young man told me his side of it, I knew what happened was my fault as much as his. Do you want me to tell you the story?"

"Yes, please do!" she said eagerly.

"I was often a very foolish little girl when I was young and sometimes my foolishness led me into awful situations. But, believe me, my dear, I wasn't bad. I just didn't know any better. I was in love . . . terribly in love! And I loved a boy of whom my parents did not approve. I saw him anyway, but only in secret. You see I didn't have the freedom that you have enjoyed. Your grandpapa was very, very strict. . . . I could go only with the boys from our church and they did not appeal to my fancy. One time when your

164

grandparents had to go to a conference and stay overnight, I thought it was a golden opportunity. I was to stay at home and be in charge of my younger brothers and sisters and they went to bed early. So I invited my boy friend to come to the parsonage and spend the evening with me. Now, I didn't know it was wrong to invite a boy over to the house when I was alone there. No one had told me. After all I had four brothers . . . and—well, I thought nothing of it. The only wrong I thought I did was to be with a boy I was forbidden to associate with. I remember how I tried to make everything as romantic as I could. I had picked flowers for the parlor and there was soft lamplight and coffee and Mama's best cookies.

"He came late; the children were all asleep and it began as a wonderful evening, but in the late hours things went out of control. My knowledge about boys and life was very limited. I was naïve and innocent despite my progress in book-learning. My parents had never told me the dangers of love. I was almost scared to death! The night had been so enchanting until suddenly my young man stopped being a good-natured, gentle companion and turned into what I thought a real devil. And he, being frustrated and with young, uncontrolled blood pulsing through his veins had completely misunderstood my invitation. In those moments of terror I remember him flinging out the angry words at me: 'For goodness' sake, what did you expect? You invited me to spend the night with you, didn't you?'

"I knew, as always when I was wrong. But I had been brought up in a God-fearing home and what was right before God mattered a lot to me. I tried desperately to think what to do. . . . There was nothing but to pray to God in my heart . . . a sorry prayer, knowing how discouraged even God must be with me . . . just hoping He would help.

" 'Please dear God,' my heart prayed, 'keep me from doing wrong. . . . I have learned my lesson. . . . I want to do the right thing. . . . I will even go out as a missionary to the heathen if you will help me to-night. . . . Oh, God . . . I am so frightened I am ready to die.'

"And the help came in a very strange way. I always marvel about the goodness of God to His erring children here on earth. The magnificence of it . . . the mercy . . . the patience. I became so calm inside it was as though I had had a cool shower; my mind was clear and my brain worked just at the time I needed it. 'Listen,' I said. 'You are so much stronger than I . . . I can't fight you any longer . . . but will you please let me tell you a story?'

" 'A story,' he gasped, hardly believing he heard right.

" 'Yes,' I said . . . 'you see the story is about you and me and it just came to me from nowhere. . . .'

" 'Go ahead,' he said. 'I'll listen to your story.'

"I spoke softly at first, as though I was feeling my way through the darkness of my brain cells. Then my voice gained in volume and I spoke clearly and with confidence as I knew it was God's help to me:

" 'It happened way off in America at the great Niagara Falls. She was a little tiny white lamb and she had gone off into the wilderness without the permission of her parents . . . she had gone swimming in the lake above the big falls although she knew it was a very dangerous spot . . . the little lamb was young and foolish, you see, and she seemed to find pleasure in disobeying her parents. But as she was swimming in the cool lake, having a wonderful time, she saw a big black eagle circling in the sky. It spotted her and soon it had its claws in the lamb's thick wool, and together they were floating with the stream. That eagle had only one thought in mind: what a wonderful meal he would have on that tender lamb! But first he would play along with her making her think that he was only riding with her down the stream of the lake. 'As soon as we reach the edge of the fall,' he said to himself, 'I will lift her and we will fly off where I can share her as a fine meal for my family.' They came nearer and nearer the roaring waterfall and just as the eagle was about to lift her, he found the lamb too heavy . . . so he tried to fly off without her . . . but it was too late; his claws were buried so deep in the white fleece of his prey that he could not get them loose and a few minutes later they both fell over the fall and were crushed to pieces in the sharp stones below.'

"I stopped. . . . What a beautiful story that was! I was thinking. And it did speak to him and to me, too. It made a very deep impression on my young man. He was himself again and begged me to forgive him for the unpleasantness he had caused.

" 'But now,' he said, 'let me tell you my side . . . the viewpoint of a man. A girl should never play with a man's emotions to the extent that he loses himself. Remember that always, my dear. Don't judge a man for what he can't help . . . when a girl willingly places him in the way of temptation, it is her fault as much as his.'

"I always remembered that and I know it was my fault as much as his, that evening so long ago. But God heard my prayer and saved us both from going over the falls of temptation. . . . That is why I ask you not to judge, before you examine your own heart before God."

She sat still a long time. Finally she looked up at me with tears in her eyes. Her arms went around me.

"Mommie," she said, "you are wonderful . . . but

not just wonderful . . . I shall always, always feel I can tell you things because you are . . . you are human."

I know my story helped her and many other young people I had told it to . . . and it also teaches that God will help us in any situation when we honestly seek His help with all our heart.

In those years I often wrote little poems. Not for any other reason than that something seemed to sing within me and I had to put it down on paper. One summer I had had trouble with the youngsters in the neighborhood who wanted to play in my cool shady yard. My children were grown up then, and I felt as do so many other mothers, this was a time in life when I could enjoy stillness and peace, and I had a right to chase the children off. But one day a strange verse came out of my pencil, and I wrote it in my letters as I felt that was a letter from God to me.

High Fences

They were too noisy, the children
    who came to play in my yard. . . .
My grass was too green,
    I had labored too hard

To let them invade to destroy
          and pull up
                 and break down. . . .
I wanted the prettiest garden in town.

Because of this sin, I became quite
    restless . . . and more . . . I couldn't stand noise
my poor head was too sore
And so came a knock
on my fancy front door
And two big blue eyes looked up at my face,
While her little sundress was an awful disgrace.

"Can I play in your garden?" said she.
"I have Billy and Ginny and Ruthy with me. . . .
We can't play in ours. . . .
My Mommie is sick. . . .
And she says: 'You go on,
Or I'll take the stick. . . .'

She smiled as she talked,
"You are pretty," she said.
"I like to play right by that
big flower bed."
And without an answer
They all ran to play.

And I stood there a moment
    as my fence tumbled down.

It might not be now . . . the prettiest place
This garden of mine . . . in life's mad race
But I am convinced . . . with my fences down
My yard is the happiest yard in our town.

Meditating in verse was so much fun! There
was no one to judge or criticize. God spoke to the
heart in many different ways. I wanted to fill my life
with Him, and I prayed that these little tryings of
mine would make lovely music in His ears, for He listens to our faintest whisper when we love Him.

December 17, 19——
Dear God,
My will is Thine, my Lord.
Take it to Thy heart
And warm it with Thy love.
It is a stubborn will
But a willing one. . . .
It is a strong will,
and it needs channeling
in the right directions.
I want it to do Thy will
completely . . . at all times
For time . . . and eternity . . .
So little I have to give . . .
But Father God, I want to live
My life just for Thee

> So create in me
> An honest sincerity. . . .

March 15, 19——

> To be filled with God's love each day
> Walk with Him every step of the way
> To sing a new song
> Of His love, all day long. . . .
> To walk
> And to talk
> And to know
> I am dear in His sight
> He is here
> As my heart . . . so near.

January 1, 19——

Dear God,

I know that what I do for others will come back to me and either bless or curse. If I don't pay my bills . . . I shall be lacking in my daily living. If I use others just to get things out of them, whatever I gain from it shall be lost in sickness or loss in other ways. How very clear the Master's words come to me now: "As ye measure to others . . . so it shall be measured unto you."

February 9, 19——

Dear God,

How wonderfully you have protected me and in my devotion I have felt close to *You*. The other day a thought came so vividly to my mind. God has cut a pattern for my earth life and my celestial garment in the world to come will be shaped from it.

June 11, 19——
Dear God,

This is my wedding anniversary day! I love to dream back. Life is surely like a story. This is our story . . . our wonderfully, happy story. It is true, we have had our ups and downs. Sometimes I have been very provoked and at times my husband had a very trying way of sulking when I displeased him. But we have grown better with the years, through understanding and learning to bear and forbear. I have learned never to make hasty decisions. When I want to tell my loved ones off, I think: If I but wait until the morrow the waves of time will have washed the anger away and the cruel words will be lost in the sea of forgetfulness instead of being uttered. I have learned with the years to delay the evil words but never to wait with the good. I love being a housewife and having a lovely home to play in. I love each little nook and corner. Dear God, I can never thank You enough for the blessings of a home and the love of a family. If I had the years that I have lived as a wife back again, I would walk up the same church aisle and say the words,

"I do," to the man I fell in love with . . . and who became my husband before God and man.

April 27, 19——
Dear God,

Last night something happened which was very hard to bear. One of my dearest friends tumbled down from the heaven where I had placed her, and she broke in little tiny pieces right before my eyes. I have to try now to put those pieces together again. It will take a long time and they will never look as beautiful as before, but if you who are the Master potter help me . . . perhaps ours will be a fine friendship again. We must learn to forgive and to forget. Friendship is too dear and rare to be broken. I am a very imperfect person, too. Sometimes one does things on the spur of the moment, and The Master said so long ago when His disciples asked Him how many times to forgive . . . not seven . . . but seventy times seventy. . . . I can't begin to count how many times You, God, have forgiven me. If I look to You for wisdom, it will come to me.

July 13, 19——
Dear God,

Today it is not just summer in nature, it is summer in my heart. Life is beautiful and I have so much to be happy for. The sun is so warm as I work among the flowers and Bob's roses bloom and bloom and sometimes in the early morning he comes in with a big red rose whose fragrance fills my whole kitchen. "From one rose to another," he says. How lucky I am. What can I wish for more? I have down here on earth all I need and still my heritage in your heaven is there for me to take possession of someday . . . when the day comes and You open that last gate. . . . Life is beautiful and so is death . . . for those who die in the Lord. . . .

❧ Chapter Eleven

I am by nature a home-loving person. A home to me is not the structure of a house put together with all sorts of materials, or the color of the wallpaper or the size of the rooms. It does not matter how modest or expensive the furniture; that is not what makes the home. When I think back on all the different places my husband and I and our two daughters have lived in during thirty-two years of marriage, I know in my heart that each place we have called home is as dear to me as the other and I feel tenderness for all of them. Year by year we have added more to our home —a little more expensive furnishing and a lot more of ourselves.

The true feeling of a home can be tested by the way strangers react to it. It has always thrilled me when people who have been guests in our home have told me in kind words that they had found something special in our home life, something they could not place their finger on. I know the secret! And it is found not only in our home, but in all homes where God has been invited to make His abode. We have always wanted our home to be a sanctuary, where HE is the most important part and where a little bit of HIS love may rub off on those who enter in.

In Papa's and Mama's parsonage there was always a special time designated for the family to gather together for worship. As soon as we children were old enough to crawl about we became part of this circle, and soon we learned to kneel with the rest of the family. Before we understood the meaning of prayer we understood that we must be silent, and when we grew older, we learned that God existed in that silence and that kneeling was to worship Him.

When I married, my husband and I followed the family tradition of having a special time set aside for God. Soon this was as dear to us as the fellowship at home had been in yonder years, and our girls felt the same security in it as I had felt as a little girl. It became a pattern for our home life.

I stand amazed and bewildered when I hear of people who are great church workers and call themselves Christians, but neglect to pray as a family unit in their own homes. "People who pray together, stay together" and they become closer and closer to each other as the years go by. There is not one problem that prayer cannot solve.

When we have house guests, we make it a rule to include them in our prayer time. Sometimes they look a bit bewildered and I hasten to make clear to them that this is not compulsory, only an invitation to them to feel that they are part of our family circle. Never has a guest refused to take part and, after it is over, they have always expressed their gratitude for being invited to share with us such a sacred tryst.

It has been a joy to know that our daughters always thought of our fellowship with love and respect and it became such a natural proceeding to them that it never caused embarrassment. I used to wonder how they would react when they brought their friends home for weekends, after they left the home, for of course there was always a houseful of young people on vacation from college and special weekends. Having girls we gradually had more boy visitors on these occasions. And I used to make a little speech to them, saying that we always had fellowship and prayer after the evening meal, and inviting them to join us. They seemed to enjoy the prayer time, too, and said they looked forward to coming back and worshipping with us again.

Once there was a young man who had taken a

fancy to our younger daughter and for the first time I hesitated about asking him to join us. He didn't seem like the type who would enjoy a prayer time. Nevertheless, I invited him as I had the others before. He looked a little surprised, but he was very sweet about it and said if this was our family routine he certainly would not want to upset it. We were happy to have him as one of us and I was ashamed afterwards to think how wrongly I had judged him.

The next time he came he told me he had been looking forward to our evening session and just as we were about to begin he said, "I have a great favor to ask of you. Would you let me conduct the family worship tonight? You see, I brought along a book my grandfather gave me years ago, I would like to read from it so we all could share its beauty."

Well, he conducted that worship as well as my Papa would have done. And though I knew he came because he took our daughter out, he surely loved this particular time we had set apart for God.

Since our family is grown up now and there are just my husband and myself at home, we have changed the fellowship period to the breakfast hour and find that time more convenient. Every morning we have a relaxed time together as we read from the Bible and some other appropriate special booklet on devotions and join in a prayer, the arms of which reach around our loved ones wherever they are. We mention them by name, one by one, asking a blessing over their lives, special protection for the day and help for us all to do God's will. And as we pray, we know that Mama is also taking all our names before God. She speaks each name sweetly and tenderly as she begins her new day. She has done this since the day we were born. Now there are fifty-one of us to pray for.

It is the prayer fellowship that gives our home that special warm something. It reaches out a joyous welcome to those who enter in, and also ties us as a family with the strongest cords on earth—the cords of love. It is the togetherness of a family that makes a home a true home.

One afternoon as I drove into my driveway there was a strange car waiting for me. I found someone sitting on our doorstep who eagerly came to meet me.

"I hope you don't mind me coming like this," she said, looking anxiously up at me. "I asked my minister to make an appointment with you for me, but he advised me just to drop in on you, assuring me you were the kind of person who wouldn't mind at all."

"He is right," I said. "I love people."

At first I thought she was a high-school girl until

I saw the wedding ring on her finger. She had a sweet, open face with wide blue eyes that smiled before she spoke.

I invited her inside my home and after we were seated on the sofa in the living room she told me why she had come.

"I have been married only a few months," she told me. "I have read both your books and I have fallen in love with Mama and the way she made such a warm, happy home for her family—but that was years ago. This might seem silly of me to ask you, but I am looking for a recipe for a perfect home life. My husband and I want to have lots of children, too. I want so much to be a real special wife and mother. Since you wrote those books with such happy home life, I'm sure you are the one who can advise me."

"I think you are very sweet," I said. "And you are on the right track. I am sure you are going to be a perfect wife because you want to with your whole heart. I have no written recipe for a happy home life, but I know how one should be lived and I will try to share with you the secret of a happy home life even in these days."

"Oh, please do!" She smiled. "I promise you I'll try it out."

"To create a home," I began, "I believe is the calling and the destiny of a woman. God gave her all the ingredients for it, but it is the mixing of them that is important if the result is to come out successfully. You know, the home is the making of a nation. When the home fails, the nation fails."

"I know," she said, looking out through the window as if she were trying to span far into the years of tomorrow, "that is the trouble with our country today . . . the home."

"It takes two to begin a family and the children to complete it, but the wife and the mother is the one who makes a home what it is. It can be a warm, dear place to live in, or just an empty shell where people spend their years together. As you have said, my Mama knew how to create a happy home. I learned the secret from her. She always said it is the little things, the small ingredients that are the most important. The wife is the first one up in the morning, having a tasty breakfast waiting for her family when they arise. A smiling face, a glad good morning, starts them out well on a new day. There is something special about a family sitting down together to begin their day with grace before they partake of food. As the children run off to school, they have a secure feeling in their hearts. They know, whatever the day may bring, this is the place they will return to, and whatever the world thinks of them, here are those who love and want them. If they have problems, they can sit down and talk them over together. Their mother makes it a point to be at home when they return from school . . . she is glad to see them. Her smile is their sunshine. Children from a happy home grow up in security and trust in life and their fellow men.

"And so with a man. If his home is right, it becomes his palace. He is King there! A man like that does not roam. He has all that he wishes for. During the day, his thoughts wander back to his dear family. It is for them that he works so hard and it is more than worth while. He remembers that morning he had that important engagement, how his wife made blueberry pancakes for breakfast because they are his favorite. He feels her embrace as he leaves in the morning and she is always at the window waving as he drives off . . . yes, he can see her many times during the day . . . standing there waving and smiling and her last words: "Have a good day, honey!" And the kids! Just good healthy kids, too full of life at times, but even though his head is tired and he longs for peace and quiet . . . it is wonderful to think of their arms around his neck . . . their wet, short little kisses. Junior will always see that the garage door is open for him at night. He blows the horn twice as he drives in . . . that's the signal to let the family know he is home. . . . How they chatter during dinner. Everyone trying to tell the happenings of the day. But Mom

manages it. She tells them all to listen and take turns
. . . she wants them to be more interested in the
others' happenings than in their own."

"That is important, I can see that!" she exclaims.
"I must remember that."

"Yes," I say. "To listen is a great art."

"And what else?" she asks eagerly.

"Oh, there are the usual things in every home. The
TV programs the children love to see before bedtime,
and also the story. It is good for Dad to read to the
little ones; he gets closer to them that way. My husband used to boast that there wasn't a fairy tale he
didn't know. He always did the reading to the girls
when they were small. And then one must see that
the children kneel to say their prayers; sometimes they
need a little help. A few moments to talk before they
are tucked in and the tender good-night kiss: 'See
you in the morning! Sweet dreams!'

"The house is still now as the husband and wife sit
down in their easy chairs. The husband loses himself
in his newspaper and the wife thinks back over the
day. It is like the pages of a book. This is a true story!
The family lives a story each day. She is satisfied because she has tried her best, and tomorrow she will
try even harder. The happiness of her family is her
whole world.

"The weekends are so important. The chores they

do together, each one taking a special interest in anything that has to do with *home*. There might be a game to see on a Saturday afternoon and at night a good movie to which they all can go together. The parents realize how fast the years go by and that soon the children will be grown up and the things they do now will be the memories they will have from their childhood days.

"I like to think of Sunday as the day that crowns them all. The husband cooking breakfast and having it ready when the rest of them wake up. This is his wife's morning off. They come up to his call blurry-eyed and stretching; they scramble to the table in nighties and pajamas and the wife says what she says every Sunday morning: 'No one can cook bacon and eggs like Daddy. Please, honey, don't ever change the Sunday-breakfast menu.'

"There is something dear about a family going to church together, dressed in their best as they drive off in the family car. The day has begun right and it will be a day of perfect fellowship . . . and——"

I stopped suddenly.

"It was a long recipe," I said, "I'd better stop now. A recipe can be too long, you know."

"Thank you," she whispered, making ready to leave. "Someday write it in a book, will you?" She clasped my hand. "I am so glad I came. I am richer now and I feel I know so much."

I waved at her from the doorway. What a wonderful little person she was! I was thinking. So young and eager to build the right kind of home. There must be many more like her. If only all brides would begin like that, searching for the key to happiness . . . true happiness, how rich our world would be!

❧ Chapter Twelve

Having grandchildren is a God-given blessing that lifts us out of the hum-drum of life and fills us with joy and fun. How wise God was to know that we needed that special gift when our years perhaps might seem duller and our pace begin to slow down a little. . . . In our children's children, we live our lives all over again. It is a different joy, though; we can share the fun without having to carry the burdens. When we get tired of their noise, we retire to our own haven of rest, so grandchildren are really ours to enjoy.

But to be a new, first-time grandmother is something else again! Thinking back now, I wish there could be a school for brand-new grannies where they could learn the first step of how not to interfere. I was not a very wise grandmother to begin with, but I learned . . . and learned the hard way. If I only had known at the start what I know now. If I had stopped to think, but most of all if I had prayed about it and let God guide my steps . . . but I didn't. This great gift I almost took for granted because it just seemed to happen to me. It is very difficult to learn that grandchildren first of all belong to their own parents. That they are ours to love and hold in our arms and lavish our affection and money on . . . but when it comes to giving advice . . . beware! We, according to our offspring, strange as it might seem, belong to a past generation. They feel things are different now. Life is a big crazy circle, for hadn't I felt the same way when I thought my parents came from the old dark ages?

Now I can smile as I think of my foolishness and forgive today's younger generation; I can do it now that I have learned. Any educated grandmother must know that you wait until you are asked for advice and that you willingly and gladly stay on the outside of the new circle of mystic fellowship until you are suddenly ushered into it.

There is a beginning to every story. Let me share mine, as, with great pleasure, I wander back and try to recapture the feeling I had when it began. This story belongs to a very young father and a still younger mother and a little redheaded chubby baby boy. Perhaps it all would not have been so complicated if our young people had not lived in our home when the great event took place.

They had met and married in college. Our daughter had just completed her first year, and her husband his third. I remember how I had dreaded that day when we would drive her out to St. Paul, Minnesota, where she was going to be enrolled in the college of her choice. It was a Swedish college, the same that so many of my sisters and brothers had attended and I had been happy and proud that she had chosen her family's old Alma Mater. What an empty household ours had been without our older daughter and how we missed her! She had been the lively, bubbling-over one, the one who couldn't wait to come rushing home from school to tell me in detail all the things that were going on. No more came the gay music from the piano she played so well and her songs that used to fill every room in the house. Her bed stood untouched and made up and my heart suffered untold agony. How soon they grew up. But this was part of life. A great adjustment that had to be made. And I was not alone in my grieving; there were millions of mothers who just now suffered the same way, and bore it bravely because this, too, was part of motherhood. But I counted the days and marked each one off with a pencil on the calendar as I waited for December and Christmas when we would see her again.

And Christmas finally came. A lovely white Christmas with evergreens and tinsel and lights and decorations shining everywhere. She came home, but not alone. Of course we had been told beforehand that a new young man would accompany her home . . . and more, much more than that . . . the newspapers on Christmas day would carry her picture with the announcement of their engagement. But when we were told they wanted a wedding the coming June, we put our foot down. Why, she was only a girl, too young to know her own mind, and we had hoped so much that she would get her education first before she began to think of marriage. But it was to no avail. Their minds were made up. All their classmates, almost, were getting married and they were to live in that cute apartment for married students on the campus. Girls did marry young nowadays and we seemed to be the only parents in the world who did not understand. I still worried about it. There had been a long high-school romance and it had seemed as if those two had been made for each other. College had changed all that! But would this love last? Did the young man know how headstrong this lovely daughter of ours could be? Would he know how she needed lots and lots of tenderness and understanding? It was so important for a marriage to be right and I felt they were too young to know, but all my talking did not even make an impression, so we gave up and I threw myself into planning the most beautiful wedding a girl could ever have.

And it was a lovely, lovely wedding. They looked so happy and everything began to seem more right. When they returned after a short honeymoon to pack their things and go back to their college town, my heart did not ache as much as the first time.

"This is life!" I told myself. Our girl had a right to plan her own life. All I could do was to pray for her happiness.

They returned to college and I settled down to housecleaning and planning of winter clothes. Then, one sunny fall afternoon, I heard a car come into our driveway. Wondering what company was arriving, I looked through the dining-room curtain, only to run quickly to the front door and open it wide, for there they were, the two of them, in their old car, waving and smiling as though they had inherited the world. It took me a while to come to my senses, but suddenly my mind was clear. What in the world were they doing home with the college fifteen hundred miles away? . . . There was no vacation now . . . they both should be in college. They saw the anxious look on my face and after our greeting my daughter told me excitedly with stars dancing in her eyes:

"Mommie, prepare yourself for a shock . . . we

are home! Home to stay for good. We have both quit college!"

"You have what?" I finally managed to get out in a faint whisper, praying in my heart I had heard wrong.

"Come, let's sit down together," said my daughter "and while my husband unpacks, you and I can talk."

We sat close together. I was trembling inside. What in the world could have happened? Had they been expelled?

"Mommie," said a small voice, so like the little girl who used to be. "I have something very important to tell you, so important that you will gladly forgive us for quitting college."

I tried to listen . . . to shut off my thoughts, to be calm, come what may, but my heart was beating like a sledgehammer and I was sure it could be heard at the end of the street.

She held my hand, and she was so very young. Her golden blonde hair curled softly around her cheeks. Her eyes so wide and blue held a mysterious light, as though two stars had lost their way and found a place in there.

"Mommie," came her voice again. "Mommie, do you know what? You are going to have a grandchild!"

My heart almost stopped. The news had come so unexpectedly. So utterly unexpectedly. Of course I had hoped that someday this would happen, but I had thought they would at least finish their education first, and have a home of their own, and my son-in-law would have a position which would enable him to support a family . . . but this . . . right now . . . two crazy kids with nothing but themselves to start with. And my little girl, only one year of college . . . and her husband only one year left and now he had thrown it over . . . just like that. I couldn't even smile. My heart was too filled with worry.

"But I thought you would graduate first," I blurted out. "I thought both of you would realize this is really not the time . . ." I stopped. My daughter's eyes began to fill with tears and she gave me a look of contempt as she left the room and rushed out to throw herself into the arms of a loving, understanding husband.

I sat in the same place for a long time. Regret filled my soul. What a fool I had been! How tenderly and sweetly she had told me, acting as though she was giving me the biggest gift in the world. And I had pushed it away. I had refused to accept it! I had no words of happiness, just an accusation, and now she had left me and something between us had been broken that would take a long, long time to mend.

It took a little while for her to give me her confidence again, but after we all had had a talk and my husband in his calm way had made me try to see things

through the youngster's eyes, the old warm relation-
ship was restored. After all, he had said, a little bride
of eighteen can't help losing her balance when she
knows she is going to bring forth a new little life. Of
course she wanted to come home to be with us. And
a husband, very much in love couldn't think of having
fifteen hundred miles between them, so he thought
quitting was the only logical thing to do. They would
have a whole lifetime to catch up on their education,
but to have their very first baby—well that was more
important than anything else in the world.

Life became calm once more. Calm and busy. We
did a lot of baby-clothes shopping and we planned
and talked and dreamed. Sometimes I almost wondered if it was I or my daughter who was having the
baby, the way it effected my whole life. It was wonderful to touch little booties and to put soft woolly
little sweaters to my cheek and to count the dozens
and dozens of diapers. And there was a brand-new
crib and a bassinet and all those tiny little ingredients
that make up that heap of things it takes to welcome
the first baby. Evenings we sat and talked in front of
the open fire and I used to relate little things from the
time my girls were babies. Where had the years gone
to? Could it really be true that soon now I would hold
a little grandchild in my arms?

As time went on we had to face facts. Our house was too small with so many in it and with the baby coming. If they were to stay with us, we had to sell our little dreamhouse and buy a bigger place. It was a sacrifice to sell it. There were so many sweet memories connected with this place where we had lived so long. But we found a fine home with two bathrooms and we moved and settled down in new surroundings in plenty of time before the great event. My husband and I gave up the big sunny master bedroom so the baby could have more sun and light and time sped by and so the day arrived.

I had everything in order. There was a private nurse waiting in the hospital when my daughter arrived there. I had had three babies without a private nurse, but something could go wrong and I wanted to take every precaution. She had no idea what it was to be in labor. And there were those long, long hours in pain and waiting. The nurse helped *me*, more than my daughter. Just knowing she was there made me feel better. When the phone rang and my son-in-law joyfully told me of the little boy, I was wild with happiness. And so that night my husband and I climbed the stairs of the hospital and stood in front of the big window to get the first glimpse of this miracle child. He was so tiny and so sweet and so redheaded, it left a warm soft glow in our grandparent-hearts. Our first grandson! He was real! I was too happy to sleep that first night. Already I was busy making plans for his future . . . for his vacations home with us and, of course, for his home-coming.

The day arrived! A beautiful sunshiny June day. The roses were blooming and I picked a big bouquet to make the house look festive. After my son-in-law had driven to the hospital to bring his wife and baby home, I sat down by the window so I could look up the street, while I waited I hummed the old lullabies. Perhaps I could sing him to sleep nights. I wanted this little boy to feel the warm welcome that awaited him in his grandparents' house. If only that car would come. I hoped my son-in-law would drive carefully. The baby was too small to be shaken up. Suddenly I saw the car! I took one last glance at the house. The crib was ready with handmade sheets and soft blankets and a big Teddy bear in one corner. When the car stopped, I was waiting on the sidewalk. I was all ready to take him in my arms for, of course, I would carry him in. I greeted my daughter with a hug and a kiss and whispered, "Put that little bundle of joy in my arms. I want him to feel so welcome!"

But my daughter just stared at me in unbelief.

"Mommie, you're not going to carry the baby. Not

this time. This is our very first baby and its Mama shall carry him in."

"But, darling," I insisted, "you are not strong enough yet! You shouldn't carry anything for many weeks."

"But I will carry my baby. I wouldn't miss it for the world. And, Mommie, I want to say this kindly, we sort of wanted to make believe we had our own home . . . would you . . . could you . . . please don't mind it, Mommie dear . . . but could we be alone with him just for the first hour?"

I was in the kitchen of my house so quick they never had time to see the hurt in my face. I heard a car door slam. They came up the walk and went slowly, slowly up the stairs. They were cooing and talking and I knew they were looking their son over, counting his fingers and toes. There was hugging and kissing and more baby-talk. It was a joyful fellowship upstairs in the intimate family circle and I, the grandmother, stood alone in the kitchen with tears streaming down my cheeks. My own daughter! How could she do this to me? I was so filled with self-pity I had no joy in my heart at all for their complete happiness in each other. All I could think of was how I had planned and dreamed and waited for this moment. And we had given up the best room in the house for them. We had sold our dear little home that we had loved so much

. . . all we could think of for their happiness we had done, and what did they give us back . . . disappointment and heartache . . . that's all. "Please, Mom, leave us alone . . . we want to be just us . . . our little family." The hurt was so big I thought I was going to die.

Finally they called me. I could come up now and see him, but I'd better have a hanky over my mouth . . . and don't go too near the crib.

Well wasn't that noble of them, I fumed inside and, feeling very old and tired, I mounted the stairs. I looked, but my heart wasn't in it. I spoke in a strange voice. "Isn't he a lovely big baby!" the voice said, but there was no music in it.

"When he gets older, you can hold him," my daughter promised generously. They didn't notice my expression or my red eyes. They hardly knew I was there. They were giving the baby its supper.

It was much later after I had cried in my husband's strong arms that it came to me how selfish and silly I had acted and the only thing that was hurt was my pride.

"I know it hurts, dear," my husband had said ever so gently, "but don't take it so hard; they are so young and so wrapped up in their happiness they have room for nothing else. Wait, and someday they will come to you. They will beg you to be part of them. Here, give me a big smile now."

But I couldn't smile. I couldn't smile for weeks. They didn't need my advice . . . they had a baby-book and if something went the least bit out of order they called their doctor.

But those awful weeks passed by somehow. I tried not to intrude . . . to remember my place. And then one night the baby had a long crying spell. They couldn't find anything in the book on how to stop it. They called the doctor. He advised them to let the baby cry until he stopped. They held him and walked with him . . . and still the cry became louder and louder. Then it happened. . . .

"Mommie," called my daughter from their room, "can you tell us what to do? Can you stop him?"

I flew into the room. "Please, God, don't let me fail," I prayed.

Gently I picked up the little bundle from the crib. I put my cool hand on his hot little face, I cuddled him close, so very close to my heart, letting all the love that dwelt there surround him. I sat in a chair and rocked slowly back and forth while a sweet old lul-laby came from my lips. He stopped crying and soon he slept peacefully in my arms.

The young parents just stared at me in unbelief.

"Why, Mommie," cried my daughter, "how did you do it? Would you want us to move the crib into your room if he starts in again? Mommie, you are a wonder! Why didn't we know you would know about babies better than both books and doctors. We should have come to you first."

That was my graduation from the school of grandmother—school of self-discipline. I had received my diploma as fast as that. I watched him that night. The minute he stirred I was beside him. I was delirious with happiness. I really, really had a grandchild.

After that night all the strict rules for the grandmother were erased. I had a chance to spoil him a little before they moved into their own home. When the second baby was due, I was trusted to come in and take care of the first one. He was a big boy by that time. I was very careful now because I knew how to act with a new grand-baby. It was just to remember . . . not to look . . . not to touch . . . not to advise and not to interfere. I didn't even go down to the sidewalk this time when they came home, and I was as happy as a lark. After all the boys were their babies . . . I had had mine. I could even understand now how important it had been for them to establish themselves that first time. I really had learned! Babies belonged to grandmothers just a little bit . . . and mostly when they cried. But as I waited for the young

parents to come up the stairs with this new baby . . .
my son-in-law came running up alone.

"We thought perhaps you would like to carry him
up," he said, a little shyly.

If I wanted to! . . . Never had a prouder grandmother carried a little dark-haired baby boy up a
flight of stairs . . . I carried him into his room and
put him down in the crib and I was personally there
to help count all his fingers and toes. A grandmother's
heart! What a strange contraption! And I was amazed
to know how soon she could forget a hurt . . . if she
only put her mind to it. Because I really felt as though
that first time had never been and I had been in that
mystic circle from the very beginning.

I have four little darlings now. Three boys and a
sweet little girl . . . and the way they hug and kiss
and love me . . . all my grandmother's pains are
over. Now I just share all their joys.

If only there were a school for new grandmothers-
to-be many others would not have to learn the way I
did. But being a grandmother is a most wonderful
thing . . . and different from all other joys . . . and
there will never be a dull moment with all those new
little lives to dream and plan for.

❧ Chapter Thirteen

As I consider our world today, I can't help but think how much young mothers could help their children build a firm foundation of faith in God if they would but practice telling them stories of the great men of the Bible. A story does something to a child's mind. It paints a picture which will be a companion in times of stress and loneliness.

As I reminisce now, I find that some of the gold nuggets from my childhood were the Bible stories Mama told me before I was old enough to read. I can hear her sweet voice still bubbling over with excitement as it placed in my mind pictures of the great men of the Bible. Let me tell you Mama's version of Enoch, the man that walked with God.

"You see," said Mama, "it happened this way: Enoch and God were very close friends, so close that every night they went walking together. One night they walked very far, because they had so much to talk about that they walked almost into the star-studded sky. And when they stopped to say good night, God held Enoch's hand for a long time smiling a wide and happy smile.

" 'We have walked so far tonight' he said. 'We are a lot nearer my home than yours. Why don't you come home with me tonight?'

"Enoch thought that this was a very good idea, so he walked along with God into the golden streets of Heaven. When he awoke the next morning and saw the beauty of God's world, he liked it so much that he never returned to earth."

What a picture of eternity that was to a little girl's mind, especially to one with a vivid imagination. Oh, I used to think so often, as I looked up at the sky, how beautiful it must be behind those clouds and how lucky Enoch was that God had invited him home to spend a night.

Another dear tale was the story of Isaac.

"It was such a terrible thing," Mama said, "and very, very hard to understand. God told Abraham to take his son, whom he loved just as much as any daddy could love his little boy, and offer him as a sacrifice on an altar far off on a mountain. Abraham obeyed, for he loved God even more than he loved his son or anything else on earth, and although it almost broke his heart, he took the things he would need and told his little Isaac that they were going for a long walk. So little Isaac kissed his mama good-bye and off they went. It was a nice sunny day with the birds singing and Isaac was singing, too. He thought it was fun going for a walk with his daddy and he ran along ahead, picking up sticks and stones, throwing the stones away but saving the sticks in case his daddy would need them to put on the altar. When they came nearer to the place, Isaac began to wonder a little. Always before, when they had gone to build an altar to offer a sacrifice to the Lord, they had had the sacrifice trotting along behind them. But now they had everything but the sacrifice. He asked his daddy about it, but Abraham only smiled a sad little smile and patted Isaac's curly black head and said almost as softly as a whisper, 'Little son, God will see that we have a sacrifice for our offering.' So Isaac took his daddy's hand and they walked the rest of the way together. When they had built the altar, Abraham lifted little Isaac up and placed him on top of it.

" 'Now,' he said, 'we will play a game. I shall tie you on this altar as if you were to be the sacrifice.' Although Isaac was a little frightened, he laughed because he saw the love in his daddy's eyes and said, 'This is a funny game, Daddy. I feel almost as though I was going to be offered.'

"Abraham had concealed the long knife behind his

back, not knowing just how he could thrust it into his laughing little boy. Finally, when he thought he had gathered up enough courage to do it, a shining angel stood behind him and took the knife from his hand.

" 'Don't touch that little boy,' the angel whispered in his ear. 'God was only testing you. He wanted to see how much you were willing to offer up for Him. You see, Abraham, you are going to be a great man and people shall know about you through all the years to come. Go out tonight and count the stars, and know that the same number of people shall come from you. And the Lord God says that He shall bless you always, and your people after you.'

"And right then and there Isaac saw a big goat caught in a bramble bush. 'Look Daddy!' Isaac cried. 'I see the sacrifice God has found for us.'

"They offered the sacrifice and praised the Lord, and then hurried home so quickly that they almost ran because they were both so happy."

I remember Mama saying to me as she looked deeply into my eyes, "You will never know what God will ask of you, my little one. But always obey Him, because He loves you more than you can ever love Him. No matter how bad things may look to you, He will never let you get hurt."

One of my very favorite stories was that of Daniel in the Lions' Den. Mama had to tell it over and over again and my heart always pounded when she told it, even though I knew the outcome.

"And they threw Daniel down into a pit of lions that were very, very hungry. They were so hungry that they could almost have eaten each other. Daniel landed on his face and when he sat up, the lions all came rushing at him as though they were trying to see who could reach him first. But Daniel wasn't a bit afraid. He knew that God had told him never to worry because He would always look after him and as he was thinking of God, he began to shine. There he sat, in a big shining ring of fire and all the animals stopped dead! They were sore afraid. Daniel sat there shining the whole night through and in the morning, looking up, he saw the King at the top of the pit and heard him calling his name in a very anxious voice. 'Daniel, Daniel! I am very glad to see that you are not hurt. You have proven to me that your God is a God of might.' As Daniel was brought up from the pit, the King wanted to know more about his God."

That story really helped me when I was afraid. Didn't God protect Daniel? Then he would take care of me. . . . Mama had told me so many times.

But my favorite of all favorites was the story of David. As a child, I had had Mama tell me often about the little shepherd boy who was so brave that he had killed a giant with a little flat stone. I never tired of

listening to all the stories she told about David. As I
grew up, I read about his life over and over again.
This was the man whom God loved in a special way,
even though David was far from perfect. He sinned
in many ways, but God always forgave him. That ap-
pealed to me because I, too, had sinned often and God
had forgiven me. David even fell in love with a married woman, taking her husband from her by placing
him in the fiercest battle where he was killed. But, oh,
how sorry David was, even though he was a King,
when he realized what he had done. God punished
David and the whole kingdom even though he loved
him. Sin did not pay—it never had and never will.
David again received forgiveness and tried to please
God. David loved God so much that he wrote many,
many beautiful psalms to God's honor and glory.

As I travel on the highways to speak in near and
distant places, I have much time to think. Sometimes
the ride is very long and I am apt to be impatient. At
a time like this, I keep my mind on God. I have read
and committed many Psalms to memory. At stop lights
and in traffic I often pray the Lord's Prayer—it takes
one Lord's Prayer for a red light. This keeps my mind
refreshed and my heart is lightened.

Often I meditate on the Shepherd's Psalm. One
special day as I was driving alone to an engagement
two hundred miles away, I felt King David very near.

I let my imagination run away with me and I had the King ride along with me. We had a wonderful conversation. I told him that, of all his Psalms, I loved the Shepherd Psalm best.

"Now, King David," I said aloud there in the car, "I hope that you don't mind if I add a little of my own version to your wonderful Twenty-third Psalm. You see, I am a writer, too, and we could sort of have this Psalm together."

And I made believe that King David told me to go right ahead, and I wrote my own words between the lines of the Psalm.

As I close this book, that has been such a joy to write, I want to share with you just what I added to the Shepherd Psalm that special day, and later wrote down on paper.

THE LORD IS MY SHEPHERD

I SHALL NOT WANT

> I shall not want anything but my Shepherd.
>> He is strong
>>> and wise
>>>> and wonderful
> And He loves me although He knows my faults,
> And even the sin and selfishness that beset me.
>> He loves me for what I am,
>> And when I am tired and weary

HE MAKETH ME TO LIE DOWN IN GREEN PASTURES

In the lush soft grass, I rest
And He stands guard over my thoughts
So no disturbing ones enter in.
I let go of my burdens and cares.
I am still and know that He is God.
When I am rested and refreshed, ready to start
my earth's journey, again

HE LEADETH ME BESIDE THE STILL WATERS.

I sit there in the quiet of the evening
And see the sun sink behind the mountains.
In that golden hour
my heart finds peace,
My striving ceases and I surrender to His will
and now

HE RESTORETH MY SOUL.

Yes, he takes my hand and holds it fast
While we walk past the many forks in the road.
How easily I could have chosen the wrong one
Had He not been with me
but,

HE LEADETH ME IN THE PATHS OF RIGHTEOUSNESS
FOR HIS NAME'S SAKE

It is a narrow path . . . but oh, so beautiful!
The birds sing in the early morning
While the grass is wet with dew;
The sun shines and the air is fresh and pure.
If I let go of my Shepherd's hand and wander off
and get lost in the deep forest
of wilderness,

YEA, THOUGH I WALK THROUGH THE VALLEY OF THE
SHADOW OF DEATH I WILL FEAR NO EVIL.

He will seek me until He finds me
And when I grow weary and faint and falter
because fear chokes me
and my vision fails me
As the shadows grow deeper and darker—then I
remember.

FOR THOU ART WITH ME
THY ROD AND THY STAFF THEY COMFORT ME.

They protect me from all ills.

THOU PREPAREST A TABLE BEFORE ME IN THE PRESENCE
OF MINE ENEMIES

Whose names are: Fear, Worry, Selfishness and
Insecurity.
When they see me drink of gladness and joy
and eat of perfect peace,
They leave me,
And then

THOU ANOINTEST MY HEAD WITH OIL.

The gentleness of His hands almost makes my
heart
burst assunder with happiness
yes, oh yes.

MY CUP RUNNETH OVER

It is too full. . . . I have room for no more
There is no limit to the abundance of gifts
which the good Shepherd bestoweth on me.
His gifts are from the best of the land.
So I shall never be lonely

He gives me companions.

and as we walk along together

one day . . . at dusk . . .

I shall come to a bend in the road,

    I shall stop,

    and far off in the distance I shall see a

        Mansion.

It is magnificent in its glory

It is a House not made by hands,

    eternal in the heavens

    And only the single eye of the soul

        can behold it.

    I shall bow down and worship

    and as I walk silently

        toward it

My heart leaps with gladness . . .

A thousand stars spring into space

All the song-birds on earth sing

    and the little children laugh

And their laughter echoes back

through God's heaven

    into the angelic chorus of the saints.

I have forgotten my yesterdays

    and all the many tomorrows

because I shall enter . . .

. . . AND EVER . . . AND EVER . . . AMEN!